102

My
Lord
Bunter

My
Lord
Bunter

By
FRANK RICHARDS

HOWARD BAKER
LONDON

(The *Magnet*, 1936, 1937)
© Copyright: The Amalgamated Press Ltd., 1936, 1937,
1938, 1972.

Originally published in single issues

Howard Baker (Greyfriars Press) hardcover edition, 1972

SBN 7030 0017 9

Greyfriars Press Books are published by
Howard Baker Press Limited,
27a Arterberry Road, Wimbledon, London, S.W.20, England
Printed in Great Britain by
Chapel River Press, Andover, Hants.

Frank Richards

The writing phenomenon known to the world as Frank Richards (real name Charles Hamilton) died at his home at Kingsgate in Kent on Christmas Eve 1961 at the age of eighty-six.

By then it is estimated that he had written the equivalent of one thousand full-length novels.

His work appeared continuously for over thirty years in those famous Fleetway House magazines *The Magnet* and *The Gem*. Most famous of all was his immortal creation Billy Bunter, the Fat Owl of the Greyfriars Remove, whose exploits together with those of the other boyhood heroes Harry Wharton and Co., delighted generations of readers from 1908 to 1940.

The war unhappily saw the end of *The Magnet* but though the post-war years brought the return of Greyfriars stories in other formats nothing ever quite recaptured the evergreen magic of the original much-loved boys' paper. It was for this reason that, two years ago, W. Howard Baker presented the first of his now world-renowned faithful facsimiles.

The brilliant character studies of boys and masters created by Frank Richards ensured his own immortality. Apart from the boys of Greyfriars, not forgetting Horace Coker, the duffer of the Fifth, there was the unforgettable Mr. Quelch, the Remove form-master ('a beast, but a just beast'), the Rev. Dr. Locke, venerable Headmaster of the School, William Gosling, the crusty, elbow-bending school porter who firmly believed that 'all boys should be drownded at birth', Paul Pontifex-Prout, the pompous form-master of the Fifth, the excitable but kind-hearted 'Mossoo' (M'sieu Charpentier, French master), the odious Cecil Ponsonby, involved in murky goings-on at The Three Fishers, and peppery Sir Hilton Popper, irascible School Governor. All these characters and many, many more are to be found in the pages of these volumes.

Each of the Howard Baker editions contains a complete series of stories from *The Magnet's* great golden age. And each is a fitting memorial to the glowing imagination, the humour, the humanity and the well-nigh incredible industry of its brilliant author.

Frank Richards loved writing for the young, and affirmed that no writer could do any better work in life than this. Certainly none did it better than Frank Richards himself.

The Greyfriars Story

A GREY old building in the trees
    From ages medieval
Has weathered all the centuries
    Of warfare and upheaval ;
A monastery of olden time,
    Its monks in Holy Orders,
Its chapter-bell would daily chime,
    And peace was in its borders.

But came a time of trouble, which
    Broke out among the tenants,
The ancient monastery grew rich,
    They suffered and did penance;
Alike from commoner and lord
    The monks took many acres,
Until the folk, with one accord,
    Defied these money-makers !

When later, the Franciscan Friars
    (As Grey Friars they were noted)
Were bringing peace throughout the shires,
    To lives of good devoted,
King Hal ascended to the throne !
    He thought the institution
Of churches ought to be his own,
    And caused the Dissolution !

The building stood till Edward's reign
    Deserted and neglected,
And then it blossomed out again,
    To honour resurrected,
" A School for Sons of Gentlemen,
    To Educate and Nourish ! "
And so it has remained since then,
    Long may it grow and flourish !

Now in its hallowed age it stands
    With years and honours greater,
With many sons in distant lands
    To praise their Alma Mater ;
While boys and Old Boys by the score
    Are swift to sing its glories,
Yet even they can't love it more
    Than we who read their stories.

E.E.BRISCOE

The Magnet

2ᴰ

Billy Bunter's Own Paper

MY LORD BUNTER !

If You Want to be Right in the Know, Consult—

The GREYFRIARS GUIDE

A TOUR OF THE SCHOOL.   The Head's Study.

(1)

"Abandon hope, all ye who enter
    here !"
Might well be carved upon
    This study door.
For some have entered, shivering with
        fear,
    And after they have gone
    Returned no more.
"Expelled from Greyfriars !" Melan-
        choly fate !
I hope I shan't earn that, at any rate.

(2)

But I myself have once experienced
    The fate of those who go
        To see the Head.
The interview was brief, and it com-
        menced
    With measured beat and slow.
        And it is said
My contributions to the argument
Were quite distinctly heard all over
        Kent !

(3)

Here sits the Head to take his share of
        ease
    When cares do not engage
        His busy mind,
Reclining in a chair with Sophocles,
    And as he turns the page
        He's sure to find
New beauties spring to light in every
        line.
That's HIS idea of fun. It isn't mine !

AFTER SCHOOL HOURS
Bunter Pays His Debts

(1)

When Bunter borrowed half-a-crown
From Clara Trevlyn in the town,
    We promised him our hardest kicks
        For trying such a game.
The half-a-crown he owed to her
He borrowed from Mauleverer,
    While Cherry lent him two-and-six,
        And Wharton did the same,
And Linley, from his meagre store,
Lent Bunter two-and-sixpence more.

(2)

From Newland, Bolsover, and Rake
Three shillings he contrived to take,
    He even hopefully appealed
        To Fishy—what a job !
Then Bull and Smithy each were
        dunned
For two-and-six towards the fund,
    And Samson Quincey Iffley Field
        Contributed a bob,
While Wibley, Morgan, Stott, and
        Brown
All helped towards that half-a-crown !

(3)

Then, going into Hall for tea,
He got a bob from Ogilvy,
    And Desmond gave him eighteen-
        pence
        With ready Irish tact ;
A bob from Bulstrode and from Todd,
And two from someone in the quad
    Who should have had much better
        sense
        (Myself, in point of fact !)
And when he put these items down
He found they made just half-a-crown !

THE GREYFRIARS ALPHABET
WILLIAM GOSLING,
The Greyfriars Porter

G is for GOSLING, the porter.
Who's not very fond of cold water
When choosing a drink for his pleasure,
But pours out a generous measure
Of something that's stronger and
        thicker,
No doubt a medicinal liquor !

He's crusty, ill-tempered, and surly,
And doesn't like chaps to be early
Returning from daily excursions ;
For one of his pleasant diversions
Is shutting the gates and reporting
Late-comers, who're fond of retorting
By ringing the gate bell, and calling
Him names which are often appalling !
So here's to his health, the old blighter,
And long may his "dooties" grow
        lighter !

ANSWER TO PUZZLE

He pushed the cork in !

GREYFRIARS GRINS

A toad was found in Loder's study
yesterday. It knew where to go !

We understand that Carne of the
Sixth intends to be a schoolmaster till
the future. It will be interesting to
know what will happen when he catches
himself breaking bounds at night.

Mr. Quelch's rheumatism is troubling
him again. As usual, it will hurt us
more than it does him.

Bolsover was seen lying on the floor
of the gym recently. It is believed he
is in training to be a heavy-weight
boxer.

Hobson's mater sent him a birthday
cake last week. In thanking her for it,
Hobson writes that, according to
Bunter, it was very tasty and cooked
just right, and he wishes he could have
tried it himself.

PUZZLE PAR

Bunter snooped a bottle of
ginger-wine, but he had no cork-
screw and couldn't draw the
cork. How did he get at the
wine without breaking the bottle,
smashing the cork, or pulling it
out ?

Answer at foot of column 2.

The Form-room clock stopped at half-
past three the other afternoon. It
wouldn't have mattered so much if
Smithy hadn't been in detention till
four o'clock. It was a quarter to five
before he realised the clock had
stopped, and the fact that he spent
three-quarters of an hour too long will
probably shorten his life.

Fisher T. Fish walked into a booby-
trap meant for Coker to-day. Good job
it wasn't wasted.

More Interesting Information in Next Saturday's MAGNET !

MY LORD BUNTER!

By FRANK RICHARDS

Playing the part of a lord at a magnificent castle, surrounded by wealth, and my-lorded by a host of servants, sounds good to Billy Bunter—and he jumps at the chance with both feet!

THE FIRST CHAPTER.
Bunter Starts First!

"BLOW!" said Billy Bunter.

Bunter looked peeved.

Most fellows, at Greyfriars School, were looking merry and bright that afternoon. It was a half-holiday, and a glorious winter's day; bright and sunny, but with a nip of frost in the air. Harry Wharton & Co. came out of the House, after dinner, looking as if they found life really enjoyable. But Bunter looked, and felt, peeved.

Standing in the quad, Bunter was going through his pockets, one after another. He searched them all with great thoroughness—and he searched them all in vain.

Not for the first time in his fat career, Billy Bunter was short of that necessary article, cash.

That morning—as had happened on many other mornings—he had been disappointed about a postal order he was expecting. And that afternoon, the need of cash was pressing and urgent.

The First Eleven were playing at Redclyffe—the last fixture before breaking up for the Christmas holidays. Quite a number of fellows were going over to see them beat Redclyffe—or be beaten by Redclyffe, as the case might be. Smithy of the Remove was taking some friends in a car—the Bounder always had money to burn. The Famous Five were going on their bikes. Billy Bunter was going by train—if cash was available for the ticket!

Not that Bunter was fearfully interested in the doughty deeds of the First Eleven. Had they been playing at home, the fat Owl of the Remove would probably not have taken the trouble to roll down to Big Side. But Smithy was standing a spread at the Rotunda, at Redclyffe, after the match. Soccer did not draw Bunter, but a spread—especially one of the Bounder's lavish spreads—drew him with an irresistible attraction!

Wherefore did Billy Bunter go through pocket after pocket, in the vain hope of discovering some forgotten or overlooked coin therein.

Deep in that urgent research, the fat Owl did not observe five juniors watching him from a little distance, with grinning faces.

Harry Wharton & Co. were quite interested. Pocket after pocket was turned out, without revealing anything in the

••••••••••••••••••••••••••••••••••••••

Amazing and Amusing Yarn of Schoolboy Adventure, featuring HARRY WHARTON & CO., of GREYFRIARS.

••••••••••••••••••••••••••••••••••••••

nature of coin of the realm. But quite an interesting variety of things were revealed. There was a handkerchief, sorely in need of a wash. There was a penknife with both blades broken. There was a stump of pencil, with half an ancient bullseye adhering to it. There was a considerable amount of fluff and dust, and some aniseed balls. There was a note-case—empty. But there was no coinage of any description—not a "bob," not a "tanner," not even a humble "brown." And Bunter, in a tone of deep feeling, said again:

"Blow!"

"Ha, ha, ha!"

Billy Bunter blinked round, through his big spectacles, as that sound of merriment fell on his fat ears. Then he spotted the Famous Five. He frowned at them.

"Blessed if I can see anything to cackle at!" he grunted. "I say, you fellows, I'm stony! I shall have to go over on a bike!"

Bob Cherry chortled.

"You'll go over, all right, if you get on that jigger of yours!" he said. "It hardly holds together! You'll go over wallop!"

"If you'd mended it for me, it would be all right!" grunted Bunter. "You can't say I haven't asked you! I've asked you a dozen times, at least! It doesn't want much doing to it, either—only the chain's broken, and the pedals are off. and one of the wheels buckled, and the mudguards twisted, and a few other things. Look here, you've got time to put it to rights before you start."

"I'll lend you a hand, if you like!" said Bob. "We don't start for half-an-hour! Come on!"

Billy Bunter did not come on. He was not looking for work.

"I think I'd better borrow a bike!" he remarked. "I say, you fellows, I've asked Smithy to lend me his—he won't want it, as he's going over in a car. He's refused. Selfish beast, you know!"

Harry Wharton laughed.

"Perhaps he doesn't want to see it with the chain broken, and the pedals off, and a wheel buckled, and the mudguards twisted, and a few other things!" he suggested.

"Ha, ha, ha!"

"Well, look here, suppose one of you

THE MAGNET LIBRARY.—No. 1,556.

fellows lend me a bike !" said Bunter.
"You're not so selfish as Smithy——"

"We are !" grinned Bob Cherry,
"Quite !"

"The quitefulness is terrific, my esteemed fat Bunter !" chuckled Hurree
Jamset Ram Singh.

"Well, I've got to go over to Redclyffe: I can't miss that spread at the
Rotunda—I mean, the last First Eleven
match of the term. If you won't lend me
a bike, lend me five bob for my fare."

"It's two bob return to Redclyffe, you
fat spoofer !" said Johnny Bull.

"Third-class," sneered Bunter.
"Travelling third may do for you
fellows. It would hardly do for me."

"You couldn't travel third?" asked
Frank Nugent.

"Hardly ! You see——"

"No good offering to lend you two
bob, then ?"

"Eh ? Oh ! Ah ! Yes ! Certainly ! Hand
it over, old chap !"

"Ha, ha, ha !"

Frank Nugent extracted a shilling
from his pocket. Harry Wharton produced another. Both were grabbed by
a fat and grubby hand.

"Thanks," said Bunter, "I'll let you
have this back out of my postal order,
when—when it comes. The fact is, I'm
expecting a good many Christmas tips
from my titled relations. Now, you
other fellows, put a bob each to this,
and——"

"Good-bye, Bunter !"

"I say, you fellows, don't walk off
while a chap's talking to you !" roared
Bunter.

But the Famous Five did walk off.
As they generally travelled third themselves, they seemed to see no special
reason why Billy Bunter should be too
fearfully aristocratic to do the same.

"Beasts !" hooted Bunter : doubtless
by way of thanks for the two shillings.

The fat junior blinked after the chums
of the Remove, through his big spectacles. Then he blinked at the window
of the school shop.

He hesitated.

It is well said that he who hesitates
is lost. The lure of the tuck was irresistible to Billy Bunter. He did not start
for the gates, to catch that train for
Redclyffe: and rolled therein.

In five minutes, Billy Bunter had
consumed jam tarts to the exact value of
two shillings.

Then he rolled out of the tuck-shop
again—jammy, sticky, and stony.

The problem of transport, which
Harry Wharton and Frank Nugent
fancied they had solved for him, still
remained to be solved.

But Bunter knew how to solve it.

Bob Cherry had said they were not
starting for half an hour. They were
not likely, therefore, to be at the bike-
shed yet. If the coast was clear, Bunter
could borrow a bike.

He did not think of going over on his
own dilapidated jigger. It was only too
likely that if he tried it on, he would,
as Bob suggested, go over wallop. He
decided on Harry Wharton's bike.

Like Moses of old, Bunter looked this
way and that way, as he approached
the bike-shed. Like Moses again, he
saw no man. The coast was clear. He
rolled into the bike-shed, and lifted
Wharton's handsome jigger from the
stand. The saddle was rather high for
Bunter : but he did not bother about
putting it down, for two good reasons.
He had no time to waste: and he was
lazy. He wheeled the machine out, and
trundled it down to the gate.

Skinner of the Remove, in the gateway, glanced at him and grinned.

THE MAGNET LIBRARY.—No. 1,556.

"Whose bike ?" he asked. "Fellow
lent you his jigger?"

"Eh? Yes ! Exactly."

"Does he know he has?" grinned
Skinner.

"Yah !"

Bunter trundled the bike out. He
mounted in the road, and pedalled away
cheerfully for Redclyffe.

What Harry Wharton was going to do
for a bike that afternoon, when the time
came to start, was a problem that was
left for the captain of the Remove to
solve. Billy Bunter really had no time
to bother about other fellows' troubles !

THE SECOND CHAPTER.

Bagging Bunter !

"WHAT the dickens——"

"What's up ?"

"Where's my bike ?"

"Eh ? Isn't it here ?"

"If it is, it's become invisible !"
grunted Harry Wharton. "My hat !
Has some silly ass had the cheek to
borrow my bike?"

"Oh, my hat !"

Four members of the Famous Five
had taken their machines; but one
member of the famous Co. was staring
round the bike-shed with an exasperated
stare.

Wharton's handsome jigger was conspicuous only by its absence.

"What cheeky ass——" roared
Wharton.

"Dash it all, it's too thick !" exclaimed Bob Cherry. "Everybody
wants to get over to Redclyffe this
afternoon, but bagging another man's
jigger——"

"Who the dickens——"

Harry Wharton stepped out of the
bike-shed, and looked up and down the
path outside. There was no sign of his
bike to be seen, however. Billy Bunter
was half an hour on his way. Bunter
was not a quick traveller on a bike, but
he was already far from Greyfriars.

Skinner, who was lounging in the
gateway, glanced at the exasperated
captain of the Remove with a grin.
After seeing Bunter start, he had rather
expected some fellow to miss a bike.
Wharton looked like the fellow who had
missed it ! Which rather amused the
amiable Skinner.

"Seen anything of my bike,
Skinner?" called out Wharton.

"Didn't you lend it to Bunter ?"
asked Skinner.

"What ? Bunter ? No !"

"Somebody lent him a jigger !"
chuckled Skinner. "He wasn't riding
his own, as it didn't sound like a jazz
band !"

"Bunter !" gasped Wharton.
"Bunter's bike's in the shed—not that
it's any good ! Did you see Bunter on
a bike ? When ?"

"About half an hour ago !" chortled
Skinner. "He's half-way to Redclyffe
on it by this time !"

Harry Wharton ran out of the gate.
But there was no sign of Bunter on the
road. Bunter was far away.

His friends joined him, wheeling their
machines. But they did not mount.
Bunter's problem of transport had to be
solved by the captain of the Remove
before they could start.

"That fat scoundrel !" gasped
Wharton. "That podgy pirate ! That
bloated brigand ! Why, we lent him his
railway fare—and now he's bagged my
bike ! I—I—I'll——"

Words failed the captain of the
Remove.

"You lent him his railway fare !"

chortled Skinner. "I noticed he
looked jammy ! Ha, ha, ha !"

"The fat villain !" exclaimed Bob.

"The blithering octopus !" said Frank
Nugent. "We'd better get after him
and——"

"He's miles away by this time. I—
I'd burst him all over the Redclyffe
road if I could snaffle him !" gasped
Wharton. "He's blewed his railway
fare on tuck, and bagged my bike !
I—I—I'll——"

"Can't borrow a jigger !" said
Johnny Bull. "Every fellow wants his
bike this afternoon. What the thump
shall——"

"You fellows get off," said Wharton.
"I shall have to go by train. I'll join
you in Redclyffe. If you catch Bunter
on the road, heave him into the ditch.
I shall have to sprint for the train,
too——"

"My esteemed chum——" began
Hurree Jamset Ram Singh.

"No time to waste, if I'm to catch
a train, Inky !" said the captain of the
Remove. "I'll cut off——"

"The English proverb remarks that
more haste is less speedy than a bird
in the bush, my esteemed Wharton. It
would be terrifically better to catch the
absurd Bunter than to catch the ridiculous train !" said the Nabob of
Bhanipur.

"But how, fathead——"

Hurree Jamset Ram Singh pointed a
dusky finger at a car that was standing
in the road. It was a four-seater, with
five fellows in it—Vernon-Smith, Tom
Redwing, Ogilvy, Russell and Peter
Todd. The Bounder had just stepped
in, and it was about to start.

"The esteemed Smithy is going to
Redclyffe," said Hurree Jamset Ram
Singh. "The absurd car will pass the
fatheaded Bunter on the road. If the
idiotic Smithy would give you a lift
to catch Bunter——"

"Oh !" exclaimed Harry.

He rushed across to the car.

"Hold on a minute, Smithy !" he
exclaimed.

"Two, if you like," answered the
Bounder. "What's up ?"

"That fat villain, Bunter, has borrowed my bike !" gasped Harry. "He
can't have done more than a couple of
miles: if you could cram me in till you
pass him——"

The Bounder chuckled.

"Not much room," he said, "but
we'll manage it. Shove up, you
fellows !"

"Thanks !" gasped Wharton.

The fellows in the car squeezed up,
and the captain of the Remove crammed
in. He waved his hand to his friends.

"Follow on, you men !" he called out.
"I'll wait for you when I've bagged my
bike !"

"Right-ho !"

The car started, and whizzed away on
the road to Redclyffe.

Bob Cherry and Johnny Bull, Frank
Nugent and Hurree Jamset Ram
Singh mounted their jiggers and followed. They were all good cyclists,
but they had no chance of keeping
Smithy's car in sight. They pedalled
after it at a good speed, but the car
soon dropped them.

But if they had no chance of keeping
up with it, still less chance had Billy
Bunter of escaping capture. In half an
hour it was probable that Bunter had
done about two miles—perhaps a little
more. And it was five miles, by road,
to Redclyffe.

Harry Wharton had no doubt of
sighting him before he had covered half
the distance.

It was undoubtedly a squeeze in the
car, with six fellows in the space

planned for four. But it was not going to last very long. Vernon-Smith had told the chauffeur to cover the ground, and the car was going all out. The miles flew under the whizzing wheels.

Its occupants watched the road, with grinning faces, for a fat figure on a bike ahead. A couple of miles from Greyfriars the Redclyffe road ran between bordering woods, winding a good deal. As the car whizzed round a bend, the Bounder pointed.

"Jolly old Bunter!" he said.

"Oh, good!" exclaimed Harry.

Ahead of the car, there was Bunter, labouring along on the borrowed bike. He was not making a great speed. At that distance from Greyfriars he was entering on the rise of Redclyffe Hill—and hills always gave Bunter trouble on a bike. Moreover, he was finding difficulties on a bike too high for him. He had to plunge at the pedals to reach them, and every now and then he missed, and the bike wobbled wildly.

Really, it would have been less trouble to get off and lower the saddle. But Billy Bunter, like many lazy people, often took a lot of trouble to save a little.

He plunged and wobbled on, happily unaware of the car rapidly overtaking him. Even at his slow rate of progress he had plenty of time to get to Redclyffe. The possibility of missing the football match did not worry him unduly, so long as he did not miss the spread which was to follow at the Rotunda. Gasping a good deal, gurgling considerably, Billy Bunter plunged and wobbled on, while the car ran him down.

Vernon-Smith called to the chauffeur. The car shot past Bunter, and stopped a dozen yards ahead of him.

Harry Wharton jumped out.

"Thanks, Smithy!" he said, as he shut the door.

"O.K.!" grinned the Bounder, and the car shot onward again, the occupants looking back with grinning faces.

They saw Harry Wharton rush at the grunting, gasping, labouring cyclist. They saw Bunter wobble wildly as he grasped the machine and pitch off. They heard a bump and a roar as he landed. Then the car shot on out of sight and whizzed on to Redclyffe.

THE THIRD CHAPTER.

Beastly for Bunter !

BILLY BUNTER roared.

He roared, and roared again. For some moments the fat Owl of the Remove did not quite know what was happening to him. He was dimly aware that somebody had jumped out of a car and rushed at him and pitched him off the borrowed bike.

Now he was sitting in the grass by the roadside, in quite a dizzy state, roaring, and blinking wildly over the spectacles, that had slid down his fat little nose.

"Ow! Ow! Ow! Yaroooh!" roared Bunter. "Beast! Rotter! Yaroop! Gimme that bike! You're not going to pinch that bike! I say, it ain't mine—a fellow lent it to me! You gimme that bike, you beast!"

Bunter tottered to his feet. Harry Wharton stood holding the bike, looking in the direction of Greyfriars for his friends. He had fully intended to boot Bunter up and down the Redclyffe road when he captured him; but the recovery of the jigger had a mollifying effect. Bunter had had a bump, and he had miles to walk, whatever the

direction he took, so the captain of the Remove left it at that.

The fat junior set his spectacles straight on his fat little nose, and blinked at him. Then he recognised the owner of the bike.

"Oh!" gasped Bunter. "Is—is—is that you, old chap?"

"Yes; you fat sweep!"

"I—I—I say, how—how did you get here?" gasped Bunter. "Mean to say you got a car to get after me, simply because I'd borrowed your bike——"

"Smithy gave me a lift, you bloated burglar!"

"The beast!" gasped Bunter. "The awful rotter! Why, I asked him to take me in his car—then I shouldn't have needed a bike. He wouldn't. And he goes and gives you a lift. The rotter! I—I say, old chap, you're not bagging that bike, are you?"

"Sort of," said Harry.

"Oh, really, Wharton! I say, what am I going to do, if you bag that bike?" exclaimed Bunter, in dismay.

"Is that a conundrum?"

"Beast! It's three miles more to Redclyffe—uphill, too!" exclaimed Bunter. "I can't walk it. I—I say, old chap, don't be a beast! Look here, you're ever so much better a walker than I am."

"I hope so," agreed Wharton.

"Well, look here, you walk it, and let me have the bike."

"Ha, ha, ha!"

"What are you cackling at?" howled Bunter.

"Your little joke."

"I'm not joking, fathead!"

"You are!"

"Beast!" roared Bunter.

Four cyclists came in sight on the road, and Harry Wharton waved his hand to them. They waved back, and came whizzing on.

Billy Bunter blinked at them through his big spectacles.

"Oh crikey!" gasped Bunter. "I—I say, Harry, old chap, I—I think you might let me have that bike. After all I've done for you, you know."

"Hallo, hallo, hallo!" roared Bob Cherry, as he came whizzing up. "Got it?"

"The gotfulness is terrific!" grinned Hurree Jamset Ram Singh.

"Booted Bunter?" asked Johnny Bull, as he jumped down.

"Oh, really, Bull——"

"The bootfulness is the proper caper."

"Oh, really, Inky——"

"Come on!" said Harry Wharton, putting a leg over his machine. "Good-bye, Bunter! Think twice before you pinch a bike next time."

"I say, you fellows, I can't stop here!" roared Bunter. "I say, it's three miles on to Redclyffe, and nearly three back to Greyfriars. I can't walk it."

"It's mostly downhill," said Bob.

"I tell you I can't walk it!"

"And I tell you it's mostly downhill! Turn over, and roll home like a barrel."

"Ha, ha, ha!"

"You—you silly ass!" gasped Bunter. "Look here, if you leave me stranded here like this, what do you think I'm going to do?"

"I think you're going to be a bit more careful about pinching a fellow's bike," answered Harry Wharton.

"Beast!"

"Look here, he ought to be jolly well booted!" said Johnny Bull.

"Yah!"

"Oh, let him rip!" said Bob Cherry.

"I don't suppose we shall ever see Bunter alive again."

"Eh? Why not?"

"He will be dead before he's walked three miles."

"Ha, ha, ha!"

The Famous Five, chuckling, remounted, and rode off for Redclyffe.

Billy Bunter glared after them, with a glare that almost cracked his spectacles.

"I say, you fellows!" he yelled.

The cyclists whizzed on.

"Beasts!" roared Bunter.

They vanished round the next bend of the road. Billy Bunter was left on his lonely own.

He was left overwhelmed with dismay.

Borrowing a bike, without the owner's leave, evidently had its drawbacks. Billy Bunter's last state was worse than his first. At Greyfriars, if only he hadn't borrowed that bike, he might have found some means of transport. Half-way to Redclyffe, on a lonely country road, there was no hope. Traffic was sparse, and there was not much chance of a lift.

Bunter was left to depend wholly on his fat little legs.

There were fellows in the Greyfriars Remove who would walk three miles, and hardly be aware that they had walked at all. But Billy Bunter was not one of those fellows. Three yards was about as much as he really cared for.

"Oh lor'!" groaned Bunter.

He blinked dismally up and down the road. He had to walk. It was an awful prospect; but there was no other. He debated in his fat mind whether to walk on, or walk back. It was nearly as far back to Greyfriars as on to Redclyffe, and at Redclyffe there was Smithy's spread at the Rotunda. That decided Bunter in favour of Redclyffe. He groaned and started.

It was awful. With every step it grew awfuller. Bunter plugged on, gasping and gurgling. Every now and then cyclists passed him. Crowds of Greyfriars fellows were going over to Redclyffe to see Wingate and his team play. But it was useless to think of asking any of those fellows to get down and walk, and let Bunter have his bike. It was a selfish world, as Bunter knew only too well.

The fat Owl was still plugging wearily on, long after the last cyclist from Greyfriars had passed and disappeared. He was still wearily plugging when they had all gathered on the Redclyffe ground, watching the Soccer match.

Harry Wharton & Co., in that cheery crowd, watched the game, and cheered old Wingate when he put the ball in—absolutely forgetful of a perspiring, fat junior plugging slowly and wearily on the Redclyffe road. Sad to relate, they had forgotten his fat existence.

THE FOURTH CHAPTER.

Bunter on the Spot !

CHUG, chug, chug!

Billy Bunter blinked round wearily at the sound of a motor-bike on the road.

Bunter was not walking now.

He was resting.

He needed a rest. He had covered a whole mile on foot. Actually it was one mile, though it seemed more like a hundred to Bunter.

In a mile, there were one thousand

seven hundred and sixty yards. Bunter could have done the sixty fairly well. But every one of the remaining thousand and seven hundred, was a yard too much.

He was going to be too late for the Soccer match at Redclyffe School. That did not worry him, so long as he was in time for the spread at the Rotunda. It was that enticing thought that kept Bunter going for a whole mile, uphill.

Now it kept him going no longer. Even at the risk of missing the Bounder's lavish spread, Bunter had to have a rest—and a long rest.

He had blinked round wearily for a favourable spot. In summer he would have disposed his fat limbs in the grass by the roadside. But in December the grass was wet and chilly. He blinked into the wood that bordered the road, and happily discovered a pile of logs left by the wood-cutters.

Sitting on a log, leaning back against the pile, the weary fat Owl rested his weary fat legs, and recovered a little from his uncommon exertions.

He was beginning to think of getting a move on again, when that chugging from a motor-bike fell on his ears. He wondered whether it might be Coker of the Fifth on his stink-bike, and whether there was a bare possibility, if it was, of Coker giving a fellow a lift.

Then his fat ears told him that the motor-bike was coming from the direction of Redclyffe. It was going in the wrong direction for Bunter, and he lost all interest in it at once.

It came down the road at great speed, and suddenly shut off. The chug, chug, chugging ceased. Then, to his surprise, Bunter heard a brushing sound, and realised that the motor-bike was being pushed off the road into the thickets.

He blinked round again.

But the pile of logs was between him and the road—the loose log on which he sat being on the side towards the deep wood. He could see nothing of the motor-bike, or its rider.

The brushing sound ceased. Only that pile of logs was between Bunter and the motor-bike. Why anyone should stop there, at the very loneliest spot on the Redclyffe road, and park his machine in the thickets was a mystery to Bunter. He was about to rise to his feet, and blink round the stack of logs, when a muttering voice fell on his ears.

"Quick! The rope—quick!"

"What's the hurry? That old fool is not doing more than twenty on his Ford, and we did nearer fifty on the jigger."

"Don't waste time, you fool!"

"O.K.! But there's some traffic on this road——"

"Not much."

"Some, anyway. We don't want to catch the wrong bird. Look here, Smiler, don't get that rope across the road till we spot the Ford. We want that old fool, Lanchester, but we don't want anybody else."

"I saw the road clear in the other direction—nobody coming up from Courtfield, Ferret."

"The road's full of turns! I tell you, get this end fixed on a tree, and watch for the Ford. I'll cut across and fasten the other end as soon as you spot it!"

There was a grunt.

"Oh, all right! Fix it on this side, anyhow!"

"O.K.!"

Billy Bunter sat perfectly still. Every word, spoken not more than ten feet from him, came clearly to his fat ears.

Obviously, the two men had not the faintest idea that anyone was at hand. The spot was lonely; the woodland dank and dreary; and no one would have expected any fellow to be sitting about in a wood in December.

They saw nothing of the fat Owl of Greyfriars—and in his alarm and terror Bunter was careful that they should hear nothing.

Billy Bunter was not quick on the uptake. But even Bunter's fat brain could not doubt the meaning of this. Those two men, within ten feet of him, were motor-bandits, planning to wreck a car coming along from Redclyffe.

Bunter's fat heart quaked.

If they spotted him there——

Two ruthless rascals, who were planning to wreck a car, by stretching a taut rope across the road, were not likely to stand on ceremony, with anyone who spotted them at this dastardly work.

Bunter felt a tremble run along his fat limbs. He hardly breathed.

Sounds came to his ears. He knew that a rope was being run round the trunk of a tree beside the road and knotted there. It was in readiness for one of the rascals to cut across the road and fasten the other end to a tree on the other side, as soon as the Ford was spotted in the distance.

Bunter suppressed a gasp of terror. The muttering voice of the man called Smiler came to his ears again.

"Stand steady with the rope, Ferret. I'll watch out."

"O.K. He won't be here for ten minutes yet. Keep your gun handy."

Billy Bunter barely repressed a squeak.

"I've got it handy, you fool!" came back the Smiler's mutter. "I fancy the sight of it will be enough for old Lanchester. The old fool is not likely to guess that there's nothing in it."

Bunter heard a chuckle from Ferret.

The fat junior breathed again.

Evidently, from the Smiler's words, he was going to hold up the motorist with an unloaded gun. The rascals were not quite so desperate as Bunter had supposed at first.

"The old fool's too valuable to plug, anyway," went on the Smiler. "But I fancy he will jump to orders with a gun looking him in the eye!"

"I should smile!" agreed the Ferret. There was a rustle in the thickets again. To Bunter's horror, the Smiler came into his line of vision, moving past the end of the stack of logs.

But he was facing towards the road, his back to Bunter, and he did not look round, or think of looking round.

Bunter, his little round eyes popping behind his big round spectacles, blinked at his back in terror.

All he saw of the Smiler was the back of a dark overcoat, and a soft hat pulled low down. But he noticed that the man was slim in build, though with rather broad shoulders, and quick and active.

Bunter saw him only for a moment or two.

Then he stepped out into the road, and the trees and thickets hid him, much to the fat junior's relief.

There was the sound of a car on the road. But it was evidently not the car they wanted, for it roared by undeterred.

Bunter heard the Ferret's voice again:

"I guess I told you, Smiler! You don't want that rope across too soon. I'm telling you!"

Only a grunt answered from the man watching the road.

Billy Bunter rose softly to his feet.

They did not know that he was there—and the sooner he was not there, the safer Bunter was going to feel.

Whether the Ford would rush on the stretched rope, and be piled up in wreckage, or whether the driver would see the danger in time, and jam on his brakes, Bunter did not know. As it was broad daylight, it was probable that the driver would see the rope, and stop in time. But the rascals were running the risk of a smash. In any case, there was going to be a "hold-up"—and Billy Bunter had no taste for hold-ups off the films. He wanted to get away from that spot, and he wanted to get away quick!

Fortunately, that was easy. He could not have reached the road without revealing himself to the two hold-up men—in which case there was little doubt that Ferret and Smiler would have grabbed him at once, and very likely knocked him on the head. But it was easy to go farther into the wood—and that Bunter did, without losing time.

He trod softly and cautiously, in dread of being heard and followed. His heart missed a beat as a twig snapped under his foot.

He heard a sharp exclamation from the Smiler.

"What's that, Ferret? Did you hear——"

"O.K.! You're all nerves, Smiler!" Grunt, from the man on the roadside.

Billy Bunter tiptoed away. It was a cold December day, but the perspiration clotted his fat face. Deeper and deeper into the wood the fat junior crept, till at last he was safe from sight and sound of the motor-bandits.

Then he turned in the direction of Redclyffe, to get back to the road at a safe distance from the ambush.

He emerged into the road, beyond a winding bend that barred him from the sight of the Smiler.

Once in the road, the fat junior took to his heels. He forgot that he was tired, in his eager haste to get to the safest possible distance from the two rascals behind him.

Puffing and blowing, gasping and gurgling, the fat junior ran. Seldom had Billy Bunter covered the ground so quickly.

Honk, honk!

A motor-horn sounded in front of him, from a car approaching from the direction of Redclyffe.

Bunter blinked at it, gasping.

Up to that moment Billy Bunter had been thinking only of his own fat and important person. Now he realised that this was the car that the two motor-bandits were watching for, beyond the bend down the road. It was a Ford car, driven by a chauffeur, with an old gentleman sitting inside, whose silvery hair showed under a shining silk hat.

Honk!

Bunter did not get out of the way. He stood in the middle of the road and waved his fat hand frantically.

"Stop!" he squeaked. "I say, stop! Danger! For goodness' sake stop! Oh crikey, stop!"

The driver stared at him and braked. The Ford car came to a halt a few yards short of the excited, fat Owl.

THE FIFTH CHAPTER.

Bunter Gets a Lift!

"OH crikey!" gasped Bunter.
The chauffeur stared at
him.

"What's up?" he demanded.
"Road up, or what?"

"Oh, no! Yes! Oh crikey!" gasped
the fat Owl. "I say, don't go on!
Stop! I say, they're watching for you!
Stop, for goodness' sake! If you run
into that rope—— Oh crikey!"

The chauffeur simply stared. Having
stared at Bunter, he stared up the road.
Nothing was to be seen as far as the
bend.

"Yes, yes!" spluttered Bunter. "I
say, you'd better turn back!"

The old gentleman gave Bunter's fat,
excited face a very keen look. The
chauffeur gave a grunt.

"You can see no one, Denham?"
asked the man in the car.

"No, Sir Peter! Shall I drive on?"

Billy Bunter realised that the old
gentleman was not Mr. Lanchester. He
was Sir Peter Lanchester.

"I say, don't go on," gasped Bunter.
"You'll run into the rope—I say, one
of them had a gun!"

Another grunt from the chauffeur.
Denham did not seem to believe in the

"I—I say, sir!" exclaimed Bunter.
This was a chance the fat Owl was not
likely to lose. "I was going to Redclyffe
—I say, sir, if you're going back, will
you give me a lift?"

"Certainly, my boy! Step in!"

Bunter fairly bolted in.

Denham backed and turned the car.

Billy Bunter blinked anxiously towards
the bend in the road, beyond which
the ambush was laid. He was in dread
every moment of seeing Smiler or
Ferret appear in view.

But neither of them appeared. Utterly
unaware of the fat junior's presence on
the spot, and never dreaming that their
intended victim had been warned, they

Billy Bunter laboured up the hill on the borrowed bike that was too high for him, happily unaware of the car rapidly
overtaking him !

"Look 'ere——" he began.

A silk hat, with a fringe of silvery
hair under it, was put out of the car.
The chauffeur did not seem much impressed by Bunter's warning. But it
was different with the old gentleman in
the car. There was a very startled
expression on his face.

"Stop, Denham!" he rapped quickly.
"Here, my boy! Come here! What is
it? Is there anything on the road
ahead? Tell me at once!"

Bunter tottered to the side of the car.

"Yes," he gasped. "Two awful
beasts—they're putting a rope across to
stop a car—— I say, are you Mr.
Lanchester?"

"My name is Lanchester, certainly."

"That's the name I heard them mention—they said old Lanchester!" gasped
Bunter. "I heard them—I was in the
wood, see? I—I came away as quick
as I could to—to—to warn you——"

"Two men, did you say?"

"Yes. One beast called the other
Smiler, and the other beast called him
Ferret!" gasped Bunter. "I heard
them——"

"You heard them speak of me by
name?"

rope, or the gun: or, indeed in the
motor-bandits at all.

"No!" said Sir Peter Lanchester.
"Turn the car, Denham! We shall cer-
tainly not go on to Greyfriars this way.
Get back to Redclyffe."

"The road looks clear enough, sir!"

"The boy has heard my name!" said
the old gentleman. "He could hardly
have guessed it, Denham. He has heard
it. Did you hear anything else in
reference to me, my boy?"

"Yes," gasped Bunter. "One of them
said the old fool——"

"Eh?"

"He said the old fool wasn't doing
more than twenty in the Ford——"

"Oh!"

"I expect you saw them pass you!"
said Bunter. "Two men on a motor-bike!
They got ahead of you and stopped."

The chauffeur gave Bunter a quick
look. Evidently, he recalled having seen
two men on a motor-bike whiz past the
car.

"Go back at once, Denham!" rapped
the old gentleman. "This is another
attempt of those scoundrels—I have no
doubt of it! Back the car and turn at
once, Denham."

"Very well, sir!"

were still waiting for the Ford to come
by—Smiler watching for the car, Ferret
holding the rope ready to cut across and
bar the road with it. Probably, after a
time, they would wonder why the Ford
did not appear—but so far, they were
waiting and watching.

They were not likely to see that Ford
now.

Having backed and turned, Denham
let the car out for Redclyffe, and whizzed away at a good speed.

The old gentleman looked back
several times with an anxious puck-
ered brow. But he settled down comfortably on the soft leather cushions at
last.

Billy Bunter blinked at him, curiously
and inquisitively.

He could see that the old gentleman,
though startled and alarmed by his
warning, was not surprised by it. His
words to the chauffeur showed that he
was not without some expectation of
danger. He had said that it was
"another attempt!" He was losing no
time in getting out of that danger.

"I am very much obliged to you, my
boy!" said Sir Peter, with a very benevo-
lent glance at Bunter. "I had no idea

that those rascals had been watching me —but they must have done so, to know that I was taking this road. I shall leave my car at Redclyffe, and take the train—do you know the station for Greyfriars School?"

"Oh, yes, rather, sir!" answered Bunter. "Change at Courtfield for Friardale. I belong to Greyfriars."

"Indeed!" said Sir Peter. "I am going there to see an old friend, whom I have not seen for very many years. Possibly you know Mr. Quelch?"

Billy Bunter grinned. He knew Mr. Quelch quite well: and had, in fact, been whacked by that gentleman, only that morning!

"He's my Form-master, sir. I'm in the Remove."

"What is your name, my boy?"

"Bunter, sir—W i l l i a m George Bunter."

"I shall remember you," said Sir Peter Lanchester. "I shall certainly mention to Mr. Quelch the service you have rendered me—the very great service." He gave Bunter a kindly smile. "Some boys would have been frightened, and would have run off—but you came to warn me of my danger! I shall not forget that, Master Bunter."

Billy Bunter opened his mouth—and shut it again.

Bunter, as a matter of fact, had been frightened, and had run off—and it was not till he saw the Ford in the road, that he remembered the motorist who was in danger.

Still, he saw no occasion for mentioning that circumstance to old Sir Peter.

If the old baronet supposed that Billy Bunter had displayed pluck and presence of mind, Bunter was not the fellow to undeceive him.

"Drive to the police station at Redclyffe, Denham!" added Sir Peter.

"Yes, Sir Peter."

"You had better come with me to the police station, and give what description you can of those rascals!" added the old gentleman. "It is possible that the police may be in time to find them and take them into custody."

"Oh!" stammered Bunter. "I—I've got to get somewhere in Redclyffe this afternoon, sir—I—I've got some friends expecting me at the Rotunda."

"I will drive you to the Rotunda, wherever that is, after we have seen the police!" said Sir Peter, with a smile.

"Oh, that's all right!" agreed Bunter.

The football match at Redclyffe School was almost over by this time, but that did not matter, so long as Bunter was in time for the Bounder's spread.

True, it was only a Ford, and as a matter of choice, Bunter preferred a Rolls. Still, it was a very nice Ford—quite different from the paternal Ford at home. And Sir Peter Lanchester was a very wealthy looking old gentleman—titled, too. Bunter did not know whether he was a knight or a baronet, yet: but anyhow, he had a title, and Bunter liked titles. Swanking up to the Rotunda in a big car driven by a liveried chauffeur was quite agreeable to William George Bunter.

On the whole, he was not sorry, after all, that Wharton had recaptured that bike. His fat face was cheery and contented, as he rolled into Redclyffe in Sir Peter Lanchester's car.

THE SIXTH CHAPTER.
And a Boot!

"HALLO, hallo, hallo!"

"Bunter!"

"The fat bounder got a lift!"

A good many Greyfriars juniors were strolling towards the tea-

shop in Redclyffe High Street, after the football match. Harry Wharton & Co. came along in time to see a handsome car stop outside the Rotunda, and the chauffeur open the door for Billy Bunter to alight.

The car rolled away leaving the fat junior on the pavement blinking round through his big spectacles. He grinned at the sight of the Famous Five.

"I say, you fellows——" squeaked Bunter.

"So you bagged a lift on the road, you fat foozler?" asked Harry Wharton.

"My friend Sir Peter offered me a seat in his car," said Bunter, loftily.

"Eh!"

"Who?"

"Which?"

"My friend Sir Peter Lanchester," said Bunter, breezily. "He's going to see old Quelch, you know—didn't you notice him in the car? An old sportsman with a white topknot. Decent old boy. You see, I saved his life——"

"You whatted?"

"Saved his life!" said Bunter, airily. "He was stopped by a gang of motor-bandits on the Redclyffe Road, and I weighed in. We've just been to the police about it."

The Famous Five blinked at William George Bunter. They were rather used to tall tales from Bunter, and they never expected him to tell the truth. But this seemed rather unusually tall, even for Bunter.

"You—you—you saved his life, did you?" gasped Bob Cherry. "You—you weighed in on a gang of motor-bandits——"

"Yes, rather! Knocked them right and left——"

"Oh crikey!"

"Dozens of them, I suppose?" asked Nugent.

"Well, to be exact, there were only two," said Bunter, "and I don't mind admitting I was glad of it—I'm not at all sure that I could have handled more than two of them—at once, you know."

"Ha, ha, ha!" yelled the Famous Five.

They were quite sure that Bunter could not have handled more than two motor-bandits at once. They were sure that he could not have handled one. Indeed, they were quite sure that he could not have handled half a motor-bandit.

"Blessed if I see anything to cackle at!" said Bunter, warmly. "You should have heard what Sir Peter said, that's all! He said 'Gallant lad! I owe you my life!' His very words."

"Did you have the neck to flag that car, and ask for a lift?" inquired Bob Cherry.

"No!" hooted Bunter. "Haven't I told you? The old johnny offered me a lift after shaving his wife—I mean, saving his life! If you fellows don't believe me——"

"The believefulness is not terrific!" chuckled Hurree Jamset Ram Singh.

"Ha, ha, ha!"

"I tell you they were holding up that car—that car that I came here in!" roared Bunter.

"Jolly obliging of them!" remarked Bob Cherry. "I suppose a car would need holding up with you in it——"

"Ha, ha, ha!"

"You silly ass! I mean they were holding up the car, with guns and—and things, and I jolly well tackled them, and then——"

"Then you woke up?"

"Ha, ha, ha!"

Billy Bunter snorted. Evidently, the Famous Five did not believe a word of it.

Had Bunter related exactly what had occurred, no doubt they might have

believed that much. But that was not Billy Bunter's way. Bunter never could tell a plain, unvarnished tale. Facts were always too commonplace for Bunter. He preferred the figments of his own fertile fancy to mere facts.

Bunter was annoyed. Naturally, he wanted the credit that was his due—in fact, he wanted more than was his due.

"Well, I fancy you fellows will hear about it at Greyfriars," he yapped. "Sir Peter will tell Quelch. He's an old pal of Quelch's, and he's going to see him. I say, you fellows, two bobbies have gone in a car to look for those motor-bandits, after what I told them at the station."

"Pile it on!"

"Sir Peter's going on by train, in case they're still after him. I'd be quite willing to go with him in the car, and see him through—after Smithy's feed, of course! But he's going by train. I fancy he's a bit nervous."

"Did anything happen on the Redclyffe road, besides a motorist giving you a lift in?" asked Johnny Bull.

"You silly fathead, haven't I told you?" hooted Bunter. "I'd walked a mile, when I came on those motor-bandits, and my legs were nearly dropping off, through your beastly selfishness in taking that bike, after all I've done for you! And that cad Smithy bringing you on in his rotten, hired car—not much of a car, compared with the one I came here in, though Smithy swanked off in it as if it was a gilt-edged Rolls-Royce——"

"Better not let Smithy hear you!" chuckled Bob. "He mightn't ask you to the spread, old fat man."

"Oh, Smithy wants a crowd at his spread," jeered Bunter. "He's asked all the Remove fellows who came over this afternoon—— Pure swank! He likes showing off his money!"

"Shut up, you fat ass!" exclaimed Harry Wharton hurriedly.

The juniors were standing outside the Rotunda, where Herbert Vernon-Smith was standing that lavish spread to a crowd of Removites. Bunter had his back to the doorway, and did not observe Vernon-Smith arrive there from within, to look out for his expected guests.

Not having, of course, any eyes in the back of his fat head, Billy Bunter did not see the Bounder in the doorway of the tea-shop. He saw, therefore, no reason for shutting up. Shutting up was not much in Bunter's line, anyhow.

"Shan't!" he retorted. "You jolly well know as well as I do that it's just swank—Smithy's swank all over! The fact is, I've a jolly good mind not to come in at all. Smithy likes to get fellows a bit above him socially, but I don't see why I should oblige him. He'd like to make the waiters think that I'm a friend of his, just to show off."

"Shut up!" hissed Bob. "Smithy is——"

The expression on Herbert Vernon-Smith's face, as he heard Billy Bunter's cheery remarks, from behind the fat Owl, was really alarming.

"Oh, blow Smithy!" said Bunter. "Fat lot I care for Smithy! I don't mind giving the fellow a leg-up, as far as that goes, but I can jolly well say I—— Yarooop! Who's that kicking me? Yarooooh!"

Billy Bunter nose-dived as a boot was planted heavily on him from the rear. As he tottered, the Bounder followed it up with another. Bunter roared, and dropped on his hands and knees.

(Continued on page 10.)

MECCANO

EVERY MODEL NEW... EVERY OUTFIT ENLARGED!

MECCANO HAS NEVER BEEN SO FULL OF THRILLS, SO FULL OF FUN!

Boys everywhere are being thrilled with the new Meccano. Every Outfit, from the smallest to the largest, is bigger. The models are all new! All more realistic. All more interesting to make. All more fun to play with. And they nearly all work just like the real thing.

With even the smallest Meccano Outfit any boy can build the most fascinating models quite easily—Cranes, Trucks, Aeroplanes, Bridges, and scores of others. He can play with them as long as he wishes, and then take them to pieces and build something else.

Meccano reproduces all the great wonders of engineering. The interchangeable strips, girders, plates and gears are made with the precision and accuracy of real engineering parts. Ask your local dealer to show you the new Outfits and new models—you will then realise how this year, more than ever before, Meccano is the most thrilling, the most entertaining and the most lasting gift a boy can possibly have!

Prices of Outfits from 2/6 to 231/-

A fine New Catalogue—

FREE TO BOYS!

Get this complete 72-page catalogue from your dealer or write direct to us for a copy, enclosing the names and addresses of three of your chums. It contains full details and illustrations of the new Meccano and all the other good things that are made in Meccanoland.

Make sure of your copy to-day.

MECCANO LIMITED DEPT. 35 BINNS ROAD LIVERPOOL 13

"Yoo-hoop! Who—— Oh crikey! Is that Smithy? Oh crumbs! I say, old chap, I wasn't talking about you! I wasn't saying—yaroooop!"

"Ha, ha, ha!"

Thud, thud, thud!

Smithy's boot landed three times with vigour before Billy Bunter scrambled out of reach and jumped to his feet.

"I—I—I say——" gasped Bunter. "I wasn't—— Beast! Keep off, will you? I say, you fellows, keep him off! If you kick me again, Smithy, you cad, I'll jolly well—yarooop!"

Billy Bunter scudded. The Bounder, apparently not satisfied yet, rushed after him, and landed two more as he fled. He did not seem to think that Bunter had had enough yet. Bunter, on the other hand, felt that he had had quite enough, if not a little too much. He accelerated, and vanished round a corner.

Smithy's spread at the Rotunda was not graced by the winsome presence of William George Bunter, after all! His boot was ready for Bunter, if that fat youth showed up again.

Bunter did not show up; he had had more than he wanted of Smithy's boot!

But it was quite a jolly spread, in spite of the absence of Billy Bunter's fascinating company. So far from missing Bunter, the Remove fellows, for the second time that day, forgot his existence

---

THE SEVENTH CHAPTER.
The Invisible Owl!

"OH, lor'!" murmured Billy Bunter.

He leaned on an automatic machine, on the platform at Redclyffe Station, and looked on life with a pessimistic eye.

Everything seemed to have gone wrong that deplorable afternoon. The one bright spot in the gloom was the two shillings' worth of jam tarts he had parked before leaving Greyfriars. But that was only a happy memory.

Bunter was hungry. He was barred from the glorious feed going on at the Rotunda. He had to get back to Greyfriars for tea—if he was going to have any tea. And the problem of transport was almost insoluble.

He had not had much luck in borrowing a bike when he was outward bound. He had no chance at all of borrowing one homeward bound. Walking five miles was an awful impossibility. The railway was the only way—and the railway, with the usual selfishness of human nature, did not carry passengers free, gratis, and for nothing.

As Bunter was as stony as the most barren tract of the Sahara desert, he had to be carried free, gratis, and for nothing, if he was carried at all!

In a little country station like Redclyffe it was not difficult for a wary fellow to wedge in on the platform without a ticket. Trains were not fearfully frequent, and between trains there were not a lot of watchful eyes about. Bunter had got on the platform easily enough to wait for the next train to Courtfield.

But the next step was not so easy.

Bunter belonged to that peculiar class of persons who believe that a railway company is "fair game." He had no objections to bilking the railway, if he could get by with the same!

But he remembered an awful occasion when a nasty railwayman had taken him by the collar. That recollection had made him realise that whether railway

companies were fair game or not, honesty was often the best policy.

Blinking up and down the platform through his big spectacles, he was in hope of spotting some Greyfriars man, returning after the football match, whom he might "touch" for his fare.

No such person was visible. Greyfriars fellows who were going back by train had gone already. Billy Bunter was the only Greyfriars fellow in the station now.

He thought of the party at the Rotunda, and groaned. But for those unfortunate remarks about the founder of the feast, he would have been scoffing good things at Smithy's expense—with a healthy chance of borrowing his fare home from one of the numerous guests.

Now there really seemed nothing for it but bilking the railway; and at that idea he seemed to feel a nasty, rough hand on his collar again.

The train for Courtfield came in, and stopped. It was not going on again for several minutes, and it was easy to pop into a carriage. But getting away undetected at Courtfield or Friardale was another matter.

"Oh!" ejaculated Bunter suddenly.

A familiar figure walked down the train and stopped at a first-class carriage. It was an old gentleman in a silk hat, with a gleam of silvery hair showing under it.

Bunter blinked at Sir Peter Lanchester

He remembered that the old sportsman was going by train, leaving his car in Redclyffe. No doubt he had been parking the car somewhere while Bunter had been walking to the station from the Rotunda. Anyhow, here he was, taking the same train.

Bunter watched him as he placed a rug and an umbrella on a seat in the carriage, and then walked down the platform. That carriage remained empty; there was not a lot of traffic on the line, especially in the first-class compartment.

Bunter's fat face brightened.

He rolled towards the train and popped into the carriage.

After the service he had rendered Sir Peter that afternoon—the very great service, as Sir Peter himself had described it—surely the old gentleman could hardly refuse to come to the rescue, if necessary, of a fellow who had "lost" his ticket!

Bunter felt that he could bank on that.

All he had to do was to sit in that carriage, and discover at the end of the journey that he had lost his ticket—and leave the rest to Sir Peter Lanchester.

He felt that this was a winner.

In a greatly relieved frame of mind he sat down in a corner seat; he blinked cheerfully from the window, at Sir Peter's shining silk hat in the distance.

Then the sight of another hat suddenly wiped the cheerful expression from his face. That hat—or, rather, peaked cap—was coming along the train, stopping at every carriage in turn.

"Oh crikey!" gasped Bunter.

A beastly inspector was looking at the tickets before the train started. Bunter remembered that beastly custom on that beastly railway. It did not always happen, but it was liable to happen any time—which was terribly discouraging to bilks.

It was all very well to tell Sir Peter Lanchester at the end of the journey that he had lost his ticket, but it was of no use whatever to make that statement to a railway inspector before the journey started.

Bunter, in his mind's eye, saw himself hooked out of that carriage.

But he was not at the end of his resources yet.

He slid off the seat, extended his fat form on the floor, and rolled under the seat, packing himself carefully out of sight.

In that deep cover he waited with a palpitating fat heart.

He heard a sound at the carriage door.

If it was the railway inspector looking in, he did not see Bunter. But the fat junior did not think of emerging. It was better to remain parked under the seat all the way to Courtfield—which was only a short run from Redclyffe—than to risk being hooked out and left behind.

The fat Owl of the Remove remained where he was.

About a minute later he had a view of a pair of shiny shoes and a pair of trouser-ends. Somebody was getting in. He had no doubt that it was Sir Peter.

The passenger sat down in the corner seat, quite unaware that there was anyone in the carriage with him.

The inspector probably had passed on by this time. But Billy Bunter did not think of emerging from cover. Really he could scarcely do so under Sir Peter's astonished eyes. A fellow who had hidden under a seat could hardly expect to get by with a story of a lost ticket; it was only too clear that such a fellow was a bilk.

After all, it was only fifteen minutes to Courtfield by rail. It was easy to remain where he was till the old gentleman had got out of the carriage; then he could follow him out and keep him in sight while he changed trains for Friardale.

Bunter settled down to it. It was not, in point of fact, the first time that he had made a railway journey parked under a seat.

Doors were slamming along the train now.

Just as the engine shrieked another passenger bolted at the last moment into the carriage

He sat down in the corner seat opposite Sir Peter Lanchester, and the door slammed immediately after him and the train started

The boots of the new passenger were only a few inches from Billy Bunter's fat little nose

The train rolled out of Redclyffe station. Bunter heard the rustle of a newspaper; Sir Peter had opened "The Times."

Of the second passenger Bunter could see nothing but the boots. Those boots stirred a little a minute after the train was out of the station. He heard a crumpling sound of paper, and realised in great surprise that the second passenger had knocked Sir Peter's newspaper aside. There was a startled and annoyed exclamation from Sir Peter.

"What the dooce——"

"Don't move, Sir Peter Lanchester!" came a voice that made Billy Bunter start and quake as he heard it. "And don't try to reach the communication cord! I shall shoot you dead if you stir a finger!"

Billy Bunter wondered for a moment whether he was dreaming. For it was the voice of the Smiler that he heard. It was one of the pair of motor bandits who had jumped into Sir Peter's carriage at the last moment before the train pulled out of Redclyffe.

THE EIGHTH CHAPTER.

Bunter Butts In !

BILLY BUNTER made no sound.
He hardly breathed.
But he listened with all his
ears.

"Good—good gracious !" He heard
the old baronet's startled voice. "Who
—who are you ? What does this mean ?
You rascal, turn that pistol away ! Is
this an attempt at robbery ? Good
gracious !"

"Nothing of the kind," came the cool,
cold voice of the Smiler. "Your note-
case is quite safe, Sir Peter. I cannot
say the same for your life. I warn you
not to make a fool of yourself !"

Sir Peter had grasped the umbrella
that lay on the seat beside him, but he
released it again. A revolver in the
hand of a man sitting opposite was
looking him in the face ; the muzzle
was hardly a couple of feet from Sir
Peter's nose ; and a pair of icy eyes in
a hard, cold face were gleaming over it.

"What do you want ?" Sir Peter's
voice was a little shaky.

"I think you know. You turned
back in your car this afternoon—but
you have been watched since," said the
Smiler quietly. "I conclude that you
have taken this train with the idea
that the roads were not safe—what ?
You could not have suited me better.
We have twelve minutes, undisturbed,
for our little interview. You are going
to answer my questions now, or it will
be the worse for you."

"What——"

"Is Lord Reynham at Greyfriars
School ?"

"No."

"Take care how you answer ! You
are on your way to Greyfriars ; that
has been ascertained beyond doubt.
Why are you going there ?"

"I am going to visit an old friend, a
Form-master in the school."

"Name ?"

"Mr. Quelch."

"An old friend—but this is your first
visit to him ?" sneered the Smiler.

"I fail to see how you know——"

"We know a good deal ! Never mind
that ! You are asking me to believe
that a Greyfriars Form-master is an
old friend of yours, and you are going
to visit him, when you have never done
so before. I've warned you to be
careful !"

"You are a rogue and a rascal, sir !"
snapped Sir Peter. "Nothing would
induce me to answer your questions, to
the harm of a boy who is under my
charge, if you blew out my brains on
the spot. But what I have told you is
the truth. I have not seen Mr. Quelch
for years, but I am going to see him
now."

"And why ?"

"To ask his advice and assistance in
the difficulties that have been brought
upon me by a gang of rascals—of whom,
I presume, you are the leader," snapped
Sir Peter

"You think a schoolmaster may help
you to deal with us ?" sneered the
Smiler, his tone very plainly revealing
that he did not believe the old baronet's
statement.

"Possibly."

"You must think of something better
than that, Sir Peter. I ask you again
whether the boy is at Greyfriars
School ?"

"You seem to be able to obtain information for your purposes," said Sir
Peter. "No doubt you could obtain a
list of the names of the boys at Grey-

friars School and satisfy yourself on
that point."

"I should not find the boy under his
own name," said the Smiler, "and none
of us know him by sight, owing to the
precautions you have taken. Wherever
he is, he does not use the name of Lord
Reynham. Is that not the case ?"

No answer

"You deny that he is at Greyfriars
School ?"

"He is not there."

"But he is—and must be—at some
such place."

"Perhaps."

"Give me the name of the school."

"I will tell you nothing !" said Sir
Peter Lanchester, and his voice was not
shaky now. "Who you are I do not
know, but I conclude that you must be
the scoundrel who has been seeking for
years to get my ward into his hands.
Where you have obtained your information I cannot guess ; I have kept my
own counsel on the subject. But it
seems that you have learned that my
ward has been placed at school under
an assumed name to protect him from
you. You will gain little by your spy-
ing. I will tell you nothing."

"I give you two minutes to cough it
up !" came the cold, hard voice. "If
you have not spoken by that time you
are a dead man !"

"I have said all that I have to say."

Sir Peter sat bolt upright, facing the
man with the gun The train rushed on
through the falling December dusk.

Under the seat Billy Bunter had not
stirred. What he had heard was Greek
to the fat junior.

But one thing was clear to Billy
Bunter's fat mind.

He had not forgotten the words of
Smiler and Ferret, in the ambush on
the Redclyffe road.

Sir Peter Lanchester, looking the
levelled revolver in the muzzle, had no
doubt that it was loaded, in a desperate
hand. Billy Bunter was aware that it
was not loaded, and that the Smiler had
no intention whatever of shooting. The
rascal was banking on the threat of
death to extract what he wanted to
know from the old baronet.

Billy Bunter did not like fire-arms,
when they were loaded. But an unloaded revolver had no great terrors,
even for William George Bunter.
Aware, from the rascal's own words to
his confederate a few hours ago, that
he was uttering only an empty threat,
Billy Bunter was not greatly scared.

"One minute !" snapped the Smiler
suddenly.

Sir Peter Lanchester breathed hard.
He did not know what Bunter knew,
and he had no doubt that he was
looking death in the face.

"One minute more," came the hard,
threatening voice, and then—— "Oh !"

The rascal broke off with a sudden,
enraged exclamation as the old baronet
threw himself forward in his seat and
grasped the revolver.

The Smiler did not fire—for a good
reason !

Sir Peter grasped the barrel of the
revolver with one hand, and with the
other, clenched, struck at the Smiler's
face. Old as he was, the baronet was
evidently game.

But the next moment the Smiler
was on his feet, grasped him ; and the
old gentleman crumpled up in that
savage grip.

The Smiler forced him back on the
seat and threw up the receiver, to use
as a club.

Billy Bunter's startled and horrified
eyes were on him, from under the other
seat.

It was fortunate that Bunter was
aware that the revolver was unloaded.
But for that, the fat junior's terrors
would probably have been too much for
him. As it was, Bunter weighed in.

He made a sudden grab at the
Smiler's ankle, from behind, and
dragged with all his strength.

The Smiler gave a startled yell and
stumbled over. Utterly unaware that
there was a third party in the carriage,
he was taken completely by surprise,
and that sudden drag on his ankle
tumbled him over headlong.

He bumped on the floor of the
carriage, spluttering wildly with amazement and rage.

Sir Peter scrambled off the seat.

He gave one astounded blink at a
fat face and a large pair of spectacles
emerging from under the opposite seat
—as amazed as the Smiler by Bunter's
sudden and unexpected intervention.
But he did not lose a moment. He
flung himself on the sprawling rascal
on the floor and pinned him down.

"Oh crikey !" gasped Bunter.

He rolled out and scrambled up.

The Smiler, on his back, struggled
furiously. He had twice the old
baronet's strength, but he was at a dis-
advantage.

"Pull the cord !" shouted Sir Peter.

"Oh crumbs !"

"The cord—the communication cord—
quick !" shrieked the old baronet.

"Oh ! All right ! Oh crikey !"

Bunter dragged at the cord. Almost
immediately there was a screech of
brakes and the train slowed.

The Smiler, with a fierce and desperate effort, hurled the old baronet off.
His own liberty was at stake now—the
train was slowing to a stop. He pitched
Sir Peter back, scrambled up, and spun
round to the door. With lightning
swiftness he threw it open and leaped
out on the line.

The train was still moving ; and the
Smiler, as he landed, rolled headlong
down an embankment. But he was on
his feet again in a twinkling, and
running.

Sir Peter, exhausted, panting, collapsed on a seat. Billy Bunter,
spluttering, collapsed on the other.
They blinked at one another. The
guard came scudding along the train,
and blinked at both of them.

THE NINTH CHAPTER.

Bunter the Life-Saver !

HARRY WHARTON & Co. put
up their bikes and cut across
to the House to join the crowd
of fellows going into the Hall
for calling-over.

A crowd of fellows were coming back
from Redclyffe, some sooner, and some
later ; but all—excepting one, were in
by the time the bell rang. But in the
ranks of the Remove, when they took
their places in the Hall, one fat, familiar face was conspicuous by its absence.

Mr. Quelch was taking the roll.
There was no answering "adsum" when
he called the name of Bunter.

Frowning, Quelch marked Bunter
absent ; and went on with the roll.

"Hallo, hallo, hallo !" murmured
Bob Cherry. "Hasn't the jolly old
porpoise rolled in yet ?"

"Not here," said Harry Wharton.
"Oh, my hat ! If poor old Bunter's
walking back from Redclyffe, he will
arrive with the milk in the morning."

"Catch him walking !" grunted
Johnny Bull. "More likely to bilk the
railway !"

"He would have got in before us, by rail!" said Nugent.

"Unless he was copped!"

"Oh crumbs!"

There was a chuckle from Skinner.

"Fancy Quelch's face, if he has to go and bail him out!" he murmured.

"Ha, ha, ha!"

"Silence!" called out Wingate of the Sixth. And the Removites subdued their merriment.

After roll there was some interested discussion in the Rag, on the subject of the missing Owl. If Bunter was walking back from Redclyffe, estimates varied as to the time he was likely to reach Greyfriars. Not before dorm, was the general opinion; while some fellows put it at midnight, and others rather thought that Bunter might arrive with the early milkman.

On the other hand, it was extremely probable that the fat Owl had made an attempt to travel ticketless on the railway—his manners and customs in that respect being very well known in his Form. In which case, as he had not turned up, it looked as if he must have been "copped."

So it was quite an interesting question whether the fat Owl of the Remove was still wearily plugging the endless miles on the Redclyffe road, or whether he was quaking in charge of a policeman—whether he would crawl in at some unearthly hour, with his fat legs nearly falling off, or arrive with a man in uniform as an escort.

Certainly no one expected him to arrive, as he actually did arrive, about half an hour later.

When a taxi was heard to drive in at the gates and come up to the House and stop, the juniors did not guess that it was Bunter coming. Some of them had heard that Mr. Quelch was expecting a visitor that day, and so they supposed that this was probably the visitor, arriving rather late. Then Skinner, looking out of the window, gave a yell.

"Bunter!"

Billy Bunter alighted from the taxi and rolled into the House. And quite an army of fellows rushed to see him. As Bunter had been left in a stony state at Redclyffe, it was quite surprising to see him arrive in a taxi! Taxicabs cost money; and Bunter was well known to be in the same state as Peter of old—silver and gold had he none!

"I say, you fellows——" squeaked Bunter. "I say——"

"Not me!" said the Bounder, grinning.

"Eh? Wharrer you mean—not you?" asked Bunter.

"I mean what I say—no good asking me to pay the taxi! Better try Mauly—he's soft!"

"Oh, really, Smithy——"

"The taxi's gone!" said Bob Cherry, looking out at the door. "Mean to say that chap gave you a free ride, Bunter?"

"Oh, really, Cherry——"

"Well, you haven't paid him, I suppose?" asked Bob. "And you can't bilk taximen as you do the railway company."

"Beast! A friend paid for the taxi at Courtfield!" said Bunter, with dignity. "One of my titled friends."

"Which, out of the hundreds?" chuckled Skinner.

"Sir Peter Lanchester!" answered Bunter calmly. "Sir Peter Lanchester, Baronet, of Reynham Castle, Sussex."

"Oh, my only hat!"

"Go it!" gasped Bob Cherry.

"You see, I saved his life——" explained Bunter.

"Oh, I remember—you were doing life-saving stunts this afternoon, on the Redclyffe road!" chortled Bob. "Knocking out gangs of motor-bandits——"

"Ha, ha, ha!"

"I don't mean that time—I saved his life again, in the train coming from Redclyffe——"

"Twice!" yelled Bob.

"Yes, twice——"

"Oh crikey! You're making a regular habit of it, then!"

"Ha, ha, ha!"

Billy Bunter blinked round at a crowd of laughing faces.

Certainly it looked as if something unusual must have happened, as Bunter had arrived in a taxi, without asking any fellow to pay the taximan. But nobody was likely to believe in Bunter's life-saving exploits—especially twice on the same afternoon. It was really rather a lot to believe!

"I say, you fellows, it's true!" said Bunter. "You see, this is how it was! After Smithy acted like a beastly hooligan, I refused to come to his spread at the Rotunda."

"You'd have got some more boot, if you had," remarked the Bounder.

"Beast! So I went to the railway station, and, as it happened, my friend, Sir Peter, was taking the same train," explained Bunter. "I—I decided to keep an eye on him, and see him safe. That was why I hid under the seat in the carriage—not because I hadn't got a ticket, you know."

"We can believe that much," chuckled Bob. "You hid under the seat of a railway carriage, because you hadn't got a ticket. You've done that before, you bloated bilk!"

"Well, Sir Peter believed me, anyhow, when I told him," snorted Bunter. "And I can tell you, it was jolly lucky for him I was there. One of the motor-bandits got into the train at the last minute. He drew a revolver——"

"Not a machine-gun?" asked Skinner.

"Ha, ha, ha!"

"No!" roared Bunter. "A revolver! I didn't know it wasn't loaded, of course. How could I? He attacked the old sportsman, and I—I—I jumped out and knocked him spinning. Felled him with a blow. Knocked him right out, you know."

"Dead for a ducat—dead!" said Wibley.

"Ha, ha, ha!"

"No, not dead, old chap," said Bunter. "I hit him pretty hard, but not so hard as all that. But he had enough, I can tell you. Then I pulled the cord, and the train stopped, and the guard came, and——"

"And got him?" grinned Bob.

"No; he jumped out and bunked."

"Then you won't be able to produce him?" chortled Skinner.

"No; you see, he got away. There was no end of a fuss guard and passengers crowding round, and all that, all wondering at my pluck——"

"At your whatter?" gasped Bob.

"Pluck!" roared Bunter. "I'd jolly well like to see you do what I did on that train, Bob Cherry, but I jolly well never shall!"

"No fear," agreed Bob. "I never travel under a seat without a ticket."

"Ha, ha, ha!"

"Beast! Well, that's why I'm late for roll," said Bunter "I came on to Courtfield with Sir Peter, and, as I'd lost my ticket in the—the desperate struggle, the old boy paid my fare, and we went to the police station, same as at Redclyffe—not that those bobbies

are much good—and then the old boy put me in a taxi for Greyfriars, and —and here I am. He hasn't come on to the school. You'd jolly well have seen him, if he had, but——"

"The butfulness is terrific!"

"Ha, ha, ha!"

"But he's phoning Quelch from Courtfield," said Bunter. "He was coming here to see Quelch, but, being a bit upset, he's putting it off till to-morrow."

"You're not going to tell Quelch that that's why you're late for roll?" asked Harry Wharton.

"Eh? Yes, of course."

"You're going to spin that yarn to Quelch?" yelled Bob.

"Of course, it's true."

"True! Oh, suffering sardines! You'd better pack some exercise-books in your bags before you try it on Quelch."

"Ha, ha, ha!"

"For goodness' sake, Bunter, tell Quelch an easier one than that!" exclaimed Peter Todd. "Can't you see that it won't wash?"

"Oh, really, Toddy——"

"Do you think Quelch will believe a word of it?" gasped Toddy.

"Don't you?" demanded Bunter.

"Eh—what? Oh crikey! Hardly!" stuttered Toddy.

"Beast!"

Billy Bunter rolled on, heading for his Form-master's study, to report his return.

The juniors stared after him blankly. What would be the result, if the fat Owl spun that remarkable yarn to Quelch, they could hardly imagine.

But Bunter seemed to have no doubts. He rolled on cheerily to Mr. Quelch's study, tapped, and rolled in.

And when he reappeared a few minutes later, without any sign of having had the whopping of his life, the Remove fellows could only conclude that he had not, after all, tried that remarkable yarn on Quelch.

THE TENTH CHAPTER.
Unsettled !

"DON'T say Christmas!"

Five voices delivered that injunction in chorus.

After dinner the following day, Harry Wharton & Co. were sauntering in the quad, discussing the Christmas holidays. As Billy Bunter rolled up, they all addressed him together.

As the time drew near for breaking-up at Greyfriars, the Christmas vacation became a favourite topic with Billy Bunter—but a topic which no other fellow seemed keen to discuss with him.

That glorious residence, Bunter Court, failed, as was usual in holiday time, to attract Bunter. He had made up his mind to spend Christmas with his old pals. But if Bunter merely said "About Christmas, you fellows," it seemed enough to make fellows remember other engagements, or pop round corners.

This was rather irritating to Bunter, who naturally wanted to get the matter settled.

The Famous Five were a little unsettled, as well as Bunter. Harry Wharton's uncle, the old colonel, and his aunt, Miss Amy Wharton, were absent from home—Aunt Amy having had to go away that winter for her health.

It had been understood that they would return to Wharton Lodge before Christmas; but the return was post-

"Stop! I say, stop! Danger!" squeaked Billy Bunter, standing in front of the oncoming car and waving a fat hand frantically. The gentleman in the car thrust out his head and inquired: "What is it, boy?" "Two awful beasts!" gasped Bunter. "They're going to stop your car!"

poned, which rather knocked on the head Harry's plans for the festive season.

Wharton Lodge not being available, the next best plan was for Harry Wharton and Hurree Jamset Ram Singh to put in the holidays with the other members of the Co.

That was the subject of discussion when Bunter rolled along, to be promptly warned off by five voices speaking in unison.

Bunter, however, was not to be warned off. Bunter could not possibly continue to leave things in this unsettled state.

"I say, you fellows, about Christmas—" he began.

"Don't!" roared Bob Cherry.

"Eh? Don't what, you ass?"

"Don't say Christmas!"

"You can shut up, Cherry! I'm speaking to Wharton about the Christmas holidays," said Bunter. "If you think I'd be found dead in your mouldy little show in Dorset, you're mistaken—see?"

"You'll be found dead, or nearly, if you're found there at all," remarked Bob Cherry.

"Yah! I say, Harry, old chap, I'd like to get this settled," said Bunter, blinking at the captain of the Remove through his big spectacles. "I've had some rather decent invitations for Christmas; but the fact is, I prefer to stick to my old pals. Mind, I can't give you the whole vacation. I have to consider my other friends. I can manage a week at Wharton Lodge."

Harry Wharton laughed.

"Only a week?" he asked.

"Well, I might make it a fortnight," admitted Bunter. "If you'd really like me to stay a couple of weeks, old chap, I might manage it. After all, we're pals, old chap."

"Are we?"

"Oh, really, Wharton——"

"Why not make it the whole vac?" asked the captain of the Remove. "No objection whatever, so far as I'm concerned."

"Ha, ha, ha!" roared the Co.

Billy Bunter blinked at them in surprise.

He had hardly expected this whole-hearted invitation to Wharton Lodge, but he could see nothing to laugh at in it. The Co., who were aware that nobody would be at home at Wharton Lodge for Christmas, could.

"Blessed if I see anything to cackle at!" said Bunter. "I say, Harry, old chap, I'll accept that invitation——"

"It isn't an invitation," explained Wharton. "What I said is, that there's no objection to your staying at Wharton Lodge all through the holidays, if you want to."

"Well, that comes to the same thing, doesn't it?" asked Bunter. "I'm on, anyhow. I hardly know how I shall put off all my other friends; but I'll do it, for your sake, old chap. Rely on me. Anybody else coming?"

"No."

"Not a party, or anything?"

"Not at all."

"I say, it will be a bit quiet, won't it?"

"Fearfully."

"Well, I'll come, all the same," declared Bunter. "I'm not going to let a pal down, because he can't afford much in the way of Christmas festivities. We'll travel down together, old fellow."

"Can't be done."

"Eh—why not?"

"Because I'm not going there."

"Eh? What the dickens do you mean?" ejaculated Bunter. "You can't ask a fellow home for Christmas if you're not going to be at home, I suppose?"

"But I haven't asked any fellow home for Christmas!"

"Ha, ha, ha!"

"Oh, shut up that cackling!" hooted Bunter. "Look here, you silly ass, do you think I'm going to stay at your place with your old uncle and aunt and nobody else?"

"No!"

"What do you mean then?"

"I mean that my uncle and aunt won't be at home."

"They won't!" yelled Bunter.

"No!"

"You—you—you silly ass!" shrieked Bunter. "Who will be there, then?"

"Nobody!"

"Wha-a-a-t?"

"I mean, as all the family will be away, most of the household will go away, too! I think one old couple will be left in charge."

"One old kik-kik-couple!" stuttered Bunter.

"Yes! I shouldn't wonder if they'd be glad to see you, Bunter!" said Harry Wharton gravely. "You'll cheer them up very likely! There won't be any festivities, of course, or much in the way of grub——"

"Eh?"

"But stay there as long as you like! If your other numerous friends will let you off, put in the whole vacation there! Go straight there when we break up and stay till first day of term. You're absolutely welcome."

Billy Bunter glared at the captain of the Remove, his very spectacles glinting with wrath.

He understood now the meaning of that unexpected permission to spend the whole of the Christmas holidays at Wharton Lodge.

(Continued on page 16.)
THE MAGNET LIBRARY.—No. 1,556.

THE BEWTY AND THE BEAK!

A Rib-Tickling Yarn of Jack Jolly & Co. of St. Sam's!"

By DICKY NUGENT

I.

" He's got it ! "

Frank Fearless of the St. Sam's Fourth made that announcement in tones of suppressed eggsitement, as he sat down at the breakfast-table

" What—the letter? Good egg ! " cried Jack Jolly, gleefully. " How do you know ? "

" I saw it in Sorter's hand when he was delivering this morning's post ! " chortled Fearless. " I reckernised my pater's fist on the envelope and I saw it was addressed to Doctor Birchemall."

" Do you think your pater did as you asked him ? " asked Merry anxiously.

" Trust the pater ! " grinned Fearless. " The moment I asked him over the tellyfone if he'd give prizes to the best dancers at the St. Sam's Ball, he said he'd do it like a shot. Our wheeze is simply bound to suxxeed. As soon as the masters hear that there are prizes to be won for dancing, they'll all want to dance."

" In which case they'll have to get a real band for the ball instead of inflicting their garstly mewsick on us ! " chuckled Jack Jolly. " Good old Fearless ! "

" Quiet, you fellows ! " hist Bright. " Here come the beaks ! "

The chums of the Fourth glanced towards the door and saw Doctor Birchemall entering with half-a-duzzen Form-masters on his heels. The Head, who held a letter in his somewhat grimy paw, was grinning all over his face, while the other masters all looked as eggsited as Second Form faggs. Putting two and two together and making five, Jack Jolly & Co. could see that Mr. Ferdinand Fearless' letter had had the desired effect !

So eggsited was the Head that he had to dip into the contents of his letter again before he dipped into his porridge bowl.

" Boys ! " he cried, standing up at the head of the Sixth Form table and waving the all-important letter above his head. " I have topping news to announce to you in regard to the grate St. Sam's Ball—news that will make you feel as pleased as Punch—and the girls of St. Lizzie's as pleased as Judy ! "

" Spill the beans, then, sir ! "

" On the bawl ! "

" I have just receeved a letter from the welthy and jennerous pater of a Fourth Form boy," went on Doctor Birchemall. " This noble-harted jentleman, Mr. Ferdinand Fearless by name, has offered two valuable trofies in the shape of cups to the cupple who dance the best fox-trot on the nite of the Ball ! "

" Hear, hear ! "

" Good old Ferdy ! "

" The cups in question," grinned the Head, " will be real imitation gold of the very finest quality and worth at least five shillings each."

" Few ! "

" This magnifficent offer, boys, is all that was needed to complete the nite of nites to which we are all looking forward so grately ! " said Doctor Birchemall. " There is only one drawback about it. My original intention that the mewsick should be supplied by Alf Birchemall and His Boys must now be abandoned for the eggsellent reason that we shall all be entering for the dancing kontest. We shall now have to rely on the Muggleton Melody Makkers, who are offered to us free of charge by Sir Gouty Greybeard."

The Head quite eggspected that the fellows would tear their hair and nash their teeth out of sheer disappointment on hearing that his band would be unable to play. But instead of that, they all grinned from ear to ear and cheered and cheered again. It quite annoyed the Head, and he wrapped the table sharply for silence.

" Silence, you disrespecktive yung cubs ! " he roared, hitting the table for all he was worth. " Stop cheering at once or—yarooo ! "

" Ha, ha, ha ! "

Doctor Birchemall broke off with a feendish yell and the fellows' cheers changed to deffening larfter. Not notissing eggsactly where he was banging, the Head had accidentally hit the edge of his porridge-bowl—with the result that the porridge had shot up in the air and landed on his face !

Doctor Birchemall's interest in the St. Sam's Ball petered out promptly when he found himself gowging hot porridge out of his eyes. He left the table and made a rush for the door, leaving the skool almost historical with larfter ; and he was seen no more at breakfast-time that morning.

Jack Jolly & Co., however, knew that he would be as keen as mustard again by the end of the morning, and they were not serprized when they came out of morning classes to see him link arms with Mr. Lickham and march the Fourth Form master away, eagerly chattering about the prizes which Mr. Ferdinand Fearless had offered.

" Let's follow the old fogeys, you chaps ! " grinned Jack Jolly. " They may put in a bit of dancing praktiss—and then we ought to see some fun ! "

" Yes, rather ! " corussed the other members of the Co.

And they followed the two beaks—and were duly rewarded by getting the larf of the term for their trubble.

Just as Jolly had suspeckted, the old fogeys were going off on the sly for a little dancing praktiss. The place they chose to do it in was the last place where people would have dreemed of looking—the cole-cellar.

The chums of the Fourth were almost busting with suppressed larfter, as they gazed down at them through air-holes at the top. Doctor Birchemall and Mr. Lickham looked as graceful as a cupple of elephants, capering about in the dim illewmination of the single electrick light.

The most commical moment was at the end. Unbeknown to the would-be dance champions, a load of coke had just arrived for delivery. The two old fogeys were so engrossed in watching their feet that they did not notiss the cole-hole open above their heads. But it opened all the same, and after a breef interval somebody above up-ended a sack of coke over the hole just at the moment when they happened to be underneeth it. Then the two old fossils woke up to what was happening and found themselves struggling on

---

"SWAT THAT— AUTOGRAPH HUNTER!"

Says GEORGE WINGATE

It's not often I condescend to write for a kids' paper. (Hi, chuck it, Wingate ! None of that Heavy Father stuff, old bean !—Ed.) But I feel that the " Greyfriars Herald " is just the right medium for an earnest appeal I want to make.

My appeal to all readers is this : SWAT THAT AUTOGRAPH-HUNTER !

Autograph - hunting was all very well when it was an innocent pastime. But since it has become a frenzied obsession with a majority of the fags, it's just a thundering nuisance.

For example, when I came away from winning the table-tennis championship the other evening, there were no less than eighteen youngsters waiting for me with autograph-books. And when I protested that I had already given most of them several autographs already, they calmly explained that those were not in their table-tennis autograph books.

The young idiots are actually specialising ! They have one book for table-tennis autographs, another for footer autographs, and so on !

The Open Debate in the Sixth Form Debating Society last week ended up in a regular riot owing to these frenzied collectors. They invaded our meeting without even waiting for the chairman to sum up, and we had to send a hurried S O S for ashplants before we could get rid of them.

As for footer—words fail me ! At the close of the last match of the term on Big Side, when we beat St. Jim's 4-2, they swarmed on to the pitch like a plague of locusts, and, as they included visitors from St. Jim's as well as home supporters, I had no alternative but to wading through their wretched books, scribbling my signature on at least a score of art-shaded pages !

There's no stopping them, either. On a recent occasion when young Paget asked me to sign, I thought I'd choke him off for good by writing " You're a silly young ass " over my autograph. Do you think Paget was choked off ? Not a bit of it ! He beamed all over his inky face and asked me if I'd mind doing the same in all his albums !

It's no longer a joke. Autograph-hunting has become a menace to the peace of mind to people in the limelight. Think it over, dear readers, I beg of you, and lend your hearty support to my pathetic appeal.

SWAT THAT AUTO-GRAPH-HUNTER !

"LET ME STAY AT SCHOOL FOR XMAS!"

Bunter's Amazing Plea

Bunter nearly brought down the house when he calmly told us the other evening that he *wanted to stay at school for Christmas!*

A sort of frozen silence descended on the Rag. One or two nervous chaps made ready to dash for a doctor as soon as the Porpoise became violent.

"*You whatter?*" was the incredulous question that was flung back at Bunter, when we had recovered our breaths.

"I want to stay at school for Christmas," repeated Bunter. "I feel I should—er—like to carry on my studies during the vac. in the proper atmosphere and all that sort of thing, you know."

"Ye gods!"

"I'm not the kind of chap that dotes on Christmas as a holiday," went on Bunter, with a disdainful sniff. "I dare say it's all right for fellows who are keen on tucking in and making pigs of themselves——"

"Great pip!"

"But there's not the attraction about it for a chap like myself. Far better for me to stay on at school and spend the time in quiet study and what not."

"Let's get this straight, Bunter," put in Tom Brown. "Do you seriously intend to stay on at the school during the vac. all by yourself?"

"Yes. I mean, no—not exactly!" corrected Bunter, hastily. "I shan't be entirely by myself, of course. Fishy's staying on, too. I'm keeping him company."

We still stared blankly. Bunter had never in the past shown any particular affection for Fisher T. Fish. Why the prospect of his company should attract the Porpoise to spending Christmas at school was utterly beyond us.

Then Fishy himself came into the Rag. There was a wide grin on his hatchet face.

"Howdo, everybody!" he greeted. "I'll tell the world it looks like being real genu-wine Christmasy Christmas for somebody this year. Yes, siree!"

"My hat! Here's another one gone off his rocker!" gasped Brown. "You've never looked forward to Christmas at school before, Fishy!"

"You've said it; but it so happens that I ain't staying at school this Christmas," grinned Fish. "You see, I happened to win a Christmas hamper sufficient for twelve in a noospaper puzzle competition——"

"Oh!" yelled the entire Rag, as the light of understanding dawned on them.

"An' I've traded that hamper with an hotel at Margate for one week's free board an' room——"

"*Wha-a-a-at?*" shrieked Bunter.

"So I guess I'll be spending my Christmas in style! Whoooooopee!"

And Fish chortled. And we yelled. Bunter's mood of studiousness was fully explained now. He had heard of Fishy's win and decided to stay on and help him out with the hamper. Apparently, that help would not be required now after all!

"Still staying on at school for Christmas, Bunter?" asked Brown.

"Beast!" said Bunter.

From which remark we gathered that he wasn't!

Molly's favers were reserved for a chosen few, among whom Frank Fearless figgered most prominently.

All were agreed that the St. Sam's Ball was proving a grate suxxess and this applied espeshally to the masters.

"It's a really ripping nite!" said Mr. Justiss.

"Topping, by Jove!" grinned Mr. Swishingham.

"Magnifeek!" was Monsure F r o g g a y's opinion.

"Hock! Hock!" cheered Hair Guggenheimer.

Mr. Lickham was not to be seen; but the others were too bizzy enjoying themselves to trubble about him. It was not till later that they realised there was more in his absence than met the eye.

Doctor Birchemall was here, there, and everywhere. He started the evening by dancing with Miss Buttercup, the headmistress of St. Lizzie's. Unforchunitly, t h e i r

dance was somewhat spoilt by misunderstandings. The Head thought it was a tango, whereas Miss Buttercup was under the impression that it was a fox-trot. In actual fact, it was a waltz.

"I wonder if he'll choose Miss Buttercup as his partner in the prize fox-trot?" grinned Jack Jolly to the charming yung lady with whom he was hopping round the ball-room.

"I shouldn't be a bit serprized!" replied the yung lady, with a trilling little larf.

But the kaptin of the Fourth and his partner were wrong. When at last the grate moment arrived for the fox-trot

kontest, they and everybody else were amazed to see the Head trot over to the door and lead in a lady nobody had ever seen before.

Even Mr. Ferdinand Fearless, who was present to judge the fox-trot kontest, stopped in the middle of his announcement to look at the Head's partner. As Jolly remarked, her appearance was enuff to stop a bus!

There was something familiar about her; but what it was, nobody could say. Before they had time to speculate on the matter, Mr. Fearless had given the signal to the band, and the fox-trot kontest had started.

Everybody was as keen as mustard on winning the prizes, and they all put their best feet forward while the judges, who had been invited from Muggleton, stood in the middle eggsercising their powers of judgment. But, concentrate as they mite on the dancing, the other competitors could not keep their eyes off the Head and his partner.

Often in the past Doctor Birchemall had cut a commical figger; but never before had he cut such a commical figger as on this occasion.

Loud and long was the larfter, as the Head careered round the ball-room; but the larfter changed to yells of pane from the unlucky dancers who came within reach of his lashing legs.

The dance came to a close at last amid loud cheers, and the crowd waited anxiously for the verdict of the judges. But Doctor Birchemall and his fair lady seemed to feel no anxiety whatever regarding the result.

They walked cheerfully up to Mr. Fearless, who was consulting the judges, boughing on both sides as though they had already won the coveted trofies.

"Well, that's that, Mr. Fearless!" grinned the Head, mopping his perspiring brow. "No need to ask for the verdict, I suppose? My partner and I have won the prizes, of corse!"

Much to the serprize of the crowd, Mr. Fearless nodded.

"Yes, of corse, my dear sir," he said. "You've won!"

The crowd gasped, and then their gasps changed to grins, as Mr. Fearless added:

"But not the real prizes, natcherally. The judges have awarded you the BOOBY PRIZES!"

"W H A - A - A T ?" shreeked the Head.

"The first prizes have been awarded to my son, Frank Fearless and your charming dawter, Miss Molly Birchemall!"

Loud cheers greeted this announcement; no verdict could have been more popular. But the Head and his partner did not cheer. They glared at each other, instead, and then, to the amazement of the crowd, the Head made a grab at his partner's nose.

"You silly ass!" he roared. "It's all your fault for not dancing well enuff!"

The next moment, a gasp of sheer astonishment went up from the onlookers. As the Head reached forward, his partner jerked her head back—and immejately afterwards, her yellow mop detached itself from her head.

"It's only a wig!" yelled Jack Jolly.

"Lickham!" shreeked Merry.

It was none other than Mr. Lickham, the master of the Fourth, disguised! Now the crowd knew why the Head's partner had seemed vaguely familiar.

"Lickham! Oh, grate pip!"

"Ha, ha, ha!"

The crowd farely yelled.

Forchunitly, the

Head's appetite for vengenz was speedily sattisfied; and the fakt that his dawter had won the prize instead of himself somewhat molly-fied his feelings. When the prizes were presented, he cheered as loudly as the rest; and he and Mr. Lickham were cheered just as hartily when they went up to collect their booby-prizes.

So everything ended up happily after all. And when the last dance had been danced, everybody declared that the St. Sam's Ball had been the jolliest affair they had ever eggsperienced —thanks, in no small mezzure, to the commical capers of the Bewty and the Beak!

MY LORD BUNTER!

By FRANK RICHARDS

(Continued from page 13.)

The expression on his fat face made the Co. roar.

"You—you—you silly idiot!" gasped Bunter at last. "You—you—you blithering fathead! Think I want to stick in a place that's shut up, with nobody there, and perhaps not even a Christmas pudding——"

"No perhaps about it; there won't be!"

"You—you—you footling fathead!" gasped Bunter. "Well, I jolly well won't go—see?"

"Please yourself, of course!" said Harry, laughing. "Now roll away, old barrel, and give us a rest."

"But I—I say, if you're not going to be at home for Christmas you'll be somewhere else."

"Fancy Bunter guessing that!" ejaculated Bob. "Did you work that out in your head, Bunter?"

"Ha, ha, ha!"

"You shut up, Bob Cherry! You needn't expect to see me at your mouldy place, anyhow! I say, Wharton, old chap, where are you going? I'll tell you what—I'll come, too, if you like!"

"Wharton's coming to my mouldy place!" chuckled Bob Cherry.

"Oh!" gasped Bunter.

"Ha, ha, ha!" yelled the Co.

"Oh!" repeated Bunter.

"And you wouldn't be found dead there, you know!" grinned Bob.

"I—I—I would, old chap! I mean, I—I'll come with—with pleasure!" gasped Bunter. "What I really meant to say, old fellow, is that I'd come to Cherry Place with—with pleasure, real pleasure, Bob, old chap!"

"Well, you might come with pleasure," remarked Bob thoughtfully, "but you'd leave without pleasure, I feel sure of that—with my boot to help you! I hardly think you'd enjoy a visit to Cherry Place, Bunter! It would be so brief—only long enough for me to boot you off the premises."

"Beast!"

"Ha, ha, ha!"

The Famous Five walked on, chuckling. Billy Bunter blinked after them—not chuckling. Bunter's arrangements for Christmas were still unsettled —and looked now like remaining unsettled.

THE ELEVENTH CHAPTER.

Expensive Eavesdropping!

MR. QUELCH stepped out of his study and walked down the passage.

He did not specially notice a fat member of his Form standing by the window, near the corner, looking out into the quad.

But Billy Bunter noticed Quelch.

His eyes gleamed behind his spectacles as the Remove master walked away to the door of the House.

Bunter knew why Quelch was going to the door. He was expecting a caller after lunch that day.

Not a fellow in the Remove believed a word of Billy Bunter's startling tale of the previous day's happenings. But Bunter knew what he knew, so to speak. He knew that Sir Peter Lanchester was going to call on Mr. Quelch after lunch that day, having put up overnight in Courtfield. Billy Bunter was extremely and intensely interested in that visit.

Bunter's besetting sin was inquisitiveness. Bunter always wanted to know. A less inquisitive fellow than Bunter might have been curious about the strange affair. He had pondered a good deal over what he had heard in the railway carriage and was unable to make head or tail of it. He was simply bursting with curiosity to know what it all meant.

He was going to know if he could.

In the way of acquiring information when his curiosity was whetted the fat Owl had no scruples whatever. So long as keyholes were made to doors Billy Bunter was always likely to learn what went on. In the Remove he had been kicked times without number for eavesdropping.

So intensely curious was Bunter to hear what old Sir Peter had to say to Mr. Quelch that he even thought of putting a fat ear to the keyhole of Quelch's study door when the visitor arrived!

But that was an awfully risky proceeding in Masters' Passage. Billy Bunter thought of it—but it was not probable that he would have done more than think of it. It was altogether too dangerous.

But when Quelch left his study to go along to the door and await his visitor there Bunter's problem was solved for him.

He blinked cautiously after Quelch, and then rolled up the passage to his Form-master's study.

By leaving his study just then the Remove master had fairly played into the hands of the inquisitive fat Owl.

Bunter popped into the study, breathlessly, and closed the door behind him. Putting a fat ear to the keyhole would have been altogether too risky when another master might come along the passage at any moment. But Bunter's present scheme seemed to him as safe as houses.

Certainly a fellow who was "copped" hidden in a master's study, lending a surreptitious ear to the conversation there, was likely to be dealt with in the most severe manner—nothing short of a Head's flogging. But Billy Bunter was not going to be caught.

In the corner of that study was a large cupboard. It had a lock and key. The upper part of the cupboard was occupied by bookshelves laden with hefty volumes. The lower part contained various odds and ends, such as a bundle of canes, and a rolled map, and other such things. But there was plenty of room for a Peeping Tom!

Bunter had it all cut and dried. He had thought out his plan—if only Quelch left that study and gave him a chance. Now Quelch had left it, and the fat Owl had his chance.

Quickly he put the key on the inside of the cupboard door. Then he parked himself inside and drew the door shut and locked it.

He was absolutely safe from discovery now.

Quelch, certainly, was not likely to guess that a member of his Form was hidden in the study. He was not likely to want anything from that cupboard while his visitor was there. But, in the remote contingency of Quelch coming to the cupboard, the door was locked and the key missing. He would suppose that the key had fallen out, and perhaps been swept up by a housemaid—as sometimes happened to keys. Whatever he supposed, he was not in the least likely to suppose that a member of his Form was locked in that cupboard.

Billy Bunter grinned over his astuteness.

After the visitor had gone Quelch would leave the study sooner or later, and the way of escape would be open to Bunter. At the worst he would have to remain parked there till the bell went for classes—when Quelch would have to go to the Form-room. It was worth while getting lines for being late for class—when he so keenly wanted to know!

To do Bunter justice, it did not occur to him that he was acting like an unscrupulous young rascal. He did not think of what these proceedings would have looked like in the eyes of other fellows. He did not, in fact, think at all.

Thinking was not Bunter's long suit. He wanted to know—and he was jolly well going to know, and that was all there was to it!

If he thought at all it was only to reflect what a clever fellow he was. Nobody else in the Remove, he was sure, would have thought of a dodge like this. On that point, undoubtedly, Bunter was right!

More than ten minutes had elapsed before Billy Bunter heard a sound in the study. Then there was the opening of a door, footsteps, and the closing of the door. Quelch had brought his visitor in.

Bunter heard a voice—the slightly wheezy, but pleasant voice of the old gentleman of the day before. To his surprise, it was pronouncing his own name. He heard it distinctly.

"Bunter——"

"Bunter?" repeated Mr. Quelch.

"The boy who was of such service— such inestimable service—to me yesterday. He told me that he was in your Form here, my dear Quelch."

"That is certainly correct."

"I should like to see him, while I am here. You will have no objection, I feel sure, to my bestowing upon him some slight token of my gratitude for services rendered——"

"Hem!"

"In my own schooldays, Quelch—a long time ago now—a little tip in addition to the usual allowance was never found unwelcome. Moreover, Christmas is approaching—a time when young people, I believe, find many roads for their money."

"No doubt. But——"

"In the circumstances, if you, as the boy's Form-master, have no objection, I should really like to make the boy a present of, say, a five-pound note! You will not refuse to permit this."

"Oh, certainly, if you so desire, Sir Peter. You shall certainly see the boy —I will send for him to come here before you leave me."

"Thank you, Quelch!"

"Pray be seated, Sir Peter."

Sir Peter Lanchester sat down.

Mr. Quelch followed his example.

Billy Bunter, in the cupboard, had a wild desire to kick himself.

That old bean wanted to tip him a fiver before he left. Bunter was to be sent for, to receive that handsome "tip." And there was Bunter, parked in the study cupboard, unable to emerge until after Sir Peter had gone.

No words could have expressed Billy Bunter's awful feelings at that moment. His remarkable cleverness in parking himself in that cupboard, to listen to what did not concern him, was going to cost him exactly five pounds.

THE TWELFTH CHAPTER.
Very Extraordinary !

"MY dear Quelch——"

"I am all attention, Sir Peter."

"I am going to surprise you very much."

"It is a surprise, and a very agreeable one, to receive a visit from an old friend I have not seen for so many years," said Mr. Quelch. "I gathered from your letter, a few days ago, that you desired to consult me upon some matter of urgent importance——"

"Very urgent, and very important, Quelch!" said Sir Peter. "It is a matter that may concern my life! You have not forgotten what I told you on the telephone last evening—my life has been in danger——"

"The police——"

"So far, they have not been able to trace the men who attacked me yesterday, and I have little hope that they will succeed in doing so," said Sir Peter. "All that is known of them is what was heard by the boy Bunter—two names, evidently nicknames, and the description I was able to give of the rascal who attacked me in the train. It is little enough for them to work upon."

"True! But—in what way can I be of assistance?" asked Mr. Quelch, evidently puzzled. "Anything, of course, that I can do——"

"I will explain. You are aware that Lord Reynham, now a lad of nearly sixteen, is my ward. He is an orphan, with no near relations, excepting his cousin Rupert. I am a very distant connection of the family; but I was appointed his guardian under the late lord's will—and I have found it a very onerous duty, Quelch. Four years ago a succession of desperate attempts were made to kidnap the boy."

"For what reason?"

"That remains unknown, unless ransom was the object. The boy will be very rich when he comes of age. Whatever the reason, William had several very narrow escapes. He is a boy of delicate health, and it told upon him severely, Quelch—so much so that I dreaded to see his nervous system absolutely shattered by a constant sense of danger. Every effort to discover the kidnappers failed—even their motive could only be guessed at—and I was driven, at last, to take very extraordinary measures for his protection."

Sir Peter paused.

"These were the measures, Quelch—he was placed at a certain school, under an assumed name, to remain there in safety till the kidnapping gang could be discovered and dealt with by the police."

"And he has remained safe?" asked Mr. Quelch.

"Perfectly so. I see him only at rare intervals, and never at the school where he boards. He has been practically adopted into his headmaster's family, spends his holidays with them, and is quite happy and contented, and perfectly safe. This, you will understand, was intended only as a temporary measure. I had no idea, at the time, that it would last over years."

"And it has?"

"It is still going on. The kidnapping gang are still at large, and I have the strongest proof that they have not abandoned their design. I had hoped, of course that they would be laid by the heels, but no trace of them has been found. On many occasions I was aware that I was watched—the rascals no doubt hoped to discover, sooner or later, what had become of Lord Reynham. It was given out that he was abroad for his health; and as it was known that he was delicate, no doubt this deluded the rogues for a time. Aware that the boy would be in danger if they were able to trace him, I have allowed this state of affairs to go on. He is still safe—under another name—but——"

"But there has been some new development?"

"Exactly!" said Sir Peter. "In some manner—I cannot even guess how—they have learned of the measures I have taken—though, fortunately, they know neither the school nor the name under which Lord Reynham passes there. This is known only to his headmaster, to myself, and to my solicitors. The boy is still perfectly safe from them; but I——"

"But you are not?"

"That is how the matter stands," said Sir Peter. "During the past few months several attempts have been made on me personally. The object, I presume, is to get me into their hands and force me to reveal the boy's present whereabouts—which, of course, I should never do.

"That demand was made yesterday, Quelch, under the muzzle of a revolver, in the train from Redclyffe—and though I doubt whether the rogue really intended to fire, I should certainly have been severely hurt in my struggle with him, but for the boy Bunter. I am an old man, Quelch, and this kind of thing is affecting me severely."

"I imagine so!" said Mr Quelch.

"What to do, in the extraordinary circumstances, has been a mystery to me," went on the old baronet. "But it happens that a short time ago Rupert returned from abroad—Captain Reynham, I should say, William's cousin and heir to the title. Rupert gave me some advice—upon which I do not care to act."

"And that advice?"

"To bring Lord Reynham home to Reynham Castle, to guard him with detectives, employed as servants in the house, and thus to ensnare the kidnapping rascals. The boy would be, as it were, a bait to draw them into an attempt, in which they might be captured."

"That is not a bad plan, Sir Peter. Sooner or later, the boy must resume his own name—the present position cannot be kept up after he comes of age, obviously. If every precaution were taken——"

"I should think of it, Quelch, if the boy were strong, sturdy, in good health. But, as I have said, he is delicate—utterly unfitted physically to go through such experiences. I do not wish to run the risk of it. His health requires care, in the best of circumstances. You will see, from that, that it is impossible to expose him to dangers and alarms."

"Quite!" agreed Mr. Quelch.

"But," went on Sir Peter slowly, "my nephew Rupert's suggestion put another idea into my mind—which is what I have to discuss with you. I have warned you that I am going to surprise you."

"Please proceed," said Mr. Quelch.

"No living soul, but yourself, has heard any whisper of this," said the old baronet. "No word of it, of course, will ever pass your lips. I have given Rupert no hint of it—he might have a careless tongue.

"If my plan is carried out, no one must have the slightest suspicion, or the whole plan would be a failure. Lord Reynham has not been seen by any of those lawless rascals for over four years—and the change from a child of eleven to a youth of nearly sixteen is very considerable, Quelch. Obviously, he would not be known by sight to anyone who saw him only as a child. Why should not another lad take his place——"

"Wha-a-t?"

"Some boy of strong character, courage, and physical fitness," said Sir Peter. "He would arrive at Reynham Castle, under the name of Lord Reynham, as if coming home for the Christmas holidays from school. I should greet him as Lord Reynham—everyone would suppose him to be the young lord—even his cousin Rupert. He would continue to play the part, in order to draw the fire, so to speak, of the kidnapping gang—Rupert's plan, but carried out by a boy able to stand the strain. That is the scheme I have formed, Quelch."

"Upon my word!" ejaculated Mr. Quelch. "Are you serious, Sir Peter?"

"Quite."

"But—but——"

"That is why I am here to consult you, Quelch. As a Form-master in this school, you must be acquainted with the characters of all the boys who come under your authority. It is possible that in your Form here there is some boy—some strong, sturdy, and courageous boy—who would be able and willing to play such a part."

"Bless my soul!" exclaimed Mr. Quelch, quite taken aback.

"Some Greyfriars boy——" said Sir Peter.

"But—but——" stammered Mr. Quelch.

There was no doubt that the old baronet had surprised him.

He had, in fact, astounded him.

"These rascals," continued Sir Peter, "already suspect that his lordship is at this school, under some assumed name. My visit to you has given them that impression; the rascal in the train yesterday said so plainly. If, therefore, a Greyfriars boy—any Greyfriars boy of a suitable age—arrived at the castle and was accepted by me as Lord Reynham, they could have no suspicion whatever that they were being deluded."

"But," gasped Mr. Quelch, "what of the boy? I certainly, as a Form-master, could never advise a boy to undertake so dangerous a task. The boy's parents would have to be consulted, and they would undoubtedly refuse their permission. My dear Sir Peter, have you not overlooked what really are insuperable difficulties in your very natural anxiety to secure the safety of your ward?"

"Possibly, possibly!" said the old baronet. "I desired to discuss the matter with you, Quelch, and should be glad if you could help me. If no Greyfriars boy is available, I must seek elsewhere. But of the plan itself, what is your opinion?"

"No doubt an excellent one, Sir Peter —if a boy can be found to play the part required of him. But I doubt very much whether such a boy can be found."

Sir Peter smiled faintly.

"Not in your Form here, at all events, I take it?" he asked.

"I am bound to say no," said Mr. Quelch. "I could not possibly advise you——"

"I shall seek elsewhere," said Sir Peter, rising from his chair. "I had hoped that you might be able to assist me, Quelch, in carrying out this plan. It appears that you cannot——"

"I regret it very much, Sir Peter—very much indeed. But really—really, I——"

"Then let us say no more about it," said Sir Peter Lanchester. "I must not trespass further on your time, my dear Quelch. If I may see the boy Bunter before I leave——"

"I will send for him at once."

Happily unaware that the boy Bunter was parked in the cupboard, only a few feet away, Mr. Quelch rang, and sent Trotter to fetch the boy Bunter.

Gladly enough would the boy Bunter have shown up, to receive the handsome tip intended for him by the old baronet.

But the boy Bunter, although blessed by Nature with an uncommon allowance of "neck," had not neck enough to emerge from the study cupboard under the eyes of Sir Peter and Mr. Quelch.

The boy Bunter had to remain where he was, while Trotter returned with the information that the boy Bunter was not to be found.

Sir Peter Lanchester, to his regret, had to go back to his car without having seen the boy Bunter—though he did not regret it half so much as the boy Bunter himself.

"Upon my word!" said Mr. Quelch aloud when the old baronet was gone. "Upon my word. What a very extraordinary idea—very extraordinary indeed! Upon my word! Most extraordinary!"

It was evident that Sir Peter's idea was a good deal too extraordinary for the Remove master of Greyfriars to have any hand in it.

Sir Peter had been gone some little time when the bell rang for afternoon class, then Mr. Quelch headed for the Form-room.

And then, at long last, Billy Bunter was able to emerge from his parking-place and scuttle out of the study—to receive fifty lines for being late in Form!

Mr. Quelch supposed that Bunter had been out of gates as Trotter had not been able to find him. Billy Bunter was more than content to let Mr. Quelch suppose so.

What would have happened to Bunter had the Remove master learned where he had spent the last half-hour would hardly bear thinking of.

———

THE THIRTEENTH CHAPTER.
Gammon!

"ABOUT Christmas——"

"Shut up!" roared five fellows.

"I was going to say——"

"Don't!"

"That I might ask you——"

"Ring off!"

"To come with me——"

"Eh?"

"To Reynham Castle——"

"What?"

"For Christmas with Sir Peter Lanchester——"

"Oh crikey!"

"Some place, I can tell you! Terrific old castle in Sussex; Norman keep and all that!" said Billy Bunter, blinking at the astonished five. "Dozens of menials, cars and things—everything of the best. Like to come if I can fix it for you?"

The Famous Five gazed at Bunter.

Tall tales from Bunter, of course, they were used to. They had heard all about Bunter Court—and had seen Bunter Villa. They had heard all about his titled relations—but had not seen them. They had heard about deeds of daring

THE MAGNET LIBRARY.—No. 1,556.

that Bunter had performed, such as terrific scraps with barges in the holidays—but they had never seen him engaged in any terrific scraps with barges in term-time. They had heard of the Bunter wealth—but had seen none of it at Greyfriars.

So they did not, naturally, expect anything in the nature of truth from Bunter.

Truth and Bunter had long been strangers, and were never expected to strike up an acquaintance by anyone who knew Bunter.

Still, even Bunter ought to have had a limit. The Famous Five felt that. And this, they could not help thinking, was a little over the edge.

"I daresay you saw the old bean who came to see Quelch yesterday," went on Bunter. "That was Sir Peter Lanchester, the old sportsman whose life I saved twice on Wednesday."

"Only twice!" gasped Bob Cherry. "Haven't you saved it again since?"

"Eh? No! He hasn't been in danger since, that I know of," said Bunter.

"Then you're not making a habit of it?"

"Oh, really, Cherry——"

"Did he ask you for Christmas while he was here yesterday?" grunted Johnny Bull.

"Not exactly——"

"I rather thought not." ·

"But the fact is——" continued Bunter.

"Oh, let's hear the fact!" said Harry Wharton, laughing. "We've never heard a fact from you before, old fat man!"

"Oh, really, Wharton——"

"The factfulness will probably not be preposterous," murmured Hurree Jamset Ram Singh.

"What I mean is I've been thinking a good bit since the old bean was here yesterday," said Bunter, "and I think I shall very likely be at Reynham Castle for Christmas. I mean, I've got pluck."

"You have?" exclaimed Bob. "Where do you pack it?"

"And why don't you ever use it?" asked Johnny Bull.

"Yah! It wants pluck—but I've got lots of that!" said Bunter. "It wants nerve—but I've got lots of nerve!"

"You must have, to spin a yarn like this," agreed Bob. "Never heard of a fellow with such a nerve."

"I don't mean that you fathead! I mean, I've got tons of pluck and nerve; and as for danger, I rather like it."

"Oh crumbs!"

"I'm jolly well going to chance it!" declared Bunter "I fancy I can fix it all right with the old bean. After all, I'm the chap to face danger."

"When there isn't any," agreed Harry Wharton. "But is it dangerous to spend Christmas with that old bean who called on Quelch yesterday? Does he bite?"

"But I should like to have a few pals with me, all the same," went on Billy Bunter, unheeding "It would be safer. Look here, you fellows, you don't seem to be settled about the hols. If I go to Reynham Castle, would you like to come?"

"If!" chortled Bob.

"The if-fulness is terrific."

"You fat ass!" roared Johnny Bull. "What are you burbling about? You don't even know that old bean who called on Quelch!"

"I saved his life——"

"Gammon!"

"Twice——"

"Fathead!"

"And I'm the man he wants. According to what he said to Quelch——"

"How on earth do you know what he

said to Quelch?" exclaimed Frank Nugent.

"Oh! Ah! Oh! I—I mean——" stammered Bunter

"You fat villain!" exclaimed Harry Wharton. "Have you been doing keyhole stunts in Masters' Passage, like you do in the Remove?"

"Oh, really, Wharton——"

"It's all gammon from beginning to end!" grunted Johnny Bull.

"Oh, is it?" yapped Bunter. "Well, look here, I'm going to drop Sir Peter a line—about Christmas. I fancy it will be all right. Now, suppose I fix it to spend Christmas at Reynham Castle, and take a few friends with me, will you fellows come? Mind, I'm not afraid——"

"What is there to be afraid of—except the butler's boot—if you butted in?"

"Ha, ha, ha!"

"Oh, don't be an ass! I'm not afraid. Still, it would be safer with a few pals round me. Now—yes or no?" snapped Bunter. "If I fix up Christmas at Reynham Castle, with Sir Peter Lanchester, will you fellows come?"

Harry Wharton laughed.

"Oh, certainly!" he answered. "We'll come—if you land yourself at Reynham Castle!"

"Quite!" grinned Nugent.

"Is there such a place as Reynham Castle?" asked Bob.

"Yes, you fathead—in Sussex."

"Not in dreamland?"

"You silly ass——" roared Bunter. "It's a magnificent establishment—just like Bunter Court, in fact."

"I fancy it's rather like Bunter Court!" chortled Bob. "Every attraction, except one—it doesn't happen to exist!"

"Ha, ha, ha!"

"Well, you'll jolly well see!" snorted Bunter. "It's settled, then, you fellows come with me for Christmas to Reynham Castle, if I fix it up."

"Ha, ha! Yes, certainly!"

"That's all right, then!" said Bunter. "Lend me a stamp, will you? I've got to write to Sir Peter."

"Oh, my only hat!" roared Johnny Bull. "Have you spun this yarn simply to get a three-ha penny stamp?"

"Oh, really, Bull——"

"Dash it all, the yarn was worth three-ha'pence!" chuckled Bob. "Here you are, Bunty, here's a stamp. Now own up that it's all gammon!"

"Yah!"

Bunter took the stamp and rolled away to his study.

Harry Wharton & Co. gazed after him in wonder.

"I suppose," said Harry thoughtfully, "that there can't, by any chance, be a word of truth in it?"

"Hardly!" grinned Bob.

"Truth—from Bunter!" grunted Johnny Bull. "Dreaming?"

Really, it did not seem probable to the Famous Five So far from believing that Bunter was going to land himself at a magnificent castle for Christmas, they did not believe in the castle—except as a castle in the air! In which circumstances, it seemed quite safe to agree to accompany Bunter to that castle—if he went.

But, as the novelists say, they little knew!

———

THE FOURTEENTH CHAPTER.
Bunter Tries it On!

"TODDY, old chap——"

Peter Todd, in Study No. 7, held up a warning hand.

Billy Bunter, sitting at the study table, with a pen in his fat paw and a thoughtful wrinkle in his fat brow, blinked at him.

"Nothing about Christmas!" warned Toddy.

Bunter gave a contemptuous snort.

"If you fancy I'd put in Christmas in Bloomsbury, Toddy——" he said, with ineffable scorn.

"I fancy you would!" agreed Toddy. "And I fancy you won't! If it's not about Christmas, you can run on."

"Beast! How many 'k's' in accident?" asked Bunter.

"Oh crikey!"

"You see, I spell better than you, Toddy—still, I don't want any mistakes in a letter to a baronet," explained Bunter.

"One of your titled relations?" grinned Toddy.

"Not exactly a relation—old friend of the family!" said Bunter airily. "I've got to get this letter off by the post, Toddy. I say, how many 'k's' do you put in accident?"

"None, as a rule. A couple of 'c's' are good enough for me."

"Oh, don't be an ass, Toddy! I know there's a 'k,' as well as an 'x,' but I want to know if there's more than one!" said Bunter peevishly.

"Ha, ha, ha!" yelled Peter Todd.

"You'll make that baronet jump if he gets 'x's' and 'k's'!"

"Well, how do you spell it?" demanded Bunter.

"A-c-c-i-d-e-n-t!" spelt out Toddy.

Snort from Bunter. He was not satisfied with that.

"Oh, you can't spell!" he snapped. "Fat lot of good asking you, Toddy! I say, look it out in the dick for me, will you?"

"Ha, ha, ha!" roared Toddy.

He did not look that word out in the dictionary for Bunter. He walked out of Study No. 7, laughing.

(Continued on next page.)

LEARN TO PLAY FOOTBALL!
BY OUR INTERNATIONAL COACH

A NARROW SHAVE !

I HAVEN'T told you a fraction of all there is to know about football, of course. If you could do everything I have told you, however, you would all be pretty good footballers by now. Some of you have improved this season. I know that a lot of you have been practising really hard ever since I told you how important practice at football is.

Anyway, you all know enough about it now to make this game of ours really interesting for yourselves. You know how you ought to be controlling and kicking the ball, what you are expected to do in your various positions and which opponents you must each mark. So let's get on and see how well you can remember all these things in an actual game.

We had reached the stage where the ball had been kicked off, and had been passed to our outside-right. It failed to reach him, because a player on the other side was doing his marking job properly, and nipped in to get the ball. Well, he has it now. He passes it to his outside-left, who runs on a bit, and then kicks it into the middle where two of his pals are waiting for it. It has gone to the centre-forward. He's shooting—lucky for us, he shot over the bar.

Let's stop the game for a moment and think about that narrow shave we had. Why was the ball allowed to get to the centre-forward of the other side without one of our players touching it? I'm afraid the answer is that we weren't marking our men as we should have been. It was a good pass which the left-half gave to his outside-left, I know, but our right-back was supposed to be marking the outside-left. It he had been in the right place, the winger wouldn't have been allowed to put the ball across so accurately that it fell right at the feet of his centre-forward.

And where was our centre-half? He was supposed to be marking the centre-forward of the other side, yet he left him with plenty of time to take careful aim and shoot. I am not suggesting that both our right-back and our

KEEP IT ON THE CARPET !

Ballooning the ball is a bad fault with a number of footballers—always keep the ball low when passing or shooting at goal !

centre-half should have got the ball before the fellows they were marking. Defenders can't be expected to do that every time. The point is, that if they had been somewhere near, the fellows with the ball would have had to hurry—wouldn't have been given so much time to think about what to do next.

SHOOT LOW !

THE second lesson of this incident concerns the "over the bar" shot by the centre-forward. Why did he do that? Simply because he did not remember the rule I gave you about keeping the ball low. If he had kicked with his instep, and had got his weight "on top," instead of behind the ball, it wouldn't have gone into the air, but into the goal.

As a general instruction for shooting—always tend to keep the ball low rather than high. It is much easier for a goalkeeper to jump up to a ball than it is for him to bend down to it. Watch a first-class player taking a penalty kick. The successful ones are the fellows who make the ball just skim the ground.

The best penalty-kicker I ever saw was Jacky Mordue, who used to play for Sunderland. In one season I think he scored fifteen goals from the penalty spot. The only one I ever saw him miss was when the opposing goalkeeper was a very small fellow. Mordue's secret of success was that he always kept the ball low. This little goalkeeper was able to get down to the low shot, and he saved miraculously. I shall have more to say about penalty-kicks later on. But what applies to them, applies to all shooting—keep the ball low.

GOAL-KICKS !

I HOPE the centre-forward who fired over the top when he had a chance to score will have learned his lesson. Now the goal-kick is being taken. Have a look at the plan of the field in your rule-book, and you will notice what is called the goal-area marked in front of the goal. For the goal-kick the ball must be placed in the goal-area. It is usually put on the corner, on the side of the goal where the ball went out of play. When the opposing centre-forward shot over the bar, the ball went rather more to the right than to the left. So the goal-keeper places the ball in that portion of the goal-area.

Two years ago it would have been permissible for a full-back to tap the ball to the goalkeeper, who could then pick it up and kick it down the field. You must have seen goalkeepers doing that when they have been taking goal-kicks. That isn't allowed now, however. A new rule says that the goalkeeper must kick the ball direct into play—must not have it tapped to him by a full-back, or pick it up in any other way. Some goalkeepers found the new way a bit hard at first. In fact, several of them, even in first-class football, couldn't kick the ball very well off the ground, so the full-back had to do it. That is allowed by the rules, but it is really the goalkeeper's job, so he should learn to take the goal-kicks.

When I say learn, I mean it, because taking goal-kicks is an art in itself. It is not just a question of kicking the ball hard. Attacks can be started by accurately placing goal-kicks. I remember a game not long ago when Ted Sagar, Everton's goalkeeper, took a goal-kick which brought a goal for his side. The wind was behind him, and so hard and straight did he kick the ball, that it went straight to one of his own forwards, who gathered it and scored without another player touching the ball. That just shows you that taking goal-kicks is all a part of football. Try, goalkeepers, to place your kicks, thus playing your part in helping your forwards.

Bunter snorted, and resumed letter-writing. He wanted to be rather particular with that letter, as it was going to a baronet, who lived in a castle. He was too lazy, however, to look out the word in the dick for himself; but, after a little reflection, he decided on one 'k.' He knew there was an 'x'

Bunter was giving that letter a lot of thought. It was—he hoped, at least—going to settle the rather urgent problem of landing him somewhere for the Christmas holidays—a problem that was growing more and more urgent as breaking-up day drew nearer.

The Peeping Tom of Greyfriars had played the eavesdropper, in Mr. Quelch's study the day before, from sheer inquisitiveness. But since then Bunter's powerful brain had been at work.

What he had heard had astonished him. It had astonished Quelch, in the study, and Bunter, in the study cupboard.

It was not surprising that Mr. Quelch had failed to play up. There was no doubt that old Sir Peter, in his keen and dutiful anxiety to secure his ward from unknown, mysterious, and dangerous enemies, had rather omitted to consider what might happen to the boy who was to take the young lord's name and place—if the plan was carried out.

Certainly, Mr. Quelch, as a schoolmaster, could not possibly have had a hand in placing any boy in such a dangerous position.

Sir Peter's visit to Greyfriars had, in fact, drawn blank, so far as Sir Peter was concerned; but it had not drawn blank, so far as Bunter was concerned.

Bunter was "on" this!

It was one of Billy Bunter's little ways to feel a lofty and scornful disregard of danger—so long as danger was not in the offing. Distant dangers had no terrors for Bunter.

What Bunter thought of, chiefly, was that the fellow who played the part of Lord Reynham would pass the Christmas holidays at a magnificent castle, surrounded by all that wealth could buy, my-lorded by a host of servants, and feeding on the fat of the land.

That was a very attractive prospect to Bunter.

It was worth a spot of danger.

Certainly, had the danger been on the spot, Bunter would have jibbed at it. At close quarters Bunter disliked danger extremely

But it was distant; and besides, the fat Owl immediately thought of the idea of taking a party of fellows with him who would rally round him and keep him safe. The Famous Five were exactly the fellows to deal with danger if it happened along. Bunter would be quite prepared to let them deal with it. They could, in fact, have it all to themselves!

The danger being remote, Bunter thought less of it than of stately halls, liveried flunkeys, turkeys, and Christmas puddings.

Plenty of fellows, with a good deal more courage than Bunter, might have hesitated to take on a part to play which exposed them to the attacks of a gang of kidnapping crooks. Bunter was, in fact, exemplifying the truth of the ancient proverb that fools rush in where angels fear to tread!

Bunter was going to rush in, anyhow—if he could!

He thought he had quite a good chance. He had already made a very good impression on old Sir Peter. Had he not tackled a man with a gun in his hand, on the train from Redclyffe? True, he had known that the gun was unloaded—but Sir Peter was not aware of that circumstance. Bunter had impressed the old baronet as a very plucky fellow.

For the rest, he was a Greyfriars fellow—and Sir Peter preferred a Greyfriars fellow, if available. And he would, of course, prefer a fine, upstanding, handsome sort of fellow, with an air of native nobility—a fellow like Bunter. Bunter was sure of that. So he was feeling fairly confident as he indited that epistle to Sir Peter.

"Deer Sir Peter,—Owing to an akxident, I happened to heer what you said to my Form-master on Thersday."

Bunter paused a little. He had to account for his knowledge of what Sir Peter required. But he realised that he could not tell Sir Peter that he had deliberately played the eavesdropper. He was aware that other people's views on the subject rather differed from his own.

But he was not long at a loss. Fibbing was Bunter's perpetual resource in moments of difficulty. It required only a short pause for Bunter to think of a fib that would serve his turn.

He gnawed the handle of his pen for a few thoughtful moments, and then grinned and resumed.

"Sum fellows lokked me up in the cubbord in Quelch's studdy for a praktical joak. Of corse, I coodn't let Quelch find me there, or it wood have got them into a row."

Bunter thought this rather good! It showed what a loyal fellow he was, willing to stand anything, rather than land his thoughtless schoolfellows in a row!

"Oweing to this, I herd what you said to Quelch, much against my will. I hoap you will excuse me, in the cirkumstances.

Of course, you may rely on me not to say a single word abowt it. I shood not think of breething a sillable.

I am riting to say that I think I am the man you want. I am perfektly willing to do what is rekwired, and if there is anny danger, I shall enjoy it. I think you must have notised that I have plenty of pluck, and I certanely cannot remember ever having bean afrade of anything.

If you wood like me to do it, I am kwite at your service. A lot of fellows here want me to go hoam with them for the hols, but I am kwite ankshus to be of service to you.

Yours truly,
W. G. BUNTER."

Billy read that letter over twice and was satisfied with it. Then he enclosed it in an envelope, addressed it to Sir Peter Lanchester, Bart, at Reynham Castle, Sussex, and stuck on Bob Cherry's stamp.

With the letter in his hand, he rolled down to the quad.

A crowd of Remove fellows were punting a footer, after class, the Famous Five among them. As Bunter emerged from the House with the letter in his hand, Bob Cherry's eye fell on him, and he cut across.

"Done it?" he grinned.

"Eh? Yes!"

"Written to the jolly old Baronet?"

"Yes: I'm just posting the letter."

"I don't think!" chuckled Bob.

Bunter blinked at him and held up the letter.

"Look!" he jeered.

"Oh, my hat!" ejaculated Bob, as he looked. There was no doubt that that letter in Bunter's fat hand was addressed to Sir Peter Lanchester, Bart, Reynham Castle, Sussex.

Bob blinked at it.

"Going to post it?" he asked.

"You silly ass!" hooted Bunter. "Think I've written it just to stuff you?"

"Sort of!" admitted Bob.

"Well, come along to the letter-box and see!" snorted Bunter.

Bob, grinning, accompanied the fat Owl to the letter-box in the school wall. To his surprise, Bunter slipped the letter in at the slot, and it dropped into the box.

"Well, what do you think now?" yapped Bunter.

"Blessed if I know what to think!" gasped Bob. "It's almost enough to make a fellow think that you've been telling the truth, old fat man. In fact, I should think so, if it wasn't impossible."

"Yah!" retorted Bunter.

And he rolled back to the House—and Bob, quite puzzled, rejoined the fellows who were punting the ball.

THE FIFTEENTH CHAPTER.
Bunter is Wanted!

BUZZZZ!
      Mr. Quelch had retired to his study, after lunch the following day, for a little rest. He had settled down in his armchair, his feet on the fender, and an entrancing volume of Sophocles in his hands, when the telephone-bell rang.

The Remove master was far from

wishing to be disturbed at that moment. But it is, of course, always at such moments that telephone-bells ring.

He laid down Sophocles and took up the receiver.

"Mr. Quelch?" came a voice over the wires; and the Remove master, who had been about to bark into the transmitter, checked that bark, as he recognised the voice of Sir Peter Lanchester.

"Speaking, Sir Peter!" he answered amicably.

"I am sorry to disturb you, Quelch——"

"Not at all!"

"But in reference to my conversation with you a couple of days ago——"

"I am afraid, Sir Peter, that I can have nothing to add to what I said at the time. I could certainly not recommend——"

"I have received an offer——"

"Oh!"

"From a Greyfriars boy——"

"What?"

"That very plucky lad, Bunter, who was of such service to me on Wednesday," said Sir Peter. "I received a letter from him this morning."

"Upon my word!"

"Owing to—to certain circumstances into which, perhaps, I need not enter, Bunter is acquainted with what I require!" said Sir Peter. "Very pluckily, he offers to play the part which I discussed with you, Quelch."

"Really, Sir Peter——" gasped Quelch.

"Before accepting this brave and generous lad's offer, I feel bound to ask your permission, as his Form-master. You have no objections, Quelch?"

"I—I—I'm quite astonished!" gasped Mr. Quelch. "Are you sure that Bunter is acquainted with the full circumstances of the case?"

"Yes, there is no doubt about that."

"And he has offered to play a part which may involve him in serious peril?"

"Precisely."

"Extraordinary!" said Mr. Quelch.

"I see nothing extraordinary in it, Mr. Quelch—a lad of courageous character like Bunter——"

"He has certainly never impressed me as a lad of courageous character!" said Mr. Quelch dryly. "Quite the reverse, I should have said."

"That is hardly in keeping with his act in tackling a man armed with a deadly weapon, Quelch, which he certainly did."

"Oh, quite! But——"

"Needless to say, I shall close with this offer from Bunter, eagerly, if you have no objection, Quelch?"

"It is not for me to object, if the boy understands what he is facing, and is willing to face it," said the Remove master. "But the consent of his father must be obtained."

"Naturally. I shall require Bunter to obtain his father's consent, as a matter of course. For the rest, you have no objection to make?"

"None!" said Mr. Quelch.

"Very good then. Subject to Mr. Bunter's consent, I shall accept the offer made by the boy. I must see him, to make arrangements. I have little doubt that I shall be watched, and, in the circumstances, I desire Bunter to be seen in my company, by any eyes that may be watching—you understand why. I think, therefore, of driving to Courtfield: and perhaps Bunter could come there—I believe it is a half-holiday to-day at the school——"

"That is the case."

"Bunter, perhaps, might like to come to tea with me, at the Hotel Royal, in Courtfield——"

"I have no doubt of it."

"Will you, then, tell him that I shall expect him at the Hotel Royal, at four o'clock, and over tea we shall have a discussion."

"Very good, Sir Peter."

Mr. Quelch sat blinking at the telephone for a whole minute after the baronet had rung off.

Sir Peter's extraordinary scheme for securing the safety of his ward had surprised him. But he was still more surprised now.

There was no doubt that the fellow who played the part of the young lord, at Reynham Castle, would be playing a dangerous game. A fellow like Harry Wharton, or Bob Cherry, might have been prepared to take the risks. But it was very surprising to hear that Bunter was prepared to take them.

Mr. Quelch was pretty well acquainted with all the fellows in his Form, and he had certainly never attributed any heroic qualities to the fattest member thereof.

He stepped to his study window, and glanced out into the frosty quad. Most of the fellows were out of the House after dinner, and among them the fat figure of Billy Bunter was visible.

Bunter was talking to the Famous Five. The five were grinning. As Mr. Quelch opened his window, Bob Cherry's face floated to his ears:

"Gammon!"

"Oh, really, Cherry——" squeaked Bunter.

"Spoof!" said Johnny Bull.

"Oh, really, Bull——"

"Bunter!" called Mr. Quelch.

"Oh!" gasped Bunter, spinning round like a fat top towards his Form-master's study window. "Oh crikey! Yes, sir!"

"Come to my study at once, Bunter!"

"Oh lor'! It—it wasn't me, sir!" stammered Bunter. That summons to his Form-master's study seemed to alarm the fat Owl. "I—I say, sir, I—I wasn't there at the time!"

"What?"

"I wasn't, really!" gasped Bunter. "I never went down to the pantry in break, sir. I—I don't know my way there. If the cook——"

"Upon my word!" exclaimed Mr. Quelch. "You have been in the pantry again, Bunter?"

"Oh, no, sir! It wasn't me. If—if there's a pie gone, sir, I don't know anything about it. I—I think it was the cat, sir——"

"Come to my study at once, Bunter!" thundered Mr. Quelch, and he closed the window with a bang.

"Oh crikey!" groaned Bunter. "I—I —I say, you fellows, do you think Quelch knows anything about that pie?"

"Ha, ha, ha!" roared the Famous Five.

"Beasts!"

Billy Bunter rolled into the House, in a very apprehensive frame of mind.

He had no doubt that he was going to be suspected of having had that pie. People always did seem to suspect Bunter of such things, somehow. It was fearfully unjust, of course. Bunter could not help feeling how frightfully unjust it was. His only consolation was that the pie, like the dear dead days in the old song, was gone beyond recall.

THE SIXTEENTH CHAPTER.

A Surprise for Skinner!

"HALLO, hallo, hallo!" roared Bob Cherry. "Enjoying life?"

"He, he, he!" chuckled Bunter. "What-ho!"

Bob was surprised.

Having seen Billy Bunter called into Quelch's study, he had naturally expected to behold signs of woe and tribulation next time he saw the fat Owl.

Instead of which Bunter was beaming. The happy grin on Bunter's fat face extended almost from one fat ear to the other. If ever a fellow looked as if he were enjoying life, William George Bunter did.

The Famous Five were going over to Highcliffe that afternoon to say goodbye to their friends, Courtenay and the Caterpillar, before break-up for Christmas. But at the sight of Bunter's beaming face in the quad they stopped, quite interested to know the cause.

Fellows did not always look so merry and bright, after being called into Quelch's study.

"Not licked?" asked Harry Wharton.

"No fear! It wasn't about the pie, you know," said Bunter. "Quelch never mentioned the pie. I've had some rather good news."

"Don't say your postal order's come?" ejaculated Bob.

"Better than that," grinned Bunter. "I rather fancy I shall have a tip of a fiver this afternoon."

"What a fertile fancy," remarked Nugent.

"Well, I mean to say, the old bean was going to tip me a fiver the other day," argued Bunter. "So why shouldn't he to-day—what?"

"What old bean?" asked Harry.

"Oh, really, Wharton, I've told you all about Sir Peter Lanchester——"

"Are you still keeping that up?" asked Johnny Bull. "Why not put on a fresh record? Tell us about your uncle, the marquis, for a change."

"Eh? I don't know any marquises, fathead!"

"I know you don't. But you know exactly as many marquises as baronets."

"Ha, ha, ha!"

"Well, you'll jolly well see!" snorted Bunter. "Guess what Quelch wanted? It was a message from Sir Peter. I'm going to tea with him this afternoon."

"Bit of a walk to Sussex, isn't it?"

"He's going to be in Courtfield this afternoon. I'm teaing with him at the Hotel Royal," said Bunter loftily. "I'd take you fellows, only—only——"

"Only you're not going?" asked Johnny Bull.

"Ha, ha, ha!"

"Only I have to be a bit particular whom I take to a swanky place like the Hotel Royal," said Bunter calmly.

"Why, you cheeky porpoise——"

"And we've got some rather private matters to discuss, too," said Bunter. "I say, you fellows, it's settled about Christmas. I shall be at Reynham Castle."

"If any——" murmured Nugent.

"Ha, ha, ha!"

"I'm going to take you fellows," said Bunter. "That's arranged, isn't it? I shall expect you to behave yourselves, put on your best manners—such as they are, you know."

"Oh crumbs!"

"I mean, I want you to do me credit," explained Bunter. "Don't let me down before a lot of liveried servants, and all that. When we're at

Reynham Castle, you'd better keep your eyes on me, and do exactly as I do."

"When?" gasped Bob.

"The whenfulness is terrific!"

"As I'm standing you a first-class Christmas holiday at a magnificent castle with my titled friends, I suppose you'll lend me my taxi fare to Courtfield this afternoon?" asked Bunter.

"Ha, ha, ha!" roared the Famous Five.

"Blessed if I see anything to cackle at!" hooted Bunter. "What are you sniggering at, you silly asses?"

"Taxi fare to Courtfield is five bob," chuckled Bob Cherry. "Anybody going to stand five bob for a holiday with Bunter's titled friends, at a castle in the air?"

"Hardly," grinned Nugent. "Dear at the price."

"But what do you want to go to Courtfield for, fathead?" asked Harry Wharton.

"I've told you that I'm going to tea with a baronet."

"Yes, I know. But what are you going for, all the same?"

"Beast!"

The Famous Five walked out of gates, laughing. Why Bunter was looking so bucked, they did not know. But they did not believe in his baronet, his tea at the Hotel Royal, or his castle in Sussex. They did not, in fact, believe a word of the whole story.

Billy Bunter snorted. Really, it was rather hard not to be believed when he was, for once in a way, telling the truth. Still, that was so unusual and unexpected, that the Remove fellows could not be expected to guess it.

A fellow who was going to tea with a wealthy baronet at a swanky hotel, naturally preferred to arrive there in a taxi, instead of foot-slogging across a muddy common. But Bunter, as usual, was short of cash.

"I say, Smithy!" He spotted the Bounder, and ran him down. "I say, old chap, will you lend me——"

"No!"

"Five bob——"

"No!"

"Only till I get back from Courtfield?" urged Bunter. "Only a couple of hours, Smithy?"

"Not a couple of years?" asked the Bounder sarcastically. "Not a couple of centuries?"

"You ass!" howled Bunter. "I say, I'm going to tea with Sir Peter Lanchester—that old bean who came to see Quelch the other day, you know. I'm spending Christmas with him at a castle in Sussex. I'd ask you, Smithy, only it would hardly do, would it?"

"What?"

"I mean, at a place like Reynham Castle, I have to be a bit particular," explained Bunter. "You're a bit too loud, I'm afraid. Otherwise, I'd really ask you there, Smithy—I would, really. You'll lend me five bob, won't you?"

Herbert Vernon-Smith looked fixedly at Billy Bunter for a moment. Then he took him by the neck, twirled him round, and planted a boot on him.

"Yarooh!" roared Bunter. "Ow! Beast! Wharrer you kicking me for, you rotter? Wow!"

The Bounder's foot was rising again; and Bunter rolled away hastily. Why Smithy had kicked him, Bunter did not know; but he could see that Smithy wasn't going to lend him the five bob, anyhow.

Up and down and round about Billy Bunter rolled for the next half hour, in quest of that taxi fare. He did not

succeed in raising it. But Skinner had a suggestion to make.

"Why not leave it to the jolly old baronet?" he asked, with a wink at three or four grinning fellows. "Mention to him that you've left all your banknotes on the grand piano in your study."

Skinner & Co. did not believe, any more than the Famous Five, in the baronet from Sussex, or the tea at the Hotel Royal. They only believed that the fat Owl was spinning a steeper yarn than usual, to raise the wind for jam tarts at the tuckshop. So Skinner was surprised by the thoughtful expression that came over Bunter's fat face.

"Oh, good!" exclaimed Bunter. "Of course, I can do that. After all, as he's asked me to tea, he can pay the taxi. Why not?"

And Bunter rolled into the House, to request permission to use a telephone to call up a taxi.

Skinner & Co. stared after him.

"Does that silly fat ass think we believe a word of it?" grunted Bolsover major.

"Blessed if I make him out!" said Skinner, in wonder.

Bunter came out into the quad again, ten minutes later, in coat and hat. He looked rather unusually well-dressed—which was accounted for by the fact that the coat belonged to Harry Wharton and the hat to Lord Mauleverer. Bunter felt that he ought to dress a little carefully, on an occasion like this.

He rolled cheerfully down to the gates, and Skinner walked after him.

At the gates, Bunter blinked up the road towards Courtfield.

"Waiting for your taxi?" asked Skinner sarcastically

"Eh? Yes!"

"Keep it up!" grinned Skinner.

Bunter disdained to answer.

He waited—and Skinner waited. A taxi came whizzing from the direction of the town. It stopped at the school gates. Skinner stared at it. Bunter clambered into it.

"Hotel Royal, Courtfield!" he said to the driver, with a vaunting blink at Harold Skinner.

"Yes, sir!"

The taxi cut away up the road, with Bunter sitting inside.

Skinner stared after it quite blankly, for a moment.

"Gammon!" he said, aloud. "Pure gammon! He's said that for me to hear—I'll bet he tells the driver something different, farther on." Skinner grinned. He had no doubt that he had it right! "By gum, I'll jolly well get after him, on my bike, and spot him—ha, ha!"

Skinner rushed for his bike.

It seemed to Skinner no end of a joke, to bowl Bunter out, and to be able to reveal exactly what Bunter had done, that afternoon when he came back telling the tale about gorgeous teas with wealthy baronets at swanky hotels!

He grinned as he shot away on the bike up the Courtfield road.

He sighted the taxi again on the road over the common. He kept it in sight. To his astonishment, it stopped at the Hotel Royal—the most expensive place in Courtfield.

Skinner dismounted on the other side of the street, and stared across.

Bunter got out of the taxi.

He rolled up the steps into the hotel entrance.

An aristocratic-looking old gentleman with silvery hair met him there, and shook hands with him. Skinner recognised Mr. Quelch's visitor of a day or two ago. He simply stared.

Bunter disappeared into the entrance,

with the old baronet. Skinner, rooted to the opposite pavement, could only stare.

A minute or so later, a gold-laced commissionaire came out, and stepped to the waiting taxi. The latter then drove away. Evidently, the taxi-fare had been sent out.

Skinner blinked.

"My only summer hat!" he murmured. "My only single, solitary, sainted aunt! It's true! Great pip!"

Skinner felt quite dazed, as he got on his bike to ride back to Greyfriars.

———

THE SEVENTEENTH CHAPTER.

Lost !

"HAD a good time?"

"How's the jolly old baronet?"

"Did he tip you that fiver?"

"Did he make it a tenner?"

"Ha, ha, ha!"

There was a ripple of merriment in the Rag, as Billy Bunter rolled into that apartment, after tea. Most of the Remove were there: and most of them seemed quite interested in Billy Bunter.

Skinner and Bolsover major, who were whispering together, did not join in the merriment. They looked curiously at Billy Bunter. But everybody else appeared to be amused. The fat Owl's antics, for the last few days, had caused quite a lot of merriment in his Form.

"I say, you fellows——" squeaked Bunter.

"Had a good spread with jolly old Sir Peter?" chortled Bob Cherry.

"Ripping!" declared Bunter. "They do you jolly well at the Hotel Royal—if you can pay, of course. Frightfully expensive place. Of course that's nothing to my friend Sir Peter."

"And where have you been this afternoon?" asked the Bounder.

"Eh? Don't I keep on telling you that I've been teaing with my friend Sir Peter, at the Hotel Royal?" yapped Bunter.

"Saved his life again?" asked Bob Cherry.

"Eh? No!"

"Why not?"

"Ha, ha, ha!"

"You silly ass!" hooted Bunter. "How could I save his life, if it wasn't in danger?"

"Well, you jolly well couldn't if it was in danger!" chuckled Bob.

"But I did—twice!" yelled Bunter.

"Still twice!" exclaimed Bob. "But it's days since you saved it twice, Bunter! Hasn't it grown since then?"

"Ha, ha, ha!"

"If you fellows cackle at everything I say, I jolly well shan't take you to Reynham Castle for Christmas!" roared Bunter, wrathfully. "Then you'll jolly well miss the time of your lives."

"The missfulness will be truly terrific!"

"Ha, ha, ha!"

"But did he tip you that fiver?" chuckled Vernon-Smith. "Wasn't there going to be a fiver? Did he forget it?"

"No, he didn't! I've got it here!"

"Wha-a-t?"

"Seeing is believing!" sneered Bunter. "The old sportsman was going to tip me a fiver, the day he came here for saving his life, only—only I wasn't on the spot. I rather thought he'd remember it to-day. And he jolly well did."

"The seefulness is the esteemed believefulness!" said Hurree Jamset Ram Singh. "Let us feast our absurd eyes on the fiver."

"Well, I've got it here in my pocket!" said Bunter. "Perhaps you'll believe it when you see it."

"Don't move!" said the bandit, knocking Sir Peter Lanchester's paper aside and levelling an automatic. "I shall shoot if you stir a finger!" Hidden underneath the carriage seat, Billy Bunter watched spellbound.

"The perhapsfulness is——"

"Preposterous!" chuckled Bob Cherry.

"Trot it out!" said Hazeldene.

"What's the betting that he'll suddenly remember he's left it in his study, you fellows?"

"Ha, ha, ha!"

Billy Bunter blinked round indignantly through his big spectacles. He slid his fat hand into his jacket pocket.

It was an actual fact, that Sir Peter had remembered that "tip." Billy Bunter had rolled out of the Hotel Royal, in Courtfield, with a five-pound note parked in his pocket. Now he was going to produce it, to overwhelm all these doubting Thomases.

He groped in the pocket.

The juniors watched him, with great entertainment. Not believing a word of the whole affair, from beginning to end, they certainly did not expect Bunter to produce a five-pound note!

They were prepared for him to keep up the game to the very last moment—to pretend to be about to produce a fiver, and then to remember, suddenly, that he had left it somewhere else, or discover that he had lost it. They were prepared for anything except the actual sight of an actual fiver.

Bunter groped.

A startled and dismayed expression came over his face. Apparently his groping fat paw failed to clutch a fiver in that pocket.

"Oh crikey!" ejaculated Bunter.

"Left it somewhere?" chortled Bob.

"Ha, ha, ha!"

"Nunno! I—I put it in this pocket all right! But——"

"Ah!" said Bob, "There's a 'but'. I was sort of afraid there would be a 'but'."

"Ha, ha, ha!"

"I—I—I say, you fellows, I—I've lost it!" gasped Bunter.

"Ha, ha, ha!" roared all the Rag.

Billy Bunter drew out the lining of his pocket. There was a hole in that lining. Bunter often had holes in his pockets—but seldom anything of any great value to lose therefrom. The fiver was gone!

"Oh lor'!" gasped Bunter, "I—I say, you fellows, it—it's lost! I—I must have dropped it somewhere, through this hole in the lining——"

"Doesn't he do it well?" gasped Toddy. "Wouldn't anybody almost believe that he'd really had a fiver?"

"Oh, really, Toddy——"

"Ha, ha, ha!"

"I say, you fellows, I never knew there was a hole in that lining when I put the fiver in that pocket!" groaned Bunter. "Now it's lost!"

"You're not much the poorer!" grinned Vernon-Smith.

"Oh, really, Smithy——"

"You fat ass!" exclaimed Harry Wharton. "Own up that you've been spoofing all the time!"

"Oh, really, Wharton——"

"Own up, you frabjous, footling freak!" grunted Johnny Bull.

"Beast! I say, you fellows, I was going to stand a study supper out of that fiver. Now it's lost. I say, who's going to lend me a quid?"

"Ha, ha, ha!"

There was a roar of merriment in the Rag. But there was no offer to lend Bunter a quid. There was no quid for the fat Owl; neither did anybody but William George Bunter believe that there had ever been a fiver.

THE EIGHTEENTH CHAPTER.

The Man in the Car!

"CARE for a lift, sir?"

"Eh? Yes, rather!" said Billy Bunter promptly.

It was Sunday morning—a bright, frosty December day. Many of the Greyfriars fellows were out on "Sunday walks" that fine morning, the last Sunday before breaking-up.

Harry Wharton & Co. had walked over to Cliff House to see Marjorie & Co. for the last time before clearing off for the Christmas holidays. Billy Bunter had something much more important than that to think of.

Bunter believed—if nobody else did—in that fiver. He nourished a hope of seeing it again.

Sir Peter had sent him back in a taxi after tea on Saturday. It was possible that that banknote, which had certainly slipped through the hole in the lining of his jacket pocket somewhere or other, had fallen in the taxi. If so, its recovery was probable.

So as soon as he was free from "divvers" that morning, Billy Bunter started walking to Courtfield. The walk across the common did not attract him, but the chance of recovering the fiver did.

So there was Bunter, rolling by the rather lonely road over the common, and, like Iser in the poem, rolling rapidly.

A car, which had been aimlessly crawling on the road for some time, slowed down behind Bunter, and the driver called to him.

Never had a voice been more welcome.

A walk of two miles was awful. Bunter remembered his walk to Redclyffe, and groaned at the idea. But there was no help for it, if he was to get on the track of that fiver. So the offer of a lift before he was a hundred yards from the school gates came like corn in Egypt, or manna in the desert. The fat junior beamed at the kindly motorist.

"I say, thanks!" he said. "I'm going to Courtfield."

"Right! That's where I'm going. Hop in!"

Thankfully Bunter rolled to the door of the car.

There was a man sitting inside who obligingly pushed the door open for Bunter to enter, and shut it again after he was in.

The car, which had hitherto been crawling, shot away at quite a good speed. The driver, of whom Bunter had seen little more than a peaked cap and a large, thick moustache, bent over the wheel, driving hard. The fat junior blinked at the other man in the car.

He was a stranger to Bunter's eyes—so far as Bunter knew, at all events. He had a pointed black beard and twisted moustache, which gave him rather a foreign look. But there was something in the rather slim form and stocky shoulders that seemed a little familiar to Bunter. He had a pair of very keen, hard, cold eyes, which fixed curiously on the fat and fatuous face of the Owl of the Remove.

"A Greyfriars boy—what?" asked the man in the car, with a smile. As Bunter had a Greyfriars cap, it was not hard to guess, if he knew the Greyfriars colours.

"Eh? Yes," said Bunter.

"I think I have seen you before," remarked the man with the pointed beard. "Were you not at the Hotel Royal in Courtfield yesterday?"

Bunter blinked at him.

"Yes. I don't remember seeing you there!" he said.

"I thought I remembered you," smiled the man in the car. "You had tea with Sir Peter Lanchester, I think."

"That's right," agreed Bunter.

"Old friend of yours, no doubt?"

"Oh, quite!" said Bunter.

"I thought so," said the man in the car, with a grimness that made Bunter blink at him. "What is your name?"

Bunter gave him another blink. He thought that rather a cheeky question from a perfect stranger. However, he answered.

"Bunter."

"Bunter?" repeated the man in the car.

"Yes, Bunter."

"You are sure your name is Bunter?" asked the man in the car, with a tone of mockery that made Bunter blink again.

"Eh? Yes, of course!" stuttered Bunter. "I suppose a fellow knows his own name. Wharrer you mean?"

The man laughed.

"Quite!" he agreed. "A fellow knows his own name, but might have excellent reasons for not mentioning it—what?"

Bunter stared at him. It seemed to him that there was a familiar tone in that mocking voice, though he had certainly never seen that face with the pointed black beard before.

"But I've told you my name!" he said. "I've mentioned it, haven't I?"

"Oh, quite! How long have you been named Bunter?" continued the man in the car, in the same tone of mockery.

"Eh?" gasped Bunter. "All my life, of course!"

He began to wonder whether the man in the car was quite right in the head. Certainly his questions were very extraordinary.

"All your life—really?" grinned the black-bearded man.

"Yes, of course!"

"You're more than five years old, I think?"

Bunter jumped.

"Of course I am!" he gasped. "Wharrer you mean? I—I—I say, I—I think I'd rather walk, after all. Tell the driver to stop, will you?"

Bunter was quite alarmed now. A man who asked a Remove fellow whether he was more than five years old, could hardly be sane.

But the man in the car certainly did not look like a lunatic. He looked like a man in a grimly sardonic and bantering humour.

"I'll tell you what I mean." He laughed again. "If you're more than five years old, my boy, you haven't been named Bunter all your life. You've been named Bunter rather less than five years. See the point?"

"I—I say, I—I want to get out!" gasped Bunter.

"Probably," assented the man in the car. "But you are not getting out just now, my lord."

Bunter bounded.

The man was mad; that was certain now.

Bunter, it was true, had a secret conviction that he looked like a lord—at least, how a lord ought to look, if he lived up to the best traditions of the nobility. Still, he was not, as a matter of fact, a lord.

A man who stated that he had only been named Bunter for the last five years, and called him "my lord," was a man Bunter wanted to get away from just as fast as he could.

He rose to his feet.

"I—I say, stop the car!" he gasped. "I—I want to get out. I—I say, I—I'd really rather walk—I would really!"

"I have not the slightest doubt of it, my lord! But your lordship is not going to walk. Sit down!"

"I—I—I say—"

"Sit down!" rapped the man in the car, so sharply and savagely that Bunter collapsed on the seat.

He blinked wildly from the window.

Lazy as the fat Owl was, he wished from the bottom of his podgy heart that he had never accepted that lift!

As he blinked out he saw that the car was turning from the main road and taking a lane that led towards the bridge over the river. That car was not, after all, going to Courtfield.

"I say, you're going the wrong way!" gasped Bunter. "I say, that way will take you to the sea!"

"You are not fond of the sea, my lord?"

"Oh, yes! No! I——"

"You would not care for a sea trip?"

"Wha-a-t?"

"I am sorry, my lord, for that is exactly what is in store for you," said the man in the car, "and though my instructions are not to hurt you in any way, if it can be avoided, I warn you that if you give me the slightest trouble I shall shoot you!"

"Oh crikey!" gasped Bunter.

The man slid his hand into the pocket of his coat. He half-drew a revolver from that pocket. He slid it back again at once, but that glimpse was more than enough for Bunter.

He leaned back in his seat in a state of utter terror and bewilderment.

"You young fool!" said the man in the car, in tones of amused contempt. "Do you fancy that I do not know who you are?"

"I—I—I'm Bunter!" stammered the fat Owl helplessly. "Bub-bub-Bunter! If you're taking me for somebody else," he added, as that idea suddenly occurred to him, "I—I can say I'm not somebody else! I—I—I'm me, you know!"

"You can bank on it that I am taking you for somebody else, my lord!" grinned the man in the car.

"But I ain't somebody else!" gasped Bunter. "How could I be somebody else? I—I ain't, really!"

"You young fool! I knew how the matter stood when the old fool went to Greyfriars the other day—and when you went to meet him in Courtfield yesterday, it was as good as telling me! Do you think that Sir Peter Lanchester was not watched yesterday?"

"Oh!" gasped Bunter.

He began to understand at last.

And, as he began to understand, it dawned on him what there was familiar about the man in the car. The black beard and the moustache and the foreign look were disguise that had deceived him—but he knew now. The voice of the man in the car was a voice he had heard before—the voice of the Smiler. It was the man who went by the peculiar name of the Smiler who was kidnapping him.

"Oh!" gasped Bunter again. "You!"

"Do you know me now?" grinned the Smiler.

"The—the man in the train——" stuttered Bunter.

"Precisely!" assented the Smiler. "The man in the train! And the old fool who refused to answer my questions need not tell me anything now—I know all that I want to know! I've got you in my hands now, Lord Reynham!"

THE NINETEENTH CHAPTER.

His Lordship Bunter!

LORD REYNHAM!

That name made it all clear —to Bunter.

That was the part he had to play at the castle in Sussex, if he carried out the compact made with Sir Peter Lanchester.

Bunter had entered on that compact with a light heart, not to mention a light head. Disregarding remote dangers, and thinking only of immediate advantages, the fat Owl had fancied that he was on to a very good thing.

It did not seem quite so good now.

He had not expected the dangers to begin, anyhow, till he arrived at the castle in Sussex. Neither, indeed, did Sir Peter.

They were starting earlier than expected.

Evidently, old Lanchester had been watched in Courtfield, and the crooks had drawn their own conclusions from Bunter's visit there. Already convinced that the young lord was at Greyfriars under an assumed name, the fact that Sir Peter had made a special journey to meet a Greyfriars boy in Courtfield was as good as proof to them.

"Oh lor'!" gasped Bunter.

He realised now that the man in the car was not a lunatic. He was the leader of the kidnapping gang who had been "after" young Lord Reynham for years; and he believed now that he had got hold of the young nobleman.

Sir Peter had expected and planned to give that impression, when Bunter arrived at the castle under the young lord's name. He had expected to be watched in Courtfield, thus setting the rascals on Bunter's track; giving colour in advance to the game that was to be played at Reynham Castle. Probably, however, he had not expected the kidnappers to get going so promptly.

Certainly, Bunter hadn't. He had not given them a thought.

Now he knew that they had set to work right on the spot. That car had been crawling on the road near the

(Continued on page 26.)

HORNBY TRAINS

"It's just like the one I drive"

—SAYS DRIVER CLARKE

Glasgow to London at an average speed of 70 m.p.h. — that was the wonderful world record non-stop run set up by "Princess Elizabeth," the magnificent 4-6-2 locomotive of the L.M.S. Railway, driven by Driver T. J. Clarke.

Here is "Princess Elizabeth," the newest and finest Hornby locomotive. This superb scale model, reproducing the real "Princess Elizabeth," in all her beauty of line and detail, is a notable landmark in the development of the Hornby Railway System. The L.M.S. have approved and co-operated in its production. Never before has so perfect a model been offered at so low a price. It has a 20-volt Electric Motor and is fitted with the famous Hornby Remote Control.

Locomotive and Tender in presentation box, 105/-

BOYS! HERE'S A GRAND NEW BOOK FOR YOU

The new Hornby Book of Trains is one of the most thrilling and interesting books on railways ever produced. It tells you all about the latest developments in railway practice, and describes vividly the thrills of building up a model railway of your own. It also includes a superb catalogue, in full colour, of all the locomotives, accessories and track in the Hornby Railway System. Every Meccano and Hornby dealer has this wonderful book, price 3d., or you can obtain it by sending 4½d. in stamps direct to Meccano Limited, Binns Road, Liverpool 13.

Boys! The greatest thrill you'll ever know is the thrill of being station-master, signalman, engine driver, guard and traffic manager of your own Hornby Railway. Just think of it! There's simply no end to the fun and the scope of the Hornby System. Models of famous expresses, "The Flying Scotsman," "The Pines Express," "The Bristolian," the "Bournemouth Limited," and many others. Powerful locomotives for every kind of work; coaches for main line and local services; wagons of all types; signals, bridges, viaducts, crossings—everything you need—and, most wonderful of all, the Hornby Remote Control by means of which a train can be started, stopped and reversed without touching it.

Begin a Hornby Railway to-day! You can start with quite a simple layout and add to it from time to time. Soon you'll be the owner of a complete system that will be the source of endless fun for yourself and your friends.

Go to your dealer to-day and ask him to show you all these wonderful Hornby Trains and Accessories.

Prices of Hornby Trains from 4/11

MECCANO LTD. DEPT. C.D. BINNS ROAD LIVERPOOL 13

school, looking for a chance to pick him up if he came out of gates, as he was likely to do on a Sunday morning.

No doubt the rascals had been prepared to grab him and pitch him headfirst into the car, if necessary. But offering him a lift had done the trick.

Neither would it have been of much use to refuse that lift, had Bunter thought of doing so. Obviously, he would have been grabbed.

"Oh lor' !" repeated Bunter.

"You understand now, my lord ?" grinned the Smiler.

"Oh, no ! Yes ! No ! Oh crikey !" Bunter gave a despairing blink from the window. The car had cut across the bridge, and was taking a lane by Redclyffe Woods, which led down to the sea, by way of Pegg, past the gates of Cliff House School.

From what the man had said, some vessel was waiting in the bay at Pegg, to take on board the supposed Lord Reynham. Evidently the plot had been carefully and elaborately laid.

The fat Owl wriggled with apprehension.

In half an hour, at this rate, he would be on that vessel, steaming out to sea. After that—what?

He could not imagine what.

He knew that this could be no ordinary case of kidnapping for ransom. Bunter was not bright, but he was bright enough to realise that !

No gang of kidnappers, for such a reason, would keep on the trail of one special victim for a period extending over years.

It was not merely a rich nobleman that they wanted: it was young Lord Reynham specially !

For some utterly mysterious reason, at which Bunter could not even guess, young Lord Reynham was marked out as the victim of this lawless gang—they wanted him, and no other member of the peerage would serve their turn.

That looked as if there was some special enmity in the case—and as if the young lord's fate, when he was got hold of, was likely to be an unenviable one !

It was no wonder that, in such strange and mysterious circumstances, old Sir Peter was anxious about his ward, and had taken extraordinary measures for his security.

But Billy Bunter, at the moment, wished that old Sir Peter's measures had not been quite so extraordinary.

Playing the part of a lord in a magnificent castle was all right ! Bunter revelled in the idea. But sitting in a car with a man who had a revolver in his pocket was not all right. It was far from all right. And the doubtful prospect of his ultimate fate was still less all right !

At the moment the fat Owl would rather have been plain Billy Bunter than Lord Reynham, owner of a great estate, a huge fortune, and a magnificent castle !

The car rushed on.

"Oh lor' !" said Bunter, for the third time.

He had one spot of comfort, now that he knew that this man was the Smiler.

That revolver, the sight of which had given him a spasm of terror, was unloaded.

Bunter knew—though the Smiler, of course, could not guess that he knew—that loaded firearms played no part in this strange scheme.

The Smiler was plainly a desperate rascal, but not desperate enough for that, and no doubt he attached an undue value to his neck. He might threaten Bunter with the deadly weapon —but he was not going to use it.

If Bunter got a chance of jumping out of the car, Bunter was going to jump—quite assured that no bullet would follow him.

But he did not look like getting a chance. In a struggle the stocky Smiler could have handled a dozen of him. And the car was going fast—too fast for a jump, if Bunter had a chance of dodging the Smiler's grasp—which he hadn't !

Bunter was "for it."

"I—I—I say, you—you're making a silly mistake !" pleaded Bunter. "I—I ain't Lord Reynham, and never was. I'm Bunter."

"That is the name the old fool gave you when he hid you at a school under an assumed name, you mean."

"Nunno. I—I never even saw old Lanchester before last week——" stammered Bunter.

"Ten miuntes ago you said he was an old friend of yours."

"Oh ! I—I—I meant that—that he wasn't——"

The Smiler laughed.

"Nothing of the kind !" gasped Bunter. "Look here, you ask any Greyfriars fellow, and they'll tell you I'm Bunter—just Bunter. I say, there's some Greyfriars chaps in Pegg this morning—you stop the car and ask them—they're in my Form—they'll tell you——"

"You mean that they know you by the name of Bunter, Lord Reynham ?"

"Oh dear ! Yes. But it's really my name !" groaned Bunter. "Look here, if you've ever seen that beastly lord, do I look like him ?"

To Bunter's great relief, that remark seemed to make some impression on the Smiler. The man's sharp eyes narrowed almost to pin-points, as he scanned the face of the hapless Owl.

"I have not seen him since he was a boy of eleven," said the Smiler slowly. "He is now nearly sixteen. In that time, he must have changed too much to be recognised. But I remember that he was very plump—in fact, a fat boy."

"Well, then, that proves it !" gasped Bunter. "I ain't fat !"

"What ?"

"I'm not skinny, like Wharton—but I ain't fat. The fellows make out that I am because they're jealous of my figure. Look at me !"

The Smiler looked at him—hard !

"I remember," he said, "that the boy seemed rather a fool ! That fits !"

"Look here——"

The Smiler scanned him—harder and harder. Bunter realised that, having watched the meeting in Courtfield, the Smiler had jumped to a conclusion—the conclusion, in fact, at which Sir Peter had intended the kidnappers to jump. But he seemed to have some doubt now, and, clearly, he did not want to risk wasting his time bagging the wrong bird.

He was about to speak again when the car slowed down. Taking his eyes off Bunter's fat face, the Smiler snapped at the driver:

"Ferret, you fool ! What——"

"O.K., Smiler ! Level-crossing !" answered the Ferret over his shoulder. "I'll mention that I can do anything with this bus except make her jump over a railway line !"

Billy Bunter's eyes gleamed behind his spectacles as the car stopped at the level-crossing in Pegg Lane. If there was half a chance——

THE TWENTIETH CHAPTER.

Removites to the Rescue !

"HALLO, hallo, hallo !"

"Jolly old Bunter !"

"The esteemed and idiotic Bunter !"

"What the dickens is he doing in that car ?"

"Looks like a foreign chap in it."

Harry Wharton & Co., on their way to Cliff House, had stopped at the level crossing. The gates were shut, and the train was signalled, so they leaned on the gate and waited for it to pass.

Not many cars used Pegg Lane; still, it was not an unusual sight to see a car slow down at the level crossing, and the chums of the Remove gave it no special heed till they caught the gleam of a pair of big spectacles flashing back the wintry sunshine, and recognised Billy Bunter in the car.

They glanced at him, and at the foreign-looking man sitting by his side, as the car slowed to a halt at the gate. They were rather surprised to see the fat Owl sitting in the car with a man who looked like a foreigner, but they supposed that he had picked up a lift, that was all.

Bob Cherry waved a cheery hand to him.

Bunter blinked out of the car.

He had had a faint hope that with the car at a halt there might be a chance of jumping out. That hope was nipped in the bud by the Smiler, who fastened a grasp of iron on his fat arm.

But as he saw the Famous Five standing by the gate, it was renewed in his podgy breast. With all the strength of his lungs, Bunter gave a sudden yell.

"I say, you fellows ! Help ! Help !"

The Famous Five jumped almost clear of the ground in their astonishment.

"What——" gasped Harry Wharton.

"Help !" yelled Bunter frantically "Rescue ! Help ! Oh, help !"

Almost petrified, the chums of the Remove stared at him.

They were so astounded that they might have supposed that Bunter was pulling their leg, or that he had gone suddenly off his "dot." But the prompt action of the man in the car was even more startling that Bunter's wild yell for help.

He grasped the fat junior and pitched him down on the floor of the car, pinning him there with his foot.

At the same moment, he almost screamed to the driver:

"Quick ! Ferret, you fool—quick !"

But the driver had no chance. The railway gates were locked in front of him; the car could not move on. High-hedged banks shut in the lane, which was narrow, and difficult for turning a car in. Backing and turning was not a quick process.

But the Famous Five were quick enough.

Amazed, as they were—utterly astounded, in fact, the action of the foreign-looking man left no doubt on the subject. Billy Bunter was in that car against his will, and was kept there by force.

It was beyond comprehension, but

Printed in England and published every Saturday by the Proprietors, The Amalgamated Press, Ltd., The Fleetway House, Farringdon Street, London, E.C.4. Advertisement offices: The Fleetway House, Farringdon Street, London, E.C.4. Registered for transmission by Canadian Magazine Post. Subscription rates: Inland and Abroad, 11s. per annum; 5s. 6d. for six months. Sole Agents for Australia and New Zealand; Messrs. Gordon & Gotch, Ltd., and for South Africa : Central News Agency, Ltd.—Saturday, December 11th, 1937.

there it was. Bunter was a prisoner in that car, in violent and lawless hands, and the Famous Five were not the fellows to leave him to it.

"Come on!" roared Bob.

They rushed at the car.

Harry Wharton and Frank Nugent grabbed at one door and dragged it open. Bob Cherry and Johnny Bull dragged at the other. Both doors flew open at the same moment as the car backed. And as the driver reached round, with a heavy spanner in his hand, Hurree Jamset Ram Singh lashed out with his walking-cane and slashed it from his hand.

"Bunter!" gasped Wharton.

"Ow! Help!" yelled Bunter. "I'm kidnapped! Help! I say, you fellows —yoooooooop!"

Bunter wriggled and gurgled under the jamming boot.

"You scoundrel, let Bunter go!" shouted the captain of the Remove, clambering into the car on one side while Bob plunged in on the other.

"Stand back!" yelled the Smiler.

The revolver came out of his coat pocket, and he brandished it at the schoolboys.

"Look out!" gasped Nugent.

"I say—help! Yarooop!" squeaked Bunter.

"Stand back, or——"

Harry Wharton, half in the car, paused as the muzzle of the firearm was almost thrust in his face. But Bob Cherry, plunging in on the other side, hit out, catching the Smiler behind the ear.

The Smiler, spluttering, rocked over on the seat. Harry Wharton hurled himself forward, grabbing at him.

His grasp closed on the black beard. To his utter amazement, the beard came off in his hand.

Up went the Smiler's right arm, the pistol clubbed in his grip. But as the desperate rascal struck at Wharton Bob grasped him and dragged him over.

He turned on Bob like a tiger, but Harry Wharton grasped his arm and twisted it so savagely that the revolver dropped to the floor.

Struggling between Wharton and Bob, the Smiler had no time for Bunter, and the fat junior wriggled away and rolled out of the car.

He bumped down in Pegg Lane, spluttering.

But he did not stay there.

Bunter's movements, which were generally modelled on those of a snail, now resembled a flash of lightning.

He leaped up like an indiarubber ball, and bolted.

In a split second Bunter was up the grassy bank beside the lane, in the wood, and running.

He vanished like a ghost at cock-crow.

It did not occur to Bunter, at the moment, to lend any aid to the juniors who had come to the rescue. All Bunter was thinking of was getting to a safe distance from the Smiler. That he did, promptly.

Wharton and Bob were still struggling with the Smiler in the car when Bunter did the vanishing act.

The Ferret jumped down and made one stride across the lane, apparently thinking of pursuing Bunter. Johnny Bull, Frank Nugent, and the Nabob of Bhanipur jumped in front of him at once.

He backed away promptly.

There was a bump in the road as three struggling figures rolled out of the car. They separated as they rolled, and jumped to their feet, the Smiler with his beard and moustache gone, and his cold, hard, clean-shaven face red and distorted with rage.

He gave a quick, fierce stare round, for Bunter was already out of sight. The Smiler stood panting with breathless rage.

His prisoner, whether Lord Reynham or not, had escaped. That meeting with the Famous Five at the level-crossing had put "paid" to the kidnappers' game. In his rage, the Smiler seemed disposed to rush on the schoolboys. They were quite ready for him.

The Famous Five drew together, barring the way Bunter had gone. For whatever mysterious reason the two rascals had bagged Bunter, Harry Wharton & Co. were quite determined that they should not bag him again.

"Pack it up, bo!" said the Ferret, who, from his choice of language, seemed to be a native of the other side of the ocean. "I'll say this lets us out! This is where we beat it!"

The Smiler gave him an angry glare for a moment, and then, with a curt nod, stepped back into the car.

Ferret resumed his place at the wheel. He backed, and turned, and the car shot away the way it had come.

The chums of the Remove watched it go. Who the two men were, why they had bagged Bunter, utterly mystified the Co. But the juniors had, at all events, rescued the fat Owl from their hands. Breathless and amazed, they watched the car whiz away and disappear in the distance.

"Well," said Harry Wharton, with a deep breath, "anybody got any idea what this means?"

"Ask me another!" said Bob.

"That blighter was got up in a false beard and moustache!" said Harry, in wonder. "And they'd got Bunter! What on earth for? What the dickens could they want Bunter for?"

"First time I've ever heard of anybody wanting him!" remarked Johnny Bull.

"Kidnapping!" said Nugent.

"But why?"

"Goodness knows!"

Bunter had vanished in one direction —the car in another. The level-crossing gates having opened, the chums of the Remove resumed their walk to Cliff House—utterly mystified by the strange affair.

THE TWENTY-FIRST CHAPTER.

Bunter's Pals!

"I SAY, you fellows!"

"How did Bunter know we had a cake for tea?" asked Frank Nugent.

"Ha, ha, ha!"

"If you think I've come to tea, Nugent——"

"Haven't you?"

"No!" roared Bunter.

On Monday afternoon, the fat Owl of the Remove blinked in at the door of Study No. 1—from which the Famous Five, who were tea-ing there, naturally concluded that Bunter had come to tea. The trifling circumstance that he had not been asked to tea, was not expected to make any difference to Bunter.

But the fat Owl, it seemed, was not, for once, in search of a free feed. He did not roll into the study. He adorned the doorway with his podgy person, blinking in through his big spectacles, with a disdainful blink.

"Keep your measly cake!" he said contemptuously.

"Thanks—we will!" agreed Harry Wharton. "Glad of the chance!"

"Something a bit better than that, up the passage!" sneered Bunter. "I've got friends who stand a fellow a decent spread."

"You're getting frightfully pally with Skinner," remarked Bob Cherry. "Does Skinner believe in Reynham Castle?"

"Ha, ha, ha!"

"You can cackle," said Bunter. "But some fellows can take a fellow's word."

"Skinner's a bit too wide, I should have thought," said Harry Wharton, laughing.

"Yah!"

It was rather a puzzle to a good many Removites. Skinner, well known to be a wary fellow, and extremely close with his money, had been pally with Bunter, ever since the fat junior had gone to tea with Sir Peter on Saturday. That very night he had stood Bunter supper in his study; on Sunday he had cashed a postal order that Bunter was expecting on Monday—but which Skinner certainly did not expect to see: on Monday he had stood him tarts in break, and dough-nuts after dinner. Now, apparently, he had asked him to tea.

Being pally with Bunter meant being Bunter's banker. Except Fisher T. Fish, Skinner was the stingiest fellow in the Form. So it really was puzzling and surprising.

True, if Skinner believed in Reynham Castle, that explained it. In that case, Skinner, no doubt, was expending a sprat to catch a whale. But as much less suspicious fellows than Skinner did not believe a word of it, it seemed unlikely that Skinner did. Still more surprising, Bolsover major, the bully of the Remove, was associated with Skinner in this new stunt.

Bolsover, as a rule, was more likely to boot Bunter than to waste a civil word on him. Now he was friendly, and had been heard to call Bunter "old chap," and "old pal."

Skinner had not mentioned his discovery on Saturday afternoon—except to Bolsover major. So nobody knew that they were in possession of private information. Had Skinner spread the news, no doubt Bunter would have found more than two friends in his Form.

"I'm going to tea with Skinner and Bolsover," said Bunter, "and I can jolly well tell you they've got something better than a measly cake. Keep that mouldy cake! Who wants it? Yah!"

"Shut the door after you, old fat man!" said Wharton politely.

"I've looked in to speak to you about the hols!" yapped Bunter.

"Like to go to Wharton Lodge?"

"Ha, ha, ha!"

"Oh, don't be an ass!" snapped Bunter. "It's arranged for you fellows to come with me to Reynham Castle——"

"If any!"

"Well, you'll believe it when you see it!" jeered Bunter. "And Skinner's coming, too—and so is Bolsover. I've invited them. And if you fellows don't like their company over Christmas, you can lump it, see?"

"We're not likely to see them over Christmas, are we?"

"Of course you will, you silly ass, as they'll be at Reynham Castle with me, and you'll be there, too!" roared Bunter.

The Famous Five gazed at Bunter. Whether there was such a place as Reynham Castle, or not, they did not know; but if there was, they had not the slightest belief that Bunter had been asked there by the silver-haired old baronet who had called on Quelch. It looked as if Skinner and his pal were more credulous than themselves.

"Now, about getting there!" went on Bunter.

"Better go by plane, I think!" said
Bob Cherry.

"By plane?" repeated Bunter.

"Yes—that's the only way to get to a
castle in the air!"

"Ha, ha, ha!"

"Will you talk sense?" roared Bunter.

"You begin, old fat bean!"

"The day we break up," hooted
Bunter, "the car will come for me. A
magnificent Rolls, with a liveried
chauffeur—I shall travel in it to
Reynham Castle. I can't take you
fellows in it. I've got reasons."

The Famous Five chuckled. They had
no doubt about Bunter's reasons—as
they did not believe in the magnificent
Rolls, any more than in the castle.

But, in point of fact, Bunter had his
reasons. He had not mentioned to Sir
Peter that a crowd of Greyfriars fellows
were coming.

As he was to be called lord at the
castle, it might be rather awkward to
have a lot of fellows there who knew
him as Billy Bunter.

This might not agree with the old
baronet's plans. He might kick. So
Bunter had sagely decided to arrive first
—and let his friends arrive a little
later.

Once he had been greeted at the castle
as the young lord, it would be too late
for Sir Peter to kick, if he wanted to,
Bunter thought this rather strategic.
There was a difference between his
viewpoint and Sir Peter's.

Sir Peter was thinking wholly of the
success of his measures for securing his
ward. Bunter was thinking wholly of
having a tremendously good time and
keeping perfectly safe all the time. His
wild adventure with the man in the car
had made Bunter quite determined on
that. Kidnappers were not going to get
another chance at Bunter—not if
Bunter knew it!

"You see how it stands?" went on
Bunter. "Sir Peter Lanchester will
come here in the car for me. I can't
have him crowded out with a lot of
noisy schoolboys. You see that?"

"Go it!" said Bob, encouragingly.
"Pile it on!"

"You'd better come by rail, the next
day or the day after," said Bunter.
"In fact, I'll let you know, from the
castle. See? I mean to say, I shall
have to be a bit tactful about it, and
those beasts can hardly start anything
the first day——"

"Eh?"

"I—I mean——"

"Well, what do you mean?"

"Oh, nothing!" said Bunter hastily.
"Nothing at all, old chap! I'll phone
you from the castle—I suppose you're
on the phone at your poor little place,
Cherry! I'll phone you up, see? That
will be best! Now, do you understand?"

"Not quite!" said Harry Wharton,
shaking his head.

"Beast! Look here, it's settled that
you come on to the castle when I phone
for you?" roared Bunter.

"When!" chortled Bob.

"Yah!"

Billy Bunter slammed the door and
rolled away. He had no more of his
valuable time to waste on those
doubting Thomases; especially with a
feast awaiting him in Skinner's study.

Bunter was annoyed—but his fat brow
cleared, when he sat down to tea with
Skinner and Bolsover major.

The only two fellows in the Remove
who believed in Reynham Castle were
very keen to visit that magnificent
abode. They pooled their financial
resources to load the study table with
good things for Bunter.

Feeding Bunter was not a light
matter. It was rather an expensive
sprat to catch the whale. But they
agreed that it was worth it. For the
next half-hour they had the pleasure,
or otherwise, of watching Bunter feed.
Judging by their polite and pleasant
smiles, it was an agreeable sight.

When the foodstuffs were finished
Bunter was finished. He rose from the
table, after a careful blink round to
make sure that nothing eatable was left.

"Thanks, you chaps!" said Bunter.
"I'll stand you something better than
that when you're my guests at the
castle."

And with that graceful acknowledgment of the spread, the fat Owl rolled
out of the study.

THE TWENTY-SECOND CHAPTER.
Bunter in all his Glory!

"WHERE did you get that hat?"

"Oh, really, Wharton——"

"Where did you pinch
that coat?"

"Oh, really, Nugent——"

"Where did you bag that suitcase?"

"Oh, really, Cherry——"

"Where did you snaffle that necktie?"

"Oh, really, Bull——"

It was breaking-up day at Greyfriars.
Harry Wharton & Co. had been busy
with packing. Coming out into the
frosty quad, they glanced at a handsome Rolls-Royce car that was standing
by the steps, with a liveried chauffeur
standing by it like a graven image.

Then they spotted Bunter.

Bunter was standing by the House
steps—remarkably and unusually well-
dressed, with a happy grin on his face.

But he looked rather worried as the
Famous Five came up. On that bright
and happy morning he did not want any
sordid dispute about the ownership of a
hat, an overcoat, a suitcase, or a necktie. Such things were below the notice
of a fellow who was about to arrive at

a castle as a lord. They were not below
the notice of the fellows to whom the
articles belonged.

"You fat, foozling, bloated burglar!"
said Bob.

"Hush!" said Bunter reprovingly.

"What! What do you mean by
hush, you fat pincher?"

"I mean Sir Peter might hear
you——"

"All the way from the castle in
Sussex?" snorted Bob.

"He's here——"

"You gammoning ass——"

"He's gone in to speak to Quelch,"
said Bunter. "He came in that car.
He may be out any minute. I'm waiting for him. You see, that's the car
I'm going in!"

"The spoofing octopus!" hooted Bob.
"Let's bump him!"

"I say, you fellows——" yelled
Bunter. "I say——"

"Scrag him!"

"Dear me! What is the matter?"
asked a voice, as a tall, silver-haired
gentleman came out of the House.

Another moment and Billy Bunter
would have been bumped. But Harry
Wharton & Co. stopped in time and
"capped" the old baronet instead.
Bunter could wait till Sir Peter Lanchester was gone.

Sir Peter gave them a nod and a
smile, and then, to their utter amazement, addressed Bunter.

"Come, my boy!"

"What-ho!" chortled Bunter.

The chauffeur lifted Bob's suitcase—
now Bunter's—on to the car. The fat
Owl stepped in with Sir Peter.

The Famous Five, spellbound,
watched, like fellows in a dream.

The magnificent car rolled away to
the gates, Billy Bunter sitting by the
side of Sir Peter Lanchester.

He grinned back at the staring five.
He waved a fat hand—probably grubby,
as usual, but nicely encased in a glove
of Nugent's.

The car turned out at the gates and
disappeared.

Harry Wharton & Co. were left staring; they could do nothing else.

Bob Cherry was the first to find his
voice.

He gasped.

"Can you beat it?"

His friends shook their heads. They
couldn't!

THE END.

*(Don't miss the second story in this
exciting series, entitled: "KING OF
THE CASTLE!" which, together with
other splendid Yuletide features, will
appear in next Saturday's GRAND
CHRISTMAS NUMBER of the
MAGNET. As there is always a rush for
this special issue, readers are strongly
advised to order their copy TO-DAY!)*

The Magnet

2ᴰ

Billy Bunter's Own Paper

Lord Bunter's Xmas Feast!

The Best of All Presents

Feeding on the fat of the land at Reynham Castle and giving orders right and left to an army of liveried flunkeys is the ideal Christmas holiday! So thinks Billy Bunter—until he takes over the reins as—

KING of the CASTLE!

By Frank Richards

A Magnificent New Long Complete Christmas Yarn of HARRY WHARTON & CO., of GREYFRIARS, starring BILLY BUNTER as My Lord of Reynham Castle.

THE FIRST CHAPTER.

Startling !

"HALLO, hallo, hallo!" roared Bob Cherry.

"What——"

"Jolly old Bunter——"

"Bunter——"

"And somebody after him! Look!" yelled Bob. He pointed from the train window.

The other members of the famous Co. stared from the windows, at the road that ran beside the railway embankment.

It was breaking-up day at Greyfriars School. The train to Lantham Junction was crowded—not to say crammed.

At the junction, the Greyfriars crowd was going to scatter to the four corners of the kingdom. But they did not seem likely to arrive there in a hurry. The train was grinding slowly up a steep gradient. Johnny Bull remarked that it was crawling; and Hurree Jamset Ram Singh declared that the crawlfulness was terrific.

The Famous Five were in one carriage, with three or four other Remove fellows. Some of them had seats—some hadn't. Bob Cherry, who was one of those that hadn't, was standing by the door, looking out into the wintry landscape.

Thus is was that he spotted the strange and startling scene on the road below.

A handsome Rolls-Royce car, going in the same direction as the train, was speeding along the road. Behind it roared a Ford.

A liveried chauffeur drove the Rolls, sitting like a graven image at the wheel. Inside were two passengers—an old gentleman with a gleam of silver hair under his shining, silk hat, and a fat Greyfriars junior whose podgy little nose was adorned with a big pair of spectacles—no other than Billy Bunter, the fat ornament of the Greyfriars Remove.

Harry Wharton & Co. had not expected to see Billy Bunter again till after the New Year. But there was Bunter—in all his glory.

True, Bunter had asked them to join him for Christmas at Reynham Castle, in Sussex. But as they did not believe that that castle existed outside Billy Bunter's fertile imagination, they had not taken the invitation seriously. They had put it down to Bunter's customary "gammon."

It had been quite a surprise when Sir Peter Lanchester turned up in that magnificent Rolls to take Bunter away.

How Bunter had wangled that, they did not know. But they supposed that the fat Owl of the Remove had wangled it somehow. Wangling was Bunter's long suit.

Anyhow—there was Bunter—sitting beside the tall, old baronet, with a cheery grin on his fat face, under a nice hat that belonged to Harry Wharton.

But what made the Remove fellows stare blankly from the train, was the obvious fact that the Ford was in pursuit of the Rolls.

That was startling, but unmistakable. The Rolls was going fast—but could

have gone faster. The Ford was going all out. The driver, bent over the wheel, was getting every ounce out of it. A man in a slouched hat sat beside him, leaning out a little, with something in his hand that glistened in the wintry sunshine.

Amazing as it was, the fellows in the train knew what that "something" was. It was a revolver !

Crack !

The sound floated up through the clear, frosty December air. It sounded like a whip cracking.

But it was not the crack of a whip. It was the report of a firearm. The man in the slouched hat was shooting at the tyres of the car ahead. In alarmed amazement, the juniors in the train saw a spurt of dust kicked up by the bullet, a yard from a wheel.

"Motor-bandits !" gasped Harry Wharton.

Crack !

The second shot knocked up the dust under one of the whizzing, rear wheels of the Rolls.

"Great pip !" exclaimed Bob. "If that villain gets a tyre, he may wreck the car—with poor old Bunter in it !"

"The awful rotter !" gasped Frank Nugent.

"But what—and why——" stuttered Johnny Bull.

"Goodness knows! He's after Bunter !"

The other fellows in the carriage scrambled across, to crowd at the windows and stare. All along the train, fellows were staring down at the road.

THE MAGNET LIBRARY.—No. 1,557.

now. At that point, road and railway ran side by side, and the speed of the cars equalled that of the train. So the strange chase of the Lantham road remained in full view of the Greyfriars crowd.

Crack!

It was a third shot.

The Greyfriars juniors stared down breathlessly. They were thankful to see that it was not a hit. Again the bullet knocked up dust near a whizzing wheel.

"Well, this beats it!" gasped Bob Cherry.

It was really an amazing scene.

There were plenty of motor-bandits, certainly; but it was amazing to see the lawless game thus played openly, in broad daylight, on a public highway.

"Bunter's taking it calmly, by gum!" said Bob.

That was most amazing of all.

At the crack of a revolver, any fellow who knew Billy Bunter would have expected him to bound like a kangaroo.

Instead of which, the fat junior sat tight, taking no heed.

Blinking up the embankment through his big spectacles, he spotted the line of startled faces along the train staring down, and grinned.

He waved a fat hand to the Famous Five.

Evidently Bunter was not alarmed—though how, and why, Harry Wharton & Co. could not begin to understand. They had, they flattered themselves, a good deal more pluck than Billy Bunter; but certainly they would have been alarmed, with a gun-man potting at the tyres of a car in which they were travelling.

And Bunter never turned a hair.

He grinned and waved at the staring juniors in the train, regardless.

But if Bunter was not alarmed, the silver-haired old baronet did not seem so easy. He was seen to half-rise, turn, and stare back from the pane of glass in the back of the car.

Then, no doubt, he spoke to the chauffeur; for the Rolls suddenly leaped into terrific speed.

It shot away like a flash, leaving the straining Ford almost standing.

Crack! Crack! Crack! came rattling from the Ford. The man in the slouched hat was pitching bullets fast. But the Rolls simply walked away from the pursuer, now that the chauffeur was letting it out, and it vanished up the road in a cloud of dust.

The Ford roared on, evidently still in pursuit, though with little chance.

A moment or two more and the road turned from the railway; and the Greyfriars crowd, rolling on to Lantham Junction in the train, lost sight of both cars.

"Well," exclaimed Harry Wharton, with a deep breath, "that beats it!"

"The beatfulness is terrific!" said Hurree Jamset Ram Singh, in wonder.

"They're after Bunter!" said Bob. "It isn't the old sportsman they want—it's Bunter. You remember, a few days ago, two blighters bagged him in a car, and we got him away from them. They must be the same two—in that Ford. But why the thump do they want Bunter?"

"Looks like kidnapping——" said Frank Nugent.

"But why should anybody kidnap Bunter?" asked Johnny Bull. "Bunter's not worth anything to anybody."

"It's a blessed mystery!" said Harry Wharton. "There can't be any doubt that they're after Bunter—though why, is a puzzle."

"He's all right now, anyhow!" said Bob. "They'll never get anywhere near THE MAGNET LIBRARY.—No. 1,557.

that Rolls again. But what the dickens can it all mean?"

Nobody could answer that question. The Famous Five could not even guess at an answer. It looked as if Billy Bunter was likely to have an exciting Christmas holiday—but what it meant was a deep mystery. The chums of the Remove had to give it up.

THE SECOND CHAPTER.
Brave Bunter!

"BRAVE lad!" said Sir Peter Lanchester.

Billy Bunter blinked at him.

"Eh?" he remarked.

"I do not think," said the old baronet, beaming, "that I have ever witnessed such courage, such steady nerve, in a boy before."

"Haven't you?" gasped Bunter.

"Never!" said Sir Peter. "I wish—ah, how I wish!—that my ward, Lord Reynham, had the same iron nerve; then it would be unnecessary for you to spend your Christmas holidays at Reynham Castle."

"Oh!" gasped Bunter.

"But he has not," said the old baronet, shaking his head. "It would be quite impossible for him to go through it."

Billy Bunter was glad to hear it.

"Such steady, unshaken courage is really remarkable," went on Sir Peter. "I see that I was not mistaken in you. Courage is required, for the part you have to play at the castle; but you have enough, and to spare."

Bunter could only blink.

What the silver-haired old gentleman was talking about was a puzzle to him.

Bunter, certainly, was brave enough, when there was no danger about. In the absence of peril, a lion had nothing on Bunter, for courage.

With danger in the offing, it would have been a different story to tell. But, so far as Bunter could see—even with the aid of his big spectacles—there was no danger in the offing.

Sitting in a luxurious car by the side of a baronet, behind a liveried chauffeur, resting comfortably on soft cushions, while the Rolls ate up the miles, suited Bunter. He was glad that a crowd of Greyfriars fellows had seen him from that passing train. It jolly well showed them that Bunter's tall tales of titled and wealthy connections were not all "gammon."

But where was the danger? Bunter had heard a sharp popping behind. He had taken it for a motor back-firing.

There was nothing alarming in that, so Bunter had not been alarmed.

Why old Sir Peter was praising him for his courage was, therefore, quite a mystery to Bunter. Still, it was quite agreeable. Bunter liked to fancy himself a doughty fellow who feared no foe.

Nobody at Greyfriars had ever praised him for his pluck. That made it all the more agreeable to hear it from Sir Peter Lanchester.

"I cannot say that I felt equally easy in my mind," went on Sir Peter. "Had a tyre burst——"

"Eh? The tyres are all right, aren't they?" said Bunter.

"Quite! But had a bullet struck one of them——"

"A—a—a bib-bub-bullet?" stuttered Bunter.

"Yes; in that case, the car certainly would have overturned," said Sir Peter. "I was far from easy. My chauffeur, Denham, has been through the War, but he was not easy. Yet you, a schoolboy, sat through it with perfect coolness. Such courage and nerve are very unusual."

Bunter blinked at him blankly.

Apparently, from what Sir Peter said, they had passed through some danger. Billy Bunter had not been aware of it. He did not even know what it was—yet.

Sir Peter Lanchester, of course, did not guess that. He supposed that Bunter knew what had happened. And the fat junior had not even turned his head, when the man in the Ford was loosing off bullets at the tyres. The cheery grin on his fat face had not changed. No wonder Sir Peter was impressed by his nerve.

"It is clear," went on Sir Peter, "that I was watched, coming to the school for you to-day. I had no doubt of it—and this is proof. That Ford was waiting to follow us when we left Greyfriars."

"Oh!" gasped Bunter. This was the first he knew of the Ford.

"I had little doubt that we should be followed on the road," said Sir Peter. "But certainly I did not look for such a desperate act as shooting at our tyres."

Bunter jumped.

"The villain fired half a dozen shots—fortunately without result. But had one struck a tyre——"

"Oh!" gasped Bunter.

He understood now.

He squirmed round and blinked back along the road. To his immense relief, there was no sign of a car behind.

He sat down again, gasping for breath.

"We have dropped them," said Sir Peter. "I have no doubt that they are still following us, but I shall take care that they get no opportunity to try such a trick again. Let them follow to Reynham Castle, if they like."

Bunter breathed more freely.

He realised now that what he had taken for some car back-firing had been the firing of a revolver. His fat heart fairly quaked at the thought of the danger the Rolls had been in.

But having thus, accidentally, as it were, acquired credit, Bunter was not the fellow to throw it away. With the danger over, and no harm done, there was nothing the matter with Bunter's nerve. If old Sir Peter made such mistakes, Bunter was not the man to set him right.

Billy Bunter's private opinion of Sir Peter Lanchester was that he was rather an old donkey. This incident confirmed him in that opinion.

That, however, was really all to the good. Only an old donkey could have thought so highly of Billy Bunter as Sir Peter did.

"I am glad that this has happened," continued Sir Peter. "It proves that, in selecting you to play the part of Lord Reynham at the castle, I have made no error of judgment, my boy."

"Oh, yes; quite!" said Bunter.

"You will be in incessant danger and——"

"Eh?"

"But you will face it with perfect coolness——"

"Oh! Ah! Yes, rather!" gasped Bunter. "The—the fact is, I—I rather like danger. A—a—a spot of danger makes a thing really enjoyable."

"I am glad you take that view,"

said Sir Peter. "That desperate act shows of what the villains are capable. And yet"—Sir Peter paused a moment—"my dear boy, brave as you are, do you clearly understand what you are about to face? I should be deeply disappointed if you decided to withdraw, and yet——"

Sir Peter broke off as the car suddenly rocked at a quick jamming of brakes.

Ahead of the Rolls, where the Lantham road ran between deep, dark wintry woods, a lorry had pulled out from a side lane across the road, completely blocking the way.

The lorry was piled with logs. It pulled right across the road. A bicycle could hardly have got by. The Rolls had to brake and halt. It halted, quivering from the sudden brakes.

Sir Peter gave a gasp.

"Trapped!"

THE THIRD CHAPTER.

Bunter Keeps Cool !

BILLY BUNTER suppressed a squeak of terror.

The log-laden lorry barred the way. Behind, somewhere out of sight, but coming on fast, was the Ford, with a desperate gunman in it. Next time Bunter heard that revolver banging, he was not going to take it for a car back-firing. He shivered with apprehension

Sir Peter Lanchester clenched his hands.

"Trapped!" he repeated. "All my plans laid for trapping those scoundrels; but I did not foresee that they would act so quickly. So near the school—before we are anywhere near Reynham Castle——"

Billy Bunter scrambled to his feet.

Like the old baronet, he had no doubt that this was a trick of the kidnappers. That lorry had been timed to pull out in front of the car and stop it—placing it at the mercy of the pursuers. As the enemy knew that they were heading for Sussex, it was easy enough to lay an ambush on the road ahead. This was it.

Billy Bunter had one idea in his fat head at that moment. Christmas at Reynham Castle ceased to appeal to him, all of a sudden. His one idea was to jump out of the car and cut.

That, certainly, would cause a quick change in the old baronet's belief in his indomitable courage. But that could not be helped. Dangers in the distance Bunter could face with unshaken nerve. Dangers close at hand were rather too much for him. He was getting away—and getting away just as fast as he knew how.

But, as his popping eyes blinked at the lorry ahead, he saw the lorry-driver staring round, and his terrors vanished.

That lorry-driver was old Joyce, the woodcutter—an ancient character well known to all Greyfriars fellows. Old Joyce was doing a great business in the last days of December, with logs for Christmas fires.

Recognising old Joyce, Bunter knew at once that it was all right.

That villain, the "Smiler," might have planned an ambush on the road; but certainly honest old Joyce was not the man to have a hand in such a thing.

That lorry had—Bunter knew it as soon as he saw old Joyce—nothing whatever to do with the rascals in the Ford behind. Old Joyce was there on his lawful occasions—trundling away a load of Yule logs

Realising that, Bunter sat down again.

Sir Peter was twittering rather like a startled chicken. He, of course, knew nothing of the local woodcutter of Friardale. He had no doubt that this was a trap. Really, it looked like it, to an old gentleman who was expecting dangers all along the road to Sussex. Bunter, who knew better, sat and smiled.

That lorry was old, cranky, and heavily laden. It moved slowly and reluctantly. It was likely to keep the road blocked for several minutes; but it was not going to stick there till the Ford came up. Sir Peter supposed that it was. Bunter knew that it wasn't. Sir Peter twittered; Bunter took it all coolly and calmly. He could afford to.

"Trapped!" repeated the old baronet. "I might have foreseen something of the kind—but I did not !"

Once more Bunter was confirmed in his belief that Sir Peter Lanchester was an old donkey.

"All my plans laid—a trap laid for the scoundrels in Sussex—but, here, we are at their mercy!" groaned Sir Peter. "They will get you—we shall not get them, as I had planned. My boy——"

"All serene, sir !" said Bunter cheerfully. "I'm not afraid of them ! There's only two men in that Ford, if—if they come up. You and the chauffeur can tackle one of them——"

"What ?"

"And leave the other to me," said Bunter.

Sir Peter stared at him.

"A desperate man—armed——" he stammered.

"That's all right, sir !" said Bunter reassuringly. "I'm not afraid of his gun ! I fancy I can handle him all right !"

"Good gad !" gasped Sir Peter.

He could only stare at Bunter. The road ahead was blocked—the Ford was coming on behind. It had been dropped —but it was certainly coming on, though at a considerable distance in the rear. Six or seven minutes would be enough—ten at the outside.

Shifting that lorry was impossible. Indeed, Sir Peter had little or no doubt that some of the kidnapping gang were

hidden by that stack of logs, and were about to leap down and surround the car.

Bunter's coolness simply amazed him.

"Keep cool, sir !" said the fat Owl cheerfully. "If this is a trap, you see, we're in it, and that's that ! Leave it to me ! I'll handle that gunman all right ! You'll see !"

As Bunter knew that old Joyce would get out of the way as fast as he could with that creaking old lorry, and that the Rolls would be speeding on again long before the Ford could come up, he could afford to take the situation calmly. And he did.

"The fact is, sir," rattled on Bunter, "I'd just as soon come to close quarters with the rotters ! Leave it to me !"

"Good gad !" repeated Sir Peter.

Denham, the chauffeur, was shouting to the lorry:

"Here ! Clear the road ! You staying there all day, grandfather ? You going to shift that lorry ?"

Old Joyce looked round at him for a moment, but did not trouble to answer. He had plenty to do, handling that heavy old creaking lorry.

It grunted, it creaked, it puffed and it blew; but slowly it obeyed the driver, and drew lengthwise along the road.

The Rolls stirred again.

Sir Peter Lanchester blinked.

"Good gad ! They are clearing the road !" he exclaimed, in infinite relief. "Is it possible that this is not a trap after all ?"

Billy Bunter winked at the back of the baronet's head, as Sir Peter stared in great surprise at the lumbering lorry —lumbering slowly out of the way.

Evidently, it was not a trap. Sir Peter realised now what Bunter had realised immediately he recognised old Joyce.

The Rolls sped on, passing the lorry and its stack of logs. Denham let it out, and it whizzed. There was still no sign of the Ford in the rear.

Sir Peter Lanchester sat down, gasping for breath.

He was immensely relieved to get clear before the Ford came into the picture again. So was Bunter, for that matter !

Sir Peter did not speak again till the

car had passed Lantham, and was speeding away to the west. He glanced several times at Bunter, however. The fat junior's cool self-possession, during those trying moments on the Lantham road, had been another surprise to him. That Bunter knew the lorry driver, and knew, therefore, that it was all right, did not occur to him. Bunter did not think of mentioning it.

"I am more than satisfied," said Sir Peter, when he spoke again at last. "Twice to-day you have proved your courage, my boy."

"My pluck's fairly well known at Greyfriars," remarked Bunter. "The fellows generally select me if there's anything a bit risky on hand."

"I have no doubt of it. And yet, what you are going to face at Reynham Castle might make even a brave boy hesitate," said Sir Peter. "It is true that I hope to trap the rascals, but I may not be successful. We are dealing with a desperate gang, I fear."

He paused.

"But I can rely on you, William. I shall call you William, my boy, as that is my ward's name."

"That's all right, sir!" said Bunter. "It's my name, too—William George."

"You will be careful, William, not to allow a single indiscreet word to pass your lips at the castle. The whole thing depends upon the utmost secrecy being observed," said Sir Peter. "Even to my nephew Rupert I have said nothing. No one at the castle will dream, for a moment, that you are not the real Lord Reynham. But a single careless word——"

"Rely on me, sir!"

"I do! I do!" said Sir Peter. "Nevertheless, be very careful. Everything depends on those scoundrels taking you for the real Lord Reynham. It is four or five years, my boy, since the first attempt was made upon my ward—and ever since he has been in danger. Only by placing him at a distant school, under an assumed name, have I secured his safety. How they discovered what I had done, I cannot even guess—but they have learned that much—though, very fortunately, they do not know the name of the school, or the name taken by my ward there."

He paused again.

"My visit to Mr. Quelch gave them the impression that he was at that school," he went on. "It was very fortunate that you heard, by accident, my conversation with Mr. Quelch, and learned how matters stood, as it led you to make the generous offer to play the part required. And yet——"

Once more Sir Peter paused.

"At Reynham Castle," he said, "you will draw the fire of that gang of scoundrels. If only my ward were a boy more like you—— But he is not—he is in delicate health, with a weak nervous system—I dare not expose him to such a strain. He must remain in safe concealment till that gang of rascals is dealt with. No one there has seen him for four or five years—and almost anyone could play the part, so far as that goes—but in view of the danger, only a boy of uncommon pluck and nerve——"

"A fellow like me!" said Bunter modestly.

"Exactly!" said Sir Peter. "Exactly, William! Mr. Quelch doubted whether I should be able to find any boy with courage and nerve to play the part of Lord Reynham, to draw those rascals into the open, and give the law a chance of securing them. But I have found you."

"Just pie to me, sir!" said Bunter breezily.

"You will be in constant danger, William, now that I have made them believe that you are Lord Reynham—that my ward was placed at Greyfriars School under the name of Bunter——"

"I rather like danger, sir."

"You will be exposed to incessant attacks while you are at the castle."

"That will make the hols a bit lively."

Sir Peter smiled.

"Well, well, evidently you are the boy I require," he said. "I should have been glad to let you bring a party of your schoolfellows with you, but, in the circumstances, that, of course, is impossible. Boys who have known you as Bunter could not be present where you are to be known as Lord Reynham."

Billy Bunter made no reply to that.

The prospect of a gorgeous time at Reynham Castle, playing the part of a peer of the realm, feeding on the fat of the land, and giving orders right and left to an army of liveried flunkeys, appealed to Billy Bunter strongly.

But the prospect of incessant danger did not appeal to him the least little bit.

For that reason he had asked the Famous Five to stay with him for the Christmas holidays, as well as Bolsover major and Skinner of the Remove.

With a crowd of Greyfriars fellows round him, Bunter calculated that he was going to be quite safe at the castle in Sussex.

But as this was not in accordance with Sir Peter's plans, Bunter sagely did not mention it.

Once he was received and acknowledged at the castle as Lord Reynham, it would be too late for Sir Peter to back out. Then Bunter's bodyguard could come along; and if Sir Peter did not like it, Sir Peter could lump it!

Such were the thoughts in Billy Bunter's fat mind, as the Rolls ate up the miles; and if Sir Peter Lanchester could have guessed those thoughts, certainly his estimation of William George Bunter would have been considerably lowered.

Fortunately for Bunter, Sir Peter was no thought-reader!

THE FOURTH CHAPTER.

His Lordship Comes Home !

"JASMOND!"

"Sir Peter!"

"Lord Reynham!"

Sir Peter was a tall gentleman, and a little slim. Jasmond, the butler at Reynham Castle, was nearly as tall as Sir Peter, and twice as wide.

Jasmond was plump, portly, and impressive. Butler at a peer's castle, he looked the part.

Billy Bunter blinked at him through his big spectacles.

Now that he stood in the vast hall of Reynham Castle, Bunter was rather glad he had made a careful selection of several other fellows' best clothes.

He realised that he had to dress his part, as much as possible, in these magnificent surroundings.

The December dusk was falling on the hills and woods of Sussex, when the car had rolled in at the immense gates, and followed a drive that seemed, to Bunter, endless, before the castle was reached.

Battlemented walls and turrets loomed up through the winter gloom as the car arrived.

Bunter had expected something on a

large scale. Sir Peter Lanchester was a wealthy gentleman: and his ward, the boy peer, was heir to an enormous fortune when he came of age. So Bunter looked for something imposing. But the old Sussex castle was far beyond his expectations.

The mere idea of staying in the superb establishment for weeks, playing the part of lord and proprietor, was dazzling to Bunter's fat mind.

It was worth a little risk. Indeed, it was worth a lot. Obviously, in such a place, the grub would be all right. If the grub was all right, everything was all right. Bunter was going to sample some. as soon as he could. He had arrived hungry. He was not thinking of danger now. Blow danger !

The massive form of Jasmond bent a little, in respectful salute to his lordship.

That nobody at the castle had seen the real lord since he was a little kid of eleven or so, Bunter knew. After four or five years on from that age the change in a fellow would naturally be very great. Almost any fellow of a suitable age could have taken up the part. Nevertheless, it seemed to Bunter doubtful whether Sir Peter's numerous staff would really take him for Lord Reynham. It seemed to him too good to be true, in fact.

But his doubts were relieved now.

Clearly the massive Jasmond had no doubts. How could he, when his master himself brought the schoolboy into the castle as Lord Reynham? Sir Peter could not have been imposed on by any impostor. That he was deliberately passing off someone as his ward, was not an idea that was likely to occur to anyone.

"May I respectfully welcome your lordship home, after your lordship's long absence?" said Jasmond, in a deep, throaty, fruity voice. "The whole staff, my lord, will rejoice to see your lordship."

Bunter beamed on Jasmond.

He liked this.

He seemed to grow about an inch taller on the spot.

Indeed as Sir Peter was presenting him as a lord, and the butler receiving him as a lord, and a dozen or so footmen standing in the hall respectfully regarding him as a lord, Billy Bunter began almost to believe that he really was a lord.

"Oh, quite !" said Bunter, airily. "Glad to see you again, Jasmond."

"Your lordship does me the honour to remember me?" asked Jasmond, with an air of great gratification.

"Oh, perfectly !" said Bunter, "In fact, I've often mentioned you to the other fellows at Greyfriars."

"Your lordship has honoured me !" said Jasmond.

"Not at all, my good fellow !" said Bunter, kindly.

"His lordship's apartments are prepared, Jasmond ?" said Sir Peter.

"Everything, sir, is in perfect order," said the butler. "His lordship's valet is in attendance."

Bunter caught his breath. He had not thought of that.

It was a joke in the Greyfriars Remove that Lord Mauleverer, who had a valet when he was at home, had wanted to bring his "man" to Greyfriars when he came. That had put it into Billy Bunter's fat head to tell the Remove fellows that he had a "man" at home at Bunter Court ! Now, however, he really was going to have a "man"—his lordship's man. This was better and better. He wondered what those beasts, Harry Wharton & Co. would say when they arrived and found him with a "man". They would not be able to make out that Bunter hadn't a valet now.

"I will take you to your rooms, William!" said Sir Peter.

"Go it!" said Bunter, cheerfully.

"Eh?"

"I mean, certainly, Sir Peter!"

Bunter followed the old baronet up one side of a vast double staircase, into a still more vast oak gallery that surrounded the hall on three sides.

Jasmond stood respectfully gazing after him as he went. So did the twelve footmen. What they thought of his lordship was not expressed in their faces. Billy Bunter had had some refreshments on the way down to Sussex, and it was possible that the staff had

Bunter. "After all, I've only been away from home a few years."

This was for the benefit of the respectful young man—evidently the valet.

Sir Peter blinked at Bunter.

Certainly, he desired that the "spoof" should be kept up, and believed in by everyone in the castle. Unless Bunter was believed to be the young lord, the kidnapping gang would give him no attention—and Bunter, as the young lord, was to be the bait to draw the rascals into the trap. So the better Bunter played the part, the better it was for Sir Peter's deep-laid scheme.

Yet the old gentleman did not seem quite pleased by Bunter's breezy self-assurance.

Deluding a gang of kidnappers was a

pression on him. Now, perhaps, he was getting a little clearer insight into the fat Owl.

Still, even if it irked him, he could hardly complain of a fellow throwing himself into a part which he had selected him to play. But he turned from Bunter a little abruptly to speak to the respectful young man.

"James!"

"Sir!"

"William, this is your valet, James Anderson."

Bunter gave James Anderson a nod.

"Dinner is at eight, William!" said Sir Peter, turning to leave the apartment.

"Right-ho!" said Bunter.

He sat down in the armchair by the

Billy Bunter sat down in the armchair and blinked at the valet through his big spectacles. "You may take off my boots, George!" he said. The respectful young man obeyed the order and then encased the fat junior's hoofs in a pair of slippers.

not expected to see a peer of the realm with a smear of jam round his extensive mouth. That smear was very evident, though Bunter had wiped off some of the jam on the sleeve of his coat.

From the oak gallery opened an immense corridor, into which Bunter rolled after the old baronet. A big oak door stood open, and the glow of a log fire came from within. Bunter rolled in with Sir Peter.

A young man who was sitting in an armchair by the log fire, bounded to his feet, at the sound of footsteps, and stood at respectful attention as they entered—looking as if he had never sat in his master's armchair in his life.

That room was immense. Bunter guessed that it was a state apartment of the castle. Sir Peter, in treating him as Lord Reynham, was going the whole hog, so to speak.

"The King's Room, William!" said Sir Peter.

"I remember it perfectly!" agreed

justifiable stratagem. But there was a spot of deception in such a scheme, of which Sir Peter preferred not to think. Bunter on the other hand, had no objection to deception. The fat Ananias of Greyfriars, in fact, revelled in it.

"The room seems smaller," added Bunter.

"Eh?"

"It's always so, when a fellow's been away a long time," remarked Bunter. "As a small kid, I thought it immense. Now it seems much smaller."

"Oh!" gasped Sir Peter.

Bunter, undoubtedly, was playing his part well. It was just such an observation as the young lord might have made, after not seeing the King's Room since the age of eleven. From the point of view of acting, it was good business. But it seemed to worry the old baronet a little.

His acquaintance with Billy Bunter was brief. Owing to certain circumstances, Bunter had made a great im-

fire, which James had so recently vacated. He blinked at his man through his big spectacles.

"You may take my boots off, George!" he said.

"James, sir!" hinted the respectful young man.

"Oh, yes! I never remember servants' names!" said Bunter, carelessly.

James gave a little start. Evidently, he had not expected this from Lord Reynham. Bunter could see that, and he wondered why. Forgetting servants' names seemed, to Bunter, frightfully aristocratic.

"Find me some slippers, Francis!" said Bunter, when the boots were off.

"James, sir!" faltered the respectful young man.

"Oh, quite!" said Bunter.

James brought slippers and encased Bunter's hoofs in them.

"Thank you, Thomas!" said Bunter, negligently.

James did not tell him again that he was called James. He left it at that.

THE FIFTH CHAPTER.
All Right for Bunter !

BILLY BUNTER blinked at his reflection in a tall pier-glass, and smiled complacently. He was pleased at what he saw.

After a rest and a little light refreshment which had been sent up to the King's Room, Bunter had dressed for dinner—with the assistance of James. He was quite unable to do it without assistance.

That morning, in the Remove dormitory at Greyfriars, Bunter had dressed unaided. But he had become a lord since then, and that made a tremendous difference. Bunter was now unable to do a thing for himself.

Already Billy Bunter was developing a complete aristocratic helplessness. Moreover, he believed in making servants work. The more trouble he gave them, the more they would be impressed—that was Bunter's idea.

Fellows like old Mauly at Greyfriars did not understand that. Lord Mauleverer never gave servants trouble that he could help. Bunter flattered himself that he knew the nobleman business rather better than old Mauly. All of a sudden, as it were, Bunter had become incapable of picking up a pocket handkerchief for himself.

With James' industrious assistance, Bunter was now in "full fig." Looking into the glass, he could hardly help being pleased.

What he saw was a handsome, well-set-up fellow, in evening clothes—whose spectacles rather added to his distinguished appearance. Probably that was not what James saw.

James, in fact, saw a fat, self-satisfied fellow, with a conceited smirk on his podgy face. However, he did not mention that to Bunter, and Bunter remained happily satisfied with what he saw.

"You can go, James !" said Bunter carelessly; and James went rather gladly. Bunter had tired him a little.

Bunter was not in need, for the moment, of his "man." And he wanted to get shut of James for a bit, while he explored his new and palatial quarters. He did not want James to watch him investigating.

His quarters were all that Bunter could have desired.

The King's Room was an immense sitting-room, with a Persian carpet worth hundreds of pounds, beautiful leather armchairs that it was a luxury to sink into, a radiogram, a telephone, and everything else that Bunter could possibly need, or fancy that he needed.

Adjoining it was a bed-room on an equally magnificent scale. Adjoining the bed-room were dressing-room and bath-room. At the last-named Bunter gave only a careless glance. He had not a lot of use for it.

But he examined with great keenness and interest the contents of wardrobes and drawers. Bunter's measurements having been supplied from the school outfitters, an ample supply of every kind of garment had been prepared for him at the castle.

He was able to discard, with contempt, the garments he had bagged from the Famous Five at Greyfriars. They could have their mouldy old things back as soon as they liked.

Sir Peter had, Bunter admitted, made his preparations with a liberal hand.

THE MAGNET LIBRARY.—No. 1,557.

The only thing he seemed to have forgotten was pocket-money. Bunter was going to remind him of it.

After all, it was up to the old bean to treat a fellow liberally, when a fellow was running such fearful risks for him—or, at all events, he fancied that a fellow was.

Bunter was not going to run risks if he could help it. He had asked Harry Wharton & Co. to the castle, to see him safe. He had asked Skinner and Bolsover major chiefly because they had fed him and pulled his fat leg—still, the more fellows he had round him, the safer he was going to be.

Considering Sir Peter's views on this subject, Bunter realised that he had to break this rather gently to the old bean. All the fellows were not coming in a bunch. Bunter's idea was to let them trickle in, as it were, one or two at a time.

Still, it seemed to Bunter now that there was no hurry about that. He felt safe enough in that crowded castle. He could phone them up when he wanted them.

The old bean, no doubt, would want him to go out and about, taking risks, to draw the attack of the secret gang who were after Lord Reynham. Bunter had his own ideas about that.

Meanwhile, he was surely safe in the

castle ! The Smiler and the Ferret, and the rest of the gang, could hardly get at him there. It was as good as being in a fortress. At least twenty-five servants, too—and his own man, with a room on this corridor. Safe enough.

Feeling so thoroughly safe, Bunter was less keen to see the Famous Five arrive. He was going to have them there—he had asked them, and he was a fellow of his word. But he jolly well wasn't going to hurry about it—in fact, he rather thought he would leave it over for a few days, to keep them on tenterhooks. That would serve them right. Finding himself so absolutely safe in the ancestral home of Lord Reynham made rather a difference to Bunter's views on this matter.

They had been cheeky—making out that they didn't really believe that he was going to Reynham Castle for Christmas—indeed, making out that they didn't really believe there was such a place.

Billy Bunter grinned, and rolled back towards the doorway from his bed-room into the King's Room. He was going to ring up Wharton on the telephone, and tell him where he was.

There was a sound of movement in that apartment.

Bunter frowned.

He had told James that he could go. Distinctly he had told James that he could go. James had no business to come back unless rung for. It was very annoying to Bunter, to think that a manservant's eye might have been upon him while he was rooting through wardrobes and drawers, gloating over his plunder. He resolved to tell James off on the spot. The sooner that manservant understood that his lordly

master was going to stand no nonsense, the better.

Frowning indignantly, Bunter rolled into the King's Room.

"Look here, James——" he rapped. In his wrath, he quite forgot to forget James' name.

He broke off, in surprise. James was not there ! He was certain that he had heard somebody, and had taken it for granted that it was James. But it was not James—nor anybody else. Nobody was there.

"Oh !" ejaculated Bunter.

He blinked round the immense apartment. Half a dozen electric lights were on, and the log fire sent out a ruddy gleam. Nobody was to be seen. Certainly, there was plenty of cover for anyone to hide, among so many massive articles of furniture. Still, James could not be supposed to have hidden himself behind the radiogram, or under one of the big armchairs. Bunter concluded that he had got out quick by the door on the corridor—or perhaps it was a falling log in the fire he had heard, and not a movement at all.

Anyhow, nobody was there—his blink round revealed only the light reflected on the walls and on polished furniture.

Dismissing the matter from his fat mind, Bunter rolled across to the table on which the telephone stood, and sat down to it.

Grinning cheerfully, he asked for "trunks," and gave the number of Wharton Lodge.

As he waited to get through, a sound fell on his fat ears, and he blinked round angrily. If that man James was butting in when he was going to speak on the telephone——

"Oh crikey !" ejaculated Bunter, in surprise.

He was certain he had heard some sound in the room. But there was no one to be seen. He almost wondered whether Reynham Castle was haunted.

However, a voice came through over the wires. He had got his number, and he gave his attention to the telephone.

THE SIXTH CHAPTER.
A Surprise for Harry Wharton !

"MASTER HARRY !"
"Yes, Wells !"
"The telephone, sir !"
"My uncle——"

Wells coughed.

"No, sir ! Master Bunter."

"Oh, all right ! I'll come down !"

Harry Wharton turned off the wireless in his "den" at Wharton Lodge. He gave Hurree Jamset Ram Singh a smile, and the Nabob of Bhanipur grinned.

Wharton Lodge had not its usual festive aspect of Christmastide. Colonel Wharton and Aunt Amy were away, and Harry Wharton was only home for a day or two, before going on with Hurree Singh to Cherry Place.

True, all the Co. had, in a hilarious spirit, accepted Bunter's invitation to the castle in Sussex. But they were not expecting to hear any more of Bunter's castle.

The captain of the Remove was not surprised, however, to get a ring from Billy Bunter. As Wharton Lodge was to be shut up over the holidays, even Wells, the butler, going away to his relations, Bunter did not want to plant himself there. But Wharton had no doubt that he would gladly have planted himself on any other member of the Co.

"Jolly old Bunter, Inky !" he remarked. "Come down and hear what he's got to say. I dare say you can guess."

Hurree Jamset Ram Singh chuckled.

"The guessfulness is preposterously easy," he answered. "The esteemed castle has fallen through, and the absurd Bunter would like to see his old pals at Christmas."

Harry Wharton laughed:

"That's it, I fancy," he said. "The old porpoise would like to roll in here, and go along with us to Cherry Place—if he rolled in there on his own, Bob would most likely boot him! Come on!"

The two juniors went downstairs.

The receiver was off the telephone, and Harry picked it up.

The nabob, with a dusky, grinning face, stood close to hear what came through.

"Hallo! Is that you, Bunter?"

"Yes, old chap!"

"You got away from those sportsmen in the Ford all right?"

"Oh, yes, rather."

"What the dickens were they after you for?"

"Kidnapping, old chap! They've heard of my wealth——"

"Bow-wow!"

"What——"

"Well, I'm glad you got away, whatever they wanted. But if they were after your wealth, why not give it to them, and have done with them? It will only cost you a few bob."

"You silly ass!" hooted Bunter from Sussex. "If you're going to be cheeky, Wharton, I shall jolly well wash out that invitation I gave you!"

"I shan't mind!" said Harry, laughing.

"I fancy you'd be jolly glad to spend Christmas at a magnificent castle, crowded with servants, and feeding on the fat of the land."

"Oh, quite! But it would have to be a real castle!"

"You fathead! I'm speaking from Reynham Castle now!" roared Bunter.

"I don't think!"

"Where do you think I'm speaking from, then, you ass?"

"Bunter Villa—alias Bunter Court."

"Beast!"

"Is that the lot?"

"No! I'm at Reynham Castle now—it's an immense, splendid place, bigger than Bunter Court——"

"Bigger than Bunter Court! It must be twenty feet long, then!"

"You—you—you blithering idiot!" howled Bunter. "The castle alone covers acres. The grounds are immense. I've got the King's Room here—you could put Wharton Lodge in the middle of the floor, and walk round it. I've just dressed for dinner——"

"Whose clobber have you pinched?"

"Beast! If you don't believe me——"

"Hardly!" chuckled Wharton.

"What do you think I was doing in Sir Peter Lanchester's car, you fathead? You saw him fetch me away from Greyfriars."

"I've wondered! I can't make out how you touched that old bean for a lift!"

"I came all the way to Sussex with him in that car. I'm at the castle now. It's magnificent. I haven't rung you up just to make you green with envy, of course——"

"Oh, my hat!"

"But I bet you've never seen such a place in your life. I've got a valet here named James. I usually call him George, because I can't remember that his name is James——"

"Ha, ha, ha!"

"Oh, cackle!" yapped Bunter. "I can't be expected to remember servants' names, being accustomed to such immense numbers of them. It's different with you, in your poor little place. I dare say you always remember your butler's name. I never can remember that it's Wells——"

"Ha, ha, ha!"

"Yah!" came a hoot over the wires. Bunter did not seem pleased by the merriment at the Wharton Lodge end.

A rather peculiar expression came over Hurree Jamset Ram Singh's dusky face, as he listened-in. He was beginning to wonder whether there really was a Reynham Castle, and whether Bunter was there.

"Well, just hear this," went on Bunter, with a snap. "I've asked you here, Harry Wharton——"

"Thank you for nothing."

"You ungrateful beast! I've a jolly good mind to wash it right out!"

"Do!"

"If you fancy I want you, you're mistaken!" hooted Bunter. "It's not dangerous, as I thought it was going to be—I mean to say, I'm not a fellow to be scared by a little danger, and if you think I want you to protect me, you're jolly well mistaken, see?"

Harry Wharton stared blankly at the telephone. Then he looked at Hurree Jamset Ram Singh.

"What on earth does the fat ass mean by that, Inky?" he asked. "I suppose there can't be a word of truth in his gas, can there?"

"The esteemed goodness knows!" said the nabob.

"I'm safe enough here," went on the fat voice over the wires. "They can't get at me in a castle like this, crowded with servants. And I can jolly well tell you that I'm not going out looking for danger. I'll watch it! So if you fancy I want you, you can go and eat coke, see!"

"Well, my hat!" said Harry Wharton, blankly.

"And you can tell the other fellows the same, when you see them," yapped Bunter. "Fat lot I want you looking after me—as if I can't look after myself!"

"This beats it!" said Harry.

"The beatfulness is terrific!" agreed Hurree Jamset Ram Singh.

It was difficult for the chums of the Remove to make head or tail of what Bunter had to say over the phone. But one thing, at least, was clear—the fat Owl was not, as usual, looking for a chance to land himself for the holidays. Wherever William George Bunter was, he was content to stay there.

"Got that?" jeered the fat voice. "Mind, I'm not turning you down! I'll have you here for a few days, as soon as I can arrange it with Sir Peter. But not unless you're jolly civil about it! See?"

"You fat ass!"

"And if you're going to be cheeky, Wharton, I can jolly well say plainly—Oh! Owl Yow-ow! Help! Help! Help!"

"Wha-a-at!"

Wharton fairly bounded, as that yelling voice came through over the telephone.

Hurree Jamset Ram Singh jumped.

"Bunter—what——" gasped Harry.

"Help!" came a howl, in fainter tones—evidently farther from the mouthpiece at the other end. Dead silence followed.

Wharton's startled eyes met Hurree Singh's. The nabob's face was grave. It sounded as if Bunter had been suddenly seized and dragged away from the telephone, and yelled for help as he was dragged. But how could such a thing be possible?

"Bunter!" Wharton fairly shouted into the transmitter. "Bunter! Answer me, you fat ass! Are you trying to pull my leg, or what?"

No answer.

"Bunter!"

Dead silence!

The instrument at the other end, evidently, had cut off. From wheresoever Billy Bunter was telephoning, and for whatever reason he had ceased to speak, he was finished with telephoning now.

Harry Wharton and Hurree Jamset Ram Singh, both utterly amazed, looked at one another with startled eyes, in silence.

THE SEVENTH CHAPTER.
Alarm in the Castle!

"HELP!" shrieked Billy Bunter—seventy-five miles away from the two startled juniors at Wharton Lodge.

Scared out of his fat wits, the Owl of Greyfriars struggled and howled.

Only a few moments ago he had been burbling on the telephone, "gassing" to his fat heart's content, in the belief that, quite safe in Reynham Castle, he did not, after all, need any protection. But now—

It was like an awful nightmare to Billy Bunter.

Who had grasped him, from behind, he had not the remotest idea. The grip that was suddenly laid on him was like iron. He had heard no footstep—whoever had crept behind him, had crept on tiptoe on the soft carpet, and grabbed him as he sat at the telephone.

(Continued on next page.)

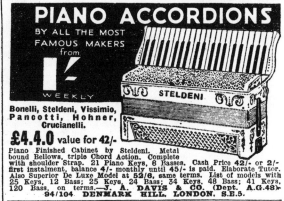

Who—what—could it be? Whoever it was, whatever it was, it was—danger! Only too well the terrified fat junior knew that.

The Smiler and the Ferret had been left a hundred miles away in the Ford —but even had they been at hand, it was unimaginable that either of them could have penetrated within the battlements of Reynham Castle. But a grip of iron was on the fat junior, who had arrived at the castle as Lord Reynham —a grip in which he crumpled helplessly. He was in an enemy's grasp!

He let out a series of sharp, wild shrieks, before he could be silenced. But a hand clapped over his mouth from behind stifled his cries.

Billy Bunter had no more chance in that powerful grasp than a rabbit in the coils of a serpent. He could not even turn his head to see who it was that had attacked him.

A sinewy arm gripped him like a band of steel—a hard hand was pressed on his spluttering mouth, and he was dragged backwards.

Hardly knowing what he did, in his frantic terror, the fat junior kicked out behind him.

By great good luck, that sudden hack landed on a shin.

Bunter heard a gasp of pain behind him, and the grasp of his unseen assailant relaxed for the moment.

That moment was enough for the frantic Owl.

He tore himself away from the relaxing grasp, and bounded.

Nobody, seeing Billy Bunter at that moment, would have suspected that his movements were generally modelled on those of a tortoise. He fairly flew!

His feet hardly touched the floor, as he whizzed for the door on the corridor.

He did not even glimpse his assailant; but he heard, behind him, a leaping footstep and a panting breath as he flew. He felt a fierce grasp just miss his fat shoulder from behind.

Then he tore the door open and bounded out of the room.

"Help! Help! Help!"

He shrieked wildly as he bounded.

"My lord!" came a startled exclamation. James appeared in the corridor.

"Help! Help! Help!" roared Bunter.

"Your lordship——"

"Help! Help! Keep him off! Help!"

Bunter, in his terror, was unaware that he had not been pursued beyond the doorway. His mysterious assailant did not show up. Bunter, by almost miraculous luck, had escaped from his grasp, and it was too late to seize him again, with help at hand and startled servants hurrying to the spot. But the fat junior, in his terror, yelled and yelled.

"What—what—what has happened, my lord?" stuttered the astonished James.

"Help!" yelled Bunter.

Many footsteps sounded in the gallery over the hall and the corridors that branched therefrom. The groom of the chambers, three or four footmen, and several other menservants arrived from various directions. More slowly, but with as much haste as was consistent with his portly dignity, Jasmond arrived. More swiftly than any of them came Sir Peter Lanchester. With Sir Peter came a rather hard-featured man with sharp eyes, dressed in black. Bunter had not seen him before, but the household knew him as Mr. Tomlinson, the baronet's new secretary.

"What——" exclaimed Sir Peter.

"Help!" roared Bunter.

"James, what——"

"Really I do not know, sir!" gasped James. "His lordship suddenly rushed out of his lordship's room calling for help, sir——"

"William——"

"Help!"

"My dear boy!" exclaimed Sir Peter. He grasped Bunter by the shoulder. "Tell me what has happened at once!"

"Oh crikey!" gasped Bunter. He pulled himself together a little as he realised that he was in the midst of a crowd and that the danger was past. "Oh lor'! Oh crumbs! I say, keep him off!"

"Him! Who?"

"He collared me from behind!" gasped Bunter.

"Who did?"

"He did! I didn't see him; he got me from behind while I was sitting at the telephone!" spluttered Bunter. "He's in my room now! Oh crikey!"

"Good gad! Impossible! What——"

"I tell you he got me!" roared Bunter. "He's there now! Tell the servants to collar him! James, go into that room at once and bag that beast! Do you hear me?"

"Yes, my lord!" gasped James.

Bunter's man went at once into the King's Room.

Sir Peter Lanchester gave Bunter a searching look, then he turned to his secretary.

"Tomlinson, search at once!"

The hard-faced, hawk-eyed man stepped quickly into the room after James. Sir Peter rapped orders to the clustering menservants. They gathered round the door of the King's Room and the door of the adjoining bed-room. If any stranger was in either room his escape was cut off; and as he had not followed Bunter out into the corridor, he was still there—if he had been there at all.

Then the old baronet stepped into the room.

Bunter rolled as far as the doorway and blinked in after him; he did not mean to enter until that mysterious assailant was secured.

Swiftly the room was searched.

There was a good deal of space to cover and a great many massive articles of furniture to look under and behind, but in five minutes Mr. Tomlinson had scanned every inch of space.

There was a slightly sarcastic expression on Mr. Tomlinson's hard face.

"No one is here, Sir Peter," he said.

"Really it seems impossible," said Sir Peter.

"Quite!" said Mr. Tomlinson.

"Don't talk rot!" roared Bunter.

Mr. Tomlinson gave a sort of convulsive jump and stared round at Bunter.

"What did you say?" he ejaculated.

"I said don't talk rot!" hooted Bunter. "That man's got to be found!"

"No one is here——"

"Rubbish!"

"Please address Mr. Tomlinson more respectfully, William," said Sir Peter. "Mr. Tomlinson is my—my secretary."

"I don't care who he is! He's talking rot!"

"Really, William——"

"That man's got to be found!" roared Bunter.

The baronet made a gesture to James, who left the apartment.

Billy Bunter, still no farther in than the doorway, glared angrily through his big spectacles. Obviously—to Bunter —the mysterious assailant was still there, and he had to be found.

Sir Peter looked inquiringly at Tomlinson. The sarcastic expression had returned to Mr. Tomlinson's face.

"No one is here, Sir Peter," he said, speaking in a low voice. "The boy has had an attack of nerves."

"You are absolutely certain——"

"I have been a detective for twenty years, and I imagine that I am capable of searching a room," answered Mr. Tomlinson dryly.

"Oh, quite, quite! But"—the baronet spoke in a whisper—"you know my plan, Tomlinson. The boy is here to draw the attacks of the kidnappers; you are here to watch for them and lay them by the heels. If there has been an attack——"

"No one is here!"

"But the boy——"

"Nerves!" said Mr. Tomlinson sarcastically. "He fancies there is danger, and he has fancied an attack!"

"On previous occasions he has shown remarkable courage and presence of mind, Tomlinson."

The detective fixed his keen, hard eyes on the fat, scared face in the doorway for a moment, then he shrugged his shoulders.

"He does not look it!" he said dryly.

"Perhaps not at the moment, but certainly he has shown great courage this very day," persisted Sir Peter. "I can hardly believe that he has been frightened at nothing."

"No one is here, sir!"

"It is inexplicable," said Sir Peter; and the detective, with another shrug of the shoulders, walked out of the King's Room, Billy Bunter giving him an inimical glare as he went.

THE EIGHTH CHAPTER.
Bunter Means Business!

"HOW the thump did he get away?"

"My dear boy——"

"He must have nipped through the bed-room——"

"But——"

"And dodged down the corridor!" said Bunter.

"Really, William——"

"That must be it, as he isn't here now," said Bunter.

Even Billy Bunter was satisfied at last that there was no extraneous person in his rooms. Having been over the whole ground himself, he could trust the evidence of his own eyes and his big spectacles.

No one was there. Bunter could only suppose that when he ran yelling into the corridor the assailant had cut through the bed-room and escaped by the door on the corridor farther along.

In that case, it was extraordinary that James had not seen him; but as it was the only possible explanation, to Bunter's mind, he settled on it.

Sir Peter Lanchester had a very doubtful look, however. James had been drawn to the spot at once by Bunter's yells. Surely he would have seen a stranger in the corridor! Besides, if the man had got clear from the King's Room where was he? Rooms and corridors up and down and round about were searched by innumerable servants without a sign of anyone being found.

Sir Peter inclined to the opinion of Mr. Tomlinson. That gentleman was an experienced detective, engaged under cover of a secretaryship to keep watch and ward in the castle while his "lordship" was there. Bunter was the bait, and Tomlinson was the trap, as it were, and between them Sir Peter hoped to snaffle the mysterious gang who were after his ward; but he had no use for a false alarm, and he was disturbed and annoyed.

"You say that you were seized from behind as you sat at the telephone," he said slowly. "In that case, how did you get free, William?"

"I hacked the rotter's shins!" snapped Bunter. "You needn't fancy that I was scared, like that cheeky secretary of yours; I was perfectly cool."

"You did not see him?"

"Think I've got eyes in the back of my head?" Bunter was annoyed as well as Lord Reynham's guardian.

Sir Peter breathed rather hard.

"But when you got loose, did you not see him?"

"I cut for the door. I wasn't frightened, but I thought I'd better get help in handling him."

"There is no sign of him to be found, William."

"What did you say?" gasped Sir Peter.

"I said rot!" retorted Bunter. "I've been attacked. The man's a fool! He ought not to have let that blighter get away if he's a detective. Fat lot of good having a silly ass like that about the place!"

"Listen to me! You know why you are here. I have every hope that the gang of rascals will make an attack upon you, and give Mr. Tomlinson his opportunity. But that can only happen outside the castle. Within the walls you are perfectly safe, and I must tell you plainly that I desire you to show more self-possession, and not to cause unnecessary alarms."

"Think I was going to let that rotter bag me?" roared Bunter. "What good would your silly Tomlinson be if that rotter had got away with me?"

this—I'm going to have some Greyfriars pals here with me."

"Nonsense!" said Sir Peter decisively. "Such a thing is impossible, as I have already told you. In the circumstances——"

"I'm having some friends here!" yapped Bunter.

"Nothing of the kind! I cannot assent to that."

"Well, I mean it," said Bunter. "I can jolly well tell you I mean business!"

"I must point out to you," said Sir Peter sternly, "that much as I am under an obligation to you, you are here under my instructions and orders."

"Oh, am I?" said Bunter defiantly. "Perhaps you'd rather I went?"

"That is impossible now. You are perfectly well aware that now that matters have gone so far it is impossible!" exclaimed Sir Peter.

"I know that. He's got away. And if he comes back again he will jolly well find me ready for him, I know that!" said Bunter, with emphasis. "He's not getting hold of me again, I can tell you!"

"Now, listen to me, William," said Sir Peter quietly. "As you know, I hope that your presence here may lead those kidnapping scoundrels to show their hand, and enable me to deal with them. Mr. Tomlinson, who is here under the name of a secretary, is actually a detective, on the watch for them."

"Then he jolly well ought to be able to snaffle that rotter who collared me!" snapped Bunter.

"His opinion is that there was no one here."

"Then he's a fool!"

"What?"

"You'd better sack him and get a better man."

Sir Peter breathed harder.

"Mr. Tomlinson is a detective of very great experience," he said.

"Is he?" sneered Bunter. "Well, they say experience makes fools wise. It hasn't done so in his case."

"I agree with his opinion," said Sir Peter sharply.

"Rot!"

"That is nonsense! Do you fancy it even remotely possible that even if an enemy penetrated to this room and seized you, he could have got you out of the castle?"

"Oh!" said Bunter.

Really, it did not seem probable.

Billy Bunter certainly had been grasped in that room by an enemy. He knew that, if Sir Peter and the detective did not. But how the rascal had hoped to get away with the supposed Lord Reynham, after collaring him in the King's Room, was quite a mystery.

Obviously he could not have carried a wriggling, squeaking prisoner down the corridors and the grand staircase, and out at the massive double doors.

"You see yourself that it is impossible," said Sir Peter severely. "A trick of the imagination."

"I know I was grabbed from behind."

"Nervousness," said Sir Peter. "Fancy!"

"I'm not a fellow to get nervous!" yapped Bunter. "Was I nervous in the car when that blighter was shooting at the tyres, and then, when that lorry barred the road, and you were jumping about like a hen on hot bricks——"

"What?" gasped Sir Peter.

"You may be nervy!" snapped Bunter. "I'm not. And I can tell you

Bunter grinned. He was quite well aware of that.

Now that he had been shown to the whole castle as Lord Reynham, he had become absolutely indispensable.

This strange game was a game that could be played only once. Obviously Sir Peter could not discard Bunter, and trot out another fellow to be called Lord Reynham—not after all the castle had seen Bunter as his lordship. Either he had to give up the whole plan, or make the best of Bunter.

"Well, not so much about instructions and orders, then," said the fat Owl independently. "I'm jolly well taking care of myself, I know that. That blighter who collared me got into the castle somehow. He may be one of the servants, for all I know."

"Nonsense!"

"Well, I'm taking jolly good care that he doesn't get hold of me again!" yapped Bunter. "Why, look at the telephone! There's the receiver hanging on the end of the cord! Think I'd have left it like that if I hadn't been collared while I was using it?"

Sir Peter compressed his lips.

"Dinner in a quarter of an hour," he said, and walked out of the King's

Room. He seemed to have had enough of Bunter, for the present.

Billy Bunter snorted as the door closed after the baronet. Then he rolled over to the telephone and replaced the receiver.

A moment later the bell rang, and he put the receiver up to a fat ear.

THE NINTH CHAPTER.
The Genuine Goods!

HARRY WHARTON gave a gasp of relief.

"We're through!" he exclaimed.

"Good egg!" said Hurree Jamset Ram Singh.

It was an immense relief to both the juniors at Wharton Lodge.

That sudden breaking off of Bunter's call, ending in wild howls for help, had naturally alarmed them.

At a distance of seventy-five miles they could do nothing. If Bunter was, as it appeared, in danger, they could not help him.

All that Wharton could do was to ring up the exchange and ask them to ascertain the number from which he had been called, and put him back on it.

That occupied some time, and even when the number was ascertained by an obliging operator, no answer came. But Wharton learned that the call had come from the Castlewood exchange in Sussex, which indicated that Bunter really had been phoning from that county, whether from a castle or not.

Then suddenly Wharton got through, and, to his great relief, a well-known fat voice came to his ears.

"Hallo! That you, Wharton?"

"Yes!" gasped Harry. "That you, Bunter?"

"You bet!"

"What did you cut off for? What did you yell for?" demanded Wharton. "You made me think something had happened to you, you fat ass!"

"Oh, really, Wharton——"

"Well, what did you mean by it, you fat blitherer?"

"I've been attacked——"

"What?"

"I was grabbed from behind while I was phoning. I should be kidnapped now, and taken goodness knows where, if I hadn't got away."

"Oh crumbs!"

"I can tell you, I'm phoning now with one eye over my shoulder, in case that blighter should show up again! I say, I ain't safe here. I thought I was, but I ain't. I say, old chap, you promised to spend Christmas with me at the castle—you know you did! I want you to come at once. Brink Inky with you."

"Oh scissors! Where?"

"To Reynham Castle, in Sussex, near a town called Castlewood. That's where I am now."

Wharton and Hurree Jamset Ram Singh looked at one another. They knew that Bunter's call had come from Castlewood in Sussex. They wondered dizzily whether there really was a Reynham Castle, and whether Bunter could possibly be there.

"Get here just as quick as you can!" gasped Bunter, over the wires. "I'm in danger every minute, day and night! You ain't the fellow to let a pal down, Harry, old chap. The other fellows can come along as soon as you like. You'll all be together over the hols. But I want some of you quick. Just hop into a car and get over here."

"Oh, my hat!" gasped Wharton. "Is

there really such a place as Reynham Castle, Bunter?"

"You silly idiot!" yelled Bunter. "I'm phoning from it! Come over at once, and ask for Lord Reynham."

"Oh crumbs! Think we can butt in on Lord Reynham without being asked, you fat chump—if there really is a Lord Reynham? What would he say when he saw us?"

"You can be jolly sure that Lord Reynham will be glad to see you! He, he, he! I can answer for that! Look here, you mayn't be able to get a train, and I dare say you've no car available. I'll send one for you."

"Wha-a-t?"

"I'll send you one of my cars from here."

"Your cars!" gasped Wharton.

"Yes, right at once! Look here, I don't know how far it is—about sixty or seventy miles, I believe—to your place in Surrey. I'll tell one of my chauffeurs——"

"One of your chauffeurs!" gurgled Wharton.

"Yes, I'll tell one of my chauffeurs to cut across just as fast as he can, and fetch you over. Some of my cars can do seventy, I fancy——"

"Oh crikey! Only some of them?"

"You'll get here to-night, anyhow. I shall stay up for you. I jolly well shan't go to bed here alone, I can tell you. I might be grabbed while I was asleep. I'll tell the man to go all out. Have your bags packed ready."

Harry Wharton gasped.

"You'll come?" asked Bunter anxiously. "I'm relying on you, you know. You said you'd come for Christmas."

"Yes; but it was all gammon——"

"Look here, you fathead, will you come if I send the car? I'll send a Rolls-Royce with a chauffeur in the Reynham livery! Will that satisfy you, you ass?"

"Oh, yes! But——"

"That's that, then! I shall have to cut off now, or I shall be late for dinner! I don't want to be late for dinner—that's important! You can expect that car under two hours."

"But——" gasped Wharton.

"Mind you're ready—you and Inky when——"

"But——" stuttered the captain of the Remove. "Look here, you fat chump, I can't make out whether you're gassing, or gone off your rocker, or what! But if that car comes for us before bed-time this evening, we'll come over."

"That's all right!" said Bunter. "I shall expect you! I shall be all right at dinner, of course—and after that, I'll keep James with me till you come."

"Who's James?"

"My valet!"

"Oh crikey!"

Bunter rang off.

Harry Wharton put up the receiver and gazed at the dusky face of Hurree Jamset Ram Singh.

The Nabob of Bhanipur gazed at him.

"Can you make all this out, Inky?" asked Harry.

"The makeoutfulness is not terrific!" answered the nabob, with a shake of his dusky head.

"Is there really a Reynham Castle, and is Bunter really there?"

"It begins to look like it, my esteemed chum."

"But how—and why—and which and——"

"Perhapsfully the esteemed and idiotic Bunter will explain when we see him," said Hurree Jamset Ram Singh. "But we know of our own absurd knowledge that some ridiculous kid-

napper has been after him, so it is not all moonshine."

"Yes, that's so—but—blessed if I can make head or tail of it! Who the thump is Lord Reynham?"

"The esteemed goodness knows."

"If he's got a castle, how the dickens did Bunter barge into it?"

Hurree Jamset Ram Singh shook his head. He had to give that one up.

"Well, if it's straight, we've got to go!" said Harry. "If Bunter's really in danger, of course, I'd be glad to stand by the fat duffer. We said we'd go to the jolly old castle for Christmas—thinking it was all spoof—but if it isn't, we shall have to play up. But, I suppose if Lord Reynham allows Bunter to send a car for us, we can take it that he's given Bunter permission to ask his friends there. That's all right. But——"

"But——" grinned Hurree Jamset Ram Singh.

"But it's all gammon!" exclaimed Harry Wharton. "I can't make it out—but it's all gammon, or most of it. Anyhow, I shall believe in that jolly old lordship's car when I see it—and not before."

"The seefulness will be the believefulness!" agreed Hurree Jamset Ram Singh.

And the chums of the Remove could only leave it at that.

If one of his lordship's chauffeurs came to fetch them in one of his lordship's cars they had to take it as genuine. But they did not expect that car to arrive at Wharton Lodge.

However, if it came, they were going in it; and they packed their suitcases ready. But they could not help feeling that they were allowing the fat and fatuous Owl of the Remove to pull their legs.

After packing, and supper, they sat down to the radio in the hall—not expecting to be interrupted by the arrival of a Rolls from a castle in Sussex—and yet wondering.

At half-past nine, which was bed-time for the Remove fellows at Greyfriars, Wharton shut off the wireless.

"Any good sitting up, Inky?" he asked.

"Let us give his esteemed lordship's chauffeur half an hour!" suggested the Nabob of Bhanipur.

But it was only a few minutes later that the grinding of a car was heard on the drive outside.

Wharton and Hurree Singh exchanged quick glances.

Then Wharton ran to the door, and threw it open. Headlights flashed through the frosty December night. The car halted. It was a Rolls-Royce—a handsome and very expensive car—driven by a chauffeur in livery.

"My only esteemed hat!" murmured Hurree Jamset Ram Singh.

Harry Wharton ran out to the car.

The chauffeur touched his hat.

"You—you've called for us?" gasped Harry.

"Lord Reynham's instructions, sir, were to call at Wharton Lodge for Mr. Wharton and Prince Hurree Singh!" said the chauffeur.

"Lord Reynham?"

"Yes, sir!"

"Any message from Bunter?"

"Bunter, sir? I have not seen any gentleman of that name at the castle. My instructions were given me by his lordship, sir."

"Well, that settles it, I suppose!" gasped Harry.

It was settled. In five minutes, the suitcases were on the car, Wharton and Hurree Jamset Ram Singh having donned coats and scarves and hats, were

A sinewy hand gripped Bunter like a band of steel and he was dragged backwards. Hardly knowing what he did in his frantic terror, the fat junior kicked out behind him. There was a gasp of pain from his assailant!

sitting in the Rolls—gliding out of the gates of Wharton Lodge.

The car shot away—the headlights glaring through December darkness.

In the car, the two juniors looked at one another in hopeless puzzlement.

"Can you make it out, Inky?" asked Harry.

"Not in the leastfully!"

"Anyhow, we're going to Reynham Castle on his jolly old lordship's instructions! I suppose Lord Reynham knows whether he wants us or not!"

"Probably!" grinned the nabob.

"But it beats me!"

"The beatfulness is terrific!"

And the two perplexed juniors could only wonder as the swift car ate up the miles for Sussex.

THE TENTH CHAPTER.

A Lordly Lord!

S NORE!

"William!"

Snore!

"Really, William——"

Snore!

The lord of Reynham Castle sat, or rather, sprawled, in a large deep arm-chair by the fireside in the great library.

The hour was late.

Late as it was, the new lord of Reynham showed no desire to go to bed—and was, in fact, determined not to go to bed. On the other hand, he was sleepy.

Being sleepy, he went to sleep. Being asleep, he snored. The deep and reverberating rumble, that was wont to wake the echoes in the Remove dormitory at Greyfriars, now woke them in the library of the great castle.

Bunter had dined well. His anticipa-

tions with regard to the food had been realised—more than realised. It was good, and it was unlimited. Dining in state, with a footman behind his chair, suited Bunter—though his attention was given more to the food than to the stateliness. How many courses there were at dinner, Bunter hardly knew; but he knew that he had made a regular meal at every one of them.

After such exertions, he needed a rest. But he was not going to bed—not till his Greyfriars pals arrived. He was not going to be grabbed again—not if Bunter knew it. Harry Wharton and Hurree Jamset Ram Singh would be at the castle that night, and as soon afterwards as he could, he was going to gather in Bob Cherry, Frank Nugent, and Johnny Bull. With the Famous Five round him, he was going to be safe. And "safety first" was Bunter's motto.

Sir Peter shook him by the shoulder at eleven o'clock. Snores were his only reward.

Sir Peter Lanchester was in rather a difficult position with regard to the new lord of Reynham. One day and evening with Bunter had rather changed his opinion of that fat youth. But he was, so to speak, "for it." Bunter was there for a special purpose—which, without Bunter, could not be carried out. He had taken it for granted that the schoolboy would carry out all his instructions with respectful alacrity. He had learned already that Bunter's idea was to suit himself; and that the fat youth had to be treated with tact.

It was rather awkward. By his own act, Bunter had been recognised as Lord Reynham, owner and master of the castle and the vast estate. True, Sir Peter had authority as guardian.

Still, a noble lord had to be allowed to have a will of his own. And it seemed that Bunter, being for the once a lord, was going to have a full lord's ticket, as it were. Bunter was, in fact, the fellow to take full advantage of the peculiar position in which he was placed.

Shake, shake, shake!

Bunter's eyes opened at last behind his spectacles. He gave the baronet an irritated blink.

"Leggo—lemme alone! Wharrer you waking me up for?" he yapped.

"William, it is long past bed-time. It is past my own bed-time!" snapped Sir Peter. "You really must go to bed!"

"Have my friends arrived yet?"

"No!" said Sir Peter, compressing his lips.

"Then I'm not going to bed!"

"I repeat——"

"You can go, if you like!" said Bunter, blinking at him. "I'm not keeping you up, am I? I'm not going till my pals arrive!"

"I had better speak to you plainly, I think," said Sir Peter. "In the circumstances as I have told you, you cannot have your friends from Greyfriars here."

"Can't I?" said Bunter, now fully awake, and giving the old gentleman a belligerent blink. "Well, I've sent a car for them, and they're coming!"

"It was a great shock to me, to learn that you had dispatched the car, William, without consulting me——"

"I suppose a fellow can do as he likes, in his own castle!"

"What?" roared Sir Peter.

(Continued on page 16.)

THE MYSTERY OF JOLLY LODGE!

First Instalment of a Rib-Tickling Xmas Serial.

By DICKY NUGENT

I.

Me-ow-ow! Yeow-ow-owl!

"Grate pip! What's that?" asked Jack Jolly, starting up from his chair at the fireside in the library of Jolly Lodge.

"Sounds like a cat concert!" remarked Frank Fearless.

"Either that or a radio set ossilating!" grinned Merry.

"Maybe it's some feroshus wild animal that has lost its way in the snow!" said Bright, with a slite shiver. "There mite easily be wolves about on a wintry nite like this!"

"Ha, ha! I think not!" chuckled General Jolly, Jack's bluff and harty pater. "Even though it's doubtful weather, it's doubtful weather it'e doubtful enuff to bring out wolves!"

"Ha, ha, ha!"

The chums of the St. Sam's Fourth larfed hartily at their host's little joak.

Larfter came easily to their yung lips now that they were at Jolly's ancestral home for the Christmas hollerdays. The snow lay thick in the eggstensive grounds of Jolly Lodge and a wintry wind howled and wissled round the towers and turrets of General Jolly's mansion; but all was merry and bright in the flickering light of the fire in the old library.

Even the Rajah of Bhang seemed to have caught the hollerday spirit. This distingwished prince, who had been a friend of General Jolly's in India, usually wore a feerce frown on his face; but he allowed himself to smile slitely, as he lissened to the cheery chatter of the Fourth-Formers.

"Our yung friends like well to be away from school, is it not, yes, no!" he cried, as he fingered the glittering diamond pin which adorned his tie—a jewel repewted to be worth a fortune. "It is releef to them to be free from burden of schoolmaster sahib, no, yes!"

"Yes, rather, rajah!" larfed Jack Jolly. "Our Head, Doctor Birchemall, is one of the biggest tirants that ever lived. It's a load off our minds to know that we've left him behind at St. Sam's."

Yeow-ow-owl! Mee-ow-ow!

"My hat! There's that awful noise again!" eggsclaimed Frank Fearless. "Is it possibul that it's a yewman being in pane?"

"Perhaps it's a ghost," said Merry, with a nervuss glance over his sholder. "I've been told that in a hysterical mansion like this there's always a haunted wing!"

"Somebody has been pullin' your leg, my boy!" larfed General Jolly. "I'll wager my life it's only a cat on the front doorstep. It's a feline howlin' that's harrowin' our feelin's!"

Yow-owl! Mee-row! Yeow-ow-ow!

"Ye gods!"

"Can't something be done about it?" asked Bright, with a shudder. "It's—it's garstly!"

"I know one certain way of stoppin' it, by gad!" grinned General Jolly. "Open the front door suddenly so as to take the dashed animal by serprize an' throw a bucket of water over it!"

"Good idea, by Jove!"

"It won't be very plezzant for the cat on a cold nite like this, but we've simply got to do something," said Jack Jolly, rising. "This way, you fellows!"

The rest of the company and followed their leader. ... didn't quite like wetting a c... cold winter's nite, but sor... had to be done to put an ... this tortcher, anyway!

Jack Jolly went down ... kitchen to fetch a pail of ... and then the quartette cre... thily across the hall to the ... front door of Jolly Lodge. ... turned back the handle a... pared to fling open the door

"Ready?" whispered Fe... Jack Jolly poised his p... nodded.

The next instant, Fearless ... open the door and Jack Jolly ... the contents of his pail thro... open doorway.

SWOOOOOOOOSH!

"Yaroooo! Yoooop! ... "What the merry dic... gasped Fearless.

Instead of the feline sq... had eggspected to hear, it v... bellowing of a yewman voi... came from the porch—and ... man voice that was very fa...

"The Head!" gasped F...

"Grate pip! So it is!"

The chums of the Fourth ... out on to the porch in sheer ... ment. It was Doctor Birc... the revered and majestick ... master of St. Sam's, wh... standing before them—not ...

"You silly yung asses ... roared. "What do you ... you're doing of?"

"Sorry, sir!" grinned ... Jolly. "We thought w... throwing water over a cat ...

The Head gowged water ... his eyes and glared.

"Do you imagine fo... moment, Jolly, that I shou... a cat to remain on a doorstep... I was singing carols?"

"Sus-sus-singing carols, ...

"Yes, singing carols!" ... Doctor Birchemall. "Sur... heard me? I was singing ... King Wence's Lass.'"

"Ha, ha, ha!"

"Dashed if I see anyt... larf at!"

"No, but we do, sir!" ... Frank Fearless. "We tho... was a cat carolling—not a y... being!"

"Ha, ha, ha!"

There were footsteps in t... General Jolly and the R... Bhang appeared from the d... of the library. The gallant ... farely blinked, as his eyes fe... uneggspected visitor.

"Gad, sir!" Surely it's ... Birchemall or his dubble?...

"It's me!" replied the ... with his usual faultless g... "Eggscuse my watery app... general; your son has just ... a bucket of water over me ... the mistake arose farely be... I was singing a carol on th...

WHEN THEY BREAK UP THEY BREAK DOWN!

Fellows Who Don't Like Holidays

You might think the Christmas hols would be greeted with delight by Greyfriars chaps.

Nothing of the kind, old pals, we assure you!

Touring the school with breaking-up day in the ofing, we found quite a number of fellows bordering on tears at the prospect of going home.

Bolsover major, for instance, was in a state of utter dejection.

"Holidays! Don't talk to me about holidays!" he groaned, when we tried to console him. "What can I do on holiday, for goodness' sake? No arms to twist, no noses to tweak, no ears to pull, no trousers seats to kick, no——"

We fled, leaving Bolsy still reeling off his list of "noes" to the air of the quad!

Soon after that we bumped into Vernon-Smith. There was a woebegone look on his hard-bitten face. "Lookin' forward to Christmas? Why should I?" he asked, twisting his lips into a cynical sneer and uttering a bitter laugh. (Don't mind Smithy—he has to do these things!) "What's Christmas to me without Quelch?"

"Without Quelch?" we yelled incredulously.

The Bounder nodded moodily.

"How can I enjoy myself, do you think, when I've no Quelchy to listen to my cool insolence and caustic wit? Without Quelchy to work up into a daily fury, I shall feel like a lost soul!"

We crept away, leaving Smithy weeping quietly against the School House steps.

Then we ran into Coker. The great man of the Fifth was wearing a frown on his noble brow.

"Blow the Christmas hols!" he snorted, when we timidly touched on them. "I'm interested in reforming the Fifth just now—not Christmas hols. And a man can't reform the Fifth when the Fifth are scattered far and wide all over the country, can he? Christmas be blowed!"

And Coker went his way snorting loudly.

Finally, there was Loder of the Sixth.

"Of course, I'm not keen on goin' home for Christmas!" he leered, when we looked round the door of his study to ask him about it. "I'm far too keen on Latin prose an' Roman history an' mathematics an' what not to want to leave the dear old school."

And Loder lit a fresh cigarette and returned to his task of marking a pack of playing-cards to the accompaniment of a roar of laughter —mirthless laughter, we concluded.

So there you are! Fellows are not all so keen on holidays as you'd think, and some of them are nearly breaking-down when it comes to breaking-up!

fore ringing the bell to tell
ad come to spend Christmas
ou, when he mistook me for
"

w, haw, haw!" yelled
Jolly. "Gad, sir, that's
call funny! Haw——"
the general broke off in the
of his larf.

at was that I heard you
he cried. "Somethin' about
' Christmas here?"

ht on the wicket!" grinned
Birchemall. "I have
to pay you the grate
of staying with you over
erday."

p!" mermered Fearless.
gad: Awfully kind of you,
re, Birchemall!" gasped
Jolly. "But I really feel
one nothin' to deserve such
ner. Can't you honner
e else instead?"

or Birchemall shook his

general; my mind is made
t's no good of you argewing
t! I know your natcheral
y makes you think that
re more worthy of this grate
; but I shall bestow it on
the same and stay at Jolly
right through the Christmas.
OO!"

gad! Well, if you must,
ust!" sighed the general.
better come inside an' dry
clothes before you catch

anks, awfully!" beemed the
And he axxepted the
on.
or Birchemall had come to

II.

Head soon made himself at
t Jolly Lodge. When Jack
Co. came down to breakfast
following day, it was to find
eady in the breakfast-room
into eggs and bacon with a
ous appetite.

hunitly, however, their first
at he mite interfere with the
joyment of their Christmas
nnished. The stony-harted
who ruled them with a rod
during the term turned out
horse of a different culler
e was on holleray.

on as breakfast was finished,
Birchemall was the first to
a run down to the frozen lake
ting. He proved to be an
luffer on the ice. While they
were cutting figgers of eight
cutting a very commical
But he took it all in good
d the juniors had to konfess
e Head possessed redeeming
rs they had never notissed

an enormous lunch, he ac-
ied the yungsters in General
Rolls-Rice to the nearest

town for a visit to the pictures.
In the evening, while the boys and
Mrs. Jolly and the rajah lissened
in to the wireless, he played snooker
in the billiards-room with General
Jolly.

It was here that a really bright
wheeze occurred to the general,
when he was watching the Head
tuck his beard under the table
before taking a difficult shot.

"I've got a rippin' idea, by
gad!" he cried gleefully. "It's
Christmas Eve an' I've been
rackin' my branes to think of a
suitable man to dress up as Santa
Claws an' take round the presents.
Birchemall! You're just the man
for the job!"

The Head jumped.

"You mean you want me to go
round in the dead of the nite,
filling up people's stockings?"

"Eggsactly!" cried General
Jolly. "With your long white
beard an' shinin' red nose, you'll
fit the part like a glove! I hoap
you won't mind?"

"Ahem! I shall be delited, of
corse, my dear general!" said the
Head. "But—er—don't you think
there's a danger that some of the
guests may mistake me for a
berglar?"

"Not the slitest, my dear
fellow!" grinned General Jolly.
"There are no valluables about
apart from the rajah's diamond
tiepin which he keeps on a table
by his bed; and in his case I can
assure you that he sleeps like a
top!"

"All screen, then, general!"
grinned the Head. "For your
sake I'll do it. You'll keep it dark
from the rest, of corse?"

"Yes, rather!" chuckled the
general. "Mum's the word!"

That nite, a bearded figger,
wearing the familiar garments of
Father Christmas, mite have been
observed flitting from room to room
on the upper floor of Jolly Lodge.
In the pail light of the moon, he
mite have been seen carrying over

his shoulders a grate sack that
simply bulged out with presents.

But although he mite have been
seen, he was not seen becawse
there was nobody awake to see
him.

Doctor Birchemall was grinning
all over his face as he went about
his task. The idea of such an important personage as himself playing the part of Santa Claws appealed to his sense of yewmer.

But his grin faded slitely when
he reached the rajah's room, and
he tiptoed across the carpet with a
grate deal of cawtion. He was not
quite sure how that grim-looking
Eastern potentate mite behave if
he found a stranger at his bedside
in the middle of the nite.

Forchunitly, there was no cause
for alarm. The Rajah of Bhang
was sleeping soundly to the tune
of a loud snoring worthy of one of
the elephants of his native land.
He never so much as moved an
eyelid when the Head leaned over
his bedside table and slipped
Christmas presents into one of his
sox.

His work completed, Doctor
Birchemall returned to his bed.

A lass! A rude awakening was
in store for the Head next morning.
Just as Jack Jolly & Co. were
laying the foundation for Christmas
Day with a good, solid breakfast,
there was a wild shout from the
floor above that sent them racing
upstairs in alarm.

Reaching the landing, they found
the Rajah of Bhang prancing up
and down, flurrishing a nife—and
looking daggers at everybody.

"My tiepin!" he shouted. "My
so-bewtiful diamond tiepin! It
is gone!"

"What?"

"Impossibul!"

"Gone! Vanished!" shreeked
the rajah. "I leave it at bedside
last nite. Now it is gone! I ask one
question: who come to my room
last nite? Yes, no?"

"Oh grate gad!" gasped General
Jolly, who had just arrived.
"Birchemall! Did you——"

A garstly pallor crept into the
Head's face.

"I never took it! I sware I
never!" he panted. "I admit that
I went into the rajah's room to
deliver presents. But I never took
his tiepin and—yarooooo! Keepimoff!"

The Head broke off—then broke
out in a cold sweat—and then broke
into a run! The rajah, rolling his
eyes furiously, ran after him.

Persewer and persewed farely
raced down the staircase of Jolly
Lodge three at a time, with the rest
in full cry behind them!

(*Looks like being an exciting
Christmas for the Head! Don't miss
the thrills and larks in next week's
spiffing instalment!*)

HERE'S FUN FOR THE FESTIVE SEASON!

Chortles HAROLD SKINNER

If there's one thing I like better than any other
it's the sound of happy laughter at Christmas.

That's why I got in touch with a pal who's a
scientific genius and very obliging. I wrote and
asked him if he could design certain models I had
already worked out in the rough. He could and did—
and, boy, am I going to
enjoy this Christmas?

I'm taking home with
me the niftiest little
bunch of surprises a fun-
lover could wish for.
When I get busy with
them on Christmas Day
I can imagine the laugh-
ter will fairly make the
welkin ring!

First, I've a rather
unusual Christmas pud-
ding. It's just an ordi-
nary common-or-garden
Christmas pud. to look
at; but wait till some-
body takes a dig at it!
He'll get the shock of his
life when it blows to
pieces in front of him!

I've also got some nice
mince pies. Nice to out-
ward appearances, at
any rate. What they're
like to eat I shouldn't like
to say. I shall never
know, either. I'm going
to take good care not to
allow my molars any-
where near them.

You see, these mince
pies are made in such a
way that as soon as any-
one attempts to eat them
a hidden spring jumps
into action and shoots
out an iron paper-grip
that gives the biter a
nasty tweak on the nose!

These brainy little
gadgets my pal has made
for me don't stop at
articles of food, by the
way. I've provided fun
for the party as well as
the meal. There are
half a dozen of those in-
flating squeakers, for instance, that blow soot
back into the user's face
as soon as he blows into
them!

As for the Christmas
tree, that's going to be a
regular mine of fun. If
I have my way, there
won't be a present on it
that doesn't squirt ink
or give an electric shock
as soon as it's touched!

Oh, yes, there'll be
fun for the festive sea-
son with a vengeance
when I take home my
little bag of tricks this
Christmas!

He'd be too Blown Out!

We refuse to believe
the yarn that Bunter
mistook Peter Todd's
football for a Christmas
pudding and ate it before
he realised his mistake.
That's too much to ask
any man to swallow.

KING of the CASTLE
By Frank Richards

(Continued from page 13.)

"You needn't yell at a fellow!" said Bunter coolly. "Am I Lord Reynham or not?"

Sir Peter glared at him.

"I sent that car," went on Bunter, "because I jolly well chose to. If you think I'm going to be grabbed in the middle of the night, you're mistaken. That's plain English! I'd rather clear off this blessed minute than go to bed without some other fellows in the room. I'm prepared to take risks—nothing wrong with my pluck, I hope—but I'm not going to be grabbed while I'm asleep——"

"No one could possibly penetrate into the castle——"

"Somebody jolly well did, this evening!"

"That was sheer imagination——"

"Rot!" said Bunter.

Sir Peter Lanchester appeared on the point of choking, for a moment.

Bunter sat up and blinked at him calmly. He was in the strongest of positions; he had, in fact, the upper hand, now that Sir Peter had announced him as his ward, William Lord Reynham.

The baronet could not undo what he had done. Only by throwing up his whole elaborate plan, could he deal with Bunter as he fervently wished to do. And that was not to be thought of.

"I know whether I was bagged or not!" said Bunter. "It's no good talking rot—I've got no use for it! I'm waiting for my friends——"

"I tell you——" roared Sir Peter.

He broke off suddenly as the library door opened. A rather tall and handsome young man in evening clothes came in, smoking a cigarette. This was Captain Reynham, cousin of the young lord: and the only near relative of Lord Reynham, old Sir Peter being a distant connection.

The young Army man glanced from his uncle to Bunter, and back again to Sir Peter. He could see that he had interrupted some dispute.

A faintly sarcastic and contemptuous smile came over his face as his glance dwelt on Bunter.

Rupert Reynham, like all the other residents in the castle, took Bunter at face value. Sir Peter had brought him there as Lord Reynham, and that was that. Nobody at the castle had seen the real lord since he was a small boy; but Rupert, as it happened, had not seen him since babyhood, having been abroad for years with his regiment. So he had not, naturally, the remotest suspicion of the trick that was being played.

But having met the young lord at dinner, he had not been favourably impressed by him—and now he seemed still less favourably impressed. There were several traces of dinner left round Bunter's mouth, and some splashes on his expansive white shirt-front, which really were not in accordance with the best traditions of the nobility.

The captain took him as Lord Reyn-

ham; but he took Lord Reynham as a fearful "bounder."

"Still up, William?" drawled the captain, lounging elegantly across the room, and leaning on the mantelpiece as he smoked his cigarette.

"I suppose I can stay up as late as I like in my own house!" snapped Bunter.

Bunter sensed, rather than saw, that the elegant young Army man regarded him with a sarcastic and amused eye.

And Bunter was not going to take any cheek from him. The son of a younger son, Captain Reynham was poor, while his Cousin William was rich. And Bunter, just at present, was his rich Cousin William!

With all his Army swank, as Bunter regarded it, the captain was, in point of fact, a hanger-on of a rich relation—it was only as nephew of the young lord's guardian that he had a footing in the castle at all. If he wanted to hang on in Bunter's castle, he was going to be civil about it, or Lord Bunter was going to know the reason why!

"Oh! Naturally!" drawled the captain. "But I suppose you did not stay up till midnight at school?"

"I can do as I like in the hols," said Bunter. "Pretty state of things, if a lord can't do as he likes in his own ancestral halls."

"Oh!" gasped the captain. "Quite!"

"I—I was just suggesting to William that it was time for bed, Rupert," stammered Sir Peter. "Now, my dear William——"

Snore!

Bunter closed his eyes behind his big spectacles, and snored. He was not asleep—but he was going to sleep. Lord Reynham was going to do what was right in his own eyes, in his own castle!

Captain Reynham looked at him, and now that Bunter's eyes were closed, did not take the trouble to conceal his contemptuous scorn. There was, in fact, a striking contrast between the fat, snoring owl, and the tall and elegant young Army man.

"Good gad!" the captain murmured in a low voice that did not reach Bunter's fat ears. "I've wondered a good many times what my noble cousin was like, Uncle Peter, but I never imagined anythin' like this! What a shockin' bounder!"

"The boy has his faults, no doubt!" murmured Sir Peter. No doubt the old gentleman was wishing that he had become rather more closely acquainted with Bunter before selecting him to play this extraordinary part at Reynham Castle.

"He was at Greyfriars, I think you told me!"

"Yes."

"He does not do the school much credit."

Sir Peter made no reply to that. He heard the sound of a distant ring, and left the library hurriedly.

Captain Reynham was left to finish his cigarette, and to regard the sprawling figure in the armchair—and Bunter, opening his eyes suddenly behind his spectacles, was startled by the black and bitter look he unexpectedly spotted on the captain's face.

But that look was gone in a moment, and the captain was smiling affably.

Bunter blinked at him suspiciously.

"Where's the old bean?" he asked.

"The—the what?"

"My guardian!"

"Oh! Sir Peter went out a few minutes ago—I think somebody has arrived——"

"My friends, most likely!" said Bunter, and he heaved himself out of the armchair. "Good!"

"One moment, William!" said the captain softly. "For some reason—I really don't know why, but I could see it easily enough when you told him about the car at dinner—your guardian does not want your Greyfriars friends here——"

"Nothing to do with you!" said Bunter.

The captain seemed to gulp.

"Oh, no! But—I thought of suggesting that you might think fit to regard your guardian's wishes in this matter and——"

"Did you?" said Bunter, blinking at him. "Well, when I want advice from poor relations, I'll ask for it. Keep it till then!"

With that, Billy Bunter rolled away to the door—leaving the captain staring after him, transfixed.

———

THE ELEVENTH CHAPTER.
An Unexpected Reception!

"BUNTER?" repeated Jasmond. "He's here, I suppose!" said Harry Wharton.

"I do not know the name, sir."

"Oh, my hat!"

Harry Wharton and Hurree Jamset Ram Singh had arrived. The car had stopped at a vast portico. A footman had let them in—but the butler swam up from somewhere. They stood in the great hall—hats and coats taken by deferential hands.

The two juniors had, naturally, expected Bunter to meet them when they came in, as he had been so eager for them to come. Still, the journey had taken time, and possibly the fat Owl had gone to bed. But when the butler stated that he did not know the name, it was something like a knock-down blow. The car from Reynham Castle had convinced them—how could it have come to fetch them, if Bunter was not there? Yet, it seemed, Bunter was not there. It seemed as if mystery was piled on mystery.

"Look here, we expected to see Bunter—a Greyfriars fellow—here!" exclaimed Harry Wharton. "Isn't he staying here with Lord Reynham?"

"There are no guests in the castle at present, sir, except Captain Reynham, his lordship's cousin."

"Who sent the car for us, then?"

"His lordship gave his instructions personally, sir."

The two juniors looked at one another. If Bunter was not there, they had no business there. But if he was not there, why on earth had Lord Reynham sent the car for them—how, indeed, did his lordship even know of their existence?

They knew nothing of him: and—unless from Bunter—he could know nothing of them! It was quite bewildering.

"Well, I suppose we'd better see Lord Reynham, as he sent the car for us," said Harry. "I suppose he's here."

"His lordship is in the library, sir! I will inform him——"

"You need not trouble, Jasmond!" It was Sir Peter Lanchester's voice as he came hurriedly from the direction of the library. "You may leave these young gentlemen to me."

"Very good, sir!"

Jasmond faded out of the picture; and at a glance from Sir Peter, the other menservants faded away. The silver-haired old baronet was left alone with the two new arrivals.

"Master Wharton, and—and Hurree Inkpot Jam, I think——"

"My esteemed name is Hurree Jamset Ram Singh, excellent and ridiculous sir!" purred the Nabob of Bhanipur.

Sir Peter blinked at him.

"Oh!" he gasped. "Exactly! William has mentioned your name to me, but I did not quite recall——"

"The rememberfulness of my absurd name is not always terrific!" assented the nabob, politely.

"Oh!" gasped Sir Peter again. "Quite! Now, my boys, I—I understand that you have come here on the invitation of a—a—a schoolfellow!"

"That's it, sir!" said Harry. "We expected to find Bunter here—but it seems to have been Lord Reynham who sent the car——"

"Oh, yes! Precisely! Lord Reynham, as I daresay you know, is my ward——" stammered Sir Peter.

"We don't know anything about him," said Harry Wharton. "We've

"If that is the case, Sir Peter Lanchester, we shall go at once," he said curtly. "But please understand that there is no fault of ours in the matter. We had a telephone call from Bunter, a chap we know at Greyfriars, and he told us he was telephoning from this house."

"Yes, yes, but——"

"We should not have come here on that alone!" snapped Wharton. "But when the car came, and the chauffeur told us that he had been sent by Lord Reynham to fetch us here, what were we to think?"

"It is very—hem—very unfortunate. I am truly sorry!" Sir Peter was confused, compunctious, but resolute. "Naturally, it is too late for you to return home to-night, I understand from William that you come from Surrey—but there is an excellent hotel in Castlewood, and the car shall take you there

There was a fat squeak, and a fat figure rolled into the hall!

Billy Bunter, with a beaming, fat face, rolled to greet his Greyfriars pals.

Harry Wharton and Hurree Jamset Ram Singh stared at him in sheer stupefaction.

They had been told that Bunter was not there; and, of course, had supposed that he wasn't. And here he was—blinking at them through his big spectacles, and beaming on them, with obvious gladness to see them.

Sir Peter Lanchester bit his lip hard. He had hoped to carry this through without Bunter coming on the scene till the juniors were gone—hoping that the fat Owl was asleep again in the library. Bunter had appeared at a very awkward moment for him.

The two juniors stared at Bunter—stared at the old baronet—and stared at Bunter again. If they had been

---

---

only seen you twice, sir, when you called at Greyfriars before break-up. We had never heard of Lord Reynham at all, except from Bunter."

"Yes! Precisely! Now, I am sorry —truly sorry—I fear that it may seem inhospitable—but—but—there is an error in this matter," stammered Sir Peter. "Owing to—to certain circumstances, it would be very inconvenient to Lord Reynham to entertain guests here this Christmas."

"Oh!"

"In these circumstances, it was—was really an error for the car to be sent for you!" explained Sir Peter. "The truth is, that—that William—my—my ward, Lord Reynham—acted without consulting me, as his guardian——"

The nabob's dusky features expressed nothing; but he looked very keenly and curiously at the old gentleman.

"I apologise profoundly!" said Sir Peter. "I cannot sufficiently express my regret, that this—this mistake should have arisen. But—but it is actually impracticable for you to stay here."

Wharton compressed his lips. His chief desire, at the moment, was to kick Billy Bunter, and kick him hard, for having placed him in a position like this.

—all expenses will be met by me, and to-morrow the car shall convey you back to your home——"

"We want nothing of the kind!" snapped Harry Wharton. "We came here believing that Bunter was here, and that the master of this place had sent specially to fetch us. If it's a mistake, the sooner we go, the better—and we can look after ourselves, and certainly we shall accept nothing at your hands, or at Lord Reynham's, either."

"My dear boy——" said Sir Peter.

"I cannot say how sorry——" His face was red with discomfort and contrition; but he was quite determined that Lord Bunter was not going to have his way, if he could prevent it.

"Never mind that," said Wharton, "come on, Inky! We can walk to the town and put up somewhere for the night. I'm sorry not to see Lord Reynham before I go, that's all. I'd like to tell him what I think of him, for playing a rotten trick like this on fellows he doesn't even know."

"The rottenfulness of the trick was terrific," said Hurree Jamset Ram Singh, "but the rapid departfulness is the proper caper, my esteemed chum."

"I say, you fellows!"

bewildered before, they were doubly bewildered now.

Bunter grinned at them cheerfully.

"I say, you fellows, I'm jolly glad to see you!" he chirruped. "I've sat up to wait for you, though I jolly nearly fell asleep. Had a good run in the car, what?"

"Bunter!" gasped Wharton. "You—you—you're here!"

"The esteemed and ridiculous Bunter!" stuttered Hurree Jamset Ram Singh.

"Eh? You expected to see me here, didn't you, when I phoned to you to come?" asked Bunter. "What are you goggling at, as if a fellow was a ghost?"

"The butler told us you weren't here —he didn't even know the name!" howled Wharton.

"Oh! He, he, he! That's all right!" said Bunter. "Don't you worry about that! He, he, he!"

"And Sir Peter Lanchester has just told us to get out, because Lord Reynham hadn't his leave to send the car for us!" hooted Wharton. "And we're going—and you can go and eat coke, you fat fraud!"

"What?" roared Bunter.

"My dear William——" gasped Sir Peter.

"You're turning my friends out?" roared Bunter. "Who the dickens are you to turn my friends out?"

"Boy!" gurgled Sir Peter.

"If they go, I go!" roared Bunter. "Got that? My hat! Of all the cheek —taking it on yourself to turn my friends away from the door! Wharton —Inky—don't go! It's all right, old fellows! Don't take any notice of that old josser!"

"Wh-a-t?" gasped Wharton.

"Stick here!" said Bunter. "I want you! I've asked you! You're my guests! Why, if you let me down, I may be kidnapped this very night, or murdered in my bed very likely! You've got to stand by a pal! I say, you fellows, it's all right!"

"But——" gasped Harry, hopelessly bewildered. "If Sir Peter Lanchester isn't in authority here, who is?"

"I am!" retorted Bunter.

"...You!" yelled Wharton.

"Yes; me."

"You howling ass! Look here, where's Lord Reynham?"

"He, he, he!"

"What are you cackling at, you fat image?"

"Oh, nothing! He, he, he! Come up to my rooms and I'll explain!"

"Don't be a silly ass! We can't stay here without being asked by the master of the place, you blithering bloater!"

"That's all right——"

"It isn't, you fathead! Look here, why doesn't Lord Reynham show up and say a word for himself? The silly ass sent a car for us——"

"Oh, really, Wharton——"

"Anyhow, if this old gentleman is his guardian, it's for him to say—and he's said! We're going!"

"You're not!" roared Bunter. "Look here, Sir Peter Lanchester, I'm fed-up with this! I refuse to stay here without my friends! If you can't be civil to my friends, I'm done with you! I say, you fellows, if you go, I'm coming with you! I'm not staying here to be kidnapped in bed!"

Sir Peter gasped for breath.

He could not let "Lord Reynham" walk off with the two Greyfriars juniors, that was clear. And it was plain that Billy Bunter was in deadly earnest. As a matter of fact he dare not remain the night at the castle unprotected, after his awful experience that evening.

"I—I—I——" stammered Sir Peter. "I—I—please remain, my boys! In the —the circumstances—I—I consent——"

"That's not good enough!" said Harry Wharton curtly. "I don't know how Bunter got here—but do you think we're the fellows to barge in where we're not wanted? Unless the master of the house asks us to stay, we can do nothing of the kind. And as he doesn't choose to show up and say a word, it's pretty clear what he wants."

"The clearfulness is terrific."

"I say, you fellows, hold on!" squeaked Bunter, in alarm. "I say, come up to my rooms and—and I'll explain."

"Please do!" gasped Sir Peter, only anxious for this extraordinary scene to be ended. "Please go with—with William, my dear boys, and—and—and I assure you that personally, on your own account, I am delighted to see you here."

The two mystified juniors exchanged glances.

"I say, you fellows, come on!" urged Bunter.

"Please go with—with William!" gasped Sir Peter.

Utterly bewildered, unable to begin to make head or tail of what it all meant, the two juniors followed "William" up the staircase And Bunter, with great relief, led them into the King's Room.

———

THE TWELFTH CHAPTER.

An Astonishing Secret!

"JAMES!"

"My lord!"

"Have you carried out my instructions about the beds?"

"Yes, my lord."

"Is everything ready for my friends?"

"Perfectly, my lord."

"Then you can cut," said Bunter. "I shall not want you again to-night, James!"

"Very good, my lord!"

Harry Wharton and Hurree Jamset Ram Singh listened to this like fellows in a dream. They stood dumbfounded, while Lord Bunter dismissed his valet.

The door closed on James. As it was nearly midnight, no doubt James was glad to be dismissed. He had been yawning his head off while he waited for his lordship.

Billy Bunter turned to the two astounded juniors with a cheery grin. He had not been a lord long, but he was very glad to show off his lordliness to his guests.

"What does this mean, Bunter?" asked Harry Wharton, finding his voice. "Why did that chap call you 'my lord'?"

"He, he, he!"

"The lordfulness of the esteemed Bunter is not terrific," remarked Hurree Jamset Ram Singh. "What is the absurd meaning of this?"

"Sit down, you men!" said Bunter breezily. "Jolly comfy armchairs here —warm your toes by the fire—help yourselves to the tuck. I've had some stuff left up here, in case I should get peckish in the night. Have some cake —or biscuits—or apples—or candied fruits—or peaches?"

"Never mind that," said Harry; "we want to know what this means, Bunter. What sort of idiotic humbug are you up to here?"

"Oh, really, Wharton——"

"What does it mean? Where is Lord Reynham?"

"He, he, he!"

"Are you going to explain or not?" demanded Wharton.

"Won't you sit down, old chaps?"

"No! If we're staying here, we're going to bed, as it's hours past bedtime. But we're not staying unless we understand what's up. What did that man James call you 'my lord' for?"

"You—you see——"

"I don't!"

Billy Bunter blinked at the two astonished and irritated juniors. It was, Bunter realised, rather a difficult matter to explain.

In his keenness to have a sort of bodyguard round him to defend him from hidden dangers, he had rather overlooked that difficulty. But he had to face up to it now.

All the castle accepted him as the young lord. But fellows who knew him quite well were hardly to be taken in.

The Smiler and his gang knew that Lord Reynham had been placed at a school under an assumed name. They had no doubt that that school was Greyfriars, and that assumed name

Bunter. But it would not have been of much use to spin such a yarn to Wharton, who knew that he was Billy Bunter, and knew his brother Sammy in the Second Form, and his sister Bessie at Cliff House.

Bunter had no strong leaning towards the truth—but even Bunter had to tell the truth sometimes, and only the truth was of any use to him now. Still he was going to tell as little as he could.

"Well, look here, you fellows!" he said. He gave a cautious blink round, and lowered his voice. "I couldn't say anything downstairs, where a lot of servants might hear—and, you see, I've got to be jolly careful. That man James might have his ear at the keyhole, for all I know."

"Is his name Bunter?" asked Harry.

"Eh? No."

"Then I don't suppose he's got his ear to the keyhole."

"You cheeky ass——"

"Are you going to explain or not?"

"Yes, you beast! Just listen!"

Bunter gave another cautious blink towards the various doors of the great apartment. Like many people, Bunter measured others by his own measure; and his own fat ear was very often near a keyhole. So he lowered his voice to a whisper:

"The fact is, you fellows——"

"Oh, let's hear the fact!" snorted Wharton. "I can tell you that we're not stopping here unless we see Lord Reynham, and he asks us to."

"He, he, he!"

"What are you cackling at, you blithering owl?"

"You see," breathed Bunter, "I'm him!"

"What?"

"I'm him!"

"Him! Who? What?"

"Lord Reynham!" whispered Bunter.

Wharton and the nabob gazed at him. They looked concerned. For one dreadful moment they feared that Billy Bunter had gone completely off his rocker.

They had not known what to expect; but most certainly they had not expected anything like this.

"I mean, I'm him, temporarily!" explained Bunter.

"Have you gone potty?"

"Oh, really, Wharton——"

"If you're not wandering in your mind, or trying to pull our legs, what the dickens do you mean, you fat idiot?"

"Don't shout!" yapped Bunter. "Don't I keep on telling you that there are keyholes to the doors? It's an awfully deep secret."

"What is?" roared Wharton.

"Don't yell!" Bunter whispered again. "I'm here as Lord Reynham. See? Now do you understand?"

"No. You can't have spoofed that old bean, if the chap is his ward——"

"He asked me to do it, you ass!"

"Rubbish! And if you're really spoofing to that extent, do you think that we're going to have a hand in it? Are you off your dot?"

"Will you shut up and let a chap explain?" hissed Bunter. "I'm going to tell you how the matter stands. I don't want to tell all the castle, you ass! Young Lord Reynham is hidden away somewhere by his guardian, because he's in danger of kidnappers. He's some sort of a weedy, seedy merchant, and old Peter is afraid of his nerves breaking down if he goes through it See?"

"But——" gasped Harry.

(Continued on page 20.)

"Stacks of gifts and hours of fun;
All good things for everyone——" says—

The GREYFRIARS GUIDE

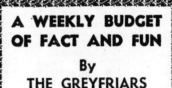

A TOUR OF THE SCHOOL.

(1)

The kitchen's full of appetising steam,
To hungry schoolboys it must surely
    seem
That working here is like a lovely
    dream,
    Devoutly to be wished !
But cooking for so many hungry boys
Means WORK—a thing which nobody
    enjoys,
As in the busy clatter, heat and noise,
    Good things are cooked and dished.

AFTER SCHOOL HOURS

Breaking-Up Night !

We're off for the vac,
    And we're not coming back
Until Christmas is done and the New
    Year begun,
    And it's fun and frivolity,
    Joking and jollity,
All the way home in the morning !
For Christmas is coming and holly is
    green,
And Greyfriars is humming with happi-
    ness keen,
So pack your portmanteau, your hamper
    and bag,
And come to the concert we hold in the
    Rag.
    We'll sing the old strains
    Of the Christmas refrains,
Till lumps of the wall break asunder
    and fall,
    We'll sing 'em unwearily,
    Happily, cheerily,
    All the way home in the morning !
The Owl is unfolding a plan to the
    Form,
A supper he's holding to-night in the
    dorm.
For once he discovers he's really in luck,
We all give him money to purchase the
    tuck.
He scuttles away very nimble
To interview poor Mrs. Mimble,
Then smuggles in pastries and pop and
    mince pies,
And joins us in eating the tasty supplies.
    Then stories are told
    Of the spectres of old,
Which make our flesh creep as we go off
    to sleep.
    To-morrow we're verily
    Travelling merrily
All the way home in the morning !

The Kitchen.

(2)

Upon the Christmas puddings and mince
    pies
Collected here, poor Bunter turns his
    eyes
Like Peri at the gates of Paradise,
    And longs to make a swoop !
Alas, he very swiftly meets his doom,
A busy cook, with still more busy
    broom,
Soon chases Master Bunter from the
    room,
    His farewell word—"Yaroop !"

(3)

On Break-up Day the staff work over-
    time
Preparing extra dishes so sublime
That all words fail me—not to mention
    rhyme !
    Ah, turkeys, puddings—come !
Come hither, oh, ye morsels of delight,
I would devour the whole of ye on sight,
Lay waste among your army, left and
    right,
    And leave no single crumb !

THE GREYFRIARS
ALPHABET
WILLIAM GREENE,
Coker's studymate in the Fifth Form.

G is for GREENE—I beg to state
He's merely Coker's studymate,
And having got that off my chest,
I'll now ignore him. For the rest,
I wish to say I'd like to know
Where all my Christmas presents go.
My Uncle Bill, so they relate,
Went out and purchased 38 !

And if he'd only thought of mine
He would have purchased 39 !
My Uncle Joe has sent away
A hundred presents, so they say,
To all the beastly family,
Except, of course, his nephew—ME.
If I lived out in Timbuctoo
I might expect a gift or two,
But while I spend my Christmas here
They'll all forget me once a year !

CHRISTMAS CHUCKLES

"Birds are intelligent creatures," says
a Nature book. You wouldn't believe
the number of local turkeys who have
committed suicide to save the farmer a
job !

Christmas comes but once a year,
    And Bunter's glad of that !
If Christmas came but twice a year,
    He'd soon be twice as fat !

Stewart of the Shell is a boon to his
relations. His birthday is on Christmas
Day, so they only have to give him one
lot of presents !

Bootles' Fertiliser Makes Plants Grow
Like Wildfire ! Having heard this,
Fishy bought a bottle—and a packet
of Christmas-tree seeds ! (They're sell-
ing at five bob each !)

Christmas waits, who sang "Christians
Awake !". under Sir Hilton Popper's
window, wished sincerely they'd left him
asleep !

Loder said yesterday he was just going
to "slip down to the village." But he
was wrong, because our slide didn't go
as far as that !

We wish "breaking-up" included
Quelchy's canes !

Fisher T. Fish has been collecting
empty match-boxes. After all, everyone
has to give Christmas-boxes, including
Fishy.

Somebody sent Gosling a bottle of
cherries-in-brandy the other day. He
didn't care much for the cherries, but
he was grateful for the spirit in which
they were sent.

A Chinese visitor to Wun Lung some
time ago called on Quelch, and bent
over in a polite bow. Fortunately,
Mr. Quelch recollected himself just as
his hand closed on the cane.

Fisher T. Fish, walking in the quad,
found a shilling, another shilling, and
yet another shilling. His beaming smile
lasted till he discovered the hole in his
trousers pocket.

"They've been after him for years—goodness knows why, but there it is! He's packed away at some school under another name!" whispered Bunter. "Old Peter's got me to come here and take his name, to draw them."

"Oh, my hat!"

"The idea is that the kidnappers will get after me, and he's got a detective in the house to nab them, if they do. See?"

"Great pip!"

"When they're snaffled, the young lord will be safe. That's the game! Old Peter's picked me out for it because I'm so jolly plucky——"

"Oh crikey!"

"They're taken in all right," went on Bunter. "You saw them after me, in the car. What I thought was a motor back-firing was a beast shooting at the tyres——"

"Ha, ha, ha! So that was why——"

"What I mean is, I knew that that beast was shooting at the tyres, and never turned a hair! You know my pluck!" said Bunter. "And so does old Peter! And one of the gang got after me again this evening, just before dinner, when I was phoning you. I had an awfully narrow escape. Old Peter thinks I fancied it—so does that silly detective of his—but I suppose I know whether a beast grabbed me round the neck or not. I'm not chancing it again, I can tell you!"

Wharton and the nabob looked at Bunter—and looked at one another.

They were utterly amazed; but they realised that this was—and must be—the truth, strange as it was.

James had called Bunter "my lord"—and that was explained now—Bunter's presence in the castle was explained—and the fact that "Lord Reynham" had sent the car to Wharton Lodge. But the explanation was really more staggering than the mystery.

"You—you—you fat spoofer!" gasped Harry at last. "You've made that old bean believe that you've got a spot of pluck somewhere, and—and——"

"Precious few fellows would have the nerve to do it, I think," said Bunter warmly. "You jolly well wouldn't, and chance it! Or Inky! I'm taking all the risk—just to oblige old Peter, and to save a chap I've never seen from danger. Plucky and generous, I call it. Facing fearful dangers——"

"Then what do you want us here for?"

"Oh, the—the fact is I—I want to give you a good time! Don't you fancy you're here to protect me! It's nothing of the kind! Being in clover like this, I'm taking you up——"

"Are you?" said Wharton grimly. "Well, you can keep your clover all to yourself, and we'll cut——"

"I—I—I mean, I—I want you here, old chap—— Don't be a beast! Look here, I've had beds put in my room for you—one on each side of my bed—and—and—and—— I say you can't let me down! Stick to a pal, old chap!"

Swank departed from Bunter on the spot at the prospect of being left alone. His fat face was deeply anxious.

"Look here, I dare not go to bed alone!" he breathed. "I—I say, you fellows, you can't leave a chap to be kidnapped! I say, stick to a pal, you know!"

Harry Wharton laughed.

"If you put it like that——" he said.

"I do, old fellow!" gasped Bunter. "Stick to me!"

"We'll stick to you for to-night, anyhow, and think it over in the morning," said Harry. "What do you say, Inky?"

THE MAGNET LIBRARY.—No. 1,557.

"The stickfulness is the proper caper!" agreed the nabob.

Really, the chums of the Remove had little choice, for, amazing as the state of affairs was, there was no doubt that Bunter was in danger at Reynham Castle. True he had, according to his own account, come there to face danger; still, the juniors did not want to leave him to it.

So for that night, at least, it was settled, and Harry Wharton and Hurree Jamset Ram Singh turned in, in the beds that had been specially placed in his lordship's room for them; and Billy Bunter, in the middle bed of three, was able, at long last, to settle down in safety and snore in comfort.

THE THIRTEENTH CHAPTER.
Booting a Nobleman !

BRIGHT wintry sunshine glimmered on the ancient walls and turrets and battlements of Reynham Castle.

It was a fine winter's morning when Harry Wharton and Hurree Singh walked out after breakfast.

They had not been up early that morning. But though they rose rather late, for once, they left Lord Bunter still in bed when they came down. James was called up to sit by his bedside till it pleased his lazy lordship to turn out. His lordship was not going to be left alone—neither was he going to turn out till the spirit moved him to do so.

At a rather late breakfast the two juniors had met Captain Reynham, whom they had found civil, but not particularly cordial. They had not seen Sir Peter Lanchester yet.

What they were going to do, in these strange circumstances, and exactly what they ought to do, the chums of the Remove did not quite know. The situation was so extraordinary that it was a little difficult to get their bearings.

"Jolly here, Inky!" Harry Wharton remarked, as they sauntered by a path in the frosty park. "No end of a show!"

"Terrific!" agreed the nabob.

"What are we going to do about it, old chap?"

"Goodness knows."

"That fat ass Bunter wants us here. I suppose he has a right to ask fellows here if the boss of the show has set him up as master of the place. But—that old bean doesn't want us."

"Hardly!" grinned the nabob.

"We can't stick on where we're not wanted. It's a queer bizney, and if that old ass has turned Bunter into a lord, to suit himself, he really ought to let the fat duffer have the game as well as the name. But——"

"The butfulness is terrific."

"That fat chump must have spoofed the old bean somehow to make him think he had the pluck for such a game. If he hasn't the nerve to carry on he will have to chuck it, that's all. We can't stick here on his account, looked on as intruders by the man who's really boss of the show. We'd better tell him so when he gets up—if he ever does."

Hurree Jamset Ram Singh nodded his dusky head. He was in full agreement with his chum.

Bunter evidently had taken on a thing beyond his powers. He was, in fact, hedging. The glorious prospect of playing the part of a lord in a magnificent castle had dazzled him and blinded him to the danger. Now that the danger had

accrued he wanted to dodge it. That, of course, was Bunter all over!

But it was not good enough for the Co. They had seen him through the dangers of the night—if any—and now it was time to clear. It was up to Bunter to stay and face the danger he had so lightly undertaken to face, or to clear off also. To remain where they were unwelcome was impossible—to fellows who did not resemble William George Bunter.

Having come to that decision, the two juniors walked back to the castle. In the vast gardens that lay between the park and the castle they spotted the tall figure of Sir Peter Lanchester. The old baronet was coming towards them, and they guessed that he was looking for them. No doubt he preferred what he had to say to be said outside the castle, safe from listening ears.

Wharton's lips set a little.

"Here's the old bean, Inky!" he said. "We may as well tell him what we've decided on and relieve his mind!"

"The soonerfulness is the betterfulness!" agreed the nabob.

They capped the old baronet politely as he came up.

Sir Peter gave them a nod and a very thoughtful and worried look.

"Good-morning, my boys!" he said.

"Good-morning, sir!" said Harry. "We're just going in to tell Bunter that we're leaving this morning, and he will have to decide for himself what he is going to do."

Sir Peter looked more worried than ever.

"Please do not act in haste," he said. "I presume that William has explained to you how matters stand here. No one was to be told; but as you are his school-fellows, and know him so well, it was unavoidable—since you are here, and——"

"You need not fear that we shall say anything about it," said Harry quietly. "It is no business of ours, and we know how to hold our tongues about matters that do not concern us."

The old baronet scanned the two youthful faces keenly. He seemed to be satisfied with his scrutiny.

"I am sure of it," he said. "You must, of course, have been very much surprised."

"Very!" said Wharton dryly.

"I must explain a little, my boy. My ward is a lad in feeble health, and has never quite recovered from the shock of attempts to kidnap him when he was a mere child—a boy of eleven. In some manner I do not understand, his enemies have discovered that he has been concealed at a school under an assumed name. If they should find him I dread the result for him. It is for that reason that I have laid this plan to entrap them."

Sir Peter paused.

"They fully believe that Bunter is Lord Reynham. If nothing is said they will continue to believe so. Their attacks will be directed against him—and sooner or later, I have not the slightest doubt, they will be caught in the act, and the law will be able to deal with them. Extraordinary as this plan may seem to you, it is the only means of protecting my ward—he will never be safe till his enemies are discovered and sent to prison."

"I understand, sir!" said Harry. "We shall not say a word of what we have been told when we leave here."

"Now that you know so much," said Sir Peter, smiling, "it is unnecessary for you to leave. I am sure you will excuse my inhospitality last night—it was due wholly to my desire to keep the secret. Now that you know the secret I should greatly prefer you to remain."

Harry Wharton smiled faintly. He could understand that Sir Peter preferred to keep them under his eye now that they knew.

"You can trust us, sir!" he said.

"I am sure of it. But please forget what I said to you last night—now that I have explained my reason. Please accept my invitation to remain at Reynham Castle for the Christmas holidays," said Sir Peter in a stately manner. "I had only one objection to your coming, which I have now explained. That objection has now disappeared. I shall be delighted if you will remain here as William's guests."

"Oh, certainly!" said Harry at once. "If you look at it like that, sir, we shall stay, of course."

"The stayfulness will be terrific!" concurred the nabob.

Sir Peter smiled.

"I am glad!" he said, and, with a stately bow, the old gentleman passed on, evidently relieved in his mind.

"Well, we're landed, Inky!" said Harry, as they walked on to the castle. "Looks as if we're going to be the guests for Christmas of Lord Bunter."

The nabob chuckled.

"But what will the esteemed old bean say when the other fellows blow in?" he asked. "Bunter has asked Bob and Franky and Johnny—as well as the esteemed Bolsover and the absurd Skinner."

Harry Wharton whistled.

"Goodness knows!" he said.

They found Bunter in the library when they went in. As it was getting near lunch-time, his lordship was down at last.

"I say, you fellows, where have you been all this time?" asked the fat Owl peevishly. "I don't expect you to go clearing off like this, and leaving a fellow alone. If that's how you're going to behave——"

"Fathead!"

"I don't want any of that, Wharton. You'd better remember that you're not in the Remove passage at Greyfriars now," said Bunter severely. "And you'd better call me my lord, too. I prefer it."

Harry Wharton looked at him thoughtfully.

"We've just told the old bean that we'll stay," he said. "We seem to be booked. But don't be cheeky, Bunter."

"Call me my lord, please," said Bunter. Evidently the terrors of the night being over, swank was supervening again. "If you can't be respectful, Wharton, I shall have to consider whether I can allow you to stay in my castle."

Harry Wharton laughed.

"That doesn't depend on you, old fat bean! We've been asked by the boss of the show, and, as he makes a point of it, we're staying on. You can go and eat coke!"

"What?" roared Bunter.

"Coke!"

"Now let's have this clear, Harry Wharton," said Bunter, with a glare of wrath and scorn. "I'm taking you up, and I'm going to give you a good time; but it's got to be understood, right at the start, that you've got to treat me in the right way. I insist on that!"

"Well, if you insist——"

"I do!" said Bunter firmly.

"All right. If you ask for it, why shouldn't you have it?"

The captain of the Remove grasped Lord Bunter by the collar, and twirled him round.

Bunter gave an apprehensive yell.

"Ow! Beast! Wharrer you up to?"

"Treating you in the right way."

"Look here, if you kick me, I'll—Yarooop!"

Thud!

Wharton's boot landed on his lordship's trousers. His lordship roared, and rolled over on a costly Persian rug.

"Yow-ow-yoop!" roared Bunter.

"Have another, my lord?" asked Harry.

"Yule" Be "Tide"

with these Greyfriars teasers

A MERRY Christmas and a HAPPY New Year To All. Which gives us Puzzle No. 1—a simple word ladder. Can you change HAPPY into MERRY in four moves, altering one letter at each move?

No. 2.   CHRISTMAS IN THE COUNTRY.—The blank spaces in the following little essay can be filled in with Greyfriars names to make sense. F'rinstance, it begins " The WALKER in the country——" Now try the others.

The —— in the country finds the grass still ——, but should he —— off the dead leaves which —— underfoot, the earth is —— like a tract of —— from the plough. He may see a bird with a —— perch on a —— of the leafless —— tree and start to —— If the farmer has forgotten to —— the gate of the —— where he keeps his savage ——, he may become a —— and have to —— —— over the hedge, but if the creature has other —— to ——, he will not chase him at any ——.

No. 3. " FOR READING HEALTHY YARNS."—Add the letters ILAU to this slogan, rearrange the whole lot and make the title of a book to which the words would apply.

No. 4.   Another little rearrangement puzzle. The following groups, rearranged, will make the names of things familiar at Christmas. The hyphenated pairs make one word each, the others two words.
SPICE MINE.   TRUE-SKY.
SPARE-IT.   AT PERHAPS.
STOLE-TIME.

No. 5.   Which Greyfriars fellow wears cherry-coloured shoes, rose-coloured handkerchiefs and gold-coloured collars?

No. 6.   BURIED FRIARS. The names of eight well-known Greyfriars characters are buried in the following four lines. Can you dig them up? (Example— " A CAP PERched on his head.")

He stood upon the stairs in ghastly glee.
" Go, sling your hook!" the rotter said to me.
" My erstwhile chum, I'm blessed if I shall go, For there's no opportunity, you know!"

(The solutions to these puzzles will be found on page 25.)

"Beast!"

"Lots more, if your lordship likes."

"Yah!"

Bunter rolled wrathfully away. His lordship, it seemed, did not want more.

THE FOURTEENTH CHAPTER.

Bunter Has To Walk!

"YOU fellows had better come."

"Oh, all right!"

Another morning had dawned on Reynham Castle. That morning Billy Bunter was up unusually early—it was only eleven o'clock when he rolled out on the steps of the great entrance.

But Bunter had his reasons for early rising that morning. Guests were coming to the castle that day. Bob Cherry and Frank Nugent were booked to arrive at Castlewood Station, and Bunter was going to fetch them in a car.

What old Sir Peter thought about it, and how Bunter fixed it with him, Wharton and the nabob did not know. It meant two more fellows in the secret, which could hardly have pleased the strategic old gentleman. But whatever Sir Peter thought, Lord Bunter had his way.

Matters were not going quite according to Sir Peter's plans. Sir Peter had an idea of lonely walks for his lordship, shadowed by Tomlinson under cover. That was the way to entrap the kidnappers.

Bunter's ideas were quite different. Lonely walks had no appeal for him whatever. No kidnappers for Bunter.

So far, he had not been out of sight of the turrets; and even in a walk in the frosty gardens, he required his two pals to walk with him, one on either side. This was not giving the Smiler and his gang much of a chance.

Indeed, Lord Bunter was liable to yap and snap, if his pals were out of his sight for a quarter of an hour. He couldn't, and didn't, forget that iron grasp that had fallen on him from behind on his first evening in the castle.

Nothing had happened since. Bunter had been in no danger, unless it was the danger of bursting at the well-spread board.

But he did not feel safe, all the same. He was going to feel much safer when he had more pals round him.

Bob Cherry and Frank Nugent were coming together; Johnny Bull, who was up in Yorkshire, was coming later. Having been informed that Wharton and Hurree Singh were at the castle, and, having ascertained that it was a fact, they had agreed to come.

Bunter's invitation had been backed up by notes from Sir Peter, and the juniors, of course, could not guess in what frame of mind the guardian of Lord Reynham had written those notes. Sir Peter, having landed himself with Lord Bunter, had, in fact, to toe Lord Bunter's line. Bunter was going to have his pals with him—and that was that!

His fat and fatuous lordship rolled out into the frosty morning, arrayed in fur-collared coat and top hat. Wharton and the nabob followed him out cheerfully. They had no objection to a run in the car, and they wanted to meet their chums at the railway station. Matters had to be explained to the newcomers, of course; and, with so urgent a secret to keep, it was better for the explaining to be done out of doors, and at a distance from all other ears.

To their surprise, the juniors found Captain Reynham sitting at the wheel of the Singer car that was waiting at the steps. There were several cars, and several chauffeurs at the castle, and though they had noticed that the captain had a car of his own, they had not expected him to bring it round to take them to the station.

Rupert Reynham gave them a pleasant smile and a nod. The young Army man was not always pleasant. The juniors had seen him several times in a gloomy, and far from cordial, mood. But he could be agreeable when he liked—and he liked now.

"Hop in, my lads!" said the captain cheerfully. "Ripping morning for a run—what?"

"Fine!" said Harry. "Are you taking us to Castlewood?"

"That's it—if my Cousin William will let me take him in my car," said Rupert, with a cheery smile at Bunter.

Bunter blinked at him.

"I told Jasmond to send round Denham in the Rolls," he said.

"Oh, quite!" agreed the captain. "If you prefer it, of course, I will return to the garage, and send Denham. But I should be delighted to drive you, William, if you will do me that honour."

"Oh, I don't mind!" said Bunter graciously.

He grinned as he packed his ample person in the car. The captain was making himself agreeable in the belief that he was dealing with his rich relative, Lord Reynham. It rather entertained Lord Reynham.

Wharton and the nabob followed the fat Owl in. The Singer shot away down the drive—more than half a mile to the great gates—and turned into the Castlewood road.

It was only three miles to the little Sussex town—a quick run in a car. The juniors expected to arrive in good time for the eleven-thirty, by which Bob Cherry and Nugent were coming.

But they were not destined to arrive so soon as they had expected.

Half the distance had been covered, when the car came to a jarring halt.

Captain Reynham stepped down, and opened the bonnet, with a knitted brow.

Billy Bunter gave him an irritated blink.

"I say, what's up?" he snapped. "What are we stopping for?"

"Engine trouble, I'm afraid," answered the captain.

Bunter snorted.

He felt that it was like any man's cheek to have engine trouble when he was carrying so important a passenger.

"Well, don't keep us hanging about," he said. "It's too jolly cold for hanging about in this weather."

"Oh, quite!" drawled the captain.

Harry Wharton and the nabob waited patiently—Bunter impatiently. But as minute followed minute, and the captain was still tinkering with the engine, they began to feel worried. Bob and Nugent expected to be met at the station, and it was close on half-past eleven now.

"I'm awfully sorry," said the captain at last apologetically. "I'm afraid this needs a more skilled hand than mine. Perhaps you boys had better walk on to Castlewood. It's hardly over a mile——"

"I'm not going to walk!" yapped Bunter.

"We can't keep Bob and Frank hanging about at the station, fathead!" said Harry. "The train's due now."

"I'm not going to walk," said Bunter positively. "Think I'm going

THE MAGNET LIBRARY.—No. 1,557.

to walk a mile and more?" He gave the captain an inimical blink. "Why the thump did you bring us on this rotten car?"

"Shut up, you ass!" breathed Wharton.

"Shan't!" retorted Bunter.

"I'm really sorry——" said the captain.

"Fat lot of good that is, after landing us here, miles from everywhere!" yapped Bunter. "Catch me letting you drive me again! Look here! As you've done it, you can jolly well walk back to the castle, and send another car, see?"

Harry Wharton glanced uneasily at the captain. He half-expected the young man to box Bunter's fat ears.

Captain Reynham's eyes gleamed at Bunter for a second. But he answered quietly:

"That is only fair. I will walk back at once. Perhaps you two boys will walk on to the station, while William remains in the car."

"Yes, that's a good idea," said Harry.

"I say, you fellows, you're not going to leave me here alone!" roared Bunter. "Suppose those kidnappers turned up?"

"Really, William, in broad daylight?" said the captain, shrugging his shoulders.

"You mind your own bizney!" said Bunter.

The captain looked at him; and then, without making any rejoinder, turned and strode away in the direction of Reynham Castle.

"You fat ass!" said Harry, when he was gone. "I wonder that chap didn't yank you out of the car and smack your cheeky head!"

"Yah! I'm not standing any cheek from him—a poor relation!" sneered Bunter. "Like his dashed cheek to bring us here and strand us! I shouldn't wonder if he's done it on purpose!"

"You fat ass! Why should he?"

"Well, he doesn't like me!" said Bunter. "He can be as jolly civil as he likes—but I jolly well know he doesn't like me."

"And you're such a likeable chap!" said Harry, laughing.

"The likeableness is terrific!" grinned Hurree Jamset Ram Singh.

"Yah! Anyhow, I'm not going to be left alone here!" snapped Bunter. "It's a beastly lonely road—that silly ass had to choose the very loneliest spot to break down in. You fellows will have to stay with me till the other car comes along."

"You can jolly well walk!"

"Shan't!"

"You fat chump, we can't keep Bob and Frank hanging about at the station!"

"Blow 'em! I'm not going to walk!" roared Bunter.

"Then you can jolly well sit there on your own, and be blowed to you!" exclaimed the exasperated captain of the Remove. "Come on, Inky!"

"I say, you fellows!" roared Bunter. "I tell you you're to stop with me—I'm not going to stay here alone! Beasts! Hold on, I tell you—wait a minute—I'm coming!"

And Bunter came!

Snorting with wrath, the fat junior rolled out of the Singer, and rolled after the other two fellows. He had to walk, or be left alone—and he was not going to be left alone. His only consolation was to walk at a snail's pace, and the more his companions were annoyed thereby, the more the fat Owl was consoled.

THE FIFTEENTH CHAPTER.

Bagging Bunter!

"I SAY, you fellows——"

"Buck up, Bunter!"

"Shan't!"

"You fat ass!" said Harry Wharton. "We've done about a quarter of a mile since we left the car—and it's past twelve——"

"I'm tired!" said Bunter, with dignity.

"Will you buck up?"

"No, I won't!"

Hurree Jamset Ram Singh grinned. Harry Wharton looked, as he felt, intensely exasperated.

It was still a mile on to Castlewood; and already his chums' train had been in half an hour. There was no sign of another car coming on behind. Rupert Reynham had a couple of miles to walk back to the castle; and it was quite probable that he was not hurrying himself on William's account.

Wharton, looking back in the hope of seeing the car from the castle, saw nothing but a bare, frosty road.

Wharton tramped on again, suppressing his angry irritation. Bunter was no walker—and he had several breakfasts to carry, as well as a heavy, fur-lined overcoat. Bunter modelled his pace on that of an old and fatigued snail, and the other two crawled in company.

A little farther on, the road dipped between high banks thickly clothed with dark fir-trees. As the three juniors trailed down into the dip, there was a rustle in the thickets on the bank at the roadside, and a figure leaped out suddenly into view.

Another second, another figure leaped out behind them, and it was followed by a third.

The startled juniors halted.

Billy Bunter gave the man in front one surprised blink, and uttered a yell of terror.

"Ow! Help! Save me! Help! Oh crikey! It's the Smiler! Help!"

"What?" gasped Wharton.

"My esteemed hat!" exclaimed Hurree Jamset Ram Singh.

Wharton and the nabob stared at the man who had so suddenly appeared before them.

They, like Bunter, knew the hard, cold face, and the gleaming slits of eyes. It was the Smiler—the rascal who had attempted to kidnap Bunter before breaking-up at Greyfriars.

The Smiler gave one swift glance up and down the road. Not a soul was in sight in either direction.

Evidently the rascals had picked the loneliest spot for their ambush. Though how they could have known that Bunter would be on the road that morning was a mystery, if the juniors had had time to think of it! Clearly they knew, for they were there—on the watch for him! But, lonely as the road was, the Smiler had no time to waste—and he wasted none.

"Quick!" he rapped. "Ferret—Ratty—quick!"

He leaped at Bunter, and grasped the fur collar of the overcoat.

" Quick ! " snarled the voice of the Smiler, as he dragged Bunter away from the lodge.   " Quick—and be silent, if you value your skin ! "   The ambushed juniors stared as the kidnapper dragged the quaking Owl along the snowy path.

The fat junior struggled and yelled.

Wharton and the nabob had no chance to go to his help. The other two rushed at them at the same moment. The burly Ferret grasped Harry Wharton, and bore him back, with a crash, to the earth. "Ratty," seized the nabob, and they struggled furiously.

"I say, you fellows, help !" Bunter yelled and roared. "I say—— Oh crikey ! Gerroff, you beast ! I ain't Lord Reynham ! Help !"

The Smiler tightened his grasp on the fat Owl's shoulder. Leaving his two confederates still struggling with Wharton and the nabob, who resisted desperately, he dragged Bunter up the steep bank beside the road.

In a few moments the fat junior would have been dragged out of sight among the dark, shadowy fir-trees.

Wharton and Hurree Singh were giving their assailants plenty of trouble. Bunter was not the fellow to give much trouble in a scrap, especially in such desperate hands as those of the Smiler.

But terror sharpened Bunter's fat wits. As the Smiler dragged him up the steep bank by the collar of the coat, the fat junior suddenly squirmed out of the coat.

The Smiler, dragging with all his strength, suddenly found himself dragging at an empty overcoat, and pitched over by his own momentum. He gave a yell of rage as he tumbled headlong in among the firs, with the fur-lined overcoat empty in his grasp.

Bunter, yelling, rolled down the bank. He bumped in the road—and bounced up again like a ball. Hitherto, since leaving the car, Bunter had crawled like a snail. Now he went up the road like a streak of lightning.

Any Greyfriars fellow who had seen Billy Bunter at that moment, would have considered that he had a healthy chance for the school 100 yards.

He flew. He fairly whizzed !

The loss of that tremendous fur-lined overcoat was a relief to his movements. His top-hat flew off in the wind—and clattered, unregarded, behind him. Bunter was not likely to stop for his hat. He would not have stopped at that awful moment for the treasures of Golconda !

He ran and ran !

Down the bank came the Smiler, with a leap, his hard face convulsed with rage. Wharton and the nabob, still struggling, were pinned down by the Ferret and Ratty—resisting as hard as they could. The Smiler did not waste a glance on them. He shot like an arrow in pursuit of Bunter.

He could have little doubt of running the fat junior down. But Bunter's escape from his hands, and sudden flight, spelled danger for the kidnapper. Lonely as the road was, cars or pedestrians might come along at any moment. Such a game needed swiftness—the Smiler had calculated on dragging Bunter into the wood, out of sight, in a few seconds, whilst his associates dealt with the other two. Certainly he had not calculated on Bunter slipping out of his overcoat and taking to his heels. It quite disconcerted the Smiler's plans.

He raced after Bunter.

Bunter charged madly on.

He heard rapid, scuttling footsteps behind him. The sound spurred him on to frantic efforts. Cold as the December day was, the perspiration streamed down Bunter's fat face. He gasped, he gurgled, he puffed, and he blew. But he pounded desperately on.

Patter, patter, patter, came the run-ning feet behind. An outstretched grasping hand touched Bunter's fat shoulder.

As if the contact electrified him, the fat junior shot on out of reach, scudding on in a frantic spurt.

The Smiler, gritting his teeth, raced after him.

Again the outstretched clutching hand touched Bunter. This time it hooked on. And the frantic Owl, as he was grasped and dragged to a halt, let out yell after yell of frantic terror.

"Ow ! Help ! Wow ! Help ! Help ! Help ! Yaroooh !"

THE SIXTEENTH CHAPTER.

Bob Cherry to the Rescue !

"HALLO, hallo, hallo !" gasped Bob Cherry.

"That's Bunter——" exclaimed Frank Nugent, in wonder.

"But what——"

"Look !" gasped Frank.

The two juniors were tramping along the frosty road, swinging their suitcases.

More than half an hour ago, the train had landed them at Castlewood Station, where they had expected to be met by a car from the castle, with their friends in it. But there was no car—and no sign of their friends; and after waiting about for ten minutes or so, they decided to walk. If the car was coming, there was no doubt that they would meet it on the road—anyhow, they expected to see something of their friends before they arrived at the castle.

But what they certainly did not expect was what they saw—Billy Bunter, coatless and hatless, charging up the road from the distance, like a runaway bull.

They stared at him blankly.

Why Bunter was charging along at that rate, without his hat, was a mystery—for a moment. But the next moment the mystery was explained as they saw the Smiler charging after him.

Even as they stared, the pursuer clutched the panting fat Owl from behind, and—dragged him backwards and over

Bob gave a gasp.

"Come on, Franky !"

He tore down the road at top speed. Frank Nugent tore after him. They were a good hundred yards off when they sighted the chase. They covered those hundred yards in record time.

Bunter, squealing frantically, crumpled up in the Smiler's iron grasp—a grasp as resistlessly powerful as that which had been laid on him in the King's Room a couple of days ago. Helpless in the kidnapper's hands, and with no second chance of slipping out of them, Bunter was dragged bodily to the roadside, and up the bank to the shadowy wood

In his haste and breathless hurry to get his prisoner out of sight, the Smiler probably had not observed the two running figures approaching.

Swift as they were, Bob and Nugent were not quick enough to collar the Smiler before he got Bunter off the road.

But, as the kidnapper dragged the hapless fat Owl up the bank, Bob Cherry reached the spot, panting. He swung up his suitcase, and hurled it.

It was rather a heavy object to use as a missile. But Bob's right arm was strong and sinewy. With a powerful swing, he sent the suitcase hurtling at the kidnapper, and it struck the Smiler in the middle of the back, just as he reached the trees with his prisoner.

Crash !

There was a gasping yell from the Smiler. That crash in his back knocked him spinning He let go Bunter, and crashed to the earth.

Bunter, released, rolled down the bank again. Bob's suitcase rolled after him.

He landed in the road, yelling. The suitcase clattered down, bumping.

The Smiler dragged himself to his feet, twisting painfully. His back had a severe pain in it.

He leaned on a tree, gasping, and glared down into the road. Bob Cherry and Frank Nugent faced him with clenched fists, ready for him if he came back. Bunter sat and yelled.

But the Smiler did not come back. He could hardly have handled the two juniors together. His game was up.

After a savage glare at them, he dis-appeared into the wood—twisting painfully as he went. It was likely to be some time before the Smiler forgot that bang on his backbone.

"Ow ! Wow ! Yow ! Help !" Bunter was roaring.

"All serene, old fat man !" said Bob, with a cheery grin. "You're all right now, old porpoise !"

"Right as rain, old fat bean !" said Frank Nugent.

Billy Bunter blinked at them dizzily.

"Oh !" he gasped. "Ow ! I say, you fellows—oh crikey ! I—I—I say, that beast—the Smiler—has he gone ? Oh dear !"

"He's gone !" said Bob. "Stick with us, old grampus, and we'll see you through ! Where's Wharton and Inky ? Didn't they come out with you ?"

"Eh ? Oh, yes ! The other beasts collared them—"

"What ?" howled Bob. "Where are they, then ?"

"Back along the road somewhere ! I say, you fellows, don't you leave me here !" yelled Bunter, as Bob and Nugent started at a run down the road. "I say, stop for me—I say—— Beasts !"

Bob and Nugent fairly flew. They were not likely to linger when they heard that "other beasts" had collared their chums back along the road.

Bunter had covered a good distance before the Smiler clutched him. There was a bend in the road, shutting off from sight what was farther on. Bob Cherry and Frank Nugent ran as if they were on the cinder-path—and Billy Bunter, in panic terror that the Smiler might show up again, rushed after them, panting

"Hallo, hallo, hallo !" panted Bob, as he tore round the bend of the road. "Here they are !"

Harry Wharton and Hurree Jamset Ram Singh were still resisting manfully. But both of them were pinned down—the Ferret had a knee on Wharton's chest, and Ratty a knee on the nabob's.

The two rascals were holding them secure, until the Smiler had got away with "Lord Reynham" — and the juniors, quite understanding what was intended, made desperate efforts to free themselves.

But their efforts were in vain. They could not help Bunter—they could not help themselves.

They were still struggling, in vain, when Bob Cherry and Nugent came speeding up—and at the sight of them, the Ferret and Ratty promptly released their prisoners, darted up the bank, and vanished into the fir wood.

Wharton and the nabob scrambled to their feet, panting for breath. They did not realise for a moment why they had been so suddenly released. Then, as they saw Bob and Nugent panting up, they understood.

"Bob !" gasped Wharton. "Franky, old man ! Oh, thank goodness ! Bun—Bunter——"

"Here he comes," grinned Bob.

"Oh, good !"

Billy Bunter came spluttering up.

"I—I—I—I say, you fellows," gurgled Bunter. "I say, let's get back to the castle—quick ! I say—oh crikey ! Oh lor' ! I say, they nearly had me this time—oh crumbs ! Come on !"

"All right now, fathead !" said Harry. "They won't tackle the lot of us together !"

"Come on, I tell you !" roared Bunter. "Where's my hat ? Gimme my coat ! Look here, you beasts, you come on, see ? I'm not going to hang about here to be kidnapped ! I say, you fellows, come on !"

Billy Bunter started. It was doubt-tackled the whole bunch of them—but ful whether the kidnappers would have Bunter was not taking chances. His little fat legs fairly twinkled down the road to Reynham Castle—and the grinning Co. had to step out—to keep pace with Bunter.

"But what," asked Bob Cherry, "does it all mean ? Those jolly old kidnappers are after Bunter—this is the third time ! You fellows got the faintest idea why ?"

"Oh, yes—we know now !" said Harry, laughing.

"The knowfulness is terrific !" grinned Hurree Jamset Ram Singh.

"Give it a name, then !" said Bob.

"It's a dead secret," said Harry Wharton. "You fellows must be told, as you're coming to the castle—but mind, not a word, not a whisper."

"You're jolly mysterious !" grinned Bob. "Cough up the deadly old secret !"

Bob Cherry and Frank Nugent stared blankly when they were told. They blinked at the captain of the Remove.

"You're not pulling our leg ?" gasped Bob.

"Honest Injun !"

"Well, my hat !" said Nugent.

"Not a syllable at the castle, even among ourselves, in case walls have ears !" said Harry. "Even Lord Reynham's cousin doesn't know—nobody's been told. His lordship's own cousin takes Bunter for his lordship !"

"But why on earth did the old bean pick out Bunter ?"

"His pluck——" said Harry, with a chuckle.

"His whatter ?" yelled Bob.

"He must have pulled the old bean's leg somehow ! Anyhow, there it is ! Mind you keep it awfully dark !"

"I say, you fellows," squeaked Bunter, "here's the car !"

Reynham Castle was in sight before Denham was seen in the Rolls. The captain seemed to have taken his time about sending out that car.

Bunter packed himself in it with great relief.

"Get in quick, you fellows !" he said. "Let her out, Denham !"

"Yes, my lord."

"My lord !" murmured Bob Cherry. "My hat !"

Billy Bunter blinked uneasily from the windows of the car until it passed in at the great gateway of the castle. Then, as it glided on up the drive, the fat junior was easy in his fat mind at last.

He was quite himself once more when he rolled out of the car at the steps of the castle door. He gave Bob and Nugent a cheery blink through his big spectacles.

"Welcome to my castle, you fellows !" said Bunter graciously.

"Thanks no end, my lord !" gasped Bob.

"Ha, ha, ha !"

And the chums of the Remove followed Lord Bunter into Bunter's castle

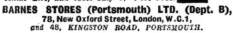

THE SEVENTEENTH CHAPTER.
The Hand of the Enemy !

"ANCESTOR of yours, my lord ?" asked Bob Cherry.

And the other fellows grinned.

Billy Bunter was showing his guests over his quarters. They were palatial quarters, and Lord Bunter naturally expected the guests to be impressed.

But Bunter, as a nobleman, seemed to appeal chiefly to Bob Cherry's sense of humour.

Bunter had, in vain, requested Wharton and Hurree Singh to address him as "my lord." But he did not need to make that request to the hilarious Bob. Bob addressed him continually as "my lord," and seemed to derive great amusement from so doing.

Looking round the spacious King's Room, Bob stopped in front of an ancient portrait let into the wall in a heavy metal frame. It was the portrait of an ancient monarch, and certainly bore no resemblance to Lord Bunter—except in one respect. The figure had a very extensive circumference. It was, in fact, a portrait of King Henry the Eighth, whose royal figure had been built somewhat on Bunter's lines.

"Oh, really, Cherry !" grunted Bunter. "If you're going to be a funny ass——"

"Leaving that to you, my lord. You do it better than I do !"

"Ha, ha, ha !"

"That's a portrait of King Henry the—the Ninth, I think," snapped Bunter. "The room's named after him. He stayed in this castle the day before the battle of—of Waterloo——"

"Oh, my hat !"

"Or—or Trafalgar; I forget which," said Bunter hastily.

"Not the battle of the Somme ?" asked Bob.

"Ha, ha, ha !"

"Well, anyhow, the old blighter stayed in this castle, and that's why this is called the King's Room," said Bunter. "I think he was the king who let the cakes burn in the neatherd's hut——"

"Oh crumbs ! Wasn't that Alf ?"

"No, Henry the Ninth, I think," said Bunter. "You don't know much about history, old chap !"

"It's Henry the Eighth, fathead," said Nugent, "the sportsman who cut off his wives' heads."

"Oh, yes, I remember," said Bunter. "I know a good bit of history. He cut off his wife's head, and she never smiled again——"

"Oh crikey !"

"James !" yapped Bunter.

"Yes, my lord ?"

"Have the beds been placed in my room, as I instructed you, George ?"

"Yes, my lord."

"Very good, Frederick ! Come and look at the bed-room, you fellows."

The juniors followed Bunter through the communicating doorway into the adjoining bed-room. Two more bedsteads were there now.

Bob and Nugent looked at them in some surprise.

There was a huge canopied bed—the historic bed in which that ferocious old gentleman, Henry Tudor, had slept some hundreds of years ago. It stood in state at some distance from the walls. Hitherto there had been a bed on either side of it. Now there was a bed at the head and a bed at the foot, also. The state bed, which was Bunter's, was quite surrounded.

"What's that game ?" asked Nugent. "Are we all camping in this room, or what ?"

"That's it !" grinned Bunter. "Lots of space ! This room is jolly nearly as big as the dorm at Greyfriars. If that blighter comes in the night he will find you fellows all round me, see ?"

"I see !" gasped Bob. "Jolly glad to be useful to you, my lord !"

"When Bull comes I'll have another bed shoved in for him, too," said Bunter. "They won't get at me if I can help it, I can tell you."

"I don't see how they could get at you at all here," said Nugent.

"Well, one of them did, the day I got here," answered Bunter. "I'm not taking chances of that happening again. Now, you fellows had a pretty good lunch, I hope."

"Fine !" grinned Bob. "Your lordship's prog is A 1."

"I dare say you'd like a rest after it. You can sit up here while I have a nap, see ?"

"Oh !"

Billy Bunter rolled back into the King's Room, and disposed his fat limbs in a deep armchair before the fire.

The four juniors looked at one another, smiling.

They were quite prepared to camp in Bunter's room and guard him from dangers, real or imaginary, but they were not prepared to sit around in the afternoon, listening to his lordship snoring.

The early December dusk was falling, but it was still light enough for a ramble round the castle, and the frosty air appealed more to them than frowsting indoors over a fire.

"Good-bye, my lord !" said Bob.

Bunter blinked round.

"I say, you fellows, stop here, will you ? I shan't want more than an hour. You'd better not talk. I don't like jaw when I'm going to sleep. Just sit round."

"Ha, ha, ha !" roared Bob.

"What are you cackling at ?" hooted Bunter.

"Your little joke, my lord ! Come on, you men," said Bob. "Lots of time for a trot round before dark."

"Beasts !" roared Bunter, as the juniors headed for the door.

"Oh, my hat ! Are the nobility all as polite as that ?" asked Bob.

"Look here, wait till I ring for James, then !" hooted Bunter. "I'm not going to be left alone, see ? I'm in danger here when I'm left alone."

"Oh, all right; buck up, my lord !"

Bunter rang, and James appeared. There was a patient, long-suffering expression on James' smooth face. A few days of his lordship seemed to have made James tired.

"Stay here, Frederick, while my friends are gone out !" said Bunter.

"Yes, my lord."

"You may sit down," added Bunter considerately. "Sit down, Herbert."

"Thank you, my lord !"

James sat down in a far corner of the vast apartment.

"You fellows can cut now !" said Bunter.

Harry Wharton & Co. cut, and his lordship was left to repose. They did not need a rest after lunch. His fat lordship did, having exerted himself at that meal much more than the other fellows. A minute after they were gone his lordship's snore awoke the echoes of the King's Room.

And in five minutes more James rose softly to his feet, stepped softly across to the sleeping beauty, and peered at him in the thickening dusk, and then softly trod out of the apartment.

The December dusk thickened in the great apartment, only the red gleam of the fire cast an uncertain wavering light. Light and shade danced on Billy Bunter's slumbering face, and the gleam was reflected from his big spectacles. His snore rumbled.

If there was another sound in the dusky apartment, Billy Bunter did not hear it.

A slight sound was not likely to waken Billy Bunter.

The sleeping fat Owl did not know that another shadow stirred, among the shifting shadows of the dusky room. He did not hear a stealthy footfall.

He did not awaken—till a sudden grasp was laid on him: and then it was too late !

As his eyes opened behind his spectacles, and his mouth for a startled yell, a thick cloth was pressed over his face, stifling his cries. With a muffled squeak of terror, the hapless fat Owl felt himself dragged bodily from the armchair.

───

THE EIGHTEENTH CHAPTER.
Struck Down !

BOB CHERRY grinned.

"James Frederick George Herbert seems to have got fed up !" he murmured.

Harry Wharton & Co. were in the old oak gallery, over the great hall of Reynham. They were looking from a tall window, over the gardens and the far-stretching park. Snow was falling—the first snow of Christmas. Thick dark clouds were banking over the park, blotting out the red glimmer of the setting sun.

Looking out into the falling snow, the juniors were debating whether to go out for a ramble, regardless of the weather, when Bob's eye fell on the neat, dapper figure of James, emerging quietly from the broad corridor on which the King's Room opened.

James passed on his way and disappeared, and the chums of the Remove grinned.

No doubt Lord Bunter had a right to command his "man" to remain while he slumbered. On the other hand, it was not surprising that James was very soon fed up with listening to his lordship's snore. No doubt he had learned, by this time, that his lordship, once asleep, was not likely to awaken in a hurry and miss him.

"Well, let's get out, you fellows !" said Bob. "Who cares for a little snow ?"

"Let's !" agreed Nugent.

Hurree Jamset Ram Sing gave a shiver.

Bob was glad to see the snow: but the delight of a northern winter had a different effect on the junior from India's coral strand.

"The freezefulness is terrific!" remarked the nabob.

"I'll warm you up with a few snowballs, old chap!"

Hurree Singh grinned.

"You fellows go outfully, and I will remain under the shelter of his lordship's ridiculous roof!" he said. "I will turn on the idiotic radio while you are gone."

"Right-ho," said Bob. "Come on, you chaps!"

Three of the Co. went down the staircase; and Hurree Jamset Ram Singh, for whom a snowfall had no attraction whatever, walked up the corridor again to the King's Room.

The radiogram was not likely to awaken his lordship—if that mattered. Nothing short of a thunderclap—and a very hefty one—was likely to awaken Lord Bunter, when he was once safe in the embrace of Morpheus.

Hurree Singh turned the door-handle, and opened the big oak door of the King's Room.

The interior was deeply dusky, with only a dancing beam from the log fire, crackling on the wide, ancient hearth.

The nabob expected to hear Bunter's snore, as he opened the door: but there was no sound of snoring in the room.

But, as he looked in, the Indian junior heard a faint muffled gurgle.

He was feeling for the lighting-switch, which was near the doorway, when he suddenly stopped, and stared, as if petrified.

Against the red glow of the fire, was a moving mass of shadow. Dumbfounded, Hurree Singh stared. Dim as it was, he could see what was happening.

Billy Bunter with a cloth twisted round his head, gurgling faintly and wriggling like an eel, was being dragged out of his armchair, in the grasp of a dark shadowy figure.

Even as the nabob stared, blankly, at the startling and unexpected vision, Bunter was dragged across the room, towards the wall where the King's portrait glimmered in its heavy frame.

But only for a second did the nabob stand amazed. Then he woke to sudden and vigorous action.

He shot across the room, like an arrow, and a dusky fist shot out, with all the force of a strong arm.

All he could see of Bunter's assailant was a dim, dark outline: but it was enough to guide his blow.

There was a sharp, savage howl, as his knuckles crashed on the side of a head.

Bunter, suddenly released, rolled on the floor.

Instantly, he tore the wrapping cloth from his face, and yelled. He yelled frantically, on his top note.

"Help! Yarook! Help! I say, you fellows! Help!"

The dark figure turned on Hurree Jamset Ram Singh with tiger-like swiftness. The dusky junior was grasped, in a grip of iron.

That grip was twice or thrice too strong for him: but the nabob gave grasp for grasp, and struggled manfully.

"Help!" he panted. "Help!"

"Help!" roared Bunter.

He scrambled to his feet. Too terrified even to realise that one of his friends was there, struggling with his unseen enemy, the fat junior bolted for the door.

He barged into the corridor, and flew.

In a split second, Billy Bunter was doing the oak gallery at about 50 m.p.h., and scuttling down the staircase, in a series of wild, kangaroo-like jumps. At every jump, he let out a yell.

"Hallo, hallo, hallo!" roared Bob Cherry.

The four juniors were in the hall below. They had been about to go out, when Bunter happened.

They stared up blankly at the fat figure bounding down the stairs. Jasmond, who was in the hall, stared up, with raised eyebrows. Sir Peter Lanchester came hurrying from the library—and Captain Reynham emerged from the smoke-room, with a cigarette between finger and thumb.

"What——" exclaimed Sir Peter.

"What the dooce——" drawled the captain.

"Bunter——" gasped Harry Wharton.

"You fat ass, what's up?" yelled Nugent.

"Help! Yaroo! Help! He got me!" yelled Bunter, as he staggered from the stairs into the hall. "I say, you fellows—yaroooh! He got me! Ow!"

"You absurd boy!" exclaimed Sir Peter. "Does this mean that you have had another fanciful attack of nerves——"

"You old ass!" yelled Bunter.

"Wha-a-t?"

"I tell you he got me! Oh crikey! He had a bag or something over my head, and was dragging me away!" gasped Bunter.

"Nonsense!"

"I tell you he did!" shrieked Bunter. "That beast James must have left me alone—I'll sack him—oh crikey!"

"Calm yourself, my boy!"

"Yarooh!"

"Inky went to Bunter's room," gasped Bob. "He can't have been larking with the fat chump, surely!"

"I say, you fellows, was it Inky? Somebody came in. I think, I—I think he's fighting with that beast now——"

"What?" yelled Wharton.

The captain of the Remove bounded up the staircase.

After him flew his chums.

The bare possibility that the nabob was in an enemy's grip was enough for them. After them, more slowly, went the old baronet. Bunter remained spluttering in the hall. Captain Reynham with a shrug of the shoulders, went back into the smoke-room.

Harry Wharton & Co. fairly flew along the oak gallery, and up the corridor to the King's Room.

"Inky!" shouted Harry, as he reached the door. It stood wide open—and the room was dark—only the firelight glimmering within.

"Inky!" yelled Bob.

But there was no answer from the Nabob of Bhanipur.

Wharton groped for the switch, and flashed on the light.

The next moment there was a cry of horror from the Greyfriars juniors as they crowded in.

On the Persian rug, at full length, lay Hurree Jamset Ram Singh—unconscious. In the light, his face was set and still, as a face of bronze.

"Inky, old man!" panted Nugent.

Harry Wharton ran to the nabob, and lifted his head.

There was a dark bruise under the dark hair, where a savage blow had been struck. That blow had stunned the Nabob of Bhanipur. His head rested on Wharton's knee—his eyes closed.

"Knocked out—poor old Inky!" gasped

ped Bob Cherry. Then—then—then there was somebody here——"

"Look for him!" panted Harry. "I'll look after Inky—you look for that villain!"

The three juniors began a hurried search.

But the mysterious assailant had had ample time to get clear. That some enemy had reached Bunter was certain now—Hurree Singh's unexpected return to the King's Room had saved him. Bunter had escaped—and the nabob, struggling with the kidnapper, had been struck senseless, while the rascal fled. There was no sign of him to be discovered.

"What——" exclaimed Sir Peter, as he strode into the King's Room. "What—why—what has happened here?" He stared down in horror at the nabob's still face.

"Nobody here!" said Bob, coming back from the bed-room. "The brute's got away. But how the thump did he get in at all?"

"Inky's coming to!" breathed Wharton, as the nabob's eyes opened, with a wild stare. "Inky, old fellow——"

Hurree Jamset Ram Singh blinked in the light. His hand groped at the bruise on his head. He tried to speak.

"Ow! My esteemed napper!" were his first words. "Ow!"

"What has happened here, my boy?" exclaimed Sir Peter Lanchester. "It is clear that you have been attacked—but how—who——"

"The ludicrous rascal had hold of Bunter!" gasped the nabob. "He gave me a terrific rap on the head while I was struggling with him——"

"But who?" gasped Sir Peter. "Did you see him?"

"Not clearfully, esteemed sahib, but I think it was that ridiculous rascal called the Smiler——"

"Good gad! But how——" stuttered Sir Peter helplessly. "One of the kidnappers—here—in the castle! Good gad!"

Leaving the nabob to his friends, he hurried from the room, in quest of Tomlinson. This was a matter for the detective to deal with.

"You think it was the Smiler, Inky?" asked Harry Wharton.

"The thinkfulness is terrific!"

"That means," said Harry quietly, "that they have a confederate inside the castle. He could not have got here without that—he could not even have known which room Bunter was in. This means that somebody inside Reynham Castle has a hand in the kidnapping."

There was no doubt about that in the minds of the Greyfriars fellows. But who, in a numerous household of forty or fifty persons, was the confederate of the Smiler and his gang, they had no means of guessing—and it was probable that Mr. Tomlinson was equally at a loss.

THE NINETEENTH CHAPTER.

Bunter the Bait!

SIR PETER LANCHESTER rubbed his hands.

His ruddy face wore a beaming smile.

It was a cold and frosty morning. Wintry sunshine gleamed on a white carpet of snow all round Reynham Castle. Standing at the great doorway which was wide open, the old baronet beamed at the wintry weather.

Captain Reynham, who was smoking an after-breakfast cigarette in the hall,

Printed in England and published every Saturday by the Proprietors, The Amalgamated Press, Ltd., The Fleetway House, Farringdon Street, London, E.C.4. Advertisement offices: The Fleetway House, Farringdon Street, London, E.C.4. Registered for transmission by Canadian Magazine Post. Subscription rates: Inland and Abroad, 11s. per annum; 5s. 6d. for six months. Sole Agents for Australia and New Zealand: Messrs. Gordon & Gotch, Ltd., and for South Africa: Central News Agency, Ltd.—Saturday, December 18th, 1937.

glanced at him once or twice curiously, but did not speak.

Harry Wharton & Co. came out of the breakfast-room, with cheery faces. Billy Bunter rolled after them, equally cheery. Meals always had a cheering effect on Bunter.

Sir Peter glanced round from the doorway, smiling.

"Ready for a walk, my boys!" he exclaimed.

"Yes, rather, sir!" answered Bob Cherry. "Ripping morning!"

"I should like to show you the old hunting-lodge in the park!" said Sir Peter. "It is about half a mile—a pleasant walk in the snow——"

"I say, you fellows, don't all of you go out!" exclaimed Billy Bunter. "I say, don't you leave me alone here."

"You are coming also, William!" said Sir Peter. "Get your coat and hat on! I insist! A walk will do you good!"

And as the Co. donned coats and hats, to walk out with Sir Peter, Lord Bunter unwillingly did the same.

He grunted as he rolled out with the cheery party. They followed a path through the frosty park, and the trees hid the castle from sight, except the tall turret dark against the steely sky.

"Christmas is close at hand now, my boys!" said Sir Peter. "I hope that we shall have a merry Christmas at the castle—a very happy Christmas." The old gentleman beamed on the juniors. "If all goes well, my ward will be able to join us at Christmas, and we shall be a very happy party."

"Oh!" gasped Bunter.

He blinked at the smiling old gentleman.

The other fellows grinned at the expression on his fat face. They did not need telling that Lord Bunter was far from keen to discard his borrowed plumes, when the time came for the real Lord Reynham to show up in his ancestral halls.

"If we are successful this morning," continued Sir Peter, "it will be unnecessary for Bunter to play the part of Lord Reynham any longer."

"Oh!" repeated Bunter.

The juniors realised that Sir Peter had some plan on hand—though they could not guess what it was. That walk in the frosty park had some special purpose.

"From what has happened," went on Sir Peter, "there is no doubt that my ward's enemies keep watch on the boy they believe to be Lord Reynham—I should not be surprised if we are watched at this very moment."

"I—I say, hadn't we better go back?" gasped Bunter.

"I am relying on your courage, William!"

"Oh! Ah! Yes! But——"

"And your nerve——"

"Oh! Yes! Certainly! But——"

"I have no doubt whatever," went on the beaming old gentleman, "that when William remains alone in the old lodge in the park——"

"Eh?"

"He will be seized by that rascal who bears the odd name of the Smiler——"

"Wha-a-t?"

"And all will be well!" said Sir Peter. "Once that scoundrel is in the grasp of the law, I shall not fear for my ward. That villain—that dastard—has been seeking to kidnap him for years—for what reason, I do not know—it is a mystery—but once his teeth are drawn, my ward will be safe. William will remain alone in the old hunting-lodge——"

"Look here——" roared Bunter in alarm.

"You need have no fear, my boy!"

said Sir Peter reassuringly. "Tomlinson is already concealed in the lodge, keeping watch. He will be on the spot. You will be in no real danger. You will simply be the bait to draw the dastard into the trap, as I planned when I brought you here under my ward's name."

"Oh crikey!"

"It's up to you, Bunter!" grinned Bob Cherry.

"Beast!" hissed Bunter.

Between Ourselves

WELL, chums, another Christmas is close upon us, and another round of festivities will shortly commence. Of all the good things you sample this festive season this splendid Christmas Number of the MAGNET will certainly be one of the best!

My staff and I wish every "Magnetite"

A MERRY CHRISTMAS!

May you have all you wish yourselves, and may the festive board groan under the weight of good things!

At Christmas-time I never fail to think of the vast army of MAGNET readers scattered all over the world, and wonder how they are spending their Christmas. I'm looking forward to enjoying myself this Christmas, and I sincerely hope that all of you will enjoy yourselves every bit as much. Have a good time, and remember that Christmas comes but once a year—so make the most of it! Be jolly—make others jolly—let the spirit of peace and good will be with you.

Meanwhile, you can look forward to another topping number of the MAGNET next FRIDAY, in which, together with our usual programme, you will find some more Christmas features. The special Greyfriars yarn is entitled:

"THE WRAITH OF REYNHAM CASTLE!"

and tells of Harry Wharton & Co.'s further exciting adventures during the Christmas vac. And you'll meet the ghost of Reynham Castle, too! Fun and thrills abound in plenty in this seasonable story, chums. Take my tip and order your copy to-day! By the way, if you've not yet got your copy of the "Holiday Annual," see your newsagent about it at the same time.

YOUR EDITOR.

Sir Peter Lanchester took Bunter's fat arm.

"Come!" he said. "We are close on the lodge now! You other boys please walk back."

"I say, you fellows, don't you leave me!" howled Bunter.

But there was no help for Bunter now; and he disappeared past the frosty trees with Sir Peter Lanchester.

The old hunting-lodge lay in a thick, secluded corner of the park. It was surrounded by thickets of evergreens, and

the leafless branches of trees almost met over it. It was partly in ruins, and only one room retained a roof, with a doorless aperture where a door once had been.

It looked dark and dismal and dreary to Billy Bunter as the hapless fat Owl arrived with Sir Peter.

"I—I—I say——" stammered Bunter.

"This is the place!" said Sir Peter, unheeding. He led Bunter in at the doorway.

There were two or three benches, but no other furnishings in the interior, which was dim and dusky. Snowflakes, blown in by the wintry wind, were scattered on the mossy stone floor.

Sir Peter glanced round.

"You are here, Tomlinson?" he asked in a low voice.

"Here!" came the rather acid tones of Mr. Tomlinson, and Billy Bunter blinked round through his big spectacles.

There was an aperture in the old stone wall—a deep, dark alcove. From that recess came Mr. Tomlinson's voice, but the detective was not to be seen.

"Very good!" said Sir Peter. "Now, you may sit down on one of these benches, William, as if you were staying here to rest after your walk. I have a newspaper here; you may read it while you wait. Do not stir from this spot for an hour. If the rogue is on the watch he will find you before that time."

"It's kik-kik-kik-cold——"

"Never mind that!" said Sir Peter cheerily.

Bunter breathed fury. He did mind it.

"Understand me," said Sir Peter, with a touch of sternness, "I rely upon you, William! You are here for a certain purpose! If you fail you are, of course, no use to me, and you may as well leave the castle at once."

"Beast!"

"What?"

"I—I—I mean, I'm ready!" gasped Bunter. "I—I—I've got pluck, I hope."

"I hope so," said Sir Peter. Possibly he was beginning to have doubts on that point. "I trust you! Mr. Tomlinson is watching over you! I will leave you!"

"Oh lor'!" groaned Bunter, as the old baronet walked out of the lodge and disappeared.

Bunter did not sit down. He did not read the newspaper. He moved about the old lodge restlessly like a fat rabbit in a cage.

Again and again he was tempted to cut. But that meant throwing up the part he was playing at Reynham Castle!

And, after all, the kidnapper might not appear. And Tomlinson was parked in the alcove only ten feet from him. Alternating between hope and terror, the unhappy substitute for Lord Reynham blinked incessantly at the doorway, and when, a quarter of an hour after Sir Peter had departed, there was a stealthy footstep on the snowy path outside, he gave a squeak of terror.

A stocky figure blocked the doorway; a cold, hard face, with a pair of glinting icy eyes, looked in at Bunter.

Bunter blinked at him, speechless.

Sir Peter, after all, had calculated well. They had been watched in the park. It was the Smiler!

THE TWENTIETH CHAPTER.

The Co. Take a Hand!

"**Q**UIET!" whispered Harry Wharton.

"Mum is the esteemed word!" breathed Hurree Singh.

Four juniors crept softly and cautiously through the thickets that surrounded the old hunting-lodge.

Sir Peter Lanchester, walking back to the castle after leaving Bunter as bait for the kidnapper, had seen nothing more of the Greyfriars fellows. No doubt he thought that they had gone for a ramble if he gave them any thought at all.

But Harry Wharton & Co., as a matter of fact, were not far away.

While admitting that old Sir Peter had a right to expect Bunter to play up in the part he had undertaken, they were not disposed to leave the hapless fat Owl to his fate.

If Bunter, as bait, drew the kidnapper into the snare, and the detective got the handcuffs on him, it was all right. But if it did not work out like that it was all wrong. And, in the latter case, the Co. decided unanimously that they had better be on the spot.

Harry Wharton had already seen the old hunting-lodge, during his days at the castle, and he knew his way about. He led the way, and his comrades followed him into the thickets in the rear of the old lodge.

Then, with great caution, they worked their way through the thickets to a spot where they had a view, between the frosty twigs, of the path that led to the doorway of the lonely lodge.

It was cold, it was damp, and it was unpleasant, standing ankle-deep in snow, with frosty twigs brushing their faces and flakes dropping on them from branches above.

But they stuck it out manfully.

As it happened, they had not very long to wait. There was a soft footstep on the path on the other side of a mass of snowy laurels.

Harry Wharton put his finger to his lips.

Suppressing their breathing, the four juniors watched and listened. They glimpsed a stocky figure in overcoat and cap passing, and it stepped into the doorway of the lodge.

"Was that——" whispered Nugent.

"Blessed if I know! Listen!" whispered Harry.

From the direction of the lodge they heard a voice in cool, mocking tones:

"Good-morning, Lord Reynham!"

"Oh lor'!" came a faint squeak.

"Is your lordship taking a little rest?" went on the mocking voice. "A somewhat dismal place for your lordship. Perhaps you will be kind enough to accompany me, and I will find you somewhat better quarters. I have a car not very far away—quite a short walk, your lordship?"

"I—I say—— Oh crikey!"

The ambushed juniors exchanged quick glances. They heard every word distinctly from the old lodge. It was the kidnapper—there was no further doubt about that.

"My lord——" went on the mocking voice of the Smiler.

He broke off suddenly. There was a sudden tramp of feet, a sound of a fierce struggle and a fall.

The juniors listened breathlessly.

Evidently the detective had weighed in. He was at grips with the kidnapper. A clink of metal reached the ears of the juniors in the thicket.

Bob Cherry gave a gasp.

"He's got him! That's the handcuffs!"

Harry Wharton nodded.

"That's it! No need for us to barge in, if he's got him—I don't suppose he'd be fearfully pleased to see us. He wouldn't be flattered at our thinking he might have made a hash of it."

Bob chuckled.

"Not likely! But—— Hallo, hallo, hallo! Look!"

An overcoated figure emerged from the doorway of the lodge. Its grip was on a fat arm, dragging Lord Bunter out.

"Quick!" snarled the voice of the Smiler, no longer mocking, but savage and threatening. "So you were watched, you fat fool—much good it has done you! Quick—and be silent, if you value your skin!"

"Oh crikey! Ow!"

For a second the four juniors stared blankly through the frosty thickets.

Evidently it was not the detective who had got the upper hand in that brief struggle.

But only for a second they stared, as the Smiler dragged the quaking fat Owl along the snowy path.

"At him!" yelled Bob.

He burst out into the path, followed by his chums. Three or four fists hit the astonished Smiler at the same moment, and he went staggering, letting go Bunter.

"Oh crikey!" gasped Bunter, his eyes almost popping through his spectacles. "I say, you fellows—— Oh crumbs!"

"Collar him!" roared Bob.

"Bag him!"

The Smiler staggered over; but as the juniors rushed down on him, he leaped to his feet. He sprang back and dodged the rush, and for a second he glared at the Greyfriars fellows, evidently more than half-inclined to spring at them. But the odds were too great, and he knew it—and he turned and bounded away.

"After him!" gasped Harry.

"I say, you fellows——"

Unheeding Bunter, the juniors dashed after the kidnapper. But the Smiler ran like a deer, and in a few moments he had vanished among the trees.

"I say, you fellows!" yelled Bunter.

The Smiler was gone.

Harry Wharton & Co. hurried back to the hunting-lodge.

Mr. Tomlinson met their eyes. His face was crimson—and a crimson stream was flowing down from his nose. His hands were joined together in front of him. The juniors wondered why for a moment. Then they saw that he had handcuffs on.

"Oh, my hat!" gasped Bob.

"Ha, ha, ha!"

The Greyfriars fellows roared. Really, they could not help it. Sir Peter had left his fat bait for the kidnapper, nothing doubting that Tomlinson would get the man if he showed up. Instead of which the detective met their eyes, handcuffed with his own handcuffs!

"When you have done sniggering," said Mr. Tomlinson, in a grinding voice, "perhaps you will kindly help me out of this!"

And Harry Wharton & Co., suppressing their sniggering, kindly helped him out of it. Without wasting time in expressing thanks, Mr. Tomlinson stalked out of the hunting-lodge, and stalked away. And the juniors did not chuckle again till he was gone.

    ·   ·   ·

"I say, you fellows!"

"Hallo, hallo hallo! Ready for lunch?"

"Blow lunch!"

"Wha-a-t?"

Bunter was frowning darkly.

He had frowned all the way back to the castle. He had frowned ever since.

"I'm fed-up!" said Bunter, as he went in to lunch. "I'm jolly well chucking it! That silly old ass—that blithering old chump—that fatheaded old josser—if he jolly well thinks I'm going to be left spotted about to be snaffled, he's jolly well mistaken! I'm going—after lunch!" added Bunter.

But as he sat down the frown disappeared from Bunter's fat brow.

He gave an appreciative sniff.

"I say, you fellows," he breathed, "it's turkey!"

And Bunter smiled again.

It was turkey for lunch.

Billy Bunter forgot narrow escapes, and kidnappers, and impending perils. Turkey filled his fat thoughts—and was soon filling his fat circumference. Bunter beamed.

    ·   ·   ·

Lord Bunter did not chuck it up! Really, it was too good a thing to be lightly chucked up. On second thoughts—proverbially the best—Bunter decided to carry on. Turkeys and Christmas puddings weighed more in the balance than kidnappers and perils—and it was going to be a Merry Christmas!

THE END.

(The next yarn in this grand Christmas series is entitled: "THE WRAITH OF REYNHAM CASTLE!" Watch out for it in next Friday's MAGNET!)

The Magnet

2ᴰ

Billy Bunter's Own Paper

When the Ghost Walks!

On a Christmas Eve some hundreds of years ago, the wicked Earl of Reynham was found murdered!
According to legend, the phantom of the wicked earl haunts the castle—and it is death to meet
him! Plucky as they are, the thought of the ghostly vision is unnerving to Harry Wharton & Co.,
of Greyfriars, who are spending the Christmas vacation at the castle.

The Wraith of Reynham Castle!

By FRANK RICHARDS

Johnny Bull stepped behind the ghostly figure in the doorway, a thick stick gripped in his hand!

THE FIRST CHAPTER.

His Lordship is Late!

"**H**ERBERT!"

"Yes, my lord!"

"My riding-kit, George!"

"Yes, my lord!"

"And buck up, Francis—my friends are waiting for me!" said Billy Bunter languidly.

"Very good, my lord!"

James, the valet, answered to the names of Herbert, and George, and Francis, without turning a hair.

Now that Billy Bunter, the fat ornament of the Greyfriars Remove, had a valet, he had become far too aristocratic to remember that valet's name.

Perhaps Bunter overdid it a little.

It was rather Billy Bunter's way to over-do things.

Fearfully aristocratic as Bunter thought it was to forget servants' names, there really was a limit.

Still, it was hardly a week since Billy Bunter had become "my lord" at Reynham Castle; so he was not quite used yet to being a nobleman.

Being a nobleman, in Bunter's happy opinion, meant swank. Of that quality, William George Bunter had lots and lots. All he ever needed was a chance to display it. Now he had the chance.

Owing to a strange series of circumstances, Billy Bunter was playing the part of Lord Reynham, in his lordship's castle in Sussex. And Bunter's idea was to play that part for all it was worth—and a little over.

It was ten o'clock on a cold and frosty morning.

This was rather early for Bunter to turn out in holiday time. But he had

arranged to go riding with his friends that morning.

Not that Bunter would have kept to the arrangement if left entirely to his own devices. Having breakfasted in bed, he had settled down to another snooze, regardless of the fact that Harry Wharton & Co. were ready, and that the grooms were holding the horses on the avenue. But his snooze had been interrupted by Bob Cherry.

Regardless of the fact that Billy Bunter was, for the nonce, a lord, and therefore to be treated with great respect by common mortals, Bob had barged in, yanked off the bedclothes, and rolled his fat lordship out of bed with a bump.

So Lord Bunter was up at that unusual hour.

It was now James' privilege to encase his lordship in his riding clothes. Lord Bunter was quite unable to do anything unaided.

Bob had announced that they would wait ten minutes. When twice that length of time had elapsed, Bunter was still in the process of being dressed by James.

There was a tramp of feet in the King's Room—the magnificent apartment honoured by Lord Bunter's occupation. Billy Bunter blinked at the communicating doorway. His guests, evidently, were coming to hurry him up.

"Shut that door, James!" he said hastily.

In his haste, he forgot to forget that James' name was James!

"Yes, my lord!"

James shut the door on the King's Room.

The next moment it burst open again with a crash. Bob Cherry tramped in. Harry Wharton, Frank Nugent, and Hurree Jamset Ram Singh looked in after him. Four members of the Famous Five of Greyfriars were at Reynham Castle. All the four looked impatient.

"Ready?" roared Bob Cherry.

"Don't yell!" said Bunter reprovingly.

"You fat ass——"

"I wish you fellows would remember that you're not in the Remove passage at Greyfriars now!" said Bunter severely. "Not so much row, Cherry!"

"You blithering bloater——"

"That will do!" said Bunter, with a wave of his fat hand. "Go down and wait for me. I may be down in a quarter of an hour!"

"We're to wait another quarter of an hour?" asked Harry Wharton.

"That's it!"

"I don't think!" remarked Bob Cherry.

"I know that, Cherry! You never do!"

"Why, you cheeky porpoise——"

"Buck up, you fat ass!" said Frank Nugent. "You can't keep the horses standing about in the cold!"

"I suppose I can do as I like with my own horses!" said Lord Bunter, blinking at him through his big spectacles. "Don't be cheeky, Nugent!"

"My esteemed idiotic Bunter——" began Hurree Jamset Ram Singh.

"You shut up, Inky!"

"Look here, fathead!" exclaimed Harry Wharton.

"I've asked you, Wharton, to remem-

THE MAGNET LIBRARY.—No. 1,558.

ber that you're not in the Remove passage now!" said Bunter calmly. "I expect rather better manners at my castle. My boots, Ronald! Shut that door first, though!"

"Is James' name Ronald now?" asked Bob Cherry.

"Ha, ha, ha!"

"I should prefer you not to be impertinent, Cherry!" said Lord Bunter. "Get out, and let Archibald shut the door!"

"Archibald?" gasped Bob.

"I mean Frederick! You are perfectly aware, Cherry, that I can't remember that my man's name is James!" said Bunter, with dignity.

"Oh, my hat!"

A faint grin flickered, for a moment, on James' usually expressionless face.

James, like all the numerous staff at Reynham Castle, from Jasmond, the butler, down to the youngest footman, believed that Bunter was Lord Reynham. His lordship's guardian, Sir Peter Lanchester, had contrived that, for his own special purposes. Even his lordship's cousin, Captain Reynham, believed the same. To all of them, Bunter was his lordship, home after a long absence. But what they all thought of his lordship was another matter.

It was possible that, in the servants' hall below stairs, there were many remarks that would have surprised and annoyed his lordship, could he have heard them.

"Now buzz off!" said Bunter. "I mean, leave me! I prefer not to be disturbed while my valet is dressing me."

"Oh, come on!" said Harry. "We'll get off, Bunter, and you can follow on; we're going through the park."

"I've told you to wait for me!" said Bunter.

The captain of the Greyfriars Remove gave him a look.

On the footing of an ordinary guest, no doubt he would have departed from Bunter's stately castle, and that would have been that. But the chums of the Remove were not on the footing of ordinary guests at the castle. They were there to protect Bunter from the kidnapping gang that were after Lord Reynham. Having promised to stay, they could hardly go and leave the fat Owl of the Remove to it.

"You fat, frabjous, foozling freak——" said Harry.

"Oh, really, Wharton——"

"You burbling bandersnatch!" hooted Bob Cherry. "Do you know that you're asking to be booted?"

"Silence!"

"Wh-a-at?"

"I said silence! You disturb me! Go away quietly, and wait downstairs till I'm ready! That's all!"

"Captain Reynham is waiting, too!" said Nugent.

"Let him wait!" said Lord Bunter. "I'm not likely to hurry myself for a poor relation."

"You silly, fat, cheeky, footling, frabjous fathead——" hissed Bob.

"Any more cheek, Cherry, and I shall order Frederick to turn you out of the room!" said Bunter haughtily. "You're not in the Rag at Greyfriars now, Cherry! I insist upon your behaving yourself."

Bob Cherry gasped. He did not answer in words. He made a sudden jump at Bunter, and grasped him by a fat neck.

There was a roar from his lordship as he twirled in Bob's hefty grasp.

"Yaroooh! Leggo! Beast!"

Thud!

THE MAGNET LIBRARY.—No. 1,558.

A riding-boot landed upon riding-breeches, and Lord Bunter went whirling. He collided with James, grabbed at him for support, and dragged him over as he went to the floor.

"Ow! Wow!" roared Bunter.

"Oh, my lord!" gasped James.

"Ha, ha, ha!" roared the Removites as Lord Bunter and his man were mixed up on the floor, with the riding-boots that James had been about to put on his lordship. It was quite a mix-up.

"Yoo-hoop!" roared Bunter. "Oh crikey! Wow!"

"Ha, ha, ha!"

Leaving his lordship and his lordship's man to sort themselves out, the chums of the Remove departed.

A few minutes later a clattering of horses' hoofs on the avenue told that they had started on the ride—which was, of course, fearful cheek on their part, and extremely annoying to that new, but important, member of the peerage, Lord Bunter.

THE SECOND CHAPTER.
A Hot Chase!

"OH, ripping!" exclaimed Bob Cherry.

Gallop, gallop!

"The ripfulness is terrific!" declared Hurree Jamset Ram Singh.

"Topping!" said Harry Wharton.

"Who wouldn't be a jolly old lord, with a jolly old castle, and jolly old tons of oof, and jolly old gee-gees in the jolly old stables!" said Bob. "Must be a jolly old life—what?"

"What-ho!" said Frank Nugent.

The keen winter wind whistled past the juniors as they rode, and stung their cheeks. The sky was like steel, banked here and there with clouds that told of more snow to come. Just before Christmas, the December day was cold and bitter, the whole landscape frosty. But it was a ripping morning for a ride, and the chums of the Remove were enjoying themselves.

There had been a fall of snow, but it had thawed away. Mists were rising, and looked like thickening later, but at the moment all was sharp and clear. It was Christmas Eve, and that day Johnny Bull was coming along to join his comrades for Christmas.

It was not wholly satisfactory in some ways to be Bunter's guests; but, having promised to see the fat Owl through the Christmas holidays, the Co. really had little choice about that. But there were compensations. This glorious ride on a frosty morning was one of them. Everything that wealth could buy was to be had for the asking at Lord Reynham's castle, and there was no doubt that wealth could buy quite a lot of very agreeable things.

The juniors had ridden through the park and out at a gate that gave on the open downs. They rode at a gallop on the frosty downs in a keen wind, with a glimpse of the sea in the distance.

The loss of Lord Bunter's society did not unduly depress them. Of that, in fact, they usually had enough and to spare. And had Bunter been with them, they would have had to content themselves with a very leisurely trot; and even at an easy trot, it was probable that his lordship would have fallen off a few times, and the other fellows would have had to dismount and pick him up—which would not have added to the enjoyment of the morning's ride.

"I suppose Bunter will be all right?" remarked Harry Wharton, with a backward glance at the mass of leafless trees in Reynham Park.

Having hung about half an hour for

Bunter, the captain of the Greyfriars Remove felt that he really had done all that could be expected. Looking after Bunter was one thing, but hanging about all the morning waiting for a lazy slacker who did not choose to get a move on was quite another.

"Captain Reynham is waiting for him," answered Bob. "He won't be alone. I suppose we couldn't leave him alone, in the giddy circs. But the captain will see him safe if anything turns up."

"Jolly good-natured of him to wait for Bunter!" said Nugent.

Bob Cherry chuckled.

"I don't think he's frightfully fond of his rich Cousin William," he said. "But, as Bunter put it with such exquisite taste, he's a poor relation, so I suppose he has to keep in with the jolly old lord."

"It's a queer business!" said Harry Wharton, with a thoughtful frown. "From what I can make out, the real Lord Reynham is a chap in weakly health, with his nervous system upset by those rotters trying to kidnap him when he was a little kid of eleven or so. His guardian's parked him at some school under an assumed name to keep him safe, and led those kidnapping blighters to believe that the school was Greyfriars and the name Bunter. And——"

"And they've fallen for it!" grinned Bob. "They're after Bunter like terriers after a rat; and if they knew he really was Bunter, they wouldn't take him at a gift!"

"But it's queer!" said Harry. "Of course, such a game had to be kept fearfully secret from everybody at the castle, or the Smiler and his gang would soon have got wise to it. But I should have expected old Sir Peter Lanchester to let the captain into it—his own nephew, and cousin of the real lord. But Captain Reynham is kept in the dark, like everybody else."

"I suppose the old bean thought he couldn't be too careful," said Frank. "He was fearfully worried, I imagine, when Bunter let us into it. He never wanted any Greyfriars fellows here with Bunter—though now we know he's glad to keep us under his eye."

"And there's more coming," said Harry. "Johnny Bull to-day, and Bolsover major and Skinner later. The old bean planned for Bunter to play at being a lord and draw the kidnappers, and give his detective, Tomlinson, a chance at them; but Bunter doesn't seem to be fearfully keen on running into danger."

"The fearfulness is not terrific!" chuckled Hurree Jamset Ram Singh.

"The fact is, that old bean, Sir Peter, is a bit of an old ass!" said Bob. "Goodness knows what that gang are going to do with Lord Reynham if they ever get hold of him! It can't be a ransom stunt; they wouldn't be after him for years on end if it was that. Whatever they mean, it would be pretty rough on Bunter if he tumbled into it."

"Well, he asked for it by coming here to play at being a lord!"

"The fat ass was thinking of swank and turkeys and Christmas puddings!" chuckled Bob. "As soon as the danger cropped up, he was in a fearful hurry to get some pals round him! Hallo, hallo, hallo! Is that a car?"

"A car—here!" exclaimed Harry.

The juniors were two or three miles from the castle by this time. The frosty, rugged downs spread round them on all sides, with no trace of a road.

It was open pastureland for mile on mile, and not even a path was to be seen. A motor-car in such a place would have been very surprising,

But Bob Cherry pointed with his riding-whip. At a distance, half-hidden by a group of frost-rimed willows, a small saloon car stood at a halt, with the driver sitting at the wheel, and a man lounging by, smoking a cigarette.

Harry Wharton pulled in his horse.

"That's rather queer!" he said quietly. "Looks like a bridle-path yonder, but it's no road for a car. I wonder——"

Bob chuckled.

"The jolly old kidnappers?" he asked.

"Well, I don't see what a car is doing here," answered Harry. "Bunter might have been with us."

"How the dickens would they know?"

"They might," said the captain of the Remove quietly. "They got at Bunter in the King's Room, in the castle, a day or two ago, and that means that they have a confederate in the place. Lots of them in the castle knew last night that Bunter was going out riding this morning, and Smiler may have got the tip. Anyhow, I think we may as well have a look at that car."

"Let's!" agreed Nugent.

And the juniors wheeled their horses and cantered towards the halted car.

They noticed that the man standing by the car stared at them intently as they approached, and, as they drew nearer, they made out his hard, cold face and glinting eyes. They knew that face. It was the face of the Smiler—the crook who, for some utterly mysterious and unknown reason, was after Lord Reynham. The man at the wheel, they had no doubt, was his associate, the Ferret.

"By gum!" said Bob, with a deep breath. "That's the rascal, you fellows, and there's not much doubt what they're hanging about here for! They've got the tip that his jolly old lordship is coming out this morning."

Harry Wharton gripped his riding-whip.

"You fellows game?" he asked. "We've got a chance of collaring those rotters!"

"Come on!" said Bob.

And the Greyfriars fellows put their horses to the gallop.

The Smiler gave them a last hard look, and then suddenly jumped into the car. The buzz of the engine followed immediately.

"They're off!" exclaimed Nugent.

"Tally-ho!" roared Bob. "After them!"

The car shot away. It jolted and rocked and bumped on the rough track over the downs, but it put on quite a good speed. After it, with a thunder of hoofs, galloped the Greyfriars fellows.

They were four to two, but a tussle with the two crooks might have been a doubtful proposition. But it was plain that the Smiler and the Ferret were not in want of a tussle—at all events, now that they had seen that his lordship was not with the other fellows.

On an open road, horseflesh would not have been of much use in chase of a car. But on that rugged bridle-path over the downs it was a different matter. The car accelerated, and then it was seen to rock wildly, and the pursuing juniors more than half-expected it to crash. But it righted again, and ran on at a reduced speed; and, getting all they could out of their mounts, the four Greyfriars fellows kept pace, and even gained a little.

The ground fairly flew under the galloping hoofs.

In the excitement of the chase, the juniors hardly noticed the distance they were covering. But mile after mile flew by, and the sea loomed nearer and nearer.

Neither did they notice at the moment that a thick mist was rising from the sea and drifting inland. They galloped hard and fast, going all out, the wind stinging their faces.

Three or four times the hard-faced Smiler was seen to lean out, and stare back, with a dark and threatening scowl. Whether the juniors overtook the car or not, there was no doubt that they were disconcerting the plans laid by the kidnapping gang. And they looked like overtaking it for a time.

But suddenly, the car turned at right angles, and shot away at a terrific speed. It had reached the road that ran along the top of the cliffs. On the smooth highway, the Ferret let it out—and it fairly walked away from the pursuers. The Greyfriars fellows, breathless, drew in their horses where the path joined the road, and stared after the car. It was vanishing in the far distance.

"N.G.!" gasped Bob. "Well, we gave them a run for their money, anyhow. They won't see anything of the jolly old porpoise this morning."

And the juniors wheeled their horses to ride back—and behind them, as they rode, the mist from the sea rolled thicker and thicker. It thickened round them in a fog while long miles yet lay between them and Reynham Castle.

THE THIRD CHAPTER.

Stranded!

BILLY BUNTER rolled out of the great portico at Reynham Castle, frowning.

James had completed his toilet at last—and his fat lordship was ready to ride. But it was clear that the other riders had not waited for his lordship: as, of course, they ought to have done, when Bunter had told them distinctly to do so.

Two grooms were walking horses on the drive—Bunter's and the captain's. Captain Reynham, a handsome figure in riding-clothes, stood talking to Sir Peter Lanchester: and the latter frowned at Bunter as he appeared.

Since Bunter had been a resident at the castle in Sussex, old Sir Peter had become better acquainted with him—which had had the result of lowering the fat Owl very considerably in his estimation. The old gentleman had, in fact, realised that the artful Owl had pulled his leg to a considerable extent.

But that knowledge had come to Sir Peter too late to be of any use to him. Having presented Bunter at the castle as Lord Reynham, Sir Peter had to stick it out, and hope for the best. But every now and then his lordship got the sharp edge of his guardian's tongue.

"William!" rapped Sir Peter.

Bunter blinked round at the old baronet, through his big spectacles. Sir Peter seemed annoyed—but Bunter was annoyed himself.

He was quite ready to give the old "bean" back as good as he gave! Perfectly well aware that Sir Peter could not part with him, now that he had announced him at the castle as Lord Reynham, Bunter was not going to stand any nonsense. Not if William George Bunter knew it!

"Well?" snapped Bunter.

"You have kept the horses standing more than half an hour!" said Sir Peter, severely.

To Sir Peter, that was a serious matter. To the fat Owl of Greyfriars, it was no more serious than keeping a bike standing.

"Have I?" said Bunter, breezily.

"That's all right: don't you worry! I say, have those rotters gone off without me?"

"Your friends have gone, some time ago!" rapped Sir Peter. "Captain Reynham has kindly waited for you."

Bunter blinked at the young Army man who gave him a nod and a smile. His fat lordship did not smile back.

Fathead as Bunter undoubtedly was, he was not such a fool as the captain, on his looks, naturally took him to be. He had his own opinion about that elegant young Army man.

When the captain made himself agreeable, Bunter regarded it as a "poor relation" greasing up to a rich relative—Bunter being, for the nonce, the captain's wealthy cousin William, Lord Reynham. And really, he had some cause: for at other times, with a wary eye behind his big spectacles, he had caught the captain fixing him with a far from friendly or affectionate eye.

Bunter knew, in fact, that Rupert Reynham regarded him, in his own mind, as a fat and offensive bounder.

"Oh, you've waited, have you?" grunted Bunter. "Well, I jolly well shouldn't go riding alone, I know that! I'm not going to be snaffled by those kidnapping rotters!"

"You may rely upon me, William, if there should be any danger!" said the captain, with a smile.

Snort, from Bunter!

"Don't fancy I want protecting!" he yapped. "I can look after myself, I hope! Still, you can ride with me!"

"I am honoured!" said Rupert, with a sarcastic inflection in his voice that he could not contrive to keep out of it.

He walked across to his horse, and took it from the groom. Sir Peter dropped his hand on a fat shoulder.

"I desire you to be more civil to my nephew, William!" he said, in a low voice. "I should be very sorry if Rupert took offence, and left the castle, instead of remaining here over Christmas."

"Rot!" said Bunter.

"Wha-a-t?" gasped Sir Peter Lanchester.

"I said rot!" answered Bunter, coolly. "He won't hike off in a hurry—you can trust him for that! He's in clover here—living on the fat of the land, and riding my horses! A ten-shilling hack would be nearer his mark, on his own!"

And Bunter rolled away to his steed, leaving Sir Peter Lanchester speechless.

With the aid of two grooms, Bunter was hoisted into the saddle. He had the stirrups altered, and then altered again—not because they needed it, but to impress on the menials that he was boss of the show. Then he gathered up the reins in a fat paw, took his riding-whip, and rode away down the avenue—looking as graceful as a sack of coke beside the elegant captain.

His lordship had given special instructions, that an extremely quiet and well-behaved "gee" should be selected for his lordly use. Those instructions, evidently had been carried out: for Bunter did not fall off his horse, all the way through the park to the gate on the downs. Moreover, he was careful not to venture on anything more than a gentle trot.

Bunter liked to tell the fellows in the Remove, at Greyfriars, about wild gallops on fiery steeds at home at that magnificent residence, Bunter Court. But when he was actually on a horse, he preferred slow motion.

Captain Reynham looked at him several times: unaware of the fact that Bunter, short-sighted as he was, caught the amused contempt in his looks.

Like so many short-sighted people,

Bunter sensed things as much as he saw them: and though the captain's face, at ten feet off, was dim to his limited vision, he was perfectly aware of the varying expressions that passed over it.

He knew that the captain disliked him—which, Bunter admitted, was natural enough, for had he been really Lord Reynham, as Rupert believed, he would have been the fellow who stood between the impecunious Army man and a great title and a great estate.

Still, it was like his cheek, Bunter considered: and he did not like it. Contempt is said to penetrate even the shell of the tortoise: and even Billy Bunter was not so thick-skinned as a tortoise.

For which reason, Bunter, generally laid himself out to be disagreeable to that cheeky "poor relation"—and he succeeded so well, that Harry Wharton & Co. had wondered, a good many times, why the captain did not leave the castle.

The juniors, when they rode out of the park, had closed the gate after them. It had to be opened again for the two riders to pass out: and as a schoolboy riding with a man, it was up to Bunter to jump down and open it.

Bunter had two good reasons for not doing so, however. Swank was one of them: and the other, a doubt whether he could have got on his horse again, once he had got off.

"Get that gate open!" said Bunter cheerily.

Captain Reynham looked at him, fixedly, for a moment. Bunter spoke to him as he might have spoken to a groom. This was Bunter's masterly way of getting his own back for the young Army man's supercilious looks.

It was not surprising that Rupert Reynham's grip closed on his riding whip, hard, for a second. During that brief second, Lord Bunter had a narrow escape of a whop across his lordly shoulders!

Then the captain dismounted, and opened the gate, holding it for Bunter to ride through.

Bunter grinned as he passed him. He was, he flattered himself, keeping this cheeky poor relation in his proper place! If he did not like it, he could clear—Bunter would not be sorry to see the last of him.

Rupert Reynham remounted and rode after Bunter. They trotted in silence over the frosty downs. Bunter blinked round several times, through his big spectacles, for Harry Wharton & Co. But the Co. were miles away, and he was not likely to see anything of them.

As the fat junior knew nothing of the ways about the castle, he left the guidance to Captain Reynham. Rupert led the way, into a bridle-path that crossed the almost trackless downs.

In the park he had been annoyed by Bunter's leisurely rate of progress; but now he seemed content to amble along at little more than a walk. His eyes which were very keen, swept the downs continually—perhaps, like Bunter, looking for the Greyfriars fellows.

A couple of miles from the castle, he scanned the ground, as he rode slowly along the bridle-path. His keen glances picked up the recent sign of motor-tyres—quite lost to Bunter's eyes. A puzzled expression came over his face—possibly he was wondering what a car had been doing there at all!

"I say—" said Bunter suddenly. "Looks to me like a fog coming on!"

The captain smiled. For the last half-hour, or more, he had been observing the thick mist rolling up from the sea, growing thicker and thicker. Looking

back, the tall turret of Reynham Castle was hidden in mist.

"I think we'd better be getting back!" said Bunter. "I can't see anything of the other fellows, and I don't want to be caught in the fog here, see?"

"Perhaps you are right, William!" said the captain.

"No perhaps about it!" yapped Bunter. "I'm right! Why, if I lost sight of you, I couldn't find my way back—I can't see the castle from here! Might wander off anywhere."

Captain Reynham gave him rather a strange look.

"Do you think so?" he asked.

"I don't think—I know! Let's get back," said Bunter. "Besides, we might be late for lunch!"

He wheeled his horse—carefully.

"Right!" said the captain cheerily. "The fact is, we're rather in danger of being caught in the fog, now you point it out, William. We had better put on a spot of speed, I think."

With a touch of the whip, the captain set his horse to the gallop.

Billy Bunter glared after him, and yelled:

"I say, hold on. I'm not going to race! Hold on! Stop! Do you hear me, blow you? Stop, I tell you!"

Perhaps, in the thunder of the hoofs, and the whistling of the wind, the captain did not hear. At all events, he did not heed. He rode on at a sharp gallop without looking back.

"Beast!" roared Bunter.

Lord Bunter did not want to gallop. He knew—as doubtless Rupert knew—what was likely to happen, if he did. But the prospect of being left alone on the lonely downs, with the fog thickening about him, was terrifying.

Bunter made the venture. He galloped after Rupert.

After so much slow motion, on a cold and frosty morning, Bunter's horse was probably glad to stretch his limbs a little. He galloped on after the captain, already far in the distance. In a couple of minutes Bunter had lost the reins—in two more, he had lost the stirrups—his riding-whip flew from his fat hand and vanished as he clutched at the horse's neck—and after rocking onward, with squeaks of terror, for about another minute, Bunter rolled off.

Bump!

"Yaroooh!"

Bunter landed on Sussex, with a concussion that almost made that county jump. He roared as he hit Sussex. The horse, possibly glad to be relieved of his lordship's uncommon weight, dashed on, and left him there.

"Ow!" roared Bunter. "Wow! Beast! Oh crikey!"

He sat and blinked after his vanishing horse. The captain was almost out of sight. In a few minutes more, he was quite out of sight—and Bunter's horse passed out of sight in its turn. And the hapless fat Owl, blinking round him over rugged, misty downs, utterly lonely, deserted and silent, tottered to his feet, and ejaculated dismally:

"Oh crikey!"

THE FOURTH CHAPTER.
In the Kidnapper's Hands!

"**H**ELP!" roared Billy Bunter.

Bunter had been tramping for twenty minutes. It seemed to him like the same number of hours.

Now he halted, gasping for breath, and blinked round him through the thickening mist that clothed the dim, rolling downs.

He had seen nothing more of his horse. Probably the animal had gone

home, knowing, better than its rider did, the way home across the downs. Neither had he seen any more of Rupert Reynham. Apparently the captain had supposed that Bunter was riding after him. Anyhow, he had disappeared without looking back—and looking back, now, would have been useless, for visibility in the mist was shortened to a matter of yards.

Stranded on the dim downs, Bunter had started to walk back, in what he hoped was the right direction. But he was soon tired of walking, and he knew that the chances were many against the direction being right. As he had not the remotest idea where the castle lay, and could not guess north from south or east from west, he might have been heading for any point of the compass. Really, exertion was rather futile, in such circumstances.

But the idea of remaining where he was, was simply terrifying. He was lost on the downs—hopelessly lost!

In clear daylight, even Billy Bunter might have arrived somewhere—but the thickening mist wrapped him almost like wool.

It was the fault of those beasts for starting without him—not, of course, Bunter's own fault for not starting when the other fellows did. But the worst beast of all was that unutterable beast Rupert Reynham, who had brought him here and left him stranded.

Harry Wharton & Co. were somewhere on the downs—but that was little use to Bunter, as they might be miles away, and would have been invisible if twenty yards away. They were not likely to help.

But surely that unspeakable beast, Rupert, would miss him, and come back for him! That was really Bunter's only hope! The beast did not like him—agreeable fellow as he was—but he could not be brute enough to leave him lost on the misty downs.

Bunter, at first, dreaded to be late for lunch—then he realised that he was going to miss lunch—and then came the awful thought that he might still be wandering on the downs when the early December darkness fell!

In one direction lay Reynham Castle; in another, the town of Castlewood, in another, a village; in another, the road by the sea. But all these directions were equally unknown to Bunter—and he was miles from any of the places, anyhow. Unless that beast Rupert came back for him, his situation was very unenviable.

Walking about at random was not much use—but if the captain, or anyone else, was in search of him, calling for help might guide them to his lost lordship! As soon as he thought of this, Bunter began to roar.

"Help! Help! Help!"

He put plenty of beef into it, on his top note. His shouts echoed and re-echoed in the mist.

"Help! Help!"

He roared till his breath was expended. But, after a little rest, he resumed roaring. Far across the downs, rang his frantic yells.

"Help! This way! Help!"

Suddenly, to the fat junior's immense relief, there came an answering call. He could see no one; but from the distance, in the clinging mist, a call came back.

"Halloo!"

"Oh crikey!" gasped Bunter, and he put all the strength of his lungs into his next yell. "Help! Here! Help!"

"Halloo!" The answer sounded closer.

"Here!" roared Bunter. "Help!"

"Coming!" called back a voice quite close at hand.

Billy Bunter galloped on, after the captain. In a couple of minutes he had lost the reins—in two more, he had lost the stirrups. Next, his riding-whip flew from his fat hand as he clutched at the horse's neck, squeaking with terror. "Yoooh! Oooch! Wooogh!"

It seemed to Bunter that he had heard that voice before; but it was not the captain's.

"Help!" roared Bunter again. "I say, mind you don't miss me! I can't see you! This way! I'm standing here!"

An overcoated figure loomed up in the mist.

Billy Bunter gasped with relief.

"This way!" he squeaked. "Don't miss me!"

To his surprise, there was a laugh.

"I'm not likely to miss you, my lord!" came the answer; and a stocky figure came towards Bunter at a run.

"Oh!" gasped the fat junior. Close at hand, he knew that stocky figure, and the hard face with its icy eyes. "Oh! Help! I say, keep off! Oh crikey!"

The Smiler, grinning sourly, grasped him by a fat shoulder. The fat Owl of Greyfriars blinked at him, his eyes almost popping through his spectacles in terror.

Too late, he realised whom his cries for help had guided to him. His fat knees knocked together.

In his terror of being lost on the downs, Bunter had forgotten the kidnapping gang. But even had he thought of them, he would not have imagined that the Smiler was anywhere at hand.

By what strange chance had the Smiler been on the downs, within hearing of his howls for help? It did not occur to him that it was not by chance, and that the kidnapper had been hunting for him, when he heard his cries in the mist.

Not that it mattered. He was in the kidnapper's grip now, and that grip fastened on his fat shoulder like a steel vice.

"You have lost your horse, my lord?" grinned the Smiler.

"Ow! Oh dear! Yes!" groaned Bunter. "I—I—I say—oh lor'!"

"It means rather a walk for your lordship, I fear! But for your meddling friends, I could have given your lordship a lift in a car!" said the Smiler. "You can thank them for having to walk!"

"I—I say, I—I don't want to go in a car, you know!" groaned Bunter. "I—I say, I—I—I want to get back to the castle! Oh dear!"

The Smiler chuckled.

"I fear, my lord, that you have looked your last on your lordship's castle!" he answered. "Come with me!"

"I—I—I'd rather not——" gasped Bunter.

"Come!" snapped the Smiler.

"Oh crikey!"

Bunter had no choice in the matter. The grip on his fat shoulder jerked him into motion. He tottered along with the hard-faced rascal. What direction the man was taking he did not know except that it certainly was not that of Reynham Castle.

The Smiler released his fat shoulder. Bunter had no chance of dodging away —had he attempted to do so, the ruffian would have clutched him again before he had taken three steps.

Quite aware of that, Bunter did not think of making the attempt. He tottered on dismally by the kidnapper's side.

The mist, which had been thickening and thickening, now blanketed the downs in a billowing fog. Alarmed and terrified as he was to find himself in the hands of the crook, Bunter realised

that if he had got away from the man he would have been utterly and hopelessly lost and helpless. He soon observed that the Smiler himself seemed to be in a little doubt.

Every now and then the man stooped and examined the ground, as if to make sure that he was on a path. The fat Owl noticed, at last, that there were tracks of motor-tyres in the damp earth.

He realised that a car must have passed that way not very long ago. It was some sort of a path over the downs, but the path itself was difficult, if not impossible, to trace in the fog. But for the indentations of the car's wheels, even the Smiler might have been at a loss to pick his way through the blinding fog, as well as Bunter.

The Smiler was, in fact, following the track of the car in which he and his associate had fled from the Greyfriars riders a couple of hours ago. That car had been waiting for Bunter; and it was, as the Smiler said, thanks to the juniors that he had to walk. Had the kidnappers' schemes that morning gone according to plan, Lord Bunter would have been whisked away in that car before the fog descended on the downs.

"Oh lor'!" groaned Bunter, as he tottered and stumbled on.

The Smiler tramped on without a word. When Bunter lagged, he gave him a look with his cold, glinting eyes that caused the fat junior to hurry on again.

Where they were heading for Bunter could not guess. Perhaps a road, where there might be a car waiting; perhaps for the sea, where some vessel might be lying off the shore to take him aboard. In a state of dismal apprehension, the fat junior stumbled on by the side of the scowling Smiler.

Suddenly, from the bank of cloud ahead came a sound—the jingling of bridles and stirrups. Unseen, but quite close at hand, horsemen were ahead in the mist.

Bunter jumped.

Instantly he thought of the Remove fellows. Instantly, also, did the Smiler, and he swung round towards Bunter and clutched.

Bunter bounded like a fat kangaroo, and the clutching hand missed him by inches. Forgetting that he was tired, the fat junior fairly bolted onward, yelling as he went.

"Help! I say, you fellows, help! Oh, help!"

A moment more, and the Smiler had clutched him.

Bunter, struggling wildly in his grasp, yelled, and yelled, and yelled!

"Help! Help! Help!"

THE FIFTH CHAPTER.
An Unexpected Meeting!

"THIS," remarked Bob Cherry, "is a go!"

His comrades agreed that it was.

For some distance, after turning back from the sea-road, where they had lost the car, the four juniors had ridden at a canter—then at a slow trot—and then they had dropped into a walk. Now, for a long time, they had been proceeding at a walk, picking their way through the fog which blanketed the downs, almost as if they were playing blind man's buff.

Thicker and thicker the mist rolled round them, and it was impossible to see more than a yard or so before one's own nose.

In their hot chase of the car, they had forgotten all else; but they wished now that they had been a little more thoughtful. It was not a light matter to be caught in the fog on the lonely downs.

But for the chase that had led them over miles, they could have ridden back to the castle before the fog thickened. Now they had to feel their way.

Harry Wharton was walking, his reins looped over his arm, scanning the earth as he went, picking up the tracks of the car. The tyre-tracks were a sure guide back to the spot where they had first seen the car—which was only a couple of miles from the castle. After that, they had to trust to good fortune and to the instinct of the horses in finding their way back to their stables.

So far, however, the tyre-tracks had guided them; but it was slow work, and the captain of the Remove had to keep a sharp eye on the ground, and stoop every now and then to make sure that he was not missing the way. Behind him his three companions sat in their saddles, walking the horses at the slowest of walks.

Missing that track meant wandering off into the wilderness of the downs. But Harry Wharton was very careful not to miss it, and the tyre-marks were deep enough to be easily picked up by a keen eye.

He little dreamed, as he followed them, that the same track was guiding the Smiler—though in the opposite direction.

"This is a go, and no mistake!" said Bob. "The fact is, you fellows, we're a set of silly asses! We ought to have kept an eye on the weather!"

"The oughtfulness is terrific, my

esteemed Bob!" murmured Hurree Jamset Ram Singh. "But the too-latefulness is also great!"

"We'll get in some time!" said Frank Nugent. "I wonder whether Bunter came out, after all?"

"Well, he'd be all right with the jolly old captain!" said Bob. "I believe Captain Reynham spent his boyhood hereabouts—he used to live at the castle as a kid, so he would know his way all right. If Bunter's with him, he won't be lost——"

"Anyhow, he'd turn back as soon as the fog came on," said Harry. "Bunter's all right! I only hope we are! We must have been a couple of hours crawling along like this already."

"Blow that car!" said Bob. "Blow the kidnappers! Blow the fog! Blow everything!"

"The blowfulness is terrific!" chuckled Hurree Jamset Ram Singh. "But we shall arrive late at the idiotic castle soonerfully or laterfully."

"Laterfully rather than soonerfully, I fancy!" grinned Bob. "This is a rotten end to a jolly ride. But what's the odds so long as you're 'appy! I say—— Why — what — what the thump——"

He broke off with a gasp of astonishment as a sudden wild yell came pealing through the fog.

Will readers please note that the next issue of the MAGNET will be on sale THURSDAY, December 23rd ?

"Help! Help! Help!"

"What——" gasped Harry Wharton.

"I say, you fellows, help!"

"Bunter!" yelled Nugent.

"Help! Oh, help!"

Harry Wharton dropped the reins of his horse and rushed forward.

He could see nothing but fog; but the wild howls of the fat Owl were just in front of him. He crashed suddenly into two figures—Bunter struggling frantically in the grasp of the Smiler.

"Help! Yarooh! Oh, help!" shrieked Bunter.

"Oh crumbs!" gasped Wharton.

He dodged a savage blow aimed at him, and grasped hold of the Smiler, shouting to his friends. Three riders loomed up in the fog, and Bob Cherry was out of the saddle in a twinkling, and springing to the aid of his chum.

Billy Bunter tore himself loose and tottered away, still squeaking for help.

The Smiler, grasping Wharton with savage hands, bore him back, and hurled him to the earth.

Then he leaped away, barely in time to dodge Bob Cherry's grasp. A moment more, and he was lost in the fog.

"I say, you fellows, help!" roared Bunter. "I say——"

Harry Wharton staggered to his feet.

"He's gone!" gasped Bob. "Who was it?"

"The Smiler, I think!" gasped Harry. "That blighter we chased in the car a couple of hours ago. How on earth did he get hold of Bunter?"

"I say, you fellows, is—is—is he gone?" gasped Bunter.

"The gonefulness is terrific, my

esteemed fat Bunter!" said Hurree Jamset Ram Singh.

"All right now, old fat man!" said Frank Nugent reassuringly. "But how the dickens——"

"Oh lor'!" groaned Bunter. "That silly fool, Captain Reynham, left me, and I fell off my horse, and——"

"Ha, ha, ha!"

"Blessed if I see anything to cackle at!" howled Bunter. "I mean, I never fell off my horse—I got down to—to—I mean, I got down, see? Only the horse ran off——"

"But why did Captain Reynham leave you?" asked Wharton.

"I suppose the silly fool thought I was riding after him! He never looked back once! I was wandering about for hours and hours and hours!"

"All those hours, really?" asked Bob.

"Yes, hours and hours and hours and hours and hours!"

"It isn't three hours since we sat your lordship down on your lordship's floor with your lordship's valet and your lordship's boots!"

"Ha, ha, ha!"

"Beast! It seemed a jolly long time, anyhow!" groaned Bunter. "Then I was calling for help, and that beast heard me and came up—oh crikey!"

"He must have cut across on foot, from another direction, after getting away in the car!" said Bob. "But how the thump did he know where to pick up Bunter? Even if some blighter at the castle told him Bunter was going out riding this morning, he couldn't have known what direction he would take! How the thump did he know?"

"Anyhow, he got me!" groaned Bunter. "All your fault for not waiting for me, as you jolly well know I told you to! You needn't deny it—you know perfectly well that I told you to wait!"

"Guilty, my lord!" grinned Bob.

"And that beast going off and leaving me!" growled Bunter. "I'll jolly well tell him off when I see him again! I shouldn't wonder if he did it on purpose—he's cad enough! I say, you fellows, let's get in! That beast might come back with some more of the gang."

"They wouldn't find us very easily," said Harry. "Not much danger of that. You'd better get on my horse, Bunter."

"Lend me a hand!"

Several hands had to be lent to get Bunter in the saddle. Thankfully he squatted there, to rest his weary fat limbs. He blinked round uneasily in the fog as the party proceeded once more.

"I say, you fellows, can't you go faster?" yapped Bunter. "We're fearfully late for lunch already!"

"We've got to keep to these tyre tracks, fathead! They're the only guide."

"Oh! That's what that beast was doing!" Bunter chuckled. "I'll bet he never thought of you fellows doing the same! That's how we ran into you! He, he, he!"

The horses tramped on with exasperating slowness. Now that he was safe in the company of his pals, Billy Bunter's fat thoughts naturally turned to lunch. They turned to lunch with deep longing.

But there was no help for it. The juniors had to proceed at a crawling pace to keep to the track, and it was nearly another hour before they reached the spot where the car had first been seen.

There the trail of the tyres ended. The bridle-path, hardly to be discerned in the thick fog, ran on, but whether in the direction of the castle or not, the juniors did not know.

There was only one thing to be done

now—to leave the horses to their own guidance, and trust to them to find their way home. And as the horses kept together, taking the same direction of their own accord, the juniors were hopeful at long last of sighting Reynham Castle looming up through the fog.

Every now and again Billy Bunter grunted. Would he reach the castle in time for lunch?

THE SIXTH CHAPTER.
Unexpected !

"LOOKS a whopping place !"

"By gum—it does !"

"How the thump did Bunter ever barge in here ?"

"Goodness knows ! I—I suppose he's really here ?"

Skinner, of the Remove, seemed

smitten with a doubt. His companion, Bolsover major, seemed more doubtful still. A taxi from Castlewood was grinding up the vast avenue at Reynham Castle, and the two Removites were looking out at the imposing facade of the old Sussex castle.

The fog, rolling up from the sea,

(Continued on next page.)

LEARN TO PLAY FOOTBALL!
OUR INTERNATIONAL COACH
BY

TIME FOR STOPPAGES

I AM afraid some of you will be beginning to think that if football matches are stopped as often as this game we are playing together has been stopped, they are not going to be very thrilling affairs. I must hasten to tell you that proper games of football do not have so many stoppages in them. Or, rather, perhaps I should say that in a real game the stoppages are not quite so long.

As a matter of fact, it has been worked out that in a first-class football match, twenty of the ninety minutes' play is taken up by stoppages—for injuries, and for the ball going out of play. The players don't notice this, of course. To them, the hold-ups are all part of the game.

The point is, that in our match the stoppages are longer because I have to keep explaining things to you. Some of them take a long time, but you can take it for granted that I never stop the play unnecessarily. I have always something to tell you, so even if you wish we could get on with the game a bit faster, cheer up, this practice match is helping to make you into good footballers.

Just to show you how often the stoppages may come, even in a real game, here is another one. When our goalkeeper took the goal-kick, as he was doing, you remember, last week, he did as I told him, and kicked the ball to one of his own players. He chose the outside-left. But the outside-left hasn't quite got the hang of trapping a ball, and it went under his foot and over the touchline.

That means a throw-in.

The throw-in is taken by a player of the opposite side from that which kicked the ball out. Our goalkeeper was the last player to touch the ball, so the other side must throw it in.

The job is usually given to the wing half-backs. It doesn't matter really who takes a throw-in, but for some reason which I can't really explain, because I don't know, it is taken for granted that the wing-half is the player for the job. The linesman will tell him where the ball went over the line, and he must stand on that spot. A part of both his feet must remain on the ground all the time he is throwing. That means that he can raise his heels, but his toes must stay on the ground. He holds the ball with two hands, taking it back over his head,

---

This week our special contributor tells you the correct way to take a "throw-in". Follow his instructions carefully.

---

and then throws it to one of his own players, keeping both hands on the ball until he finally leaves go. Do you see how I mean?

THE THROW-IN

THE action is the same as when you are doing a touch-toes exercise, raising both your arms above your head, and then bringing them down. Do that exercise with a ball in your hands, and you have got the proper throw-in. There are three things to remember. First of all, the feet on the ground rule. Secondly, the arms must be taken well back over the head; and, thirdly, the ball must be thrown with both hands. If you break any of these rules, and the referee sees you, you lose your chance, and the throw-in is taken by the other side

Too many footballers think that the throw-in is unimportant, and so long as the ball gets back into play nothing else matters. That's where they are wrong. The throw-in can be very useful. One of the first players in first-class football to realise just how useful it could be was Sam Weaver, the former Newcastle man who now plays for Chelsea. He practised and practised at throwing-in until he got so good at it that he could throw from the touchline right into the middle of the field.

Imagine what this means when Weaver takes a throw-in near his opponents' goal. He can throw the ball right into the goalmouth. Although a goal cannot be scored direct from a throw-in, it gives the forwards a jolly good chance to score. Other players have learnt this trick since Weaver thought of it. Tom Gardner, of Aston Villa, and Jack Crayston, of Arsenal, are two which come to mind. Believe me, many goals have been scored from their throws.

SURPRISES ARE USEFUL

DON'T expect you to be able, just yet, to throw a ball from the touch-line right into the goalmouth; but I have told about these players to show you that first-class players think the throw-in is worth a good deal of thought and practice. And here's another little dodge in connection with the throw-in. It will sometimes pay for the fellow who is standing nearest the ball when it goes out to throw it in quickly, before the other players gather round.

I remember seeing Eric Brook, the Manchester City outside-left, do this in a match. He doesn't usually take the throws-in, of course, but on this occasion he picked the ball up quickly and threw it in to one of his colleagues, who caught the defence by surprise and went on to score a goal.

I think I see a mischievous sparkle in the eye of one wing-half who is reading this. He thinks he has worked out a good way of taking a throw-in. He imagines himself taking the throw-in in the proper way, but instead of throwing the ball to another player, he throws it to himself—in other words, he drops it at his own feet, so that he can have a free-kick at it. I like to see you fellows working out ideas for yourselves, but I am sorry to say that this chap will have to have another think, because he is not allowed to do that. The law says that he mustn't touch the ball again until it has been played by another player.

Incidentally, this goes for all free-kicks as well. A player who kicks off from the centre of the field, who takes a goal-kick, a corner-kick, a penalty-kick, or a free-kick, must not touch the ball a second time until it has been touched by another player.

Here's a bit of luck. Just to prove what I have been saying about the importance of the throw-in, look what has happened! The half-back of the other side took the throw-in, but the ball went to our inside-left. He wasn't marked, you see, because the player who usually marks him was taking the throw-in, and, foolishly, nobody had come to take the half-back's place. Therefore, our inside-left was able to get the ball, and he went right through to finish off with a nice low shot into the net. The goalkeeper tried hard, but he couldn't stop the ball, and we have scored a goal.

THE MAGNET LIBRARY.—No. 1,558.

across the downs, had not yet reached the castle, though wisps of it were drifting across the park. Battlemented walls and tall turrets glimmered in the wintry sunshine. Bolsover major and Skinner had a good view of the castle, and they were duly impressed—and a little uneasy.

Before break-up at Greyfriars School, Billy Bunter had told all who wanted to listen, and a good many who didn't, about the gorgeous Christmas holiday he was going to have at Reynham Castle. Few of the Remove fellows believed a word of it—being too much accustomed to Bunter's castles in the air to believe in his castle in Sussex.

But Skinner, having looked into the matter, and witnessed a meeting of the fat Owl with Sir Peter Lanchester, had satisfied himself that it was all right. He had confided his belief to Bolsover, and the two of them had pulled Bunter's fat leg to the extent of extracting an invitation from him to join him at the magnificent castle.

Since break-up, however, they had not heard from Bunter.

Possibly the fat Owl had forgotten them. Anyhow, he had not taken the trouble to write.

Still, he had asked them to come—and, after waiting in vain to hear from Bunter, they had come.

They had expended a good deal of tuck on Bunter to extract that invitation from him. Having thus expended a sprat to catch a whale, they did not want to lose the whale!

So here they were, on Christmas Eve, coming up the drive in a taxi from Castlewood—hoping for the best, but feeling more and more dubious, as the magnificence of the castle impressed them more and more.

Knowing nothing of the extraordinary part Bunter was playing there, they could not guess how, or why, the fat Owl of the Remove had contrived to barge into such an establishment.

The idea that he had, after all, pulled their leg, and was not there at all, was quite dismaying.

"You said you knew for certain, you ass!" said Bolsover major, with a glare at Skinner. "You told me you'd seen him and the old bean——"

"So I did!" snapped Skinner. "I saw him meet Sir Peter Lanchester, and I could see that he knew him all right. And the old bean came and fetched him away when we broke up—a lot of fellows saw him."

"Well, that looks all right," said Bolsover. "But Bunter's such a fearful spoofer—he might have wangled a lift in the old bean's car on break-up day—and never gone with him at all!"

"I don't think so!" Skinner shook his head. "I fancy it's all right—though I simply can't imagine how Bunter ever wangled himself into a place like this. But he must be there!"

"Well, we shall soon see, anyhow!"

The taxi rolled on, and stopped at last at the great granite steps at the entrance of the castle.

Leaving their suitcases in the taxi, the two Removites ascended the steps to the great door.

A footman admitted them, and they entered a vast hall, adorned with figures in glistening armour. If Bunter were there, he was not visible. And the footman, to their dismay, did not know the name.

However, he called the butler, and the two uneasy visitors hoped for better news from the butler.

Jasmond, the portly butler of Reynham, swam towards them, after they had waited a few minutes. He eyed them rather curiously. They were not

the first callers at the castle who had inquired for that unknown person, Bunter. Harry Wharton had asked for Bunter, on his first arrival, not being then aware that the fat Owl had become Lord Reynham.

"Isn't Bunter here?" demanded Bolsover major gruffly.

"I do not know the name, sir," answered Jasmond. "No one of that name, certainly, is staying at the castle!"

"Not here?" breathed Skinner.

"No, sir!"

"Oh crumbs!"

"Look here!" growled Bolsover, major. "We've been asked here by a Greyfriars chap named Bunter, who told us he was staying here for Christmas. See? He came here with an old gentleman named Sir Peter Lanchester."

"There is some mistake, sir!" said Jasmond politely. "No one of the name of Bunter came here with the master!"

"He jolly well started in the car with him, I know that!" said Skinner.

"Indeed, sir!"

"Didn't anybody come here with Sir Peter?" asked Skinner.

"Only his ward, sir."

"His ward?"

"Lord Reynham, sir!"

"Not Bunter?"

"No, sir," said Jasmond, with a faint smile. "Only his lordship, sir."

"That fat frog was pulling our leg!" muttered Bolsover major. "We'd better get out of this, Skinner!"

"Is Sir Peter Lanchester at home?" asked Skinner.

"No, sir! The master has gone out to look for his lordship, who went riding this morning, and did not return when expected."

"You're quite sure that nobody named Bunter is staying here?"

"Quite, sir!"

"He hasn't been here at all?"

"No, sir!"

Percy Bolsover and Harold Skinner looked at one another, with feelings too deep for words.

They were unwilling to believe that the fat Owl of the Remove had pulled their leg to the extent of causing them to undertake a long journey, and present themselves at an establishment where they were not expected. But there seemed no doubt about it now.

If Bunter was not at the castle, and had never been there, and his name was unknown to the butler, it was hardly possible to doubt that the whole thing was spooff.

"By gum, I'll make him sit up for it, next term!" breathed Bolsover major. "The fat rotter, making fools of fellows like this!"

Skinner set his lips hard. He thought of all those jam tarts, all those dough-nuts that had been wasted on Bunter to extract that invitation from him.

A faint smile flickered over Jasmond's portly face. He showed the two unhappy fishers for invitations out with great politeness.

They went back to their taxi.

"Get back to the station!" grunted Bolsover to the driver. And the taxi buzzed away down the avenue to the gates.

"You silly ass, Skinner!" growled Bolsover, as they went.

"I jolly well thought——"

"You silly fathead!"

"By gum—wait till I see Bunter next term!" breathed Skinner.

The taxi rolled away down the road to Castlewood. Up that road the fog was now rolling in thick banks. The taxi-driver slowed down to a crawl. Visibility was only a couple of yards.

"Oh crumbs!" said Bolsover major, glaring out into the rolling fog. "This puts the tin lid on! We shall lose the train back!"

"And the next after it, at this rate!" groaned Skinner.

"That fat scoundrel——"

"That podgy blighter——"

"Oh, won't I give him jip next term!"

"Won't I burst him all over the Remove!"

"Blow him!"

"Bother him!"

The taxi crawled through the thickening fog.

Bolsover major and Skinner had one consolation—and one only—the prospect of dealing with Billy Bunter next term at Greyfriars. Judging by their remarks, Bunter was booked for a really fearful time next term!

THE SEVENTH CHAPTER.
Better Late Than Never !

SIR PETER LANCHESTER, in those same moments, was peering over the gate from the park, into the dim, swirling mist that enveloped the downs beyond.

Through the smoky mist came the sound of plodding hoofs, much to the relief of the baronet.

He had been rather alarmed when he was informed that his lordship's horse had been found by a keeper, coming back without its rider. That looked as if his lordship had had a fall—which, considering what sort of a horseman his lordship was, was not surprising. It was a great relief to Sir Peter to hear horsemen approaching from the foggy downs. He held open the gate for them to ride in.

"What!" ejaculated Sir Peter, as they came into view.

He stared at the party—Harry Wharton walking, Bunter on Wharton's horse, and the other three fellows following.

"Here we are again!" said Bob Cherry cheerfully. "The jolly old gees knew their way home all right! They've taken their time—but here we are!"

"I am glad to see you safe again, my boys!" exclaimed Sir Peter. "I was afraid you had ridden too far, and been lost in the fog."

"Exactly what happened, sir!" said Wharton. "But we left it to the horses, and they've brought us back all right."

"But where is my nephew?" asked Sir Peter. "You seem to have picked up William—his horse came back some time ago—but Captain Reynham was with him."

Snort from Bunter.

"Hasn't he got back?" he demanded.

"He has not returned yet, William!"

"He, he, he! I dare say he's lost in the fog, then!" Bunter chortled. "Serve him jolly well right!"

"William!"

"Oh, you needn't William me!" yapped Bunter. "That beast——"

"Who?"

"That beast!" hooted Bunter. "That beast cleared off, and left me to it, when I fell off my horse—I mean, when I dismounted, and that beastly kidnapper got me, and if these fellows hadn't found me, where should I be now?"

"Good gad!" ejaculated Sir Peter. "But——"

"Serve him jolly well right, if he's lost himself!" yapped Bunter. "I jolly well hope he has! I hope he'll be out all night, so yah!"

"Shut up, you fat ass!" breathed Bob.

"Shan't!"

"Kindly tell me what has happened, Wharton!" said Sir Peter Lanchester, as the party moved on by the path through the park.

He listened to the tale of the morning's happenings.

"It is extraordinary!" he said. "William has had a narrow escape! It is unfortunate that Tomlinson was not on the spot—he might have——"

"Fat lot of good he would have been!" grunted Bunter. "You'd better sack that detective and get a better one!"

"That will do, William!" said Sir Peter, breathing hard.

Grunt from Bunter.

"I'm fearfully hungry!" he snorted. "It's nearer tea-time than lunch-time, I know that! I'm glad that beast has missed his lunch, anyhow!"

"Captain Reynham is most likely searching for you on the downs!" said Sir Peter severely. "That must be why he has not returned."

"Lot he cares whether I'm lost!" grunted Bunter. "I believe he jolly well left me stranded on purpose!"

"Nonsense!" said Sir Peter sharply.

"Well, he must have heard me calling to him, and he cleared off, all the same—never looked back once!" snorted Bunter. "Just like he did with the car the other day—stranding me half-way to Castlewood, and making me walk! I jolly well shan't go out riding with him again, I can tell you. I'm fed-up with him leaving me spotted about for those kidnappers to get hold of!"

"You had better say no more, William!"

Grunt!

The weary party arrived at the castle at last.

Harry Wharton & Co. went up to change; but Billy Bunter did not bother about changing.

His lordship could do as his lordship jolly well liked, in his own castle, and his lordship jolly well did. In riding-breeches and muddy boots, his fat lordship made a bee-line for the dining-room—heedless of the lifting of Jasmond's eyebrows.

What Bunter wanted was grub—and he wanted it quick! And he had it quick—and piled into it without delay!

He was going strong when the other fellows came down, newly swept and garnished—more than ready for that very late lunch.

Sir Peter had lunched long ago; and he was very anxious and worried about his nephew. The December dusk was falling, thickening and darkening the fog that now wrapped the castle like a blanket, and the captain had not yet returned.

"By gum, if that chap's still out on the downs looking for Bunter——" said Bob Cherry uneasily.

"Rot!" said Bunter.

"Why hasn't he come in, then, fathead?"

"I jolly well know he wouldn't look for me!" said Bunter. "He doesn't like me. He knew jolly well he would lose me, when he galloped off like that, all of a sudden!"

"That's rubbish!" said Bob. "As if a man would play a rotten trick like that on a schoolboy! Bosh!"

"The boshfulness is terrific!"

"Oh, is it?" snorted Bunter. "If he makes out that he was looking for me, when he comes in, he'll be telling whoppers, see? I know he jolly well cleared off, and left me to it—that's the sort of

cheeky cad he is! And I'll jolly well tell him so, too—a cheeky poor relation! Yah!"

"Oh, shut up, you fat ass!"

"Beast!"

Bunter had started first; but he was still going strong at the late lunch when the other fellows had finished.

The Greyfriars Ghost

Being ye True Storie of ye Haunted Class-room at Grey Friars Schoole, discovered and tolde by DICK PENFOLD.

The boy sat at the class-room desk
Whence all but he had fled;
The college, old and picturesque,
Was silent as the dead.

The school had broken-up and gone,
The Christmas Vac. begun,
Yet still that schoolboy lingered on,
The last and only one.

The day before the Christmas Vac.
He'd been detained to stay
Until the master should come back
And let him go away.

The master, busy in his den,
Forgot the hapless boy,
And all the other Greyfriars men
Were far too full of joy.

Throughout a long and sleepless night
He sat in silence grim,
And in the morning's wild delight
No fellow thought of him!

His eyes were fixed with longing gaze
Upon the open door,
But boys and masters went their ways
And silence fell once more.

"Oh, tell me, can I go now, sir?
Please, master, give the word!"
The master, then at Winchester,
His voice no longer heard.

"Oh, master, this is past a joke—
Oh, heed my frantic call!"
His voice rang wildly, and awoke
The echoes—that was all.

Day after day, though cold and numb,
He sat with sinking heart
Still waiting for his Beak to come
And tell him to depart.

Day after day in silence passed
Without his master's leave,
Until the village bells at last
Rang out for Christmas Eve.

"A Merry Christmas, everyone!"
He found the strength to say,
And then, his earthly labour done,
He gently passed away.

And when re-opening day came round,
They wondered where he'd gone,
Until inside that room they found
A dusty skeleton!

And now at Christmas this uncouth
Young spectre we behold—
The Ghostly figure of the youth
Who Did as He was Told!

(Other youths take warning!)

Leaving Billy Bunter still parking the foodstuffs in great quantities, the four juniors went back into the hall, where Sir Peter Lanchester was staring from a window into dusky fog.

They were a little worried themselves, not so much on the captain's account, as on Johnny Bull's. Johnny was booked to arrive that day; but trains were a little uncertain on Christmas Eve; and at what time Johnny would land at Castlewood Station they did not know.

It was arranged for Johnny to ring up, when he did arrive, when a car would be dispatched for him at once. But now that a fog like a blanket lay on the whole vicinity, trains would be more uncertain than ever; and it was quite possible that Johnny might blow in very late.

The four juniors were very anxious to hear from Johnny; and it was a great relief when a footman came to inform Wharton that he was wanted on the telephone. He ran to the telephone-cabinet.

"Hallo!" came Johnny Bull's deep voice over the wires. "That you, Harry?"

"Yes, old chap! Jolly glad you've got through all right!"

"It's as thick as pea-soup here, and the trains are all at sixes and sevens! But I've got in—I'm speaking from the station! Don't let them send a car—it would take half an hour to crawl here through the fog. I'll pick up a taxi here."

"Right-ho!"

"They tell me it's about two miles! I shan't do it under the hour, in this pea-soup! See you later, old chap!"

"Right-ho!"

Johnny Bull, at the station, cut off, and Wharton went back to his friends. They were relieved about Johnny, now. But old Sir Peter was still anxious—peering from the windows in the hope of seeing Rupert Raynham. But whether the captain was searching for his lost lordship on the downs or not, he remained absent, and the old baronet watched in vain.

THE EIGHTH CHAPTER.

Voices in the Mist!

JOHNNY BULL looked out of the station entrance, into the old High Street of the Sussex town, rather grimly.

He was warmly wrapped against the cold, with a scarf tucked under his coat-collar; but it was chilly and damp and dismal. He could not see across the street in the fog; and he was wondering whether he would be able to get a taxi to take him to the castle. Not a vehicle was to be seen.

He debated in his mind whether he had better walk. It was a direct road of a little more than two miles, he had learned, and he could hardly miss his way; and he was likely to walk as fast as a car could venture to move in the blinding fog. He was thinking it over, when a gleam of headlights came dimly through the vapour, and a taxi stopped—and, to his astonishment, two Greyfriars fellows got out.

He blinked at Bolsover major and Skinner. They did not observe him standing there for the moment. Both of them seemed in fearfully bad tempers.

"Oh, that fat rotter, giving us a time like this!" said Skinner. "I believe we've been a couple of hours crawling back here."

"Won't I smash him, when I see him again!" hissed Bolsover.

"Hallo, you fellows!" said Johnny Bull.

The two spun round and stared at him. Skinner bestowed on him a rather unpleasant grin.

"Oh! You here to visit Bunter at the jolly old castle?" he jeered.

"That's it!" said Johnny, with a nod.

"Well, you won't find him there; it's all spoof!" said Bolsover major. "He asked us as well as you, the fat scoundrel: and it's all gammon—we've been there, and that fat spoofer's not there at all!"

"Not!" exclaimed Johnny in astonishment.

"Never been there—they didn't even know his name!" said Bolsover major, and having paid the taxi-driver, he tramped into the station, snorting fog.

"But I say—what the dickens!" exclaimed the astonished Johnny. "Bunter must be there—I'm going to stay with him, with my friends—look here, Skinner, what the dickens do you mean?"

Skinner laughed.

His amiable nature found a little consolation in another fellow getting the same disappointment.

"So you let him take you in, too!" he said. "Well, it's all gammon—pure gammon! You've had your little trip for your pains—same as we have! We've been to Reynham Castle, and the butler had never even seen Bunter—he told us that nobody of that name was staying there, or had been there at all."

"But Wharton——" said Johnny, in bewilderment. "Wharton must know, and he said——"

"Ha, ha,!" chortled Skinner. "His Magnificence taken in, too! Well, he won't find Bunter at Reynham Castle, any more than we did! By gum, I'll punch the fat porpoise next term, though! Won't I boot him!"

"But—I say——"

"I've got to get a train!" said Skinner, and he tramped away after Bolsover major, leaving Johnny Bull staring in bewilderment and surprise.

What this meant was beyond Johnny's comprehension. Evidently Bolsover major and Skinner had been to the castle, had failed to find Bunter there, and had cleared off again—anxious to get a train home.

But whether Bunter was at the castle or not, it was certain that Harry Wharton & Co. were there; for Johnny had been on the phone to Wharton ten minutes earlier.

He stepped out to the taxi in which Skinner and Bolsover had arrived at the station.

"Think you could get to Reynham Castle through this?" he asked.

"You'd walk quicker, sir," said the taximan, evidently very unwilling to repeat the trip. "It's too thick for a car, sir! I've been over an hour doing two mile, and me 'eart in me mouth all the time. There ain't a car on the roads."

"Oh, all right!"

Johnny Bull started to walk, swinging his suitcase. Outside the lights of Castlewood, it was thick and dark on the road. But he had inquired the way carefully at the station, and he only had to keep on the main road—and he tramped away quite cheerfully.

About a mile out of the town, he had been told, the park wall of the Reynham estate commenced; and after that he had only to keep on along that wall, to reach the great gates. He had been tramping about twenty minutes, when

he glimpsed a high wall on his right, over-topped by ghostly, frosty, branches, dim in the clinging vapour. This, evidently, was the Reynham park wall; and he tramped along under it.

A glimmer of light came to his eyes at last. He looked in at a great gateway, where the gates stood wide open. The light came from the window of a lodge within.

Johnny Bull turned in at the gateway, and tramped up a vast avenue, lined with tall, leafless trees that loomed spectre-like.

He kept to the middle of the broad avenue—but every now and then found himself almost walking into the trees, on one side or the other, and once he bumped his nose on a frosty trunk.

"Blow!" murmured Johnny, rubbing his nose.

After that he trod on more slowly and cautiously. How long that avenue was, he did not know—but it seemed endless; and he began to wonder whether he would ever sight the lighted windows.

Suddenly from the dense, foggy darkness round him came the sound of a voice—so startling, in the silence, that Johnny stopped dead as he heard it.

Someone else was on the dim avenue, though he had heard no footstep and had not had a glimpse of anyone.

"You fool, Smiler, you fool!"

It was a low voice, in tones of intense anger and irritation.

Johnny Bull almost wondered whether he was dreaming.

The voice was quite strange to him; he had never heard it before. But the name, or rather the nickname, that it uttered, was not strange to him.

He knew that the Smiler was the name of one of the mysterious rascals who had attempted to kidnap Bunter before break-up at Greyfriars; and who, from what he had heard from his friends since, was still after Bunter at the castle in Sussex.

Johnny Bull stood quite still.

The speaker, and the man to whom he was speaking, were both hidden from him, in mist and darkness; but they were quite close at hand.

He had, in fact, almost walked into them—and might have done so, had not that sudden sound of a voice caused him to stop. They were not ten feet away—standing under one of the trees by the side of the avenue.

Johnny Bull had plenty of pluck; but his heart beat a little faster as he realised that it was the kidnapper, with some confederate, who was so close to him in the fog.

"You fool!" went on the passionate, angry voice. "Are you always going to fail? What is the use of this—failure after failure?"

"Not my fault, guv'nor!" came another voice. "That fat young covey seems to have all the luck! Hold on, guv'nor—did you hear something?"

"Don't be a fool! Do you think anyone would be out in this weather—I can hardly see my hand before my face!"

"I thought I heard——"

"Don't talk nonsense!"

Johnny Bull hardly breathed. He could see nothing; but he felt, and knew, that the Smiler was peering round suspiciously in the mist. Some faint sound of the junior's footsteps had reached him, probably before Johnny stopped.

"I thought I heard——" Johnny caught the muttering voice.

"The wind, you fool!"

"Well, this ain't the weather for a walk, that's a cert." The Smiler seemed to be satisfied. "Look here, guv'nor, it's no use ragging a man. Everything

was ready this morning—all ready for that fat bird to drop into the trap, if he had come along without his friends, as you reckoned you could fix it——"

"The fat fool saved me the trouble of fixing it. They started without him, as he was late, like the lazy, fat, slacking young rotter he is."

Johnny Bull grinned. Had he not known that they were speaking of William George Bunter, he would have guessed it now.

"That was how it was, was it?" said the Smiler. "Well, we never saw him, but the others came on us in a bunch, and we cleared off in the car——"

"I know all that. But when the fat fool was left alone on the downs, I got word to you where to find him——"

"And I did find him, guv'nor! I got him all right! But the fog had come down by then, and I had to pick my way, and I ran right into that bunch of young blighters, and——"

"I know you failed; I know you have always failed! Five years ago you failed, and old Lanchester parked him somewhere where he could never be found. Now that he has come out into the open again it is easy work—or should be. But you have only a tale of failure to tell."

"If them young coveys wasn't here with him——"

"Yes, yes; that has saved him—again and again that has saved him. There is a detective in the house watching over him, but he has given us no trouble. If those schoolboys were not here——"

"We'd have had him easy, but for that! Next time——"

Johnny Bull heard an angry, scoffing laugh.

"Next time! Always next time! I am tempted to throw up the whole game. Fortune is against me—failure after failure."

"You can't afford to do that, guv'nor. There's too big a thing at stake for that, and I fancy there's three of us would have something to say about that. We ain't in this game for our health, guv'nor."

"You dare to threaten me, you dog? You dare——"

"Keep cool, guv'nor! I tell you, next time——"

"Bah! I have waited here—how long?—for you to come and tell me that the fat fool was safe in your hands—that he was already out at sea. And this is the news I have waited for!"

"Not my fault, guv'nor. In this fog it wasn't easy for me to get here at all——"

"And all you have to tell me, is another failure—when all seemed certain at last! Bungling fools, all three of you! This will end with you and Ratty and Ferret in the prison cells—and perhaps myself after you! A fat, stupid, obtuse fool, and you cannot handle him!"

"If his friends wasn't with him——"

"They are with him, fool!"

"Couldn't they be got shut of, guv'nor? There's ways——"

"I have been thinking of that. It may be possible, but it is useless to discuss it longer. And I must get back to the house. I shall have to explain already. You had better go. I will get you on the phone when I want you."

Johnny Bull had not stirred—in dread of the two unseen rascals hearing him again if he moved. But as those words reached his ears he stepped back as softly as he could.

But, softly as he stepped, there was a sound, and he heard the quick, snarling voice of the Smiler.

"What's that? Who's that? I told you—— There's somebody——"

Billy Bunter lighted up—puffing out smoke with a great air of enjoyment. "Dash it all, put on a smoke, you fellows!" he said. "Quelch hasn't got his eye on you now! Be men for once—like me!"

Johnny Bull heard a quick footstep, and he knew that a hand was groping. He dashed up the avenue at a run.

"Good gad! Who——" It was the unknown man's voice, in startled tones. "Has someone—who——"

A dim shadow loomed in the fog. A figure, hardly seen, collided with the junior as he ran. It was the "guv'nor"—whoever the "guv'nor" was—and he bumped into Johnny without seeing him.

Without even stopping to think, Johnny Bull hit out with his free hand, and felt his clenched knuckles crash. There was a gasping cry as the man staggered, and Johnny Bull raced on.

In a few seconds the fog swallowed him, and whether the Smiler and his mysterious companion hunted for him or not, he never knew. He saw and heard nothing more of them.

Not till he bumped into a tree did he drop into a walk again, and at length, to his great relief, the lighted windows of the castle gleamed out into the December dark in front of him.

THE NINTH CHAPTER.
A Surprise for Johnny Bull!

"HALLO, hallo, hallo!".
"Here he is!"
"I say, you fellows——"
"Here you are, Johnnny, old bean!"

Johnny Bull grinned cheerily as his friends greeted him in the brightly lighted hall of Reynham Castle. They were glad to see him, and he was very glad to get in. A footman took his suitcase, another his coat, another his hat and gloves. Johnny warmed his hands at the crackling log fire, grinned at his friends, and looked round him.

"Some show!" he remarked. "Jolly glad to see you fellows again! Hallo! Is that Bunter? You're here, then, old fat man?"

"Eh? Of course I'm here!" said Bunter, blinking at him through his big spectacles. "Haven't I asked you here for the hols, fathead? Welcome to my castle!" added Bunter loftily.

"Wha-a-t?"

"Getting deaf? I said welcome to my castle!"

Johnny Bull blinked at him.
"Your castle?" he repeated. "Potty?"

"Oh, really, Bull——"

"Is that fat ass off his chump?" asked Johnny Bull, looking round at his friends in wonder. "Look here, you chaps, I'd like to know what all this means. You've told me in a letter that you're here, and that it's all right, but I'm blessed if I can make head or tail of it."

Harry Wharton laughed.

"No wonder," he said. "You're going to have a surprise, old bean, same as we had when we got here. Couldn't put it in a letter; it's a dead secret."

"The deadfulness of the esteemed secret is terrific!" grinned Hurree Jamset Ram Singh.

"Who's the boss of this show?" asked Johnny. "I don't know what you fellows are talking about, but I suppose I'd better see the boss of the show as I'm here. Who is it?"

"Me!" said Bunter.

"Fathead!"

"Look here, you cheeky ass," hooted the fat Owl indignantly, "I jolly well tell you——"

"Chuck it, ass!" said Johnny Bull. "I've heard that Reynham Castle belongs to Lord Reynham. Is he around?"

"Yes, and no!" said Harry, laughing.

"Well, that's lucid, at any rate!" said Johnny, staring.

"Better speak to Sir Peter," said Harry. "He's really boss of the show, being Lord Reynham's guardian——"

"Oh, really, Wharton——"

"That old bean who came to Greyfriars to see Quelch last week of the term," said Nugent. "You remember him? Here he comes!"

Sir Peter Lanchester had gone into the library. Now he appeared at the doorway, looking into the hall. There was a worried frown on the old gentleman's face. He was still worried about his nephew's absence. But he summoned up a kind and hospitable smile as Johnny Bull was presented to him and shook hands with the latest arrival at Reynham Castle.

"You are very welcome, my boy," he said. "William will explain to you how the matter stands, and I am sure I can rely on your discretion."

"Eh? Oh, yes!" stuttered Johnny, quite mystified.

"Come up to my rooms, old man," said Bunter. "I'll put you wise. He, he, he! I can jolly well tell you, I'm boss of the show here!"

"Rats!"

"Beast!"

"Bunter's king of the castle!" grinned Bob. "Every day I'm expecting to see him bursting all over his ancestral halls with importance!"

"Oh, really, Cherry——"

(Continued on page 16.)

THE MAGNET LIBRARY.—No. 1,558.

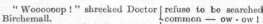

BIRCHEMALL AT BAY!

Another Rollicking Instalment of Dicky Nugent's Great Xmas Serial;

"THE MYSTERY OF JOLLY LODGE!"

III.

Mrs. Duff, the cook at Jolly Lodge, stood in the doorway of her kitchen, with her arms akimbo. She dropped a curtsey, then lifted up her voice.

"Beg parding, but would anyone like to stir the pooding for luck ? " she bawled up the stairs in her rich and fruity voice.

As if in answer to her invitation, there was a deffening clatter of footprints down the stairs. It was accompanied by frenzied yells and wringing war-woops.

Mrs. Duff was not aware that it was the Rajah of Bhang, chasing Doctor Birchemall in the beleef that he had taken his diamond tiepin. At the sound of the clattering footprints she beemed all over her fair, though fatty feetchers.

"Lawks-a-mussy ! What a rush they're in, to be sure ! " she cried. "They must be looking forward——"

Then the cook broke off with a shreek.

Evvidently, Doctor Birchemall at all events was not looking forward, for he came galloping round from the stairs as if he saw nothing in his path.

Biff ! Thud ! Wallop !

"Ow-ow-ow ! Save us ! "

"Yarooooo ! Help ! "

When she invited the guests of Jolly Lodge down to stir the pooding, Mrs. Duff had been looking forward to a good mix-up ; but she got a bigger mix-up than she had eggspected when the Head biffed her backwards into the kitchen and brought down a projecting tray-load of washing-up from the dresser at the same time !

Cups and saucers, plates and dishes crashed down on to the pair, as they collapsed on the floor. There was the very dickens of a din for a few seconds. And then there came a different kind of din, as the Rajah of Bhang reached the doorway and uttered a peercing war-cry. The dusky Oriental flurrished his nife and performed a dance of triumph when he saw that he had Doctor Birchemall at his mersy.

"Har, har ! " he cried. "Now you give back my so-bewtiful tie-pin ! "

"Help ! Perlice ! " roared the Head. "Keepimoff ! Yoooooop ! "

Doctor Birchemall jumped to his feet with a wild howl, and leaped across the kitchen like a kangarooo, as the rajah hopped into the kitchen. As for Mrs. Duff, she gave one shreek, then went off into a feint.

Forchunitly, General Jolly arrived in time to prevent his eggsited guest from doing any dammidge.

"Jentlemen ! Jentlemen ! What on earth are you doing of ? " he cried, his refined voice rising to a note of shocked serprize. "Rajah, I must request you to hand me that nife at once ! "

"But my so-bewtiful diamond tiepin——"

"Tiepin or no tiepin, I allow no man to flurrish a nife like yours in Jolly Lodge—on Christmas Day above all days ! Eggscuse me, rajah, for being blunt—but that nife looks a lot too sharp ! "

Such cutting words, coming from a jentleman of General Jolly's stamp, projooced an emmejate effect even on the irate rajah. He came to a stop and boughed.

"Thowsand pardons, my dear general ! " he cried. "I forget myself in my terrifick anxiousness ! "

He handed over the nife without further argewment. And Doctor Birchemall leaned back against the kitchen table, breething sighs of releef and mopping his fevered brow, while the cook came out of her feint again.

Jack Jolly & Co. hawled her to her feet.

"Feeling all right, cook ? " asked Jolly, as they deposited her in a chair.

"Right as ninepence, thankee kindly, Master Jack, so long as no furrin jentlemen go gallivantin' about with their daggers in my kitchen ! " answered Mrs. Duff. "Now, what about all givin' the pooding mixture a stir for luck ? "

"A good idea, by gad ! " cried General Jolly, who was anxious to pore oil on trubbled waters. "Will you go first, rajah ? "

"To please you, general, I do it—but I think more of diamond tiepin than Christmas pooding ! " sighed the rajah.

With these words he seezed a wooden spoon which was lying on the table and dipped it into the pooding mixture.

He found his task a somewhat meenial one. To go in for a dig at pooding-mixture seemed infra dig to him, and after a cupple of meer jabs at it he passed the spoon to General Jolly, who stirred it with millitary zest.

Jack Jolly & Co. then took it in turns to have a stir, and after them came Doctor Birchemall.

The Head almost caused a disaster. He was too nervuss of the rajah to pay much attention to the pooding, and the first mistake he made was to dip his beard into the mixture. Only when he started stirring viggerously and got his face funguss tangled up round his spoon did he realise what he had done, and by that time his beard had receeved a tugging that almost wrenched it from its roots.

"Woooooop ! " shreeked Doctor Birchemall.

He almost carried the pooding mixture away with him as he jumped back. Luckily, however, Mrs. Duff saw the dangwer, and with a litening-like movement detached it from the Head's wiskers in the nick of time.

"Bravvo, cook ! " larfed Jack Jolly. And there was a cheer from the rest of the Co.

"And now to return to the subject of the tiepin ! " said General Jolly, as they quitted the kitchen and tramped up the stairs again. "The tiepin must be found by hook or by crook ! "

"Perhaps it has been found by a crook already ! " sujjested Bright brightly.

"I think we not far look for the crook ! " hist the Rajah of Bhang, with a glare at the Head. "We search Birchemall sahib and then we find it, har ? "

"Let's search the bed-room first, my dear fellow ! " urged General Jolly. "It may be lyin' on the floor all the time, and it would be sheer folly to have Doctor Birchemall on the carpet if it's to be found on the rug ! Come ! "

The general led the way back to the rajah's bed-room, and the rajah reluctantly followed, muttering to himself as he did so.

Arriving at the scene of action, everybody searched for all they were worth. They looked in the firegrate and up the chimbley and round the picture-rail and carefully eggsamined all the other likely places, but no sign of the missing tiepin could they find.

"Nothin' doin', my dear rajah ! " said General Jolly at last, with a sad shake of his head. "Your preshus possession has vannished just as though the earth had opened and swallowed it up ! "

"But I do not swallow that ! " said the rajah, fixing a glare on the Head. "I insist that we search Birchemall sahib ! "

Doctor Birchemall eyed the door longingly.

"I refuse ! " he cried. "I never took that tiepin, I tell you, and I

refuse to be searched [
common — ow - ow !
alone ! "

The Head's protes[t]
a feendish howl as th[e]
patience eggshausted,
like spring. Doctor B[i]
bowled over like a nin[e]
rajah, with a look of [deter]-
mination on his dial, [
sit on his chest to ke[ep]
while he made his sea[rch].

The next moment [the]
rajah's turn to yell. [
on the Head's beard[
anattermy peerced b[
sharp and pointed, a[
leaped up as though [
electrified, clutching [
seat of his trowsis.

He eggstracted the [
that had stabbed hi[m]
samined it closely, [
shout escaped his lips [
"The pin of my ti[epin]
THE DIAMOND IS [

IV.

Every eye was tu[rned]
Head.

The rajah's annow[nce]
come like a bomshell [
That Doctor Birc[hemall]
several sorts of a ras[cal]
them would have bee[n]
agree, but nobody ap[
Rajah of Bhang h[
considered him capabl[e]

Yet what else were [we]
now ?

The Head was th[
who was known to h[
the rajah's bed-roo[m]
nite.

The fakt that he [
General Jolly's rekv[
guise of Father Christ[mas]
prove him innersen[t]
been the only known [
rajah, right enuff, and [
of the missing articl[e]
found consealed in h[
minus the diamond ! [

Small wonder that [
the rajah's bed-roo[m]
Doctor Birchemall wi[th]
akin to horror in thei[r]

"Gad, sir ! " cried G[
uneezily. "What hav[
about this ? "

"Only that I am [
was the Head's wringi[ng]
never sneaked that spa[
the vulgar mite put it[
the insinuation that [
priated that article [
Someone must have p[
my wiskers to put [
scent ! "

"A likely story ! " [
rajah. "Where yo[
diamond, har ? Tell q[
I send for perlice ! "

The culler faded fro[m]
face.

"P-p-perlice ? " h[
"Surely you are not [

r the perlice ? Let's wait and get
ir Christmas dinner over first ! "
But the rajah had made up his
ind, and he hurried down the
airs to the tellyfone in the hall.

Doctor Birchemall waited only
ng enuff to hear him start speak-
g to the perlice-station.

From that moment his manner
nderwent a startling change. In-
ead of cowering and cringing and
ining and fawning, he started
icking up for himself in no un-
rtain way.

"Very well, then, rajah ! " he
id, between his tightly clenched
lse teeth. " Send for the splits !
o your worst ! I shall fight them
the last ditch ! ' Defiance ' not
Defence ' is my motter from now
1 ! "

There was a gasp from his
sseners.

" Grate gad ! Do you mean that
ou will resist arrest ? " asked
eneral Jolly.

The Head grinned and nodded.

" Yes, rather ! I'll resist till the
tter end—and I bet I shall give
m a run for their munny, too !
tand aside ! "

Instincktively they parted to
ake way for him. There was a
ell from the rajah, who had just
placed the receever of the telly-
ne.

" Stop him ! You not let him
o ! "

But Jack Jolly & Co. had no
tention of standing in the Head's
ay. Inwardly they rather ad-
ired him for putting up a fight,
nd in any case they could see some
n coming out of this before the
orning was out. They jumped
side and Doctor Birchemall
alloped past them.

A moment later, the Rajah of
hang followed him at the dubble.

The two vannished out of the
ont door, and General Jolly led
he way after them. The general
as frowning feercely.

" Egad ! A nice how-do-you-do
his is for Christmas Day ! " he said,
gging at his mistosh as they went
ut on the porch. " I wonder what
irchemall intends to do ? "

General Jolly soon learned. As
e led the way into the snowclad
rounds of Jolly Lodge, he heard
he Head's voice raised in a chortle
f triumph.

" Hip-hip-hip-hooray ! I'm the
ing of the castle ! Let 'em arrest
e now if they can ! "

" What the merry dickens ! "
jackulated Frank Fearless.

The general and the St. Sam's
uniors broke into a run.

On the other side of a clump of
rees, an amazing site met their
yes. There sat Doctor Birchemall
n the roof of a summer-house,
athering up handfuls of snow and
naking them into snowballs ! The
ewcomers were just in time to see

him herl a snowball with deadly
aim at the Rajah of Bhang, hitting
the rajah on the boko !

Plop !

" Yaroooooo ! "

" Plenty more where that one
came from ! " yelled the Head,
cheerfully. " Now bring the perlice
to arrest me if they can ! Yah ! "

Doctor Birchemall was at bay
with a vengenz—and how he was
going to be dislodged from his perch
looked like providing a pretty problem for Christmas Day at Jolly
Lodge !

(*Don't miss the grand finish of this
yarn next week !*)

SPOOKS, SPECTRES OR SPIRITS!

Hoskins Revels In 'Em, BUT—

Hoskins has another claim to
fame besides his prowess on
the piano.

He's a specialist in spooks,
spectres and spirits !

When asked by a " Grey-
friars Herald " representative
in Hobson's ancestral home,
where he is staying over Christmas, whether he ever felt nervous during his ghost-hunting
stunts, the music-maker of the
Shell laughed heartily.

" Me nervous of ghosts ? Not
likely ! I've seen too much of
'em to feel nervous of 'em ! "

Hoskins ran his fingers re-
flectively through his lank locks
and chuckled reminiscently.

" I could tell you tales of my
experiences with spooks and
spirits that would make your
hair stand up on end ! " he said.

Our representative, knowing
something of Hoskins' keen
imagination, winked at the
ceiling and said " Really ? "

" Why, only last week, when
I stayed a night with young
Temple of the Fourth, the
ghost of one of his ancestors
appeared," said Hoskins, drama-
tically. " We spotted it standing by a window on the landing
when we were on our way up
to bed. It was dressed in
armour and it was surrounded
by a weird, phosphorescent
light."

Our representative shuddered.

" Was Temple scared ? " he
breathed.

" Scared ? Why, I've never
seen a man in such a blue funk !
He grabbed my arm in a sort of
frenzy. ' Look, Hoskins !
Look ! ' he said, in a voice that
was hoarse with horror ! Then
he turned and ran for dear life."

" And you, Hoskins ? "

" Oh, I was as brave as a
lion, of course ! I didn't go
too near the ghost—it doesn't
do to upset them, you know.
I just retreated at my own
pace."

" Ahem ! Exactly ! "
grinned the " Greyfriars Herald " representative. " And
what other weird adventures
have you had with denizens of
the spirit world ? "

" Lots and lots," answered
Hoskins, cheerfully. " Mostly
at Christmas time, you know,
in the houses of Greyfriars chaps
with whom I've been staying.
It's queer, but that's always
where it seems to happen."

" I saw a headless figure
stalking down a corridor in
Stewart's house, and a shrouded
phantom at Rayner's place, and
a ghastly object that moaned
and clanked chains, as it glided
across the moonlit hall at
Robinson's."

" And were you equally
brave each time ? " asked our
representative.

Hoskins nodded eagerly.

" Oh, absolutely ! Ghosts
have no terrors for me—none
whatever ! Why, if I saw a
ghost now, I'd——"

What Hoskins was about to
say he would be will never be
known.

But what he did do on the
appearance of a ghost was
made quite clear to our representative the next instant.

Hoskins had stopped speaking
because a ghost had appeared !

It loomed up out of the
shadows of the library where
the interview had been taking
place—a white, spectral shape !
Hoskins took one good look at
it, let out a howl of terror, and
then just flew out of the library !

Hoskins may revel in the
company of spooks, spectres
and spirits, as he boasts. But
if his reaction at Hobson's
place is anything to go on, he
believes in revelling in their
company for a period not exceeding one split second !

Discussing the matter afterwards with the ghost, the
" Greyfriars Herald " representative was assured that Hoskins
was always the same. The
ghost declared emphatically
that any of Hoskins' other
ghosts would say the same.

The ghost, by the way, was
Hobson and his ghostly pre-
decessors were Robinson, Rayner, Stewart and Dabney.

We always thought there
must be something besides his
piano-punching that made
Hoskins so popular as a Christmas visitor !

The Wraith of Reynham Castle!
By FRANK RICHARDS

(Continued from page 13.)

Johnny Bull, quite mystified, accompanied his friends up the stairs into the King's Room.

James was there, and Bunter rapped out an order. Bunter could never see his man without giving him an order.

"Robert!" rapped Bunter.

"Yes, my lord?" said the patient James.

"Put some logs on the fire, Archibald!"

"Yes, my lord!"

"Then you can clear, Frederick! Shut the door after you, Henry!"

Johnny Bull listened to this rather like a fellow in a dream. He found his voice, when James-Robert-Archibald-Frederick-Henry had retired, and closed the door after him.

"Am I dreaming this, you fellows?" he stuttered. "What was that chap mylording that fat ass for?"

"This is where you hear the history of the jolly old mystery!" grinned Bob Cherry. "Bunter's Lord Reynham."

"Eh?"

"Positively for one occasion only!" chuckled Bob.

"Ha, ha, ha!"

"Blessed if I see anything to cackle at!" snorted Bunter. "Fat lot of good all of you fellows trying to pass for a lord, anyhow! Old Peter knew what he was doing when he picked me for the part!"

"What the thump do you mean?" howled Johnny Bull. "Trying to pull my leg?"

"Honest Injun!" said Harry Wharton, laughing. "Bunter's a giddy nobleman now! Up to last week he was only one of nature's noblemen——"

"Ha, ha, ha!"

"Now he's the genuine article—for a time! A temporary lord! After the hols he will be plain Bunter again!"

"Very plain!" grinned Bob.

"The plainfulness is terrific!"

"But what——" howled the amazed Johnny.

"Listen, and I will a tale unfold!" chuckled Bob. "Old Peter's got a ward, a rather sickly kid, the real Lord Reynham, parked in a school somewhere under an assumed name, to keep him safe from kidnappers——"

"Who've been after him for years!" said Nugent, taking up the tale.

"Nobody knows why or wherefore!" went on Bob. "But that's how it stands. Somehow the Smiler's gang spotted that dodge, though they never spotted the school or the name—see? But they were hunting for 'em——"

"So old Peter got the bright idea of letting them think that the school was Greyfriars," said Harry.

"And the name Bunter!" grinned Bob.

"So the esteemed and absurd Bunter was brought here as a ridiculous lord!" chortled Hurree Jamset Ram Singh.

"Keeping Smiler & Co. off the right track, and on the wrong one!" explained Harry Wharton. "And Bunter plays the part like one to the manner born. Don't you, Bunter?"

THE MAGNET LIBRARY.—No. 1,558.

"I rather fancy so!" assented Bunter. "Easy enough to me, you know."

"Ha, ha, ha!"

"The old bean's got a secretary, Tomlinson, who is really a detective, watching for the blighters to get after Bunter!" went on Harry. "Some day he will get them—perhaps!"

"The perhapsfulness is terrific!"

"Then the real lord will be able to show up——" said Nugent.

"As safe as houses!" said Bob Cherry. "Got it now, Johnny?"

"Oh crumbs!" gasped Johnny Bull.

"They've been after Bunter, thinking him the jolly old lord—I mean the jolly young lord——"

"Ha, ha, ha!"

"Lots of times! And we've no doubt that they've got a spy in the house, from what's happened—the kidnapper's tried to bag him in this very room!"

"Oh!" exclaimed Johnny.

"Of course, it's a deep and deadly secret; even his lordship's cousin Rupert doesn't know!" said Harry. "Not a word—not a giddy syllable. We're as good as certain that there's a confederate in the household——"

"No doubt at all about that!" said Johnny Bull, with a grin. "And the confederate in the house is the man who is bossing the business; the other three just carry out his orders!"

"Eh?"

"What?"

The juniors stared blankly at Johnny.

"How the thump do you know, when you've only just set foot in the place?" demanded Bob Cherry.

Johnny Bull grinned, and related what had happened on the foggy avenue as he came.

THE TENTH CHAPTER.

A Startling Suspicion!

"ANOTHER of them?"

There was a sarcastic inflexion in Captain Reynham's drawl. He was standing in the hall, a handsome and elegant figure in evening clothes, when the Greyfriars party came down, talking to Sir Peter. His glance turned on Johnny Bull, the latest addition to the Greyfriars party.

Perhaps he did not intend his remark to reach the ears of the schoolboys. But it did reach them, and while the Famous Five affected not to hear it, Billy Bunter gave the young Army man an inimical blink through his big spectacles.

The captain, evidently, had returned at last; for there he was, changed for dinner. He had, in fact, come in very soon after Johnny Bull's arrival, much to Sir Peter's relief, and explained that he had been looking for "William" on the downs—a statement which Sir Peter did not dream of doubting, though Billy Bunter certainly would have doubted it.

Bunter had a strong suspicion that that supercilious young man had stranded him on the downs on purpose that day, in which case it was improbable that he would have spent hours in hunting for him again.

"Another?" repeated the captain, as his uncle did not answer. "Is William bringing all Greyfriars here for Christmas?"

"William naturally desires to have some of his friends about him at Christmas-time, Rupert!" said Sir Peter. "They seem very nice boys—very nice boys indeed. I like them all!"

Rupert shrugged his elegant shoulders. Bob Cherry winked at his friends. All the juniors knew that Rupert Reynham did not like their presence at the castle—though why, was rather a puzzle, for they could hardly see how it concerned him in any way. Certainly, he had no reason to like Lord Bunter; but the other fellows had given him no offence that they knew of.

But they had observed already that the captain was a moody, discontented man, with an irritable temper. They kept clear of him as much as possible, though at times he took the trouble to make himself agreeable, and at such times he could be very pleasant.

"Who's that sportsman?" asked Johnny Bull, in a low voice.

"My cousin Rupert!" grinned Bunter. "Uppish sort of cad—a poor relation, you know. Thinks no end of himself; but I jolly well know that he hasn't got a bean, and——"

"It's Captain Reynham," said Harry. "Old Peter's nephew——"

"That's how he's hanging on here," sneered Bunter. "I never asked him here, I know that."

The juniors grinned. Lord Bunter seemed to be taking himself very seriously in his lordship's role! Really, the fat Owl seemed to imagine, by this time, that it really was his castle!

The Greyfriars fellows crossed the hall, to where the old baronet and his nephew were standing by the fire. After discussing the matter, they had decided that Sir Peter had better be told of what Johnny Bull had seen and heard on the avenue as he came.

Captain Reynham moved off a little and lighted a cigarette as the juniors approached.

Johnny Bull looked at him curiously. He had never seen Lord Reynham's cousin, but, hearing his voice, it seemed to strike his ear with a familiar note, as if he had heard it before.

"We've got something to tell you, sir—at least, Bull has!" said Harry Wharton. "He ran into those rotters, coming up the drive in the fog——"

"Is it possible?" exclaimed Sir Peter. "Please tell me, my boy."

Captain Reynham, who turned away, turned back quickly. His eyes fixed sharply on Johnny Bull.

He did not speak, but it was clear that he was keenly interested in what Bull had to say.

Johnny Bull told succinctly what had happened on the avenue. Old Sir Peter listened with the closest attention.

"You did not see either of them?" he asked.

"I couldn't, sir, in the fog," answered Johnny. "But the one who was called the Smiler must have been the kidnapper—and the other——"

"The other, his confederate, here!" said Sir Peter, knitting his brows.

"A pity you did not see him, my boy!" drawled the captain. "Haven't you any idea what he was like?"

"Only that he was tall," answered Johnny.

"Oh! You noticed that, foggy as it was, although you could not see him?" said Rupert.

Johnny Bull looked at him rather grimly. He did not like the captain's sarcastic tone.

"There was a sort of shadow in the fog, as he bumped into me," he answered quietly. "He was a good bit taller than I am, that's all. And I hit him; and I think my fist landed on his chest. I know he was a good many inches taller than I am. That's all!"

"It is little—but it is something," said Sir Peter, with a nod. "You saw nobody on the drive, Rupert? From the time you came in you must have passed the spot very soon after this lad."

"Nobody!" said Captain Reynham.

"Not even a shadow in the fog." He laughed. "You are sure that you did not fancy this mysterious encounter, my lad?"

"Quite sure!" answered Johnny Bull, staring at him. "I'm not a fellow to fancy things, Captain Reynham. We don't fancy things in Yorkshire. Facts are good enough for us."

The captain shrugged his shoulders and turned away.

Johnny Bull's eyes followed his tall, elegant figure with a grim stare.

Sir Peter left the hall, the juniors guessing that he was going to pass on this latest piece of information to his private detective, Mr. Tomlinson.

"I say, you fellows," said Billy Bunter, "if Bull's sure about that blighter being tall——"

"Of course I'm sure!" rapped Johnny.

"Well, then, we ought to be able to spot him," declared the fat Owl. "If we go over the whole place, sorting out all the tall ones——"

Bob Cherry grinned.

"There's forty or fifty people about the jolly old place—tall and short, and middle-size," he remarked. "Some sorting out."

"Well, whoever it was, must have been out of the house at the time," argued Bunter. "We can make Jasmond find out who was out at that time."

"By gum! Might be something in that," said Frank Nugent. "If it's one of Jasmond's army, he might know——"

"Make up a list of every tall chap in the place, and jolly well make him say where he was at the time—what?" said Bunter.

"Fathead! That list would include your jolly old Cousin Rupert," said Bob, laughing. "He's tall, and he was out at the time."

And the juniors laughed.

But Johnny Bull did not join in the laugh. He gave a little start, and drew in his breath sharply.

He turned from the group of juniors, and looked across the great hall at the captain, lounging and smoking his cigarette.

For a long moment Johnny's eyes remained fixed on that tall handsome figure—and his thoughts were racing.

It was impossible—impossible! But where had he heard the captain's voice before, when he had never seen the man until ten minutes ago?

The juniors chatted on till the gong went for dinner; but Johnny Bull did not join in the talk. Johnny was thinking, and strange and startling thoughts were in his mind.

THE ELEVENTH CHAPTER.

The Legend of Reynham Castle!

"SMOKE?"

"Yes, rather!" said Billy Bunter promptly.

He stretched out a fat hand towards the cigarette-case.

Four juniors said nothing. A faint grunt was audible from Johnny Bull—that was all.

It had been a jolly evening.

The Greyfriars party were gathered in the music-room. Sir Peter had joined them there, and, somewhat to their surprise, Captain Reynham.

Hitherto, the captain had displayed little taste for cheery boyish society. Now, however, he seemed to like it, and there was no doubt that he succeeded in making himself very agreeable. Even Billy Bunter thought that

he was not, after all, such a beast as he had seemed to be.

Rupert sat at the piano and played. The schoolboys enjoyed a "sing-song" —Christmas carols and school songs, especially the Greyfriars School song. And then Bob sorted out a volume of Gilbert and Sullivan. Even Billy Bunter contributed a fat squeak, though his musical efforts were a little marred by the fact that he had forgotten the words, and did not remember the tunes.

But it was quite a merry evening, and the captain made himself very useful at the piano, and sat with a paper cap on his head, evidently in the best of tempers. Sir Peter left them to themselves, after a time. And, as it was holiday-time, all the fellows stayed up a good deal past their usual bedtime.

But the captain rose from the piano at last, and stretched himself, and took out his cigarette-case. As if unthinkingly, he offered it to his companions— apparently forgetful of the fact that they were schoolboys.

Billy Bunter helped himself to a smoke at once. That was one of Billy Bunter's little ways. Bunter would always smoke a cigarette, if he could get the same for nothing. He was not ass enough to spend money on smokes, but he liked to be, as it were, an inexpensive man of the world.

"Got a match, Wharton?"

"Fathead!" answered Harry politely.

"Yah!" retorted Lord Bunter, forgetting for the moment that he was a peer of the realm, and answering like a common mortal—a very common one, in fact.

Harry Wharton looked rather curiously at the captain. Rupert had made himself very agreeable that evening; but it was difficult to know what to think of a man who offered cigarettes to schoolboys.

Bunter was the only member of the party who accepted a smoke.

Bunter found a match, and lighted up, puffing out smoke with a great air of enjoyment.

"Dash it all, put on a smoke, you fellows!" said the fat Owl. "Quelch hasn't got his eye on you now. No prefects about. He, he, he! Have a smoke, Bob, old chap! Be a man for once—like me!"

"A man—like you!" gasped Bob. "No, thanks!"

"Ha, ha, ha!"

"Sorry," said the captain; "my mistake." He slipped the cigarette-case back into his pocket, and helped himself to a cigar. "I'm hardly used to juvenile society. Really, I quite forgot. Of course, you boys don't smoke."

"No," said Harry politely.

"The smokefulness is terrifically bad for the esteemed and ridiculous wind," explained Hurree Jamset Ram Singh. "It has a spoilful effect on a fellow's form for Soccer. Likewise, it produces retardfulness of the idiotic growth."

"Oh, exactly!" gasped the captain. "Quite! Perhaps you had better not finish that cigarette, Cousin William."

"I'll watch it," grinned Bunter.

"Christmas Eve," remarked the captain. "A famous date in the history of this ancient place. Probably you boys are unacquainted with the legend of the castle, except, of course, William."

"Eh?" said William.

William knew very little about Reynham Castle, except that the food there was remarkably good.

"Ghost story?" asked Bob, with interest. "Let's hear it before we go to bed. What's Christmas without a jolly old ghost?"

"If you'd like to hear——"

"Yes, rather!" said Nugent. "The ratherfulness is terrific!"

"William, of course, knows the story," said the captain. "He must have heard it a good many times in his childhood here."

Harry Wharton & Co. made no rejoinder to that. The captain was not in the secret. He took "Lord Bunter," at face value, as it were, never dreaming of suspecting that the youth was not his Cousin William.

The juniors, of course, could tell him nothing, as they had promised the deepest, strictest secrecy to Sir Peter. But it made them feel a little awkward.

Captain Reynham believed—as Sir Peter had made all the castle believe— that the young lord had been placed at Greyfriars School under the name of Bunter, to protect him from kidnapping.

The astute old gentleman had allowed Smiler & Co. to discover that "fact," and Bunter's presence at the castle under his lordship's name made it scarcely possible for them to doubt it.

Such a scheme, strange as it was, was justifiable, to protect a weak and sickly lad from dangerous enemies. But the juniors would have felt more comfortable if Sir Peter had let his nephew into the secret. He seemed, to them, to be carrying caution to excess.

"You remember the story, William?" asked Rupert.

"Oh, yes! Quite! What is it?" asked Bunter.

The captain laughed.

"You have forgotten it in your long absence from home," he remarked. "But if there is any truth in the legend, you might be reminded of it when you go to bed to-night."

"Eh? How's that?" asked Bunter.

"According to the legend, the stain of the murdered earl's blood is renewed on the floor of the King's Room on the anniversary of his death."

"Gorroogh!"

"We'll look for it when we go up," chuckled Bob Cherry. "I fancy it will want some looking for."

The juniors gathered round the fire to listen to the ghost story.

Billy Bunter finished his cigarette, and threw the stump in the fire.

Outside, the wintry wind was howling round the ancient chimney-pots, and snowflakes were dashing against the windows.

Captain Reynham sat with his half-smoked cigar in his hand, listening for a moment or two to the howl of the wind round the old turrets.

"It was such a night as this," he began. "A wild winter's night—a Christmas Eve many hundreds of years ago. The Lord Reynham of that time was said to be a very wicked nobleman. It was whispered that he had slain his cousin, the old earl, in the forest, and thus succeeded to the title. It was on the eve of Christmas that the old lord had been found, run through the body, under the ancient oaks of Reynham. And when the anniversary came——"

The captain paused, to take a pull at his cigar.

"That night the new lord of Reynham was feasting high in his ancient hall," he resumed. "The wine flowed freely, and all was merriment and roystering. But as midnight chimed, a sudden silence fell on the festive hall. A chill spread through the assembled guests, and the wicked lord was seen to pause with the wine cup half-raised to his lips, and then suddenly in the midst of that deathly and eerie silence, was heard——"

Snore!

The captain was interrupted by that cheery sound from the deep armchair in which Lord Bunter was sprawling.

"Wake up, you fat ass!" said Bob Cherry, shaking his fat lordship. "You're missing the ghost story!"

"Urrggh! I'm not asleep! I heard all you fellows were saying!" mumbled Bunter. "Lemme alone!"

"William is not interested," said the captain, with a smile. "But if you boys would like to hear the rest——"

"Please go on, sir! Never mind jolly old William!"

"In the midst of the deathly silence," resumed the captain, "was heard a strange and terrible cry from the wicked earl. He started to his feet, the wine from his goblet spilling over his ruff and trunk hose. His eyes were fixed in a dreadful stare on the door. All eyes turned in the same direction, and the great oak door was seen to swing slowly open, but none was seen to enter. The door swung shut, and all were conscious of a cold and chilly presence in the crowded hall; but nothing could be seen, unless Lord Reynham saw it. His eyes, starting from his pallid face, remained fixed, following, apparently, the motions of an unseen figure that was slowly approaching him——"

Snore!

Bunter was going it again.

"Suddenly, as if at the touch of an icy hand, the Lord of Reynham leaped to his feet and fled from the hall. As he fled up the stairs, he looked back, with ghastly fear in his face, and all knew, though none could see, that some strange shape followed him——"

Snore!

"The guests and the retainers stood petrified by fear and dread. Above, a crash was heard as the door of the King's Room closed, then the jarring of locks and bolts. The wicked earl had shut himself in the King's Room——"

Snore!

"With trembling footsteps, they followed up the stairs, and gathered in an affrighted crowd outside the door of the King's Room. From within was heard the clash of steel—clash on clash, as of two desperate enemies fighting to the death. It died away at last, and there was a groan! Then deep, deep silence, broken only by——"

Snore!

"Broken only by the wail of the winter wind round the snowy turrets. At length the retainers forced the door, and penetrated, trembling, into the King's Room. And by the light of torch and cresset they saw the wicked earl lying on the floor, run through the body, in a pool of——"

Snore!

"In a pool of blood, slowly spreading over the ancient oak, glistening in the light! But of his assailant and slayer nothing was to be seen. Doors were locked and barred; the fire burned in the ancient chimney; none had entered, none had left. Yet the wicked lord had been slain in fight; he lay dead in the pool of blood, slain by a phantom hand."

Snore!

"From that day the phantom of the wicked earl has haunted the scene of his death," went on Rupert. "Every Christmas Eve the stain of blood is renewed on the oak, and every night from then till the New Year the spectre walks—and it is death to meet him!"

"Seen him?" grinned Bob.

"I have never put the matter to the test," said Rupert. "But others have

THE MAGNET LIBRARY.—No. 1,558.

done so, keeping watch in the King's Room on Christmas Eve. I have been told that such a watcher was found dead —that another fled from the room a raving maniac; but of my own knowledge, I can say nothing."

The captain's voice was very quiet and grave. The schoolboys looked at him curiously. It seemed impossible to them that the Army man could possibly attach the least belief to such a legend of his ancestors.

"Come with us, and let's look for the jolly old stain!" said Bob.

Rupert shook his head.

"It is absurd, of course, but I do not care to do so," he answered. "Really, I should not have told you the legend, but——"

"Oh, that's all right! We're not scared!" said Harry Wharton, laughing. "We'll certainly look for it ourselves, but we don't expect to have much luck!"

And Billy Bunter was heaved out of his chair and shaken into half-wakefulness, and the Famous Five marched him off to bed, after saying "Good-night!" to the captain.

THE TWELFTH CHAPTER.
The Stain on the Oak!

"JAMES!"

Billy Bunter was sleepy—fearfully sleepy. Generally ready to go to sleep, the fat junior seemed readier than ever to-night. He was so sleepy that he forgot to call James "Frederick" or "Herbert."

"Yes, my lord!"

"Take my shoes off, James! I'm sleepy!"

"Yes, my lord!"

The Famous Five did not need, like Lord Bunter, the assistance of a valet to go to bed. And, unusually late as the hour was for them, they were not thinking immediately of bed.

Bunter had heard little of the ghost story, and was not in the least interested in ghostly bloodstains on ancient oak. Bunter was sleepy, and wanted to turn in. But the Famous Five were going to give the King's Room the once-over, looking for that ghostly stain.

Not, of course, that they dreamed for a moment of believing in spooks. But, as Bob Cherry remarked, it was only sporting to give the giddy ghost a chance of showing whether he was the genuine goods or not. Certainly, as they scanned the polished oak floor of the King's Room, they had not the faintest anticipation of discerning any stain that had not already been on the old time-blackened oak.

Billy Bunter turned into the big canopied bed—once, it was said, occupied by no less a person than King Henry the Eighth, who had visited the castle in ancient days. From that stout monarch the great room took its name, and his life-size portrait was on the wall, staring down from a huge metal frame.

Ranged round the canopied State bed were five other beds, which belonged to Harry Wharton & Co. That was Bunter's scheme for keeping safe from night attacks, and so far his lordly slumbers had not been troubled.

It was, indeed, a little difficult to see how the kidnappers were to get at his lordship, with the other fellows camped all round his bed; certainly it could not have been done without giving the alarm.

First, there had been two extra beds in that room, then four, and now there were five. As fast as his guests arrived, Lord Bunter gave orders for beds to be

prepared for them in his room. Fortunately, there was plenty of space, apartments in Reynham Castle being of immense size.

Bunter was snoring as soon as his head touched the pillow. He remained happily unconscious of the proceedings of the other fellows.

They moved about the King's Room, adjoining the spacious bed-room, and scanned the old hard oak floor. They smiled as they did so—at the absurdity of the idea of looking for ghostly bloodstains.

But Bob Cherry came to a sudden stop, with a startled ejaculation.

"Hallo, hallo, hallo!"

"Found it?" grinned Nugent.

"Look!"

Bob pointed to the floor midway between the King's portrait on the wall and the communicating doorway in the bed-room.

A dark stain on the polished oak had caught his eye.

There were many stains on the old oak, trodden by countless feet through the centuries. But there was a strange freshness about that stain that startled the juniors as they looked at it.

"What the dickens——" muttered Bob.

"James!" called Harry Wharton.

"Sir!"

The valet appeared in the doorway between the rooms. He had finished with his lordship, and was about to go.

"I suppose you've heard the story about the wicked lord who was murdered in this room, James?" said Harry.

"Oh, yes, sir! It is very often told in the servants' hall at Christmas-time, sir," answered James.

"Then I dare say you know the exact spot where the bloodstain is supposed to be?" asked Harry.

"Oh, certainly, sir! Just where you young gentlemen are standing!" answered James.

"Oh!"

The juniors exchanged glances.

James glanced from face to face, and then looked at the oak floor. He gave a start, and his face paled.

"Good-night, gentlemen!" he said hurriedly. "Now that his lordship is in bed, I will go——"

"Hold on a minute!" said Harry quietly. "Look at that stain, James! Have you seen it there before?"

"No, sir!" faltered James.

"Do you mean that it is a new stain?"

"It was not there this morning, sir. I am sure of that. I was present when the maids were doing the room." James moved away towards the door while he was speaking, his eyes uneasily on the dark stain on the oak. "I—I—I don't quite understand it, sir! I—I will go, if there is nothing more, sir!"

And James went.

"Now what the thump," said Bob, in a low voice, "does this mean?"

"Goodness knows!"

Harry Wharton stooped, and rubbed the stained oak with his finger. He gave a slight shudder as, lifting the finger to the light, he saw a faint reddish stain on it. His heart beat a little uncomfortably.

"James can't have been playing tricks here, surely!" muttered Nugent. "He looked quite scared—you could see what he thought——"

"It's a trick of some kind," said Harry, "because it can't be anything else. The idea of a blood-stain renewing itself on the anniversary of a murder is—is——"

"Bunk!" said Johnny Bull.

"The

(Continued on page 20.)

READY, YOU FELLOWS? Then off we go again with—

The GREYFRIARS GUIDE

A TOUR OF THE SCHOOL. Masters' Corridor.

(1)

The Masters' Studies here are situated,
  They're studies full of gravity and gloom,
And here your breath is permanently baited,
  So let us take a peep in every room.
The first is Prout's, with many curious features,
  His Winchester repeater's seen at once,
With stuffed and mounted carcasses of creatures,
  The relics of his bygone thrilling hunts.

"I SAW THREE SHIPS COME SAILING IN!"

A Verie Olde Carol, as warbled by W. G. Bunter.

I hope my ship comes sailing in,
Comes sailing in, and brings some tin,
And if I get it, I shall grin—
  That Christmas postal order!

I've been expecting it for years,
For years and years (excuse my tears!),
I'll shout with joy when it appears,
  That Christmas postal order!

Perhaps some titled relative,
Some relative will surely give
The thing for which alone I live,
  That Christmas postal order!

Alas, the postman's gone away,
He's gone away, and sad to say
He didn't hand to me to-day
  That Christmas postal order!

Perhaps, at length, it will arrive,
It will arrive, if I'm alive,
By Christmas, 1985,
  That missing postal order!

* * *

Why are the stars like star-gazers?
  Because they have studded the sky for ages.

(2)

In Quelchy's room a typewriter is noted,
  And reams and reams of manuscripts he's done,
That glorious work, to which his life's devoted,
  "The History of Greyfriars, Volume One"!
And Wiggins has a heavy window curtain
  To make a dark-room for his photographs,
Whatever the result, it's fairly certain
  He'll be annoyed if anybody laughs.

(3)

Mossoo has lots of books in foreign lingo,
  While Capper's study's very neat and prim,
And Hacker's foreign curios—by jingo!
  Those swords and spears are typical of him!
And Larry Lascelles boasts of many a trophy,
  With cups and caps and silver shields galore,
While Twigg's content with poetry and coffee;
  It's very quaint—the Masters' Corridor!

THE GREYFRIARS ALPHABET

PATRICK GWYNNE, The Irish Sixth Form Prefect.

G is for GWYNNE—an Irish coon,
And, faith, he's not a bad gossoon!
No, on the whole, he's not so bad,
And that is kind of me, bedad!
For here's a thing I'd have you know:
He gave me six a week ago!
Six whistling wallops on a spot
Where every pain feels extra hot!

And on the Christmas vac I take
A most uncomfortable ache!
Yet, notwithstanding this, I say
He's not so bad—the pesky jay!
He's second prefect, Wingate's chum,
And always smiling, never glum.
At sport he's grand and plays to win,
So here's a MERRY CHRISTMAS,
  Gwynne!

XMAS GRINS

It seems a strange way of accepting a Christmas present to want to whop somebody. Luckily Loder doesn't know who sent him the cigars! (I bet he smokes one though, all the same.)

A famous London store is advertising "Fifty New Lines in Christmas Gifts." That's nothing—Quelchy's just given me five hundred!

One of this year's Christmas bargains is a model railway so true to life that the trains are always late.

Our local railway is offering "Reduced Fare for Christmas." As long as our kitchen staff don't copy 'em that's O.K. by me.

Quelchy's so fond of dishing out lines this Christmas that some of us are wondering whether he will go a bit further and leave us a few lines in his will!

PARTY PUZZLE

A Christmas traveller was heard whistling "Good King Wenceslas" to the tune of "Home, Sweet Home." What was his profession?

Solution at foot of column.

Fisher T. Fish doesn't trust anyone, not even Father Christmas. He is putting a padlock and chain on the stocking he will hang up on Christmas Eve.

Peter Todd says the weather is too cold to put your nose outside the door. Of course, in Toddy's case, when his nose is out most of him is out, so this may be true.

ANSWER TO PARTY PUZZLE

A magician! Nobody else could whistle words!

ANOTHER JOLLY JAUNT WITH OUR JOVIAL GUIDE NEXT THURSDAY!

"The bunkfulness is terrific!" murmured Hurree Jamset Ram Singh. But his dark eyes dwelt on the stain with a gleam of uneasiness in them.

"But what silly ass can have played such a trick?" said Bob. "Why, we should never have looked for the beastly thing at all, if Rupert Reynham hadn't happened to tell us the ghost story this evening! We'd never have heard of the jolly old wicked lord till an hour ago."

"And we certainly shouldn't have noticed it on the dark oak if we hadn't specially looked for it!" said Harry.

"That's a cert! If anybody played this trick, he must have played it for nothing—he couldn't have known that we were going to hear about the beastly thing.——"

"Blessed if I can make it out," muttered Nugent.

"If the fellow who put it there fancied that we should see it, it might be a trick to scare us!" said Harry slowly. "One of the kidnapping gang is a member of this household—and from what Johnny heard, it seems that that one is their leader. He can't like us here protecting our prize porpoise—in fact, Johnny heard him say so. If he did this——"

"That's it, of course!" said Nugent, relieved. "Why, of course! It's a rotten trick to put the wind up Bunter's bodyguard. I dare say he thinks we knew all about the ghost story—Lord Reynham would naturally know, and the old porpoise is Lord Reynham now——"

"Well, he won't frighten us very easily, if that's the case!" said Harry. "I suppose the rascal, whoever he is, could have sneaked in here and done this. It's a trick, at any rate."

"Let's get to bed," said Bob. "We shall be fancying next that we hear the jolly old wicked lord groaning."

Groan!

The five juniors started violently, and stared round them. The sound that reached their ears was a low, faint groan coming from whence they could not guess.

"Did you hear——"

Harry Wharton ran to the door, opened it, and looked out into the bed-room—with a suspicion that Bunter might be playing a trick. But his fat lordship was in the canopied bed, fast asleep, and snoring.

Harry Wharton set his lips.

"You fellows all heard that?" he said. "There's no doubt about it now—some blighter has set out to give us a scare. By gum! I wish he would show up in reach of a fellow's knuckles!"

"Better see that all the doors are safe before we turn in," said Bob. "Bunter generally goes to that—but he's gone off to sleep to-night, and forgotten it."

The Famous Five made a careful round, looking to all the outer doors. There were three doors on the corridor; from the King's Room, the bed-room, and the dressing-room. Each one of them was carefully locked and bolted.

The locks on the doors were heavy, old-fashioned, and very strong; but Lord Bunter had on his first day in the castle, ordered bolts to be put on, and Lord Bunter's orders had been carried out.

The juniors were rather glad of it now. Locks might be picked; but bolts were a different proposition. When they went to bed, they did so in the absolute certainty that no one could enter without waking them.

But, late as the hour was, they did not fall asleep so easily as usual.

That strange story of the ghostly fight in the King's Room ran in their minds; and, though they were sure that a trick had been played, the bloodstain on the oak, and that ghostly groan were uncanny, and a little unnerving. It was long after the chimes of midnight that they slept at last.

THE THIRTEENTH CHAPTER.

The Spectre of Reynham Castle!

HARRY WHARTON awoke suddenly.

He had been dreaming.

In his dreams was pictured the strange tale he had heard of the spectre of the castle. He seemed to see the hall door opening to an unseen hand, as the captain had related, and the wicked earl, starting up with spilling wine-cup, gazing at the dread figure that no other eyes could see. In the visions of slumber he followed the desperate man in his flight to the King's Room, and heard the crash of locks and bars—the clash of steel—the dying groan. He awoke with a start and a shiver, and stared into the darkness about him.

Was he dreaming still?

He sat up, staring in the gloom. There had been a fire in the room, but it had long ago died out, and all was dark.

But a red gleam of glowing logs met his eyes, glimmering through the dark. It came from the ancient hearth in the King's Room adjoining.

He gave a start and a shiver.

All the outer doors of the rooms had been locked and bolted. The communicating door between the King's Room and the bed-room had been closed, but not fastened. There was no occasion to fasten an inner door, when no one could possibly obtain admittance to any of the rooms.

But that door, which had been closed, was now partly open. Through the gap came the glimmer of the fire in the King's Room.

Harry Wharton gazed at it fixedly.

The door could not have opened of its own volition. Yet it was partly open—and, as he gazed, he saw that it was slowly opening wider.

The darkness was deep. But the fire-light in the adjoining room, glimmering through the aperture, showed it growing wider and wider.

Wharton heard a gasp from the darkness. It came from one of the other beds.

He whispered, a faint, husky whisper.

"Is that you, Frank?"

"Yes! Did you hear?" breathed Nugent's voice.

"I woke——"

"Something woke me," whispered Nugent. "I—I think it was a—a groan! I—I'm sure I heard——"

"So did I!" came a whisper from Bob Cherry.

Harry Wharton, his heart beating hard, peered round in the gloom. In the faint glimmer that came from the next room, he could dimly make out his comrades—all of them sitting up in bed, their eyes fixed on the slowly opening door.

Bunter did not stir. His deep snore went on uninterrupted. But the Famous Five were all wide awake.

"Can you see?" came a startled whisper from Bob. "That door——"

"The wind!" muttered Johnny Bull.

"It was latched, and there's no wind —the windows are shut——"

"Then what——"

The whispers died away. The five

schoolboys sat and stared as if fascinated at the door—slowly, slowly pushing open.

Wider and wider the space grew; clearer the red glimmer from the crackling logs in the King's Room.

It was strangely, eerily, like the ghost story they had heard—and what, in the name of all that was horribly mysterious, could it mean? No one was in the King's Room—no one could be there, unless he could pass through solid walls or solid doors, locked and bolted. Yet that door was opening to an unseen hand.

Spellbound they watched with throbbing hearts.

The door stood wide open at last, and the doorway was no longer vacant. The juniors could not believe what they saw. Yet they saw it.

A figure in the ruff and doublet and trunk hose of Tudor days, but all a spectral whiteness, stood there.

The face was in shadow, as it looked towards them; but they could make out that it was a ghastly, lifeless whiteness, with two eyes that gleamed and glittered as if from a dead mask of white.

The blood seemed like ice in their veins as they gazed.

It was strange, ghastly, unbelievable —but they had to believe what their eyes saw. Backed by the ruddy glimmer of the logs, the figure stood there—silent, spectral, blood-curdling.

Unable to stir, hardly able to breathe, the horrified schoolboys watched petrified.

It seemed to them that the gleaming, glittering eyes passed from face to face, watching them, scanning them. For a long minute, that seemed an hour to the juniors, the spectral figure stood, their amazed eyes glued to it.

The fire in the King's Room, behind the figure, blazed up; the sudden flame throwing into relief every detail of the ghostly form.

Then it died down again, and for a moment there was darkness.

Petrified, the blood seeming to congeal in their hearts, they watched the dark doorway, the spectral figure growing dim and disappearing.

The firelight blazed up again.

The doorway was empty.

Like a bodiless phantom the spectre had vanished during those few moments of darkness.

They could see into the King's Room; the fire blazed up, showing empty space. They did not stir. The horror of what they had seen froze them.

A long, long minute passed. Then at last Harry Wharton made a movement. With set teeth, he slipped from his bed.

"Harry——" whispered Nugent.

"It's a trick!" muttered Wharton. "I tell you it must be a trick! I'm going in there——"

"Don't!" muttered Frank. "Don't!"

"I tell you it's a trick!"

"It—it must be!" stammered Bob. "But—but—but how did anyone get in? How could anyone get in?"

"I'm going to see!"

Wharton grasped a stick from his bed-side and stepped towards the doorway.

In a moment his comrades were out of bed and following him. Every nerve in their bodies shrank from the horror of what they had seen—but they were not letting him go alone.

They reached the doorway and gazed into the King's Room. The fire died down—all was dim shadow.

Wharton reached to a switch and flashed on the electric light.

Sudden illumination flooded the great room. It showed the King's Room as they had left it—empty; it gleamed on the walls, on the polished furniture, the

King's portrait looking down from its great metal frame—but nothing more. There was no sign of the spectre.

"Come on !" muttered Harry.

He stepped through the doorway. His friends followed him. In silence, with beating hearts, they searched the room.

No one was there. They examined doors and windows. The door on the corridor was locked and bolted, as they had left it; the windows were fastened.

They gathered again in a bewildered group. No human being could have entered the King's Room by door or window. Was it, then, a supernatural vision that they had seen?

"What——" muttered Nugent. His face was white.

Harry Wharton stared round at the walls. Reynham Castle was an ancient building, and the thought of secret passages and secret doors came into his mind.

But it came only to be dismissed. The walls of the King's Room were of oak over solid stone blocks. But that ancient oak, black with age, had been papered over and covered with a cheerful tint.

Oak panels might have moved to a secret spring, but papered walls would have shown a break.

The captain of the Remove passed slowly round the room, scanning and examining every wall, and his friends, as they guessed his thought, followed him.

But there was no sign of a break in the wallpaper to be detected—there was no secret panel in the wall.

Solid walls, bolted doors, fastened windows at a great height from the ground, surrounded them. Yet they knew what they had seen.

In spite of reason, in spite of common sense, they seemed to be driven to the belief that the spectre of Reynham Castle had appeared to their eyes, haunting the scene where the wicked earl had been slain in that ghostly combat long years ago.

In silence they returned to the bedroom. Bunter, undisturbed, was still snoring. They looked at him. The ghostly groan that had awakened them had not awakened Bunter.

The chums of the Remove were deeply shaken, but had Bunter's eyes seen what they had seen there was no doubt that the fat junior would have been paralysed with terror, and they were glad that he had slept through it.

They said nothing; even Johnny Bull, hardest-headed member of the Co., had nothing to say. They returned to their beds—but not to sleep. The light was left on—but sleep was impossible. Pale and weary, they were glad, at last, when the dim dawn of Christmas Day glimmered in at the windows.

THE FOURTEENTH CHAPTER.

A Bump for Bunter !

"**M**ERRY CHRISTMAS !" chirped Billy Bunter.

He blinked at the juniors in the other beds.

It was ten o'clock.

Billy Bunter, sitting up in bed to breakfast, was merry and bright. The Famous Five were neither.

Generally the juniors were up and out long before his lazy lordship thought of turning out in the morning. They never had the least inclination to follow Bunter's example of slacking in the holidays.

Bunter had had, as a rule, to be satisfied with James and a couple of footmen remaining with him after the juniors had gone down, his bodyguard abso-

lutely refusing to stay until his fat lordship rolled out of bed at ten or eleven.

This morning, however, they were still in bed at ten o'clock. They had dropped off to sleep after dawn, after hours of dismal wakefulness.

"I say, you fellows, you're jolly slack this morning !" said Bunter, blinking round at them. "I had to get out of bed to let James in. I called you, Wharton, and you didn't answer. What's the matter with you all ?"

"We were up in the night !" said Harry curtly.

"Eh ?" A well-laden fork stopped half-way to Bunter's capacious mouth. "I say, I never woke up ! What's happened ! The kidnappers——"

"No !"

"Oh, all right, then ! I say, you look a peaky lot !" Bunter grinned. "That chap Reynham was telling us a ghost story last night, wasn't he ? Been seeing ghosts ? He, he, he !"

What would have happened, had Bunter awakened and seen the spectre of the castle, the juniors knew well enough. It was doubtful whether all the attractions of playing the part of a nobleman would have kept him at the castle, had he seen that awful apparition.

But he had not awakened and he had not seen it, and that made all the difference. In broad daylight Bunter feared no phantoms.

The Famous Five, turning out of bed, looked at one another. Frosty sunlight gleamed in at the windows. The fog of the day before had rolled away and Christmas morning came fresh and bright. In the clear, fresh morning their strange and terrible experience of the night seemed like some ghastly dream.

Yet it had been real !

One fellow might have dreamed, or fancied, that fearful vision—five fellows could not have done so. Whether it was a trick that they could not understand, or a vision from another world, they had seen the spectral figure in the doorway of the King's Room.

With the return of daylight, belief, or half-belief, in the supernatural seemed absurd. And yet——

"Let's get out !" said Bob. Out-of-doors, in the fresh air, was Bob's cure for all worries and troubles.

"But I say, you fellows, what's happened ?" asked the fat Owl. "Did you dream that you saw a ghost, or what ?"

"No, fathead !"

"Well, you're looking fearfully peaky !" grinned Bunter. "I can see that you've had a scare ! He, he, he !"

The juniors compressed their lips. They had no doubt that their faces betrayed the strain they had been through.

"You fat ass !" growled Johnny Bull. "I wish we'd woke you up now, and you'd have seen it, too."

"Then you did see something ?" grinned Bunter.

"Yes, fathead !"

"Well, what was it ?" asked Bunter. "Tell me ! I say, you fellows, why didn't you call me ? I'd have snaffled the ghost. He, he, he ! It would take a bit more than a spook to frighten me ! He, he, he !"

"You podgy, pernicious porpoise !" exclaimed Bob Cherry. "If you'd seen it you'd have woke the whole castle with your howls."

"He, he, he ! Tell me about it," grinned Bunter, with his mouth full of kidneys and bacon. "What was it frightened you ?"

"We weren't frightened, fathead !"

"You look as if you were !" chuckled

Bunter. "You're as white as a sheet, Nugent, old chap."

"Ass !"

"You're all of a tremble, Wharton !"

"Fathead !"

"Somebody's been larking with you, I can see that ! I say, you fellows, I was so sleepy last night I forgot to lock the doors. I suppose somebody came in and gave you a scare !"

"We locked and bolted all the doors, idiot !"

"Then how did you get a scare ?" asked Bunter. "Think a ghost came down the chimney ! He, he, he !"

"Oh, shut up, you cackling ass !" growled Johnny Bull. "Look here, you fellows, it gave us a turn, and no wonder; but it's all gammon—a rotten trick of some sort ! There ain't such a thing as a ghost !"

"Of course not !" chortled Bunter. "I dare say you saw a shadow or something. What was it like ? Gurrrrrrgh ! Urrrggh ! Wurrggh !" Chortling, with his capacious mouth full of kidneys and bacon, caused trouble. Bunter choked and gurgled. "Ooogh ! Grooogh ! Wooogh ! Bother you—making a fellow laugh when his mouth's full ! Groogh !"

Bunter cleared his fat neck, and chortled again.

"I say, you fellows, cough it up !" he urged. "Do you really fancy you saw that ghost that Reynham was telling us about ?"

"Yes, we saw it, fathead !" snapped Harry. "Now dry up !"

"He, he, he !"

"We saw it," said Johnny Bull, glaring at the gurgling fat Owl, "and it was some sort of gammon. Now shut up !"

"He, he, he ! Wake me up when the ghost walks again !" chuckled Bunter. "I'm fearfully keen on ghosts ! He, he, he !"

"Well, according to the tale, it will walk again—every night from Christmas Eve to the New Year !" said Bob. "And we'll jolly well wake you up next time, you fat, gurgling gargoyle."

"Oh, do !" grinned Bunter. "I'll protect you ! You won't find me looking peaky in the morning, after seeing a ghost ! I'll jolly well get it with a bolster. Why didn't you shy a pillow at it ?"

"Shut up, you ass !"

"He, he, he ! I say, you fellows, do you call this plucky ?" asked Bunter. "Look at me going through all sorts of dangers here, without turning a hair—and you fellows conk out like that, because you see a shadow or something ! This will make them laugh when I tell them in the Remove studies next term ! He, he, he !"

The Famous Five glared at the chortling fat Owl. But glares had no effect whatever on Lord Bunter. Bunter had the advantage now; and when Bunter had an advantage, he was the fellow to use it.

"You needn't scowl at a fellow because he's got pluck and you haven't," grinned Bunter. "If you'd woke me up, I'd have shied a pillow at it ! Next time you see something awful and horrible, chuck a pillow at it !"

"That's a tip !" said Bob Cherry.

He stepped to his bed, and picked up the pillow therefrom. As he swung it in the air, the fat lord of Reynham Castle blinked at him in alarm.

"Here, I say, wharrer you up to ?" gasped Lord Bunter.

"Chucking a pillow at something horrible !" answered Bob.

"Ha, ha, ha !"

"I say—yaroooooh !" roared Bunter, as the pillow flew, and crashed.

It caught Lord Bunter under his fat chin, and spun him out of bed.

There was a heavy bump on the floor, and a crash and a clatter as Bunter's well-laden tray landed on Bunter. Bacon and eggs, kidneys and tomatoes, jam and marmalade, toast and grape-fruit, fell over Bunter like leaves in Vallombrosa of old.

"Yarooop!" roared Bunter. "Beast! Wow! Beast!"

"Ha, ha, ha!"

"Ow! Oh crikey! Wow!"

Billy Bunter sat up amid the wreck of his breakfast, like Marius in the ruins of Carthage. He sat up and roared.

"Ow! Beast! Wow! I'll jolly well have you turned out of my castle! Yarooh! Wow! That kidney's gone down my back—urrgh—I'm all jammy—groogh—ow! You beast—wow! Ow!"

"Ha, ha, ha!"

"Ooooooooogh!"

Billy Bunter did not chortle any more. For the next quarter of an hour, his remarks were chiefly "Ow!" and "Wow!" and "Beast!"—and he was not feeling in the least inclined to chortle.

THE FIFTEENTH CHAPTER.
Christmas Night!

"LEAVE the light on!"

"What?"

"That's all—leave it on!"

Christmas Day had passed pleasantly enough at Reynham Castle, but the Greyfriars fellows were looking forward to Christmas Night with mixed feelings.

So, it appeared, was Bunter—when the night came.

During the day, the fat lord of Reynham had made quite a number of playful remarks about fellows who were frightened by ghosts. Bunter had been, in fact, fearfully amused on that subject. But when he rolled up to bed, his amusement seemed to be gone, and he was observed to blink round him a little uneasily.

Bunter was sleepy. He was, in fact, yawning his fat head off when the juniors went up to bed. There was a whiff of cigarette smoke about Bunter. His last proceeding, before going up, had been to smoke one of the captain's cigarettes—not, certainly, because he wanted to, but just to show what an independent man of the world he was.

Sleepy as he was, he was not too sleepy to remember the ghost story. And the fact that the spectre was, according to the legend, due to reappear every night till the New Year, seemed to haunt the fat junior's mind. Dark, wintry night, it appeared, made the ghost story less amusing to his fat lordship.

"You bloated blitherer, what do you want the light left on for?" demanded Johnny Bull.

"Well, you fellows might be frightened again!" explained Bunter. "Better leave it on! You haven't got my nerve, you know!"

"The nervefulness of his esteemed lordship does not seem to be terrific," remarked Hurree Jamset Ram Singh.

"I'm only thinking of you fellows, of course," said Bunter. "I don't want to be disturbed in the night by a lot of duffers getting into a blue funk! Just you leave that light on!"

And Bunter dropped his fat head on to the pillow, and snored.

Doors were locked and bolted, as on the previous night; but the Famous Five were quite aware that locks and bolts would not keep out the spectral visitant.

THE MAGNET LIBRARY.—No. 1,558.

"Might as well leave the light on!" said Frank Nugent. "The fact is, I should like it left on, as well as that fat ass!"

Harry Wharton nodded.

"Might as well!" he agreed.

Johnny Bull looked round at his comrades. There was a deeply thoughtful expression on Johnny's face.

"Better turn it off!" he said.

"Bunter will make a fearful row, if he wakes up and finds himself in the dark," said Frank, "and if he saw that spook he would go into a fit."

"Blow Bunter!" Johnny Bull sank his voice to a whisper. "Just turn in as usual, I'll turn off the lights. I've got a reason."

The four looked at him. In the strange circumstances, they would have felt more comfortable, with the fires banked up high in both rooms, and all the electric lights left on. But they nodded assent.

There was no objection from Bunter—he was already fast asleep and snoring. Four of the juniors turned in, and Johnny Bull was left to turn off the lights.

None of them was likely to sleep. The more they thought about that ghostly visitation, the more convinced they felt that it was some sort of eerie trickery, though they could not explain it. But trickery or not, there was little doubt that the ghost would walk again.

Whether it was some ghastly trick to frighten them away from the castle, or whether it was the phantom of the wicked old earl, the spectre was due to reappear. And four members of the Co. would have been glad to have the light on.

But Johnny Bull, after turning off the lights and seeing that the fires were too low to illumine either room, did not go to bed.

Harry Wharton started, as he felt a tap on his shoulder.

"What——" he began.

"Quiet!" whispered the voice of Johnny Bull. "That jolly old ghost who can walk through solid walls may be able to hear through them! See?"

"But what——"

"Get out and dress," whispered Johnny. "We're sitting this one out, old bean. I'm going into the next room—now it's dark—to watch——"

"Oh!" gasped Wharton.

"If that ghost walks again, I've got a pretty thick stick, and I'll see whether he's solid enough to bang it on!" came Johnny's whisper. "You fellows stay here—and if he shows up in the doorway, I'll get him from behind! See?"

"Oh!" repeated Harry.

"After last night, he fancies he's got us scared stiff. The fact is, we were scared—no good denying that. But we're not going to be spoofed twice in the same way. If the ghost walks again to-night, I'm getting him."

Johnny's whisper was quiet and steady. The practical, hard-headed Yorkshire junior had thought the matter out, and resolved on his line of action. He did not believe that the ghostly visitation was supernatural; he believed that it was a trick, and he was going to act on his belief.

Wharton shivered a little. He had plenty of courage, and plenty of nerve, but the thought of that ghastly vision in the dark was unnerving.

"Look here, you're not going alone!" he whispered. "I'll come——"

"Two's a crowd—one's enough! We've got to be jolly careful they don't spot anything. The ghost wouldn't walk if he knew!"

"But——"

"Leave it to me. You keep close to

a switch, and be ready to turn on the light. Tell the other fellows."

"Oh, all right!"

Johnny Bull glided noiselessly away in the darkness.

Wharton, his heart beating, crept out of bed, and in a few minutes he had whispered Johnny's plan to Bob Nugent and Hurree Singh.

The three juniors turned out at once, and they dressed quietly in the dark. Bunter snored on undisturbed. In dense darkness, the four waited. They heard no sound from Johnny Bull.

Johnny had opened the door of the King's Room, and, leaving it wide open, crept into the adjoining room. There was not even a glimmer from the fire—he had taken care of that.

In what way the mysterious visitant obtained entrance to the King's Room he did not know, and could not guess; but he did not doubt that there was a way in—there had to be, unless the spectre was a visitor from another world. And by that way, it was more possible that observation could be kept on the room.

In that case, a mere glimmer of light would have been enough to warn the trickster. If Johnny had been seen on the watch, the real spectre might have walked, but certainly a trickster would hardly have made the venture.

The sturdy junior made his way noiselessly in the dark apartment. He had mapped out what he was going to do. Two big armchairs had been left standing with the high backs near together. Between those high chair-backs Johnny Bull crouched, on his knees, with a stick grasped in his hand.

All was silent and still.

Long, long minutes passed—the time seemed endless. Every minute seemed an hour in the darkness and the silence of midnight. It was eerie, creepy, waiting there, in deep silence, unable to see his hand before his face—waiting for a ghostly form to loom in the gloom.

But Johnny had his nerves well in hand.

The winter wind wailed round the ancient turrets. From the bed-room came Bunter's unceasing snore. There was no other sound—as dreary, endless minute followed minute.

And then at last there came, suddenly, a faint, faint sound in the silence.

Johnny Bull felt the blood rush to his heart.

He could see nothing, but he knew that he was no longer alone in the King's Room in Reynham Castle.

THE SIXTEENTH CHAPTER.
Laying the Ghost!

JOHNNY BULL did not stir.

He waited.

His heart was thumping. In the blackness, in the eerie silence of the haunted room, something like a superstitious thrill ran through him.

In that room, with bolted doors and fastened windows and solid walls, there was some strange presence. Earthly or unearthly, it was strange, thrilling. But he kept cool and waited and listened.

Only blackness met his eyes.

But his ears were on the alert. Again a faint sound came to him. Then there was a faint red glow in the darkness.

Johnny Bull's face set grimly. He knew what that meant. Whoever was

"I say—yarooooooooh!" roared Billy Bunter, as the pillow flew, catching him under his fat chin and spinning him out of bed. There was a heavy bump on the floor, and a crash and a clatter as Bunter's well-laden tray landed on his fat person.

in the room was stirring the embers of the fire, softly and cautiously. The reason hardly needed guessing. Some sort of light was necessary to make the spectre visible—proof enough that it was no phantom.

The red gleam from the stirred embers grew brighter. A dim glow spread through the room.

Something white and spectral glimmered in the gloom.

Johnny Bull lifted his head, silently, cautiously, and peered at it. In the dim red glow he could see the open doorway from the King's Room to the bed-room. In that doorway stood a figure—the spectral figure in doublet and hose and ruff—white as the driven snow.

Four juniors in the bed-room were facing it—but Johnny Bull, from the King's Room, saw it from behind.

Silently he rose to his feet.

He stepped swiftly out of cover behind the ghostly figure in the doorway, a thick stick gripped in his hand. That stick was uplifted as he stepped behind the ghostly form that stared into the bed-room.

It came down with a crashing blow.

But it did not pass through a bodyless phantom. It crashed on something solid—and there was a loud, startled, savage cry as the spectral figure lurched over and crashed.

At the same instant there came a sudden flood of illumination, as the electric light was switched on in the bed-room.

"Look!" yelled Bob Cherry.

Just within the doorway sprawled the phantom figure on its hands and knees. Johnny Bull's blow had caught it across the shoulders, hurling it over. The juniors gazed at it as it was

revealed in the sudden blaze of bright light.

Only for a moment the spectral figure sprawled. Then it bounded to its feet, gasping, and spun back to the doorway.

Grimly and ruthlessly, Johnny Bull lashed at it again with the stick, and the blow landed on the spectre's head.

The strange figure staggered back, with a yell of rage and fury.

Harry Wharton & Co. were springing on it the next moment.

There was no hint of the supernatural now—the cheat was revealed. It was a solid and living body that had caught the crashing blows from Johnny's stick—and in a moment the four juniors were grasping it, and they found it solid enough.

"Bag him!" gasped Bob.

Four pairs of hands grasped the spectre of Reynham Castle. Johnny Bull's were added the next moment.

The white-clad figure struggled madly. It was evidently a very powerful man who was in the grasp of the Famous Five, and he fought desperately for his freedom.

But, powerful as he was, he was no match for five determined fellows. Grasped on all sides, he was dragged to the floor.

Bob Cherry's knee was planted on his chest. Nugent and Hurree Singh had hold of his arms. Wharton's arm gripped his neck—Johnny had him by the doublet. He wrenched and heaved and struggled; but he had no chance.

Still, for several long minutes the struggle went on. The strange intruder of the night did not yield until he was breathless and almost exhausted. But the juniors did not let go for a

moment, and he lay helpless in their grasp at last.

"Got him!" panted Bob.

"We've got the rotter!" said Harry Wharton breathlessly. "Get hold of something to tie his paws. He's as strong as a horse! Bunter! Bunter! Turn out, you fat duffer!"

Only a snore answered from Bunter.

It seemed strange enough that the noise of the struggle had not awakened even a hefty sleeper like Bunter. But he did not wake. Deaf to the sounds around him, deaf to Wharton's shouting voice, the fat lord of Reynham Castle snored on.

"Wake up, fathead!" bawled Bob Cherry.

Snore!

"By gum! That fat ass can sleep!" gasped Bob. "Hold the brute while I get something to fix him!"

Bob ran to the nearest bed, grabbed a sheet, and wrenched it into strips. The spectral visitant was still struggling; but he was held fast, and in a minute or less strips of sheet were bound and knotted round his wrists.

Then he was allowed to rise to his feet.

He stood gasping and panting in the midst of the juniors. His eyes were blazing with fury from the dead whiteness of his face.

That face was unknown to the juniors—but Wharton, as he scanned it, burst into a laugh. It was a close-fitting white mask that covered the face from forehead to chin, giving it its ghastly aspect; and it was through eyeholes that the fierce eyes glittered and gleamed.

The captain of the Remove grasped the mask and peeled it off. Then the light shone on a hard-featured face that all the juniors knew.

"The Smiler!" yelled Bob.

"The kidnapper!" gasped Nugent.

The Smiler spat with rage. Strange enough, the dark, evil face of the crook looked, over the Tudor ruff round his neck. It was the Smiler who had played the part of the spectre of Reynham Castle!

"And now," said Johnny Bull, "we'll see how this beauty got in! He won't get out again the same way in a hurry!"

Bunter snored on, as the Famous Five led their enraged prisoner through the doorway into the King's Room. Harry Wharton switched on the electric light there, and they looked round the room with eager eyes. It was now certain that there was a secret way into the room—the presence of the kidnapper was a proof of it.

"Hallo, hallo, hallo!" yelled Bob. "Look!"

He pointed to the portrait of King Henry VIII. The juniors stared at it. One side of the big metal frame jutted from the wall.

The tall picture-frame was a door, opening on hidden hinges. The intruder had left it a few inches ajar for his retreat.

"Oh, my hat!" said Wharton.

He ran to the picture, grasped the thick metal edge, and pulled it wider open. Beyond was a dark cavity; and he had a glimpse of a narrow spiral stair leading downwards through the massive thickness of the ancient wall.

"By gum!" ejaculated Bob. "That's it, is it? That's how they got at the jolly old porpoise the other day!"

"And that's the way he was going, if they got hold of him," said Harry. "There must be an outlet at the other end, or this rascal couldn't have got in. If the fat ass had been here alone——"

"They'd have had him all right!"

"No doubt about that!"

"Now we'd better call old Peter, and see this rotter fixed up for the police to call for him!" said Bob. "Your game's up now, Mr. Smiler—no more kidnapping stunts for you!"

The Smiler stood scowling and gritting his teeth, as the juniors proceeded to give the alarm. His game was up—the ghost had been laid: and the spectre of Reynham Castle had walked for the last time!

THE SEVENTEENTH CHAPTER.

Mysterious!

SIR PETER LANCHESTER blinked, in amazement. His startled eyes seemed almost to pop from his face.

Loud ringing of bells, and calling voices startled the whole household. A crowd gathered in the corridor outside the King's Room.

Sir Peter entered, in his dressing-gown, a thick malacca in his hand—after him came Mr. Tomlinson, the detective, and Captain Reynham. Jasmond hovered in the doorway, half-dressed—behind him a startled crowd of menservants. Almost all the castle had been roused.

"What—what—what——" stuttered Sir Peter.

He stared at the Smiler, in his Tudor costume—considerably ruffled and rumpled by his struggle with the juniors. He stared at the picture standing open like a door from the wall. He seemed hardly able to believe his eyes. Indeed, he hardly could.

Mr. Tomlinson was equally astonished. Neither did he seem wholly pleased.

The detective was there to watch over his lordship and snaffle any kidnapper who came after him. So far, he had done no snaffling. But the Greyfriars fellows evidently had.

Captain Reynham was a little pale, seeming more startled than any other of the startled crowd.

The juniors did not give him any special attention—excepting Johnny Bull. Johnny had not forgotten the familiar note in the captain's voice, which reminded him of the voice he had heard in the fog on Christmas Eve.

Johnny Bull's eyes were on the captain: and he saw Rupert Reynham's startled glance fix on the prisoner: and the steady look that the Smiler gave him in return.

Only for a second, however, did the captain look at the captured man. Then he walked across the room to the King's picture, and stood looking into the cavity behind it—his back to the others in the room.

"What—what——" Sir Peter seemed hardly able to speak. "What—what—what has happened here?"

"The ghost walked—and we laid him, sir!" said Bob Cherry, grinning. "Meet the spectre of Reynham Castle!"

"But what—what——" stammered the old baronet. "How—what——" he pulled himself together. "Who is this man?"

"The Smiler!" chuckled Bob.

"The kidnapper!" gasped Sir Peter.

"That very identical bean! We've tied him up to keep him out of mischief —but a pair of handcuffs would come in useful."

Mr. Tomlinson seemed to wake from his amazement. He stepped towards the Smiler, and there was a clink of metal. The kidnapper's eyes gleamed as the handcuffs were snapped on his wrists. Johnny Bull noted, grimly, that his glance shot round to the captain for an instant. But Rupert Reynham was still standing with his back to the rest. Johnny would have liked to see his face at that moment—but only his back was to be seen.

"Tell me——" gasped Sir Peter.

The juniors related what had happened in the night.

Sir Peter listened in amazement, but with great satisfaction dawning in his face.

This was the success of his deep-laid scheme. He had planned that Bunter, playing the part of the young lord, should draw the kidnapping gang into the trap. True, he had planned that his detective should be on hand when the attempt was made, and lay the rascal by the heels. That part of his scheme had not worked. But the Greyfriars juniors had played the part Mr. Tomlinson had been intended to play. Here was the kidnapper—a prisoner!

"Amazing!" said Sir Peter. "I had no knowledge of a secret door into this room—none whatever! Did you know anything of it, Jasmond?"

"Nothing!" gasped the butler.

"There is a legend that an ancient lord of Reynham was slain in this apartment, and that the murderer escaped, though the doors were locked and barred," said Sir Peter. "Evidently that secret door was known in the old days—and someone has discovered the secret since to make this use of it. You knew nothing of this, Rupert?"

Captain Reynham turned round from the secret doorway. If he had had a shock, as Johnny Bull strongly suspected, he had recovered—and his manner was as cool and nonchalant as usual.

"Quite a surprise to me," he drawled. "Who would have thought it?"

"Someone, certainly, must have made

the discovery, and passed on the knowledge to this rascal!" said Sir Peter. "It is proof, if one were needed, that he has a confederate in this household. Only some inmate of the castle could possibly have made such a discovery."

"Really, it almost looks like it!" said the captain with a nod. "Perhaps the good man will tell us how he came by the knowledge!" He fixed his eyes on the Smiler's scowling face. "Now your game is up, my good fellow—you may as well make a clean breast of it!" he went on. "How did you find out about this secret door into Lord Reynham's room?"

"Answer!" rapped the baronet.

"Find out!" snarled the Smiler.

"If you have a confederate in this household," said the captain, sternly, "you may as well name him. It may make things easier for you."

The Smiler looked at him, a strange gleam in his eyes.

"I ain't saying anything!" he grunted.

"Well, we have you safe enough, at all events," said Captain Reynham. "I suggest, uncle, that this man should be safely locked up for the night, and the police informed. They can get here early in the morning to take charge of him. I will myself sit up till dawn and keep guard over him."

"Mr. Tomlinson will take charge of the man, Rupert!" said Sir Peter.

"Now that my cousin William's enemy has been taken, I am rather unwilling to lose sight of him, until he has been handed over to the police," said Captain Reynham. "If Mr. Tomlinson takes charge of him, I will share his watch— we cannot make too sure of him."

"Very well, if you wish, Rupert."

Johnny Bull drew a deep breath.

He had been wondering whether Captain Reynham would make any suggestion of that kind. Now he had made it.

But he said nothing.

"Where is William?" asked Sir Peter, glancing round. "Surely William has not remained asleep during all this disturbance?"

Harry Wharton laughed.

"He's a pretty good sleeper, sir!" he answered. "He hasn't woke up!"

Sir Peter Lanchester smiled.

"Well, well, if that is the case, there is no need to disturb him," he said. "Mr. Tomlinson—Rupert—take that man away!"

The Smiler was led out of the room, walking—with a scowling face between the captain and the detective.

Sir Peter crossed over to the secret door and examined it with much surprise and interest.

"You never knew anything about that, sir?" asked Johnny Bull.

"Nothing!" said Sir Peter. "Its existence might have been guessed, from the old legend of the castle, however. To-morrow those recesses shall be explored—Mr. Tomlinson may find some clue that might be useful to him."

The juniors smiled. They had already made up their minds that they were going to explore the secret passage behind the wall of the King's Room, on the morrow.

"There is a bolt on the inner side," said Sir Peter, scanning it. "Recently oiled, as you see. There appears to be no other fastening." He pushed the heavy picture frame into its place,— it closed without a sound. "Perhaps you had better place some heavy article of furniture against it. for the rest of the night—it cannot be fastened on this side. My dear boys, I do not quite know how to thank you for the service you have rendered."

Sir Peter beamed at the juniors.

"I admit," he added, "that I was a— a little disconcerted, when William proposed to bring his Greyfriars friends here—in the circumstances—but it has turned out very fortunately. Very fortunately indeed. We now have the leader of the gang in our hands—and I have little doubt that once he is in the hands of the police, his accomplices will be found, and my ward secured from danger at last. I thank you, my boys— I thank you most heartily for this great service."

And Sir Peter left the juniors to themselves.

He was feeling very pleased with them: and they were feeling very

"Well, if Bunter had woke up, he would have been scared more than any of us. He would very likely have cleared out of the castle—at least, he would have changed his rooms, and they'd have had no more chance of getting at him by the secret passage."

"I suppose so! But——"

"So it didn't suit them for him to wake up!" said Johnny.

"I suppose they banked on the fat ass being a heavy sleeper," said Bob. "They'd know that much about him."

"They couldn't have banked on us not waking him up. They had to be certain that he slept through it."

"How could they be, fathead?"

"They had to be, or the whole game

result of the shaking. He showed no signs of waking up.

"Good heavens!" breathed Harry.

"Look here, we've got to make sure about this!" said Nugent. "Roll him out of bed! That will wake even Bunter, if——"

"It won't—this time!" said Johnny Bull calmly.

Johnny was right. It did not. For five minutes the juniors tried to wake Bunter—and failed. He was in a deep, and evidently drugged, sleep, from which it was impossible to awaken him. They left him at last, and as his fat head rested on the pillow again, he snored.

GROANS for CHRISTMAS!

THE MOANING MONK. (Ghost to Greyfriars School, by appointment): "Christmas is a snare and a delusion. I'm a hard-working ghost, anxious to earn my living — or non-living — by haunting as many people as the Ghosts' Trade Union permits. Yet what happens? Just as I'm ready to put in a good night's haunt, the boys break up for Christmas, and I'm reduced to haunting Master Fish, who spends his holidays at the school.

"Mind you, I haunt Master Fish very thoroughly. Indeed, I keep his hair permanently on end during the Christmas vac. But it is a waste of talent.

It is small satisfaction to me to drive Master Fish nightly up the nearest chimney when I might be spreading dismay and terror through an entire school. I feel that my moans are of really first-class quality. Let me give you a sample moan — there's no charge——" (But I left hurriedly at this point.)

THE RED EARL. (Ghost of Mauleverer Towers): "Speak not to me of Christmas, thou scurvy malapert. I could a tale unfold whose lightest word would harrow up thy soul, were I not infringing the copyright of Hamlet's ghost—the varlet! Ha, ha! So that scurvy Monk would groan at driving one pestilent numbskull up the chimney! What would he say to a job like mine?

"Grammercy, sir, I tell thee this. He should try haunting a lord who could sleep peacefully through the veriest

> Our Special Reporter has the fearful job of finding out what ghosts think of the Festive Season.

earthquake. Time after time, beshrew me, have I roared myself hoarse by the rogue's bed. I have haunted him so terribly that, odd's my life, I've frighted myself and fled in terror. And not an eyelid, sir, has the fool batted. He might have been sleeping in a hammock beneath the whispering trees for all the notice he took of me. Beshrew me, it's wearing me to a shade!"

OUTSIZED OSWALD. (The awe-inspiring spectre of Bunter Court): "I say, you fellows, Christmas is awful. It's the worst time of the year. It's all very well for these Moaning Monks and Red Earls to grouse, but they don't know what hardship means.

"I first became a ghost one Christmas when I thought I had room for just one more mince pie. I crammed it in and burst on the spot. Well, as soon as I was a ghost, I started haunting the kitchen. Most Bunters do that without waiting to become ghosts.

"The agony is fearful. You see, old fellow, ghosts can't eat, and to see all those turkeys, puddings and pies simply asking to be wolfed is more than flesh

and blood can bear — or ghosts, either. I have to watch Billy and the others shovelling the stuff away, and I can't get so much as a mouthful. I'm sure it will be the death of me.

"By the way, old fellow, did you say you have five bob you don't want? I'm expecting a ghostly postal order in the morning. Don't walk away while a fellow's talking to you—) BEAST!"

AWFUL ALGERNON. (The blood-curdling phantom of Popper Court): "Don't talk to me of Christmas, sir. Dashed impudence. I know you, boy—I saw you pulling down one of Sir Hilton Popper's 'Trespassers Will Be Prosecuted' boards. Don't blame you, either. Last Christmas, after I'd haunted him, he put a 'Ghosts Will Be Prosecuted' board on his bed-room door.

"Gad, sir, I'm fed up with haunting Sir Hilton at Christmas-time. He believes in looking on the wine when it's red—looks pretty hard, too. Consequence is, he takes things like me as a matter of course. The room being full of spotted eagles, he doesn't notice a mere ghost. Good mind to resign, sir, and haunt a temperance hotel—only I'd have to sign the pledge, and that's a thing no Popper would ever do!"

And if Sir Hilton Popper sees this, the next ghost to be interviewed will be Terrible Tom Brown, the Phantom Reporter, slain by a Bad Baronet!

pleased with themselves, as they went back to the bed-room where Bunter was still snoring.

"By gum! He can sleep!" said Bob, grinning at the fat Owl in the canopied bed. "Fancy even Bunter not waking up with all that row going on."

Johnny Bull stood by the fat Owl's bedside and looked hard and keenly at Bunter's sleeping face. Then he looked at his friends.

"Bunter didn't wake up last night," he said quietly, "and he's not woke up to-night. If he had woke up it would have spoiled the game of those rotters."

"Eh?"

"What?"

"Look at it!" said Johnny, in the same quiet tone. "That ghost business was meant to scare us away and leave Bunter unprotected. It can't have had any other object."

"That's so, but——"

was no good," answered Johnny Bull stolidly. "So they made sure of it. Bunter's been drugged!"

"Drugged?" gasped Bob.

"He was drugged last night, and he was drugged again to-night," said Johnny. "It won't hurt him. He woke up all right this morning, and he will wake up all right to-morrow morning. They're kidnappers, not murderers. But you couldn't wake him now, at any price."

The Co. looked at Johnny, with startled faces. Then Bob Cherry stepped to the canopied bed, grasped the sleeping Owl by the shoulder, and shook him.

Bunter's eyes did not open.

Shake, shake, shake!

"Gurrrrggh!"

The fat junior's snore changed to a stertorous grunt. But that was the only

"By gum!" said Bob. "This is awfully thick! He's drugged!"

"The drugfulness is terrific!"

"But who——" said Nugent.

"The leader of the gang—the man in the castle—the man I heard talking to the Smiler in the fog!" said Johnny Bull.

Harry Wharton looked steadily at the Yorkshire junior.

"I don't quite make this out!" he said slowly. "It seems to me, Johnny, that you know something you haven't told us."

"I think I do," assented Johnny, "but I've got to be sure. I think there will be proof in the morning, and then I'll jaw fast enough."

"How do you mean?"

"If the Smiler is gone in the morning I shall be sure!"

"Fathead! How could he get away,

with the handcuffs on him, and Tomlinson and Captain Reynham watching him?"

"Well, we shall know in the morning!" said Johnny Bull enigmatically. "If the Smiler is still here, safe for the police to take him away, I've made a mistake, and the least said the soonest mended. If he's gone, I shall know where to put my finger on the scoundrel who is after Lord Reynham, and I'll jaw as much as you like. Now I'm going to bed."

And Johnny Bull went to bed, and his puzzled and perplexed comrades followed his example.

THE EIGHTEENTH CHAPTER.

Gone !

BOXING DAY dawned frosty and bright.

Harry Wharton & Co. were up early that morning, regardless of the fact that they had missed a great deal of sleep the previous night.

Billy Bunter was still fast asleep when they went down, but James and a footman were left in attendance, as usual, to watch over his fat lordship till it pleased him to wake.

Neither Sir Peter nor the captain was to be seen when the Famous Five went down. The portly Jasmond presided over breakfast, in the breakfast-room overlooking the snowy terrace.

"They haven't come for that kidnapping sportsman yet, Jasmond?" asked Bob Cherry.

"No, sir. I understand that Sir Peter intends to telephone to the police station at Castlewood as soon as he comes down," answered the butler. "The master is not down yet."

"Man still safe—what?" asked Bob, with a wink at the Co.

Johnny Bull's extraordinary suspicion that the prisoner might be gone in the morning rather amused Bob.

"Eh? Yes. I presume so, sir!" answered Jasmond. "He was placed in the gun-room, and Mr. Tomlinson, I understand, remained the whole night with him, and is still there."

"And Captain Reynham, too?"

"No, sir; I think Captain Reynham went to bed, after all; his breakfast has been taken up to his room," answered Jasmond.

Four members of the Co. smiled. Rupert Reynham had seemed very keen to keep a watchful eye on the captured kidnapper; but it seemed that he had soon got fed-up with it, and left it to Tomlinson.

But Johnny did not smile. He looked very thoughtful.

Having finished breakfast, the Famous Five went out into the hall.

Harry Wharton glanced at Johnny Bull's thoughtful face with a faint smile.

"Now——" he said.

"What about going and waking him up?" asked Johnny.

"Bunter? Why?"

"No; not Bunter."

"Who, then?" asked Harry, staring. "Tomlinson!"

"Are you trying to be funny, or what?" asked Bob Cherry. "Do you fancy that a detective went to sleep, with a dangerous prisoner to guard?"

"Yes."

"Then you're a silly ass!" said Bob. "Look here, what is it you've got in your fat head, Johnny? You're too jolly mysterious."

"The mysteriousness is truly terrific!" said Hurree Jamset Ram Singh, turning his dark eyes in wonder on the Yorkshire junior.

"Look here, Johnny——" began Harry.

"I told you," said Johnny stolidly, "that if that sportsman got away I should have something to tell you. Let's go and see."

"Tomlinson is there. Jasmond said so."

"What's the good of that, if he's asleep?"

"But he isn't, fathead, and can't be."

"Why not?" asked Johnny. "Bunter was made to sleep pretty sound last night. Why not Tomlinson?"

"Oh!" exclaimed Harry, startled.

"Hallo, hallo, hallo! Here's the old bean!" murmured Bob, as Sir Peter Lanchester came down the staircase.

The old baronet greeted the juniors with a kind and cheery smile. He was evidently in great spirits that morning. The capture of the kidnapper had been an immense relief to him. He beamed on the Greyfriars chums.

"I am now about to ring up the police station," he said. "You boys will be required to make a statement when the police arrive for that scoundrel. Please do not be too far away."

"Hadn't you better give him a look-in, sir, before you phone?" asked Johnny Bull. "If he happened to have got away——"

Sir Peter laughed.

"That is very unlikely," he said. "My nephew tells me that he remained with him till three in the morning, and when he went to bed Mr. Tomlinson remained on the watch. He is still with him, my boy."

"Johnny thinks he may have bolted in the night, sir!" said Bob, grinning.

"Impossible!" said Sir Peter. "However, I will certainly go and make sure that he is safe."

The old gentleman walked away to the gun-room, and Johnny Bull followed him. The other fellows followed Johnny, smiling a little. The idea that a handcuffed man, watched by a detective, could have escaped, seemed to them too absurd to be entertained.

Sir Peter opened the door of the gun-room and stepped in.

The next moment the cheery smile was wiped from his ruddy face, as if by a duster. He uttered almost a roar of surprise and rage.

"Gone!"

"What?" gasped Harry Wharton.

The Famous Five fairly leaped into the room after the old baronet. The gun-room had one occupant. That was Mr. Tomlinson, sprawling in a deep armchair, fast asleep.

A window was open—snowflakes drifting in on the wind. That told the way the Smiler had gone. But of the Smiler there was no sign.

THE NINETEENTH CHAPTER.

Johnny Bull Surprises the Co. !

HARRY WHARTON & CO. walked under the leafless, frost-rimed branches in the park.

Light snowflakes whirled on the wind, and fell around them. Johnny Bull walked in silence, and his friends waited for him to speak. What Johnny had to say, he meant to say out of reach of possible listening ears.

They had left Sir Peter in the gun-room—shaking the startled Mr. Tomlinson into wakefulness. The old baronet had been very angry and excited, which was not surprising, and the detective absolutely overwhelmed with confusion and dismay. If he had, as Johnny had hinted, been drugged, like Bunter, the effect had worn off. He awakened when Sir Peter shook him. The juniors, unwilling to witness his humiliation, left at once—not envying the hapless detective what he was going to hear from Sir Peter.

Four members of the Co. were puzzled and perplexed. What Johnny Bull knew, they could not guess; but it was clear that he knew something. They were eager to hear what it was.

"Cough it up, old bean!" said Harry, as they entered the frosty park. "Nobody here to listen, if that's what you're thinking of."

"Just that!" said Johnny. He glanced round, scanning the snow among the frosty trunks, and seemed satisfied. "All right! I've found out who's the nigger in the wood pile—the man behind this kidnapping business. Now I know who he is, I know why, too! I couldn't be sure till——"

"Till you found that the Smiler had got away," said Harry. "Yes, you said so. But I don't see——"

"Blessed if I do, either!" said Bob. "If poor old Tomlinson was drugged, as Bunter seems to have been, he doesn't know it—and I'm dashed if I can see how he was got at! Captain Reynham was with him, too, up to three o'clock, from what old Peter says. So it must have been after that. But how?"

"Before that!" said Johnny.

"Fathead! Think somebody got at Tomlinson while the captain was sitting with him in the gun-room?"

"Yes!"

"Well, that beats it!" said Bob. "You're dreaming, old man! Think the captain would have left him going off to sleep?" He laughed. "Do you really think that a drug could have been shoved at Tomlinson without his knowing, and under Captain Reynham's eyes?"

"He may have smoked a cigarette with the captain," said Johnny Bull calmly. "There was a cigarette-end in the ashtray at his elbow."

"I dare say he did—why shouldn't he?" said Bob. "What the thumping dickens are you driving at, Johnny Bull? Can't you keep to the subject?"

"Keeping to it, old bean," answered Johnny.

"Seems to me you're talking out of the back of your neck," said Bob rather crossly. "Tomlinson went off to sleep—but it's practically impossible for him to be got at with a drug. I'm blessed if I understand how Bunter was got at, either, if you come to that. We eat and drink the same as he does, though not so much—and they've never got at us!"

"That beats me," said Harry slowly. "If they could drug Bunter, why couldn't they play the same game on us? Then they needn't have played that ghost business to scare us away—they simply had to put us to sleep, and walk Bunter off under our noses by the secret passage."

"The tricky blighter couldn't get at us as he did at Bunter!" answered Johnny Bull.

"Why not?"

"We don't smoke!"

Printed in England and published every Saturday by the Proprietors, The Amalgamated Press, Ltd., The Fleetway House, Farringdon Street, London, E.C.4. Advertisement offices: The Fleetway House, Farringdon Street, London, E.C.4. Registered for transmission by Canadian Magazine Post. Subscription rates: Inland and Abroad, 11s. per annum; 5s. 6d. for six months. Sole Agents for Australia and New Zealand: Messrs. Gordon & Gotch, Ltd., and for South Africa: Central News Agency, Ltd.—Saturday, December 25th, 1937.

That reply caused Johnny's companions to come to a sudden halt, stand round him, and stare at him. If Johnny had suddenly turned into a griffin, they could not have stared at him harder.

There was a long moment of silence. The captain of the Remove broke it.

"What do you mean?"

"What I say!" answered Johnny Bull. "We don't smoke! If we did, we should have been served with drugged cigarettes, sent to sleep, and Bunter would have been walked off."

"Drugged cigarettes?" gasped Nugent.

"Yes. As we declined the jolly old smokes, the only thing was to take advantage of Bunter being a silly ass, let him smoke one, and send him to sleep, and spring the ghost business on us."

"It was Captain Reynham who gave Bunter a cigarette," said Harry Wharton, in a low, tense voice.

"I know!"

"You don't mean—you can't mean that——"

"I do!"

"Johnny!" gasped Nugent.

"Potty?" inquired Bob Cherry.

Johnny Bull smiled faintly. He had astonished his friends—or, rather, he had astounded them. They looked at him as if they fancied that he was wandering in his mind.

"Unless you're potty, old man, you've spotted something," said Harry, at last. "Cough it all up, for goodness' sake."

"You remember the evening I came, what happened in the fog on the drive. Talking in the hall, Bob mentioned that Captain Reynham was a tall man, and had been out at the time——"

"That was a joke, you fathead!" exclaimed Bob. "Just a joke, because it would put the captain on Bunter's list, if——"

"I know! But it made me think of something," said Johnny. "The captain's voice seemed familiar to me, as if I'd heard it before—though I'd never seen him. That remark of yours, Bob, put it in my mind where and when I'd heard it."

"Not——" breathed Nugent.

"Talking to the Smiler in the fog!" said Johnny, with a nod. "He was the sportsman who bumped into me, and who I knocked over."

"You—you think——"

"I know—now!" said Johnny stolidly. "Up in Yorkshire we don't jaw till we know a thing for certain. I had to be sure before I jawed—a thing like this is too jolly serious for idle chatter."

"I should think so!" breathed Harry.

"Hearing a voice once, and in the fog, too," said Bob, "you couldn't be sure—you couldn't possibly——"

"Haven't I said so? I banked it in the back of my mind, meaning to make sure before I opened my mouth too wide."

"Are you telling us that you've made sure that Captain Reynham, nephew of our host here, is a dastardly villain in league with kidnappers?" breathed Wharton.

"Yes!"

"Oh crumbs!" gasped Bob. "I fancy old Peter would want a lot of proof before he swallowed that! Dream again, old man!"

"Let us hear the esteemed rest, my excellent Johnny!" said Hurree Jamset Ram Singh. "There is some morefulness to come."

"Lots!" said Johnny Bull. "I wasn't sure, as I said, only wary! I had my eye on the captain. That was all. It might have been a similar voice I heard

in the fog. Still, there was something to go on. From what he said, he was clearly one of the household—he was tall —and he was out of the house at the time—all these details apply to Rupert Reynham, as well as the man in the fog. But—it seemed fearfully thick——"

"It did—and does!" said Bob.

"If I'd been sure, I should have known why he gave Bunter cigarettes. I simply thought, like you fellows, that he was rather a blackguardly, careless ass to offer cigarettes to schoolboys. But when we found out last night that the fat ass was drugged, I guessed. I knew he was drugged before we looked at him —the row we had made scrapping with that brute would have awakened Rip van Winkle. I knew he was drugged— and knew why."

"Yes, but——"

"He would have preferred to give us the dose—but we weren't taking any. So Bunter was sent to sleep, while they put up the spectre game to frighten us. It was in that cigarette. He couldn't get at the food—how could he? Dozens of servants about—and a man in his position trying to mess about with the grub! The cigarette did it."

"It's only suspicion——"

"Is it?" said Johnny. "When they came to the King's Room last night, I waited for the captain to suggest that he should take charge of the Smiler—his pal. He did!"

"Oh!"

"Old Peter put it up to Tomlinson, and Rupert had to stand for it. But it didn't worry him a lot," added Johnny sarcastically. "He sat up with Tomlinson in the gun-room, and they smoked a cigarette in company. He left him at three, to be safely off the scene when the Smiler cleared—knowing that Tomlinson would be fast asleep. I fancy he came back later, and helped his pal to get clear of the handcuffs, before he dropped from the window, too. Tomlinson was fast asleep then, of course."

"Oh!"

"I knew, or as good as knew, that the Smiler would be gone this morning," said Johnny. "I left it at that, for proof. I knew that if he were gone, the captain must have shut Tomlinson's eyes somehow. Easy enough to offer him a cigarette—same as Bunter. Tomlinson did smoke a cigarette—one of the captain's——"

"I noticed the fag-end in the ashtray at his elbow," said Harry slowly. "But you can't tell that it was one of the captain's."

"I can," said Johnny calmly. "I looked at it. It was the same brand as the one he gave Bunter."

"Oh!"

"Now," said Johnny quietly, "I've told you. Now run over in your minds the times Bunter has been in danger here. What was the captain doing at the time? From what you've told me, they nearly had him on Christmas Eve morning, out riding on the downs. Who left him alone there?"

"Captain Reynham," said Harry, in a low voice.

"You've mentioned that last week they nearly had him on the Castlewood road—after a car broke down, and you had to walk. Whose car was it?"

"Captain Reynham's," repeated Harry.

"Who told us the ghost story the night the ghost walked for the first time?"

"Captain Reynham."

"He's the man!" said Johnny. "The man in the fog told the Smiler there might be a way of getting rid of Bunter's friends. The same night, the

captain spun us the ghost story—and then the ghost walked. If we'd helped ourselves to his smokes, it would have saved him a lot of trouble. Lucky we're not jolly old men of the world like Bunter!"

"But——" gasped Bob. "If—if—if— you're right—my dear chap, he's young Lord Reynham's own cousin—his only near relation."

"That's why!"

"Eh?"

"He will step into the whole bag of tricks if anything happens to Lord Reynham!"

"Oh!" gasped Bob.

"It beat me," went on Johnny, "why crooks who tried to kidnap a kid of eleven should keep up the game years on end—it couldn't be for ransom! They wouldn't and couldn't stick to it for years for a reason like that. But the next man on the list for the earldom had a good reason for sticking to it. I'll bet you Tomlinson has thought of that. Any detective would. He hasn't said so to old Peter—he couldn't—but I'll bet that he advised leaving the captain out of the secret—letting him believe, like all the rest, that Bunter was the real lord."

"But——" Harry Wharton gasped. "Johnny, old man, do you know what you're saying? Kidnapping wouldn't do the trick. The next heir couldn't step in, unless Lord Reynham was dead!"

"I know that. But he isn't villain enough for that!" said Johnny Bull. "He's a discontented, hard-up son of a younger son; but he's not an awful villain. I think very likely he doesn't think himself a villain at all. Our beautiful laws give landed property to the eldest son—it's law, but it's no good calling it fair play, because it isn't! I imagine that a lot of younger sons feel anything but brotherly when their eldest brother walks off with all the boodle, and leaves them without a bean."

"Well, yes; but——"

"There's a big property, and it all goes to young Lord Reynham. Rupert gets next to nothing. I fancy he's brooded over it till he's worked it out in his own mind that, if the law won't give him his share of the family loot, he's going to help himself, if he can! That means that he's a reckless, discontented, unscrupulous adventurer! But knocking his cousin on the head would be a horse of another colour! So he banked on kidnapping—and if young Lord Reynham ever falls into the hands of that gang, he will disappear—and never be heard of again!"

"But——"

"After a time, death would be legally presumed, if the chap never showed up again, of course. Or they might fix up evidence of something of the kind—spoof evidence—which would be good enough if the young lord was never seen again. And you can bet that they've a safe place ready to park him in if they get him. When they had hold of Bunter, thinking he was the young lord, they let out that he was to be taken across the sea!"

The juniors stood silent, heedless of the snowflakes falling round them.

Johnny had given them a shock.

It was a new idea to their minds; but now that it was there, a crowd of little circumstances cropped up in their minds that gave more and more colour to it.

There was a long silence.

Johnny Bull broke it.

"That's the lot!" he said. "I couldn't speak out till I was sure—I'm sure now. The captain put that gang after young Reynham when he was a little kid—and when he was abroad, himself, clear of suspicion of anything that happened. Old Peter beat them by parking the kid at a school somewhere under an assumed name. They spotted that trick—lately. It's only lately that Captain Reynham came home—and he found that much out. Lucky for the poor kid that he never found out more—or they'd be after the real lord instead of that fat ass Bunter. What do you fellows think about it?"

"Blessed if I know what to think!" said Harry.

"Same here!" said Bob.

"The samefulness is terrific!"

"Leave it at that," said Johnny. "No good saying anything, anyhow. All we can do, so far, is to carry on—watching over Lord Bunter. But we know whom to watch now—and if we can catch him on the hop, old Peter's ward will be safe from him. That's what we want. Leave it at that!"

The juniors walked back in silence to the castle.

Johnny Bull had no doubt—but his friends, though they, too, had little doubt, could not quite make up their minds to it. In fact, they hardly knew what to think—but they had, at all events, plenty of food for thought!

THE TWENTIETH CHAPTER.
Bunter Knows!

"I SAY, you fellows!"

Billy Bunter was down when the juniors came in. He seemed to be waiting for them. He frowned at them impatiently over his big spectacles.

"I wish you fellows wouldn't go marching off when I want to speak to you!" said Bunter irritably.

"Did you want to speak to us?" asked Bob mildly. "If we'd only known!"

"You wouldn't have gone out, I suppose?"

"Wrong! We shouldn't have come in!"

"Ha, ha, ha!"

"Oh, really, Cherry! Look here, you fellows. I've jolly well found something out—I fancy I've spotted the man!" said Bunter, sinking his voice to a mysterious whisper. "The confederate of those rotters in the castle, you know!"

"Wha-a-t?"

The Famous Five stared at Bunter, startled.

Bunter nodded.

"They've been telling me about what happened last night," he explained. "I think you fellows might have woke me up. But never mind that. You got that villain, the Smiler, and he got away again. I suppose you've heard?"

"Sort of," agreed Bob.

"Well, that settles it!" said Bunter. "His confederate has helped him to get away," of course—and I jolly well know who it was, too! Think I'd better tell old Peter?"

The Famous Five gazed at Bunter.

Johnny Bull had, or believed that he had, spotted the man; and his chums had little doubt that he was right. But they certainly had never dreamed of Bunter spotting the man. They gazed at him—and Mr. Tomlinson, looking out of the doorway of the smoke-room, gazed at him, too.

Bunter, as he stood facing the surprised five in the hall, had his back to the door of the smoke-room, and did not observe Sir Peter's detective looking out.

Mr. Tomlinson had a view of the back of Bunter's fat head. He stared at it, evidently surprised by the fat Owl's words.

"You see, the awful rotter's pulling old Peter's leg!" went on Bunter. "Taking his pay, you know, and pulling his leg all the time!"

"Oh!" ejaculated Harry.

And he smiled! Bunter evidently had been thinking it out, and was satisfied that he had made a discovery. But from his words, it was clear that his discovery was not the same as Johnny Bull's.

The fat Owl's suspicions were fixed upon some person who was taking Sir Peter's pay—evidently someone employed in the castle.

Of what they knew, or believed that they knew, the Famous Five had resolved to say nothing. They had no proof to offer; and obviously Sir Peter Lanchester would have required the clearest and strongest proof to convince him that his nephew was the young lord. It was a case where the least said was the soonest mended—until actual proof transpired.

So, in the circumstances, it was rather a relief to find that Billy Bunter had not come to the same conclusion. Evidently he hadn't.

"Who's the jolly old sportsman, then?" asked Bob Cherry, with a grin.

"I should have thought you fellows would have guessed!" grinned Bunter. "But, of course, you haven't my brains! Clear enough to me! That man Smiler was snaffled last night—well, who was left to guard him in the gun-room?"

"Mr. Tomlinson and Captain Reynham! But what—"

"Well, the captain went off to bed, and left Tomlinson alone with him," said Bunter. "Old Peter believes that Tomlinson went off to sleep—"

"So he did!"

"He, he, he! Old Peter's been ragging him for going to sleep and letting the man get away!" grinned Bunter. "Of course, he never really went to sleep."

"What?"

"Spoof, of course!" said Bunter. "He's the man!"

"He—he—he's the man!" gasped Harry Wharton.

Bunter grinned and nodded. Behind him, quite an extraordinary expression was coming over the face of Mr. Tomlinson. As the Famous Five were facing him, they could see him, though Bunter couldn't—having, of course, no eyes in the back of his fat head!

Mr. Tomlinson's look was quite alarming!

"Tomlinson's the man!" said Bunter.

"Shut up, you ass!" gasped Nugent.

"Tomlinson——"

"Shan't!" said Bunter.

"I tell you, Tomlinson——"

"He's the man—taking old Peter's pay, you know, and accomplicing—I mean confederating—with the kidnappers all the time," said Bunter. "Letting that man Smiler go is proof of it! You fellows would never have guessed that."

"No fear!" gasped Bob Cherry. "Look out, you fat ass—oh crumbs—look out!"

"Eh? Look out for what?" asked Bunter. "Wharrer you mean? Now, what I want to ask you fellows is, do you think I'd better go to old Peter, and say—whooop! Yarooop! Whooop! Who's that?- What—yarooooop!"

Billy Bunter roared as a sudden grasp was laid on him from behind.

Mr. Tomlinson, with a face red with wrath, had made a jump out of the doorway of the smoke-room!

Bunter's remarks seemed to have annoyed the detective. Perhaps that was not surprising.

Mr. Tomlinson had never treated Bunter with the respect due to a noble lord; perhaps because he knew that he wasn't one! But now he treated him less respectfully than ever.

He grabbed Bunter with his left hand and spun him across a chair. His right hand rose, and descended in a series of terrific smacks on his lordship's lordly trousers.

Smack, smack, smack, smack!

"Yaroop!" roared Bunter. "I say, you fellows—yoo—hooop!"

"Ha, ha, ha!"

Smack, smack, smack!

"Yow-ow-ow-ow! Help! I say—yarooop!" yelled Bunter. "Leggo, you beast! Yow-ow! Oh crikey!"

Smack, smack, smack!

"Whooooop!"

"Ha, ha, ha!"

Two or three startled servants came running into the hall; and Mr. Tomlinson, releasing Bunter, stalked back into the smoke-room. Bunter was left yelling.

"Ow! Wow! I say, you fellows—yaroooh!" roared Lord Bunter. "I'll have him sacked—I'll have him booted out of my castle—I'll—yoo-hoo-hoooop!"

"Ha, ha, ha!" roared the Famous Five.

"Beasts! I say—wow! Wow! Wow!"

"Ha, ha, ha!"

There was quite a roar in the stately hall of Reynham Castle. Harry Wharton & Co. roared with laughter. Billy Bunter roared—not with laughter! But he roared the loudest! Indeed, just then, the Bull of Bashan, famed for his roaring, had nothing on Lord Bunter—not a thing!

THE END.

(The final story in this splendid Christmas series is better than ever, chums. It's entitled: "LORD BUNTER'S BODYGUARD!" Watch out for it next THURSDAY!)

The Magnet

2ᴰ

Billy Bunter's Own Paper

LORD BUNTER *takes the* PLUNGE!

SPECIAL CHRISTMAS WEEK ISSUE OF—

The GREYFRIARS GUIDE

A TOUR OF THE SCHOOL.
By a HOLIDAY ANNUAL.

(1)

'Twas only just a month ago
  That I was newly bought and splen-
    did,
But now I'm torn and smudged and
    worn,
  And my career's completely ended.
With spotless pages, colour plates,
  And stories, humorous and pleasant,
Bob Cherry thought the book he bought
  A most delightful Christmas present.

CHRISTMAS CRACKERS

Old Inky doesn't worry
  When he goes out carolling,
For he can always "Hurree"
  If the folk won't let him "Singh."

It's a lovely Christmas dinner—
  Lick your tongue!
Bird's-nest soup and tender snails,
Choice rat-pies with puppies' tails,
Curried cats and frog and whales—
It's a lovely Christmas dinner
  For Wun Lung!

When Skinner sent an almanac
  At Christmas to his Uncle Ned,
Although the dates were printed black,
  His birthday date was marked in red!

My legs looked just like nutcrackers
  When I was skating—but
It was the ice on which I fell
  That really cracked my nut!

When I went out carolling
  A dog began to howl,
He howled so loud I couldn't sing,
  The noise he made was foul!
And then, from out his cottage door,
  Appeared old Gaffer Jones;
Said he: "We've heard you sing before
  And recognised your tones!"

Christmas Greetings from the Greyfriars Rhymester

I wish the best of health and luck,
  The best of Christmas cheer,
To everyone who has the pluck
  To read ME through the year!
    (They deserve it.—ED.)

(2)

Frank Nugent borrowed me next day,
  And lent me to his minor, Dicky;
From him I met, to my regret,
  Young Sammy Bunter, fat and
    sticky;
His major Billy took me back
  And sold me to a Fishy rotter,
Who sold me for a shilling more
  To Coker as a gift for Potter.

(3)

George Wingate borrowed me from
    him,
  And Tubb, his fag, annexed me
    gladly;
Then from the fags, reduced to rags,
  To Trotter I went very sadly.
He left me on a window-seat
  Where Nugent found me and returned
    me!
Bob took one look at me, his book,
  Then silently and sadly burned me!
Thus ended, full of fire and flame,
My tour of Greyfriars College—Shame!

THE GREYFRIARS ALPHABET

HORACE HACKER, M.A.,
master of the Shell Form.

H is for HACKER, a master we hate,
He lives in an almost perpetual bate.
His features are acid and so is his
  tongue,
We do not imagine he ever was young.
To think of old Hacker an inky-faced
  boy
Makes Shell fellows chuckle with daring
  and joy.

It cannot be true that he ever was
  pressed
To bend himself over for six of the best!
He'd certainly answer the master:
  "How dare
You tell me to bend myself over that
  chair?
This insolence, sir, you shall dearly
  repent,
To meet your requirements I cannot
  consent!
The whole situation's unparalleled, sir,
A thing that should not be allowed to
  occur!"
An hour or so longer he'd stand there
  and speak,
And probably finish by caning the
  Beak!

CHRISTMAS GRINS

Bolsover majo. had nightmare on
Christmas Eve. He dreamed he was
kissing Quelchy under the mistletoe!

Fisher T. Fish is going to have his
Christmas pudding X-rayed before
taking a slice. There's a threepenny-
bit in it somewhere.

Cecil Ponsonby, of Highcliffe, is
spending Christmas at Dartmoor.—At
last!

Quelchy has been asked to carve the
turkey in his hotel. He is bound to
"cut up rough."

PUZZLE PAR

Here are parts of a tree. ROOT,
STEM, BRANCH, BOUGH,
SPRIG, LEAVES, and FRUIT.
Each of these words is associated
with one of the following, though
not in this order—BAY, GINGER,
HOLLY, LICORICE, LAUREL,
MISTLETOE, GRAPE. Can
you pair the correct words
together?

Answer at foot of column.

There was much handshaking and
congratulation among the fellows who,
after a long and stern fight, succeeded
in not having Bunter for Christmas.

Among the big-game hunting trophies
in Mr. Prout's study will shortly appear
the stuffed head of a savage wait, which
he shot as it howled beneath his window.

Mr. Hacker's cook forgot to put the
stuffing in his turkey. The unfortunate
woman is now too busy writing 500 lines
to worry about Christmas.

ANSWER TO PUZZLE

Licorice-root, Stem-ginger Laurel-
branch, Mistletoe-bough, Sprig of holly,
Bay-leaves Grape-fruit.

Playing the role of Lord Reynham in a magnificent castle, Billy Bunter fancies he's miles above' his old schoolfellows.   But when danger threatens, the Owl of the Greyfriars Remove clings to Harry Wharton & Co. closer than a brother !

LORD BUNTER'S BODYGUARD!

By Frank Richards

Under cover of the tree, Harry Wharton watched the two ruffians lift the unconscious form of Bunter from the trunk at the back of the car !

THE FIRST CHAPTER.

Bunter All Over !

"NOT a step !"

"Look here——"

"Not a step !" repeated Bunter firmly.

Five fellows gave Billy Bunter exasperated looks.

But exasperated looks had no more effect on the fat Owl of Greyfriars than water on a duck's back.

"We've got to walk !" hooted Bob Cherry.

"Rats !"

"Look here, you fat ass——" said Harry Wharton.

"Not a step !"

Walking never appealed to William George Bunter at the best of times. And this was, really, one of the worst of times. Snow had been falling for an hour or more, thick and fast; and it was coming thicker and faster. Traffic in the High Street of Castlewood had completely stopped. The old Sussex town was buried under a blanket of snow. A taxi could not be had for love or money.

Harry Wharton & Co. were good walkers, and not afraid of a spot of bad weather, but a walk of two miles through a snowstorm did not attract them. But as there was nothing else to be done, they made up their minds to it.

Billy Bunter hadn't, and wouldn't !

What was going to be done, in the circumstances, Billy Bunter did not know. But he knew what was not going

to be done. He was not going to walk through the snow.

"You bloated chump——" breathed Johnny Bull.

"Yah !"

"My esteemed idiotic Bunter——" murmured Hurree Jamset Ram Singh.

"You needn't jaw !" said Bunter. "I'm not going to walk through this ! I ordered them to send the car ! I'll sack that chauffeur !"

"You howling ass !" said Frank Nugent. "How do you think a car could get through this ?"

"I'm not accustomed to being kept waiting for my car !" said Bunter loftily. "This sort of thing won't do

Exciting Yuletide Adventures of HARRY WHARTON & CO., of GREYFRIARS.

for me ! They ought to manage it somehow !"

"Fathead !"

"Beast !" retorted Bunter.

Really, it was a difficult position. Billy Bunter's party at Reynham Castle had run across to Castlewood in the car to see the pictures. The car had been ordered to return for them.

But while they were watching the pictures the snowstorm had come on. It had been snowing all the while they watched. They emerged into a snowy

universe, in which it was impossible for any car to shove along.

The Famous Five realised very soon that it was no use waiting for the car, which couldn't come for them. Even had it been there, it could hardly have carried them away. Billy Bunter declined to realise it. He insisted on waiting—and they had now been waiting half an hour. And five of the party were not going to wait any longer.

"Better start !" said Johnny Bull. "If Bunter wants to hang on here, we're not stopping him."

"I say, you fellows, you're not going without me !" howled Bunter.

"Come on, then !" said Harry Wharton.

"Shan't !"

"You blithering, blethering, blathering bloater——" hissed Bob Cherry.

"Beast !"

"We can't stick here till we turn into icicles, Bunter !" said Harry Wharton. "Get a move on, and don't be such a fat slacker !"

"Boot him !" suggested Johnny Bull.

Billy Bunter turned his big spectacles on the exasperated five, with a blink of wrath and disdain.

"I'm not walking it," he said. "It's over two miles to the castle, and I can't, and won't, and shan't, see ? And you fellows ain't going without me, either. I've stood you a topping Christmas holiday at my castle——"

"Whose castle ?" asked Bob.

"Mine !" roared Bunter. "My castle, you cheeky ass ! I've fed you on the THE MAGNET LIBRARY.—No. 1,559.

fat of the land! My hosts of servants have waited on you! You've used my horses and my cars! All I've asked you to do, in return for my munificent generosity, is to stick to me and keep those beastly kidnappers off! That's the least you can do, I think!"

"I'm going to kick him!" said Johnny Bull, breathing hard. "Bunter has to be kicked—and he needs it more when he's playing at being a lord than he ever did before."

"Behave yourself, Bull!" rapped Bunter.

"What?" roared Johnny.

"You're not in the Remove passage at Greyfriars now! I keep on telling you so! Have a spot of manners when you're a nobleman's guest in a magnificent castle!"

"The kickfulness is the proper caper!" grinned Hurree Jamset Ram Singh.

"No cheek, Inky! Shut up!"

"You fat, frabjous ass——" exclaimed Harry Wharton. His temper was very near to failing him.

"That will do, Wharton! Hold your cheeky tongue!"

"Why, I—I—I'll——" gasped the captain of the Greyfriars Remove. "I'll——"

"You'll do as I tell you!" said Bunter. "Shut up! I've heard enough from you!"

"If you want to be booted all the way back to the castle——"

"You won't come back to the castle if you don't mind your manners! I've got my position to think of, before the servants! I think you fellows might try to do me a little credit! After all I've done for you! I really think that!"

The Famous Five gazed at William George Bunter as if they could have eaten him.

This was Bunter, all over!

Playing the part of Lord Reynham, at Reynham Castle, had got into Bunter's head! He was, for the nonce, somebody; and kept on forgetting that he really was nobody!

Old Sir Peter Lanchester had picked him to play that part, while the real lord was kept safe from the Smiler and his kidnapping gang; but since Bunter had been at the castle, it was probable that the old Sir Peter wished that he had picked somebody else!

He had come to know Bunter better during the Christmas holidays, and the better he knew him, the less he admired him!

Sir Peter had to stand for it, having presented the fat Owl at the castle as his ward, young Lord Reynham.

But the Famous Five did not have to stand for it—excepting for the circumstance that they had promised to see the fat Owl safely through the vacation. Often and often, they had become fed-up. When Bunter was in danger, he was wont to cling to his old pals closer than a brother. When he was not in danger, swank supervened—and Bunter was hard to stand.

And really it seemed sometimes that the fat Owl, having played the part of a lord for a couple of weeks, really fancied that he was a lord, and monarch of all he surveyed.

"What I want you fellows to do," said Bunter victoriously, as the Famous Five glared at him, "is to remember your position—and mine! Be respectful! Do as you're told! I don't want to be hard on you! I've taken you up, and I mean to treat you well! But I don't want, and won't have, any cheek! If I have any more cheek, I tell you plainly that I shall have to consider
THE MAGNET LIBRARY.—No. 1,559.

whether I can let you stay any longer at my castle."

Harry Wharton breathed hard.

"We've promised to see you through, you fat chump!" he said. "You let old Sir Peter suppose that you were ready to face danger here—and at the first spot of it, you got us here to protect you! But that does it! We'll clear. No need to walk to the castle, you fellows—they can send our bags after us! It's only a short walk to the railway station! Come on."

"Good egg!"

"Good-bye, Bunter!"

"Say good-bye to Sir Peter, and Captain Reynham, for us!" grinned Nugent. "Ta-ta, old fat bean!"

Billy Bunter blinked at his Christmas guests. He was quite satisfied, in his own fat mind, that the gorgeous glories of Reynham Castle were an irresistible attraction to the Famous Five—as they were to his fat self. So he was surprised, as well as annoyed, when the five juniors started to walk away through the thickly falling snow.

"I say, you fellows——" he yelled.

"Good-bye!"

"You're not going!" howled Bunter. "I—I say, you fellows, why, that kidnapping beast Smiler may be watching us this very minute, for all I know! I say, you ain't leaving a pal in the lurch!"

"You fat idiot!" roared Bob.

"Oh, really, Cherry——"

"You blithering dunderhead——" hooted Johnny.

"Oh, really, Bull——"

Harry Wharton paused. Really it was a little difficult to decide how to deal with Lord Bunter.

"I say, you fellows, what are you getting your backs up about?" demanded Bunter. "Have I said anything to offend you?"

"Wha-a-at?"

"Oh, my hat!"

"I shouldn't think of turning you out of my castle to go back to your poor little homes——"

"You burbling idiot!"

"Oh, really, Nugent! Look here, it looks as if that car isn't coming, and—and if you like I—I'll walk. There!" said Bunter, in a burst of graciousness.

The Famous Five looked at one another.

Harry Wharton burst into a laugh.

"Oh, come on," he said, "we've got to stick to the fat frog! Come on, you fat ass! We're seeing you through; but if you ask to be booted again, you'll get what you ask for! Get a move on, fathead!"

And, Lord Bunter getting into motion at last, the Greyfriars fellows tramped away through the thickly falling snow, and headed for Reynham Castle.

THE SECOND CHAPTER.
A Lift for One!

"OH lor'!"

"Buck up, Bunter!"

"Beast!" groaned Bunter.

"Only another mile or so!" said Bob Cherry encouragingly.

"Oh dear! Oh crikey! Oh lor'!"

It was not an easy walk for any fellow in thick snow, which clung to the soles of the boots, and made walking hard and heavy. But if it was not easy for the Famous Five, it was fearfully hard for Billy Bunter.

The winter darkness had fallen. There was hardly a gleam of a star through the snow. Mist hung over trees and hedges. A cold wind blew from the sea, whirling snowflakes. Nobody was

enjoying that walk, but five fellows realised that grousing would not help.

Neither was it necessary for the Famous Five to grouse. Billy Bunter did enough grousing for the whole half-dozen.

Bunter grunted and gasped and grumbled and groused. It was a sort of perpetual melody all the way. And his pace, which had not been rapid to begin with, dropped to a snail-like crawl.

"How long are we going to be getting in, at this rate?" asked Johnny Bull, with deep sarcasm.

"The longfulness will probably be terrific!" sighed Hurree Jamset Ram Singh. The junior from India's coral strand was enjoying the weather even less than Bunter, though he did not grouse.

"I'm tired!" snorted Bunter indignantly.

"You'd better put it on a bit, old fat man!" said Bob.

"Shan't!"

"The sooner we're in, the better. Suppose those jolly old kidnappers dropped on us?" suggested Bob.

"How would they know we'd been to the pictures at Castlewood?" yapped Bunter. "You can't scare me!"

"Might be tipped by somebody at the castle. We jolly well know they've got a confederate in the place."

"Oh, rot!" said Bunter.

A hint of the kidnappers, as a rule, was more than enough to alarm the fat Owl; but Bunter was too tired and too peevish to think of kidnappers now. All he could think of was that weary tramp through the snow. His fat little legs were feeling as if they were going to drop off. Bunter had twice as much weight to carry as any other fellow in the party, and it was telling on him.

"If a fellow could only get a lift!" he groaned.

"Not likely—in this!"

"Oh dear!"

"Put your beef into it, old porpoise!"

"Oh lor'!"

"Save your breath for walking!"

"Beast!"

Bunter crawled on wearily.

Harry Wharton glanced back in the shadowy, misty lane. Two or three times he had thought that he had heard a sound on the road, and now he was sure that he heard the clink of harness.

Some sort of a vehicle was coming up the road from Castlewood. It was not a car; no car was likely to venture out in a foot of snow. Nor would he have expected to see any vehicle at all. It was slow and hard work for a horse to pick a way along. Still, the rattle of harness showed that some country cart was coming up the road behind; and slow as its progress must have been, it was moving faster than the walkers, for it was evidently overtaking them.

"I say, you fellows!" Bunter caught the sound and stopped. "I say, that sounds like a horse and cart. I say, hold on!"

He blinked back through his big spectacles, in the misty gloom. A moving light glimmered, evidently on the vehicle that was approaching. Billy Bunter blinked at it with deep thankfulness.

Since he had been a lord, Billy Bunter had grown fearfully aristocratic, and hardly deigned to step into anything but a first-class car. But at the present moment, with his fat legs dropping off, aristocratic prejudices were forgotten. He would have been glad of a lift in a cart or a wagon, or even a wheelbarrow. Anything that went on wheels was good enough for Billy Bunter at that weary and dreary moment.

The juniors halted and looked back at the approaching light. It was not likely that a vehicle could give a lift to six, unless it were a wagon; but a lift for Bunter would solve the chief problem. Once relieved of the crawling fat Owl, the Famous Five could put on a brisker pace. At the present rate of progress they seemed likely to be a couple of hours covering the remaining mile to the castle.

It was a small cart that loomed up in the dim snowy dusk. A man dressed in corduroys, with a hat pulled down over his face, and his collar turned up against the weather, was driving it. The cart was piled with a load of faggots, and it could be seen at a glance that no space was available for passengers, except for one sitting beside the driver.

"I say, stop, will you?" squeaked Bunter, as the cart came plugging through the snow.

The driver looked down at the bunch of shadowy figures in the gloom, but he did not stop.

"What's wanted?" he asked, in a gruff voice. "If I stop my 'orse he will want some starting again in this 'ere! What do you want?"

"Look here, stop——"

"Ain't I said I can't stop?" grunted the carter. "I got to get these faggots to the lodge at the castle. Wish I 'adn't started now."

"You're going to Reynham Castle?" asked Harry, walking beside the tramping horse, followed by his friends.

"Ain't I jest said so?" The carter seemed surly, but the weather was not of a kind to make any carter good-tempered.

"I say, if you're going to the castle, give me a lift?" exclaimed Billy Bunter anxiously. "We're going to the castle."

"'Ow can I give you a lift—'arf a dozen of yer?" grunted the carter. "The 'orse couldn't do it, even if I 'ad room in the cart."

"I say, you fellows, as you're so keen on walking, you can walk the rest," said the fat Owl. "I say, my man, you give me a lift! I'll stand you five shillings."

The carter eyed the party.

"I could give one bloke a lift, and I'd do it for five bob," he said.

"I say, you fellows, help me up!" gasped Bunter.

So long as he got a lift for his fat self, Bunter regarded the matter as satisfactory. And the Famous Five, who were more than fed-up with crawling like snails, regarded it in the same light.

"Up you go!" said Bob.

The cart drew to a stop, and Billy Bunter was bunked into the seat beside the driver.

The cart plugged on again, the fat Owl grunting with satisfaction as he rested his weary limbs.

The driver gave the horse a touch of the whip, and the cart moved a little faster than before.

The Famous Five walked on behind it.

"Thank goodness for that!" grunted Johnny Bull. "Now we can walk!"

"Best foot foremost!" said Bob cheerily.

Crack, crack, crack! came the sound of the carter's whip in advance. Possibly Bunter was urging the carter to make haste. He was, at all events, making haste, and, in spite of the difficulty of pulling the cart through deep snow, the horse was putting on more speed.

The tail-light winked farther and farther ahead of the tramping juniors. Now that they were relieved of the crawling fat Owl, they tramped on a good deal more briskly. But they did not keep the cart in sight, and the tail-light, winking from the gloom ahead, suddenly disappeared.

THE THIRD CHAPTER.

Bagging Lord Bunter!

BILLY BUNTER gave a sudden squeak.

"Here, hold on! Keep to the road, will you? Where are you turning off to?"

The carter made no answer. He had put out the tail-light, unnoticed by Bunter. But a quarter of a mile from

the spot where he had picked up Bunter a dark lane jutted off the road. To Bunter's surprise and annoyance, the carter was turning his horse into it.

As he had stated that he was taking his load of faggots to the castle lodge, all he had to do was to keep to the high road, which passed the gates of Reynham Castle. Instead of which, he was turning off the main road into the dark lane that led in the direction of the sea.

"That's not the way to the castle!" yapped Bunter. "You said you were going there! Look here, keep straight on!"

Still without answering, the carter swung his vehicle round into the lane and drove on into deep darkness.

In the narrow lane, between high hedges, the snow was thicker and deeper than on the high road. The driver lashed his horse, but it dropped to a mere walk.

Billy Bunter, in amazement and annoyance, grasped the man's arm.

"Can't you hear me?" he snapped.
"I tell you that ain't the way to Reynham Castle! That leads down to the shore, five miles away! Do you hear me?"

"I hear you, my lord!" answered the carter, with a change in his voice that made the fat junior jump.

While with the juniors, the carter had spoken like any other country carter, only rather gruffly. Now his voice was quite different. It had a mocking tone in it that Bunter knew.

The fat Owl blinked at him in startled terror. He could hardly make out the man at his side in the dimness, but he guessed. His fat heart almost stood still. Then, with a squeak of terror, he half-rose to jump down from the cart.

An iron grip on his arm forced him back into his seat.

"Sit where you are, my lord!" went on the mocking voice—the voice, as the hapless Owl knew now, of the Smiler; the mysterious kidnapper who had haunted the pretended Lord Reynham all through the Christmas holidays. "I cannot part with your lordship yet!"

"Oh crikey!" gasped Bunter. "I—I say, I—I'm going to get down! I—I say, I—I'd rather walk!"

"No doubt!" grinned the Smiler. "But I could not think of letting your lordship walk! I should be sorry to knock your lordship on the head with the butt of this whip; and no doubt you would be sorry, too, my lord! If you'd rather not, you had better keep still!"

"Oh lor'!" gasped Bunter.

He kept still.

"I have had some difficulty in getting hold of you, my lord!" chuckled the Smiler, evidently very elated with his success. "I shall not part with you again in a hurry! Thank your lordship for helping me!"

"Eh?" gasped Bunter. "How did I help you?"

The Smiler chuckled.

"I dare say you can guess that you and your friends were watched in Castlewood," he said. "The snowstorm gave me this chance—with your lordship's help. You hung about long enough for me to make my arrangements; and I was aware, my lord, that if I came along with room only for a lift for one, which one of the party would claim that lift. You see, my lord, I am acquainted with your lordship's kind, unselfish, and considerate nature!"

And he chuckled again.

"Oh crikey!" groaned Bunter. "I—I wish I'd let one of the other fellows have the lift now! Oh crikey!"

Billy Bunter groaned dismally. He was in the trap this time. His fat lordship had played fairly into the enemy's hands.

Obviously, the kidnappers' confederate at Reynham Castle had put the Smiler wise—probably by telephone—that the Greyfriars fellows had gone to the pictures at Castlewood that afternoon.

The Smiler & Co. had been on the watch, ready to seize any chance that might turn up to get Bunter away from his bodyguard.

The snowstorm had given them the chance, and the cunning and wary Smiler had made the best use of it—with, as he mockingly pointed out, his lordship's help. Had not Bunter insisted on waiting so long for the car that could not come, had he put on speed on the way home, had he not bagged the lift and left the other fellows to walk, the Smiler's task would not have been easy. Bunter had made it easy for him.

"Oh, those beasts!" groaned Bunter. "Letting you get me off like this right under their noses——"

The Smiler chuckled again. He had assumed a surly gruffness in talking to the juniors, to prevent suspicion that he had any wish to give his fat lordship a lift. But he was in great good humour now.

"I say, where are we going?" mumbled Bunter.

"This lane leads, as your lordship has mentioned, to the shore," answered the Smiler. "It is not easy going, but that's not a matter of choice, in the circumstances; I can assure your lordship that I should have preferred to offer your lordship a lift in a car. But the weather did not permit, my lord, and your friends might have smelt a rat, I fancy. They had no suspicion of a carter—taking a load of faggots to the castle. But we shall arrive sooner or later, my lord, and you will have quite a comfortable trip in a motor-boat——"

"Oh crikey!"

"Merely a short trip!" grinned the Smiler. "I can promise you quite a comfortable cabin on a very good vessel, which will convey you, my lord, to a much pleasanter climate than this. I hope, my lord, that you will like the climate when you arrive there—you are booked for a very long stay!"

"I—I say, I—I've got to go back to Greyfriars at the new term, you know!" gasped Bunter.

The Smiler chuckled again at that.

"Look here, I ain't Lord Reynham!" said Bunter desperately. "It—it's all a mistake! I—I never was, you know!"

"It is hardly worthy of a nobleman to tell barefaced falsehoods, my lord, especially such palpable ones!" grinned the Smiler.

"I tell you I ain't!" wailed Bunter. "You only think I'm Lord Reynham because you haven't seen him since he was a kid of eleven, when old Peter parked him away to keep him out of your clutches. Old Lanchester knows all——"

"That will do, my lord!"

The Smiler cracked his whip and lashed the horse. The cart was going at a mere crawl now, the horse hardly able to drag it through the thick snow that was banked up in the narrow lane.

But lashing the horse was useless; the animal was doing its best, and could do no more.

The Smiler muttered an oath.

He had taken the first turning off the high road, anxious to get his prisoner away. But the going was much harder in the narrow lane than on the highway, and progress much slower. Several times the horse stumbled, and the cart lurched.

Had they still been on the high road, Bunter might have hoped that the Famous Five would have overtaken him. But there was no chance of that now.

He had no doubt that they had already passed the corner where the cart had turned off, and gone tramping on towards the castle, never dreaming that he was no longer ahead of them.

Bunter was captured, and he could not even hope to make his captor believe that he was not really Lord Reynham. He was received and acknowledged at the castle as the young lord; he had been taken there by the young lord's

THE MAGNET LIBRARY.—No. 1,559.

guardian, Sir Peter Lanchester. Even the young lord's cousin, Rupert Reynham, never dreamed of doubting that he was the genuine article. To the kidnapper, his denial seemed the most absurd of falsehoods—an absolutely fatuous attempt to get out of the trap by denying his own identity.

The horse stumbled again, and the Smiler rapped out an oath. He laid down the whip and drew a cord from his pocket.

He grabbed Bunter's fat hands, knotted the cord round the podgy wrists, and tied the end to the back of the seat.

Then he stepped down from the cart to lead the horse.

Billy Bunter groaned.

Had the Smiler left him at liberty, he would have jumped down and taken his chance of dodging away in the darkness.

But the wary rascal had taken care of that.

The fat Owl blinked round him dismally through his big spectacles. Hope of help there was none. Frosty, snowy hedges shut in the lane; dimly through the gloom loomed spectral branches of trees. The snow was still falling heavily. No one was likely to be abroad in the lonely lanes in such weather.

The Smiler, leading the horse, tramped on, muttering an oath now and then. The wild weather had served his turn; but it was causing him trouble now. He had a good many miles to cover, and it was hard going.

"Oh lor'!" groaned Bunter.

From the bottom of his fat heart he wished that he had never played at being a lord. A gorgeous Christmas holiday in a magnificent castle had tempted him, and he had banked on escaping the danger by surrounding himself with Greyfriars fellows. Again and again they had saved him from the clutches of the kidnappers, who were after Lord Reynham. But they could not save him now.

Billy Bunter had enjoyed being a lord. He had spread his lordliness all over Reynham Castle. Now he would have asked nothing better than to be Billy Bunter again! And even that was denied him. He had played at being Lord Reynham—to the kidnapping gang he was undoubtedly Lord Reynham—and now he was booked for the unknown fate intended for the young lord; and in those dismal moments Billy Bunter was the unhappiest daw that had ever strutted in peacock's feathers!

THE FOURTH CHAPTER.

The Track in the Snow!

HARRY WHARTON came to a sudden halt.

Tramping up the snowy road, collars turned up and heads down to the bitter wind, the Famous Five were putting on all the speed they could. The thought of the crackling log fire in the hall at Reynham Castle was very attractive.

But the captain of the Remove halted at the turning. Dark and misty as it was in the lane, the deep tracks of the cart that had gone ahead of them were visible enough—indeed, so deep were those tracks in the thick bed of snow that every now and then some of the juniors stumbled in them.

"Stop a minute, you fellows!" called out Harry.

"By gum!" exclaimed Bob, in a startled tone. He had noticed what Harry had noticed a moment earlier.

"What——" began Nugent.

"Stop and look at this!" said Harry. He bent down, scanning the thick snow.

Save where the cart had trundled through, it was undisturbed and smooth. Beside the deep tracks of the cart it lay glistening in a smooth sheet. Those deep tracks were powdered with newly falling flakes, and in a short time they would have been filled up, leaving no sign.

The heavy furrow in the snow did not run straight on, on the way to the castle. It swept round in a curve, leading away into the side-lane.

In a light snowfall the juniors would not have noticed it, and would have gone tramping on, past the end of the lane. But a furrow dragged in snow seven or eight inches deep was quite another matter.

"That cart turned off here," said Harry. "Look!"

"What the dickens!" exclaimed Johnny Bull, staring at the snow. "I suppose that carter knew his way——"

"He said he was going to the castle!" said Harry. "He must have known the way. It's a straight high road to the castle."

"Then why——" said Nugent.

Harry Wharton, with a knitted brow, stood staring up the dark lane, black as a hat, between frosty hedges, up which ran the track of the cart.

His friends gathered round him, staring, too.

"Blessed if I make this out," said Bob. "Bunter knew the way, if the carter didn't. Why didn't he tell him?"

Wharton set his lips.

"There's only one answer to that," he said quietly. "We've been spoofed! That cart followed us out of Castlewood specially to pick up Bunter."

"Oh crumbs!" breathed Bob. "The jolly old kidnappers——"

"It can't be anything else! I thought that tail-light disappeared rather suddenly. That was why he was hurrying on, too, after picking up Bunter."

"He didn't seem keen to pick up anybody——" said Nugent.

"If he had been, we should have suspected him at once!" answered Harry Wharton. "I never dreamed that a carter, with a load of faggots—— But there's only one reason why he's turned off the road, and why Bunter didn't stop him from turning! And that's——"

"They've got him!" said Bob.

"And we're going to get him back!" said Harry. "Come on! If we hadn't noticed the track turning the corner—and I suppose he never expected us to—he would have walked the fat ass off easily enough. We should never have missed him till we got to the castle. But now——"

"Now we're not ten minutes behind him," said Bob. "And it will be pretty hard going for a cart up that lane. Come on!"

The Famous Five turned into the lane.

They tramped in the furrow left by the horse and cart, in dense darkness, amid whirling flakes.

It was possible, perhaps, that the carter had mistaken the way, and that Bunter had not noticed it in the dark. In that case, they had to overtake the fat Owl and turn him back.

But they did not think that such was the case. It seemed to all of them clear enough that this was another move on the part of the kidnapping gang, who believed Billy Bunter to be Lord Reynham.

They tramped on as fast as they could. In the thick snow, the cart could not be very far ahead of them, but they saw no gleam of the tail-light.

"Yurrrrrrrrrgh! Beast! Urrrrrgh!" spluttered Lord Bunter, as a snowball aimed by Bob Cherry landed on the side of his fat head. "Wharrer you up to, you silly idiot? Larking with snowballs—gurrggh!" Squash! Another snowball landed on the same spot as the first.

They could guess that it had been put out. The cart had vanished in darkness, but it could not be far ahead.

For a quarter of an hour the juniors tramped on, making the best speed possible; and then, on the wind, a sound came to their ears from the darkness ahead—the sound of a horse labouring through the snow and the creak of the jolting cart dragging after it.

"That's it!" breathed Bob.

"That's it!" repeated Harry. "The tail-light's out; and the man can have had only one reason for taking in the light. He never expected us to spot that he had turned the corner, but he was not taking chances."

"Plain enough now!" said Johnny Bull. "It's the Smiler, or Ferret, or Ratty—one of the three! We can handle him, whoever he is! Put it on!"

The juniors broke into a trot. It was rough going, and they could not have kept it up long. But it needed only a few minutes.

Before their eyes, looming up in the gloom like a dark shadow, was the cart, with its load of faggots.

Their footsteps made little sound on the snow, and that little was drowned by the creaking and jolting of the cart and its load.

As they reached the cart they separated, Wharton and Nugent passing it on the left, Johnny Bull and Bob and Hurree Singh on the right.

In the deep gloom they saw a fat figure perched up in front, and caught a gleam of spectacles.

But they noted that the driver was not in his seat. The next moment they discerned that he was leading the horse, jerking and dragging at it savagely, to urge the animal on. His muttering voice came back to them, muttering an angry oath.

The Smiler did not look round, and was evidently quite unaware that pursuers were close on him.

But Billy Bunter, blinking down from the cart, spotted the shadowy figures that came panting up on either side of the vehicle.

He did not recognise his friends in the gloom; it did not occur to his fat brain that they had spotted the tracks and turned the corner in pursuit. But he saw several running figures, and that was enough for Bunter. He yelled the moment he saw them.

"Help! I say, help! I say, I'm Lord Reynham! I've been kidnapped! I say, I'm tied to this seat! Help! Help!"

The Smiler, at the sound of that frantic yell, ceased to drag at the horse and turned back, with a savage glare, towards Bunter.

"Quiet, you fat fool!" he snarled. "Do you think there's anybody in this wilderness to hear you? Be quiet, or I'll stick a gag in your mouth! You—you——"

"Help!" yelled Bunter.

The Smiler, with a savage face, made a step back. Then he saw what Bunter had seen—a bunch of running figures, level with the cart.

"Get him!" panted Bob, putting on a spurt.

But for Bunter's yell, the juniors would undoubtedly have "got" the Smiler, collaring him before he knew they were there.

But the fat Owl had unconsciously warned the kidnapper in time.

For a split second the Smiler stared blankly; then, with Bob's grasp almost on him, he made a desperate leap backward.

"Bag him!" panted Harry.

There was a yell of rage from the Smiler. He made another spring back —and another. Then, as all the juniors plunged at him together, he turned and tore away, disappearing through the frosty hedge.

Bob Cherry, leaping after him, slipped in the snow and fell. His hand touched the Smiler as he tore out of reach.

The rascal's escape had been narrow. He owed it to Bunter. But he was gone, vanishing in snow and darkness.

Harry Wharton & Co. gathered round the cart. The horse had come to a halt of its own accord.

"I say, help!" yelled Bunter. "Help! I say——"

"Shut up, fathead!" grunted Johnny Bull.

"Oh! Oh crikey! Is that you fellows!" gasped Bunter. "I say, you fellows, I'm tied to this seat! Oh crikey! I say, is that beast gone?"

"The gonefulness is terrific."

"Oh crumbs! I—I say, you fellows, did you come after me?" gasped Bunter.

"Oh, no!" grunted Johnny Bull. "We got here without coming after you!"

"Ha, ha, ha!"

"Beast! Why did you let him get hold of me?" yapped Bunter. "Letting that beast walk me off under your silly noses, when I'm standing you a splendid holiday at my castle just to keep him off. If that's what you fellows call

gratitude, I can jolly well say——
Gurrrrrrrrrrggh !"

A snowball, landing on the side of Bunter's fat head, caused him to complete his remarks with a wild, spluttering howl.

"Gurrggh ! Wurrggh ! Beast ! Oooooogh !"

"Ha, ha, ha !"

"Have another ?" asked Bob Cherry.

"Yurrrrrrrrrrggh ! Beast ! Urrrggh !" spluttered Lord Bunter. "Wharrer you up to, you silly idiot ? Larking with snowballs—— Gurrggh ! After letting me be walked off by that kidnapping beast—— Yaroooooh !"

Squash !

Another snowball smote in the same spot as the first. Bunter spluttered and roared.

"Go on !" said Bob encouragingly, "I'll keep it up as long as you do, Bunter !"

But Bunter did not go on. He realised that his rescuers did not find his observations grateful or comforting, and that replies would take the form of snowballs. He spluttered, and gasped, and grunted, but he said no more.

THE FIFTH CHAPTER.

Unexpected !

SIR PETER LANCHESTER stood in the great stone porch at the stately entrance of Reynham Castle, and looked anxiously down the drive, thick with falling snow, winding away between lines of leafless trees.

Beside him stood Captain Reynham, his nephew, cousin of the young lord whose part the fat Owl of the Remove was playing at the old Sussex castle.

The young Army man was smoking a cigarette, and there was a faint smile on his handsome face, as he looked out into the whirling snow.

But that smile vanished, and he looked grave as the old baronet turned a worried glance on him.

"The boys have not returned from Castlewood yet, Rupert !" said Sir Peter. "It is quite impossible for a car to get through this snow ! If they have walked——"

"A rather severe walk for my Cousin William !" drawled Rupert. "He is not, I think, much of a walker. He will be tired."

"If they get in safely—that matters little !" muttered Sir Peter, with another anxious glance down the long avenue.

"Why should they not ?" drawled the captain. "Even William will manage it, given time—and the others are hardy young rascals—they will not turn a hair."

"I cannot help thinking of the kidnappers !" said the old baronet. "It is a lonely road—it must be absolutely deserted in this weather——"

"Even kidnappers would hardly be tempted out in this !" said Rupert Reynham. "I cannot picture them strolling about in this snowstorm, on the chance——"

"They may have been given word !" said Sir Peter, with a troubled brow. "You know, as well as I do, Rupert, that they have some confederates in the castle."

Rupert shrugged his shoulders.

"I know that you think so, Uncle Peter," he answered; "but I cannot believe so, myself. Jasmond has faith in all his staff——"

"There can be no doubt about it. Someone discovered the secret door into

the King's Room occupied by William," said Sir Peter; "but for his schoolfellow friends being on the watch, he would have been taken away by the secret passage. I knew nothing of it—and it can only have been discovered by some occupant of the castle."

"Possibly from outside !" suggested the captain. "Your detective, Tomlinson, has explored it, and found that there is an outlet in the park. It may have been discovered from that end."

Sir Peter Lanchester shook his head.

"It is possible," he said, "but it is far from probable. Besides, the knowledge those rascals have shown of William's movements proves that they have a spy within the household who conveys information to them."

"But who ?" said the captain.

"I have not the remotest idea !"

"But your detective——"

"Neither has he !" said Sir Peter. "There is someone here who cannot be trusted; but I can see no clue to his identity."

"And you think that he may have tipped his confederates that William is hung up at Castlewood with his friends ?" asked the captain thoughtfully. "In that case, you have only to inquire who has left the castle during the last couple of hours."

Sir Peter shook his head again.

"I have no doubt that the telephone was used," he said.

The captain started a little.

"You think so ?" he exclaimed.

"One of the telephones could be got at, I have no doubt," answered Sir Peter. "We know quite well that such a method of communication is used by them. You remember when the boy Bull arrived here on Christmas Eve, he almost ran into two of the rascals, in the fog, on the avenue—the villain who is called the Smiler, and the man he addressed as the 'guv'nor'—and the boy heard the latter say that he would get his confederate on the phone if he was wanted——"

"I know the boy said so !" sneered Captain Reynham. "I rather thought, myself, that a fertile, boyish imagination had something to do with it."

"I don't think so, for a moment. They are all very sensible lads, and Bull appears to me especially level-headed—a very sensible and practical lad !"

"If anything should happen to William, I should be sorry that you adopted my suggestion of bringing him here, instead of leaving him in his safe concealment."

Sir Peter made no answer to that.

He coloured faintly as he turned his head away, to stare down the shadowy avenue again.

Captain Reynham believed that his suggestion had been acted upon—but it had been acted upon only in part.

The captain had suggested that Lord Reynham, hitherto hidden safely from his mysterious enemies, should be brought openly to the castle, and a detective engaged to watch over him there; thus tempting the kidnapping gang to make some attempt, which would give the law a chance at them.

As he had not seen his cousin William since the latter was a small child, he had no doubt that Sir Peter had adopted his suggestion when Bunter arrived at the castle, announced there by Sir Peter as Lord Reynham.

He did not know his cousin by sight, and all he remembered of him was that he was plump. Like the rest of the household, he had received the pretended lord as the genuine article.

It was his suggestion that had put

that extraordinary idea into Sir Peter's mind.

Sir Peter regarded it as a good idea; but he had no intention of exposing his ward, a weak and sickly lad, to danger, and constant alarms.

For that reason he had looked for someone to play the part of his ward; and Billy Bunter was the lucky man !

Only the detective, Tomlinson, knew the facts—until Bunter had brought the Famous Five in; they, of course, knew that Bunter was Bunter, and not William Lord Reynham.

But they had been as discreet as the old baronet could have wished; the secret was safe with them.

More than once, old Sir Peter had been tempted to let his nephew, at least, know how the matter really stood. But the detective had urged upon him with such earnestness that not a single soul should be told, that the captain, like the rest of the household, was left in ignorance of the facts.

It was, therefore, rather an awkward topic; and Sir Peter, instead of replying to his nephew, moved a little farther off, to the entrance of the porch, to stare out into the falling snow.

His plan was, that if the kidnappers made an attempt on "Lord Bunter," Tomlinson should be on the watch for them; but at the present moment the detective was in the castle, and the sudden snowstorm gave the enemy an unlooked-for chance.

With deep uneasiness, he watched for a sign of the returning juniors—heedless of the bitter wind that scattered flakes round him.

Suddenly he uttered an exclamation.

"They are coming ! Thank goodness for that !"

Shadowy figures loomed out of the falling snow and dusky darkness into the bright electric light from the porch.

Sir Peter stared—and stared again.

Captain Reynham threw away the stump of his cigarette, stepping quickly forward.

"What—what——" ejaculated Sir Peter.

"Good gad !" said the captain.

It was a rough-looking cart, drawn by a weary horse, that loomed up the dim avenue—such a vehicle as had never, probably, approached the grand entrance of the castle before.

Harry Wharton and Bob Cherry, thick with snow, were walking one on either side of the horse, Johnny Bull tramping a little ahead. In the cart could be seen Frank Nugent and Hurree Jamset Ram Singh.

The captain's eyes flashed over them as they came into the light. The Famous Five were all in view; nothing was to be seen of Billy Bunter.

"What——" exclaimed Sir Peter Lanchester.

"Anythin' happened ?" drawled the captain.

"Yes !" Harry Wharton's eyes fixed curiously on the handsome young Army man as he answered.

"William has not returned with you ! You don't mean to say that the kidnappers have got my Cousin William !" exclaimed the captain. He breathed quickly and hard. "Tell me at once—have you seen anything of them ?"

"Yes—the man called the Smiler——"

"Good heavens !" breathed Sir Peter. "I feared it—I——"

"They've got William !" rapped the captain. His face was keen with excitement. "The Smiler—he got William ?"

"He got him by offering him a lift, and——"

"Oh ! They have him, then !" exclaimed Captain Reynham. "Uncle Peter, you seem to have been right—they——"

From the interior of the cart a fat figure rose to view, and a pair of big spectacles gleamed in the light.

"I say, you fellows, are we there? You might have woke me up! I say, help me out of this beastly cart!"

Captain Reynham gave a violent start and the colour wavered in his cheeks at that unexpected apparition, and he

stared blankly at Billy Bunter—alias Lord Reynham!

THE SIXTH CHAPTER.
A Little Liveliness'!

BILLY BUNTER blinked down through his big spectacles.

Sir Peter Lanchester's face registered relief at the sight of him. Bunter, evidently, had been sitting down in the interior of the cart and had

gone off to sleep there, and the halting of the cart had jolted him awake. That was the simple reason why he had not been visible at first.

But the expression on Captain Reynham's face caused the Famous Five to fix their eyes upon him, keenly, sharply. Bunter's unexpected apparition had evidently given the captain a shock.

He was so startled that for the moment he was quite off his guard. In

(Continued on next page.)

LEARN TO PLAY FOOTBALL!
BY OUR INTERNATIONAL COACH

THE IDEA IS GOOD BUT—

WHEN a goal has been scored—you remember we scored one in this match of ours last week—the game has to be re-started in just the same way as it began—that is, with a kick-off from the centre spot.

The only difference is that the ball is kicked-off by the opposite side from that which has just scored. Therefore, in this instance, the centre-forward of the opposing side will go through the process which our centre-forward went through at the start of the game. The referee waits to see that the players of both sides are ready—they should take up their positions as before—then he blows his whistle. The centre-forward kicks-off, and the game is in progress once more.

As the ball is passed to the inside-left of the opposing side, our inside-right dashes forward and tackles him for the ball. There is a bit of a mix-up, they both fall over, and the ball rolls wide. That was a good move on the part of our inside right. He was wide awake, and he didn't give the fellow he was marking a second in which to get control of the ball before he tackled him.

I must say that it wasn't a very correct tackle, but that was because I haven't told you anything about tackling yet. The idea was very good, and it stopped the opponent from doing something useful with the ball. If the tackle had been more correctly done, the ball would not have rolled wide, but would have come out of the mix-up at the feet of our inside-right. So I think this is a good time for me to let you into a few of the "secrets" of tackling an opponent.

THE ONLY WAY

YOU remember, when we were talking about anticipation, a few weeks back, I remarked that the easiest and most effective way to take a ball from an opponent was to intercept the pass. Don't think I am going back on what I said then, because it still remains true; but there are occasions when the only way to get the ball from the man in possession is to tackle him for it. Anticipating what an opponent will do next, and nipping in to intercept the pass, is not always possible. Let me explain.

> When tackling an opponent don't set about the job half-heartedly. Go in with all your might, using your body as well as your feet. It's the only way to come out on top!

Supposing our inside-right, instead of "going for" the player with the ball after it had been kicked-off, had stayed back and waited for him to pass it. The inside-left of the other side wouldn't have passed it at all. Seeing no one near him, he would have started to go through on his own, and our inside-right would have been left looking rather silly, waiting for a ball which did not come.

When the player with the ball saw he was going to be tackled, however, he could do one of two things. He could pass to a colleague before the tackle came, or he could hang on to the ball, and try to beat our inside-right. He tried the latter method, and on this occasion he failed. Our inside-right did very well to take the ball from him, but for his benefit and for everybody else's, let me explain the correct way to tackle.

When I was thinking about the most important things to tell you on this subject, I had a chat with Joe Nibloe, the famous full-back of Sheffield Wednesday. Nibloe is one of the few players who have won winners' medals for the English and Scottish Cup, and, being a full-back, he knows all about tackling. He told me that when he goes into a tackle he repeats to himself subconsciously the words: "That ball is mine."

In the opinion of Nibloe, the most important thing in tackling is to go for the ball without worrying about anything else. "That ball is mine," is his slogan. Why not make it yours? Go into a tackle determined that you are going to get the ball. Don't worry about whether you will get hurt.

POINTS TO REMEMBER

WHEN you have taken the ball from the fellow in possession, however, you have won only half the battle. The thing is to take it away from him in such a way

that you can do something useful with it yourself—in other words, you must try to come out of a tackle with the ball at your feet. You will be the most likely to do this if you tackle a player not only with your feet, but with your body as well. Don't just stick your feet out, hoping to kick the ball away from the other fellow's toes. Put your feet in the way of the ball, and put the weight of your body behind your feet.

You see what I mean? When you tackle, throw your weight towards the player you are tackling rather than away from him. It takes a bit of courage, I know, especially if you are a little 'un up against one of these hefty fellows.

Here is another point which our inside-right would have watched, if he had known about it, when he made that tackle which has given us much to talk about. He did not know, when he decided to go for it, that the player with the ball wouldn't pass to a colleague. If the player had passed, the obvious place would have been to his outside-left, because the middle of the field is well packed with players, as you may imagine, just after the ball has been kicked-off. In order to prevent the ball being passed to the outside-left, our inside-right should have tackled his opponent from the left side—in other words, from the side to which he was going to pass the ball. That would have compelled him to pass inside rather than outside.

Perhaps this point is not very important in a case like this. It is important for the purpose of tackling near goal. Suppose a wing man is running along with the ball, waiting for a chance to centre it. The important thing is to prevent him getting the ball into the middle where one of his colleagues is waiting to have a shot at goal. Therefore, the player who goes to tackle him must do so from the "inside," forcing the man with the ball to pass outwards, where there is less likelihood of danger being caused.

I hope you have understood all this. It is really quite advanced stuff, but I feel that by now you will be ready to "tackle" the more intricate things in football. I haven't finished with tackling yet, either. You will hear more about it next week.

THE MAGNET LIBRARY.—No. 1,559.

that brief moment his face told what the Famous Five already suspected—that he had not expected his fat lordship to return to the castle. He had not been surprised to see that he was missing—but he was surprised to see that he was present!

For a long moment the captain stared at the fat schoolboy in the cart, his eyes starting—so utterly confounded by his sudden appearance that even the short-sighted Owl of the Remove noticed it and blinked at him curiously.

The next moment savage anger flashed into the captain's face. He made a stride forward, caught Harry Wharton by the collar, and shook him violently.

"You young rascal!" he thundered. "You lying young rascal! How dare you lie to me—you——"

Wharton, taken by surprise by that sudden outburst of rage, sagged in his grasp for a moment. The next, with flashing eyes, he gave the captain a violent shove on the chest that sent him staggering backwards.

"Hands off, please!" he snapped.

The captain, staggering back, slipped in the snow outside the porch and fell. As he rose on his elbow his face expressed such bitter rage and fury that Johnny Bull and Bob Cherry jumped to Wharton's side, and Frank Nugent and the nabob leaped down hastily from the cart. For the moment it looked as if Rupert Reynham was about to jump up and spring at Wharton like a tiger.

He might have done so, but as he sprang to his feet Sir Peter Lanchester hastily interposed.

In angry amazement, he waved the captain back.

"Rupert, are you out of your senses?" he exclaimed. "What do you mean by this—laying hands on a guest here? Are you mad, or what?"

Captain Reynham panted.

"That young rascal——"

"I say, you fellows, what's up?" squeaked Bunter from the cart. "I say, what's he getting his rag out for?"

The Famous Five did not answer Bunter. They stood in a group, eyeing the captain grimly.

"Rupert," exclaimed Sir Peter, "control your temper, sir! What do you mean by this—I repeat, what do you mean?"

With a visible effort, Captain Reynham pulled himself together and controlled his anger. His face reddened under the old baronet's astonished and angry glance.

"Sorry," he said. "But, really, it was too bad of the boy to play upon my—my anxiety in such a way. He led me to believe that my cousin was in the hands of those scoundrels—a schoolboy idea of a joke, I suppose! Is it a matter for jesting?"

"I did nothing of the kind!" said Harry Wharton curtly. "I was answering your questions."

"You young rascal!" The captain's temper flamed out again. "You said that the kidnapper had got him by offering him a lift—a foolish falsehood——"

"The kidnapper did get him by offering him a lift!" said Harry. "We got him back again, and here he is!"

"Oh!" panted the captain. "You—you——"

"Calm yourself, Rupert!" said Sir Peter severely. He turned to the juniors. "Please excuse my nephew; we have both been alarmed at your long absence, and feared that something had happened. Tell me what has happened to William."

"The Smiler picked him up in this cart—we took him for a carter," answered Harry. "But we spotted that

the tracks turned off the road, and guessed. We followed on and got him back. The Smiler got away—and we tipped the load out of the cart and used it to get back here. That's all!"

"I say, you fellows, give me a hand down! Do you want me to stick here all night?" squeaked Bunter.

"We've been a long time getting back here through the snow," went on Harry. "Bunter fell asleep in the cart—that's why Captain Reynham did not see him till he got up!"

The captain caught his breath.

"Sorry!" he muttered. "I—I supposed from what you said that William was in the hands of those rascals—and—and—I suppose you can understand my anxiety——"

He broke off abruptly, turned, and walked back into the hall. He brushed past a lean man dressed in black as he went in, hardly noticing him. But Mr. Tomlinson's hard, sharp eyes were very keenly on the captain, watching him curiously as he walked hastily across the hall and disappeared into the smoke-room.

"Come in, come in, my boys!" said Sir Peter. "Thank goodness you have all returned safely, at all events. Please do not take offence at what Rupert said—he was anxious about William, and naturally upset by such a misunderstanding."

"Blessed if I ever noticed that he was anxious about me before!" said Bunter.

"That will do, William!" said Sir Peter rather sharply. "Please come in at once, my dear boys! I will send a servant to take the horse away. Come, come!"

The Greyfriars fellows were glad enough to get in and to warm their chilly limbs at the blazing log-fire. It had been a long and weary tramp through the heavy snow—though, had they not borrowed the kidnapper's cart for the transport of William George Bunter, they might not have been in for two or three hours yet.

Jasmond and his myrmidons came to relieve them of snowy coats and hats, and they gathered gladly before the fire.

There Sir Peter elicited from them a fuller account of the adventure in the snow; an account to which Mr. Tomlinson listened also, in silence, but with keen attention.

"Evidently that scoundrel had information from his confederate in the castle, Tomlinson!" said Sir Peter.

"It would appear so!" said the detective.

"But who——" muttered the old baronet.

Mr. Tomlinson did not answer that question.

The Famous Five, looking at his expressionless face, wondered whether he could have answered it.

Many times in the last few days they had wondered whether Mr. Tomlinson shared their own suspicions of Rupert Reynham. But Mr. Tomlinson's cold and self-contained countenance never gave any clue to his thoughts.

Billy Bunter blinked at the detective.

"Yes, who?" said Bunter. "I'd jolly well like to know who! If I paid a detective I should expect him to find out!"

"Shut up, you fat ass!" whispered Bob.

"Shan't!" retorted Bunter. "What's the good of a detective if a crook carries on his games right under his nose?"

"Be silent, William!" said Sir Peter.

Grunt from Bunter.

Mr. Tomlinson's face did not reveal that he heard Bunter's remarks at all. But the tips of his ears were growing red.

He left the group in the hall abruptly.

Bunter gave a snort as he walked away.

"That man's no good!" he said loudly enough for Mr. Tomlinson to hear as he went. "Look at what happened the other day—you fellows copped that villain Smiler when he got into my room by the secret door, and Tomlinson let him go!"

"He did not let him go, William!" rapped Sir Peter sharply.

"Well, as good as," said Bunter. "He sat up to guard him till the morning, and the man got away in the night, didn't he? Tomlinson went to sleep and let him get away. Snoring while the man escaped! Fat lot of good having a detective like that about!"

"That will do, William!"

"Looks jolly suspicious to me!" said Bunter. "How do you jolly well know that Tomlinson ain't the man here who gives them the news?"

"You absurd boy!"

"Well, going to sleep, and letting the Smiler get away looks like it to me!" said Bunter. "My advice to you is to sack him, and get a better man!"

Harry Wharton & Co. wondered for a moment whether Sir Peter Lanchester was going to smack the head of the fat junior who was playing the part of Lord Reynham at Reynham Castle.

His look showed that the thought was in his mind, and that he would have derived satisfaction from the same.

However, Sir Peter restrained his natural desire to give Lord Bunter what he was asking for, and walked away after the detective.

Billy Bunter's fat head had had a narrow escape—not for the first time since he had been lord of Reynham Castle.

THE SEVENTH CHAPTER.

Bunter Plays Billiards!

CLICK! Click!

It was the sound of a billiard ball meeting another, and then another.

Harry Wharton looked in at the doorway of the billiards-room at Reynham Castle.

It was the day after the adventure in the snow. The afternoon was bright and frosty, and the Famous Five were going out. So they looked for Bunter. Wharton had his skates over his arm as he looked into the billiards-room.

The lake in the park was frozen hard, and the chums of the Remove were going to skate. It was improbable that Bunter was keen on joining them in skating; skating was a form of exertion, and therefore had little appeal for his fat lordship. Still, they did not want to walk off without telling him.

But it was not easy to find Bunter.

It was after the whole party had been looking for him for some little time that Wharton glanced into the billiards-room, hardly expecting to see Bunter there, but to make sure that he wasn't there.

Bunter, however, was there. Cue in hand, he was leaning his well-filled waistcoat over the table, blinking carefully through his big spectacles, and taking a shot. He brought off a cannon as Harry looked in.

From which it might be deduced that the balls had been left in a remarkably easy position, for otherwise Billy Bunter certainly would not have brought it off.

"Good man!" said the voice of Captain Reynham. "You've played a lot of billiards, William, I fancy. You seem to have had chances at school!"

"Well, not a lot, you know," said Bunter. "But I'm rather a dab at billiards—I am at most things, really!"

Harry Wharton, standing at the door, simply stared.

Captain Reynham and Billy Bunter were playing billiards, apparently on the best of terms.

This was the first time that Rupert had been seen on friendly terms with his "Cousin William."

The captain's opinion of "William" was no secret to the Famous Five; indeed, Billy Bunter, obtuse as he was, had observed that the handsome young Army man regarded him as an offensive bounder; and, in return, he regarded the captain as a cheeky and supercilious beast.

More than once, Lord Bunter had told the juniors that he was going to give the fellow a hint to go. His lordship had no use for cheeky poor relations in his castle.

However, his fat lordship had stopped short of that. Rupert, it was true, was a "poor relation" of the real Lord Reynham. But he was nephew to the young lord's guardian, and until the young lord came of age, Sir Peter Lanchester was master of the place. Even Bunter lacked the nerve and impudence to think of taking advantage of his peculiar position to the extent of turning Sir Peter's nephew out.

As a poor relation, Rupert might have been expected to make himself agreeable to his fat lordship; but very rarely had he done so. He seemed, very often, unable to conceal his dislike and contempt.

Bunter did not like it. He disliked it very much. And he got his own back, as he expressed it, by being offensive to the captain in many ways—especially by making allusions to poor relations in his hearing when Sir Peter was not about.

Many times, the juniors had expected the irritable, moody young man to box Bunter's ears, or boot him, for his impudence. Still, he could hardly box his lordship's ears, or boot him, in his lordship's own castle—so long as he could control his temper. But as it was quite obvious that he had an angry and passionate temper, the juniors would never have been surprised had he lost control of it when Bunter was making himself particularly offensive.

So it was simply astonishing to Harry Wharton to see the two of them on what seemed the best of terms.

They were playing billiards together, and the captain was not only smiling and agreeable, but he was taking the trouble to flatter Bunter.

He had only to see the fat Owl with a cue in his hand to see that he was a rotten player, and the remark that Wharton heard, as he came in, was sheer humbug. Not only had Bunter not made a good shot, but he could not have made the cannon at all unless his opponent had left the balls nicely placed for an easy one.

Bunter, of course, was quite satisfied. He fancied that he could play billiards, just as he fancied that he could play football and cricket. Bunter had a fertile fancy.

He proceeded to take aim for another shot with the ease and grace of a hippopotamus. The captain, a little behind him, looked at him—with a sarcastic sneer that was not visible to Bunter, but clearly visible to the junior looking in at the door.

They had not seen Wharton, and he paused a moment, looking on.

Bunter made his shot, and missed. Indeed, it was a safe bet that Bunter would miss every time, unless his opponent played his game for him.

Captain Reynham stepped to the table to take his shot.

Wharton, with a frowning brow, still watched. The captain, he could easily see, was a good man at billiards—he was, in fact, the type of man who would be good at that game. He did not score, but his shot left the balls in such a position that Bunter could scarcely fail to pot the red at his next shot. It was left almost hanging over the edge of a pocket. That this was done intentionally, Wharton knew as well as if Rupert Reynham had told him.

"Coming out, Bunter?" he asked abruptly.

"Eh?" The fat junior blinked round. "No, don't bother!"

"We're going skating."

"Well, go, then, and don't bother!" said Bunter.

Wharton breathed rather hard.

"Look here, Bunter, hadn't you better come? It's a lovely day, and the lake's frozen, and——"

"I wish you wouldn't interrupt me when I'm playing billiards, Wharton! Do clear off and give a fellow a rest!" yapped Bunter. "If you spoil my shot, you ass, you may cost me a fiver!"

"What?"

"A fiver! Now shut up!"

Harry Wharton came farther into the room. From what he saw, he could guess that Rupert Reynham had decided on a change of tactics, and was bent on making himself agreeable to the fat junior whom he believed to be his cousin, Lord Reynham. But he had naturally supposed that it was a game for "love," and Bunter's words startled him.

Captain Reynham turned his head away, a flush in his cheeks. He was not lost to a sense of shame, and he knew very well what Wharton must think of his playing for money with a schoolboy.

"Are you playing for money, Bunter?" asked Harry very quietly.

"We've got a fiver on the game," said Bunter breezily. "Why not?"

"Plenty of reasons why not, I think," said Harry.

"Quelch isn't here," jeered Bunter. "Think a prefect is going to squint in at the window! Don't be an ass, old chap!"

Wharton was silent for a moment.

He had no doubt that Bunter, in the part of Lord Reynham, had succeeded in extracting pocket-money from Sir Peter on a liberal scale, but he hardly supposed that it ran into fivers. Bunter was not, as Rupert believed, a wealthy nobleman; he was the impecunious Owl of Greyfriars, and he certainly could not afford to play for such stakes.

"I shan't ask you to lend me the money if I lose," said Bunter sarcastically; "and if you look at the score you'll see that I'm winning."

"Fathead!"

"Ninety already out of a hundred, and Rupert's only made fifty!" grinned Bunter. "What about that?"

Harry Wharton did not state what he thought about that. What he thought—or, rather, knew—was that Rupert was allowing the fat Owl to win—or, rather, he was working hard at losing.

"Look here, you fat ass, stop it!" said Harry at last. "What would Sir Peter Lanchester think if he saw this?"

"What do I care? I'm master in my own house, I suppose?"

Wharton breathed hard.

"Will you come out?" he asked.

"No, I won't."

"You frowsy, fat Owl!" exclaimed

Harry angrily. "I've a jolly good mind to boot you round the billiards-table!"

The captain looked round at last.

"Is this specially your business, Wharton?" he asked, with a sneer. "I understand that William has you and your friends here to keep a sort of guard over him, but hardly to set up in judgment upon him."

"I should jolly well think not!" exclaimed Bunter hotly. "Mind your own business, Wharton! Who the deuce do you think you are, setting up in judgment on your betters?"

"You fat chump——"

"Yah!"

"Come, come!" said the captain. "Run away and get on with your skating, my lad. William does not want you here."

"No fear!" said Bunter. "Get out, Wharton!"

Wharton's eyes flashed at the young Army man.

"You ought to be ashamed of yourself!" he rapped.

"Wha-a-at?"

"You wouldn't dare to lead that fat fool on like this if Sir Peter was about!" exclaimed Harry scornfully.

Captain Reynham's handsome face became crimson. He gripped his cue as if about to lay it on Wharton hard; and Harry clenched his hands. But Rupert restrained his temper; he gave the junior a bitter look and turned to Bunter.

"Is that how you allow your friends to talk to your cousin, William?" he asked quietly. "I am your guest here."

"No, it jolly well isn't!" roared Bunter. "Get out of it, Wharton! Do you hear? By gum, if you don't clear out I'll ring for a footman to put you out!"

"You fat fool——"

"Shut up and get out!"

Harry Wharton looked at him and looked at the captain; then quietly he turned and left the billiards-room.

THE EIGHTH CHAPTER.
Fed-up!

"HALLO, hallo, hallo!"

"My esteemed Wharton——"

"Harry, old man——"

Four juniors in the hall stared at Wharton in surprise as he joined them. His face was pale with anger. He threw down his skates.

"Not coming out?" asked Bob.

"No! I don't know what we'd better do!" Wharton was breathing hard, and his eyes were glinting. "I've a jolly good mind to clear right off this minute——"

"We can't do that, and leave Bunter to it," said Johnny Bull quietly. "What's happened now?"

Wharton glanced round.

"We've got to talk this over. Come up to the King's Room."

"But what——"

"I can't tell you here—can't tell all the castle!"

"Oh, all right!"

The Co., puzzled, followed the captain of the Remove up to the King's Room. In that magnificent apartment Wharton slammed the door, and then looked into the adjoining bed-room to make sure that no listening ears were about, and shut the communicating door.

His chums waited in silence for him to speak. They had seldom seen him look so intensely angry.

"Look here, you fellows," said Harry abruptly, "we've got it clear in our minds that Captain Reynham is at the bottom of this kidnapping business. We're all agreed on that?"

"I think so," said Bob slowly. "But there's nothing to go on if you're thinking of that, old chap. We've got proof enough for ourselves; but old Peter would simply snort if we told him that his nephew——"

"Well, look at it," said Harry. "Johnny is certain that the rotter he heard speaking to the Smiler in the fog on Christmas Eve was the captain. He's sure it was his voice, though he didn't see him."

"Quite!" said Johnny Bull.

"We know that we got the Smiler when he got in here by the secret door, and the captain insisted on joining Tomlinson to keep guard over him till morning. We know that the captain gave the detective a cigarette, and that he went to sleep, and the Smiler got away. We jolly well know that it was a drugged cigarette."

"We can't prove it," said Nugent.

"We know that Bunter was twice got hold of by the Smiler when the captain contrived to leave him stranded by himself——"

"Yes, but——"

"We know that that kidnapping gang aren't after Lord Reynham for ransom, or anything of that kind. They started on him when he was a kid of eleven, nearly five years ago. Old Peter only protected him from them all these years by parking him at a school under an assumed name. They've been hunting him ever since. That doesn't mean ransom; that means a special motive—it means, as we all know now, that Lord Reynham is to disappear, and his death to be legally presumed, so that the next heir can step in."

"We know it—at least, we're sure of it!" said Bob. "But——"

"The butfulness is terrific," murmured Hurree Jamset Ram Singh.

"Since we've found it out," went on Harry, "I've had an eye on Tomlinson. And, having an eye on him, I've got the impression that he has an eye on Captain Reynham. I suspect very strongly that his suspicions are the same as ours."

"Well, he doesn't know what we know; but I suppose a detective would naturally think of the man who stands to gain," said Nugent—"and that's Captain Reynham, of course."

"Well, then," said Harry, "what about putting the whole thing up to Sir Peter Lanchester and leaving it at that and getting out?"

Four heads were shaken together.

"N.G.!" said Johnny Bull. "We know what we know, but old Peter doesn't. He's not going to believe very easily that his nephew is a scheming, plotting scoundrel. Most of it rests on my recognising the captain's voice in the fog, and old Peter would think I'd made a mistake."

"Look here, old chap," said Frank Nugent quietly, "it's no good putting it up to old Peter without proof. You've agreed to that yourself till now. What's made you change your mind?"

Harry Wharton paused.

"Well, I suppose you're right," he said slowly. "But—but I can't stick it any longer with that fat fool. That plotting rascal has changed his tactics now; he's making up to Bunter."

"He can't stand him," said Bob.

"I know he can't; he loathes the sight of him—and no wonder, if it comes to that! Before we spotted his game we wondered how he could stay on here, with that fat fool insulting him nearly every time he sees him. Well, we know now why he stays on; he's staying on till he lands the fat chump into the clutches of his confederates, thinking that he is Lord Reynham. But he's on a new dodge; he's playing billiards with Bunter now and letting him win, with a fiver on the game."

"Oh, my hat!"

"And Bunter ordered me out!" said Wharton, breathing hard.

"The fat chump!"

"We've promised to see him through; but there's a limit," said the captain of the Remove. "That's the limit. We should have cleared off before—or rather, we should never have come here at all—but for protecting that blithering owl. He spoofed old Peter into believing that he was the kind of chap to take on a risky job—and he got us here to keep off the risks. I don't mind that, but we're not standing his silly cheek—at least, I'm not. We've got to keep the secret. And we can't boot the fat chump all over the castle that's supposed to belong to him. But——"

"We can't go and leave him to it," said Nugent.

"I tell you there's a limit! They can't work that secret door stunt again. It's been screwed up, and the passage behind is blocked. He's got dozens of footmen at his beck and call, and he can have them sleeping round his bed at night, instead of us. I can tell you I'm fed-up!"

"But——"

"Oh, but—but—but——" growled Wharton.

Bob Cherry laughed.

"We didn't expect Bunter to have good manners when we came here, old bean. He's only a silly idiot; but he's really in danger. I think it's up to us to stand it as long as we can. Let's get out of doors."

"You silly ass! You think out of doors is a cure for everything!" grunted Wharton.

"So it is—or nearly," said Bob cheerfully. "We can't stop Bunter blagging in his own jolly old castle. Let the fat frump rip, and blow him! Let's get out——"

"Oh, rats!" growled Wharton. "I've a jolly good mind to pack my bag, and clear off by the next train!"

"You couldn't please the captain better," said Johnny Bull dryly. "If you want to please that rotter, and leave him a clear field, go ahead!"

There was a pause.

"Oh, let's get out!" said the captain of the Remove, at last. And the Famous Five went out with their skates.

And as they skimmed merrily over the frozen surface of the lake in Reynham Park, the clouds cleared from Wharton's brow. Bob Cherry's usual recipe for trouble was, after all, a good one—out of doors was a cure for a good many worries and troubles. In the sharp, frosty air, skating on the frozen lake, Harry Wharton soon forgot Billy Bunter, and all his works.

THE NINTH CHAPTER.
Once Too Often!

"GIVE you your revenge!" grinned Billy Bunter.

"You're too good for me, William."

Bunter grinned complacently.

From the interior of the cart a fat figure rose to view and a pair of spectacles gleamed in the light. "I say, you fellows, are we there? You might have woke me up! I say, help me out of this beastly cart!" Captain Reynham gave a violent start as he stared blankly at Billy Bunter.

He was quite willing to believe that he was too good for Rupert Reynham on the billiards-table.

Indeed, there seemed proof of it to Bunter—as he had in his pocket a five-pound note, won at the game from Cousin Rupert.

Sprawling in a deep leather arm-chair in the billiards-room after the game, Bunter was smoking a cigarette, and feeling no end of a man of the world.

He was revising his opinion of Rupert.

Hitherto, he had regarded him as a supercilious, unpleasant beast, who looked at a fellow as if a fellow wasn't there, which was frightful cheek on the part of a poor relation. He had, he flattered himself, given the beast back as good as he gave, too.

Now, however, the captain had turned up a much more agreeable side of his character. There was no trace of superciliousness. There was no hint of dislike or disdain.

Even Bunter did not suppose that the captain had discovered, all of a sudden, what a nice fellow he really was. But he did suppose that Rupert had come to the conclusion that it was worth his while to "grease" up to a rich relation.

Which made Bunter chuckle inwardly, in view of the fact that he was not Rupert's relation at all; and, so far from being Lord Reynham, had never even seen the young lord in his life.

Of that, of course, Bunter was not going to give a hint—friendly as he was getting with the captain.

Bunter was not good at keeping a secret; but he could keep the secret on which his position at Reynham Castle depended. He was by no means tired of playing the part of a noble lord.

What the captain thought of him was not revealed in his smiling face. His thoughts could not have been flattering, of an egregious young ass, who did not even suspect that he had been allowed to win that fiver on the billiards-table, and who sat smoking a cigarette, when he would immensely have preferred to be sucking a stick of toffee.

"What about a stroll when you've finished your smoke?" asked the captain. "A turn or two on the terrace would——"

"It's cold," said Bunter.

"I'll ring for your coat."

"Oh, all right."

The captain rang. Bunter was arrayed in hat and overcoat by menial hands, being much too aristocratic to put on a coat unaided.

Captain Reynham opened the french windows, and they stepped out on the terrace.

It was carpeted with snow, and Bunter grunted. Fresh air did not appeal to Billy Bunter very strongly. Still, as he had not yet been out that day at all, even the lazy fat Owl was willing to put his fat nose outside for ten minutes or so.

"Shall we walk and meet your friends?" asked the captain. "They will be coming back from the lake, I fancy, by this time."

"It's a jolly long walk," objected Bunter.

"There's a short cut by a corner of the park—under ten minutes."

"Oh, all right!"

They entered the park by a narrow path that ran between thick, frosty trunks. Leafless branches met over their heads, like a network against the steely sky. No snow was falling, but there was a thick carpet of it on the earth, in which the two pairs of foot-prints were clearly imprinted.

Mist hung among the frosty trees. Billy Bunter, on his own, could never have found his way to the lake. But the captain, of course, knew the ways about the park, and Bunter rolled on contentedly by the side of the tall, slim young man.

Captain Reynham paused abruptly, and fixed his eyes on a dusky opening among the trees.

"Did you see someone?" he asked quickly.

"Eh? No!" Bunter blinked round. "Where?"

"I think he dodged behind that old beech." The captain pointed. "Wait here a minute or two, William. I had better see——"

"I—I say, I—I think I'll be getting back," squeaked Bunter. The mere hint of someone lurking in the park was enough for Bunter. "I say, you come back with me——"

"I think I had better see who it is," said the captain gravely. "Perhaps you had better turn back, though. You must not run risks, William."

On that point, William was in full agreement.

The captain turned off the path under the trees, and William George Bunter revolved on his axis, and started back towards the castle.

It was easy enough for even Bunter (Continued on page 16.)

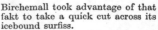

THE PROOF OF THE PUDDING!

Last Laughable Instalment of Dicky Nugent's Great Christmas Serial

GREYFRIA

No. 273.

EDITED BY HARI

V.

" The coppers are coming ! "

Frank Fearless spoke these words in a horse whisper. His fourfinger trembled with eggsitement, as he pointed across the snow towards the gates of Jolly Lodge.

Jolly and Merry and Bright followed his gaze. They wissled as they saw two podgy perlicemen plodding ponderously up the path.

" Few ! The Head's in for it now right enuff ! " remarked Jolly, with a rye grin. " Fansy the poor old buffer being carted off to a perlice station before he's had a chance to eat his Christmas dinner ! "

" They've got to catch him first, old chap," said Bright. " Perhaps they won't find that an easy task ! "

As if in support of Bright's view, a snowball came whizzing across at that moment from the roof of the summer-house on which Doctor Birchemall had perched himself. It missed the Rajah of Bhang by inches and found a billet on General Jolly's chin.

Plop !

" Ow ! Yooooop ! Oh, gad ! " gasped the general.

" Sorry and all that, general ! " came a cheerful chortle from the Head. " I meant that one for the rajah ! "

" You—you——"

" Now, then, wot's all this 'ere ? " broke in a stern official voice as the officers of the law arrived on the seen.

The rajah pointed dramattickally to the roof of the summer-house.

" I order that you arrest that man ! " he cried. " He rob me of my so-bewtiful diamond tiepin ! "

" Mite I hask wot proof you can projooce, sir ? " asked one of the officers.

For answer the rajah whipped out the bare pin and flurrished it before their eyes.

" See ! Here is the pin with diamond missing ! " he hist. " When I sit on his chest, it pierce my trowsis. Becawse why ? Becawse he hide it in his beard ! "

" But wot's 'appened to the diamond, sir ? "

" Ha ! That is for you to answer ! " snapped the rajah. " First step towards it—arrest that man ! "

" Ho, werry good, then, sir ! "

The two perlicemen salooted and plodded through the snow towards the Head's improvised fortress. But they had hardly taken half-a-duzzen steps before two snowballs came sailing through the air.

One of the officers stopped one with his nose ; and the other stopped the other with his right ear ; and they both came to a stop with feendish yells.

" Ow-ow-ow-ow-ow ! "

" Yaroooo ! 'Elp ! Yoooop ! "

" Ha, ha, ha ! Merry Christmas, officers ! " roared Doctor Birchemall. " Try a few more while you're here ! Coming over ! "

" My h a t ! The Head's going it this time and no mistake ! " gasped Fearless. " If he goes on at this rate, he'll earn himself a good long stretch in chokey ! "

" It will be rank injustiss if he does," declared Jolly. " It's my beleef that the Head is innersent."

" Same here ! " corussed Fearless and Merry and Bright.

" I hoap you're right, boys," sighed General Jolly. " But I must say that the evvidence is overwhelming."

" Har ! The perlice will soon drag the truth from him when he is in their klutches," said the rajah with a sceptical smile. " See ! They arrest him ! "

But the rajah spoke too soon.

Just becawse the perlicemen had climbed up the side of the summer-house to the roof level, the rajah imagined that it was all over bar shouting. But Doctor Birchemall was by no means at the end of his tether yet.

He farely rained snowballs on them as they started crawling up the sloping roof on their hands and neeze. And finally, when they continued towards him with tunicks d e n t e d, but curridge undawnted, he made a desprit bid for liberty.

With a sudden, litening-like movement he stepped off the roof-top, sat down and started sliding straight at them !

The constables tried to stop him as he swept towards them ; but they mite just as soon have tried to stop the advance of a juggernought ! By the time he reached them, the Head had turned into a regular avalanche that swept everything from its path, and the unforchunit officers were sent flying off the roof amid torrents of cascading snow !

Crash ! Thud ! Wallop !

" Ha, ha, ha ! "

Jack Jolly & Co. farely yelled. The site of Doctor Birchemall's would-be captors disappearing in the snow under the summer-house was too commical for words. Even General Jolly had to hide a grin, while a feint chuckle escaped the lips of the Rajah of Bhang !

But Doctor Birchemall had no time to spare for lafter. While the perlicemen were struggling out of the mitey snowdrift that now surrounded them, he was hopping to his feet again. And by the time they had got free, he was galloping away in the direction of the ornamental lake on the other side of the drive.

The lake was frozen, and Doctor

Birchemall took advantage of that fakt to take a quick cut across its icebound surfiss.

But at that point misfortune overtook him. Although he did not know it, the ice was dangerously thin on the far side of the lake ; and the Head's galloping feet were more than it could stand !

Just as the officers of the law reached the side of the lake, there was a sharp, omminous cracking sound.

The next moment, with a feendish yell, Doctor Birchemall vanished into a hole in the ice !

VI.

Clang ! Clang ! Clang !

" Grate pip ! There goes the dinner-gong ! " eggsclaimed Merry. " Our Christmas dinner is ready, you fellows ! "

" Who cares about Christmas dinner when the Head's in danger ? " asked Jolly. " Our first task is to reskew him ! "

The chums of the Fourth were racing towards the lake. Christmas dinner would have to wait, they thought, till the Head was saved. At least, that was what Jolly and Fearless and Bright thought. Merry seemed to have his doubts.

" Can't we leave the Head till afterwards, you fellows ? " he asked. " After all, we only get a Christmas dinner once a year ! "

" True enuff. But it's up to us to see the old josser righted first," panted Jolly. " I couldn't enjoy my pooding knowing that the Head was in this lake. Hallo ! There he is ! "

Doctor Birchemall had appeared once more. Forchunitly, the water in the lake was quite shallow, and when he regained his feet he found that it only came up to his waist.

But the Head seemed to find this cold comfort. His face was blue with the cold as he crunched his way through the icy water to the shore.

" Brrrrr ! It's kik-kik-kik-cold ! " he groaned.

The Head always had been a talkative sort of person ; and now his teeth were chattering. He was shivering and shaking like a jelly,

as the perlice-officer helped to terra firma again.

" L-l-l-lemme change n kik-clothes ! " he gasped stood in the snow with ice ar flowing off him.

" Ho, no, you don't ! " one of the constables. " you in the name of the lor

But General Jolly, who kind-hearted jentleman, going to allow this.

" I have an idea," h " What about you two staying to dinner with postponing the arrest til finished ? That will give 'hem !—prisoner time to ch clothes and warm him again."

The two officers licke chops and rubbed their tions.

" My heye ! That's wo a good idea," said one of t " Wot do you say, Bill ? "

" Yuss ! " grinned his pa

" Then come along at o gad ! " cried General Jolly, " Birchemall, my dear fell must have a rub down bed-room and a change of c and then you too must for Christmas dinner."

" Thanks awfully, ge grinned the Head. " I'll self in next to no time, you. There's only one di I have no other clothes to into, apart from the Santa outfit you lent me last nite

" Egad ! Why not wea then ? " asked the general, twinkle in his eye. " It v a seasonable touch to a da has so far been somewhat in the Christmas spirit ! jentlemen ! "

General Jolly led the wa to the house, where Mrs was waiting at the grate fro to hurry them up for dinne

Mrs. Jolly knew nothing the missing diamond ; but as she saw the perlice he woman's intuishun told h something was wrong.

" Oh, I do hoap nothi happened to spoil our Ch party, jentlemen," she ripp they came up the steps.

" A meer trifle, m answered General Jolly, as as he could. " The rajah that Doctor Birchemall ha his diamond and the perl here to arrest him. Docto emall has been unforchun to fall through the ice when across the lake to escape."

" Bless me ! What trilled Mrs. Jolly, throwing hands in horror. " You n upstairs at once and change, Birchemall. I will postpone till you are ready."

Now that the Head was

HERALD

STOP PRESS NEWS

January 1st, 1938.

his Christmas dinner, no-
seemed to trubble him.
the prospect of being taken
dewrance vile as soon as it
ver did not damp his en-
asm. He hurried into the
nd raced off up the stairs
; a time, leaving a trail of
behind him.

rest adjerned to the dining-
to await his return.

rybody looked a lot happier
sight of the dining-room.
: a very cheery specktacle,
huge fire burning in the
and the table already groan-
der the weight of good things.
the Rajah of Bhang seemed
.x a little as he axxepted a
f sham pain from the butler.
is grate pity about Birchem-
hib,'' he remarked, with a
'' I like to beleeve that he
eal my diamond. But the
nce——''.

t's forget the evvidence,
and eat, drink and be merry,''
General Jolly, gaily. ''Per-
omething will turn up to put
rs right. Who knows ?''
ody knew—just then. But
ntionally General Jolly
himself a profit before the
had ended !

vas a gay and carefree party
at down to dinner half an
.ter. Nobody looking at that
dinner-table would have
ed for a moment that a
v lay over the Christmas
rations at Jolly Lodge.

m pain and ginger-beer corks
d and crackers eggsploded.
turkey was done to a turn
le guests had to konfess that
so many helpings they had
left room for the Christmas
ıg.

ertheless, they all waded
heir steeming portions with
. And then, suddenly—
v-ow-ow ! My tooth ! I
ɔmething in pooding !''
vas a yell from the Rajah of
;. General Jolly larfed.
on't worry, rajah ! I eggs-
it's the lucky threepenny-

rajah put his hand to his
nd drew out something from
en his teeth. Then a gasp
eer amazement went round
ıble.

vas not a threepenny-bit that
d found in his portion of
ng. It was something far
valluable than that.

he missing diamond !'' yelled
: Fearless. '' It's the missing
ɔnd—in the Christmas pood-
Hooray !''

ut how it come here ?'' asked
mistified rajah above the
d cheers of the Christmas

know !'' cried Jack Jolly.
as plain as a pikestaff !''

Remember how the Head got his
beard tangled up in the pooding
when he was stirring it ? That
was when it fell out of its setting—
and that eggsplains why the pin
was found in his beard without
the diamond !''

'' Egad ! Then the pin must
have been in your beard intact,
Birchemall, when you went to
stir the poodin' !'' gasped General
Jolly. '' The whole thing's as
clear as mud now. IT GOT
CAUGHT UP IN YOUR BEARD
WHEN YOU LEANED OVER
THE RAJAH'S BEDSIDE
TABLE TO FILL HIS STOCKIN'
AN' YOU CARRIED IT ABOUT
WITHOUT KNOWIN' IT TILL
THIS MORNIN' !''

'' Bless my sole !'' gasped the
Head. '' Then I shan't have to
go back with these perlice officers
after all ?''

'' Ha, ha ! Not likely, my
friend !'' larfed the rajah. '' I do
you grate injustiss. I am sorry !
But never mind. We give you
now, to make up, the best Christmas
you ever have, eh ?''

And they did. And, strangely
enuff, when they looked back
afterwards on that ripping Christmas party, everybody agreed that
it could not have been half so
suxxessful without the Mistery of
Jolly Lodge !

'' Let's go to a
panto !'' suggested
Wibley on Boxing Day.
'' What-ho !'' I
answered promptly.

Going to a panto with Wibley would make a jolly good
jaunt, I imagined. A panto
on Boxing Day is a good treat,
anyway. In this case there
was an added attraction.
Wibley, owing to his pater's
influence in theatrical circles,
is in the happy position of
being able to get the best seats
for nothing !

I felt in fine fettle by the
time we reached the West
End. There was a lot to look
forward to—bright lights,
catchy choruses, mirth-mak-
ing comedians, for instance. I
thought I was in for a topping
time !

My mistake—I wasn't ! And
right here and now I'm going
to broadcast a warning.
DON'T GO TO A PANTO
WITH WIBLEY !

It was Wib. who spoilt it
for me. The frabjous chump
would spoil it for any man !

Like most other Greyfriars
chaps, I go to a panto to get
a good laugh.

Not so Wibley ! He goes to
criticise.

Whenever I grinned, he
frowned. Whenever I laughed,
he groaned. Whenever I
slapped my sides, he tore his
hair !

Once, when I yelled '' En-
core !'' he yelled '' No more !''

In a short time Wib. was
reduced to a picture of despair. His chin was buried
deep in his shirt-front and a
scowl was on his face. When
the lights went up at the end
of the first act and I said,
'' Good show, what ?'' his
looks would have killed.

'' Good?'' he gasped. '' Why,
they broke down six times in
that act !''

'' My hat ! Did they ? I
didn't notice them !'' I said
in surprise.

'' Great pip ! They don't
even know their lines ! Apart
from that, look at the cos-
tumes, the scenery, the dancing ! Why, they're simply
ghastly !''

'' Are they really ?'' I
asked, blinking.

'' Awful ! Terrible !'' said
Wib. '' If it goes on like this,
Rake, I don't mind telling you
it will drive me off my onion !''

Unluckily for us both, it
did go on like that. And it
nearly drove Wib. off his
onion, and Wib. nearly drove
me off mine ! Yet without him
I should have enjoyed it no
end.

I seriously advise you
people never, under any circumstances, go to a panto
with Wibley !

OLD RIVALS IN NEW SPORT!

Friars v. Saints at Ice-Hockey

We thought we'd played St.
Jim's at every game under the
sun. But we've just discovered
that we had not thought of
everything under the arc-lights !

In the past, we've met Tom
Merry and his men at football,
cricket, swimming, rowing, running, hurdling and boxing. Now

we have been able to celebrate
the Christmas vac by adding one
more sport to this imposing list
—ice-hockey !

We take off our hats to Arthur
Augustus D'Arcy of St. Jim's
for introducing us to a really
thrilling sport !

Arthur Augustus, you see, has
a brother, Lord Conway, who
happens to be a director of a
London ice-rink. And it so happened that the ice-rink of which
he was a director was lying idle
on Monday mornings. It occurred to Arthur Augustus that
it would be a bright idea for a
little crowd of us to give the
game a try-out one Monday
morning ; and he put it up to
Lord Conway.

Result : Wharton received a
cordial invitation from Tom
Merry and St. Jim's and Greyfriars indulged in a really hot
tussle on the ice !

The game was played at top
speed throughout, and if science
was absent there was no lack of
enthusiasm to make up for it !

We are quite willing to admit
that the passing was not exactly
machine-like in its precision.
Nor were the rules of the game
always observed in all their
niceties. But as for speed, we
humbly claim to challenge com-
parison with the pick of the pro-
fessionals.

There were one or two bumps
—or, more accurately, one or
two hundred bumps ! Collisions,
too, were painfully plentiful,
and at one period no less than
eight players were piled up in a
heap in midfield.

But we had a tip-top morning, and if it was a little too
strenuous for everybody's taste,
at least it gave us all an appetite
for the lunch with Lord Conway
that followed.

The result was a draw of four
goals apiece. The opinion of the
Greyfriars men was that we
were a little unlucky not to win.
On the other hand, St. Jim's
unanimously agreed that on the
run of the play they should have
been just ahead of us at the
finish. So you can take your
choice.

Anyway, win, lose or draw,
it was a great game !

(Continued from page 13.)

to find the way, as the footprints were deep and clear in the soft snow.

He hurried on, anxious to get out of the park, and in sight of the castle. The captain had disappeared among the trees, and he was alone.

"Oh!" gasped Bunter, suddenly coming to a dismayed halt.

He had taken hardly a dozen paces, when a figure leaped from behind a tree by the path, and grasped him by the shoulder.

Bunter's little round eyes almost popped through his spectacles in alarm. He opened his mouth for a yell, and a hand was clapped over it instantly.

"Quiet!" snarled the Smiler.

"Urrggh!"

The fat junior gurgled under the gripping hand. The captain, and probably the Greyfriars fellows, might have been within hearing. But the Smiler was taking care of that.

Bunter blinked at him in horror.

How the Smiler had happened to be lurking by that particular path, just when he had gone out for a walk with Captain Reynham, he did not guess; but there he was, and Bunter was in his grasp once more.

Swiftly the Smiler knotted a scarf over Bunter's mouth. Then, with a grip of iron on a fat shoulder, he dragged him off the path into the trees.

What happened next was a surprise to the Smiler, as much as to Billy Bunter. A figure appeared with a sudden spring from apparently nowhere, and, before the Smiler knew what was happening, he was grasped, and tipped over headlong.

He went down on his back with a crash and a grunt, Bunter staggering away, blinking in bewilderment.

Like a fellow in a dream, the fat Owl watched Mr. Tomlinson. It was Sir Peter's detective who had appeared so suddenly and unexpectedly from nowhere. He was kneeling on the fallen ruffian, and even as the astonished Smiler began to struggle, his hands were dragged together, and the handcuffs clicked on his wrists.

Mr. Tomlinson rose, a faint grin on his hard face. The Smiler, mad with rage, wrenched furiously at the handcuffs.

"This time," said Mr. Tomlinson cheerfully, "I think you will not get away. Not this time. It was once too often, my man!"

Billy Bunter dragged the scarf from his mouth. He gasped for breath, and ejaculated:

"Oh crikey!"

THE TENTH CHAPTER.

With the Handcuffs On!

"HALLO, hallo, hallo!" roared Bob Cherry.

"Great pip!"

"The jolly old Smiler!"

The Famous Five were coming back

from the lake, their skates swinging on their arms, when they spotted the group in the stone porch. They broke into a run at once, and arrived breathless.

"Tomlinson's got him!" gasped Nugent.

"The gotfulness is terrific!"

"Hurrah!" chortled Bob.

Mr. Tomlinson glanced at the Famous Five and smiled faintly. His usually expressionless face betrayed his elation at his success.

The Smiler stood there—handcuffs on his wrists, rage in his face, and the detective's hand on his arm. Sir Peter Lanchester stood rubbing his hands with great satisfaction. A dozen servants looked on. Billy Bunter was gasping for breath.

The detective had walked his prisoner back to the castle at a good speed—and Bunter had had to put on pace to keep up.

"Excellent—excellent!" Sir Peter was saying as the juniors arrived. "My dear Tomlinson, excellent! Take care that he does not escape again!"

"I shall not go to sleep again, sir, while this man is in my charge!" said Mr. Tomlinson very dryly. "I shall take remarkably good care of that!"

Harry Wharton & Co. exchanged a quick, involuntary look.

To their ears, there was a significance in the detective's tone that was lost on the old baronet. They wondered whether he suspected—as they strongly did—that he had been drugged the night the Smiler had escaped after his capture in the haunted room.

"I say, you fellows, he's got that beast!" squeaked Billy Bunter. "I say, he had me—collared me in the park——"

"You went into the park alone, fathead?" asked Bob.

"No fear—I went with Captain Reynham——"

"Oh!" exclaimed all the five together.

They were not surprised that the Smiler had been on hand, in that case.

"Only the captain saw somebody dodging among the trees, and I started back," explained Bunter. "This beast got me only two or three minutes after I'd left the captain, see?"

"I—I see!" gasped Bob.

"The seefulness is terrific!" murmured Hurree Jamset Ram Singh.

All the Famous Five "saw"—much more clearly than Bunter did. They suspected that Mr. Tomlinson "saw" also.

"Then Tomlinson popped up!" grinned Bunter. "I had no idea he was there—and that beast hadn't, either——"

"How very, very fortunate!" exclaimed Sir Peter, rubbing his hands. "We have the scoundrel at last. This is the same man——"

"The Smiler!" grinned Bunter. "He ain't smiling now—— He, he, he!"

"My dear Tomlinson, this is splendid!" exclaimed Sir Peter. "I congratulate you, Tomlinson! How did you happen to be on the spot? It was remarkably fortunate, but how did it happen?"

"It did not 'happen,' sir!" answered Mr. Tomlinson, in the same dry tone. "As his—hem—lordship went for a walk in the park, I considered it my duty to keep him in sight—without getting in sight myself. That is all."

"Oh, quite!" said Sir Peter, perplexed. "But as he was in company with my nephew——"

"I thought it possible, sir, that they might happen to part company, in which case his lordship might be in danger, sir."

Again the Famous Five exchanged a quick look. This remarkable foresight on the part of Mr. Tomlinson indicated only one thing to their minds —that his suspicions took the same line as their own.

"Well, well, it appears that you were right, as it actually occurred," said Sir Peter. "Possibly one of the rascals allowed my nephew to see him, to draw him away from William—from what William says. He may have caught the other—we must hope so. At all events, we have this scoundrel!"

"We have him, at all events, sir," assented Mr. Tomlinson. "If you will order a car, Sir Peter, I will take him directly to the police station at Castlewood. The sooner he is under lock and key the better."

"Oh, certainly! Ah, here comes my nephew!" exclaimed Sir Peter Lanchester, as Captain Reynham came in sight, approaching from the direction of the park at a rapid run.

Harry Wharton & Co. watched him curiously as he came. That he had led the fat Owl into a trap, and that he had believed that Bunter was still in the trap until he sighted the group before the porch, they had no doubt whatever.

The Smiler's eyes turned on him, as he came up, panting for breath.

Captain Reynham looked at him, at the detective, at Sir Peter, and at the juniors, in turn. The juniors did not fail to note that Mr. Tomlinson's eyes were fixed very keenly and curiously on the captain's flushed face.

"You—you—you have——" Captain Reynham stammered. "What has happened—who—what——"

"You know this man Rupert," said Sir Peter. "It is the same scoundrel who was caught in the King's Room a few days ago and escaped——"

"Oh! Yes! Now—now you say so, I seem to recognise him!" gasped the captain. "But what—how——"

"He seems to have been lurking in the park, and he seized upon William when you left him," said Sir Peter. "You did not find the other?"

"The—the other?"

"William says that you left him to look for some man you saw among the trees——"

"Oh! Yes! He—he dodged me in the park," stammered the captain. "One—one of this rascal's associates, I have no doubt."

Harry Wharton & Co. stood silent. Knowing what they knew, they could guess the terror and dismay under which Rupert Reynham was struggling at that moment.

The Smiler, his right-hand man in the kidnapping scheme, was a prisoner again—he had not only failed once more, but he stood in the detective's grip with the handcuffs on.

They wondered whether Rupert was in dread of the rascal telling what he knew! The Smiler was, at all events, banking on his secret confederate to save him, as he had saved him before. His eyes were fixed on the captain, with an expression that the juniors understood.

"Tomlinson, fortunately, was on the watch!" said Sir Peter, with intense satisfaction, which he had no doubt his nephew shared. "The scoundrel is a prisoner again. This time——"

"This time we must make sure of him," said the captain. He was recovering his coolness. "Let him be taken into the house and the police telephoned for——"

Bob Cherry winked at his comrades. The juniors were wondering what move the captain was going to make with a view to getting a chance of releasing his confederate. This was it!

"Tomlinson is going to take him directly to the police station, Rupert," answered Sir Peter.

"Is that safe?" asked the captain. "The man has confederates—there might be an attempt at a rescue, and it is a lonely road. Surely it would be wiser to keep him here and send for the police."

"Perhaps so," assented the baronet. "Yes, perhaps you are right, Rupert. The rascally gang might resort to desperate measures, for all we know."

"I think, sir, that I can undertake to place the man safely in official hands!" said Mr. Tomlinson.

"Well, perhaps——" The baronet paused, looking from the detective to his nephew and back again. "No doubt——"

"With your permission, Sir Peter, I will convey this rascal to the police station at once," said Mr. Tomlinson dryly.

"One moment!" cut in the captain. "I do not want to rub it in, Tomlinson, but the last time this man was in your hands, he escaped. I think it very unwise, uncle, to run the same risk again."

Mr. Tomlinson flushed faintly.

"He will not escape this time!" he said briefly.

"I should be glad to be assured of that!" said Captain Reynham. "Please do let the man be kept here till the police can take him away, uncle. It is much the safer plan."

"Well, if you think so, Rupert——"

"I do most decidedly."

"Really, sir——" said Mr. Tomlinson, biting his lip.

"After all, Tomlinson, it is certainly the fact that the man escaped the last time he was in your hands," said Sir Peter. "Let him be taken into the gun-room, and I will telephone at once for the police."

"But, sir——"

"Please do as I say, Mr. Tomlinson!" said Sir Peter Lanchester, with a strong hint of command in his voice.

Mr. Tomlinson compressed his lips.

"Very well, sir; it is for you to give orders here!" he said.

And he led the handcuffed rascal into the building, and all the spectators of the curious scene followed.

THE ELEVENTH CHAPTER.

Harry Wharton & Co. Take a Hand!

"LEAVE him to me!" said Captain Reynham.

The Smiler stood in the gun-room, scowling, the handcuffs on his wrists. Mr. Tomlinson stood quite close to him—watchful as a cat. Harry Wharton & Co. looked in at the doorway.

Sir Peter Lanchester had gone to the telephone, and was already ringing up the police station at Castlewood. In half an hour, probably, a police-car would be at the castle, with constables to take charge of the kidnapper.

That half-hour was all the Smiler had—and all his secret confederate had. Once he was taken away in official hands, his confederate could do nothing to save him—and could only hope that the prospect of an ultimate share in the plunder would keep him silent.

The juniors could not help wondering, with keen interest, what steps Rupert Reynham would take this time. On the previous occasion, it had been late at night, and he had, as the juniors believed, succeeded in planting a drugged cigarette on the detective. Mr. Tomlinson, at all events, had gone to sleep on the watch, and the Smiler had escaped.

The captain's problem was not so easy now. And Harry Wharton & Co. had made up their minds that, whatever measures he might take, those measures were going to be defeated.

To the schoolboys, the captain paid no heed. It was the detective with whom he had to deal.

"Leave him to me!" repeated the captain. "I think, Tomlinson, that you are losing time—the man I saw in the park is undoubtedly a confederate of this scoundrel—you may get him yet, if you lose no time——"

"I have little hope of it, sir," said Mr. Tomlinson dryly, "and I certainly prefer not to leave my prisoner. Please share my watch if you so desire."

Sir Peter Lanchester came in from the hall. The old gentleman was rubbing his hands with gleeful satisfaction.

"The police will be here soon, very soon!" he said. "We must take care that the scoundrel does not escape this time."

"I shall take care of that, sir!" said Mr. Tomlinson.

"I was suggesting, uncle, that the man should be left to my care," said the captain. "There is another of the gang lurking in the park, or was a short time since, and it may not be too late for Mr. Tomlinson to secure him."

"Excellent!" exclaimed Sir Peter, at once. "I will accompany you, Tomlinson—let us go at once. You will not leave the rascal alone for one moment, Rupert, till the police are here?"

"Not for a second!" said the captain. "Rely on that."

Mr. Tomlinson drew a deep, deep breath.

"Sir Peter Lanchester, I prefer to remain in charge of my prisoner!" he said very distinctly.

"He will be quite safe in my nephew's hands, Tomlinson," said Sir Peter, staring at him.

"I will undertake not to go to sleep!" said the captain, in a sarcastic tone. "Rely upon me for that."

"Come, Tomlinson!" said Sir Peter, rather sharply.

To the juniors in the doorway, Tomlinson's face was an interesting study at that moment. His unwillingness to leave his prisoner in Rupert's hands had, to their minds, only one meaning—he distrusted the captain. But if that was the case, he certainly could not state what he thought to the captain's uncle.

He was in an extremely difficult position; for if there was, as the captain stated, another of the gang lurking in the park, it was up to the detective to get after him, if he could.

"Come!" repeated Sir Peter. "I am waiting, Tomlinson! You are losing time—losing, perhaps, another prisoner!"

There was no help for the hapless detective. He could not speak out; and he was under orders at Reynham Castle.

"Very well, sir!" he almost gasped. "Perhaps these young gentlemen would like to remain here till the police come!" he added, like a man catching at a straw.

"Thank you—I do not desire the help of schoolboys in taking care of a hand-cuffed man!" said the captain.

"We're quite willing——" began Bob Cherry.

"Nonsense!" said the captain.

"Please do not butt into matters that do not concern you, my boy!"

Mr. Tomlinson's face did not express his feelings—but the juniors could guess that they were deep, as he followed the baronet from the gun-room.

Harry Wharton & Co. lingered at the doorway, and the captain calmly shut the door in their faces. The key turned inside—perhaps as an additional precaution against the escape of the prisoner—more probably, in the opinion of the Co. to leave the captain uninterrupted while he devised ways and means for releasing the prisoner, while concealing his own part in the release.

The Famous Five walked back into the hall.

"Well," said Bob, "this is a go!"

Harry Wharton set his lips. Looking out of the doorway, he could see the unhappy Mr. Tomlinson going into the park with Sir Peter—the old baronet quick and eager, the detective lagging.

"That villain's not getting by with this, you fellows" said the captain of the Remove, in a low voice.

Johnny Bull grunted.

"He's got by!" he answered. "It's the same game as before—that kidnapper will get out of the same window! The spoofing rotter will make out that he got loose somehow, and knocked him down with a chair or something—anyhow, the man will be gone when the bobbies get here. That's the game."

"That's the game," agreed Harry," and it's a game that we're going to put paid to!"

"How?" asked Nugent.

"The Smiler can't be let out by the door—running the gauntlet of a dozen servants—the captain's got to keep up appearances. It's the window, or nothing. That window looks over a shrubbery——"

"Just what he wants!" said Bob. "Plenty of cover——"

"And just what we want!" said Harry. "We're going to stick in that shrubbery, and watch that window till the police get here!"

"Oh!"

"I say, you fellows!" Billy Bunter rolled over to the Famous Five. "I say, what about tea?"

"We're going out——"

"Silly asses—I'm going to tea!" And Bunter went.

Harry Wharton & Co. went out. They strolled casually along the terrace, and then quietly made their way to the shrubbery under the gun-room window.

There was, as Bob had said, plenty of cover; thick banks of evergreens, loaded with snow.

Keeping in cover of the evergreens, the Famous Five approached the gun-room window, as near as they could, without revealing themselves to watchful eyes within.

Then they waited.

It was not likely to be a long wait. The kidnapper and his confederate had no time to lose.

They had no doubt that the captain was already releasing the Smiler from the handcuffs. What story he would tell, when he had to account for the prisoner being gone, they could not guess, but they had no doubt that he would invent some plausible explanation. In the position in which he now found himself, the schemer had to take risks, and there was little or no doubt that he would take them.

"Hark!" whispered Bob suddenly.

There was a sound of a casement cautiously opening. It was followed by the "plop" of feet landing in the snow.

A second later, the evergreens were shaking, as a figure plunged into their cover, to escape observation from other windows.

The Smiler, most assuredly, never dreamed that those evergreens were already populated.

He made that discovery suddenly and unexpectedly as unseen figures suddenly pounced on him and bore him to the ground.

The Smiler gave a startled gasp, and struggled. He fought almost like a wildcat. But every one of the Famous Five had hold of him, and he was pinned down helplessly. His eyes fairly burned with rage, as he glared up at the Greyfriars fellows.

Bob Cherry gave him a cheery grin in reply to his savage glare.

"Waiting for you, old bean!" he said. "It's jolly cold here—much obliged for not keeping us waiting long."

"The obligefulness is terrific, my esteemed and execrable Smiler!" chuckled Hurree Jamset Ram Singh.

The Smiler, with gritting teeth, wrenched and wrenched. But he wrenched in vain; the Famous Five had him, and they kept him. The handcuffs were gone—but Bob Cherry produced a whipcord from his pocket, winding it round the thick wrists, and knotting it again and again. The Smiler, panting with rage, lay a helpless prisoner.

"Now sit on him!" said Bob cheerily. "We've got him, and we're keeping him till the bobbies come! Sit on him till we hear the car!"

The Smiler spat out furious curses. He ceased to do so as Bob crammed a handful of snow into his mouth. After that he lay, in savage, vindictive silence, while the juniors listened for the sound of the police car from Castlewood.

THE TWELFTH CHAPTER.

Not Gone!

INSPECTOR SHUTE, of Castlewood, stepped from the car as it stopped at the castle door.

A constable followed him up the steps, where Jasmond let them in. The butler led them directly to the door of the gun-room.

He tapped on that door, and turned the handle.

The door did not open.

Jasmond knocked again, and called: "Please open the door, sir! Inspector Shute from Castlewood!"

There was no reply from within.

"The prisoner is there?" rapped Mr. Shute.

"Yes, sir," said the perplexed butler. "Captain Reynham remained in charge of him, and he appears to have locked the door. It is very odd that he does not answer."

"Very odd indeed!" rapped Mr. Shute. He knocked sharply on the door with his knuckles. "Captain Reynham! Please open this door!"

There was no reply, but from within a sound was heard, as of someone struggling.

The inspector knitted his brows.

"Something is wrong here!" he rapped. "Captain Reynham! Will you answer? Can you answer?"

"Here is the master!" said Jasmond.

Sir Peter Lanchester came in, a little breathless. He was followed by Mr. Tomlinson.

"What is it?" asked Sir Peter. "What——"

"I understood from you, sir, on the telephone that the man called the Smiler had been secured, and that I was desired

THE MAGNET LIBRARY.—No. 1,559.

to take him into custody!" rapped the inspector. But——"

"That is the case," said Sir Peter. "My nephew is guarding him till your arrival. He is in this room. Why—what——" Sir Peter turned the door-handle, and knocked. "Rupert! Open this door, Rupert! What has happened?"

There was a sound again from within, but no reply, and the door did not open.

Mr. Tomlinson set his lips hard.

"Something has happened!" exclaimed the old baronet in an agitated voice. My nephew—alone with that ruffian—— Rupert! Rupert!"

"The man was handcuffed!" said Mr. Tomlinson, between his set lips. "The man was quite powerless."

Inspector Shute stared at him.

"This does not look like it!" he rapped. "This door must be forced!"

"Jasmond!" exclaimed Sir Peter. "James! Thomas! Francis! Lose no time! Force this door at once! Good gad! What may have happened to my nephew? Yet the ruffian was handcuffed; he appeared perfectly safe!"

There was a swift hammering and clanging on the lock of the gun-room door. In a very few minutes it was forced open.

Sir Peter hurried in the moment it was open, with deep and intense anxiety in his face. Inspector Shute stepped in swiftly after him, Mr. Tomlinson following, his lips hard set.

The casement stood open. The Smiler was gone. On the floor lay Captain Reynham, bound hand and foot and gagged. He was struggling with his bonds.

"Rupert!" gasped Sir Peter.

Inspector Shute stooped over the bound man and quickly removed the gag—a twisted handkerchief—from his mouth.

The captain gasped for breath.

His hands and ankles were tied with a cord snapped from the curtains. In a few seconds the inspector had released him.

"Rupert! What has happened here?" exclaimed Sir Peter. "The man—has he escaped?"

"I fear so, uncle!" gasped the captain. "I am sorry—truly sorry, but I think I can say that it was not my fault! I had no doubt—no doubt whatever—that he was secure!"

"He was handcuffed!" grunted Mr. Tomlinson.

"So I supposed!" snapped the captain. "But your handcuffs, Mr. Tomlinson, can hardly have been secure. The man, at all events, succeeded in releasing his hands. Either the handcuffs were not securely locked, or else he was able to slip his hands out of them."

"They were securely locked!" said Mr. Tomlinson grimly.

"He got his hands free, at all events! Believing him to be secure, I was looking from the window when I was suddenly struck down from behind!" snapped the captain. "I was dazed by the blow—almost stunned—and could make no resistance while he made me a prisoner, as you found me. I have been struggling to get loose and cry out ever since, but——"

"The man is gone!" grunted the inspector.

"He escaped by the window while I lay helpless," said Rupert. "I am more sorry than I can say, uncle; but——"

"Thank goodness it is no worse, Rupert!" said Sir Peter. "You might have been severely injured, as the man was not, after all, secure! Really, Mr. Tomlinson, I trusted you——"

Mr. Tomlinson's thin lips shut harder, but he made no rejoinder.

The Castlewood inspector glanced at him—a grim glance. That glance told very plainly what Inspector Shute thought of private detectives.

"Well, the man is gone!" grunted the inspector again. "We have come here for nothing! How long since, Captain Reynham?"

"About twenty minutes."

"We may pick up his track in the snow. There may be a chance yet," said Mr. Shute. "I shall lose no more time, at all events."

He hurried back into the hall, followed by the constable.

As he strode towards the door he suddenly stopped, with a gasp.

Five juniors were coming in, and in their midst they led a man with his hands tied behind him.

Inspector Shute blinked at them. The constable blinked. Jasmond and a dozen footmen blinked.

"Who—who is this?" gasped Mr. Shute.

"The man you want, sir!" said Harry Wharton.

"The jolly old Smiler," chuckled Bob Cherry—"not at the moment smiling, but the genuine Smiler, sir!"

"The smilefulness is not terrific, but it is the esteemed and execrable Smiler!" grinned Hurree Jamset Ram Singh.

"You—you boys—you stopped him?" gasped the inspector.

"We did, sir!" said Johnny Bull. "We thought you'd like to find him here when you came! Here he is!"

"Here he is, as large as life!" said Frank Nugent.

The Smiler stood, silent and scowling. His game was up now with a vengeance.

Mr. Shute, grinning with satisfaction, clapped the handcuffs on his wrists.

"What——" came Sir Peter's voice.

He came out of the gun-room, followed by Mr. Tomlinson and Captain Reynham.

The captain's face whitened at the sight of the Smiler. He stood gazing at him, transfixed.

Mr. Tomlinson's face lighted up.

"This is the man!" he exclaimed.

"This is the man, Mr. Shute!" said Sir Peter.

Mr. Tomlinson glanced at the smiling faces of the Famous Five. He smiled himself. The corner of his eye was on Rupert Reynham's white face.

"But how——" exclaimed Sir Peter. "Is it possible that you boys saw the rascal escaping and stopped him?"

"Just that, sir!" said Harry. "As he got away last time, sir, we rather thought he might get away again, so we parked ourselves in the shrubbery under the gun-room window and watched for him."

"And he walked right into our hands, sir!" said Bob. "Very obliging chap!"

Mr. Tomlinson shot a swift, penetrating look at the captain of the Greyfriars Remove.

"This is excellent!" said Mr. Shute. "These boys have been very useful, sir; they deserve great praise! We have the man. I shall take him into custody on your charge. I must warn you, my man, that anything you may say will be taken down, and may be used in evidence!"

The Smiler said nothing.

He stood silent, scowling, his eyes lingering on the face of Rupert Reynham.

"Before you take him away, inspector," said Sir Peter, "I wish to put a question to the man."

"He is not bound to answer," said Mr. Shute.

SING, BOYS, SING these—

GREYFRIARS CHRISTMAS CAROLS!

Specially Written for College Carol Parties by HAROLD SKINNER.

You All Know This One

Good old Quelchy once looked out
On the Feast of Yuletime,
While his class sat round about,
Fed with beastly school-time!
Brightly shone the fire that night,
Though the cane was cruel,
When a porpoise came in sight,
Singing to the schoo-oo-el!

"Hither, Wharton, stand by me!
If thou know'st it telling,
Yonder person, who is he?
What is that he's yelling?"
"Sire, we know him!" Wharton
grinned.
"He's a human barrel,
Trying now to raise the wind
With a Christmas carol!"

"Bring my cane, and bring it well,
Bring my birch-rod hither!
I will teach him how to yell
When I journey thither!"
Quelch and Wharton forth they went,
Forth they went together,
Through the fat boy's wild lament,
And the wintry wea-ea-ther!

Hark, the song grows fainter now,
Bunter's sight grows stronger!

Fails his heart, he knows not how,
He can sing no longer!
But Good Greyfriars men be sure
He will soon be starting
Quite a different kind of roar
If he's slow depar-ar-ting!

Merry Christmas Bells

*A very old carol with modern
improvements.*

Oh, how we hate the rising-bell,
It's never late, and who can tell
The agonies we have to bear
When rising in the wintry air?
But—ring the merry, merry, merry
Christmas Bells,
Yes, ring 'em till the echo roars!
While their happy music on the breezes
swells
We'll join our merry, merry snores!

Oh, dismal din—the classes bell!
We trickle in, and know full well
We'll soon be getting Quelchy's cane
And shrieking like a parrot in pain!
But—ring the merry, merry, merry
Christmas Bells,
Yes, ring 'em till the welkin blinks!
While their happy music on the breezes
swells
We'll have another forty winks!

It makes us sad—the assembly bell,
To some poor lad it means a knell,
For on the platform in Big Hall
His pride will have a terrible fall!
But—ring the old etcetera Christmas
Bells,
Yes, ring 'em till they all turn red!
However much their music on the
breezes swells
They'll never get us out of bed!

The Mistletoe Bough

*This famous carol, all about Lord
Lovel's Bride, is all about Mr. Bunter's
Son for a change.*

The Doctor stood in the college Hall.
"Be silent there!" they heard him call.
"Last night in bed, beneath the sheet,
I found—and with my naked feet—
A hidden Mistletoe Bough!"

And when the chuckles died away,
The Reverend Head went on to say,
"The culprit will be brought to book,
I hear a certain junior took
This spreading Mistletoe Bough!"

"That boy, named Bunter, will stand
out,
And tell me why he stole about
Beneath my bed-room window, and
Why he was holding in his hand
A certain Mistletoe Bough?"

"Oh, really, sir!"—in tones of woe,
"I'm so short-sighted, as you know.
It was an absolute mistake,
I really never meant to take
That beastly Mistletoe Bough!

"You see, I put it there instead
Of holly, sir, inside your bed!
For I was certain I had got
A bough of holly, sir, and not
That rotten Mistletoe Bough!"

At this, the Doctor's features took
An extraordinary look.
"Bend over, boy!"—his birch-rod gone,
He cast a frantic eye upon
That hefty Mistletoe Bough!

And when the grisly scene was done,
Said Bunter: "It's not everyone,
Who can declare with truthful eye
That they've been firmly walloped by
A stinging Mistletoe Bough!"

Christmas Is Coming

Christmas is coming, and Gosling's getting fat,
If you put a penny in the poor man's
hat,
He'll give you a look that is terrible
and grim,
Nothing less than half-a-quid will do
for him!

"Oh, quite, quite! My man," said
Sir Peter, fixing his eyes on the sullen,
scowling face, "you are now in the
hands of the law. It is perfectly well
known here that you have some confederate in this household who has
helped you in your dastardly attempts
to kidnap Lord Reynham. Will you
give his name to Inspector Shute?"

Captain Reynham pulled himself
together.

"The man is hardly likely to do that,"
he said. "I have no doubt that he still
expects assistance from his confederate,
and that he feels that he can rely on
him to give any help he can in the present circumstances."

"Possibly, possibly," said Sir Peter.
"But now that he is faced with a long
term of imprisonment——"

"There are many ways in which his
confederate can still assist him, though
not in the way of regaining his liberty,"
said the captain. "Such as secretly
paying lawyers for his defence, and
helping him when he comes out after
serving his sentence."

"Really, Rupert, you are encouraging
the man to keep silent by such
remarks!" exclaimed the old baronet
testily. "Pray say no more! Now, my
man——"

"I ain't saying nothing!" said the
Smiler stolidly, breaking silence for the
first time.

"Rascal!" exclaimed Sir Peter indignantly. "A member of my household is
in collusion with you—some servant that
I have trusted! Now that you are in
the hands of justice——"

"You can sort over your servants

yourself, and find the man, old feller!"
said the Smiler.

"That is an admission, at least, that
it is one of the menservants!" said Captain Reynham.

"Yes, yes; no doubt, no doubt! Mr.
Shute, I leave this scoundrel to you."

The Smiler was left in safe hands.
Sitting in the car between Inspector
Shute and a constable, with the handcuffs on his wrists, the Smiler was
booked. Sir Peter Lanchester's ward
was relieved of one, at least, of his
enemies; and relieved of him for good!

But Rupert Reynham gave no hint of
what he was thinking. His face bore a
cheerful expression, and only the chums
and perhaps Mr. Tomlinson—detected
a trace of strain in his bearing.

THE MAGNET LIBRARY.—No. 1,559.

THE THIRTEENTH CHAPTER.

Something Like a Shindy!

"GREAT pip!" ejaculated Bob Cherry.

It was the following morning.

The Famous Five had been up, and out, for some hours before Lord Bunter thought of stirring—as usual!

Now they had come in again, and Bob Cherry had come up to the King's Room to see whether Bunter was up, and to lend a friendly hand at rolling him out of bed if he wasn't up.

Bunter was up!

He had had breakfast—more than one; and turned out of bed. He was not dressed yet; but he was sitting in the King's Room, enveloped in a voluminous dressing-gown. With him sat Captain Reynham. Both of them were smoking cigarettes.

Bob Cherry stared at them.

A few days ago it would have surprised him to see the captain on pally terms with the fat Owl. But the Famous Five were aware that Rupert had changed his tactics towards his supposed cousin. He was on the very best terms with Bunter now.

If he hoped that it would lead to the fat junior taking another walk in the park, he was disappointed. Bunter had not stirred out of sight of the castle since the Smiler had grabbed him in the park.

Certainly, it had not occurred to his fat mind that Rupert Reynham had led him into a trap on that occasion. But he was not taking any chances.

In view of the new state of affairs, Bob was not surprised to see the captain in the King's Room with Bunter. But he was surprised to see how the two were occupied.

They were sitting at a card-table: the fat, untidy Owl sprawling in his dressing-gown; the captain handsome and fastidiously dressed, as usual. Cards were on the table, and little heaps of half-crowns, and a small pile of currency notes. That was how Bunter was spending his morning!

He blinked round at Bob through his big spectacles.

"Don't come in!" he said.

"What?" gasped Bob.

"I'm busy! Don't interrupt the game! Go out and skate, or something—anyhow, don't worry!" said Lord Bunter.

"You fat, frowsy, frabjous, foozling frump!" roared Bob.

Captain Reynham glanced at him. There was a faint flush in his cheeks. The fat and fatuous Owl of the Remove regarded this sort of thing as "sporting," and was quite satisfied with himself and his companion. But Rupert was no fool, and, utterly unscrupulous as he was, he winced at the disgust and scorn in Bob's ruddy, honest face.

He had his own game to play, and he was playing it by any method that came to hand. The fatuous folly of the fat Owl gave him an opportunity; and he was using it without scruple. But he flinched under Bob's eyes.

"You rotter!" exclaimed Bob. He was speaking, not to Bunter, but to the captain. "You rotten rascal!"

Rupert's eyes glittered at him.

"Are you speakin' to me?" he drawled.

"You know I am! Look here, stop that!" roared Bob. "You rotten rascal, leading that fat fool on to gamble! You ought to be booted!"

The captain's face flushed, and then whitened.

Billy Bunter became as red as an enraged turkey-cock.

"You cheeky fathead!" he roared. "Get out! Shut up! By gum, if you think I'm going to stand manners of that sort in my castle, Bob Cherry——"

"You fat idiot!"

"You cheeky beast!"

"Stop that at once!" roared Bob.

"You silly chump!" howled Bunter. "Can't I do as I like in my own house? If you don't like it, clear off! Who wants you here, I'd like to know?"

"You do, you fat rascal! You're afraid of a shadow, if you haven't got somebody to protect you!" roared Bob savagely.

"Yah!"

Bob Cherry strode into the room, his eyes blazing. He strode straight at the card-table, and kicked it.

The table flew. Cards and coins and currency notes showered over the polished oak floor of the King's Room.

Captain Reynham sprang to his feet with a gasp of rage. Billy Bunter blinked in speechless wrath through his big spectacles.

"You impudent young cad!" roared the captain. "William, shall I throw that young hooligan out?"

"Yes, rather!" gasped Bunter. "Kick him out! Cheeky rotter! Sponging on a fellow, and kicking up a shindy! Chuck him out, Rupert!"

"Hands off, you blackguard!" roared Bob.

But the captain's angry grasp was on him the next moment.

Bob Cherry, with flashing eyes, hit out.

Bob was a hard hitter. Rupert staggered under the blow. But he grasped the junior, and whirled him towards the door.

Strong as he was, sturdy, and full of pluck, Bob was no match for a grown man. But he resisted every inch of the way.

A chair went crashing—a table rocked. Billy Bunter, spluttering with wrath, blinked on, through his big spectacles.

There was a pattering of feet in the corridor without. The other members of the Co. coming up after Bob, heard the din, and hurried on to see what was the matter.

They stared into the King's Room in amazement at the sight of Bob Cherry struggling in the grasp of Rupert Reynham.

"Bob!" gasped Wharton.

"My esteemed Bob——"

"Lend a fellow a hand!" panted Bob. "The brute's too big for me! Will you lend a fellow a hand?"

"I say, you fellows, you keep out!" squeaked Billy Bunter. "I don't want you here! Rupert's chucking that cheeky cad out by my orders! Look what he's done to my card-table!"

Harry Wharton & Co. did not heed Bunter. They rushed at the captain together, grasped him, and dragged him away from Bob.

Rupert Reynham went sprawling and gasping on the floor. Bob Cherry stood panting.

"But what—what——" gasped Nugent.

"Can't you see?" snapped Bob. He pointed to the scattered cards and money on the floor. "Look!"

"None of your business!" howled Bunter. "Pretty state of affairs, I think, if a chap can't do as he likes in his own castle!"

"Shut up, you fat fool!"

"Beast!"

Rupert staggered to his feet. His immaculate clothes were considerably dishevelled, by the struggle, and he panted for breath. He made a stride towards Bob Cherry, and the Co. closed round their chum at once.

"Get out!" said Harry Wharton tersely.

"You cheeky cub——"

"Get out, or you'll be thrown out!" said the captain of the Greyfriars Remove.

"Look here, Wharton, you cheeky ass——" squealed Bunter.

"Shut up, Bunter!"

"Shan't!" roared the indignant fat Owl. "Look here! If you can't be civil, I won't have you staying in my castle, so there!"

"Kick him!" said Harry.

"Yaroooh!"

"Now, Captain Reynham, get out!" said Wharton. "You can go out on your feet, or on your neck, whichever you prefer! Sharp's the word!"

"You cub——"

"That's enough! Are you going?"

"I say, you fellows——"

"Shut up, you bloated blitherer!"

"You cheeky beasts——"

"Kick him again, Johnny!"

"Yow-ow—wooop!"

"Now chuck that cad out, you men!" said Harry, as the captain stood panting and glowering.

But Rupert Reynham backed to the door. He had handled Bob, but the Famous Five together could have handled him easily, and it was clear that they were going to do it. He breathed rage as he backed.

"Sir Peter will hear of this!" he panted.

"Would you like Sir Peter to hear of that, too?" asked Harry Wharton, scornfully, pointing to the scattered cards and money on the floor. "You cur, your uncle would kick you out of the place himself, if he knew! You don't dare to let him know! Get out! You make me sick!"

And the captain stepped out of the King's Room, and Wharton slammed the door after him.

THE FOURTEENTH CHAPTER.

A Bath for Bunter!

BILLY BUNTER glared at the Famous Five with a glare that might have cracked his spectacles.

The fat Owl was spluttering with rage.

"You—you—you cheeky cads!" he gasped. "You—you cheeky rotters! You—you cads! You—you swabs! I'm fed-up with you! Meddling in a fellow's business, you—you—you cheeky rotters——"

Bunter gasped for breath.

"Shut up!" said Johnny Bull, in a deep growl.

"Shan't!" roared Bunter. "Get out, the lot of you! I've been kind to you fellows—taking you up, and asking you to my castle for Christmas, and all that—and this is how you repay my generosity!"

Harry Wharton & Co. looked at him.

Bunter waved a fat hand at them.

"Just get out!" he said. "I don't want you here! I never wanted you, if you come to that! You make out that you came here to protect me! Yah! I'm not a fellow to want protecting, I hope!"

"Well, my hat!" said Bob.

"I've been kind to you, and you're ungrateful—just as ungrateful here as you are at Greyfriars," continued Bunter scornfully. "I've given you a splendid time in my castle! After all that, you can't even be civil! Well, I'm done with you!"

The Famous Five stood looking at him.

"You make out that I want you here," went on Bunter. "Well, I don't! I'm all right now! I mean, I'm not afraid of a little danger! They've got that beast Smiler—he's safe in prison! They've screwed up that secret door; nobody can get at me here now. I'm pretty sick of having you fellows about, making out that you're protecting me! If I want any protection—which I don't—I've got a friend here, see?"

"A friend?" repeated Wharton. "Who?"

"My Cousin Rupert!" said Bunter, with dignity. "He's offered to sleep in the dressing-room next to my bed-room, if I like, instead of having all you fellows camped round my bed. You've been a lot of trouble and nuisance camped in my room——"

"You fat villain!" shrieked Bob. "You made us camp in your room to protect you, you fat funky freak!"

"Did I?" sneered Bunter. "Well, I don't want you there, I can tell you. In fact, I won't have you! If you fellows want to stay on here we've got to come to an understanding. You've got to behave yourselves, and kick up no more rows, and you've got to be civil to Rupert. I shall expect you to apologise to Rupert——"

"You fat idiot!" ·

"I shall insist on that," said Bunter firmly. "Otherwise—I'd better put it plain—I expect you to go. You've barged in here, sticking on to a chap because he knows you at school. It's a bit thick, I must say, that! But I've been pretty decent to you. This is how you repay me!"

"I suppose," said Johnny Bull thoughtfully, "that he would burst all over the castle if I punched him."

"Yah!"

Harry Wharton drew a deep, deep breath.

"This does it!" he said. "Bunter will have to take his chance. We're getting out of this."

"I know I am!" said Johnny Bull grimly.

The Co. all nodded assent to that. They had come to Reynham Castle, at the fat Owl's urgent and almost frantic request, to protect him from the kidnappers. Clearly Bunter believed that he was safe now.

The most determined and dangerous of the gang, the Smiler, was under lock and key. The secret passage into the King's Room had been discovered and blocked up, and Captain Reynham had undertaken the role of protector.

The schemer's game was to get rid of the schoolboys, who had hitherto protected the supposed Lord Reynham. His fat lordship was playing the schemer's game for him.

"Go as soon as you like," sneered Bunter. "The sooner the better! My kindness has been repaid with ingratitude! Go back to your poor little homes! I can jolly well tell you, I don't want you here!"

"You think you will be safe with Rupert Reynham on hand?" asked Harry, with a curious look at the fat Owl.

"You think he will protect you?" grinned Bob.

"I don't want any protection that I know of," answered Lord Bunter loftily. "I hope I can protect myself. I'm not a fellow to funk a little danger, like some fellows I could name. Still, if I wanted any help, I jolly well know that

Rupert would be more useful than a lot of silly schoolboys."

"Oh, my hat!"

"Your manners have been rotten all along," went on Bunter. "I've stood it! I asked you here, meaning to give you a good time, and I've put up with your rotten manners; but there's a limit. You can't expect me to stand this sort of thing, barging into my apartments like a mob of hooligans, when I'm playing a quiet game of poker with a friend. It simply won't do. You fellows aren't accustomed to expensive places and good society. I am. You'd better go."

"We're going, you fat fool!" said Harry. "But——"

Bunter waved a fat hand.

"That's enough!" he said. "Pack and go! You can stay to lunch if you like. I shall expect you to catch a train this afternoon. After kicking up such a shindy, you can't expect anything else. You needn't say any more. I'm going to dress now!"

Lord Bunter rolled into the adjoining bed-room with his fat little nose in the air. He shut the door after him emphatically.

"Well," said Bob, with a cheery grin, "that's that! Are we going to tell Bunter before we go that his new protector is the skunk who is on his trail?"

"Can't leave even that fat idiot in the dark about that," said Nugent. "I suppose he's too much of an idiot to believe it; but we're bound to tell him."

Harry Wharton shook his head.

"No good telling that to Bunter," he said. "He hasn't sense enough to understand, and he would think we were stuffing him, to make an excuse for staying on here. He's fool enough."

"Oh crikey!"

"Ten to one he would tell the scoundrel, and Rupert would simply be warned and put on his guard," said Harry. "Bunter wouldn't believe it, and he hasn't sense enough to keep his mouth shut."

"Yes; but——"

"No good telling Bunter, but we can tell Tomlinson, and put him wise to all we know," said Harry. "I'm certain now that he's got his eye on the captain; you saw how unwilling he was to leave the Smiler in his hands yesterday. He knew as well as we did that something would happen and the man would get away."

"I believe so," said Nugent, with a nod. "And the way he followed them when they went into the park, it's pretty clear that he didn't think that fat fool was safe there with the captain."

"The fact is, he's a pretty capable man, though he hasn't had much chance of showing it, so far," said Harry. "We'd better compare notes with Tomlinson, and then clear. We promised to see Bunter through; but we're let off that now, and I can't stand any more of him, for one."

The bedroom door reopened, and Billy Bunter blinked out into the King's Room.

"I've rung for Frederick," he said crossly. "He hasn't come up. He's kept me waiting a whole minute—or more! Does the fellow think I can dress without the assistance of a valet, or not?"

"You fat Owl——"

"Oh, really, Cherry—— I say, you fellows, this is dashed annoying!" said Lord Bunter, blinking very seriously at the Famous Five. "Francis must have heard the bell. Is it possible that he has the impudence to keep me waiting?"

"Fathead!"

"I think I shall have to sack that

man Ronald," said Bunter, shaking his head. "One thing I can never stand, and never will, is impudence from menials."

"Perhaps he's getting tired of being called Frederick, and Ronald, and Francis," suggested Bob. "He might like to hear his own name for a change."

"I never can remember servants' names, Cherry. The man can hardly expect me to remember that his name's James."

"Ha, ha, ha!"

"Blessed if I see anything to cackle at! James—I mean Frederick—hasn't come up. Go and look for him, Cherry."

"Eh?"

"Go at once, and tell him I'm waiting."

Bob looked at the fat junior. Lord Bunter was evidently in his lordliest mood—common mortals only existed to carry out his lordly behests.

"I'm waiting, Cherry," said his fat lordship, with dignity.

"Well," gasped Bob, "I won't go and hunt up James; but perhaps I can be of assistance to your lordship. I'll try. Your lordship hasn't had your lordship's bath yet, I think. Your lordship isn't fearfully keen on baths. But I'll help you this time——"

"I'm not taking my bath this morning," said Lord Bunter hastily.

"Your mistake," said Bob; "you are!"

He made a jump at Lord Bunter, and grasped him by his fat neck.

His lordship gave a yell as Bob spun him back into the bedroom.

"Ow! Leggo, you beast! I say, you fellows—— Ow! Wow! Ooogh!"

"Ha, ha, ha!"

"Leggo!" shrieked Bunter.

Bob Cherry did not let go. He whirled Lord Bunter across the bed-room to the door of the bath-room. With his left hand he opened that door.

Bunter struggled wildly. Of all the luxurious appointments of Reynham Castle, the bath-room was the one that Bunter patronised least. But he was going to patronise it now—with Bob Cherry valeting his lordship.

"Ow! Beast!" roared Bunter, as he was whirled into the bath-room. "Wow! I tell you I ain't going to bath this morning!"

"And I tell you your lordship is!" grinned Bob. And he bumped Billy Bunter headlong into the marble bath, and turned on the cold tap.

Splash!

"Gurrrrggh!"

"Ha, ha, ha!"

"Oh, sir!" gasped James. James had arrived at last. James gaped in at the bath-room doorway. "Oh, sir! What——"

"Too late, James-Frederick-Ronald-Thomas-Francis-Herbert," said Bob. "I'm valeting his lordship this morning. His lordship is taking his lordship's bath."

"Urrggh! Grooogh! I'm all wet! Gurrggh!"

Bunter struggled up.

Bob Cherry shoved him down again. His fat lordship collapsed in streaming cold water, and roared and spluttered.

"Yarooh! Urrgh! Beast! Wooooogh!"

"Ha, ha, ha!"

"There!" gasped Bob. "You can carry on now, James. Don't give his lordship any soap. His lordship doesn't like soap. His lordship hates it, in fact—don't you, my lord?''

"Gurrrgh! Beast! Lemme ger-roat! Urrggh!"

Bunter wallowed and splashed and spluttered. Bob Cherry, chuckling, left him to the grinning James.

Splashing and spluttering followed the Famous Five as they departed, leaving his lordship wallowing in his lordship's bath for the first time since his lordship had arrived at his lordship's castle.

THE FIFTEENTH CHAPTER.

Cards on the Table!

HARRY WHARTON tapped at the door of Mr. Tomlinson's room, which was at the end of the corridor on which the King's Room opened.

The detective opened the door, and lifted his eyebrows a little at the sight of the Famous Five.

"What——" he asked.

"We're leaving this afternoon, Mr. Tomlinson," said Harry. "We want a few words with you before we go."

The detective gave him a very hard, keen look.

"Please come in!" he said curtly: and the juniors entered, Mr. Tomlinson closing the door after them.

He waved his hand to chairs.

"You are leaving?" he asked, in the same curt tone. "Why?"

"You may guess why," said Harry. "That fat fool is having his leg pulled by a man here who wants us to leave him unprotected."

Mr. Tomlinson's keen eyes had a sudden gleam in them.

"Meaning?" he asked quietly.

"Captain Reynham," replied Harry.

"You do not mean to say that you suspect——"

"I mean to say exactly that—and that, I believe, you have the same suspicion in your mind, Mr. Tomlinson," said Harry bluntly. "You need not confide in us if you don't want to, but I want you to listen to what we have to tell you. It may be of use to you in nailing that scoundrel."

"I am bound to listen to anything you may have to tell me, of course," said Mr. Tomlinson primly.

He listened without an interruption, while the juniors told him what they knew. Every now and then that alert gleam came into his eyes. When they had finished, he asked a few curt questions:

"You are sure it was Rupert Reynham's voice you heard speaking to the Smiler in the fog on Christmas Eve, Master Bull?"

"I wasn't sure at first, but I was afterwards," said Johnny. "I know now that he was the man."

"Sir Peter, of course, would suppose that you were mistaken."

"That's why he hasn't been told."

"Oh, quite! And, after that——"

"After that I had an eye on him, and when I was satisfied that he was the man, I told these fellows—and they're all satisfied," said Johnny. "Look here, the night the Smiler was caught in the haunted room, the captain sat up with you to watch him. You went to sleep after the captain left you——"

Mr. Tomlinson coloured faintly.

"And I believe," said Johnny, "that you guessed afterwards why. I did, anyhow. Captain Reynham gave you a cigarette before he left you."

"He did," said Mr Tomlinson, very grimly.

THE MAGNET LIBRARY.—No. 1,559.

"It was drugged," said Johnny Bull. "That's why you went to sleep, and the Smiler got away. I believe you guessed it."

"What makes you think that?"

"The way you kicked at leaving the Smiler to him again yesterday. You knew the man would get away."

"You, also, apparently, as you watched for him, and caught him going," said Mr. Tomlinson, smiling. "Well, my boys, I am glad you have come and told me all this. I knew that you knew something when I heard that you had watched for the man under the gun-room window yesterday. Certainly I never dreamed that you knew so much. This is very useful to me. But——" He paused.

"You needn't tell us anything, sir," said Harry. "We've a pretty clear idea of what you've got in your mind. What we want is to help you all we can to keep that fat chump out of danger after we're gone."

"That is the idiotic sine qua non," agreed Hurree Jamset Ram Singh.

"From what you have told me," said the detective quietly, "I judge that you are able to keep your own counsel. If you are going, I will say nothing. But are you bound to go?"

"Bunter asked us here, and he's given us the order of the boot," said Wharton. "We've only been here on that fat fool's account, and he thinks he's safe without us now. It's happened to-day; but it was bound to happen, now that the captain is taking the trouble to pull his leg. His game has been to clear us off the scene all the time."

"Exactly so," assented Mr. Tomlinson. "And by going, to play into his hands, as that stupid boy Bunter is doing."

"Well, yes," said Harry slowly. "But I don't see how we can help it, Mr. Tomlinson. The fact is, we can't stand any more Bunter."

"Which is the captain's object and intention," said Mr. Tomlinson.

"Ye-e-es, I suppose so, but——"

"I quite understand your feelings, but you must remember that Master Bunter, with all his nonsense, is nobody here," said the detective. "He has no right either to invite guests or to dismiss them. He was brought here for a certain purpose, having deluded Sir Peter Lanchester into the belief that he was a courageous lad, willing and able to play a dangerous part. Sir Peter understands him better now, and has been very much annoyed by his fatuity and impudence—as I have no doubt you have observed."

"Sort of leaped to the eye, didn't it?" grinned Bob.

"I think," said Mr. Tomlinson, "that you would be well advised to take no heed of Master Bunter's absurdity, and to remain here."

"Oh!" said the juniors together, dubiously.

"Sir Peter Lanchester, who is master of the house, likes you, and makes you thoroughly welcome," said Mr. Tomlinson. "That being the case, you can surely disregard the absurdities of a foolish boy who is taking an unwarrantable advantage of the position in which he is placed."

"Yes, I suppose so," said Harry. "But——"

"And, foolish and offensive as Bunter is, you would not really wish harm to befall him!"

"Of course not!" said Harry. "We stand for his silly rot at school, and I suppose we could stand it here, if you

come to that. Of course, we're really Sir Peter Lanchester's guests, not Bunter's. But do you mean that you, as a detective, think we are useful here, in beating that rascal?"

"That is precisely my meaning!" said Mr. Tomlinson quietly. "As Bunter's schoolfellows and friends, you have many opportunities of watching over him that do not, of course, come my way. This has been proved, I think, by various occurrences here."

"No doubt about that! But——"

"If you choose," said Mr. Tomlinson, "you can be of immense help to me in one of the most difficult tasks I have ever undertaken as a detective. You have proved that you can be discreet, which is all that is necessary. I am alone here, pitted against an unscrupulous and keen-witted scoundrel who has authority in the house, and the complete confidence of the man who has employed me to defeat him. It is a very extraordinary position, and I am naturally anxious to obtain all the help I can."

"We couldn't speak to Sir Peter about his nephew," said Harry. "But a word from you, as a detective——"

Mr. Tomlinson shrugged his shoulders.

"So far from venturing to breathe a word to Sir Peter, against Rupert Reynham," he said, "I have not found it easy to keep him from placing complete confidence in his nephew, and thus ruining the whole scheme."

"Oh!"

"I can say nothing without absolute proof," said Mr. Tomlinson. "My position in that respect is, indeed, precisely the same as your own. You saw what happened yesterday! I could not tell Sir Peter Lanchester that his nephew was planning to set that scoundrel free. That was impossible. I had to take the chance—or rather, the certainty, of seeing my work undone. But for you boys, the man would have escaped again."

"Yes, I see that!" said Harry.

"If you remain, and continue to be as discreet as before, you may be of the greatest service," said the detective. "And Bunter is in very real danger."

"I suppose those brutes would let him go again, if they got him, when they found out that he wasn't really Lord Reynham?" said Bob.

"Possibly! Possibly not! He might know too much, after being in their hands, ever to be allowed to go free again," said Mr. Tomlinson. "My own belief is that they would keep him safe—in the same very secure spot that is already planned and arranged to receive Lord Reynham."

"Oh crumbs!" said Bob. "I—I suppose they would!"

"I do not think that his life would be in danger—because if the rascals were prepared to go to that length, they would have done that already, in dealing with the supposed Lord Reynham. But I am quite assured that he would remain a prisoner in some remote spot, probably thousands of miles from this country."

"We shall stick to him!" said Bob.

"Blow him!" grunted Johnny Bull. "After that, I don't see that we've got much choice! After all, we can boot him when he's cheeky!"

"The bootfulness can be terrific!" agreed Hurree Jamset Ram Singh.

Mr. Tomlinson smiled.

"Another point is this," he said. "You have never seen the real Lord Reynham. I have seen him—he is a weak and somewhat sickly lad, and he has never recovered from the attempt to kidnap him when he was a child—

Bob Cherry sent the card-table flying with his foot, and cards and coins and currency notes showered over the polished floor. Captain Reynham sprang to his feet, with a gasp of rage, while Billy Bunter blinked in speechless wrath through his big spectacles.

several attempts, rather! I feel sure that you must sympathise with him, and would be glad to help in relieving him of a danger that makes it necessary for him to be hidden, under an assumed name."

"You bet!" said Bob. "Poor kid! We'll do anything we jolly well can, Mr. Tomlinson—you can bank on that!"

"Then you will remain here," said the detective.

"Certainly, if you make a point of it," said Harry Wharton, at once. "If we're going to help save the real lord, we shan't be scooted off by the dummy lord, you can be sure of that."

"Cards on the table, then!" said Mr. Tomlinson, with a smile. "My own suspicion, or rather certainty, is precisely the same as your own. When Sir Peter first consulted me, I knew nothing of Captain Reynham; but the fact that he was next heir to the property and title indicated possibilities, that was all. The fact that he was abroad when the first attempts were made, years ago, seemed to tell in his favour—but that, of course, might simply have been a matter of cunning arrangement—an alibi established in advance. Without suspecting him, but regarding him simply as a possibility, I insisted with Sir Peter that he, like everyone else, should be kept in the dark—on the grounds of general caution. Sir Peter, fortunately, agreed —though reluctantly."

"Of course he never dreamed——" said Nugent.

"Neither then—nor now!" said the detective. "In point of fact, I found later that he had let the captain know that Lord Reynham was placed at

school under an assumed name. Fortunately he never mentioned the name, or the school—his pledge to me prevented that. Otherwise——"

"Otherwise, Rupert wouldn't be getting pally with jolly old Bunter just now!" grinned Bob.

"Scarcely! I made a few inquiries about the captain—learning that he was the son of a younger son, with nothing beyond his Army pay, except an allowance from his uncle—and that he was in debts of which Sir Peter knew nothing. I found that he had returned to England, taken up his residence here, and advised Sir Peter to bring Lord Reynham openly to the castle, as the best method of getting at his enemies. After which," added the detective, dryly, "I had a very keen eye open for the captain."

He paused.

"When I found that the kidnappers knew that the young lord was at a school under an assumed name," he went on, "I asked Sir Peter whether he had mentioned that fact to anyone— and learned that he had mentioned it only to Captain Reynham."

"But he never guessed, all the same——"

"He did not. He still wonders how the Smiler and company found it out. But——" Mr. Tomlinson paused again. "I did not feel sure, until the night I went to sleep, and the Smiler escaped. Then I remembered that I had smoked one of the captain's cigarettes before he left me."

"And then you knew?"

"Then," assented Mr. Tomlinson quietly. "I knew—what I could not prove, and what Sir Peter would not have listened to for a moment."

"A bit of a problem, and no mistake!" said Bob.

"The man is as cunning as a fox, and as unscrupulous as a wolf!" said Mr. Tomlinson. "Yet he has his limits! Nothing, I am assured, would induce him to commit the last and greatest of crimes. His cousin's life is in no danger. Short of that, he is prepared to use any and every means of robbing him of his property. Lord Reynham, once in his power, will disappear for ever— his death will be legally presumed, after a time, and Rupert Reynham will step in. That is the game—which I am going to defeat!"

The detective's eyes gleamed again, for a moment.

"Apart from professional considerations, and my desire to earn Sir Peter's very generous fee," he said, "I am determined that such scoundrelism shall not succeed—that a poor, persecuted boy shall not be sacrificed to the greed of an unscrupulous rascal! In that, I feel sure, you agree with me."

"What-ho!" said Bob. "All the jolly old way, Mr. Tomlinson."

"We're staying!" said Harry. "Whenever we can be of any use, Mr. Tomlinson, you've only to say the word. And we can keep our mouths shut—as you've seen already!"

And that was settled, and fixed, when the Famous Five left Mr. Tomlinson's room. Which, possibly, might be a surprise to Lord Bunter—and displeasing to his lordship—so it was fortunate that Lord Bunter did not matter!

THE SIXTEENTH CHAPTER.

Sticky !

"I SAY, you fellows !"

"Hallo, hallo, hallo !" said Bob Cherry affably.

And his comrades grinned.

After lunch that day, Billy Bunter had had his usual nap—requiring his usual rest after his usual exertions. Then he had played a game of billiards with his new pal, Rupert Reynham, and smoked a cigarette or two with that valuable friend. Then—declining the captain's invitation to accompany him on a stroll—he looked for the Famous Five—with the amiable intention of speeding the parting guests.

He found them in the hall, having just returned, fresh and ruddy, from skating—and with no signs of departure about them.

"What train are you fellows catching ?" asked Bunter.

"Ha, ha, ha !" roared Bob.

This was rather a reversal of a state of affairs usual in the "hols." Every member of the Famous Five had been landed with Billy Bunter, more than once or twice, in the hols, and when Bunter was a guest, the most difficult thing about him was to get him to catch a train.

Now Bunter was—or fancied he was—the host; and the Famous Five were the fellows who wouldn't catch the train.

"What are you cackling at, fathead ?" asked Bunter, blinking at Bob.

"The old order changeth, giving place to the new !" quoted Bob.

"Ha, ha, ha !"

"Blessed if I can see anything to cackle at !" grunted Bunter. "Look here, you're pretty sticky—but you're going, Rupert's fed up with you."

"Bad taste on Rupert's part !" said Bob, shaking his head. "He can't know what really nice chaps we are."

"Well, you can't expect him to get over the way you treated him this morning," said Bunter. "I may as well tell you plainly, that he wants you to go. He makes a point of it."

"Dear me !" said Bob, "Rupert makes a point of it ! Do you make a point of it too, old fat man ?"

"I do !" said Bunter, firmly. "Sorry, and all that, but I'm fed up ! Meddling when a chap's having a quiet smoke over a game of poker—you can't expect a fellow to stand for it ! Besides, your manners are jolly bad—they let me down before my servants, you know——"

"Whose servants ?" asked Nugent, grinning.

"Mine !" roared Bunter. "I don't want any cheek, Frank Nugent. Just get out when a fellow tells you he doesn't want you. You can have one of my cars to the station——"

"Whose cars ?" chuckled Bob Cherry.

"Mine !" howled Bunter. "Don't give me any cheek, Bob Cherry ! Look here, when are you fellows going ?"

"The whenfulness is terrific."

"I suppose you're not sticking on where you're not wanted !" said Bunter contemptuously.

"Hardly !" said Harry Wharton, laughing. "We couldn't have come here at all, if old Peter hadn't backed up your silly gas. Old Peter's invitation still holds good—and we're staying on it."

"I've told you I don't want you here——"

"Several times. Now we'll mention that we don't want you here."

"What !" yelled Bunter.

"Are you going ?" asked Bob chuckling.

"Me !" gasped Bunter. "Why, you silly ass ! Look here, I didn't come along here to talk rot——"

"What are you doing it for, then ?"

"I fancied that you were going to turn out sticky," said Bunter. "I noticed that your things weren't packed. They've been taken out of my rooms, though——"

"We're not camping in your rooms any more, old fat man. We've heard enough of your snore to last us till next term at Greyfriars."

"You're going !" hooted Bunter.

"Guess again !"

"Mean to say you're not catching a train ?"

"Not the least little bit in the world !"

"Why I'll have you chucked out !" gasped Bunter, in almost speechless wrath. "I'll have you chucked out of the castle by my menials !"

"Let's put it up to Sir Peter !" suggested Bob. "Let's go and explain to him that you want us to clear out, so that you can smoke and gamble in peace with his nephew ! I'm sure the old sportsman would be interested."

"Ha, ha, ha !"

"I—I—I don't want you to mention anything of that kind to old Peter !" said Bunter, hastily. "He would very likely get waxy. He's an old-fashioned old fossil. Of course, I'm master here—still, I don't want that old donkey to go off at the deep end. Rupert would get a ragging, too. Look here, you beast, don't you get sneaking to old Peter."

"Fathead !"

"I've told Rupert you're going——"

"Go and tell him we're not !"

"But you are !" urged Bunter. "I don't want you here—see ? Rupert makes a point of it, and I make a point of it ! Got that?"

"Suppose you and Rupert go and eat coke together ?" suggested Bob.

"You silly ass ! Will you get out ?" hooted Bunter. "This is my castle, ain't it ?"

"About as much as it's mine !" grinned Bob.

"Look here, I'm not asking you to stop any longer—see ?

"We're not asking you to stop any longer—see ? "

"Ha, ha, ha !"

"We've exactly as much right to ask you, as you have to ask us !" explained Bob Cherry. "And we don't like you here ! You're not good company ! You're lazy, and fatheaded, and you don't wash ! Get out—see ?"

"Ha, ha, ha !"

Billy Bunter blinked at the Famous Five in intense exasperation. Often and often he had been a sticky guest himself. But he had never expected the chums of the Remove to be so sticky.

But they were. They were fearfully sticky—and they were sticking.

"Well, of all the cheeky cads !" gasped Bunter. "Sticking in a fellow's castle whether he likes it or not ! That's the limit ! Look here, you cheeky beasts, what are you going to do?"

"I'm going to bump you for your cheek !" said Bob, cheerily.

"Same here !" said Johnny Bull.

"The samefulness is terrific."

"Hear, hear !"

"I say, you fellows—leggo !" roared Bunter, as he swept off the polished floor in the grasp of five pairs of hands.

"I say——yaroooop !"

Bump !

"Yaroooooooop !"

Bump !

"Oh crikey ! Ow ! Wow ! I say, you fellows——"

Bump !

"Ow ! Beasts ! Wow ! I say, old beasts —I mean old chaps——"

Bump !

"Yuroooooooooop ! "

Bunter sat and roared.

Harry Wharton & Co. strolled away to the music-room, and left him roaring.

———

THE SEVENTEENTH CHAPTER.

A Mysterious Move !

"GOING !"

"Rot ! "

"He's fed up with you fellows—and no wonder !" said Billy Bunter scornfully, "He can't stand you ! "

"Fathead ! He's not going !"

"He jolly well is ! Pretty thick I think, for my friend Rupert to have to go, because you fellows won't ! " said Bunter, contemptuously.

It was a couple of days later.

During those days, the Famous Five had had little of Billy Bunter's fascinating society—and had not missed it a lot.

But their eyes had been on Bunter, all the same.

They had rooms of their own now, and were no longer camped in Bunter's room round the canopied bed where the fat Owl slept and snored.

Bunter's new pal, the captain, occupied the dressing-room attached to Bunter's bed-room, and was, in Bunter's happy opinion, a sufficient protection,

For which reasons, the Famous Five had their eyes open by day; and Mr. Tomlinson, they were aware, prowled a good deal by night.

As the secret door into the King's Room was no longer available, the juniors did not quite see how Rupert's new move was going to benefit him much; but they were wary all the same.

Indeed, now that the captain had lost his right hand man, the Smiler, they knew that he had to depend chiefly on himself—the other two members of the kidnapping gang, Ratty and the Ferret, were merely ruffians who could carry out orders, quite different from the cunning and resourceful Smiler.

What move the schemer was going to make, was rather a puzzle to them; but they had no doubt that he would make one, and make it soon—for he had to act before the end of the holidays.

At the new term, the fat junior whom he believed to be Lord Reynham would return to Greyfriars—and the kidnappers' task would be infinitely more difficult to carry out in a crowded school, than at the castle in Sussex.

But this new move, announced by Billy Bunter astonished them. They could not believe that the captain was leaving the castle, as stated by the fat Owl.

Leaving the castle meant giving up the game—and they could hardly believe that Rupert Reynham was abandoning the scheme upon which he had been concentrated for years.

"He's going !" said Bunter, "This afternoon ! Didn't you see that big trunk come yesterday? He's packing it now."

"Rot !" said Bob Cherry. "He's not going !"

"You can ask old Peter !" sneered Bunter, "He's told him ! Look here, you fellows, if you clear off——"

"Fathead!"

"You see, he can't stand you——"

"He seems to be able to stand you!" said Bob. "If he can stand you, old fat man, he can stand anything."

"Beast!"

Bunter snorted and rolled away. His indignation was deep—at fellows hanging on at "his" castle against his wish. Sir Peter Lanchester did not seem somehow to regard it as Bunter's castle, however; and so long as old Peter made them welcome, the Famous Five were staying on.

And old Peter liked them there much more than he liked Bunter there—very much more. Bunter was, in fact, only there because the peculiar circumstances made him indispensable; while the old baronet really liked the cheery faces of the Famous Five about.

"It can't be true!" said Harry, in

he's not catching a morning train. And that means——"

"That means that the car will pull out after dusk," said Bob. "And that means that something's booked to happen on the way that dear old Rupert doesn't want anybody to see."

"All the samefully, the seefulness will be terrific!" declared Hurree Jamset Ram Singh.

The juniors were rather curious to see Captain Reynham at lunch that day. Since the shindy in the King's Room, he had hardly spoken to any of them, or seemed to have noticed that they were in the castle at all.

At lunch he ignored them, as usual; but from his talk with Sir Peter, they ascertained that Bunter's news was correct. The captain was leaving. He was catching the six o'clock train at

and as they supposed that the captain would go in his own car, that would place the fat Owl completely in his hands—if they did not intervene.

In Bunter's present truculent mood, it might be a difficult matter for any of the party to go in the car also. But that did not apply to Mr. Tomlinson, whose duty it was to keep an eye on his lordship.

Wharton had a word with the detective in the afternoon, and learned that it was Mr. Tomlinson's intention to go with Bunter, if Bunter went with the captain.

Indeed, as the captain was well aware that Bunter would not be allowed out of the castle unwatched, Harry Wharton wondered whether this was, after all, the game. But he could think of nothing else

---

Lots of fellows talk about Santa Claus (or Father Christmas) and know nothing at all about him, except that he manages to keep his face clean while sliding down chimneys. Now I've been looking into his history, so lend me your ears and I will a tale unfold.

Once upon a time a poor old beggar was wandering through the snowy steppes of Russia. Climbing the steppes made him footsore and weary, and the only bit of luck he'd had in twelve years was when the snow froze his feet so he couldn't feel his corns.

He couldn't afford a shave, so his face was hidden in a long white beard—which was probably all for the best. And because he had a fat and jovial appearance, nobody would believe he was starving, and when he begged for alms, the passers-by would cast one eye on his girth, then smite him on the boko with ye brick.

"I say, you fellows," he whined, holding out his hat, "can you lend a fellow a groat until to-morrow? I'm expecting a postal order from a titled relation in the morning. The postal order will be for ten roubles, so if you lend me that, I'll hand you—I say, don't walk away while a fellow's talking to you—beasts!" And he got no alms—only boots!

He did everything he could think of to get money, except work—he didn't think of that—and when Christmas came round, he was without a bean.

The Story of Santa Claus

Discovered after years of tremendous research

By BOB CHERRY

Even a Russian farmer, who found Claus with a chopper in his turkey-shed, didn't believe he was there to chop up firewood.

"Thou varlet," he snarled. "Thou didst come after my turks. To pay for thy cheek thou canst go and gather me some firewood, or dadblame me, I'll pop ye in gaol for the festive season."

So poor old Claus tottered out, groping with numbed hands in the snow for bits of wood so small and rotten that a sparrow would have scorned to perch on them. He passed through a neighbouring park, belonging to a rich king, and as it was the Feast of Stephen, this king followed the custom of his house and looked out. Kings in those times always had to look out. It paid.

"Hither, page," roared this king, "come stand by me. Dost thou see what I seest? Or have I got them again? Bring me flesh and bring me wine, we'll ask this codger in to dine."

Santa Claus was very interested in the flesh and wine—especially the wine—but what he liked most was the lavish gold and silver plate which adorned the table. So when the king turned his back, he stuffed the lot in a sack, pinched the royal reindeer sledge, and vanished like smoke. And King Wenceslas swore a mighty oath he'd never be such a sap as to ask a peasant into the palace again.

Being in a hurry, Santa Claus exceeded the speed in a built-up area until he was gonged by the Reindeer Corps. The cops cast a suspicious eye on his sack.

"Wotcher got in there?" they asked, and when they saw the contents, they whistled softly and took out their manacles.

"Presents, that's all," said Santa, banking on his jovial appearance. "I'm going to leave them at the houses of poor people!"

"Oh, yeah? We'll come with you and watch!"

There was no help for it, so Santa drove round, stuffing costly gold and silver plate in the peasants' cottages. Then the cops shook his hand and wished him a Merry Christmas.

"Merry Christmas? Har, har, har!" And poor old Santa drove straight off to the workhouse and rang the visitors' bell.

And that, my beloved 'earers, is the story of Santa Claus.

More or less!

---

a low voice when Bunter was gone. "The man can't be going."

"May be chucking it," said Nugent doubtfully.

Wharton shook his head.

"He's not chucking it. If he's going, it's some trick—some new move! I can't make it out yet—but that's it!"

"Maybe going to get his pal Billy to go in the car!" suggested Bob, with a grin. "If that's it, his pal Billy will go farther than he expects."

"By Jove! That might be it—the simplest of tricks!" said Harry, with a nod. "Bunter might go to the station to see him off—thinking he would come back in the car——"

"And he wouldn't jolly well come back!" grinned Bob. "Rupert would explain that he wanted to walk, or something——"

"That's it!" said Johnny Bull.

"Well, if Rupert really goes, some of us will be on the watch when the car starts for the station," said Harry. "If that fat fool goes in the car, we shall have to keep him in sight somehow. Bunter says it's this afternoon—

Castlewood; which, at that time of the year was well after dark.

Once or twice the juniors caught Mr. Tomlinson's eyes fixed on the captain's face with a penetrating look.

They could guess that the detective was perplexed by the latest move of the schemer.

After lunch, the captain and Lord Bunter went into the billiards-room, where the click of the balls was heard.

Sir Peter, no doubt, fancied that they were playing a harmless game; but the Famous Five had no doubt that the captain was taking the shortest cut to Bunter's fat heart—letting him win money on the game.

Harry Wharton & Co. had intended to go out skating that afternoon. The snow had cleared off, but the lake was still frozen hard. But they gave up that idea since they had learned of Rupert's impending departure.

They remained in the castle; and five pairs of eyes were going to be very much on the alert when the captain went. They had little doubt, by this time, that the big idea was for Bunter to go in the car to the station—

After tea, Billy Bunter made one more effort. He followed the Famous Five into the hall, and fixed his big spectacles on them, with a very serious blink.

"I say, you fellows——" he began.

"Don't!" said Bob Cherry.

"Eh? Don't what?" yapped Bunter.

"Don't say! Don't jaw! Just shut up!"

"Look here, you cheeky beast, will you clear off! You're practically turning my friend Rupert out by sticking here!" hissed Bunter.

Harry Wharton laughed. Evidently the captain had his fat lordship just where he wanted him. Never had Bunter, if he had only known it, been more in need of the protection of which he was so anxious to be rid.

"William!"

Bunter blinked round.

"Coming up to help me finish packing?" asked Captain Reynham, with a smile, taking no notice of the Famous Five.

"Oh, certainly, old chap!" said Bunter.

And he rolled up the staircase after Rupert.

In the oak gallery, over the hall, Mr. Tomlinson was seated with a newspaper, which he was probably not reading. He was ready, if there was any sign of Bunter going in the car. Four members of the Famous Five remained by the fire in the hall. Harry Wharton put on his coat and cap, and went out on the avenue. He was quite puzzled; but if there was, at the very last moment, some unforeseen trickery, the captain of the Remove was there to watch for it.

With one fellow out on the drive, four fellows in the hall, and the detective in the gallery over the hall, his fat lordship was not likely to go unseen—if he went. Never, in fact, had Lord Bunter been so well guarded. And yet——

THE EIGHTEENTH CHAPTER.

Harry Wharton on the Spot!

HARRY WHARTON was deeply perplexed.

He stood on the dusky avenue, under one of the frosty trees, invisible in the winter gloom, but able, from where he stood, to watch the brightly lighted entrance of the castle.

The captain's car had been brought round.

Two or three footmen were carrying out his baggage; several suitcases and a gun-case and a large, heavy trunk.

A luggage grid, at the back of the car, had been let down for the trunk, and the footmen were strapping it on. There was no sign of Bunter.

Captain Reynham was to be seen, in the lighted doorway, saying good-bye to Sir Peter Lanchester.

When his baggage was on the car he came down the steps.

Wharton watched, puzzled.

Obviously, the scheme was not to get Bunter to drive to the station with him. Bunter was not to be seen at all.

Captain Reynham sat at the wheel and started up. From the deep dusk Wharton watched him in perplexity.

Was he, after all, giving up the game, or had he spotted the fact that he was suspected, and decided to go while the going was good? Or was he, after all, taking his departure in the ordinary way of things?

Wharton could not guess.

The car got into motion, and the headlights flashed down the drive. It rolled past the spot where Harry stood.

In a few more moments it would have been gone.

Harry Wharton glanced again at the lighted doorway.

He saw his friends looking out; but Bunter was not with them. He had, it seemed, remained upstairs, and had not troubled to come down to see his friend Rupert off.

It was rather instinct than thought that caused a sudden, startling suspicion to flash into Wharton's mind—as the car glided by with the big trunk strapped on behind.

His eyes fixed on that big trunk.

He remembered Bunter's remark—that it had arrived at the castle the day before. Why had the captain sent for a special trunk for his baggage? A special trunk—a very large one—and he had asked Bunter to go up and

help him finish packing—Bunter had been alone with him there—and he had not come down to see him off!

As if by a lightning flash, Wharton saw it. And as the car glided by, he ran out from the darkness of the trees, and grasped at the baggage strapped on the grid behind.

He hung on.

It was all he could do on the spur of the moment. It was easy enough to hang on the strapped trunk; and the captain, looking ahead as he drove, had seen nothing of the shadow suddenly flitting from under the trees and darting behind the car.

He drove on fast.

Harry Wharton hung on to the strapped trunk on the grid. He felt—he knew—what was in that big trunk.

That was the scheme.

That trunk had been carried down under the nose of the watching detective, under the eyes of the juniors in the hall—and that trunk, Wharton felt in his very bones, contained the kidnapped fat Owl.

Easy enough when Rupert had had him alone; the rascal who had drugged the detective with a cigarette had something at hand to silence the hapless fat Owl. Drugged, senseless, Bunter was packed in that trunk, and the supposed Lord Reynham was being carried off, unseen and unsuspected, under the eyes of the whole crowded castle.

Left without the aid of the Smiler, the plotter had been compelled to act for himself. This was how he had done it.

Wharton, once the idea was in his mind, was as sure of it as if he could have seen the unconscious fat face of Bunter through the locked lid of the trunk.

The car gathered speed on the drive, and at the gateway it almost flashed past the lodge and turned into the Castlewood road; it roared away down the dark road.

Wharton was sure. But he knew that he would soon know for certain. The captain would not drive to the station if he had a kidnapped schoolboy in the trunk. He would never risk such baggage on the railway—neither did he need to. His confederates were at hand, and his aim would be to hand the kidnapped boy over to them at the earliest possible moment.

Harry did not expect the car to keep on the direct road to Castlewood—and it did not. Half a mile from the castle it turned into a dark lane and bumped on over rutty ground.

Obviously the captain was not going to the station—that was a certainty now.

The car jolted on fast, though the lane was jutty and rugged. Harry Wharton had his arms and shoulders over the strapped trunk; he hung on easily enough. Obviously the captain never dreamed that anyone was hanging on behind the car; he drove steadily on. Wharton could do nothing but wait and watch events; he hung on and waited.

The boom of the sea fell on his ears. The car slowed down on a road that ran by the seashore. Through the gloom white spray glimmered. Far out on the water burned a light. Thick frosty trees and bushes lined the landward side of the road.

The car slowed and slowed. Harry Wharton heard a shrill whistle from

the direction of the sea. The car stopped.

He knew then that this was the rendezvous. He dropped off the strapped trunk and backed quickly into the deep shadow beside the road.

Captain Reynham stepped down. No doubt the headlights on that lonely road were signal enough to the men who waited on the shore.

Two dusky figures came tramping up the sand. Wharton glimpsed their faces in the car's lights and knew Ratty and the Ferret.

He backed deep in cover.

He was powerless to act. Discovery meant that he would share Bunter's unknown fate—and could not help him. He could only watch. Any one of the three rascals could have handled him. But he watched with the knowledge that if he escaped unseen he had proof now—proof that would overwhelm the plotting scoundrel and save the kidnapped schoolboy.

"You got him, guv'nor?" It was the Ferret's voice.

Wharton heard a sarcastic laugh.

"Yes. It was easy, once I had the matter in my own hands. Smiler bungled and bungled; I have not done so. The fat fool is in the trunk."

"By gum!" said Ratty, with a deep breath.

"He came up to help me pack the trunk," went on the captain in the same sarcastic tone. "He did not guess how he was intended to help. The fat fool hardly squeaked when I jammed the chloroform pad on his foolish face. But lose no time; get him down to the boat. The sooner the better——"

"Nobody about here, guv'nor——"

"Lose no time, I tell you!" snapped Captain Reynham.

The two ruffians stepped round behind the car. The trunk was unstrapped, unlocked, and opened. Dimly Harry Wharton saw a fat, insensible figure lifted out, and caught a gleam of spectacles.

"Pack a few rocks in the trunk; it must not weigh less when I return to the castle," said Captain Reynham.

"You're going back, guv'nor?"

"I have forgotten some things, and have to return for them, losing my train," said the captain. "I have that all cut and dried. When I return I shall find that Lord Reynham is missing, and shall, of course, cancel my intended departure, in those painful circumstances."

Wharton heard a chuckle.

The fat Owl was lifted between the two ruffians and carried away down the beach to the unseen boat. Captain Reynham stood watching them as they went. When they were out of sight he sat at the wheel and backed and turned the car.

The big trunk had been strapped on again, locked on the rocks that had been placed in it to give it the necessary weight. Every point had been guarded by the cunning and wary plotter.

The car got into motion, passing the junior who was blotted from sight under the dark trees.

As it passed, Harry Wharton slipped out and caught hold of the trunk and hung on again. Captain Reynham was driving back to the castle—and driving back in a mood of complete and triumphant satisfaction. Probably he would have felt neither so triumphant

Printed in England and published every Saturday by the Proprietors, The Amalgamated Press, Ltd., The Fleetway House, Farringdon Street, London, E.C.4. Advertisement offices: The Fleetway House, Farringdon Street, London, E.C.4. Registered for transmission by Canadian Magazine Post. Subscription rates: Inland and Abroad, 11s. per annum; 5s. 6d. for six months. Sole Agents for Australia and New Zealand: Messrs. Gordon & Gotch, Ltd., and for South Africa: Central News Agency, Ltd.—Saturday, January 1st, 1938.

nor so satisfied had he been able to guess who was driving back with him.

Not till the car was nearly at the castle door did Harry Wharton drop off behind; then he walked on after the car as it ran up to the castle entrance.

THE NINETEENTH CHAPTER.

Denounced!

"YOU cannot find him?"

"No, sir."

"It is very extraordinary! Tomlinson——"

"It is very extraordinary indeed," said Mr. Tomlinson between his closed lips.

Sir Peter Lanchester was in the library. The Co. were there with him, and Tomlinson. Sir Peter looked worried and anxious, so did the juniors and the detective.

"But he should not go out alone, especially after dark," said Sir Peter. "Neither can I understand his having done so. You have looked——"

"We've looked everywhere, sir," said Bob Cherry. "Bunter doesn't seem to be in the castle at all. I can't make it out."

"He never went with Captain Reynham," said Nugent.

"No. I saw my nephew off at the door," said Sir Peter. "That was an hour ago. Where is Wharton? He may have seen something of William, and——"

"He hasn't come in," said Johnny Bull. "He—he went out just before Captain Reynham started."

"But if William is not in the castle, where can he be?" exclaimed Sir Peter. "There are a dozen doors by which he may have left. But why should he? He was, in fact, very nervous about going out, especially alone. What do you make of this, Mr. Tomlinson?"

"I cannot understand it," said the detective. "It appears that the foolish boy has gone out. But why——"

The library door opened, and Captain Reynham stepped in.

All eyes turned on him—Sir Peter's in surprise mingled with relief.

"Rupert!" he exclaimed. "Then you have not caught your train!"

"No," said the captain. "I found that an attache-case had been overlooked and came back for it. But I have just heard a very startling thing from Jasmond. He says that William cannot be found."

"That is so. And I am thankful that you have returned, Rupert; you may be able to help."

"It is very odd," said Captain Reynham. "I saw William only ten minutes before I went. He was in the King's Room. The secret door—— But that has been screwed up; it is impossible——"

"That is quite impossible!" said Mr. Tomlinson.

The captain glanced at him.

"Well, it is your task to find him, Mr. Tomlinson," he said. "I will render any assistance in my power. In the circumstances, uncle, I shall not return to London this evening. Possibly William has only gone out for a stroll——"

"Catch him!" said Bob.

"If it is certain that he is not in the castle——" said Rupert.

"That appears to be certain," said Sir Peter. "If he has, after all, gone out, Wharton may have seen something of him. Wharton appears to be out of doors——"

"Possibly they have gone together," suggested Rupert.

"It is possible, of course. But——"

"Hallo, hallo, hallo! Here's Wharton!"

The library door opened again, and Harry Wharton came in. His face was flushed, and he was breathing hard.

"Harry!" exclaimed Frank Nugent, taking a step towards him. He could see at a glance that something had happened.

Harry Wharton shut the door.

Then he came across to the group by the fireside.

Mr. Tomlinson gave him a rather startled glance.

"Wharton," exclaimed Sir Peter, a little testily, "it appears that William is missing from the castle! You have been out. Have you seen anything of him?"

"Yes," answered Harry quietly.

Quietly as he spoke, his voice had the effect of a thunderclap on Captain Reynham.

The young Army man gave a violent start, and made a swift step towards Wharton.

"You have seen him?" he exclaimed.

"Yes!" repeated Harry, looking him steadily in the face. "I have seen him, Captain Reynham, and know where he is now."

The strange pallor that came over the captain's face caused even Sir Peter to give him a sharp and curious look.

The blow was so sudden, so unexpected, that it was scarcely possible for the plotter to be on his guard. His look at Harry Wharton was almost wild, his eyes burning from a white face.

"You know?" he gasped.

"Yes, I know."

The effort that Rupert Reynham made to pull himself together was visible to all eyes. A grim expression came over Mr. Tomlinson's face.

"Well, if you know, my lad, tell my uncle at once and relieve his anxiety," said Captain Reynham, in an attempt to speak casually. "From what the boy says, uncle, it appears that there is no—no cause for alarm."

"Please tell me at once, Wharton!" said Sir Peter.

"I am going to," said Harry. "But, first, I had better say that I have proof now of the kidnapper's identity, and that your handcuffs will be wanted, Mr. Tomlinson."

"They are ready!" said Mr. Tomlinson grimly.

"Do you mean proof of the identity of the kidnapper's confederate in the castle?" asked Sir Peter.

"Yes, sir!"

"That is excellent, if correct!" exclaimed the old baronet. "His name?"

"He is here!" said Harry. "You fellows stand ready to collar him, if necessary. You are ready with the handcuffs, Mr. Tomlinson? I tell you that I have proof—as an eye-witness."

Mr. Tomlinson moved a little nearer to the captain. The Co. watched their leader, in breathless excitement.

All could see that Harry Wharton had made a discovery during his absence from the castle. It was as clear to Rupert Reynham as to the rest, and his face went paler and paler.

He lighted a cigarette, but his hand was shaking so that he could hardly get the match to it. Yet what, he was asking himself, could the boy have seen? What could he know? He could have seen nothing of what had happened on that lonely road by the beach; he had not been absent long enough to cover the distance on foot. What could he know?

Sir Peter Lanchester started to his feet.

"You say that he is here, Wharton!" he exclaimed blankly. "You do not mean in this room?"

"I mean in this room, sir!" answered Harry.

The old baronet glanced round the spacious library.

"Concealed in this room!" he ejaculated.

"No, sir!"

"Then what do you mean?" exclaimed Sir Peter testily. "You appear to me to be talking in riddles, boy!"

Captain Reynham burst into a laugh. It sounded so cracked, so false, that his uncle turned to look at him.

"Evidently our young friend considers this a matter for jesting!" said Rupert.

But, with all his effrontery, he could not speak in his usual easy drawl. His voice was shaking.

"You must get ready for a shock, sir!" said Harry. "I am sorry! It will be a very painful surprise to you. But I must tell you, if only to get Bunter out of the hands of those scoundrels before they put to sea with him!"

"Where have you seen him?" rapped Mr. Tomlinson.

"On the beach some miles from here, handed over to the two rascals called Ratty and the Ferret by the villain who took him away from this castle!" answered Harry.

The cigarette dropped from Rupert's fingers.

"And who was it?" exclaimed Sir Peter.

Harry Wharton lifted his hand, and his finger pointed at the white-faced man, who stood stricken, almost stunned.

"That was the man," he said—"Captain Reynham!"

THE TWENTIETH CHAPTER.

The Game's Up!

"CAPTAIN REYNHAM!"

"Yes!"

"My nephew!" gasped Sir Peter. "Are you mad?"

"Look at him, sir!" said Harry quietly. "He knows the game is up now!"

Sir Peter Lanchester turned his eyes on his nephew. He stared at the white, stricken face, from which every vestige of colour seemed to have drained.

What he read in that face caused his own to pale.

He made a step towards the young Army man.

"Rupert"—his voice was husky—"deny this! The boy is mistaken—or mad! Why do you not speak, Rupert?"

The captain found his voice.

"It is false—false!" He panted out the words. "Let him prove——"

Sir Peter Lanchester gave him a long, long look, and his old face seemed to grow older and greyer. He turned quietly to Wharton.

"Speak!" he said briefly.

"I am sorry, sir!" said Harry. "I know this must be an awful shock to you. We've suspected Captain Reynham for a long time, but there was no proof. We were on the watch to-day, to see if he tried to get Bunter away in his car. I was watching on the drive when he went, and it suddenly flashed into my mind why the big trunk was on the car."

"Oh!" breathed Mr. Tomlinson.

"That big trunk!" muttered Bob.

"We never thought——"

"I hung on behind the car, holding on to the trunk," said Harry. "Captain Reynham never knew, of course. I dropped off when he stopped at a lonely place by the sea. I got into cover. I saw them take Bunter from the trunk—heard what Captain Reynham said to his accomplices. He told them he had chloroformed Bunter and packed him in the trunk, and told them to take him to the boat. They packed rocks in the trunk, in case the servants should notice any difference in weight when he came back here. I hung on behind again when he started; he gave me a lift, without knowing it, almost to the door."

"Then Bunter——" exclaimed Bob.

"He has been taken out to some vessel lying off shore in a boat. That vessel can be stopped, Sir Peter, if you telephone to Mr. Shute. And when Bunter is here again, he can tell you who seized him in the King's Room and put the chloroform pad over his face."

A deep silence followed Wharton's words. It was broken by a clink of metal.

Mr. Tomlinson had taken the handcuffs from his pocket.

Captain Reynham stood as if petrified, the perspiration thick on his brow. Sir Peter Lanchester waited for him to speak. He did not speak.

"A clear case—at last!" said Mr. Tomlinson. "I could not speak before, Sir Peter; like the boy, I could not speak without proof. But I have known for more than a week that your nephew was the man!"

"My nephew!" breathed the old baronet. "Good heavens! But why—why——"

He could not grasp it yet.

Mr. Tomlinson smiled faintly.

"The next heir to Reynham!" he said.

"Good heavens!" repeated Sir Peter.

"It is for you to say, sir, whether I take this man into custody, to be handed over to the police!" said Mr. Tomlinson.

He made a motion with the handcuffs.

Sir Peter Lanchester shuddered.

"No, no! Even if he is guilty—no! Rupert, speak! Have you nothing to say—nothing?"

The captain breathed hard and deep. He was recovering something of his coolness.

"Yes," he said; "I have something to say." His voice was even. "You believe what the boy has said. Believe it if you choose; it will not be so easy to prove in a court of law! Lord Reynham is gone. I stand in his place. If you believe what this boy has said, you may believe also that Lord Reynham will never be seen again! If you choose to drag our name through the law courts, I do not think that you will be able to shake my position. I defy this man—a private detective without official authority—to arrest me! If Lord Reynham is not found—and you can take it from me that he will not be found—I am master here!"

He spoke quietly, deliberately.

Sir Peter gazed at him in silent horror, the juniors almost in wonder. He stood out now, to all eyes, as what he was—the unscrupulous, ruthless adventurer.

"If that vessel is stopped I doubt whether a prisoner will be found on board!" said Captain Reynham, in the same icy tone.

The meaning—the terrible meaning—of his words was plain.

"William is gone!" he went on. "A

lazy, frowsy, self-indulgent, good-for-nothing fool! Let him go! Dead or disappeared, he is gone, and I stand here as master of Reynham Castle!"

Sir Peter gazed at him, dumb.

"Leave it at that!" said Rupert, with bitter coolness. "This detective is in your pay. Silence him! The boys will keep the secret if you ask them; or they may chatter as they will. I care little! You do not desire futile disgrace to our name, which is all you can achieve now. I am master of Reynham Castle."

Sir Peter found his voice.

"And now," he said, "I know you as you are—rascal, villain, plotting villain! Now, I will tell you where you stand, master of Reynham Castle, as you fancy yourself. Traitor and dastard, the boy you have kidnapped is not Lord Reynham. You have heard these lads call him Bunter, and fancied that it was the name under which my ward passed at Greyfriars School. Fool, as well as villain, it was his own name, and he was not Lord Reynham!"

"Hardly!" murmured Bob Cherry.

"He was brought here," said Sir Peter, "to draw the attacks of the kidnappers, in my ward's name. To draw the scoundrels, of whom I never dreamed that my own nephew was one, into the trap! The plan has succeeded perfectly, chiefly owing to these Greyfriars boys. Scoundrel! The boy you have kidnapped has no connection whatever with the Reynham family! His name is Bunter: these boys know his parents and other relatives! Lord Reynham, my dear ward, is safe from you. Do you understand? Safe!"

Captain Reynham stood quite still.

For a moment or two, perhaps, he did not believe it. But he looked from face to face, and knew!

"Not Lord Reynham!" he said at last, in a gasping voice.

"Not quite!" grinned Bob Cherry. "You wouldn't think so if you knew his sister Bessie, and his brother Sammy, and his people at Bunter Villa."

"The boy," said Sir Peter, "is Bunter! If he is kept a prisoner it will not serve you. Do you understand now, scoundrel?"

"I understand," said Captain Reynham, in a low voice. "I have been fooled all along the line! I knew you were hiding something, though I never knew what. So it was this! Taken in—by an old fool and a set of school-boys. If that fat fool goes to an island in the Pacific, or if they throw him overboard, Lord Reynham remains! And, after this, I have no chance!" He burst into a harsh, bitter laugh. "The game's up! I give in!"

He shrugged his shoulders with an air of indifference, and lighted a cigarette.

"Yes," said Sir Peter, "the game is up, Rupert Reynham! Now that I know who my ward's enemy is I shall know how to guard him, and to-morrow he will resume his own name, and his rightful place. And you——"

He paused for a moment.

"You," he said, "will leave England this very night. First you will bring Bunter here, safe and sound; then you will go. If you are in this country at noon to-morrow you will be arrested on my charge, and prosecuted for kidnapping, and sent to the prison you deserve. If you ever return to England

the handcuffs will be on your wrists the same day. Now go!"

Mr. Tomlinson, with obvious reluctance, slipped the handcuffs back into his pocket. Rupert Reynham cast one look of bitter malice at the Greyfriars juniors and walked out of the library.

   ·   ·   ·

"I SAY, you fellows!"

"Hallo, old bean!"

"I've got a bit of a head-ache!"

"How's that?"

"Blessed if I know! Have I been asleep?" Billy Bunter sat up, groped for his spectacles, jammed them on his fat little nose, and blinked at the juniors round the canopied bed.

"What's the time?"

"Nearly nine!"

"Why, we're late for dinner!" exclaimed Billy Bunter. He sat up. "I say, you fellows, I seem to have been asleep a jolly long time! Funny thing is, I don't remember lying down—Oh!" Bunter gave a yell as a rush of recollection came. "I say, you fellows, stick to me! Keep him off—that beast Rupert! I say, he stuck something over my face. He got me! I say—keep him off!"

"All right now, old chap!" said Bob Cherry soothingly. "The rotter brought you back before he went—and he's gone now for good! You won't see him any more."

"Sure he's gone?" gasped Bunter.

"Gone for good—order of the boot—catching the Channel boat to-night, and never coming back again!" said Harry Wharton.

"Oh, good!" gasped Bunter. "I say, you fellows, he got me! It jolly well looks to me, now, as if he had a hand in that kidnapping business——"

"Think so?" grinned Johnny Bull.

"Well, it looks like it to me, now," said Bunter. "You fellows mayn't be able to see it—you're not very bright—but that's what it looks like to me——"

"Ha, ha, ha!"

"Blessed if I see anything to cackle at! I say, you fellows, we shall be late for dinner at this rate! Ring for James—I mean Frederick! I say, you can stay on in my castle——"

"Really and truly?" chuckled Nugent.

"Ha, ha, ha!"

"Oh, don't cackle at everything a fellow says!" yapped Bunter. "I'm inviting you to stay on in my castle for the rest of the hols——"

"We'll see what Lord Reynham says to-morrow!" chuckled Bob.

"Eh? Who? How——"

"Lord Reynham will be here to-morrow—the genuine article!" grinned Bob.

Bunter blinked at him.

"Oh crikey!" he said.

That was all he could say. That unexpected—and apparently unwelcome news seemed to have taken Lord Bunter's breath away. The jackdaw was going to lose his borrowed plumes. It was the last of Lord Bunter!

THE END.

(Frank Richards commences the New Year well with the finest yarn he's ever written. It's entitled: "BUNTER'S BIG BLUNDER!" Watch out for it in next Saturday's MAGNET.)

The Magnet

2D

CRA-A-SH!

COME INTO the OFFICE, BOYS - AND GIRLS !

Your Editor is always pleased to hear from his readers. Write to him : Editor of the "Magnet," The Amalgamated Press, Ltd., Fleetway House, Farringdon Street, London, E.C.4. A stamped, addressed envelope will ensure a reply.

I PICKED up the first letter from my mail this week, and got quite a thrill when I saw that it was signed " Inquisitor." I had horrible ideas about the Spanish Inquisition and fancied myself being placed on the rack, or shoved in boiling oil, and things of that sort.

However, " Inquisitor," who hails from Manchester, only wanted to ask me a few questions. The first concerns

THE TORTOISE.

He wants to know when tortoises hibernate. As a matter of fact, this depends largely on the weather and local conditions. I happen to have a couple of tortoises myself. One of them buried itself in my garden over a couple of months ago. The other one I put in a box filled with grass, which I placed in a warm corner in the house. As soon as the weather begins to get cold, tortoises look out for a warm spot. If you keep tortoises, the best plan is to put them in a box with plenty of grass or hay, let them bury themselves in it, and then see that the box is kept in a warm spot. A corner near the kitchen fire is best. After that, don't worry about them until next spring. When the weather becomes warm enough for them, they'll come out—and be just as lively as they were before they went for their long winter's sleep.

In reply to the other questions " Inquisitor " asks : Billy Bunter weighs 14 stone, and Harry Wharton and Bob Cherry are both 15 years of age.

Now for a letter from " R. F. F.," of Richmond, Surrey.

HE MAKES YOUR EDITOR BLUSH

with pride, because he says so many complimentary things about THE MAGNET.

With regard to his query about Claude Rains, the film actor, he will be pleased to know that this actor is British, and appeared on the stage for many years before he went into films. Like many other British actors, Claude Rains went to Hollywood, but it will not be long before he is seen in quite a number of films, including British ones. If my chum cares to write to the managers of his local cinemas, they will be only too pleased to tell him when they are screening the next film in which this particular actor appears.

I AM afraid that " W. A." and " F. E.," of Englefield, near Reading, will find a little difficulty if

THEY WANT TO JOIN THE " MOUNTIES."

There are so many anxious to join this wonderful corps that the waiting list is a long one. Recruiting is not carried out in this country for the " Mounties." It's not easy for anyone who has been used to our British climate to face the rigours of the North-West. My chums would have to go to Canada in order to join—and the chances are that they would find themselves unsuitable.

So far as the Grenadier Guards are

concerned, any post office will be pleased to supply particulars of recruiting in this or any other corps, In most big towns there is an Army Recruiting Office, with an official in charge who will give full particulars of any branch of the British Army in which one may be interested.

Now comes a query from a West Hartlepool reader, who asks me if I can tell him what is

THE WORLD'S DEEPEST DIVE.

This was made by an American diver who was working on the construction of the San Francisco-Oakland Bay Bridge. The actual depth of the water was only about forty feet, but it was necessary to go down another 200 feet in order to find a solid foundation. A caisson with a false bottom was used to dredge into the mud, until the depth of the hole was 245 feet under the surface. Then the diver went down, thereby establishing a world's record for deep water diving on any construction work.

An American reader has sent me along some particulars of what is claimed to be

THE MOST LUXURIOUS BUS

in the world. We've got some pretty good night-travelling buses in this country, but we'll have to " go some " if we want to beat the new cross-country sleeper-bus which has been started on a run between Los Angeles and Kansas City. This bus carries twenty-five passengers, each of whom has a sleeping berth. There are five compartments all told, in the bus, and they are equipped with wireless, a mirror, hot and cold running water, and a portable table. A corridor runs the entire length of the bus down one side. In the day-time the sleeping berths are converted into cushion lounge seats. The walls of the bus are insulated to guard against changes in the weather. The power plant is placed at the back of the bus, to eliminate noises. There is, however, a false radiator front, and behind it is a spacious luggage compartment. Besides the driver, there is a porter, who has a " kitchenette " from which light lunches and other refreshments can be supplied to the passengers. " Some " bus, eh ?

NOW for a few

RAPID-FIRE REPLIES

to other questions fired at me by readers : **What is the World's Greatest Power Plant ?** The hydro-electric plant at Dnieproges, on the Dnieper River in Russia. It cost about twenty-two million pounds to construct.

What is the Longest Canal in the World ? Russia also claims this record. The Baltic-White Sea Canal, recently opened, is 141 miles in length. The longest river route for navigation connects Moscow with Archangel, and is 2,100 miles in length.

Who Was " Sixteen-String Jack "? A highwayman, whose proper name was Jack Rann. He received his nickname

because of the blue ribands with which he used to decorate himself. He was a most audacious criminal, and managed to keep the Bow Street runners at bay for a long time. But they got him in the end, and he was executed.

Has a Toy Balloon ever Crossed the Atlantic ? Yes. One was released from New York, and was subsequently picked up at Edale, in Derbyshire.

What is the Lowest Part of North America ? Death Valley, in California. It is 250 feet below sea level. It is also the hottest place in North America.

Is there such a thing as an Automatic Revolver ? No, an automatic is a pistol, not a revolver. In a revolver, the barrel revolves as the shots are fired. With an automatic the bullets rise up into the barrel from the magazine.

How Many Ribs has a Python ? It has been calculated that a python 30 feet in length has no fewer than 600 ribs !

Are any Horse Races Held without Jockeys ? Yes. In Mexico riderless horse races are frequently held. The horses compete against each other without carrying any jockeys.

Here is a curious little paragraph which I have unearthed for you :

WHO WANTS TO BUY A PRISON ?

Do you realise that this country is becoming so law abiding that some prisons have been standing empty for years—and are frequently sold at " bargain prices " to anyone who wants them ? Just a little while ago the disused Cambridge Prison was sold for a few pounds. The gallows, in perfect working order, were sold for only one guinea ! But prisons are not the only buildings which sell cheaply nowadays. Some years ago an entire South Country resort was auctioned for £1,250—and it cost nearly a hundred thousand pounds to build !

One of the biggest bargains ever made was by a man who bought

A CASTLE FOR 2s. 6d. !

It was the thirteenth-century Castle of Montemale in Italy. Just a short while ago the biggest bid at an auction sale was seven lire, which is worth approximately two shillings and sixpence. So the castle was " knocked down " for that amount ! In this country castles are worth quite a lot of money, although I know one famous old castle where you can rent one of the towers, furnished, for as little as two guineas a week. In many places abroad, old castles are standing derelict, and can be bought quite cheaply. If you don't want a castle, what about an entire village ? There's one up for sale now—the village of Horton, near Northampton. If you happen to possess a rich uncle, what about dropping him a hint that a village would make a most useful and attractive birthday present !

As space is getting rather short, I must hold over a number of other paragraphs and answers to queries until next week and tell you what is in store in next week's issue of the MAGNET. First of all comes :

" THE OUTSIDER ! " By Frank Richards

the second yarn in our grand new series featuring Eric Wilmot. Mr. Hacker thinks he has done a big thing for his nephew in obtaining for him admission at Greyfriars. But the master of the Shell has made the biggest mistake in his life, for Wilmot is most unhappy in his new surroundings, which is somewhat mystifying to Harry Wharton & Co. When you've finished this first-rate yarn, you'll find thrills galore in our super sea and adventure story. And just to round off this super issue, there'll be a " Greyfriars Herald " supplement, another contribution from our pet Rhymester, and another chat with

YOUR EDITOR.

The BOY who WOULDN'T MAKE FRIENDS !

By FRANK RICHARDS

In the opinion of Harry Wharton & Co., of Greyfriars, one Hacker in the school is enough and to spare ! Now, like a bolt from the blue, comes the Shell master's nephew, Eric Wilmot . . . whose room is voted better than his company !

THE FIRST CHAPTER.

Bunter Asks For It !

"START at two !" murmured Bob Cherry.

Bob spoke in a low voice—which was far from his usual custom. Bob's voice, as a rule, had rather a megaphonic quality, and his remarks could easily be heard by all whom they might concern, and a good many whom they did not concern.

But in the Remove Form Room, during class, it was necessary for a fellow to be cautious.

Mr. Quelch was looking in his desk for a book, and had his back turned momentarily to the Form. His gimlet eyes were not on his class; but his ears were equally sharp. So Bob whispered.

Harry Wharton nodded.

It was safer not to speak. Talking in class was frowned upon severely by Herry Samuel Quelch. Quelch liked to see his boys, in class, concentrated unremittingly on their lessons. That liking was seldom wholly gratified.

"On the bikes——" went on Bob.

"Quiet !" breathed Frank Nugent.

"Quelch can't hear ! We shall get to St. Jude's before three—"

"Yes ; shut up !"

"Putting it on a bit, you know. Ripping day for a ride."

Mr. Quelch glanced round from his desk. Perhaps a faint murmur of a voice had reached his keen ears.

Bob was promptly silent.

A fellow might get a detention, for talking in class. And a detention that afternoon would have been simply awful.

It was a clear, bright, frosty, January day, and that afternoon was a half-holiday. On such a day, Bob, more than any other fellow in the Greyfriars Remove, felt the call of the open spaces. Detention would have been an awful disaster.

However, Mr. Quelch turned back to his desk, and resumed his quest of the book he wanted. He was not likely to find it in a hurry, as Vernon-Smith, just before third school, had transferred it to the wastepaper-basket under the desk. Happily unaware of that little jest of the Bounder's, Quelch turned over the papers in his desk, growing puzzled and irritated, while Smithy winked at Redwing, and grinned.

The rustle of papers in the Form-master's desk broke the silence of the Form-room. Under cover of that rustle Bob went on, still in a cautious whisper :

"St. Jude's have a match on to-day, you know—they're playing some school —I forget the name—"

"Topham !" said Harry.

"Yes, that's it, Topham ! We want to see how St. Jude's shape, as we're playing them later in the term—"

Mr. Quelch glanced round again.

"Is anyone speaking in class ?" he inquired, in a rumbling voice.

Dead silence.

A pin might have been heard to drop in the Remove Form Room.

Nobody answered the question.

Mr. Quelch resumed the search for the vanished volume. He was surprised and annoyed by his failure to find it in his desk. He grew more and more annoyed as he continued the search. It was not a judicious moment for any Removite to take risks.

Bob Cherry was silent for a full minute. Then, after a cautious glance at Quelch, he resumed, in a still lower whisper :

"We shall see the game at St. Jude's, and then we can bike over to Lantham or Courtfield for tea. See ? Tea out."

"You won't tea out if Quelch catches you wagging your chin, fathead !" murmured Johnny Bull.

"My esteemed Bob," breathed Hurree Jamset Ram Singh, "speech is silvery, but silence is the cracked pitcher that goes longest to the well."

"I say, you fellows——" whispered Billy Bunter.

Billy Bunter had heard the whispering with absolute indifference, till Bob mentioned teaing out.

Then Billy Bunter sat up and took notice.

Teaing out—or in, for that matter—was always an interesting matter to William George Bunter.

A football match at St. Jude's did not interest Bunter. He did not want to know how they were shaping at Soccer at that school. He had no desire whatever to stand about, on a cold and frosty afternoon, watching fellows kicking a ball. His opinion of the Famous Five was, that they were a quintet of silly asses, to think of passing a half-holiday in that fatheaded way, when they might have been frowsting over a study fire.

But if tea was to follow the match, that put a different complexion on it. Bunter was willing to watch a football match, if it was to be followed by a spread at the Pagoda, in Lantham, or the bun-shop in Courtfield.

He leaned over his desk, his little round eyes quite eager behind his big round spectacles.

THE MAGNET LIBRARY.—No. 1,457.

"I say——"

"Shut up, ass!" murmured Bob.

"But, I say, I'll come!" said Bunter. "I'm fearfully keen on football, as you fellows know——"

"Oh, my hat!"

"Quiet!"

"But if you're going on the bikes, make it a bit later," suggested Bunter. "Mine's got a puncture, and I shall have to get one of you fellows to mend it."

"'Ware, beaks!" hissed Bob.

Mr. Quelch was looking round again. He was quite exasperated by that time by his failure to find the vanished volume. His gimlet eyes fixed on Billy Bunter.

"If anyone is talking in class——" rumbled Mr. Quelch.

Silence!

The Remove sat like stone images under Quelch's gleaming eye. Then, once more, the Remove master turned to his hopeless quest.

Bunter only waited till his head was turned. Bob Cherry had realised the value of discretion, and he said no more. But discretion was not numbered among the many gifts of William George Bunter.

"I say, you fellows——" whispered Bunter. "I say, it's a pretty long step to St. Jude's on the jiggers! I can do it all right, of course, but you fellows would very likely crock up. What about a taxi?"

No answer!

Harry Wharton made Bunter a sign to be silent; but he did not venture to speak. Even from the back of Quelch's head, an observant eye could detect that he was getting dangerous!

"I'll stand the taxi!" went on Bunter. "That's all right! I'll stand you fellows a taxi with pleasure. One of you can lend me five bob—it won't run to more than that! What?"

Silence!

"If I stand the taxi, you fellows can stand the tea!" went on Bunter. "That's fair! Better have it at Lantham—they have jolly good prog at the Pagoda. Leave it to me to order the spread, if you like! I'm rather a dab at that sort of thing!"

"Bunter!" Mr. Quelch whirled round from his desk and rapped: "Did you speak, Bunter?"

Bunter jumped. In his keen interest in teaing out, he had almost forgotten Mr. Quelch. Now he was reminded of him.

"Oh, no, sir!" he gasped.

"I heard you speak, Bunter!"

"Oh, no, sir! Not a word!" gasped Bunter. "I was only saying to Cherry that——"

"It appears," said Mr. Quelch, in a deep voice, "that my class cannot maintain silence even for a few moments, while I am occupied. Bunter, you will be detained for one hour this afternoon."

"Oh crikey!"

"You will return to the Form-room at two o'clock, Bunter——"

"Oh lor'!"

"And if you speak again, I shall cane you!"

Bunter did not speak again.

Quelch gave up the search for the missing book, and carried on without it. Billy Bunter sat with a fat, dismayed face through the remainder of third school.

That detention washed out the trip, so far as Bunter was concerned. Which dismayed Bunter—and, no doubt, ought to have dismayed the Famous Five. But, to judge by their cheery looks when

the Remove was dismissed at last, they were able to bear the loss of Billy Bunter's company with considerable fortitude.

THE SECOND CHAPTER.
Sticky!

BOB CHERRY cut down to the bike-shed immediately after dinner.

A recently repaired puncture on his jigger had shown signs of giving more trouble, and Bob wanted to make sure that it was all right, before he started with his friends on a long spin, up hill and down dale.

His chums waited for him to rejoin them with the news that it was all right. After a quarter of an hour had elapsed, however, they began to entertain a misgiving that, instead of being all right, it was all wrong!

So they walked down to the bike-shed, to see how Bob was getting on, and found him with his jigger up-ended, his face red with exertion, and his usually sunny expression quite absent.

"Puncture?" asked Johnny Bull.

Bob looked at him over the upside-down jigger.

"Oh, no!" he answered, with biting sarcasm. "I've turned the bike upside down because I prefer to ride it that way! Makes a bit of a change."

Sarcasm was not, as a rule, one of Bob's failings. It looked as if that puncture was giving him some trouble.

Harry Wharton, Frank Nugent and Hurree Jamset Ram Singh smiled, and were silent. They knew when silence was golden.

But Johnny Bull grunted.

"No need to be shirty about it!" he remarked.

Tact was not Johnny Bull's long suit.

"Who's shirty?" inquired Bob.

"Sounds as if you are! I think——"

"You do?" asked Bob. "Oh, don't pile it on, old chap! Tell us an easier one! I don't want to doubt your word, of course; but do you seriously expect any fellow who knows you to swallow that?"

Johnny Bull stared at him.

Then he grinned, and was silent.

He was not, perhaps, quick on the up-take, but he realised by that time that the least said the soonest mended.

Bob Cherry had a tube of solution in his hand. He seemed to have been using it rather liberally. There was some on his fingers, a dab on his nose, a smear or two on his trousers. He laid it down, while he made an examination of the tyre. That examination did not seem to encourage him. His brow wrinkled deep and dark.

"All right now?" asked Nugent.

"No!" said Bob curtly.

"Can we help?" inquired Harry.

"Thanks; but it's trouble enough already!"

"Hem!"

Bob's sunny temper undoubtedly was deteriorating. A minute or two later he stared round as if in search of something. He murmured expressively as he stared, without finding what he sought.

"Looking for something?" asked Johnny.

"Not at all! I'm just twisting my neck about to exercise it! Good for the neck muscles!"

"Oh, don't give us any more sarc, old chap! If you're looking for that solution——"

"Fancy Bull guessing that, when it's as plain as daylight!" said Bob. "Well, I am looking for the solution! If you know where it is——"

"You're kneeling on it."

"Wha-a-at?"

Bob Cherry bounded up.

A squashed tube was exuding the last remnant of its contents on the knee of his trousers.

Bob gazed at it.

So did his chums! With heroic efforts they suppressed a desire to chuckle. Bob's expression showed it was no time for chuckling.

In silence—his feelings being too deep for words—Bob went into the bicycle shed for more solution. Still in silence, he came back with it.

"I say, you fellows!" Billy Bunter rolled up. "I say, got a puncture, Bob, old chap?"

Bob did not waste any "sarc" on Bunter as he had on Johnny Bull. It was a very, very troublesome puncture, and his feelings were growing deeper and deeper—too deep for sarcasm.

"Rotten old tyre!" said Bunter. "Why don't you buy a new tyre, old chap?"

Bob breathed hard and deep. Bunter was right. It was an old tyre, and really a new inner tube was needed. But a new inner tube cost certain shillings, which, at the moment, Bob did not happen to have in his possession.

"Lots of trouble for nothing," said Bunter, blinking at him. "I shouldn't mind spending a few bob on a bike, old fellow."

"Will you shut up, Bunter?" asked Bob, with ferocious calm.

"Oh, really, Cherry! If you're hard up I'll lend you enough to get a new tyre—when my postal order comes! I'm expecting it to-morrow."

Bob dabbed solution, and made no answer.

"I say, you fellows," went on Bunter, "I've got to get into the Form-room at two. You heard what that beast Quelch said! What about waiting for me?"

"Ripping idea!" said Frank Nugent. "We're going over to St. Jude's to see them play Topham, and the game will be over by the time your detention's up. I suppose that wouldn't matter?"

"Well, no!" said Bunter. "After all, what's the good of standing about getting your feet cold? My idea is, cut that right out, and go straight over to the Pagoda at Lantham for tea."

"Fathead!"

"Better still—the bunshop in Courtfield," said Bunter. "It's nearer—see?"

"Ass!"

"Look here, Wharton, are you going to wait for me, or not?"

"Not!"

"Well, I dare say you won't have started, if you're going to wait for Cherry to get through with that puncture," said Bunter. "He, he, he! Looks as if he's going to make a day of it!"

"Shut up, ass!"

"He, he, he!"

Bob Cherry rose from beside his exasperating jigger. He gave Billy Bunter a rather deadly look.

"That's done!" he said.

"Oh, good!" said Harry Wharton cheerfully. "We shall be off in lots of time, old chap!"

"The lotfulness will be terrific!" declared the Nabob of Bhanipur.

"I think it's all right now!" said Bob. "Shan't have to wait long for it now, and——"

"I say, now you've done yours, Cherry, what about doing mine?" asked Bunter. "I shall have to have my bike—to come after you, you know."

"Idiot!"

"If you're going to be a selfish, lazy beast——"

"I'm going to kick you if you don't shut up!" roared Bob. "Can't you roll away, and give a fellow a rest, you blithering owl?"

"Well, I think you might mend a chap's puncture," said Bunter. "I've got detention! It won't be so much trouble as yours; mine isn't such a putrid old tyre! I can afford a new one when I need one—see? You could do it in ten minutes."

After more than twenty minutes on his own puncture, Bob Cherry did not seem, somehow, keen on spending another ten on Bunter's.

"Rotten slacker!" said Bunter. "I say, Nugent, are you going to mend my puncture for me?"

"I don't quite think so, old fat bean!"

"What about you, Bull?"

"Rats!"

terrific crash and clang, and Bob gave a roar of wrath.

"You clumsy ass! If that puncture's busted again——"

"He, he, he!"

Bob jumped at his bike! He glared at the mended tyre! He pressed it and squeezed it—and breathed fury.

"Oh my hat!" said Johnny Bull. "Another bust?"

"What do you expect of a rotten old tyre like that?" argued Billy Bunter. "Besides, you can't mend a puncture, Cherry! You're too clumsy! You— I say, here—what—— Keep that stuff away! Oh crikey! Yaroooooooh!"

Bob Cherry hurled himself on the Owl of the Remove. With one hand he grasped him by the collar. With the other, he squeezed solution over his fat face. He squeezed it liberally.

—more, in fact! He did not want any down his fat neck! He gurgled, he spluttered, and he flew!

By the time Bob came out of the shed Bunter had disappeared over the horizon. And Harry Wharton & Co., feeling that Bob would be better left to himself at such dire moments, judiciously took a walk round the quad —and Bob Cherry wrestled manfully with that puncture, till, at long last, he won the victory.

THE THIRD CHAPTER.
Coker's Catch!

"SEEN Potter?"

"No!"

"Seen Greene?"

"No!"

Coker of the Fifth snorted.

"Puncture?" asked Johnny Bull. "Oh! No!" answered Bob Cherry, with biting sarcasm. "I've turned the bike upside down because I prefer to ride it that way!" A minute later, Bob stared round as if in search of something. "If you're looking for the solution," said Johnny, "you're kneeling on it!" "Wha-a-at!" gasped Bob, suddenly noticing the squashed tube exuding the last remnant of its contents on the knees of his trousers.

"What about Inky?"

"The ratfulness is terrific."

"Well, of all the rotten slackers!" said Bunter. "Never seen such a lazy lot. Did you say you'd do it, Wharton?"

"If I did, I never noticed it!" answered the captain of the Remove.

"Well, if that puncture isn't mended, I mayn't be able to come over and join you at St. Jude's," said Bunter crossly.

"Oh, good! If anybody mends that puncture for Bunter, I'll punch his head!"

"Ha, ha, ha!"

"Yah!"

Billy Bunter turned away with an angry grunt.

Perhaps it was by accident that he barged into Bob's up-ended bike as he turned. Perhaps it was not by accident. Anyhow, the bike went over with a

"Urrrrggh!" gurgled Bunter, as some went into his mouth. "Gurrgh! Beast! Leggo! I say, you fellows—— Yoooooooch! Grooogh! Ooooch!"

"There!" gasped Bob. "Take that!"

"Urrrgh!"

Billy Bunter staggered away, clawing at a sticky face with sticky hands. He spluttered and gurgled as he clawed.

"Ow! I'm all sticky! Wow! I say —grooogh—beast—oooogh——"

"Ha, ha, ha!"

"Look at me!" shrieked Bunter. "I say—urrrgh! Beast!"

"Wait till I get some more!" gasped Bob. "I'll let you have some down your silly neck——"

He rushed into the bike-shed.

Billy Bunter rushed in the opposite direction.

He had as much solution as he wanted

He was standing beside a bicycle, in the road, when Harry Wharton & Co. wheeled their machines out.

They were rather in a hurry; Bob's puncture had a little delayed starting. Still, they paused to answer Coker as he called to them.

The Famous Five were looking, and feeling, merry and bright. They had sketched out quite an enjoyable afternoon.

A swift ride through the clear, frosty air, then watching a good game of Soccer, and exchanging friendly greetings with old acquaintances at St. Jude's, then another spin, and tea at the Pagoda, at Lantham—and then another ride round till they had to get in for calling-over. It was not a programme that appealed to Billy Bunter—

with the single exception of the episode of tea at the Pagoda—but it seemed a very cheery sort of half-holiday to the strenuous heroes of the Remove.

But there was no time to lose now. At the best, they did not expect to arrive at St. Jude's in time to see the kick-off. So, really, they had no time to waste on Coker.

Ignorant of that fact, Coker went on crossly:

"The silly asses! I told them plainly to wait for me here! I didn't mean to be more than a few minutes, and I told them so! That ass Hacker stopped me and jawed, you see! The way beaks jaw!"

Harry Wharton & Co. were aware of the way beaks would "jaw." At the present moment, however, it was the way Coker jawed that mattered! Really and truly, they had no time to listen to Coker.

"Just because I punched Hobson!" said Coker. "Fancy the Shell beak jawing me for that! Pretty state of things Greyfriars is coming to, when a Fifth Form man can't punch a cheeky fag in the Shell! I jolly nearly told Hacker what I thought of him."

Coker snorted angrily. Evidently he had not enjoyed the conversation of Mr. Hacker, the master of the Shell.

"Hold on!" he rapped, as the juniors began to mount. "Look here, Potter and Greene must be somewhere about. I distinctly told them to wait, and I wasn't much over half an hour! What are you grinning at?"

"At a silly ass, if you want to know, old bean?" said Bob Cherry affably. "Come on, you fellows!"

"I said hold on!" rapped Coker. "Look here, young Wharton, cut into the House and see if they've gone in."

"Eh?"

"Deaf?" snorted Coker.

Harry Wharton laughed.

"Sorry, old man, I've no time to listen to your little jokes!" he said, and he put a leg over his machine.

"You young ass!" hooted Coker. "I'm not joking!"

"You are, old man! You're an unconscious humorist!" explained Wharton. "No end funny, if you only knew it!"

And he pushed off. Coker of the Fifth never could quite understand that he could not give orders to the Remove fellows, though really they did their best to make it clear to him.

"Look here——" he roared.

"Rats!" said Wharton, over his shoulder.

The next moment that shoulder was grasped, and he was hooked off his machine. He gave a yell as he came down on the road with a bump, and his bike went jangling.

"Now——" roared Coker.

Coker got no further.

Like one man, the Co. left their jiggers and jumped at Coker! Five bikes sprawled as five pairs of hands were laid on Horace Coker—and the next moment Coker was sprawling, too. He was also bawling!

Bob Cherry seized Coker's large ears as he sprawled and bawled, and tapped his head on the road.

Tap, tap, tap!

"That will do for Coker!" remarked Bob. "Now let's push off!"

Leaving Coker strewn and roaring, the chums of the Remove picked up their bikes, mounted, and rode off.

Coker scrambled up.

He was dusty. He was untidy. He was crimson with wrath. He forgot Potter and Greene, who so unaccountably had not waited half an hour for him. He grabbed his bike, put a long leg over it, and shot off in pursuit of the Famous Five.

"Hallo, hallo, hallo! Jolly old Horace is after us!" chuckled Bob Cherry, as he gave a glance back over his shoulder.

"Cheeky ass!" growled Johnny Bull. "Let's stop and mop up the road with him!"

"No time!" said Harry. "We shall be late at St. Jude's as it is! Let old Coker run on."

The chums of the Remove spun swiftly away on their machines. After them, going strong, rushed Coker of the Fifth.

Coker was anxious to get to close quarters.

Previous experiences with the heroes of the Remove might have warned Coker that getting to close quarters with them was likely to prove neither grateful nor comforting.

But experience which is said to make fools wise, never had that effect on Coker of the Fifth.

Besides, the juniors were going all out, which looked as if they were fleeing from the wrath to come! In point of fact, they were in a hurry to get over to St. Jude's, but to Coker's eyes they seemed to be in panic flight. And he charged after them as fast as his long and brawny legs could drive the pedals round.

Several miles slid by under the whirling wheels; and Coker had not gained.

But now Redclyffe Hill lay ahead of the riders, and on that rather steep rise Coker counted as a certainty on the juniors crocking up, or at least slowing down.

"Carry on!" said Harry Wharton, as the bikes came up the rise. It was rather usual for cyclists to wheel their machines up that hill, but there was no time to lose now.

They pedalled hard up the hill.

It was rather rough going, and it was hard work, but they did not slow down. Coker, behind them, was gasping a little. He expected to see the five jump out of their saddles any minute—when Coker was going to rush them down and mop them up, as they so richly deserved.

Pop!

"Oh, crikey!" gasped Bob.

"What's that?" asked Johnny Bull, glancing round.

Bob Cherry slowed and dismounted. The rough going on Redclyffe Hill had done it. That wretched puncture had broken out again.

"Oh!" said Johnny, comprehending.

The Co. came to a halt and jumped down. Bob Cherry stuck his bike against a wayside tree and made an examination. His face grew longer and longer as he did so. His chums watched him. In the stress of this new disaster, they forgot all about Coker of the Fifth—coming up hand over hand.

"Bad?" asked Harry, at last.

"Putrid!" grunted Bob.

"We shall see a lot at St. Jude's at this rate!" remarked Johnny Bull.

Bob gave him a glare.

"Nobody's asked you to stand around and stare, like a cow at a train!" he pointed out. "You're no use, and you can't be ass enough to suppose that you're any ornament! Get on to St. Jude's, and leave me to it!"

"Look here——"

"Well, why don't you go?" hooted Bob.

"Because I'd rather stay with you, old chap!" answered Johnny affably

"Your company's better than a football match, any day."

Bob stared at him. But the soft answer turneth away wrath, and Bob's clouded face broke into a grin.

"Well, it's rotten," he said. "I don't believe I can do anything with that putrid tyre. I'll try, of course. But you men had better push on—I don't want to muck up your half-holiday."

"Rot!" said Harry.

"The rotfulness is terrific, my esteemed and idiotic Bob."

"Well, here goes, then!" sighed Bob. "I—— Hallo, hallo, hallo! I forgot that mad idiot Coker—here he is!"

Horace Coker came up with a rush. He knew nothing about the puncture, and he supposed that the steepness of the hill had stopped the juniors. He felt that he had calculated well.

"Now, then——" panted Coker, as he jumped off his machine.

And he rushed at the Famous Five.

They still had no time to waste on Coker—but they had to waste some, in the circumstances. Coker started in to mop up the cheeky juniors—and for some wild and whirling minutes Harry Wharton & Co. had to forget all about punctures, and football matches, and concentrate on Coker.

They concentrated.

The mopping-up duly took place. But not as planned by Coker—the difference being that it was Coker who was mopped.

The chums of the Remove collected some damages. But the damages collected by Coker of the Fifth were beyond numeration, at least, without going into very high figures.

After five hectic minutes a breathless, dizzy, and dismantled Coker was deposited in a dry ditch, where he rolled in nettles. Leaving him there, the juniors returned to Bob's bike.

Bob got busy on that bike.

The other fellows kept a wary eye open for Coker, when he crawled out of the ditch and the stinging nettles.

But Coker of the Fifth required no further attention. Mopping-up no longer had any appeal for Coker. Without even a word, the breathless and dusty Horace picked up his jigger, and wheeled it away. He was feeling too used-up even to mount it. He limped and lurched away, and the chums of the Remove were left to themselves—and the puncture.

The puncture, really, gave them enough to think about. Bob Cherry wrestled and strove with it, and his friends watched him with silent sympathy, and their chances of seeing anything of the football match at St. Jude's grew smaller by degrees, and beautifully less.

THE FOURTH CHAPTER.

Bunter the Hunter !

BILLY BUNTER was released from detention at three o'clock. He rolled out of the Form-room, with a frowning fat brow.

He had not the slightest expectation that the Famous Five had waited for him. Only too well he knew the selfishness of human nature!

Harry Wharton & Co. had planned a cycling afternoon, with a visit to St. Jude's thrown in, and Billy Bunter had cheerfully sought to turn it into an expedition to a teashop, and a spread, for the single and sole behoof of W. G. Bunter. And they had not been taking any, which was not, perhaps, surprising—but very annoying to the fat Owl.

Now that he was out of detention the fat junior had no time to lose. He had

to get to St. Jude's before the game was over.

Not that he cared two straws or one about the game, or whether St. Jude's beat Topham or whether Topham beat St. Jude's. But after the match was over the fellows who had gone there to see it, would remount their bikes and ride—and Bunter had to catch them, if he was to accompany them to the real and important function of the afternoon—tea!

If he had known exactly where that important function was to take place, he might have headed direct for the spot—but he did not know! All depended on getting to St. Jude's before the Famous Five left.

Biking was out of the question. Apart from Bunter's bike being in its usual dilapidated state, he was far from keen on a ride of ten miles—moreover, if Bunter had had to ride ten miles, he would have been more likely to arrive at St. Jude's, in time for their next football match, rather than the present one.

Getting a train from Courtfield was no resource. No train would have landed him there in time, not to mention the difficulty of travelling on the railway without the preliminary proceeding of buying a ticket.

Any fellow but Billy Bunter would have felt that it was rather a hopeless case. But the fat Owl had his own methods.

There was only one way—taking a taxi. Bunter had thought it out while under detention in the Form-room.

It was generally easy to bag a telephone on a half-holiday when many of the staff were taking their walks abroad.

It was easy to phone for a taxi, and buzz off in the same. That was what Bunter had decided to do.

Having ascertained that Mr. Hacker, the master of the Shell, was out, the fat Owl cheerfully proceeded to Hacker's study and rang up the taxirank at Courtfield.

Then he donned hat and coat, rolled out of the House, and out of the gates, and walked up the road to meet the taxi on its way.

He had hardly covered a hundred yards when the taxi came buzzing along the road over Courtfield Common, and Bunter held up a fat hand.

"St. Jude's School, as fast as you can go!" he said, as he stepped in.

"Yes, sir!"

Bunter sat down, and the taxi whirled on.

He grinned cheerfully as it ate up the miles.

Lots of fellows in Bunter's place would not have grinned. The fare was likely to be about seven-and-six. Bunter had the sum of exactly one penny in his pocket.

But he had thought it all out. Bunter was, he flattered himself, the fellow to think things out. He was one of those clever fellows.

He was going to offer the Co. a lift in the taxi to the teashop; they could park the jiggers somewhere. If they accepted, they would naturally be responsible to the taximan.

But that was only the first string to Bunter's bow. If they declined the lift, as was extremely probable, he had another card to play.

The taxi-driver, if not paid, was certain to make a fuss. Bunter knew, from a lot of experience of that kind, that taxi-drivers, in such circumstances, always did. Could the Famous Five, before a lot of St. Jude's fellows, let the man kick up a fuss about his fare? Hardly! They would have to lend

Bunter the necessary sum to satisfy the man.

Bunter counted on that as a certainty. Harry Wharton & Co. would not want an angry and indignant taximan rooting about St. Jude's for a Greyfriars fellow who had bilked him.

So it seemed to Bunter he was all right.

Bunter had told the driver to go as fast as he could, and the man obeyed instructions. The taxi fairly flew. There was no doubt that Bunter would be in plenty of time for the finish of the match, even if he did not see the whole of the second half. So long as he glued himself on to the Famous Five before the finish, it was all serene.

Had not the taxi been going so very fast, and had not Billy Bunter been so short-sighted, he might have noticed something of interest, as he shot up Redclyffe Hill.

That was a group of schoolboys gathered round an up-ended bike, under a tree near the road.

But the fat Owl did not even see them as he shot by, let alone recognise them.

He sped on towards St. Jude's, happily unconscious that he was leaving Harry Wharton & Co. farther and farther behind, with every revolution of the wheels.

Neither did the Famous Five observe the taxi or its occupant. Their attention was given to Bob and his bike, and too many cars passed on the road, to draw their attention.

Bunter sped on, in a cheerful mood.

A sound of shouting greeted his fat ears, as he drew near St. Jude's. He distinguished the word "Goal."

Evidently the game was on.

The taxi jarred to a halt at the school gates. Bunter alighted.

"Wait here," he said breezily, "I shan't be long."

"Yes, sir."

The taximan backed his car to the roadside, away from the gates, and waited, as bidden. Bunter rolled in.

He was no stranger to St. Jude's; he had gone over with the Greyfriars team on occasions of the matches. Most of the Lower School of St. Jude's seemed to be gathered on the football ground, watching the game. Among so many fellows, packed round the ground, it was not surprising that Bunter did not spot the Famous Five in a hurry. He had, as yet, no suspicion that they were not there.

They had had plenty of time to get to St. Jude's, long before Bunter, so he naturally supposed that they were there—little dreaming that they were still halted halfway, while Bob Cherry wrestled and strove with a rebellious puncture.

"Goal !"

It was a roar.

"Good old Wilmot! Goal!"

Billy Bunter gave a careless blink at the game.

He noticed that it was a small bunch of fellows who shouted "Good old Wilmot!" not the St. Jude's crowd. Apparently they were Topham men, who had come over to cheer their team, and Wilmot was one of the Topham footballers.

Wilmot, whoever he was, had just bagged a goal, and his friends roared and cheered.

"They've got a good man there!" Bunter heard a St. Jude's man remark, as the players went to the centre of the field.

"Jolly good!" remarked another. "That's his third goal! That sportsman brought his shooting-boots with him from Topham!"

Billy Bunter blinked at Wilmot of Topham. He saw a handsome and athletic lad, whose face looked very bright and happy. Wilmot of Topham was evidently enjoying his success in the match.

The ball was kicked off again; but Bunter gave its career no further attention. He blinked round in search of Greyfriars fellows.

They were not to be seen.

He rolled here, and he rolled there, but he failed to spot the Famous Five—which was very annoying.

Bunter was short-sighted; but he would have needed telescopic vision to spot the Famous Five just then, as they were five miles away!

Bunter did not suspect that. He suspected that they had spotted him and were keeping out of view. It had happened, more than once, that fellows were not so anxious to see Bunter, as Bunter was to see them.

He had to find them. Apart from the urgent and important consideration of a spread at the teashop, the taximan had to be paid. He simply had to find the elusive five.

"I say, you fellows, have you seen any Greyfriars men about?" he asked, addressing a group of St. Jude's juniors.

'No; none here, I think," was the answer.

"Some friends of mine came over to see the game," explained Bunter. "I know they're here."

"Sorry—haven't seen them."

Bunter resumed his search.

"Goal!"

"Hurrah!"

"Wilmot! Wilmot!"

The little bunch of Topham men were yelling again. Wilmot had bagged his fourth goal, which was rather a remarkable performance, for St. Jude's were quite good men at Soccer. The Topham skipper clapped him on the back, in the field; and the Topham followers roared and cheered.

"Time for another yet," Bunter heard one of the Topham men remark, looking at his watch. "I say, four goals to one is something to tell the fellows when we get back! Isn't Wilmot a corker?"

"It's Wilmot's game!" remarked another. "Hurrah!"

"Bravo, Wilmot!"

"Give us one more, Eric old man!"

"Hurrah!"

One of the Topham crowd yawned.

"I say, it's jolly cold here!" he remarked.

None of the others answered that remark. Their eyes were glued on the game. Bunter was blinking at the Topham group, to see whether he could spot a Greyfriars cap among them. He had hunted everywhere else.

"Only five minutes to go!" went on the fellow who had spoken. "Thank goodness for that!"

One of the other Tophamites turned his head at that, and snapped:

"Oh, shut up, Crawley! What the thump did you come over for, if you didn't want to see the game? What do you care for footer, anyhow? Backing horses is more in your line!"

"Look here——"

"Rats!"

Bunter grinned at the expression on the face of the fellow called Crawley.

He had a rather narrow, and far from pleasant, face—and it looked less pleasant than ever, as he scowled at the fellow who had snapped at him. That fellow, however, ignored his existence.

THE MAGNET LIBRARY.—No. 1,457.

ence—his eyes were on Wilmot, in the field.

Crawley, scowling, left the group, and lounged away towards the school buildings.

"I say," Bunter addressed him as he paused—"I say——"

The Topham man stared at him.

"What the dooce do you want?" he snapped.

"Have you seen any Greyfriars fellows about?"

"Never heard of Greyfriars, and shouldn't know one if I saw one!" grunted Crawley, and he lounged on.

"Beast!" breathed Bunter.

Crawley, of Topham, certainly did not seem a very agreeable sort of fellow.

He disappeared into the House, and Billy Bunter resumed his hapless hunt for the Famous Five. He was beginning to feel a deep misgiving now.

A sudden commotion among the crowd drew his attention. The game was over.

The Topham men, cheering, gathered round Eric Wilmot as he came off the field with the other players. Bunter gave the handsome, flushed, happy face one blink—but not a second one! Now that the game was over, and the crowd on the move, he made a last, desperate search for the Famous Five. Wilmot, and his four goals, filled the thoughts of the Tophamites, but mattered nothing whatever to Billy Bunter.

Up and down and round about, the Owl of the Remove sought for the five and found them not.

And it was borne in on his fat mind, at last, that they were not there!

Why they weren't there, was a mystery; but it seemed clear, at last, that they weren't!

And Bunter, with a sinking heart, thought of the taxi waiting in the road—and from the bottom of that sinking heart he wished that he had not been so fearfully clever. For, as the chums of the Remove were not there, it was a certainty that they were not going to pay the taximan! It was equally certain that Bunter wasn't, as he hadn't any money! On the other hand, the man had to be paid—that was another paralysing certainty!

"Oh lor'!" said Bunter

———

THE FIFTH CHAPTER.

Luck for Bunter!

"SEEN anything of my friends?"

"No, sir!"

"Five fellows on bikes, one of them a darkey."

"No!"

Billy Bunter breathed hard.

The taximan had seen nothing of the Famous Five. If they had dodged Bunter, and left, they could hardly have got away unseen. The driver, standing by his car, chewing a cigarette, would assuredly have noticed them. It was Bunter's last hope—had the man seen them go, he could have driven in pursuit. Now his last hope was gone.

It looked as if they had never been there at all. It was inexplicable, as they certainly had intended to see that match at St. Jude's. Something had happened to stop them, apparently.

Bunter could have groaned.

In other circumstances, the fat Owl might have dodged away, leaving an infuriated taximan to stew in his own juice, as it were! But that would have been futile, in the present circumstances. He had telephoned the man

from Greyfriars, and if he did not see his passenger again, the man would simply drive to the school to ask for his due. If there was going to be a row, it was better to have it here than at Greyfriars—with his Form-master, and perhaps the Head, barging in!

The taximan was waiting cheerfully enough. As he charged for waiting, he was in no hurry to get going. And as he knew that Bunter belonged to Greyfriars, he had no doubt about his fare—as yet!

Bunter opened his lips—and closed them again! A "row" was better there than at Greyfriars, doubtless; but it was horribly unpleasant, all the same.

Indeed, he could hardly hope that a "row" would be the end of it. Taximen have to live, like other men, and they cannot live on rows! Suppose, after the "row," the beast drove to Greyfriars to complain and demand payment!

It was awful to contemplate!

"I—I think I'll look round for them!" stammered Bunter at last; and he rolled away from the taxi.

That was simply a trick to gain time, to try to think out this new and awful problem. Bunter knew that it was useless to look round for them—he knew that they were not anywhere about St. Jude's.

In the stress of this unlooked-for worry, Billy Bunter actually forgot the spread he was missing! He would have been willing to give up all idea of sharing in that spread, if only he could have thought of some way out of the fearful difficulty in which his cleverness had landed him.

But he couldn't!

Possibly he realised, in those distressful moments, that honesty was the best policy! But that discovery, though useful for future reference, did not help him now.

What was he going to do?

That question, with Bunter, generally meant, whom was he going to do? But now there was nobody to be "done."

Bunter ambled about the road, in distressful thought and anxiety. The taximan chewed his cigarette and waited, with undiminished cheerfulness. The fat young gent was running up a bill, but the taximan did not mind, if the fat young gent didn't!

"Oh crikey!" moaned Bunter.

The desperate idea even came into his mind of trying to raise the wind from a St. Jude's man. Lunn, the junior skipper there, was rather friendly with Harry Wharton & Co., and no doubt he had seen Bunter, and knew him by sight. But——

Bunter had plenty of cheek—it was indeed his greatest gift! But even more than Bunter's cheek was required to barge in on Lunn at St. Jude's and ask him for a loan of ten shillings.

But what was he going to do?

He blinked at a fellow who came along from the direction of the school. The taxi was parked by the roadside, at some little distance from the gates.

Bunter supposed that it was a St. Jude's fellow coming along, and he almost made up his fat mind, if the fellow turned out to be an acquaintance, to make the desperate attempt to "touch" him for a loan.

He blinked at the junior as he approached, and gave a snort of disappointment and disgust.

It was not a St. Jude's fellow at all; it was a Topham man—that fellow Wilmot, who had taken the goals.

It was rather odd that the Topham

"Hold on!" shouted Coker. "Sorry, old man," said Wharton, putting a leg over his machine, "I've no time to listen to your little jokes!" The next moment, his arm was grasped, and he was hooked off his machine. "I said hold on!" roared Coker. "And I mean hold on!"

goal-getter should be walking away from St. Jude's by himself. But Bunter was too deep in his own problem to think or care about that curious circumstance.

But even Bunter, with his fat thoughts concentrated on himself, could not help noticing a strange and startling change in Eric Wilmot's looks, as the Topham fellow came nearer.

Half an hour ago Bunter had seen him come off the football field, flushed and bright and cheery, surrounded by enthusiastic friends. Now his handsome face was white as chalk, his lips were trembling, his eyes drooping, and he walked on blindly, like a fellow so deeply under the stress of emotion that he did not know or care where he was going.

Bunter gave him a second blink—and a third! Then he fairly fixed his eyes and his spectacles on the Topham fellow in amazement!

What on earth could be the matter with the chap? Only half an hour had elapsed since his happy triumph, and he looked like a fellow who had "taken the knock," and been completely knocked out.

So white and worn, and utterly disheartened did the Topham fellow look, that the waiting taximan looked at him very curiously, as well as Billy Bunter.

As he came past the spot where the taxi was standing, the Topham junior seemed to come out of a daze at the sight of it. He stepped towards the vehicle.

"Taxi," he said. "Good! Take me to Redclyffe station—quick!"

"Sorry sir; engaged!" said the driver.

Bunter rolled up.

"It's my taxi!" he said, blinking curiously at Wilmot's pale, stricken face.

"Oh! Sorry!"

The Topham fellow was turning away.

"Hold on!" said Bunter. "I can give you a lift, if you're in a hurry."

Wilmot paused.

That, for some unaccountable reason, he was anxious to get away as quickly as he could from the spot where he had played so great a game and from his friends was quite clear.

It was an utter mystery to Bunter, but the fat junior saw in it a gleam of light in the deep darkness of his own problem!

"Jump in!" he said encouragingly.

Wilmot did not look like a fellow keen on accepting favours from strangers.

In spite of his desire to get away, he was evidently unwilling to accept a lift from a fellow he had never seen before.

But at that moment another fellow appeared from the school gateway. It was the narrow-faced fellow, Crawley.

He glanced down the road, and Wilmot saw him. A sudden red came into the pale cheeks, and Wilmot turned quickly to the cab.

"Thanks!" he said, and stepped in.

Bunter followed him in.

"Redclyffe station!" he said to the driver.

"Yes, sir."

The taxi buzzed. Wilmot had fallen, rather than sat, in a seat. Bunter squatted by his side, blinking back with a grin at Crawley in the road.

Why Wilmot had suddenly made up his mind to accept the lift, rather than encounter one of his own schoolfellows mystified Bunter more than ever. But it rather amused him to see Crawley come along at a run, and then stop as the taxi dashed off.

The narrow-featured Topham fellow was left in the road with a scowl on his face.

St. Jude's was out of sight in a couple of minutes. It was not a long run to Redclyffe station, but it was long enough for Billy Bunter to get going on his plan of action.

Wilmot sat, a drooping figure, almost hunched on his seat. Whatever it was that had happened since the football match—and it was clear that something must have happened—it had crumpled him up. The fellow who had looked so fit and keen on the football field, had a dazed and helpless look now. Billy Bunter would have felt sorry for him if he had had time to bother about anyone but himself.

"Feeling the strain—what?" he asked breezily.

Wilmot did not answer, but he looked at the fat junior.

"Hard game!" said Bunter. "I watched it, you know! I'm rather a whale at footer, at my school."

A faint smile glided for a second over Wilmot's harassed face. But it was gone at once.

"You want to keep fit for the game," said Bunter sagely. "I never get knocked up by a game as you are now."

Wilmot gave him another look, but did not speak.

"Glad I was able to offer you a lift," went on Bunter. "I can tell you, you're looking pretty sick. But, I say, I hate to mention it, but I'm rather short of tin, and going out of my way like this will put something on the fare! You won't mind standing your whack?"

"Glad to!" said Wilmot, with great dryness.

"That's all right, then," said Bunter affably. "To tell you the truth, I'm in rather a fix! I left my money behind when I came out. Look here, as you want the taxi, you can have it if you like, and I'll hop out. What?"

"Eh! Yes! Anything you like."

It was clear that the Topham fellow was hardly listening to what Bunter was saying. But Bunter wanted it plain. He did not want a disgruntled taxi-driver calling to see him at Greyfriars later.

"You don't mind settling the fare?" he asked.

"Eh! No! If you don't want the cab, I'd be glad to have it to myself!" muttered Wilmot.

That was not exactly complimentary, but it was welcome. Evidently the Topham fellow wanted to be alone—even Billy Bunter's fascinating company seemed to have no charms for him! But that suited Bunter—in the peculiar circumstances!

"Well, if you're willing to pay what the man's got on the clock——" said Bunter.

"Yes, yes!"

It seemed that the Topham junior was not only willing, but eager, so long as he got rid of Bunter!

"It's over ten bob now——"

"That's all right!"

Bunter was glad to hear it.

"Well, if you don't mind——"

"Not in the least! Leave it to me! Thanks!"

He was actually thanking Bunter for landing the taxi on him! Wilmot seemed to have taken the knock that afternoon in some mysterious way; but there was no doubt that Billy Bunter was in luck!

Bunter told the driver to stop. He stepped out, and the driver looked at him.

"My friend's taking on the taxi and paying the fare," explained Bunter airily.

The driver glanced at his new passenger.

"That all right, sir?" he asked.

"Yes, yes! Drive to the station—quick!"

"Yes, sir."

The taxi buzzed away with Eric Wilmot.

Bunter was left on the Redclyffe road, blinking after it—his awful problem solved!

His last blink at the parting taxi showed him a white, tortured face; then Eric Wilmot was gone from his sight; and Billy Bunter, having wondered for about a minute what was the matter with the fellow, dismissed him from his mind, and in about another minute forgot his existence!

THE SIXTH CHAPTER.

Bunter Borrows a Bike!

"HALLO, hallo, hallo!"

"Bunter!"

Five juniors walked bicycles up the last slope of Redclyffe Hill.

Over the crest of the hill, from the other side, came rolling a fat, tired, breathless, and disgruntled Bunter.

How long Bob Cherry had spent on that wretched puncture his chums did not really know. It seemed like hours and hours and hours.

Bob was determined. He had, so to speak, got his teeth into that tyre, and he was going to mend it, or "bust."

THE MAGNET LIBRARY.—No. 1,457.

As it turned out, it was the tyre that "bust."

Long and patient labour did not set that puncture right. Once, hopefully, Bob fancied it was all right, and the bike a going concern again. Mounting it proved otherwise. The tyre flattened again—worse than before. Bob's chums exercised patience while he had another "go."

But when Bob discovered that the inner tube was split, beyond the power of repairing, even Bob gave it up. Wheeling the bike was the only resource.

By that time, the football match at St. Jude's, if not already over, must have been near the finish; and it was quite certain to be long finished before the juniors could reach the spot on Shanks' pony.

They had to give up St. Jude's as a bad job. Which was the reason why Bunter had not found them there.

Still, there would be time for a spin before lock-up at Greyfriars, if they walked on to Redclyffe, and got the bike put in order at the cycle-shop there. That was better than nothing.

As there was nothing else to be done, they did that.

Five fellows, keeping resolutely cheerful, walked up Redclyffe Hill, pushing the bikes—Bob's going far from easily on a flat tyre.

Thus it was that they met Billy Bunter face to face. Bunter had started to walk home.

It was a long walk, a weary walk, and a woeful walk. Bunter, at first, had been so immensely relieved at getting out of the difficulty with the taximan that he had hardly given a thought to the walk home.

But by the time he had covered half a mile, he gave it many thoughts—all of them dismayed and disgruntled and dismal.

Half a mile was enough for Bunter—if not too much! And four more weary miles lay between him and Greyfriars School! Unless he could pick up a lift of some sort, Bunter was likely to crawl into Greyfriars in a state of collapse.

So it was a happy meeting to Bunter. He blinked at the five through his big spectacles, and came to a gasping halt! Among the five, he could hardly doubt that he could borrow the railway fare to Friardale.

"I say, you fellows!" he gasped.

"Taking a long walk, old fat man?" asked Harry Wharton, puzzled. It was quite surprising to see Bunter so far from home on foot.

"Oh, really, Wharton!"

"Tired?" grinned Nugent. Bunter looked tired.

"Ow! Yes!" groaned Bunter. "I say, you fellows, it was pretty thick to let me down like that!"

"Who's let you down, fathead?"

"I looked for you at St. Jude's!" snorted Bunter. "You told me you were going to be there, and you never turned up!"

"Oh, my hat! Have you been to St. Jude's?" exclaimed Bob. "You saw the footer match, while we missed it! Did St. Jude's win?"

"Blessed if I know!" answered Bunter. He had already forgotten that trifling detail.

"You must have watched the game pretty keenly, if you don't know who won!" remarked Johnny Bull.

"Oh, blow the football match!" grunted Bunter. "You let me down! I say, if you're going to tea in Redclyffe, I'll walk back with you."

"We're not!" said Harry Wharton, laughing. "Tea's washed out, old fat

bean. We're going to spend the money at a cycle-shop instead."

"What utter rot!" snorted Bunter. "Well, look here! Lend me my fare home. I can walk to the nearest station, then, see?"

"You shouldn't have come over if you hadn't your fare back!" grunted Johnny Bull.

"Beast!"

"Oh, let's see what can be done!" said Harry Wharton resignedly. "If Bunter waddles down the hill to Redclyffe Station, he can get home for a bob, third——"

"If you think I'm going to travel third-class, Wharton——"

"I think you're going to travel third, if you travel at all, you fat idiot! But if a third-class fare's no use to you, say so—I can find something else to do with the bob."

"If you're going to be mean, Wharton, hand over the bob, and I'll get off!" grunted Bunter.

Wharton handed over the necessary "bob." Bunter sniffed, doubtless by way of thanks, and dropped it into his pocket.

"I say, you fellows, it's a quarter of a mile down the hill to the station," he grunted. "One of you lend me a bike to do it on, will you?"

"Eh?"

"I'll leave the bike at the station for you to fetch. See?"

The Famous Five gazed at Bunter.

Having already walked the bikes up that long, long hill, one of them was to walk a bike up again, for a distance of a quarter of a mile—to save Bunter's fat little legs a walk downhill!

That was Bunter's idea!

But it was nobody else's! The fact was, of course, that nobody but Bunter mattered in the least! But the chums of the Remove were unaware of that fact, as it happened!

"Come on, you men!" said Johnny Bull, and he started. And Frank Nugent and Hurree Singh grinned, and wheeled after him.

"I say, you fellows," squeaked Bunter. "I say, Wharton——"

"Roll off, you fat ass!" said Harry Wharton, and he followed his friends.

"I say, Cherry——"

"Fathead!" answered Bob.

"Lend me your bike, old chap?"

"I don't think you'd enjoy riding it, if I did!" chuckled Bob. The fat Owl had not noticed the flat tyre. "Anyhow, I'm going on! Ta-ta, fatty!"

Billy Bunter's eyes gleamed behind his spectacles.

He was not going to walk that quarter of a mile if he could help it! And it seemed to him that he could help it. His cleverness came to the fore again!

The hill was rather steep. A fellow once started on a bike, going downhill, would go like an arrow, and be instantly beyond recapture. It would not be necessary to pedal—it was a free-wheel run all the way. As if to help Bunter in that masterly strategic scheme, four of the Co. had gone on, and that gave him a start, ahead of possible pursuit from Bob's comrades.

"Hold on, Cherry!" gasped Bunter. "I say, I want to tell you—I remember now—that football match——"

"Well, I don't want to be left behind," said Bob, glancing after his comrades, and unaware that that was exactly what Bunter did want. "Cut it short, old man!"

"Topham won!" said Bunter.

"By gum, did they?" said Bob, interested. "They must be a pretty good team, then. I know St. Jude's are shaping jolly well. Did old Lunn bag anything?"

"I never noticed."

"What was the score?"

"I forget!"

"Oh, my hat! You seem to know a fat lot about it!" said Bob. "Is that all you've got to tell a chap?"

"I—I saw some jolly good goals taken," said Bunter. "There was a Topham chap who played up wonderfully—chap named Wilson, or something, I forget—quite in my style, you know—bagging goals right and left—"

"Ha, ha, ha!"

"Blessed if I see anything to cackle at! Let's see, I think I remember the score—two to one—or three to one—or four to one, perhaps—either that, or something else—"

"Oh crumbs!"

"Or something of the sort," said Bunter. "I say—"

"Thanks for giving me such an accurate description of the match, old bean. I'll get on now," said Bob. His friends were disappearing over the crest of the hill ahead.

"I'll wheel the bike a bit of the way for you," said Bunter.

"Don't trouble."

"Pleasure, old chap!" declared Bunter, and he took hold of the bike.

Bob Cherry was an unsuspicious fellow. He had not the remotest idea of Bunter's felonious designs on that bike. But he was surprised!

It was so utterly unlike Bunter to offer to take trouble on anyone else's account that it was a little difficult to believe.

Still, when Bunter grasped hold of the bike, as if to wheel it, it seemed genuine, and Bob let go the machine. He had done all the wheeling he wanted, if it came to that, and certainly it would have been rather a relief to have that rocky jigger wheeled for him a bit of the way up the hill.

"Ow!" he ejaculated suddenly, as a pedal banged on his leg.

"Better walk clear, old chap!" said Bunter.

Bob gave him six feet of space. He did not want another bang from a pedal. It did not occur to him that Bunter wanted room to turn the bike—now that the other fellows were at a safe distance.

That occurred to him a few seconds later—as Bunter, suddenly and swiftly, whirled the bike round. With unusual activity, the fat junior bounded into the saddle, and the bike shot away down the hill.

Bob stood almost petrified.

"Bunter!" he gasped "My bike! Why, you fat villain! Stop!"

He leaped in pursuit.

But on the steep slope the bike shot instantly far from reach, as the astute Owl had calculated.

But there was one thing upon which Billy Bunter had not calculated, and that was a flat front tyre. He had that discovery yet to make.

He made it suddenly and painfully.

Had the bike been in good order, there was no doubt that Billy Bunter's strategic scheme would have succeeded. He would have raced away to the railway station, and would have been gone in the train before Bob could have covered the distance on foot.

But the bike wasn't in good order. It shot away down the hill a dozen yards, but so rockily and bumpily that Bunter realised that, even in that brief space of time, that something was wrong.

Rough going on a steep slope was no place for a fellow to try riding on the rim. The bike rocked and bumped and waddled, and suddenly crashed.

Bunter flew.

What happened he hardly knew. But he knew that he was sitting in the grass beside the road, with more aches and pains distributed over his fat person than he could have counted. And he was yelling wildly.

"Ha, ha, ha!" roared Bob.

He came along at a run and picked up the bike. Bunter sat and roared.

"Yoop! Yarooh! I'm killed! My neck's broken! Wow! My leg's smashed! Whoooooop! I say—— Yarooop!"

"Can't you get up?" asked Bob.

"Ow! No! Wow!"

"Then I shall have to kick you where you are!"

Bunter found that he could get up. He got up quite quickly.

"Beast! Keep off! Ow!"

"Ha, ha, ha!"

Bob Cherry grasped the jigger and wheeled it up the hill again.

Billy Bunter gasped and spluttered, and rolled away on foot for the railway station. It was an aching and painful Bunter that got into the train, and rubbed bumps and bruises all the way back to Greyfriars.

THE SEVENTH CHAPTER.
What's Happened to Hacker?

JAMES HOBSON of the Shell breathed hard and deep as he came out of the House on Saturday afternoon.

Hobby, generally a very cheery and good-tempered fellow, looked grim and gloomy, almost fierce.

Which was a surprise to Harry Wharton & Co. as they sighted him in the quad. That afternoon the Remove were playing the Shell in a Form match; and when football was on Hobby generally looked merry and bright.

"Hallo, hallo, hallo! Enjoying life, old bean?" asked Bob Cherry, giving the captain of the Shell a smack on the shoulder.

"Fathead!" said Hobson.

"My esteemed and absurd Hobson, what——" murmured Hurree Jamset Ram Singh.

"Br-r-r-r!" said Hobson.

"What's up, old scout?" asked Harry Wharton.

"Hacker!" said Hobby, in concentrated tones. "Hacker! My beak! If you men ever hear of Hacker being brained with a ruler in our Form-room, you'll know that he asked for it a lot of times before he got it!"

Whereat the chums of the Remove grinned. Hobby, evidently, was boiling; but they did not think it probable that so tragic a fate would ever fall to the lot of his Form-master.

"Hacker biting this morning?" asked Bob sympathetically. "He's a bit of an acid drop, I know."

"The acidity is terrific!" agreed the Nabob of Bhanipur.

"All in the day's work, old chap!" said Johnny Bull, very comfortingly. "We get the sharp edge of Quelch's tongue pretty often in the Remove. Taking 'em wide

and large, Hacker doesn't bite oftener than Quelch."

"Something's up with him," said Hobson glumly. "He's like a bear with a sore head to-day. I've heard that he bit Prout in Common-room. He's generally pretty civil to the Fifth Form beak, but I've heard that he shut him up like a pocket-knife at brekker."

"Old Prout shutting up at times!" remarked Nugent. "Quelch snaps at him every now and then. Beaks will be beaks, you know!"

"I fancy he's had a letter that's upset him," said Hobson. "I know he's pulled a letter out of his pocket in the Form-room six or seven times this morning and looked at it, with a face as black as—as—as yours, Inky!"

"My esteemed idiotic Hobson——"

"Income-tax, perhaps!" said Bob. "These elderly sportsmen often let off steam when they get a pleasant little note from the Inland Revenue Department. I've heard my pater sometimes."

"Well, whatever it is, it's upset him," said Hobson, "and he's passed it on to us! We've had just one long rag this morning in the Shell!"

"Rough luck!" said Bob.

"Brace up, old bean!" said Harry. "Hacker has his little ways—they all have—but he's not a bad old bean, really."

"Oh, I know that!" grunted Hobson. "Only the other day he barked in when that silly idiot Coker was being cheeky and jawed him—not that I wanted him to, you know; still, he did, and it was amusing to watch Coker's face. Hacker's an acid drop, but a man can stand him, as a rule. But now——"

"Well, it's a half-holiday to-day, and you're done with Hacker," said the captain of the Remove.

"That's all you know!" groaned Hobson. "We've got detention!"

"What?"

"Hacker got worse and worse!" groaned Hobby. "He caned Stewart and Hoskins, and gave me lines. That was bad enough! I tell you, he handed out lines in tons—chucked 'em over like confetti! Some of us started shuffling our feet—not stamping, as he chose to call it; but perhaps we did make a bit of a row. Well, we thought it was time to let him know where he got off—see? Then he squealed out detention."

"Oh crikey!"

The Famous Five looked grave enough now.

Detention for the Shell that afternoon meant washing out the Form match. Evidently Mr. Hacker must have been in a very truculent mood that morning.

"Well, you seem to have asked for it," remarked Johnny Bull. "We shouldn't stamp in the Remove-room, whatever Quelch did."

"Perhaps you haven't the nerve!" suggested Hobson.

(Continued on next page.)

"We haven't the fatheadedness, any-how."

"Look here, you cheeky, silly, gab-bling Remove tick——"

"Order!" said Harry Wharton. "No rags, old beans! That won't do any good. I say, Hobby, Hacker may feel better after dinner, and let you off. Dinner often has a soothing effect on beaks."

"That's the idea! Ask him nicely after dinner, and point out that there's a football fixture!" said Frank Nugent. Hobson shook his head.

"I'd no more go to his study than I'd go into a tiger's den!" he said impressively. "I'm barring Hacker till he gets over this, whatever it is!"

"But, my dear chap, we're going to play football!" urged Wharton.

"Looks as if we're not!" groaned Hobby.

"Dash it all, if you won't try it on, I jolly well will!" said Harry. "I've a right to point out to him that he's mucking up a football fixture when we're playing in it!"

"Try it on, if you like!" said Hobson. "Guard with your left when you tackle him, that's all!"

And James Hobson, driving his hands deep into his trousers pockets, tramped away in the quad, looking like a fellow who had collected most of the troubles of the universe in a big bunch.

"Well, this is rather thick!" said Bob, with a whistle. "We're getting rotten luck in footer this term, my beloved 'earers! Last Wednesday we were dished over seeing the game at St. Jude's, and now our Form match is washed out owing to Hacker getting out of bed on the wrong side!"

"It's not washed out yet," said Harry Wharton. "Hobby ought to speak to him after dinner. But if he won't, I will."

When the bell rang for dinner, and the juniors went in, Harry Wharton & Co. turned their eyes on the Shell table. Mr. Hacker lunched when his Form dined, like most of the staff, and he was in his usual place.

But he was not, as Bob remarked in a whisper, looking his usual bonny self.

His face was grim and glum—an expression reflected in the countenances of most of the Shell fellows.

Whatever it was that disturbed Mr. Hacker, it seemed that it was still going strong. He had, at the best of times, rather an acid temper, though he was, like all the masters at Greyfriars, a dutiful beak, and a good and conscientious man in his own way. But his looks betrayed the fact that his temper just at present was not merely acid, but pure vinegar.

However, Harry Wharton hoped that dinner might have its usual ameliorating effect. Certainly he was not going to scratch the Form match that afternoon if it was possible to induce Mr. Hacker to rescind his sweeping edict.

Moreover, that Form match was of unusual import, as it happened. For it happened that Vernon-Smith, who had been a tower of strength in the Remove team last term, had turned up for the new term quite off colour—a thing that may happen to the best and keenest footballer. The captain of the Remove was going to give his chum, Frank Nugent, a trial in the Bounder's place, and the game with the Shell was an excellent opportunity.

Naturally, Wharton wanted to know how Frank was likely to shape in the eleven before meeting such teams as Highcliffe, Rookwood, St. Jim's, or St. Jude's. He was very keen on that match with the Shell taking place as scheduled.

And so, having waited awhile for dinner to produce the hoped-for soothing effect on Hacker, the captain of the Remove made his way to Masters' Studies, and tapped at Hacker's door—gently and respectfully.

He knew that Mr. Hacker was in his study—and he hoped that he was not taking a nap in the armchair. He hoped to find him, soothed by a good dinner, taking a brighter and happier view of the universe and the things therein—and prepared to make concessions to anxious footballing fellows!

Having delivered that gentle tap, Wharton opened the door and gave quite a jump.

Hacker was there, as he expected. He was not napping in the armchair. Neither, unfortunately, was he in a soothed state, taking brighter views. He was standing at the telephone, barking into that instrument, having apparently just got his man at the other end.

"I should say so! Yes! Shocked! Shocked indeed! Amazed—dismayed! I can find no words to describe my feelings! Of course, I will come! I am bound to stand by Eric, even——"

Hacker ceased to bark, suddenly, as he spotted a face at the door. Harry Wharton was quite taken aback. He realised that this was an unfortunate moment for calling on Hacker!

Undecided whether to back out and close the door, or to step in, he was hesitating, when Hacker spotted him, and barked:

"What! Who—— Wharton! What do you want here? How dare you walk into my study? Go away at once! I shall complain to your Form-master of this intrusion! Shut that door instantly!"

Harry Wharton, with deep feelings, stepped back, and shut the door. Obviously, it was useless to ask favours of Hacker just then.

His friends were waiting for him in the quad.

"What luck?" asked Bob.

"What did Hacker say?" asked Frank Nugent.

Wharton made a grimace.

"He bit! He was on the phone, jawing somebody! I shall have to leave it till later. Dash it all, the man can't keep on being shirty permanently, because he's got some family trouble on his mind."

But leaving it till later proved no resource. For within ten minutes, the chums of the Remove beheld Mr. Hacker, in coat and hat, striding down to the gates. He strode out, and was gone.

—— ——

THE EIGHTH CHAPTER.

It's An Ill Wind——

"I SAY, you fellows!"

"Oh, shut up, Bunter!"

"But I say, what's up with Hacker?"

"Blow Hacker!" said six or seven fellows at once.

The Famous Five, and several other Remove men, were consulting with Hobson, and Hoskins, and Stewart, and some other Shell fellows.

Football was in all their thoughts. But Mr. Hacker was gone out, leaving his Form under the sentence of detention.

It was impossible now to ask him to wash out that sentence—and it was scarcely possible to get on with the game, with the sentence still in force. If Hacker walked in, and found his Form playing football, it meant something in the nature of an earthquake—in Hacker's present mood.

On the other hand, if he was gone for

the afternoon, the risk could be taken. It looked as if he had forgotten having detained the Shell—he had not taken the trouble, at all events, to see them into detention before he went out. Still, they were not due for detention till two o'clock, and he might come whisking in before two, if he had only gone for a walk.

In such a doubtful and worrying state of affairs, the footballers had no use for Bunter's chin-wag! They waved him impatiently away.

"But, I say," persisted Bunter, "old Hacker looks fearfully upset. He will have to run to catch that train, too!"

"Train! Has he gone to catch a train?"

All faces brightened. If Hacker had gone to catch a train, it looked as if he was gone for the afternoon. Wharton remembered that he had been saying on the phone that he would come—somewhere or other.

"How do you know, Bunter?" demanded Hobson.

"I heard him asking Quelch about trains," explained Bunter. "Quelch told him that there was an up train at two, from Courtfield."

"By gum! If that's where he's gone——"

"He was asking Quelch about the trains to London!" said Bunter. "I say, Quelch looked at him! He could see that he was fearfully upset! So could I. I wonder what's happened? say, you fellows——"

"If Hacker's gone off to London——" said Hobson, with a deep breath.

"Looks like it!" said Hoskins.

"Forgotten that he's kept us in!" remarked Stewart. "Unless he's spoken to a prefect about it——"

"What a bit of luck!" said Bob Cherry. "We're all right, you men. Hacker's gone for the day."

"We're under detention, all the same!" muttered Hobson. "But—but I think—in the circumstances——"

"Wait till two o'clock," said Stewart sagely. "If Hacker's tipped a prefect, we shall hear by then. If not——"

"If not," said Hobson, "even Hacker won't expect us to detain ourselves. He will be disappointed if he does."

"We've a right to wait till our beak walks us in," said Stewart, "and we've a right to play footer while we wait."

"Hear, hear!"

"I say, you fellows——"

"Bunter, old fat bean, there's a packet of toffee in my study," said Harry Wharton, laughing. "Buzz off and bag it!"

The captain of the Remove felt that Bunter had earned a reward.

Bunter rolled off promptly. The Remove and Shell fellows waited rather anxiously for two to strike.

It looked as if Mr. Hacker, in his upset state, had rushed off to catch the train for London, utterly forgetful of the sentence on his Form. But it was so unlike Hacker, as a rule, to forget such things, that it seemed rather too good to be true. The footballers were hopeful, but anxious. If Hacker had left instructions with a prefect, there was nothing doing. But if he hadn't, and it looked as if he hadn't, all was serene.

Wingate of the Sixth came sauntering across the quad with Gwynne of that Form. Wingate, as a rule, was very popular with the juniors—so was Gwynne. But now the juniors eyed the two seniors with deep distaste. Both of them were prefects—and either or both might have been left the task of herding the Shell into detention.

But Wingate and Gwynne walked on, unheeding the anxious group. Remove

Wharton opened the door of Mr. Hacker's study, and was quite taken aback to see the master of the Shell standing by the telephone. "I should say so!" barked Hacker into the transmitter. "Yes! Shocked! Shocked indeed! Amazed—dismayed—I can find no words to describe my feelings! Of course, I will come—I am bound to stand by Eric——" Wharton hesitated whether to back out or stay in.

and Shell breathed freely again. Two was striking now.

"Hallo, hallo, hallo! Here comes Loder!" breathed Bob Cherry.

Loder of the Sixth came along. He came directly up to the group, and their hearts sank. Were all their hopes to be crushed at the last moment? If the execution of Hacker's sentence had been left in the hands of the bully of the Sixth, there was no hope.

"Hobson!" rapped Loder.

"Yes, Loder!" almost groaned Hobby.

"Where are your lines?"

"Lines!" repeated Hobson, with a start.

Loder smiled sarcastically.

"Forgotten that you had a hundred lines?" he asked. "I believe you're playing football this afternoon! Well, no football till you've handed in your lines."

Loder, as usual, was making himself unpleasant. To his astonishment, Hobson's face brightened up. Loder stared at him. It was the first time, in his experience, that a junior had looked bucked on being asked for lines.

He did not know that Hobby had been expecting something much worse! But the juniors, seeing now that Loder knew nothing about the detention, all smiled cheerily.

"Oh, all right, Loder!" gasped Hobson. "I've nearly done them—I'll bring them to your study in a quarter of an hour."

"No football till you do!" grunted Loder, and he walked away again, quite puzzled.

The juniors exchanged happy glances.

"Right as rain!" said Harry. "Hacker hasn't left word! Cut off and finish your impot for that tick, Hobby—lots of time before kick-off!"

"What-ho!" grinned Hobby.

There was another alarm when Walker of the Sixth was seen coming out of the House with Carne. But Walker and Carne went down to the gates, and walked out. At a quarter past two, Hobby handed in his lines to Loder—and by that time it was clear that all was well. Hacker, utterly contrary to his usual custom, had forgotten a punishment. It was a plain proof that he was fearfully upset.

The two teams gathered on Little Side, in cheery spirits. Hacker was in the London train, safe off the scene. No person in authority had been left to carry on with the detention. The Shell were perfectly within their rights in staying out till they were shepherded in. And, as the canny Stewart had pointed out, they had a right to play footer, if they liked, while they waited for Hacker.

So they played footer.

It was real luck. It was indeed so very lucky that Mr. Hacker was so fearfully upset that they rather forgot to sympathise with him in his unknown and mysterious trouble.

Clearly something very startling must have occurred to upset Mr. Hacker so much and to take him off to London, forgetful of a sentence passed on his Form.

But the juniors were not thinking of that—they were thinking of Soccer.

Bad luck for Hacker was, in the circumstances, good luck for his Form —as the proverb declares, it's an ill wind that blows nobody good! The ill wind for Hacker was a favourable breeze for the Shell!

James Hobson had the additional satisfaction of winning that game. That was not, of course, quite so satisfactory to the Remove. They had played the Shell once already that term, and

beaten them—now, as Hurree Jamset Ram Singh remarked, it was a boot on the other leg! Frank Nugent, in the Bounder's place in the front line, played up his hardest; and he played quite a good game—but he was not in the same street with Smithy, when Smithy was at his best. The Shell were an older Form, and it would have been a hard tussle at the best of times—now it proved a little too hard.

Vernon-Smith stood and looked on, with rather a sneer on his face.

Smithy was well aware that he was off colour, and that his skipper had no choice but to try a new man in his place; but it irritated him, all the same, to hang about while other fellows played football. And probably he was not wholly displeased to see that Frank, with all his efforts, failed to fill the vacant place satisfactorily.

"Sorry, old man!" Frank remarked to his captain when the game was over, the Shell having been victorious by two goals to one.

"My dear chap, we can't win every match!" answered Harry.

"Smithy may pull up in time for Rookwood!" said Nugent.

Wharton nodded, without replying. He was very keen to keep his best chum in the Remove team if he could; but he had to bite on the fact that Frank was not the man for the Rookwood match, if a better could be found.

Hobson & Co. went off, bucked and cheerful. Mr. Hacker had not come in, and everything had gone well. Hobby had a lingering uneasiness about the view Hacker might take of the matter when he did come in. Still, they had had the game; and that was that.

(Continued on page 16.)

LOOK TO YOUR LAURELS, KIPPS!

Says PETER TODD

Kipps will have to look to his laurels. Nobody has ever challenged his right to the title of Champion Conjurer of the Remove in the past, but now our one-and-only Prize Porpoise is out to wrest it from him!

And when Bunter gets going, you know, there's no stopping him! He's already Form champion in voice-throwing, gorging, fibbing, boasting and slacking, so if he really puts his mind to it, what's to prevent him gaining similar honours in conjuring?

The display he gave in the Rag the other evening was most impressive.

He started by drawing yards and yards of coloured paper strips from his mouth. From a distance of a hundred yards or so, it would have been impossible to see that the paper was coming from his sleeve instead of his mouth.

Several other clever tricks followed—performed with such dexterity that a blindfolded man wouldn't have stood an earthly chance of seeing through them.

But Bunter's greatest triumph was reserved for the end. For this trick he borrowed Hazeldene's gold watch.

"I say, Hazel, you don't mind if I smash it up, do you?" he asked.

"Not at all!" grinned Hazeldene, knowing how safe gold watches are in conjurers' hands.

"Good! Here goes, then!"

And Bunter wrapped up Hazel's watch in a handkerchief and started to hit it good and proper with a heavy hammer, afterwards making the handkerchief and its contents disappear.

"Now look in your pocket and you'll find the watch there—entirely undamaged!" said Bunter proudly.

And, sure enough, Hazel dived a hand into his pocket and, amid loud applause, drew out a watch!

There was only one snag about it. It happened to be the toy watch Bunter had actually intended smashing up. By an unlucky mischance, due to his short sight, Bunter had smashed up the real watch instead of the dud!

Still, as he told Hazel, accidents will happen even amongst the most expert conjurers—and, anyway, Hazel had said before he began that he had no objection to his watch being smashed!

No kid about it, chaps—if Bunter goes on as he has started, Kipps will soon have to play second fiddle!

His Acting Was "Hole"-ly Good!

Wibley accidentally fell through a trapdoor on the stage while acting in a holiday panto., yet he was still carrying on with his part, even as he vanished from sight.

Critics are agreed that his performance at this point was absolutely "floor-less!"

To The Domestic Staff

Horace Coker wishes you to know that it's quite unnecessary for you to sweep up the gym next Monday morning, since he intends to mop up the floor there with Blundell in the afternoon!

Japes Unlimited—

Offer their unique service to intending japers. Booby-traps fixed, studies wrecked, notices pinned to victims' backs, banana-skin slides carefully prepared. Tell us what you want. We do the rest! Expert advice free of charge. Estimates on request.—JAPES UNLIMITED, Study No. 11, Remove.

GREYFRIA

No. 172.   EDITED BY

The MASKED MARAWDERS!

By DICKY NUGENT

"We want more tuck!"

Mr. I. Jolliwell Lickham's voice rang out across Masters' Common-room like a thunder-clap. Like listening, his listeners, the other masters of St. Sam's, chimed in with a loud "Hear, hear!"

Dr. Birchemall, who was presiding over the first Masters' Meeting of the New Term, glared at them. Picking up his chairman's mallet, he brought it down on the table with a deffening crash.

"Jentlemen, jentlemen!" he barked. "What are you doing of? Why, this is rank mewtiny!"

"Mewtiny or not, sir," said Mr. Lickham doggedly, "the fakt remains. The rashuns we are living on at present would hardly keep a cat alive! We want more tuck!"

"Hear, hear!"

"Well, there's no sattisfying some people," remarked the Head, with a shrug. "Only a minnit or two ago you were saying you were fed up; and now you say you want more tuck. Why don't you make up your minds which you mean?"

"Eggscuse me, sir!"

It was a weak, wining voice coming from the direction of the door. Turning round, Doctor Birchemall perseeved that Toadey minor of the Fourth was poking his head into Masters' Common-room.

"Toadey minor!" cride the Head, in his refined voice. "How dare you bust into a private meeting like this here?"

"Begging your pardon, sir, but it's important!" gasped

Toadey minor, who was the biggest sneak in the skool. "Something's arranged for to-nite which I feel I ought to report to you, sir. The Fourth are going to hold a dormitory feed!"

Doctor Birchemall gave a violent start. A cunning gleem came into his beady eyes, as he looked from Toadey to the mewtinous masters.

"A dorm feed, eh?" he said. "This is a jolly serious statement to make, Toadey. Are you sure of your fakts?"

"Certain, sir!" wined Toadey. "I saw Jolly and his pals carting up the grub!"

"Kindly refrain from using slang eggspressions, Toadey. What you mean, presumably, is 'lugging up the tommy'?"

"Yes, sir; that's right, sir!" wined Toadey, who always agreed with anything a beak mite say. "Please, sir, I hoap you're pleased with me for tipping you the wink!"

The Head frowned.

"No, Toadey, I am not pleased. Take a thowsand lines for being a sneak and a cadd!"

"Wha-a-at!"

"I regard it as a kontemptible thing for you to split on your Form-fellows!" snapped the Head. "Go—and don't forget that thow-

sand lines birch you and blew!

"Oh, cr Toadey almost tott of Master mon-room

When t had closed him, D Birchemall to the grinning a his dial.

"Well, jentlemen," "Toadey's informe couldn't have come at time. You want tu the Fourth Form h All that remains is fc konfiscate it. How take it, though, withou knowing who we are?

Mr. Lickham winke

"Quite easily, sir we need do is to wear and raid the dorm a the tuck by sheer armed, let us say, with and nottid towels!"

"Oh, grate pip!"

For a moment the gasped. But whe thought it over they chortled.

"Gratters, Lick grinned Doctor Birc "It's a jolly good They'll never guess being raided by n They'll think we're Formers or Sixth Form like as not!"

"Glad you like it Mr. Lickham, blushin destly. "Now what preparing for the fra tlemen? It's nearly b and it won't be lon before they begin their

The masters' meetin broke up on a note of optimism.

But the beaks mi have been so optimist they known what was

WOULD YOU BELIEVE IT?

Fisher T. Fish, displaying an invention of his own to Removites—a calculating machine—asked them to put coins into it to be added up. Vernon-Smith, however, soon spotted that Fishy's calculating machine was calculating in its owner's favour! Another "calculating" trick of Fishy's! "No change"!

Bob Cherry possesses a signal drum, given him by Major Cherry, like those used by native tribes, by which they send out a call to arms. Bob used it to call the Remove to arms when Temple & Co. raided the Remove passage—and the response was so strong that Temple & Co. were "drummed" out in no time!

Dicky Nugent was very the billy-goat which h allowed to keep as a pet. Bunter, however, teased he "got its goat"— butted him! As soon Head heard that Dicky had developed into a "b he would listen to no "b but sent it away

HERALD

STOP PRESS NEWS

...RTON.   **January 18th, 1936.**

...nd the scenes. Toadey felt so wild about his ...nd lines that he lissened ...he keyhole, after the ...ad sent him packing. ...n as he knew what ...he wind, he rushed off ... Junior Common-room ...d Jack Jolly & Co. all the masters' plot—— ..., of corse, mentioning ...l spilled the beans !

... was dismay in the ...f the Fourth when they ...he news. Some were ... of putting up a fight ...ir feed, and others ... to call it off com-

...ack Jolly had different ...together.

... got a better plan," ...nned. "Lissen, you ...!"

...ank his voice to a ... as he eggsplained his ... When he had ..., there was a burst of ...from the Fourth.

...ly good idea, Jolly !" ...nk Fearless.

... jape of the term, bai ... chuckled the Hon.-Guy de Vere. "Let's ...ay right away !"

...e mistick hour of ten ... out from the old ...wer of St. Sam's, ...d masked figgers, wear-...ssing-gowns, and carry-...ows and nottid towels, ...lled in Big Hall.

... signal from their ...they filed up the stairs ...nded their way to the ... Form dormitory. ...the leader pawsed, ...s hand on the door-

...dy, you men ?" ...dy, I, ready !" ... in charge !" ...r Birchemall—for it ...—flung open the door ... the way in, and in ... jiffy the masked

marawders were charging into the dorm.

They couldn't have come at a better moment—or so it seemed ! The Fourth were all out of bed, and Jolly and Merry and Bright, in the centre of the dorm, were just on the point of opening two wacking grate hampers of tuck. The site of those hampers farely inspired the raiders !

Towels and pillows whirled fewriously, as they waded in, and the Fourth Formers scattered in all directions. With ringing war-woops, the attackers seezed the tuck-hampers, and then retreated, lashing out right and left as they did so. And in less time than it takes to relait, they were scampering glee-fully down the stairs again,

with their booty in their midst !

Back in Masters' Common-room, they flung off their masks and opened the tuck-hampers.

"Ham-patties, s o s s i d g e-rolls, döenutts—my hat ! This is a feed to write home about !" cried Doctor Birchemall. "Help yourself, jentlemen !"

The masters didn't need a second invitation. They started skoffing the raided tuck ravvenously.

For a few ticks, no sound was heard save the champing of many jaws. But then :

"Woooo00p !" yelled the Head suddenly.

"Grooooo0 !" howled Mr. Lickham.

"Yarooooo0 !" roared Mr. Justiss. "Help ! I'm poi-soned !"

Yells and shreeks and moans and groans began to echo and re-echo across Masters' Common-room. Staid and vennerable masters began to roll about on the carpet, holding their tummies.

"Ow-ow-ow ! It's a hoaks !" cride Doctor Bir-chemall horsely, as he eggs-amined the hampers more closely. "There's nothing but rubbish underneeth—and the tuck on top has been filled with ink and glew and soot ! Grooooo0 !"

"Ha, ha, ha !"

From the doorway came a yell of larfter. The Fourth Formers had come down to see the fun, and they simply couldn't help themselves. They shreeked.

"Ha, ha, ha !"

"You—you—you——"

The Head tried to make a rush—but before he could do so, an aggernising pain in his little Mary made him collapse again, moaning feebly.

"Come on, you chaps !" grinned Jack Jolly. "We'll get back to the dorm now and start on the REAL feed ! Good-nite, sir !"

"Ha, ha, ha !"

And the Fourth Formers, still larfing historically, re-turned to their dorm and had a jolly good tuck-in—feeling quite sure that they wouldn't have to worry any more about the Masked Marawders !

WILL COKER BECOME TRAPEZE STAR ?

Asks GEORGE BLUNDELL

Coker has come back to school with a new ambition. He wants to be a trapeze artiste ! During the vac. he went to a couple of circuses where trapeze acts were featured, and the sight of the performers flying through the air from one trapeze to another filled him with envy. He took the first opportunity to start practising in the gym when the new term began.

I need hardly say that he's an unqualified success at trapeze work. A chap like Coker could hardly be otherwise, could he ? I can already foresee the day when his name will be featured in big letters outside the massive marquee of some world-famed circus, and when his dizzy deeds in midair will hold audiences spellbound !

But before he achieves these heights of fame, he'll certainly have to get himself a more attentive pair of assistants than Potter and Greene !

When I looked into the gym yesterday morning, Potter and Greene were just waiting to catch him as he did a daredevil dive from the top of a lofty horizontal bar. Of course, Potter and Greene should have been so wrapped up in the job as not even to notice my arrival. But they both turned round when I walked in, and both fixed their eyes on the box of chocs. I had just bought at the tuckshop.

"Have one ?" I asked, not noticing Coker up aloft.

"Thanks !" said Potter and Greene.

They reached for the chocs. At the same moment Coker dived. A moment later three fiendish yells rang out, and Potter and Greene hit the floor—hard—with Coker on top of them !

The best advice I can give to Coker, if he really wants to become a trapeze star, is to advertise for a couple of really efficient catchers—chocolate-eaters barred !

Still A Photographer !

Frank Nugent asks us to deny the yarn that he has abandoned photography for debating. He points out that in joining the Remove Parliament, he is merely " deve-loping " his powers of speech !

OH, FOR AN IDEAL REPORTER !

Sighs HARRY WHARTON

We welcome new blood on the " Herald." But good new reporters are jolly rare birds !

Take the two I tried out this week—Skinner and Alonzo Todd.

Within an hour of his appointment, Skinner had turned in a dozen news items of the most exciting kind. The Head, he said, had resigned, and was to be replaced by one Doctor Hokum, who had just served seven years in Dartmoor for forgery. The governors had decided that all boys should have brekker in bed for the rest of the term. Mr. Prout had just shot a Second Former, under the mistaken impression that he was firing at a sparrow. And so on ! It was juicy copy—but it wasn't true !

'Lonzy was just the opposite. He stuck grimly to the truth—but he didn't put a penn'orth of pep into it. Several juveniles, he said, had recently engaged in highly diverting games of chess. Students were again getting into their scholastic stride. We've had a lot of rain. And lots more like that !

What's an editor to do ? I can't print sensations that aren't the truth—and I can't print the truth when it's not sensational ! Yet the chaps who want to join the " Herald " staff always give me one or the other !

GREYFRIARS FACTS WHILE YOU WAIT !

...Ogilvy, the Scots junior, ...l at putting the weight, ...s to represent his country ... at the Highland Games. ...ting the Remove, he ... heavy iron weight a ... a half further than C. R. ... the Upper Fourth ...n. But Temple does not ..., on Ogilvy, on Scotch oats !

A grinning face chalked on the top of Mr. Twigg's mortar-board caused recurrent giggles in the Second Form Room. Only when, in dire wrath, Mr. Twigg threw his mortar-board on the floor, did he perceive the cause of the merriment ! Twigg suspects Dicky Nugent. But Dicky is keeping what he knows " under his hat " !

Horace Coker was firmly con-vinced he was cut out to be a film star, and he actually got a job as an " extra " last vac. When it was explained that he was to " double " for a fellow who had to be pushed into a pond, however, Coker was speechless with indignation. He refuses to " speak " of his " non-speaking " part !

(Continued from page 13.)

THE NINTH CHAPTER.

Quite A Surprise For Hobby!

"HOBBY, old man——"

Harry Wharton looked into Hobson's study in the Shell after prep.

Hobson and Stewart and Hoskins were there. Hoskins had produced his fiddle—which was a signal for his study-mates to find sudden and pressing business elsewhere. Hobson was just remarking that he had to see Temple of the Fourth about a Form match when Wharton looked in.

"Hacker——" said Harry.

"Has he come in?" asked Hobson. "He wasn't in at tea-time. Hacker's been making a jolly day of it."

"He came in some time ago, and went to the Head!" answered Wharton. "He's been with Dr. Locke a long time."

"Does he still look shirty?" asked Hobson anxiously.

"Well, no! But he's just asked me to look for you, and send you to his study."

"Oh gum!"

Hobson looked dismayed.

"Look here, it's all right," said Harry. "Even Hacker wouldn't expect fellows to walk into detention without being told."

"But you say he's been to the Head——"

"Can't have been about that; he would see you first, if he was going to report you to the Big Beak."

"Yes, that's so," said Hobson, relieved. "And—and you say he doesn't look so shirty as he did?"

"No; he looks a bit worried, I thought; but not crusty! He seems to have got over his tantrums," said Wharton encouragingly.

"Well, I'm glad of that, at least," said Hobson. "I suppose I shall have to go and see him. Anyhow, we had the game."

James Hobson proceeded to his Form-master's study—not in a happy mood.

It was a relief to hear that Hacker no longer looked shirty; but even at his best, he was rather an acid gentleman. And though all the Shell fellows felt that they had acted quite within their rights that afternoon, they did not feel sure that Hacker would see eye to eye with them!

Hobby, in fact, was expecting trouble; and he wondered whether it meant only a "royal and imperial jaw," or lines, or a whopping! It was not a happy Hobson who tapped at Hacker's door and entered.

Mr. Hacker was seated in his arm-chair by the fire, gazing into the latter with a clouded and thoughtful brow.

He did not look bad-tempered now; but he did look like a man who had found serious trouble of some sort, and upon whose mind it weighed.

He glanced round at Hobby.

THE MAGNET LIBRARY.—No. 1,457.

"Come in, Hobson," he said. "You may shut the door."

Hobson shut the door.

He stood before his beak, waiting for the storm to burst. But Mr. Hacker did not seem in a hurry to begin. He gazed at Hobson in a thoughtful way and seemed to be undecided how to get going.

"If you please, sir——" ventured Hobson. He felt that it might be judicious to get in his defence first.

"What?" barked Mr. Hacker.

"I mean, sir, as you went out——" stammered Hobson.

"What?"

"I—I mean, we had to wait for you, sir," explained Hobson hopefully. "And —and we just played footer while— while we were waiting——"

"You played football!" repeated Mr. Hacker. "Indeed!"

"Our match with the Remove, sir— and—and in the circumstances, sir, I— I think, as we had to wait, that—that it was all right—and—and——" Hobby's voice trailed off under Mr. Hacker's frigid stare.

"I don't understand you, Hobson," said the master of the Shell testily. "Why should you not play football on a half-holiday?"

Hobson almost jumped.

That, certainly, was not the reply he had expected from Mr. Hacker.

"I—I mean——" he stuttered.

"Well, what do you mean, Hobson?"

"I—I mean—the—the detention——"

"Upon my word!" said Mr. Hacker. "Oh, quite so, quite so—I fear that I must have forgotten, in the stress of other matters. Upon my word! It quite slipped my mind, Hobson."

Hobson breathed hard. He could see now that the sentence of detention had slipped Hacker's mind so completely that he had forgotten it altogether—till Hobby reminded him now!

Evidently, that was not why he had sent for Hobson. Hobby could have kicked himself for having reminded him. Still, how was a fellow to know?

"Quite!" said Mr. Hacker. "Is it possible, Hobson, that because this matter slipped my attention, you——"

Signs of "shirtiness" were only too clear in Hacker's face. Hobson suppressed a groan! It was coming now!

But it did not come!

Mr. Hacker checked himself.

"Well, well," he said, amazing Hobby, "as I forgot the matter, Hobson, possibly my boys felt entitled to forget it also. You appear to have acted somewhat thoughtlessly, Hobson, but—well, well, we will say no more about the matter."

"Oh, thank you, sir!" gasped Hobson.

It was rather difficult for Hobby to believe his ears! The upsetting of Hacker that day seemed to have done him good, Hobby thought!

"It was on quite another matter that I sent for you, Hobson!" went on Mr. Hacker.

Hobby realised that now. He could only wonder what the "other matter" was. Not a row, evidently, for Hacker was looking amiable—as amiable as Hacker could look!

"The fact is——" Mr. Hacker paused for a moment.

"Yes, sir!"

"The fact is——" Mr. Hacker began again. He still seemed undecided how to begin, and Hobby's wonder increased. "The fact is——" He coughed. "Hem! You were speaking of—of football! As it happens, my nephew is a very keen footballer, and no doubt it will—er——" Hacker paused again. He was rather unused to being amiable, and the new

mood came rather jerkily. "I believe he is a very good footballer indeed!" he added.

"Is he, sir?" said the wondering Hobby. He had never heard of Mr. Hacker's nephew before—never thought of Hacker having one, indeed he had hardly thought of the stiff, acid master of the Shell as a human being at all, with ordinary human ties.

And what Hacker's nephew had to do with Hobby was a mystery. Hobby, so far as he could see, was never likely to meet the kid.

"My nephew Eric," went on Mr. Hacker, "is coming to Greyfriars on Monday, Hobson."

"Oh!" said Hobson.

He began to understand.

It was much to Hobby's credit that he did not allow his face to betray the dismay he felt.

One Hacker was enough, in Hobby's opinion! Two Hackers would be altogether too much of a good thing! And a young Hacker in the Shell—some beastly little tick, of course—it was absolutely rotten!

"You will meet him on Monday, probably!" said Mr. Hacker.

"Yes, sir," said Hobson, trying to look as if he liked the prospect. "I— I—I shall be—be glad to meet Hacker, sir."

"Eh! What do you mean? Oh! My nephew's name is not Hacker," said the master of the Shell. "His name is Wilmot—Eric Wilmot."

"Oh!" said Hobby. "I shall be glad to meet Wilmot, sir! Is—is—is he coming into the Shell?"

Hobson hardly dared to hope for an answer in the negative!

But his luck was in that day! The answer came—in the negative!

"No, Hobson!"

"Oh!" said Hobson.

A minute or two ago Hobby had been trying not to look dismal. Now he tried not to look glad!

"He was in the Lower Fourth Form at his last school," said Mr. Hacker. "He will go into the Lower Fourth here—the Remove! I have arranged the matter with the Head to-day. I——" He broke off, as if he realised that he was saying more than was necessary to Hobson. "Eric—I mean, Wilmot—will arrive on Monday."

"Yes, sir!"

As the new fellow was not coming into the Shell, Hobby did not quite see how it concerned him at all. Neither would he have expected a man like Hacker to bother much about a schoolboy nephew. Still, as Hobby admitted, you never could tell! Hacker might have had lots and lots of deep family affection bottled up under his crusty exterior.

Anyhow, it was clear that he was concerned about this chap Wilmot, or he would not have sent for Hobby to speak to him on the subject.

"I think you will probably like Eric —I mean, Wilmot, Hobson," said Mr. Hacker. "I believe he is very popular —a very agreeable boy."

"Greasy little tick!" was Hobson's unspoken comment.

Aloud he said:

"Oh, yes, sir!"

"He will be new here," said Mr. Hacker. "Of course, he has been to school before; but—as I say—he will be a stranger among us! If you are able to do anything, Hobson, to make his first days at Greyfriars—er—easier—I should say—er—pleasant—I am sure, Hobson——"

"Certainly, sir!" said Hobson. "We don't see much of the Remove, in the Shell, as a rule; but if I come across young Wilmot, I'll be decent to him, sir."

Hobby meant that, quite sincerely. There was a chance that Hacker's nephew was not a tick—he might be quite unlike Hacker ! But, tick or not, it seemed to be this chap Eric who was the cause of Hobson escaping trouble over the detention. One good turn deserved another.

"Thank you, Hobson," said Mr. Hacker, very graciously. "The fact is, Hobson, I shall feel obliged if you find any way of showing my nephew some little friendly attention. You might, perhaps, speak to your friends in the Remove on the subject. I very much desire my nephew to be happy here."

It was borne in on Hobby's surprised mind that Hacker really was a human being after all ! There was real feeling in his voice as he spoke. Hobby, who had the kindest heart in the world, quite warmed.

"I'll do anything I can, sir ! I'm sure I shall like the chap ! I'll look for him on Monday, sir."

"Thank you, Hobson," said Mr. Hacker.

And Hobby left his Form-master's study, greatly relieved, rather puzzled, but resolved to do his best for the new fellow—even if, as Hobby feared, he turned out to be a greasy little tick !

THE TENTH CHAPTER.

A Spot of Mystery !

"KINDLY remain a few moments, Wharton."

"Certainly, sir !"

Head boy of the Remove was not wholly his own master like other fellows. When the Remove was dismissed in break, on Monday morning, they went out joyfully into keen, frosty air—and head boy had to say what his Form-master had to say.

In point of fact, Wharton would have been glad to scuttle out after the others. But as Mr. Quelch asked him kindly to remain, there was no choice in the matter ; and he had to remain, whether kindly or unkindly. Hoping that Quelch would cut it short, he stood by the master's desk.

Mr. Quelch looked at him over the desk.

"A new boy comes into the Remove to-day, Wharton," he said.

"Oh, yes, sir !" said Harry.

"You were aware of it, Wharton?" asked the Remove master, raising his eyebrows a little.

"Hobson told me, sir—his Form-master's nephew is coming," said Harry. "Mr. Hacker told him so on Saturday."

"Oh ! Quite, quite !" said Mr. Quelch. "Well, Wharton, this boy—er —Wilmot—joins us to-day."

Quelch pursed his lips, and his brows knitted a little. Wharton, noticing it, wondered whether Quelch disliked the idea of having another beak's relative in his Form.

Hobson had told Harry about it. Loyal old Hobby, willing to do all he could, had asked the captain of the Remove to give the new kid a friendly word, if he happened to see him, and to refrain from kicking him for a day or two, even if he asked for it.

To which Wharton, grinning, had assented at once. Wharton had not had an easy first term at Greyfriars himself, and he remembered how much a little kind help meant to a new boy in a new world. He was prepared to be

quite decent to Hacker's nephew, even if he asked to be kicked !

Mr. Quelch was silent for a moment or two, and Wharton waited. The impression strengthened in his mind that Quelch did not want Hacker's nephew in the Remove. If that was the case, however, Quelch was certainly not likely to confide the fact to his head boy. Still, it was clear that he had something to say to Wharton about young Wilmot.

"Wilmot—er—arrives to-day," said Mr. Quelch, overlooking the fact that he had already told Wharton that. "And—er—I have decided to place him in your study, Wharton."

"Oh !" said Harry.

He looked as equable as he could. There were only two fellows in Study No 1 in the Remove—himself and Nugent.

There were three or four in most of

the studies. So there was nothing to grumble at in Hacker's nephew being landed on him. True, he did not want a new kid in the study—but he was a reasonable fellow.

"I trust, Wharton, that you will make Wilmot welcome," said Mr. Quelch, answering Wharton's unspoken thoughts.

"Certainly, sir !" said Harry. "I dare say we shall like him all right."

"Yes, yes, probably !" said Mr. Quelch, as if he doubted it himself. "I believe he is a rather keen footballer, Wharton—I understand that he was considered so at his former school—and that, doubtless, will recommend him to you, as football captain in the Form."

"Oh, yes, rather, sir," said Harry, with a cordiality that made his Form-master smile.

It occurred to Wharton, at once, that if this chap Wilmot was really hot stuff,

(Continued on next page.)

GREYFRIARS INTERVIEWS

It's nice to get up in the morning, but it's nicer to stay in bed . . . especially these cold mornings ! And none knows it better than the junior chosen by the Greyfriars Rhymester this week in his series of interviews,

LORD MAULEVERER,
the aristocratic slacker of the Remove.

(1)

"Once upon a time," so runs the story,
  "A certain lord named Mauly went berserk,
Perhaps in search of novelty or glory,
  He actually started on some work !
For nearly five whole minutes he was busy,
  And then, when sheer exhaustion made him wince,
He turned and fell asleep, completely dizzy,
  And in that state he's lasted ever since ! "

(3)

This limp and lazy lord is not a dullard.
  No fear ! His brain is very sharp and cute.
He never lets his view of life be coloured
  By prejudice which reason may refute.
He gives his judgments honestly and fairly,
  No matter what discomforts they may make,
And as his friends acknowledge, Mauly rarely
  Has known the pain of making a mistake.

(4)

With little fear of violence or booting,
  I went along and knocked at Mauly's door.
There came no answer, save a kind of hooting,
  Which I at once decided was a snore !
So in I went, and found the fathead dozing,
  Full length upon the sofa he had lain.
His mouth was gently opening and closing,
  And from his nose there came a sound of pain !

(2)

This may be false, but there is no denying
  That Mauly spends his life in slumber deep ;
A decent chap, whose only vice is lying !
  Yes, lying on his sofa fast asleep !
While other fellows chase the bounding leather,
  Or dive into the river for a swim,
Old Mauly sleeps, and never minds the weather,
  Which makes so little difference to him !

(5)

I took a hefty grammar from the table,
  And, with a tear, I dropped it on his map !
The howl he gave was like the Tower of Babel,
  As he was thus awakened from his nap !
"Oh, gad ! You dangerous ruffian ! " he chanted,
  And then, extremely wrathful, I suppose,
He swiftly clutched that grammar up and planted
  The volume fairly on my Roman nose !

(6)

"Yarooh ! " I roared, my merriment forgotten,
  As tenderly I nursed the damaged place ;
For you'll agree, I think, it's simply . . rotten
  To bung a grammar at a fellow's face !
It made me wild, so I picked up the grammar
  And went to throw it—when I heard a cough !
And saw old Mauly flourishing a hammer—
  And so, on second thoughts, I let him off !

(7)

"And now a word with you," I said severely,
  "I've come here for an interview—don't rag ! "
But Mauly yawned, and turning over, merely
  Replied in feeble tones : "It's too much fag ! "
I prodded him a little with my finger,
  Said I : "Wake up, you limp and lazy lord ! "
He said : "I'm goin' to sleep, you needn't linger ! "
  And as I watched him angrily, he snored !

(8)

I must have woke the fathead times unnumbered,
  But every time I woke him, he said : "Scat ! "
And then he simply closed his eyes and slumbered,
  As if he thought me satisfied with that !
At last I had to own myself defeated.
  With mournful brow I walked toward the door.
The last I heard from him as I retreated
  Was—just a single loud defiant SNORE !

he might solve that little difficulty about filling the Bounder's place in the Remove eleven.

"In other respects," said Mr. Quelch, "I do not know how you will find him. I have, of course, never seen him, so far; but Mr. Hacker, his uncle, has—er—a high opinion of him, I believe."

Wharton listened respectfully, wondering more and more.

It was perfectly clear that there was something in Quelch's mind which he was not going to utter. For some reason, he was perturbed about that new kid coming into the Remove. Why, was rather a mystery, for the fact that he was another master's nephew could hardly account for it.

"I have a special reason for placing this boy Wilmot with you, Wharton," went on Mr. Quelch.

Then he stopped quite suddenly. It was just as if he had approached perilously near to the secret thought in his mind, and was alarmed at the danger of giving it utterance.

"Yes, sir," said Harry. "That's all right, sir! We can't grumble at having him in our study—Bob has four fellows in Study No. 13, and——"

"Oh, yes, yes!" said Mr. Quelch. "Quite so; but that is not the reason. You are a sensible boy, I trust, Wharton."

"Thank you, sir!" said Harry blankly.

"Nugent, also, is a boy of very steady character," said Mr. Quelch musingly. "I have a very good opinion of both of you."

Wharton hardly knew what to say. This was quite pleasant hearing, of course. It was gratifying to learn of Mr. Quelch's excellent opinion of him and his chum. But it was surprising and perplexing. Quelch could hardly mean that Wilmot was some sort of a "bad hat," likely to have a bad influence on any but boys of steady character. But really it sounded like it. Certainly he had never spoken in such a strain before, on the occasion of new fellows coming into the Form.

Mr. Quelch opened his lips again, and Wharton waited with considerable curiosity to hear more. But the master of the Remove closed them, with what he had been going to say unuttered.

He drummed on the desk with his fingers. Wharton suppressed a smile while he waited.

He knew, just as if Mr. Quelch had told him so, that there was something on his Form-master's mind with respect to the new boy, Wilmot. It was something he could not tell, but which made him secretly uneasy.

Was the chap some untrustworthy tick? But surely he must be all right if Dr. Locke let him come to Greyfriars at all! And a master's nephew, too! But there was something—that was clear.

Again Mr. Quelch opened his lips. Again he closed them. Then he said abruptly:

"Thank you, Wharton! You may go!"

Wharton went.

He glanced back, without thinking, as he left the Form-room, and was quite surprised by the expression he caught on Mr. Quelch's face. Quelch was frowning darkly and his lips were set in a tight line. That glimpse was more than convincing. Quelch, for some reason, hated the idea of Hacker's nephew in his Form! Whatever it was he had been unable to tell his head boy, it weighed deeply and heavily on his own mind.

Wharton hurriedly went down the passage.

THE MAGNET LIBRARY.—No. 1,457.

His friends were waiting for him outside the House, and they gave him inquiring looks.

"You've been a jolly long time!" said Nugent. "Not a row with Quelch, I hope?"

"Oh, no! Far from it," said Harry, laughing. "Quelch has been telling me what a nice chap I am."

"Lots of Form-masters don't know much about chaps in their Forms!" grinned Nugent.

"Oh, quite—he has been telling me what a nice chap you are, too!"

"Oh! In that case a Daniel come to judgment!" said Nugent, laughing.

"But seriously, I can hardly make Quelch out," said Harry. "He's planting that new kid in our study—you remember I told you that Hobby said his beak's nephew was coming into the Remove to-day——"

"I say, you fellows——"

"Shut up, Bunter! We're getting him in our study," said Harry. "Quelch seems worried about it somehow—blessed if I can guess why."

"I say——"

"Roll away, Bunter!"

"I say, you fellows, my postal order hasn't come!" said Bunter, blinking solemnly at the chums of the Remove through his big spectacles. "I've looked in the rack, but there's no letter for me. If one of you fellows has got half-a-crown he doesn't want——"

"There's one thing," said Harry, "Quelch says that Wilmot was a good footballer at his last school——"

"What was his school?" asked Bob.

"Quelch never said! But if he's good at Soccer he may come in useful," said Harry. "You see——"

"I say, did you say a new kid's coming?" asked Billy Bunter, with some interest. Bunter had a natural interest in new kids. New kids hadn't heard of his celebrated postal order! And a fellow who hadn't heard of it was more likely to cash it than a fellow who had! "I say, what did you say his name was?"

"Wilmot!" answered Harry.

"I believe I know somebody of that name," said Bunter, wrinkling his fat brow in thought. "I've heard that name somewhere lately."

"Poor old Bunter!" said Bob Cherry commiseratingly.

"Eh? What do you mean, 'Poor old Bunter'?" demanded the fat Owl, blinking at him.

"I mean, if you know the new chap he knows you—and he won't be likely to lend you anything if he does."

"Ha, ha, ha!"

"Beast!" yapped Bunter. "I say, you fellows—about my postal order——"

Harry Wharton & Co. walked away to join other Removites in punting a footer about—apparently quite uninterested in Bunter's postal order.

When they went in for third school Wharton noticed that Quelch still had a very thoughtful frown on his brow, and wondered whether he was thinking about Hacker's nephew. He was feeling very curious about that youth by this time, and rather interested to see him to see what sort of a merchant he was.

Towards the end of third school there was a tap at the door, and Mr. Hacker glanced in.

"If you can spare a moment, Quelch——" he said.

Mr. Quelch did not like sparing moments while class was on. But he went to the Form-room door.

The two masters spoke together in a low tone that did not reach the Remove. But Mr. Quelch's voice came to their ears suddenly as he spoke with some emphasis.

"Really, Mr. Hacker, I see no reason for a Remove boy to miss a whole lesson this afternoon."

"Oh, very well, sir!" said Mr. Hacker snappishly.

He went away, and Mr. Quelch came back to his Form. His lips were tightly compressed. What Hacker had wanted was a mystery to the Remove—though if he had wanted a Remove fellow to cut a class any Remove fellow would have been extremely willing to oblige him. However, whatever he had wanted, it was clear that Quelch had declined, and that was that!

THE ELEVENTH CHAPTER.

Hobby in Luck!

"HOBSON!"

James Hobson jumped.

"Oh! Yes, sir!" he gasped.

It was close on the finish of third school, and Mr. Hacker had left his Form-room. He had gone down the corridor, in point of fact, to speak to Quelch at the door of the Remove Room. The Shell did not know why he was gone, but they were naturally pleased at his going—it gave them a little welcome relaxation.

Hobby's relaxation took the shape of dropping an ink-ball down the neck of Chowne of the Shell. Chowne's antics, when he felt that ink-ball sliding down his back, entertained Hobby.

Then Hacker's voice barked as he came in at the door.

Hobby gazed at him in dismay.

He had no doubt that Hacker had spotted his little jest on Chowne, and was going to make it clear, perhaps with the aid of the cane, that a Form-room was not a proper place for jesting. Instead of which Mr. Hacker merely said:

"I wish to speak to you, Hobson, after this class. Remain here."

"Yes, sir."

Mr. Hacker glanced at the Form-room clock. It still wanted one minute to time for dismissal. Hacker was not the man to dismiss his Form even one second ahead of time. So the Shell stared when he dismissed them—sixty seconds before they were entitled to escape from Hacker and class.

Unexpected as it was, it was very welcome, and the Shell scuttled away cheerfully. Hobson remained to hear what Hacker wanted.

"I think I mentioned to you, Hobson, that my nephew arrives to-day," said Mr. Hacker.

"I remember, sir!" said Hobby.

"I should like him to be met at the station at Courtfield," said Mr. Hacker. "You might care to go, Hobson."

Hobby looked at him.

If Mr. Hacker supposed that Hobson might "care" to waste his time on a benighted new kid Mr. Hacker showed very poor judgment.

Hobby certainly was going to be kind to the little beast when he came. He had a kind heart, and he was a fellow of his word. But going down to meet a train at Courtfield was rather too much of a good thing. Hobby, naturally, had his own occupations, quite enough to fill up his time before the bell rang for afternoon class.

It was scarcely possible to refuse the request of a Form-master. But Hobson did feel that it was rather thick!

"Oh, of—of course, sir!" he stammered. "But—but as Wilmot is going into the Remove, sir, perhaps if a Remove chap went——"

"I have thought of that, Hobson!" said Mr. Hacker.

"What I mean is, sir, it would be

During Mr. Hacker's absence from the Form-room, Hobson took advantage of the welcome relaxation by dropping an ink-ball down the neck of Chowne. He jumped the next moment, however, as the Form-room door was thrown open and a voice barked: "Hobson!" It was Mr. Hacker returning!

more pleasant for him—a fellow of his own Form——" said Hobson hopefully.

"Quite so, Hobson, but it appears to be impracticable!" said Mr. Hacker. "Mr. Quelch is not prepared to allow a Remove boy to miss a class for the purpose."

Hobson started.

It flashed into his mind, from Hacker's words, that the new tick was going to arrive while class was on!

That put an entirely different complexion on the matter!

Hobby, naturally, did not want to use up his own fully occupied leisure between dinner and school by rotting about at a railway station, meeting a new kid! But he was willing—more than willing—to sacrifice a class for that purpose!

Hobby was prepared to cut a class to meet a new kid—or for any other reason whatsoever! The reason mattered less than cutting the class! Hobby would willingly have gone to Courtfield, or anywhere else, to meet Hacker's nephew, or Hacker's great-grandfather, for that matter—in lesson-time! Hobby bucked up at once.

"My nephew," resumed Mr. Hacker, "will arrive at Courtfield Station by the two-thirty train, Hobson."

Hobson smiled genially.

At two-thirty that afternoon the Shell would be in the Form-room, and doing Roman history with Hacker.

Hobson was going to lose the knowledge he might have acquired of the Twelve Cæsars. But he did not mind.

He was, in fact, in luck, and he knew it. Any other man in the Shell would have jumped at the chance.

"I'll be awfully glad to meet the chap, sir," said Hobson, sincerely enough. "I'll bring him safe to Grey-friars, sir. It will be a real pleasure to me, sir," added Hobby, with un-doubted sincerity.

Mr. Hacker smiled quite genially. Perhaps he did not realise how much "cutting a class" had to do with Hobby's enthusiasm.

Anyhow, he was pleased.

"Thank you, Hobson!" he said.

"Not at all, sir," purred Hobby.

"No doubt you will find my nephew easily enough," said Mr. Hacker. "He is, of course, a stranger to you, but he——"

"Oh, easy, sir!" said Hobson. "I'll spot him all right. Rely on me, sir."

"Very well, Hobson."

Hobson went joyfully away. He quite liked Hacker at that moment, and was prepared to like his nephew.

The crusty old beak certainly seemed fond of his nephew, and, owing to that, Hobby was going to have a pleasant trot on a fine frosty afternoon, while less fortunate fellows were grinding in class. So Hobby fully approved of crusty Form-masters being fond of their nephews.

"Hallo, hallo, hallo! Enjoying life?" roared Bob Cherry, catching sight of Hobby's bright face as he came out of the House.

Hobson grinned.

"I'm in luck," he said. "I say, I've got leave from class this afternoon to go and meet that new tick, Wilmot—old Hacker's nephew, you know. I get out of a whole class. You can tell Quelch when you see him again that I'm jolly glad he wouldn't let off a Remove man."

"Oh!" exclaimed Harry Wharton. "So that was what Hacker wanted!"

"Look here! That's not cricket!" exclaimed Bob indignantly. "Wilmot's a Remove man, and a Remove man ought to be sent to meet him—if any-body. I'd be quite glad to go myself."

"Same here!" grinned Frank Nugent. "We've got Latin grammar this afternoon."

"The samefulness is terrific!" agreed Hurree Jamset Ram Singh. "The esteemed Quelch might have stretched a point."

"I'd have gone, if he'd asked me," remarked Johnny Bull, with a nod.

"Bet you would!" chuckled Hobson. "But I'm jolly well going! You can tell Quelch I'm much obliged to him. Ha, ha, ha!"

"Quelch is a bit of a sweep," said Bob. "He might have obliged another beak. It's pretty plain that's what Hacker came to ask him. Crusty old merchant to refuse to oblige another beak!"

"Jolly glad he did!" grinned Hobson. "You kids can stick in class with Quelch, and think of me trotting over to Courtfield. Ha, ha!"

"Gentlemen, chaps, and sportsmen!" said Bob Cherry. "Quelch seems to me a disobliging old sweep. We can't tell him what we think of him. But it's too thick. Hobson's bagged a jaunt that properly belongs to the Remove, and, as we can't bump Quelch, I think we'd better bump Hobby."

"Hear, hear!" said the Co. at once.

"Hold on! I say!" yelled Hobson, as the grinning five collared him. "I say—— Whoop! You cheeky fags! Yaroop! You bump me, and I'll jolly well—— Yurrggghh!"

Bump!

Hobson was rather a hefty youth. But he was no use in the grasp of five pairs of hands.

He swung off his feet, and earth and sky reeled round him. Then he tapped on the quad, and roared wildly.

"Give him another!" said Bob.

Bump!

"Yaroop!" roared Hobson. "Oh, my hat! I'll jolly well—— Yoooop!"

THE MAGNET LIBRARY.—No. 1,457.

"One more for luck!" said Bob.
Bump!

"Whooop!"

Then the Famous Five walked away, chuckling, leaving James Hobson sitting on the earth, gasping for breath, crimson and winded.

It was quite some time before Hobby recovered sufficiently to rush off in search of Hoskins and Stewart to tell them of his good luck.

THE TWELFTH CHAPTER.
Meeting Eric Wilmot!

A HANDSOME face looked out of a window of the train that stopped at Courtfield Junction at two-thirty.

Handsome as that face was, it had on it an expression of sullen despondency that considerably marred its good looks.

Eric Wilmot, Hacker's nephew, the new fellow for the Greyfriars Remove, looked out gloomily on the platform.

He saw that it was Courtfield, his destination. Yet oddly enough he seemed in no hurry to alight from the train.

He sat and stared glumly.

His eyes fell on a rather burly fellow in a Greyfriars cap with a rugged, good-humoured face standing on the platform, gazing along the train.

But he had never seen Hobson of the Shell before, did not know him, and was not interested in him. He gave him only a cursory glance.

Other passengers alighted—but not many. There was no rush of traffic at Courtfield.

Hobson watched them all.

But none of them could have been Hacker's nephew. There was a stout farmer, a nurse with a child, a young lady typist from Chunkley's Stores, Mr. Pilkins, the estate agent, Mr. Lazarus, the second-hand merchant, and a couple of men who looked like commercial travellers. Hobby did not know Hacker's nephew by sight; but he could see that none of this collection could possibly be Hacker's nephew.

He wondered whether the new tick had lost his train.

Hobby did not mind if he had. He was willing to fill in the time at the pictures while he waited for the next train.

Still, Hobby was a conscientious chap. He was going to make sure. Hobby knew what a silly ass a new kid might be—he had been a new kid himself. If the young tick was on the train, it was Hobby's duty to see that he got off at Courtfield.

So he walked along the carriages, staring into one after another. Thus he came to spot the handsome, sullen face that looked out of a window.

He halted.

This fellow looked as if he might be the man. The train stopped several minutes at Courtfield, and it was not restarting yet. Still, if the tick did not know that he had got to his station, it was time he was told. Hobson jerked open the carriage door.

"You happen to be Wilmot?" he asked.

The sulky face stared at him.

"That's my name!" came the curt answer.

"Going to Greyfriars?"

"Yes."

"Well, this is your station. Hop out! You'll get carried on goodness knows where if you stick in!"

Wilmot made no answer. Neither did he stir. Hobson stared at him, puzzled.

"This is Courtfield!" he said.

"I know that."

"Oh, you know it!" said the mystified Hobby.

"Yes."

"Why don't you get out, then?"

"You're asking a lot of questions for a stranger," said Wilmot, with the same sulky look and tone. "May I suggest that you mind your own affairs, and leave me to look after mine?"

Hobby breathed rather hard.

"I've been sent here to meet you," he said. "I'm Hobson of the Shell at Greyfriars. Hacker's my Form-master."

"Oh!"

"Well, are you getting out?" demanded Hobby.

Wilmot seemed to be considering it. What there was to consider was a mystery to Hobson. The fellow knew that he had got to his station, and did not seem to care whether he was carried on past it or not. Which was a frame of mind absolutely incomprehensible to James Hobson.

"The train will be going on in a tick," said Hobby.

"I don't care!"

"You don't care?" ejaculated the astonished Hobby.

"No."

"Well, my only summer hat! Your uncle will care, I fancy, if you don't turn up at school!" gasped Hobson. "And the Head may have something to say, and your Form-master, too—old Quelch. Are you off your rocker, or what?"

"Oh, don't bother!"

Hobby regarded him grimly.

He had arrived at Courtfield, full of the kindest intentions towards his Form-master's nephew. He was prepared to be very decent indeed to the fellow who had got him out of a class with Hacker. Now his feelings changed. He was conscious of a keen desire to plant a set of knuckles in that sulky handsome face.

However, he refrained from doing so. He stepped back.

"Well, please yourself," he said. "Hacker sent me here to meet you, but I suppose he wouldn't expect me to yank you off the train by your ears."

Wilmot shrugged his shoulders. But he seemed to make up his mind, and stepped from the carriage.

There was a scream from the engine. The new boy had made up his mind only just in time. The train rolled on, leaving him standing on the platform with Hobson.

Taking no notice of the Shell fellow, he walked along towards a box that had been dropped out by the guard.

Hobson followed him.

"I say, Wilmot——" he began. Hobby was puzzled and mystified and far from pleased, but he wanted to be as decent as possible to this very unusual new kid.

"Yes—what?" Wilmot spoke curtly over his shoulder without turning his head.

"They'll send your box on—you needn't bother about that!" said Hobby. "I'll speak to the porter."

"I can take it with me on a taxi, I suppose."

"You can if you like, of course, if you've got tin to blow on taxicabs!" said Hobson. "But I say, it's a ripping walk over the common! Topping afternoon for a walk!"

"I don't care for it."

"Well, look here," said Hobson restively, "I don't see taking a taxi! It will get us to the school in next to no time!"

"I've got to get there, haven't I?"

"Yes. But there's no blessed hurry! If you're keen on seeing Quelch, I can

tell you I'm not keen on getting back to the Shell Form-room!", said Hobson warmly. "I shall have to go into class again when I get back, of course!"

Wilmot stared at him.

"Do you mean that you don't want to come in the taxi?"

"Yes, I jolly well do!"

"Well, I haven't asked you, have I?" Hobson crimsoned.

"Hacker's sent me for you!" he exclaimed. "I shall have to stick to you, of course!"

"What utter rot!"

"Oh, quite!" said Hobson savagely. "It doesn't matter to me, I can tell you, if a new kid goes mooning about missing his station and getting lost! If you think I care two straws, you're jolly well mistaken—see!"

"I don't think so!"

"Well, you'd be jolly well mistaken if you did! And I've got to carry out Hacker's orders—see?"

"Rubbish!"

Leaving Hobson rooted to the platform, the new fellow went along to the porter and directed him to have the box placed on a taxicab.

Hobson rejoined him as he went off the platform. Wilmot was taking no notice of him, but Hobson was not to be ignored. He was keeping his temper with great difficulty.

"Look here, Wilmot," he said, "be a reasonable chap! Let your box be sent on, and let's walk."

"I don't care to."

"I shall have to come in the taxi if you do. It's pretty rotten. Look here, new kids are not supposed to put on roll like this!" said Hobson. "Fellows who put on roll at Greyfriars get kicked for it!"

"Bother Greyfriars, and you, too!"

"Don't you want to come to Greyfriars?" asked Hobson blankly. That obvious fact dawned on Hobby's rather slow brain at last.

"No, I don't!"

"Well, you're all sorts of an ass!" said Hobson. "Chap has to go to some school, and if he has to go to school, it's rather a catch to get into the best school going!"

Wilmot stared at him and laughed—not a pleasant laugh.

"Is that what you think of Greyfriars?" he asked.

"Of course it is!"

"Then you're more sorts of an ass than I am! I wouldn't be found dead in the place if I could help it!"

"You wouldn't be found dead at Greyfriars!" repeated Hobson dazedly. "No!"

"You cheeky tick!"

"That's enough!"

Wilmot walked out of the station. Hobson, with a red and frowning face, tramped after him.

Kind-hearted Hobby had never ragged a new kid. But he felt powerfully tempted to rag this one bald-headed! Only by a very powerful exercise of self-control did he restrain himself from collaring Eric Wilmot there and then and mopping up the slushy pavement with him.

The box was placed on the taxi. Evidently Wilmot intended to take the cab, regardless of Hobby's wishes in the matter. But Hobby made another effort.

"Look here, Wilmot——"

"I'd rather you left me alone, if you don't mind," said the new junior. "If you've come here to meet me, I'm obliged, and that's an end of it! But I don't see any reason for my uncle to send a fellow to meet me here—I know my way about, and I'm not going into

his Form, either! Do you take me for a kid that's never been to school before?"

"Oh, you've been to school before, have you?" grunted Hobson. "Well, I don't know what school it was, but I can see they didn't kick you enough!"

Wilmot gave a shrug of the shoulders, which had a very irritating effect on the Shell fellow.

"Well, look here," said Hobson, "I think you're a rotten tick, Wilmot! And if you weren't a new kid, I'd jolly well punch your head—see?"

Wilmot looked at him.

"Never mind my being a new kid!" he retorted. "Get on with it as soon as you like! I'm feeling like punching somebody!"

"By gum!" said James Hobson. He came very near taking the fellow at his word. But he made an effort and refrained. "Well, the Remove are getting a prize-packet in you, and no mistake! I dare say they'll take some of the cheek out of you before you're many days older. You're going to take this taxi?"

"I've said so!"

Wilmot settled the matter by stepping into the vehicle.

"Well, I call it rotten!" said Hobson. "This means that I shall be landed in the Form-room again. I never saw such a tick! But if you're going in the dashed taxi, I shall have to, as Hacker sent me for you!"

"You've forgotten one thing!" said the new junior, staring at him icily from the taxi.

"What's that?"

"That I haven't asked you!"

"Look here——"

"Drive to Greyfriars School, please!" said Wilmot to the taximan; and he drew the door shut with a slam.

Hobson stood staring.

The taxi whirred away down Courtfield High Street, leaving Hobson standing on the pavement and still staring. He stared after the vanishing vehicle as if fascinated. It disappeared in the traffic of the High Street.

"Well, I'm blowed!" said Hobson.

It was all he could say.

THE THIRTEENTH CHAPTER.
Uncle and Nephew!

HARRY WHARTON & CO., grinding Latin grammar in the Remove room, heard a taxi drive up to the House. They wondered whether it portended the arrival of the new fellow, Wilmot.

No doubt the same thought occurred to Mr. Quelch, for he was observed to pause and listen for a moment. But Quelch carried on, apparently indifferent to the fact that a new member of his Form might, or might not, have arrived.

But if Mr. Quelch was not interested, another beak was. Mr. Hacker left the Shell room at once when he heard the taxi stop.

He was on the step of the House when Eric Wilmot descended from the cab. His eyes fixed on the handsome sulky face.

Wilmot paid the taximan and glanced round him with a cold, careless, indifferent glance. Then, as he saw his uncle, he coloured a little, and came up the steps.

Mr. Hacker frowned as he saw that his nephew was alone. He shook hands with Wilmot, without much cordiality on either side.

"Where is Hobson?" he asked.

"Hobson!" repeated Wilmot.

"I sent a boy of my Form to meet you at the station. Has he allowed you to come here alone? I shall——"

The look on Mr. Hacker's face hinted of trouble to come for Hobson. But Wilmot broke in at once.

"Oh, that fellow! He met me at the station!"

"Why did he not return with you, then?"

"I didn't want his company!"

"What? I sent him specially to meet you. He should have returned with you. I shall punish him——"

"He's not to blame," said Wilmot.

"He is very much to blame!" snapped Mr. Hacker.

"I mean, I wouldn't let him come in my taxi."

"What! And why not?"

"I didn't want him."

Mr. Hacker looked at his nephew.

"Did Hobson tell you I had sent him to meet you, Eric?"

"Yes."

"And you chose to leave him behind?"

"Yes."

Mr. Hacker breathed hard through his nose.

"Wait here, while I speak to Gosling about your box!" he said curtly.

"Very well!"

Eric Wilmot waited, with an expressionless face—save for the cloud of sullenness that seemed habitual to it. He hardly gave a glance about him, indifferent to the place in which he found himself. When his uncle rejoined him, and signed to him to follow, he followed the master of the Shell to the latter's study.

There Mr. Hacker surveyed him, with a look that was a little puzzled, and still more displeased.

"You seem to have treated Hobson very uncivilly, Eric," he said at last.

"I didn't mean to be uncivil!"

"He is a very good-natured boy," said Mr. Hacker. "He was prepared to be friendly with you."

"I don't want him to be."

Mr. Hacker compressed his lips.

"Are you so sure of making friends that you can afford to be rude and uncivil to the first Greyfriars boy you meet?" he snapped.

"I'm not keen on making friends here?"

There was a long pause. Mr. Hacker stood staring at the handsome face, as if trying to penetrate through the mask of sullen indifference that hid Eric Wilmot's thoughts and feelings.

"This will not do, Eric!" he said at length. "A sullen and sulky temper will not help you here."

Wilmot made no reply.

"You have little cause to display such a temper," said the master of the Shell warmly. "You should be grateful and thankful, Eric. You have such a chance, as you could not possibly have expected after what happened at Topham. You must be aware of that."

"I know!" said Wilmot, in a low voice.

"It is only the fact that I, your uncle, am a member of the staff here, that has obtained admittance for you to this school!" said Mr. Hacker sharply.

Wilmot winced.

"I know!" he repeated.

"You may look upon it as a small thing!" said Mr. Hacker, with a note of angry indignation in his voice. "But I can assure you, Eric, that my interview with the headmaster on the subject was far from pleasant. I am not a man to ask favours—and I had to ask a favour —a great favour—and Dr. Locke found

THE MAGNET LIBRARY.—No. 1,457.

difficulty in granting it. Do you imagine that it was agreeable to me?"

"It was good of you, uncle!" said Wilmot. "I'm grateful! I know it must have come hard—I'm no fool!"

"You might, then, show a little better feeling, and a better frame of mind, I think!" said Mr. Hacker acidly. "But for my intervention, your school career would have ended when you left Topham!"

"I wish it had!" muttered Wilmot. "I never wanted to come here!"

"What—what?"

"I know it was a big chance—and I can understand why the mater jumped at it. But—but—" He broke off.

"That is nonsense! It is a great chance for you, and you must make the best of it. Judging by appearances, you seem bent on making the worst. Think of my position!" snapped Mr. Hacker. "The headmaster was doubtful—only my earnest assurance of my faith in you moved him, at last, to give you this chance. It was intensely humiliating to me to have to explain the position to your future Form-master, Mr. Quelch——"

Wilmot started, as if an adder had stung him.

"Does he know?" he panted.

"He had to be told, as your Form-master, naturally. Dr. Locke made a condition of that, and I could hardly object."

The handsome face was flooded with crimson.

"What's the use of my trying to make a fresh start here, if it's tattled all over the school?" muttered Wilmot.

"Have a little common sense!" snapped Mr. Hacker. "Do you suppose that your Form-master will tattle, as you disrespectfully term it? No one knows anything of you, with the exception of the headmaster, your Form-master, and myself. The boys know nothing, except that you are my nephew. They have probably never even heard of Topham School; and you, naturally, will make no reference to it. You start here with an absolutely clean sheet—and it is such a chance as you can have had no right to expect."

"I know! But——"

"Mr. Quelch is not pleased—you can understand that. But you have it in your own hands to win his good opinion. He is a just man, and will judge you by your conduct here."

"How can I face him, if he knows about——"

"You have, I hope, a clear conscience!" snapped Mr. Hacker. "All that I have done for you has been done on the understanding that your conscience is clear, in spite of appearances, of the terrible cloud you are under!"

Wilmot lifted his head proudly.

"My conscience is clear enough!" he answered firmly. "I've never done anything that I'm ashamed of!"

"I hope so—I believe so!" Mr. Hacker's voice was earnest, yet with a lingering dubiety in its tone. He was not by nature a trusting man—he was a little distrustful and suspicious. Something in his tone struck Wilmot, and the boy's handsome face crimsoned again.

"If you don't believe me, uncle——"

"I have said that I do!" said Mr. Hacker acidly. "That suffices! But, as I have said, it is by your conduct that you will be judged here. Your conduct, Eric, must be absolutely exemplary. You owe that, at least, to me. And my advice to you is to forget that you ever were at Topham—to dis-

miss from your mind all that may have happened there——"

"As if I could!"

"You will make new friends here——"

"I don't want to make friends here!" muttered Wilmot. "My friends are at Topham—and what must they be thinking of me now!"

"Dismiss that from your mind! What cannot be cured, must be endured! Make the best of your new life, not the worst! Surely you can see that that is good counsel, Eric?"

"Yes, yes! I'll try!"

"Very well! I must return to my Form now—I have left them too long! But I will take you to the House-dame first. Later, when Mr. Quelch is disengaged, I will take you to him. Come!"

Eric Wilmot followed his uncle from the study.

THE FOURTEENTH CHAPTER.
Where's Wilmot?

"I SAY, you fellows! Seen that new chap—Wilson, or Wilkins, you know——"

"Wilmot, fathead!"

"I mean Wilmot!" said Billy Bunter. "I say, seen him? I've been looking for him! What are you grinning at, I'd like to know!" added Bunter warmly, as the Famous Five smiled broadly.

"Give him a rest, his first day here!" suggested Bob Cherry. "Tell him about your postal order to-morrow, old fat man."

"Ha, ha, ha!"

"Oh, really, Cherry! I say, I think I know the chap!" said Bunter. "I told you fellows I'd heard the name of Wilmot lately. I can't quite remember where it was, or when—but——"

"Looks as if you know him a lot!" grinned Bob.

"Well, not a lot, perhaps!" admitted Bunter. "But well enough to——"

"To ask him to lend you half-a-crown?"

"No!" roared Bunter. "Nothing of the kind! To speak a civil word to a new kid—that's what I mean. I believe in being kind to a new kid!" added Bunter loftily. "You know what I did for you, your first day here, Wharton!"

"I remember," assented Wharton. "You borrowed a bob! And now I come to think of it, you never squared. I'll have the bob now!"

"I don't mean that, you ass!"

"I do!" said Harry. "Bob, please!" He held out his hand.

Billy Bunter snorted, and rolled away, leaving the chums of the Remove chuckling.

"By the way, where is the new kid?" asked Nugent. "He must have come."

"Must have," said Harry Wharton. "But I've seen nothing of him. Hacker may have had him to tea, as he's his nephew; but he wouldn't be keeping him all this time, unless he's fearfully fond of his company."

After class, the juniors had expected to see something of the new fellow. Wharton and Nugent had some little interest in him, as a new member of their study; also, they were mildly curious about the fellow. With the intention of being nice and agreeable, they had laid in a rather decent spread at tea-time, intending to ask Wilmot to share it, and at the same time to make him better acquainted with themselves and their friends.

But Wilmot had not turned up at tea-time, and the Famous Five tea'd in Study No. 1 without him. Certainly

they did not miss him; and, in point of fact, forgot him. Now they were reminded of him, and they began to wonder what had become of him.

"Might look round for him," remarked Wharton. "We told Hobby we'd be civil to him. Hacker put it to him, and he put it to us. If he's wandering about somewhere and doesn't know how he got there, we might take him in hand."

"Let's!" assented Nugent.

"Hallo, hallo, hallo, there's Coker!" exclaimed Bob Cherry. "Looking as if the earth belongs to him, as usual! What about knocking his hat off?"

"We're going to look after Wilmot."

"Oh, bother Wilmot! You look after Wilmot while I look after Coker, then!" Johnny Bull and Hurree Singh accompanied Bob, to look after Coker. Harry Wharton and Nugent went to look for Wilmot.

"Seen a new kid about, Smithy?" asked Wharton, as they came on the Bounder.

"No."

"Seen a new kid about, Toddy?"

"No."

"Bless him!" said Wharton. "Perhaps he hasn't turned up, after all! Hallo, Skinner! Seen a silly ass mooning about?"

"Eh? Yes!" answered Skinner, at once.

"Oh, good! Where is he?"

"Speaking to me now!" said Skinner blandly.

"You silly fathead!" roared Wharton, and he walked on with Nugent, leaving Harold Skinner grinning.

"Hobby will know," said Nugent. "He went to the station for him, you know. Let's ask Hobby."

"Good egg!" assented Wharton, and they went into the House and proceeded to Hobson's study in the Shell.

There they found James Hobson. He was talking in rather emphatic tones to Hoskins and Stewart, when the Removites arrived.

"Did you pick up that new sheep at the station, Hobby?" asked Harry.

Hobby frowned darkly.

"Don't talk to me about him!" he said. "Blow him!"

"The kid's put Hobby's back up!" explained Stewart, with a grin. "Hobby hasn't taken a fancy to him."

"I was just telling these fellows about him," said Hobson. "Only I can't think of a word for him! The tick!"

"Then you did meet him?"

"The worm!" said Hobson.

"Did you bring him in?"

"The rotten sheep!"

"Where is he now?"

"The cheeky cad!"

Evidently Hobby had met the new fellow, and had not taken a liking to him.

"Hobby, old man, you never ragged a kid on his first day!" exclaimed Wharton.

"No, I didn't!" growled Hobby. "But if he hadn't been a new kid, I'd have mopped up Courtfield with him! The sneaking outsider!"

"But what did he do?" asked Nugent, in wonder.

"Cheeked me!" said Hobson. "Took a taxi, and left me standing! Of course, I was glad to be left. I wanted to walk it! But the cheek, you know! After I went to the station to meet him! Lucky for him that he's not in the Shell—we'd lynch him! You can have him in the Remove! He may suit you—a rotten, cheeky, uppish, sulky cad, asking all the time to have his head punched!"

"You don't want to come to Greyfriars?" asked Hobson, the obvious fact dawning on his rather slow brain at last. "No, I don't!" snapped Wilmot. "I wouldn't be found dead in the place if I could help it!" He walked out of the station, Hobson, with a red and frowning face, accompanying him.

"Sounds nice!" said Harry. "But where is he now, if he came?"

"Don't know, and don't care!" answered Hobson. "I haven't seen him since he left me standing on the pavement at Courtfield and buzzed off in his blessed taxi! Blow him!"

"If he took a taxi to the school, he must have got here."

"I suppose so! Tell him to keep out of my way, if he doesn't want his nose pushed through the back of his head!"

Wharton and Nugent left Hobby's study. They exchanged rather curious looks as they went.

"What sort of a sportsman can the fellow be?" murmured Wharton. "Hobby isn't the chap to take a dislike for nothing. Everybody gets on with Hobby. Hacker's nephew must be a bit of a tick."

"More than a bit, I should think," said Frank. "Nice to have him in our study! Hallo, there goes the bell! We shall see him in Hall."

It was the bell for calling-over. Wharton and Nugent looked round when they joined the rest of the Remove in Hall. But there was no unfamiliar face in the ranks of the Remove.

"I say, you fellows, that new chap isn't here!" squeaked Billy Bunter. "I say, did he come, after all?"

"He came all right!" said Hazeldene.

"Seen him?" asked Harry.

"I saw Hacker taking a chap to Quelch's study just after class. Looked a sulky sort of brute."

"He's cutting roll!" said Nugent.

"Oh, a beak's nephew can do as he likes!" sneered Skinner.

"Rot!"

Roll was taken by Prout, master of the Fifth. Mr. Quelch was present, and Wharton noticed that his eyes were keenly on the Remove. When the name of Wilmot was called, and there was no answer, Mr. Quelch compressed his lips very tightly. Whatever might be the reason of Wilmot's absence, it was clear that his Form-master had expected him to be present, and was annoyed.

After call-over, Mr. Quelch signed to his head boy, and Wharton stopped as the others went out.

"Do you know where Wilmot is, Wharton?" asked the Remove master.

"I haven't seen him yet, sir."

"It is very singular," said Mr. Quelch. "If you see him, Wharton, tell him to come to my study."

"Certainly, sir."

Wharton left the hall in a state of surprise. In the Rag, he found a good many fellows discussing Wilmot and his proceedings. It was known that he had arrived at the school; that he had had an interview with his Form-master—after which he seemed to have vanished.

Apparently he had gone out of gates. Smithy remarked that the young ass was getting Quelch's rag out, to begin with.

When the Remove went up to their studies for prep, the new boy had not turned up. Wharton and Nugent sat down to prep in Study No. 1 without the company they had expected there.

Billy Bunter gave them a blink at the doorway on his way to No. 7.

"Wilmot here?" he asked.

"No, ass!"

"He can't be out of gates now!" said the Owl of the Remove.

"Looks as if he is!"

"Well, I'm jiggered!" said Bunter. And he rolled on to his own study and prep.

THE FIFTEENTH CHAPTER.
The Wet Blanket!

"COME in, ass!"

Prep had been going on for half an hour, when there was a tap at the door of Study No. 1. Wharton called out without looking up as the door opened.

Fellows were not supposed to leave their studies during prep, but, like other imperfect mortals, Remove fellows often did what they were not supposed to do. So Wharton took it for granted that his visitor was a Remove man who preferred conversation to preparation, by way of a change.

But he jumped up the next moment, with a crimson face, realising that it was not a junior who had entered.

"Oh!" he gasped. "Sorry, sir!"

Mr. Quelch took no notice of his head boy's rather unfortunate greeting.

"This is Wilmot, Wharton!" he said.

"Oh, yes, sir!" stammered Harry.

Wharton and Nugent looked at the boy who followed Mr. Quelch into the study.

Wilmot had turned up at last. The chums of Study No. 1 regarded him with some curiosity. They saw a slim, but athletic fellow, with handsome features, and dark blue eyes, and dark wavy hair. Wilmot was a good-looking fellow. But a cloud of sulky depression was on the good-looking face.

They had no doubt that Quelch had "jawed" him for his extraordinary conduct. He was not likely to have caned a new boy; but he was certain to have spoken to him very plainly. The look on the Remove-master's face was very grim.

"Wilmot," he said, coldly and formally, "this is your study! This is Wharton, the head boy of your Form: the other is Nugent. You will remain here during preparation; but you need do none yourself your first evening."

With that Mr. Quelch left the study.

The door closed after him, and Wilmot was left standing, looking at his new study-mates.

There was an awkward pause.

"So you're Wilmot?" said Harry, breaking the silence.

"Yes."

"Did Quelch jaw you?" asked Nugent, with a grin.

"Yes."

"You don't seem to mind."

"No."

"I say, it was rather thick, walking off like that," said Frank. "The beaks are rather particular about fellows turning up for roll, you know."

"They are at most schools, I believe."

"You've been to school before?"

"Yes."

"Then you knew you were asking for a row?"

"Oh, yes!"

"Quelch didn't whop you, did he?" asked Harry.

"No."

"Well, he wouldn't your first day, and I expect he would go as easy as he could with another beak's relation. But what on earth did you cut roll for?" asked the captain of the Remove.

"I went out."

"I guessed that one!" said Harry, with a smile. "But I suppose you knew that you had to get in for calling over?"

"Yes."

"But you didn't turn up."

"No."

It was rather difficult to establish a friendly atmosphere with a fellow who answered only in curt monosyllables. Not that Wilmot looked as if he desired to be friendly. He looked tired, as if he had covered a great distance in that walk out of gates, and he looked sulky. That was all.

"Did they teach you any words except 'yes' and 'no' at your last school?" asked Frank.

Wilmot stared at him for a moment and coloured. He did not answer. He crossed over to the fire, and stood leaning on the mantelpiece, with his hands in his pockets.

Wharton and Nugent looked at him, and looked at one another, and resumed prep. There was deep silence in the study.

After a time Wharton glanced round at the new fellow. He had not moved. Tired as he looked, he had not sat down. He stood leaning on the mantel, his eyes fixed before him in a gloomy stare.

"Squat in the armchair, kid," said the captain of the Remove. "There's a 'Holiday Annual' on the shelf, if you'd like it."

Wilmot started, as if roused out of a deep reverie and brought suddenly back to his surroundings. He nodded, and sat down in the study armchair, but he did not seem to want to read. Now that he was sitting down his gaze fixed on the embers of the fire in the grate.

Prep was resumed. Exactly what to make of that unusual new fellow was a mystery to the two Removites. Wharton put aside his books at last. He had never had any experience of such an absolute wet blanket as this fellow before, but he could feel for a boy who was down in the mouth on his first day at school. And if the fellow was going to stick in that study, it was for the general comfort to establish friendly relations.

"Like Greyfriars?" he asked, by way of a beginning.

"No!"

Wharton coughed.

"You'll like it all right when you shake down," he said.

"I doubt it."

"Um! I've heard that you play a good game of Soccer."

The hard, indifferent face brightened a little, as if the right chord had been touched. But it set again as dark and sulky as before.

"I shan't play Soccer here," said Wilmot briefly.

"Why not?"

No answer.

"We're pretty keen on it here," said Harry. "We run a team in the Remove, and have regular fixtures. Anyhow, you'll have to play in games practice—that's compulsory, unless a fellow's a crock. Did you play for your school?"

"You're asking me a lot of questions."

Wharton stared.

"Can't you answer a civil question?" he said. "As I happen to be football captain in the Form, I should have to see how you shape at the game, anyhow."

No reply.

"Look here, Wilmot," said the captain of the Remove quietly, "you're put in this study, and we're landed together for the term. Civility costs nothing."

The new fellow, staring into the fire, did not seem to hear him. Wharton's cheeks flushed.

"You seem to have put Hobby's back up," he said, "and no wonder——"

"Who's Hobby?"

"The chap who met you at the station——"

"Oh, that fool!"

"Hobby's not a fool," said Harry. "He may not be very bright, but he's a good chap, one of the best at Greyfriars."

"I don't care what he is."

Wharton breathed hard.

"I don't know where you've been to school before, Wilmot," he said, "but they don't seem to have taught you much in the way of manners."

"If you don't like my manners, you can leave me alone."

"You won't have to ask that twice!" said Harry curtly, and he rose to his feet. "Coming down, Frank?"

Nugent nodded, and put away his books. The study door opened, and a fat face and a large pair of spectacles loomed in.

"I say, you fellows," squeaked Billy Bunter, "has Wilmot come?"

THE SIXTEENTH CHAPTER.
A Surprise For Two!

ERIC WILMOT started violently. He sat bolt upright in the armchair, his eyes fixed on the fat face of Billy Bunter in the doorway.

Every vestige of colour drained from his cheeks.

So startled was his look that Wharton and Nugent could hardly have failed to notice it. They stared at him blankly.

He did not heed them. He gazed at Bunter as if the fat junior in the doorway had been the ghost of William George Bunter instead of William George in the flesh—and plenty of it.

The fat Owl blinked round the study through his big spectacles. Eyes and spectacles landed on the junior in the armchair.

"Oh, here you are, Wilmot!" said Bunter affably. "You've turned up, what?"

Wilmot did not speak. He only regarded Billy Bunter with the same fixed stare.

Why the sight of Bunter produced such an effect on him, made Wharton and Nugent wonder. Bunter, certainly, was not a pleasing object to look at. But even Bunter was not, as a rule, calculated to produce this startling and dismaying effect on the beholder.

Bunter rolled in.

"I say, you fellows, that's Wilmot, isn't it?" he asked.

"Yes, that's Wilmot," said Harry Wharton. "You said you knew him—and it looks as if he knows you, Bunter."

"Well, I fancy we've met," said Bunter. "I heard the name only lately somewhere, and——"

Bunter broke off suddenly.

He stared at Wilmot, his eyes almost popping through his spectacles. At closer range, he recognised the junior at once.

He remembered now where he had heard the name of Wilmot. He had heard it, shouted by the Topham men, on the football field at St. Jude's.

He had seen Wilmot before—on the St. Jude's field, happy and triumphant, enthusiastically cheered by his friends. He had seen him again, white and harassed and dazed, looking as if he had "taken the knock," and been knocked out.

And now he saw him—Wilmot, of Topham, in Study No. 1 in the Remove —a new fellow at Greyfriars! Only last week he had been a Topham man, playing football for his school at St. Jude's. Now he had come to Greyfriars as a new boy! The astonished Owl blinked at him in blank amazement.

"You!" he gasped.

Wilmot found his voice. It came husky:

"You!"

"Great pip!" said Bunter.

Wharton and Nugent looked from one to the other. What this could possibly mean, beat them hollow.

"You!" repeated Wilmot. "I'd forgotten your existence. I never knew you belonged to this school. If I'd known——"

He checked himself.

"So you know Wilmot, Bunter?" said Frank Nugent.

"Oh! Yes, rather!" said Bunter. "At least, I met him last week! Didn't I, Wilmot?"

Wilmot did not answer. His brain, at the moment, was in a whirl. His uncle had warned him—for good reasons —not to mention the name of his last school, at his new school. If the Greyfriars fellows learned that he had been at Topham, they might learn, also, why he had left Topham so suddenly, in the second week of the term. And here was a fellow whose existence he had forgotten till this moment, who knew that he was a Topham man! Little had he dreamed, when he met that fat and fatuous fellow near the gates of St. Jude's, that he would meet him again in a few days—at Greyfriars!

Bunter blinked at him.

"I say, fancy meeting you here, Wilmot!" he said. "I knew I remembered your name, when I heard it, but I never thought it was you, of course! I say, why did you leave your last school?"

Wilmot winced as if he had been struck.

Wharton and Nugent exchanged a look. Whatever this mysterious affair might mean, it was no concern of theirs, and they did not want to butt into another fellow's affairs. And, little as they liked the new fellow, they could not help taking pity on the dumb misery in his face. They left the study and went down the passage.

"You left jolly suddenly, didn't you?" Bunter was going on, as they left. "Fancy you being here, you know, when only last week——"

Slam!

The study door closed, cutting off the rest of Bunter's remarks.

Wharton and Nugent knew that it must be Wilmot who had slammed it. They went down in silence to the Rag.

(Continued on page 28.)

DAN of the DOGGER BANK!

By DAVID GOODWIN.

The Sham Derelict !

KENNETH GRAHAM, son of a millionaire shipowner, is rescued off the Dogger Bank by the crew of the fishing trawler, Grey Seal.

His past life a blank, he is given the name of "Dogger Dan," and signed on as fifth hand under Skipper Atheling, Finn Macoul, Wat Griffiths and Buck Atheling.

Aware of his nephew's fate, and knowing that he will be heir to the shipowner's money when his brother dies, Dudley Graham engages Jake Rebow and his cutthroats of the Black Squadron to get Kenneth out of the way for ever.

Following a fruitless attempt on their lives by Rebow's confederates, Dan and Buck Atheling catch the crew of the Adder, the Black Squadron's flagship, smuggling. Boarding the trawler, they imprison the two men left in charge and make for port.

Caught in a hurricane, they are wrecked on a sandbank, the only occupant of which is a wealthy old Dutchman named Jan Osterling.

After leaving the old man for a time, they return to find him dying as the result of a brutal attack made on him by the two prisoners from the Adder.

Before breathing his last, Jan asks the boys to hand over his savings to his nephew Max, in return for which he hands them a chart disclosing the whereabouts of a hidden treasure worth £5,000 to be divided between them.

Dan and Buck eventually rejoin the Grey Seal, which is saved from destruction by the timely intervention of a German gunboat chasing the smugglers.

. . . . . .

"Whew !" said Buck, as a distant humming in the air rose to a shriek, and swept down upon the Seal. "Here's the squall at last !"

"Round with her !" cried Atheling. "Haul down a pair o' reefs, an' quick about it !"

A snorting, tearing wind—the sudden gale of the North German coast—struck the stout trawler nearly flat. Her quick, handy crew had all they could do to get her under control, and by the time she was reefed down the sea was rising angrily, and she plunged and bucked wildly, smothered in stinging spray, with a dead lee-shore under her.

"We must claw off an' get sea-room !" said Atheling. "Sheet your jib home !"

"Dad," cried Buck, making his way along the reeling deck to where his father stood at the helm, "don't put to sea ! Run her into the gatway. There's treasure on that island—five thousand pounds in gold ! An' if we leave it now, we may lose it for good !"

Atheling, braced at the kicking tiller, stared at his son in speechless surprise.

"Did ye get a knock o' the head when ye were ashore there ?" he said.

"Ay, an' plenty of 'em !" replied Buck. "But it's the truth, dad ! Tell him it's true, Dan !"

"It is, cap'n," said Dan. "There's five thousand pounds lying in the sand there, and I've got the title-deed and plan for it in my pocket !"

Swooping round, the Wasp crashed full into the Narwhal, striking her in the bows, and tearing the forestay right out of her. Down came the Narwhal's mast with a crash !

Hurriedly, raising his voice above the roaring gale, wiping the spindrift from his eyes, Dan told, in as few words as possible, all that had happened on that grim island, whose deadly shore the Seal was even then trying to claw away from. It sounded a wild tale as Dan told it, jerkily and hastily, through the roar of the salt wind.

Atheling listened as best he could while intent on his work. The eager earnestness of the boys impressed him. All the same, it was plain he did not believe the story.

"You're mad, both of ye !" he growled at last. "Go below an' quit this foolishness !"

"It's true, dad, on my honour !" pleaded Buck. "Do, for Heaven's sake, turn her, and run into the gatway ! We'll pilot you in !"

"The gatway !" roared Atheling. "Risk my smack on an unknown bar in a gale o' wind an' darkness ! Ye're raving mad, both o' ye ! Not a word more—go !"

When John Atheling gave an order that way, there was no more to be said. Dan and Buck went below.

"We'll wait till this infernal gale dies down," said Buck to Dan, "and then we will try again to convince him. We're not going to let five thousand pounds lie in a sandhill for want of takin' it out !"

As the Seal thrashed her way to open sea, and left the grim island behind, the two chums made up their minds to return and unearth the treasure, whatever danger stood in the way.

Hour after hour passed as the Grey Seal made her way north-westward, and the gale, like many summer storms, blew itself out as quickly as it had arisen. The trawler, having won good sea-room, hove-to under small canvas for the rest of the night. By daybreak the wind had almost ceased.

When the opportunity presented itself, the boys once again tackled the skipper about the treasure.

Atheling, however, could not be induced to take any interest in the matter.

Buck and Dan were beside themselves with helplessness and impatience.

"When we're ashore again I'll have you overhauled by a doctor, Dan," said Atheling. "That head o' yours ain't right yet. All this time you don't know who you be, or where you come from. An' now you've got this mad idea in your bonnet, an' persuaded this cub o' mine to believe it, too."

"But it's all true, captain, every word of it," said Dan, almost weeping with vexation. "The Squadron killed

THE MAGNET LIBRARY.—No. 1,457.

Jan Osterling, and the money's there. Why did the gunboat come out after them if it isn't true?"

"Don't tell me!" said Atheling. "She was after them for some fish-poachin' game they're wanted for!" As a matter of fact, this was a good shot of Atheling's, for the gunboat had orders from Cuxhaven, and knew nothing of the raid on the island. "You've made a smart trawlerman since we've had you, Dan. There ain't a better or pluckier one on the Dogger. But there's places in your figurehead that ain't quite caulked."

"But won't you go and see, dad?" pleaded Buck. "The Vulture's spiked in the gatway for anyone to see. Why, Dan's showed you the plan Jan Osterling gave him before he died."

"A bit o' parchment with some scribbling on it!" grunted Atheling. And then he showed signs of being aroused. "Clear out o' here, both o' you, with your cock-an'-bull story, or I'll start you with a rope's-end!"

Buck pulled Dan's sleeves, and they went out.

"It's enough to make a chap mutiny," growled Dan, when they were alone.

"Don't worry about it," said Buck. "We ain't beat yet. We'll bring him round sooner or later, but it's got to be done tactfully. Let's think out a plan."

"Suppose we paddle off in the boat to do a bit of hooking and talk it over? I've got a notion."

That evening the two chums launched the boat and pulled about a mile away from the Seal.

The day had been hot and close, and there was a mutter of thunder in the air.

Laying the long-line took some time, but when it was done Dan delivered himself.

"We took some topping hauls of fish to-day," he said. "We'll work those long-lines all night, an' if we do as well three or four days running we'll have a rare load. Prices are still big at Amsterdam and Rotterdam. If we get enough fish, the skipper'll run in there. Then, if he still don't believe, we'll take French leave and go to Baltrum ourselves after the treasure."

"That's it," said Buck. "Dad'll be savage about it, but he'll cool down when we turn up with the five thousand pounds. An' then—— Hallo!"

Buck broke off suddenly with that exclamation, turned, and stared ahead.

Dan uttered an exclamation and followed his gaze.

Drifting along, about half a mile away, came a large, unkempt-looking trawler. There were no signs of life on her deck. Her sails were slatting and banging as she rolled in the swell. The peak of the mainsail was dropped, ropes and halliards were swinging about loose, and it was plain she had no living hand to control her. She rolled along helplessly, coming to the wind, and then falling off again.

As the boys watched attentively, wondering what it might mean, a flash of lightning showed her plainly against the clouds behind.

"A derelict!" said Buck, running out his oars. "Great Scott, it's the Wasp!"

"Deserted," cried Dan, "or I'm a Dutchman! Her boat's gone! What does it mean? By Jove, I know! The gunboat caught her an' arrested the crew—I'll bet my wages on it! They tried to tow her, but the rope broke in the storm, an' they took the crew an' abandoned her."

"That's about the size of it!" cried Buck. "Anyway, she's derelict. We'll board her an' salve her. No, we'll run her back to Baltrum an' snaffle the treasure, by George!"

"Come on!" cried Dan.

Another flicker of lightning lit the abandoned craft. The thunder growled threateningly, and big drops of rain began to fall.

Making the painter fast to the shrouds, the boys leaped aboard the craft. The decks of the smack looked forlorn and deserted.

"She seems down by the head," remarked Dan, stepping forward. "Shouldn't wonder if there's some water in her. She's—— Ah!"

Swiftly as the strike of a snake a slip-noose shot out of the darkness and settled around him. In an instant it was pulled tight, pinning his arms to his sides. A jerk at the rope brought him down heavily, only to find that Buck was in the same plight.

"So, ma beauty," said a hissing voice close in his ear, "ye've walked into the trap!"

Bending over Dan was the lanky figure and mean, cruel features of Foxey Backhouse, a grin of triumph playing round his pale lips.

Again the lightning glared. Before it died Dan caught sight of a trio of sharp topsails in the distance. It was a trap indeed. The Wasp, leaving the remainder of her crew with the Squadron, had left Foxey and his companion to manœuvre her, in the condition of a derelict, close to the boys. They knew the bait would be taken, and the trick was well carried out.

"The Seal's seen us!" cried Buck. "She's after us!"

"Ay, it's true," said the man who was bending over him.

An oath escaped him as he glanced at the trawler.

Atheling, who had been watching through his night-glasses, scenting something wrong, had headed the Seal straight for the sham derelict.

"Put ye knife intil him, Foxey, an' mak' sure!"

"Na! Hold your hand!" cried Foxey, springing to the helm. "Leave the cubs an' trim sail! They're tae be taken alive tae the skipper! That's Rebow's orders! They're tae be knifed if there's any chance o' their getting free, but no' otherwise!"

"We've nothin' but ourselves to blame!" muttered Buck bitterly.

Dan did not answer. With a thrill of hope he felt the slip-noose give. The tempest swept down upon the vessel with a rush of wind and a patter of heavy rain, giving the two men all the work they could handle.

"Hold yourself ready, Buck!" whispered Dan. "I can get my right arm free!"

Buck said nothing, but quivered with expectation.

A fierce shouting came from the Seal astern, but ahead, the Squadron vessels were rushing down at full speed towards the quarry.

Dan's pistol was aboard the Seal, but he had his knife. His right arm was free at last. He waited till the flickering lightning left the sea in gloom, and then leapt forward to the mast.

One slash with his knife severed the peak halliard, and the gaff came down with a run. Another slash sent the jib tearing from its hold and clapping over the bows like a winged seagull. The smack was crippled. A vivid flash showed the ruin those two slashes had wrought.

Before Dan could turn, however,

Foxey was upon him. A lurch sent the boy, still half-bound, into the scuppers, and the knife was torn from his grasp. Dan had fallen upon his free arm and for a moment was utterly helpless.

With a scream of rage, Foxey stood over him, his hand grasping his long French knife. The steel gleamed as he threw his arm upwards for the fatal blow, and Dan shut his eyes.

But even as the cold steel glinted, the sky split open with a crash that shook the crippled smack from stem to stern. A blinding chain of white-hot flame seemed to leap from the riven clouds on to the point of the murderous blade as Foxey raised it.

Then followed a splutter of molten metal, and a seared, blackened object that a second before had been a man rolled heavily into the scuppers and lay there silently.

The End of Foxey Backhouse!

AFTER the fearful glare and the crash came a silence and a darkness that weighed upon the eyes and covered all things. Then a low moan sounded from the scuppers, followed by the roar and hiss of the rainstorm.

"Dan—Dan," cried Buck, "where are you?"

There was no answer. The black water washed against the sides of the vessel, and the rain drummed on the deck.

Again the lightning shimmered, farther away this time, and lit up the craft.

Buck saw his comrade lying in the scuppers, white and still.

Close to him, rolling gently from side to side with the swaying of the vessel, was a blackened, shrivelled object twisted into a kind of knot. A smell of burnt cloth arose from it, for a serge coat that it wore was smouldering, till the thresh of the rain put it out.

A fused, melted steel blade lay beside, and a shower of molten drops had burnt into the deck-planks as though a leaden bullet had been melted in a ladle and scattered around.

It was the end of Foxey Backhouse! He had raised the knife aloft to deal the blow that was to end the hunt of the Black Squadron after Dogger Dan, and the lightning had struck him through the very weapon itself and hurled him into the pit in the fraction of a second.

"Dan's dead!" groaned Buck, tugging furiously at the bonds that held him. "The lightning has killed them both!"

He was flaying his wrists till the blood ran, and with perseverance he soon freed himself.

As he flung the rope from him the second Squadron man, who had lain dazed and stunned since the deadly flash, struggled to his feet. Seizing a stretcher, Buck rushed at the ruffian and dealt him a blow that sent the man on his back into the scuppers once more.

"Lie there till I tell you to rise!" said Buck grimly. "There's another change o' skippers on this craft!"

He turned to Dan anxiously. The boy opened his eyes and looked round in a stunned, helpless way.

"Thank Heaven you're alive, Dan!" said Buck. "Are you hurt much?"

"I don't know," said Dan. "I feel as if I'd been hit with a steam-hammer. No," he continued, struggling up, "I b'lieve I'm all right."

Printed in Great Britain and published every Saturday by the Proprietors, The Amalgamated Press, Ltd., The Fleetway House, Farringdon Street, London, E.C.4. Advertisement offices: The Fleetway House, Farringdon Street, London, E.C.4. Registered for transmission by Canadian Magazine Post. Subscription rates: Inland and Abroad, 11s. per annum; 5s. 6d. for six months. Sole Agents for Australia and New Zealand: Messrs. Gordon & Gotch Ltd., and for South Africa: Central News Agency, Ltd.—Saturday, January 18th, 1936.

He felt himself carefully, and Buck rejoiced. The lightning flash—that strange, unaccountable power that can slay a crowd of living creatures at one blow, or pick one out of a crowd and leave the rest unhurt—had stricken the destroyer, but saved the victim.

By good fortune Foxey Backhouse had not been in contact with any part of Dan when he raised the knife, the flash had leaped through him and then through the iron bolts of the smack to her keel, passing away into the deep sea.

"Is that Foxey?" said Dan, looking at the shrivelled bundle, with a shudder. "Poor brute!"

"Thank your stars for that flash!" returned Buck. "It saved you! To work now! The fleet's closing on us!"

In the dazed silence following the stroke they had forgotten the existence of the enemy, whose vessels were racing up with the storm. Two of them were yet a long way off, but the other was almost upon them, racing at full speed.

"That's the Narwhal," cried Buck—"the fastest they've got left in the Black Squadron. Rebow'll be aboard her; but here's the Seal close up to us. Get hold o' those jib-halliards an' run the jib up again!"

"But what can we do?" said Dan, obeying. "She's got rifles."

Atheling was bringing the Grey Seal up rapidly, and a great shouting arose from the decks of the Narwhal.

"I'll show you!" said Buck, running up the peak again, so that the big red mainsail showed its full surface to the wind. "It's risky, but we've got ourselves an' the Seal into this mess, an' we've got to get out of it. They don't know on the Narwhal that we're in command here. They think we're prisoners!" Then he turned to the man in the scuppers. "Lie down, you!" he cried.

Buck rapidly ran the fall of the mainsheet round the body of the ruffian, and bound him tight with a couple of half-hitches. There was no time to do more. The jib-halliard that he had cut during the chase had not pulled right out of the block, and he sprang aloft and got hold of it.

In the whistling squall it was all the boys could do to set the jib again.

"Ahoy!" came a hail from the Seal, as she raced up. "Buck! Dan! Are ye alive yet?"

"Ay, an' kicking!" cried Buck. "Up your helm, Dan! Get her round!"

"It's more than ye deserve!" hailed Atheling. "Heave her to, an' jump aboard as we run past ye. It's your only chance. Here's the Narwhal close on to us!"

Buck hailed the Seal.

"Don't do that, dad; there isn't time! They'll cut you down while we're gettin' aboard. We're goin' for them. Run past when we hit 'em, and stand by to pick us up!"

"Obey orders, ye whelps!" roared Atheling, in reply.

"It's a rope's-ending anyway," said Dan, "if we're not shot! The skipper's got his monkey up!"

"I reckon this is our command," said Buck. "I ain't sailed a vessel o' my own before, bar the old Adder, an' I'm going to run her till she busts. We must risk ourselves to cripple the Narwhal. We've walked into the trap, an' we must pay the piper!"

Buck was afraid the fast-arriving Narwhal would open fire on the Seal at close quarters if something were not done to cripple her.

All unwarily, the Narwhal came sousing along at her best pace. She was to windward, and had naturally heard nothing of the hails that passed between the Seal and the Wasp.

"Lie low!" ordered Buck. "Turn up the collar of your jumper, an' shove your sou'-wester over your eyes. They won't recognise us, then. Ah, dash the lightning! It's been a good friend to us, but another flash like that will give us away!"

The storm was at its height, but the flashes were playing some distance to leeward, and lighting up sea and sky like noonday, leaving a jagged seam imprinted on the eyeballs as it subsided into darkness again.

The Grey Seal rushed past, veered round, and came up again, Atheling savage with rage at the disobedience of his "cubs."

"Wasp ahoy!" screamed Jake Rebow. as the Narwhal came within hailing distance. "Jack! Foxey! What are ye aboot? Rin her up head tae wind, an' we'll jump aboord as we pass!"

The Wasp's crew, save the two who had been left aboard her to trap the boys, were on the Narwhal, Rebow among them.

"Ease her up a bit, Dan," said Buck, helping to handle the kicking tiller.

Up towards each other ran the two vessels, the Seal close behind. A few scattered shots were fired at the Seal from the Narwhal, but without effect. The latter's crew were too busy getting ready to board the Wasp.

Short-handed as the Wasp was, it was essential to put more men on her before the two vessels could tackle the Seal together, and it would be touch-and-go, as they knew, jumping aboard her in the dark.

"Ready?" whispered Buck.

"Ay, ready!" answered Dan, his hands tightened on the tiller.

"Up wi' her!" cried Rebow to the Wasp. "Now's your time!"

"Now!" cried Buck fiercely, and the boys forced the tiller hard down.

A roar arose from the Narwhal as the Wasp, swooping round, crashed full into Rebow's vessel, striking her in the bows, and tearing the forestay right out of her.

Down came the Narwhal's mast with a crash!

A Queer Capture!

"GET your guns going!" shrieked Rebow to his men.

Out over the Wasp's bulwarks plunged the boys, headlong into the inky water. It was their only chance. The sudden shock of the collision had thrown most of the Narwhal's crew off their feet, and the boys were overboard before aim could be taken.

The water roaring in their ears, Buck and Dan shot to the surface and struck out strongly, shouting lustily to let the Seal know where they were.

Atheling was ready, and on the lookout.

"They're givin' us the slip!" screamed Rebow. "Plug them while they're in the water!"

Plut! Tut-tut-tut!

Bullets spattered around the two boys. They dived like dabchicks, swam under water as far as they could, and shot up again alongside the Seal.

Atheling luffing his vessel, had let her tremble in the eye of the wind before paying off on the other tack long enough to take the boys aboard. In a moment strong hands seized Dan and Buck, and they were on the deck of the old Seal once more.

"Smartly with those jibsheets!" cried Atheling. "Pay her off, and away!"

The two Squadron smacks were too hard pressed to fire. A gaping hole had been cut in the Narwhal's bow above the water-line, and it was all her crew could do to keep her afloat.

The smacks, locked together, were pounding each other with a force that threatened to send both of them to the bottom out of hand, and the crews were struggling for dear life to get them apart.

A last random shot and a volley of curses followed the Seal as she raced along into the smother and the darkness.

The other Squadron vessels were urgently hailed as they came up, and put off at once to render aid to the injured vessels.

Dismasted, helpless, the Narwhal rocked upon the waters.

"Bring the cubs here!" ordered Atheling, as the Seal rushed to the southward. "Now, my lads, what have you to say?"

Buck told his father the whole story.

A rope's-ending was the least the boys hoped for. But when the tale was finished, the captain stood silent at his helm for a full minute before he spoke.

"Ye did right," he said at last. "I ought to be taking the hide off both of ye with a piece o' tarred hemp this moment. But ye've saved your skins. Ye were running your own ship."

"We've never questioned orders aboard here, under you, dad," said Buck.

"I reckon not," said Atheling, a twinkle in the corner of one eye—"not when I'm handy to look after ye. It was a smart trap o' Rebow's, an' an older man than either o' ye might ha' fallen into it. But I don't know what to do wi' you cubs. Just so sure as ye go out on your own, somethin' o' this sort happens. I'll have to separate ye, an' put one out under Long John for a spell!"

The boys went below, feeling somewhat floored. Such a threat was sobering.

"Still, it's a good night's work," said Dan, as he settled down in his bunk. "D'you reckon the Narwhal's sunk?"

"They may save her," returned Buck. "They're good at that sort o' work. But we've taken the edge off the Blacks. It was fine while it lasted. What worries me is that we ain't any nearer the treasure. Dad don't believe in it any more, an' after this last shindy we'll be kept at the fishin' day and night for a spell."

Buck was right. The Seal was kept trawling diligently for four days, all hands working at breaking strain day and night by watches. The soles were "on," and there was lost time to be made up.

The boys were refused all boat leave, and though, as a rule, they gloried in the fishing, they were chafing incessantly at being unable to make for the hidden hoard on Baltrum Island.

One idea dominated them without ceasing—the treasure. It seemed written on every fish they caught, and between the hiss of wet trawl-ropes they heard the voice of the lost island calling them.

Atheling refused to hear anything about it, and threatened a rope's-ending if it were mentioned again. He thought it purely an idle fancy of Dan's unbalanced mind, and that Buck had heard so much about it from his chum that he believed it, too.

The two chums did not confide their knowledge to the rest of the crew, knowing that Skipper Atheling's decision was final, and that they would only be laughed at.

They obtained leave to go hand-lining in the boat once or twice after the trawling slackened a little, and talked over many a plan for bringing their disbelieving skipper to reason. But nothing turned up for a week.

Finally, they went off in the boat with the hand-lines after cod, and Buck expressed his intention of getting away, if possible, to follow the search.

"W h a t—desert?" asked Dan anxiously.

"Not quite that," replied Buck, grinning. "But dad would soon sing another tune if we came back with that five thousand, an'——"

"Hallo!" broke in Dan. "What's that?"

He looked away over the swells, where a large, pale-green mass, like a curiously coloured sankbank, lay above the water.

"What on earth is it?" he queried. "There are no banks out here, surely?"

"By gosh!" said Buck. "That's a dead whale! It's been hit by a steamer or something. Let's have a look at it."

"Is it any good?" asked Dan, as they pulled up to the carcass.

"It ain't a sperm whale," replied Buck. "They're worth tons o' money, and we don't get 'em about here. This is a killer, an' he'd be worth maybe twenty pounds if he was in order. But he's a dead'un, an' has been so some time, no doubt. I wonder the dogfish an' gulls ain't pulled him to pieces."

The boat touched the creature. The part of it above water was about twenty feet long, and how much there was below the water-line could only be guessed.

"Rum-looking beast!" said Dan, staring at the great jelly-like mass. "Why, there's room for a picnic on his back! It must have been a pretty smart knock that killed him. I thought whales were dark-coloured."

"They go like this when they're dead," said Buck. "Pity; he'd be worth something if he were alive."

"Let's board him, just for fun," said Dan.

Before Buck could object, Dan had stepped out on to the great flat back.

The sea was calm as a pond, and there was hardly any ground-swell.

Dan walked up and down the whale's back with a rolling gait, while Buck grinned. Suddenly Dan's face changed, and Buck shouted anxiously:

"Look out! He's moving!"

"Great Scott!" exclaimed Dan.

The big green mass gave a heave under him, and he ran back towards the boat hurriedly.

But he did not reach the boat. The whole of the creature sank under him

like a stone, and vanished, leaving him struggling in the water.

"Ha, ha, ha!" laughed Buck, rowing up and hauling his friend out, spluttering and coughing. "Got a free bath that time, didn't you?"

"The brute's alive, after all," said Dan, as he got aboard.

The whale's back broke the surface once more, and rested motionless, not more than fifty yards away.

"He's mighty sick, or he'd ha' gone right away. If we could get him, an' scoop in twenty pounds!"

"How are you going to do it?" grunted Dan. "You want harpoons an' a whale-boat, an' all sorts of gear."

"For a sperm-whale, in the pride o' his sweet young life, you do," agreed Buck, rapidly untying a big coil of anchor-line that lay in the bows. "But this gentleman ain't feelin' very fit, an' we might get the better of him.

"There's the boathook, with a sharp spike point, an' the hook below it. That'll serve as a barb if we can drive it in over the bend o' the hook, an' it ought to hold. There's plenty of thin line. We'll have a shot at it, anyway. The Seal can come up an' tow him off, but we'll bag him to our own cheek."

They fixed up the gear busily. Dan cut a deep notch in the boathook handle, and fastened the line securely. The affair made a rough but very passable harpoon.

When it was ready, Buck sculled the dinghy gently and quietly up to the motionless creature. Dan, poised in the bows, kept the line all clear, and took careful aim. Throwing was impossible—the only chance was to drive the boathook in with both hands at close quarters. The whale, being off colour, was not scared away.

When he was right over the monster, Dan raised his ready-made harpoon and drove it into the great soft mass with all his force. It sank in half-way up the handle, through the blubber.

There was a flap and a jerk that nearly upset the boat. Down went the whale, and the line began to whistle out over the stern-head. When it ran out, there came a jerk that nearly snapped the cord and upset the boys in a heap on the floorboards. But the boat gave to the pull, and began to tear along through the water at a frantic rate.

"Don't get up—you'll capsize her!" cried Buck. "Sit on the floor, as far aft as you can get, an' keep her nose up!"

"This would beat a torpedo-boat on steaming trial!" said Dan. "The harpoon's holding."

(*Dan and Buck are booked for something new in sea trips this time, what? Be sure you read next week's exciting chapters of this powerful adventure yarn, chums.*)

THE BOY WHO WOULDN'T MAKE FRIENDS!

(*Continued from page 24.*)

There, Frank spoke to his chum in a low voice.

"That chap did something at his last school, and got booted out, Harry!"

He spoke with conviction.

Harry Wharton nodded.

"Looks like it!" he muttered.

"And Hacker's got him in here—his uncle! That accounts——"

"For a lot of things," said Harry. "But I'm dashed if I understand how that fat ass, Bunter, knows anything about him."

"He does!"

"Yes, he does! But mum's the word. Frank—the fellow seems to be a sulky tick, but——"

Frank Nugent laughed.

"If Bunter knows anything about him, it will be all over the school!" he said. "Trust Bunter!"

"I suppose so!" assented Wharton.

It was about a quarter of an hour later that Billy Bunter rolled into the Rag. Apparently, he had stayed in the study for a talk with the fellow he knew. There was a fat smirk on his face as he rolled in, as if something entertained Bunter.

"Hallo, hallo, hallo!" roared Bob Cherry. "Bagged the new kid, Bunter?"

"Oh, really, Cherry——"

"Haven't you found Wilmot yet, old fat man?" grinned Johnny Bull.

"Oh, yes, I've seen the chap!" answered Bunter carelessly. "He's not the fellow I know, after all."

"Not the fellow you know, Bunter?" exclaimed Harry Wharton.

Bunter gave him a blink.

"No! As it turns out, I've never seen him before!" he answered breezily. "Not the same chap at all! Quite another chap, you know!"

"Oh, my hat!" murmured Nugent.

His eyes met Wharton's. But neither of them spoke. If the new fellow had a secret, and Bunter, contrary to his usual custom, was going to keep it for him, they certainly had no desire to barge in and spill the beans.

But they rather wondered how long Bunter was likely to keep it. If Eric Wilmot, with a secret to keep, was relying on the discretion of the most talkative ass at Greyfriars, he was leaning upon a very rotten reed.

THE END.

(*Be sure you read the second yarn in this grand new series featuring Eric Wilmot. It's entitled: "THE OUT-SIDER!" and you'll vote it a real good 'un!*)

HANDS OFF!
MUSTN'T PUNCH ERIC !
BEWARE OF Mr HACKER!

THERE'S A GOOD TIME COMING! So——

COME INTO the OFFICE, BOYS ~ AND GIRLS!

Your Editor is always pleased to hear from his readers. Write to him: Editor of the "Magnet," The Amalgamated Press, Ltd., Fleetway House, Farringdon Street, London, E.C.4. A stamped, addressed envelope will ensure a reply.

I SUPPOSE most of you at some time or other have heard a conjurer say: "There is nothing up my sleeve. boys and girls." Well, I'm going to start the ball rolling this week by saying just the opposite. Boys and girls there is

SOMETHING UP MY SLEEVE

—and what's more this something is going to make you all sit up and take notice!

Now put your thinking caps on, chums, and try to imagine the stupendous surprise which I've fixed up for you. I guess you'll all say

"MORE FREE GIFTS!"

Right in one! But what kind of Free Gifts? Ah, that's where I've got you all! It's my secret at the moment, and it's a secret I am going to keep to myself for this week, at any rate. I'll tell you this much, though, these coming Grand Free Gifts are going to be something really extra special. Doesn't that whet your appetite?

The best thing you can do, chums, is to ask your newsagent to deliver or reserve a copy of the good old MAGNET for next week. Because next week, as Fisher T. Fish would say, I'm going to "spill the beans"! Believe me, chums, these Free Gifts will be something out of the ordinary. If you miss 'em, you will feel like asking your pals to give you a kick. And when you see the——

Ah, I nearly gave the whole secret away then; and I don't want to do this until next week. Look out, then, chums, for next Saturday's MAGNET and full particulars of the ripping Free Gifts coming your way very soon.

———

ONE of my readers, who signs himself "Fatty," of Peckham, writes me this week to ask a few questions concerning New York, and, in particular

THE STATUE OF LIBERTY.

How high is it? he asks. The statue itself is about 200 feet high, and is one of the largest in the world. It was made by a French sculptor, who was commissioned to do so by the French Government. The statue was then presented to the American government in commemoration of the centenary of American independence. It was completed in 1884, and erected two years later on Bedloe's Island at the mouth of New York harbour.

"Fatty" also wants to know the height of the Empire State Building, in New York. This is the highest building in the world, and towers 1,248 feet above street level. Previous to the building of this enormous skyscraper, the record for height was held by the Crane Building, of Chicago, which is 1,022 feet. Next comes the Woolworth Building in New York, with a height of 792 feet.

THE MAGNET LIBRARY.—No. 1,458.

THERE are many of my readers who are like "Marcus Aurelius," who writes to me from Coventry.

HE WANTS TO GO ABROAD,

and asks me to tell him how he can get a job abroad on a coffee or tobacco plantation. Coffee plantations are not doing very well at the moment, and vast crops have had to be burned, owing to very poor demands. Many big coffee plantations have been closed down, with the result that experienced men have been put out of work. So I am afraid that my Coventry reader doesn't stand much chance in the coffee business.

Neither is there much scope on tobacco plantations. What is happening nowadays, especially in countries like Australia, is that men are settling on the land and farming their own tobacco. A system of small tobacco farms, with a co-operative marketing plan, has been carried out. Each smallholder farms his own tobacco, so there is not much chance for a youngster. There are many big tobacco plantations in various parts of the world, of course, but local native labour is generally used. The executive positions are filled by experienced men.

The best way for this reader to get information regarding a situation abroad is to write to the Crown Agents for the Colonies, 4, Millbank, Westminster, S.W.1. This department acts as business agents for the Governments of the Colonies, Protectorates, etc., and naturally knows all particulars of conditions abroad, the chances of employment, and so on.

———

My remarks, a little while ago, regarding curious place-names, have brought me a letter from a Northumberland reader, who sends me a list of

MORE QUEER PLACE-NAMES.

Near Newcastle-on-Tyne, he tells me, there are places called Wide Open, Pity Me, and Windy Nook. Make-em-Rich is another village in Northumberland. Here are some others: Tadley God Help Us (in Hampshire); Dead Maiden (Hampshire), Ugley (Essex), New Invention (Staffordshire), Fryup (Yorkshire), Cold Roast Hamlet (Bucks), and Come to Good (Cornwall).

I reckon that list will take a bit of beating! But if there are any curiously-named places round about your neighbourhood, send them along to me, and I'll publish them in this little chat of mine.

Towns and villages aren't the only things with names that are out of the ordinary. Quite a number of people have peculiar surnames. Here is another list of

CURIOUS SURNAMES AND THEIR MEANINGS.

I wonder if any of my readers bear these unusual names?

Whalebelly. Originally a nickname for the man who played the part of Jonah in medieval dramas.

Venus. Comes from "Fenhouse," meaning a dweller in the house by the fen.

Bacchus. The original bearer of this name must have been a baker, for the word is derived from "bakehouse."

Bannfird. Comes from the Anglo-Saxon. It meant the chief horn blower to a king.

Tredger. Comes from the word "treader," meaning a walker.

Cogman. Was originally a sailor on a small vessel which was at one time known as a "cog."

Woolway. Despite its mild sound, comes from Anglo-Saxon words meaning "wolf-warrior."

That's sufficient to be going on with. I'll look up a few more for you in the near future.

Here's a curious bit of information which has just been unearthed. You'll find it hard to believe, but

THE GREAT WAR ISN'T FINISHED!

Seventeen years ago, peace was signed, and everybody imagined that everything had been squared up. But, by a curious error, the tiny republic of San Marino, in Italy, was not invited to join in the peace negotiations with Turkey. San Marino joined the Allies in 1915, and declared war on Turkey. As no peace negotiations have been carried out between these two countries, they are still technically at war with each other!

A little while ago a Turk who had paid a visit to San Marino was arrested, and charged with being a member of a country that was at war with San Marino. Needless to say, this state of affairs will doubtlessly be rectified soon, but it is certainly amazing to think that the Great War is still on!

———

JUST to finish up my chat, here is a selection of

RAPID-FIRE REPLIES.

to questions which have been fired at me by various readers.

Is there any Rocket Postal Service in Operation? Yes, in Austria, where rockets are used to fire a postal service over a high mountain. This service has its own particular postage stamps.

How does an Octopus Swim? It uses the "rocket" principle. It draws water in and then ejects it violently, thus pushing itself along in a similar manner to the way in which a rocket pushes itself through the air.

Which is the best Medium for Carrying Electricity? Gold. A gold thread will carry as much electricity as a four-inch copper cable.

Does Sound Carry Faster on Hot or Cold Days? On hot days. For every degree the temperature is raised there is a difference in the speed of sound of two feet per second. The air molecules are in more rapid movement and carry the sound waves faster.

Who Invented Unbreakable Glass? It was invented during the regime of the Roman Emperor Nero. The secret was then forgotten, but modern scientists have succeeded in rediscovering it.

Before space runs out, I must tell you what is in store for next week. First and foremost is

"THE FORM-MASTER'S FAVOURITE!" By Frank Richards,

another tip-top story of the chums of Greyfriars, featuring the new boy, Eric Wilmot. The title will give you some idea of the plot without my saying more. There will be another full-length instalment of David Goodwin's popular adventure story, not to mention the "Greyfriars Herald," our clever Rhymester's contribution and another cheery chat with your Editor. And don't forget the stupendous surprise I've promised to tell you more about next week!

YOUR EDITOR.

The OUTSIDER! By FRANK RICHARDS

Having been forced to leave his last school, one would naturally expect Eric Wilmot to lie low and say nothing. But Mr. Hacker's nephew is something new in new boys . . . bent on making himself as unpopular as he can in his new surroundings !

THE FIRST CHAPTER.
Orders are Orders !

"LEAVE me alone !"

"Sorry," said Harry Wharton, with sarcastic politeness; "but, you see, it can't be done."

Eric Wilmot, the new fellow in the Greyfriars Remove, stared at the captain of the Form for a moment, and then turned his back on him and walked across to the study window.

Wharton was standing in the doorway of Study No. 1 in the Remove. He had a coat on over his football rig, and a Soccer ball under his arm.

His face flushed, and a gleam came into his eyes as Wilmot turned his back. Really, that was hardly the way for a new fellow to treat the captain of his Form. Even Billy Bunter would have been offended. And the captain of the Remove was not to be treated like Billy Bunter ! Not quite !

"Wilmot !" he rapped.

The new junior stood looking out of the window. His handsome face was marred by the expression of sullen sulkiness that seemed habitual to it. Harry Wharton stared at the back of his head.

"Wilmot !" he repeated, in rising tones.

"I've asked you to leave me alone !" answered the new junior over his shoulder, without looking round.

"You don't seem to catch on," said Harry. "It's games practice to-day. You're wanted."

"I've told you I shan't play Soccer here."

"That's not a matter of choice," explained Wharton. "A fellow can slack and frowst about if he chooses, instead of playing games, but games practice is compulsory on certain days. This is one of the days. Now do you catch on ?"

No answer.

"You see, you can't do exactly as you like here," said the captain of the Remove. "If you want to be as free and irresponsible as a stray dog, you shouldn't have come to Greyfriars."

"I never wanted to come."

"I guessed that one some time back," said Harry, smiling a little. "But you're here now, Wilmot. Why not make the best of it ? You seem to have the rottenest, sulkiest temper ever. I've never met a fellow who asked so often to have his head punched. But——"

"Are you wound up ?" inquired Wilmot, still over his shoulder and without turning his head.

"I'll cut it short," said Harry. "You've got to come down to games practice, whether you like it or not; and as captain of the Form, I have to see that you do. So come."

"I'm not coming !"

Harry Wharton breathed hard and deep. He wanted to be patient with a new fellow, especially a fellow who had been put in his own study. But his patience was very near the limit.

Frank Nugent came up the passage. "Everybody's ready !" he said. "What are you waiting for, Harry ?"

"His Highness, Eric the First of Greyfriars," answered the captain of the Remove, "doesn't care to come, and the fact that he has to doesn't make any difference to his serene mightiness !"

Nugent stared for a moment, and then burst into a laugh. He looked into the study—at the back of Eric Wilmot's handsome head.

"Come on, Wilmot," he said good-naturedly. "Can't keep all the fellows waiting, you know."

No reply.

"If the chap's seedy, you can let him off, Harry," suggested Frank. He was always good-natured and tolerant.

"Are you seedy, Wilmot ?" asked Wharton sarcastically.

"No."

"I've just heard from Bunter that he's got a pain and doesn't feel up to footer. Have you got a pain like Bunter ?"

Nugent chuckled. Wilmot did not answer, or turn his head, but his ears were seen to redden. Apparently he did not relish being compared to the fat slacker of the Remove.

"Only cheeky, what ?" went on Wharton.

Silence.

"Or is it funk ? Are you afraid of getting a rap, or a tap ? If you're a footer funk, you can say so."

THE MAGNET LIBRARY.—No. 1,458.

Wilmot's ears were burning now. Evidently he was not enjoying this conversation, addressed to the back of his head! But with the sulky obstinacy that seemed a part of his nature, he remained at the window, staring out into the quad.

"Hallo, hallo, hallo!" came Bob Cherry's roar from the Remove staircase. "You men ever coming? Taken root, or what?"

Bob came tramping up the passage. Johnny Bull and Hurree Jamset Ram Singh followed him. They all looked into the study—at the back of Eric Wilmot's head.

"Forgotten footer, Wharton?" asked Bob.

"No. I'm trying to persuade Wilmot to come."

"Eh? Doesn't he know he has to?" demanded Bob. "Wilmot, old bean, get a move on! You're not changed yet! Buck up!"

Harry Wharton glanced at the back of an immovable head—and then at his friends. He was getting very angry, and he was also perplexed. There were slackers in the Remove, and the football captain sometimes had a little trouble with them. Billy Bunter generally had a pain, or an ache, just in time for games practice. Skinner and Snoop would dodge it whenever they could. Still, they knew that they had to toe the line. This chap didn't seem to have assimilated that elementary fact.

Neither did he seem to be exactly a slacker, and he did not give anyone the impression of being a funk. It seemed to be sheer, sulky, wilful obstinacy—a thing rather new in Wharton's experience.

"What's a fellow to do, you chaps?" asked Harry. "He won't come. If I let him off, I shall get rowed by old Wingate! I can't let him off."

"If you let him off," said Johnny Bull, in a deep voice rather like the growl of the Great Huge Bear, "you'd better resign the captaincy. You ought not to keep on the job if you can't handle it."

"Do come along, Wilmot, and don't play the goat!" urged the pacific Nugent. "Wharton can't let a man off; he's responsible to the captain of the school. Every other slacker in the Form will be complaining if he's made to turn up and another man let off."

"What's the good of talking to him?" grunted Johnny Bull. "He's a cheeky ass! I suppose he fancies he can do as he likes because he's a beak's nephew!"

"Oh," ejaculated Wharton, "is that it, Wilmot?"

Wilmot made a movement. The contemptuous tone in Wharton's voice had stung him. He was nephew of Mr. Hacker, the master of the Remove, and it was said in the Remove that his uncle, crusty old stick that he was, was very much attached to that nephew. But if the new junior was thinking of banking on that relationship, he was not likely to have much success.

"Rotten tick," said Johnny, "and a fool, too! Hacker won't back you up in this sort of thing, Wilmot. He couldn't."

Wilmot turned from the window at last. His handsome face was flushed with anger.

"Nothing of the kind!" he snapped. "I want to be left alone, that's all. I never wanted to come to this rotten school. I'm fed-up with the place, and with you, too! You don't want me at the footer. I've no friends here, and don't want any. Leave me alone, then."

THE MAGNET LIBRARY.—No. 1,458.

"Wouldn't touch you with a barge-pole, you sulky tick!" retorted Bob.

"Nobody wants you, if you come to that," said Harry quietly. "Nobody could be expected to want a sulky brute with a rotten temper. But you've got to come down to games practice, because I've no power to let you off, if I wanted to. Will you come down and change?"

"No, I won't!"

"That does it," said the captain of the Remove. "You'll either walk, or you'll be taken. Choose!"

"Oh, shut up!"

Wilmot turned his back again.

Wharton's eyes glinted.

"Help him along!" he said.

And the Famous Five stepped into the study, grasped the sulky fellow standing by the window, and hooked him across to the door by main force.

Wilmot struggled and panted.

"Hands off, you rotters!"

"Get him along!"

Five pairs of hands were on Wilmot, and they were sturdy hands. But even so, it was not easy to hook him out of the study. He was a fellow of slim and graceful build, but there was plenty of strength in him.

He struggled fiercely in the doorway, and again in the passage. The whole half-dozen went whirling and scrambling across the landing to the stairs. Wilmot's face was crimson with passionate temper, and Wharton's dark with anger; but the other fellows were grinning.

"Heave ahead, my hearties!" chuckled Bob.

"The heavefulness is terrific!" gasped Hurree Jamset Ram Singh.

"Will you come now, Wilmot?"

"No!"

"Yank him along!"

On the landing the obstinate fellow put up a last fierce resistance. There was a scuffle, a scramble, a bumping and a thudding, and the whole mob of struggling juniors went rolling down the Remove staircase to the landing below.

- - -

THE SECOND CHAPTER.

Hacker Barges In!

MR. HACKER, master of the Shell at Greyfriars, gave an angry grunt.

He was standing near the big staircase talking to Prout, master of the Fifth, when there were loud sounds of uproar from somewhere above.

Whereupon Mr. Hacker grunted, and Mr. Prout shrugged his plump shoulders.

The din sounded as if it proceeded from the Remove quarters, and neither master doubted that it did. Both of them believed that they could have improved on Mr. Quelch's management of that Form.

Scuffling, bumping, gasping, shouting, sounded in the upper regions. Neither master doubted that a "rag" was on, or that Quelch's Form were mixed up in it.

"Scandalous!" remarked Prout.

"The Remove!" said Hacker bitterly.

"As usual!" said Prout.

"Oh, quite as usual! I wonder Quelch does not intervene. He must surely be aware that this din is going on."

"I believe he is out," said the Fifth Form master. "I think I saw him going with Dr. Locke——"

"His boys should not create this disturbance during his absence."

"Most certainly not!"

"Someone should intervene," said Mr. Hacker. "You, sir, as a senior master——"

Prout shook his head.

"Mr. Quelch is so—er—excessively touchy on that subject," he remarked. "He dislikes intervention by another master in the affairs of his Form. More than once, sir, Quelch has answered with acerbity—I can only call it acerbity—when he has been given well-meant counsel——"

"Is the House to be turned into a bear-garden?" snapped Mr. Hacker.

"Apparently, sir," answered Prout. "I shall not intervene. But you, sir, have a relative in Quelch's Form, I understand—a nephew, a new boy—you may consider that that gives you a right to intervene. Certainly this disturbance should end."

"It sounds," said Mr. Hacker, "as if a number of boys were rolling bodily down the upper stairs."

"It does," said Prout.

"My nephew, I am assured, would never take part in any such uproar," said Mr. Hacker. "He had the best of reputations at his last school. I have no doubt that he is the best-conducted boy in the Remove, which, certainly, is not saying very much."

"Quite!" agreed Prout.

Prout rolled ponderously away. Hacker stood listening to the din with a frowning, knitted brow.

Hacker was a conscientious and dutiful master, but afflicted with an acid temper and a somewhat interfering disposition. The sound of rolling downstairs was followed by a sound of scuffling on a mid-way landing. Certainly it was time the uproar was stopped. Quelch might be "touchy" on such matters—most Form-masters were. Hacker did not want any trouble with Quelch, especially as his nephew, Wilmot, was in that master's Form. But he was not going to let this go on.

He whisked up the stairs.

On the upper staircase a number of Remove men were gathered, most of them grinning. They were ready for football, but seemed more interested in what was going on below. Some of them looked rather startled as they saw the master of the Shell whisking up the stairs.

"Oh, gad, here's Hacker!" exclaimed Vernon-Smith.

"Oh, my hat!" murmured Peter Todd.

"'Ware beaks, you men!" called out Hazeldene.

Frowning, Mr. Hacker made his way through the cluster of juniors, who gave him room to pass. He reached the landing.

On that landing something like a dog-fight seemed to be going on. One fellow was wriggling and struggling in the grasp of five others.

Mr. Hacker glared at the scene.

"Cease this disturbance immediately!" he thundered.

He recognised Harry Wharton & Co., but he did not recognise the fellow they were grasping, for the simple reason that Eric Wilmot's head was gripped under Bob Cherry's arm, and his face invisible.

Harry Wharton, panting for breath, looked round. He, like the fellows on the staircase, looked a little startled at the sight of Hacker. In the circumstances, Wilmot's uncle was not wanted on the scene.

However, it could not be helped. If Eric Wilmot had been related to the whole staff at Greyfriars, from the Head down to the French master, he would still have had to toe the line in the Remove.

"Did you speak, sir?" asked Harry politely.

"I did, Wharton! I ordered you to cease this unseemly disturbance, and to cease it at once!"

Wharton looked at him.

"Who is that boy you are bullying?" asked Mr. Hacker acidly.

Wharton reddened.

"We are bullying nobody, sir, and we are not taking orders from any Form-master but our own!" he answered, very distinctly.

"What? Do you dare to be impertinent, Wharton?"

"Eric!" he exclaimed.

Wilmot panted for breath.

"So it is my nephew you are bullying, Wharton!" exclaimed Mr. Hacker, his face almost white with passionate anger.

"I've said that this fellow is not being bullied, sir," answered the captain of the Remove. "He knows why he was handled, and he can tell you, if he likes."

"There is no need for my nephew to tell me anything. What I can see with my own eyes is enough for me!" exclaimed Mr. Hacker. "Lay a finger on him again—any of you—if you dare!"

he was utterly winded, and could only gasp.

"Come with me, Eric," said Mr. Hacker. "I shall take you away from these young ruffians. I shall lay a complaint of this before Mr. Quelch. I shall allow no repetition of it!"

Wilmot, gasping, found his voice.

"It's all right, sir!" he panted. He was always careful never to address Mr. Hacker as "uncle" before others.

"What do you mean, Eric?" exclaimed Mr. Hacker sharply.

"Dear little Eric!" came a voice from the staircase. "Sweet little Eric!"

There was a laugh.

With a sudden wrench, Wilmot tore himself loose, and his flushed face and untidy hair came out from under Bob Cherry's arm. Mr. Hacker gave a jump as he recognised his nephew. "Eric!" he exclaimed, his face almost white with passionate anger. "So it is my nephew you are bullying, Wharton!" "He knows why he was being handled, sir," said Wharton, "and he can tell you, if he likes!"

"I'm ready to answer to Mr. Quelch, sir," said Harry. "You fellows, get on with it! Get him down to the changing-room!"

There was a chuckle on the lower stair.

"Meddlin' ass!" came a voice from the crowd, which was very probably the Bounder's.

"Go home, Hacker!" came another voice.

Mr. Hacker stood red and wrathful. He was exceeding his authority; and his position was very awkward if Quelch's boys did not choose to regard him. At that moment Eric Wilmot, with a sudden wrench, tore himself loose, and his flushed face and untidy hair came out from under Bob's arm. In the presence of a beak he was not held so tenaciously as before.

Mr. Hacker gave a jump as he recognised his nephew.

Harry Wharton stood undecided. His comrades waited for his word. The fellows on the staircase gazed on with breathless interest at the scene. A "row" with a beak was uncommonly exciting.

Wharton was acting within his rights —indeed, he was doing his bounden duty as everyone knew but Mr. Hacker. But a beak was a beak, all the same. It was a delicate matter, rowing with a beak.

There was a tense pause.

Eric Wilmot, crimson, untidy, panting for breath, stood untouched. Many eyes were on him—all of them contemptuous. A fellow who took advantage of relationship to one in authority was an object of scorn; and Hacker's interference was tactless—the worst thing he could have done for the fellow. Everyone expected Wilmot to make the most of it, and despised him accordingly. He tried to speak, but

Wilmot's face, already crimson, seemed to grow redder, if possible. Hacker never seemed to understand that he ought to call him Wilmot.

"It's all right, sir," he answered. "I don't want to be protected. It was all my fault, too. I only got what I asked for. There's no need for anyone to interfere."

"Oh!" ejaculated Mr. Hacker, taken quite aback.

"My hat! The chap isn't such a greasy tick as he makes himself out to be," murmured Bob Cherry.

"Oh, come on, you men!" said Harry Wharton abruptly. "We can't waste any more time. Leave Wilmot to do as he likes."

"Rot!" grunted Johnny Bull.

But he followed his Form captain, as Wharton went down the stairs. It was an unpleasant pill for the captain of the Remove to swallow. But handling Wilmot under his uncle's eyes was rather too much of a good thing; and he gave it up at that. The rest of the Removites followed on, and Wilmot was left panting and gasping on the landing, under the acid stare of Mr. Hacker.

"Eric——" began the master of the Shell.

"I can't stop, sir; I've got to go and get changed for footer."

Wilmot went down the stairs, leaving Mr. Hacker staring. He hurried at once to the changing-room.

The rest of the Remove were changed already, and going down to Little Side. They arrived there, not expecting to see the new junior arrive in his turn. But two or three minutes later a slim but athletic figure in football garb came cutting down the field.

"I say, you fellows, here comes Wilmot!" squeaked Billy Bunter.

Everybody looked round. Wilmot came up, flashed and panting. Harry Wharton gave him a look.

"So you've changed your mind?" he said.

"Can't you see I have?" retorted Wilmot.

"Well, all right, so long as you're here."

"I shouldn't be here if my uncle hadn't barged in!" answered Wilmot, with a curl of the lip. "I don't suppose you understand it, but that's why!"

Wharton smiled.

"I think I do," he answered. "Get going, you men!"

It was clear enough that Wilmot had changed his mind because he disdained to reap advantage from his relationship to a beak. That, undoubtedly, was a point in his favour. Mr. Hacker's interference had had quite an unexpected result.

Now that he was on the football ground, however, Wilmot did not seem to be of much use there. He played Soccer, as Bob Cherry described it, like a sack of coke. The juniors had heard from Hobson of the Shell, who had heard it from Mr. Hacker, that Wilmot had been considered a great footballer at his last school—wherever that was! But the fumbling and foozling show he put up now did not seem much like it. It seemed that he took no interest in the game whatever, and was only anxious to get away.

When the practice was over he got away—by himself! And there were few fellows in the Remove who were not glad to see the last of him.

THE THIRD CHAPTER.
Very Mysterious!

"I SAY, you fellows!"

Billy Bunter blinked in at the doorway of Study No. 1, and blinked round the study—with a disappointed blink. Wharton and Nugent were there—but their study-mate, the new fellow Wilmot, was not.

"I say, where's Wilmot?" asked the fat Owl of the Remove.

"Don't know!" said Nugent.

"And don't care!" added Wharton.

"Isn't he coming up to tea?" asked Bunter.

"Don't know!" said Nugent again.

"And don't care!" repeated Wharton.

Billy Bunter blinked at them through his big spectacles. Wharton and Nugent, being busy, took no further heed of the fat Owl. Nugent was poaching eggs for tea, Wharton was buttering toast. The rest of the Co. were coming to tea, but had not yet arrived.

"I say, you fellows——"

"Look here, your precious pal Wilmot isn't here!" rapped Wharton. "If you want him, go and look for him!"

"I wish you fellows wouldn't row with my pal because he's in your study!" said Bunter peevishly. "I was going to ask him to tea in Study No. 7, but I've been disappointed about a postal order. Is he teaing in Hall?"

"Most likely; he's not likely to have been asked into any study in the Remove!"

"Well, I don't want to tea with him in Hall," said Bunter. "He can have all the doorsteps and dishwater! I say, you fellows, I'll tea with you, if you like, though Wilmot isn't here."

"We don't like!" Wharton pointed out.

"He, he, he!"

Billy Bunter decided to take that remark as a joke. He rolled into the study.

Having been disappointed once more about his celebrated postal order, which had caused him so many disappointments, Billy Bunter had to bag a tea somewhere. Toddy of Study No. 7 was teaing out, and when Toddy tea'd out, there was nothing for Bunter in Study No. 7.

"I'll make some more toast, old chap!" he said. "All right, I'll slice the loaf; don't you take any trouble! I hope you've got plenty of butter—I like it on thick! I say, got any jam?"

"No!"

"Measly sort of tea to ask a fellow to——"

"Anybody asked you?"

"I mean, I don't care much for jam—it's not much I eat, as you know, at any time. Any marmalade?"

"No!"

"Well, look here, Ogilvy's got a jar of marmalade. I saw it in his study. One of you cut along and bag it, while I make the toast!"

The chums of Study No. 1 seemed deaf to that suggestion. Bunter did not act on it himself. He did not want to be the fellow responsible, when Robert Donald Ogilvy inquired later what had become of his marmalade!

He proceeded to make toast—a mountain of it! Wharton patiently buttered the mountain. Frank Nugent dished up five poached eggs—and added one more, for the additional guest. Bunter blinked at the dish.

"Good!" he said. "But aren't you fellows having any?"

"We are!" said Harry Wharton grimly. "Five of us are having one each. Shut up!"

"I think you fellows are silly asses to row with Wilmot," said Bunter crossly. "He's got lots of money!"

"Do you think we want his money, you fat tick?"

"Well, it comes in useful at tea-time," said Bunter. "You might think of me! But you fellows always were selfish! That's why I changed out of this study—I never could stand selfishness! Not that Toddy's much better, in Study No. 7. He's gone out to tea to-day, and never even asked me whether I was fixed up for tea! Selfishness all round! I wonder sometimes that I don't grow selfish myself."

"Oh crikey!"

There was a tramp of feet, and Bob Cherry, Johnny Bull, and Hurree Jamset Ram Singh came in. Wharton and Nugent gave them welcoming grins—Bunter an uneasy blink. There seemed to be only poached eggs and toast for tea—and not too much of that! In these circumstances, Bunter would have been satisfied with a smaller party.

"Hallo, hallo, hallo!" roared Bob. "Here you are!"

He slammed a pot of jam on the table. It was customary, on such occasions, for contributions to be made from all quarters.

"Oh good!" said Bunter. "I say, you fellows, I'll stand a pot of marmalade! You don't mind if I do, Wharton?"

"Not at all!"

"Lend me eighteenpence, then——"

"Eh!"

"And you cut down to the shop for me, Bob——"

"Ha, ha, ha!"

"Blessed if I see anything to cackle at! Look here, are we having that marmalade, or not?" hooted Bunter.

"Not!"

"If Wilmot were here, he'd lend me eighteenpence——"

"Go and look for him!" suggested Wharton.

"I wish you fellows wouldn't row with him! Look at the way you were dragging him about yesterday!" said Bunter. "You can't expect him to tea with you in the study after that."

"He gave up teaing in the study before that!" said Frank Nugent. "And I've a jolly strong suspicion that he did it because you came to tea so often, Bunter!"

"Oh, really, Nugent——"

"Not much doubt about that," said Harry. "It was plain enough—though why he didn't kick Bunter out, I don't know! Nobody here would have stopped him, I know that."

"Oh, really, Wharton——"

"It's pretty queer," said Johnny Bull, as the juniors sat down to tea. "Wilmot's made no friends here, and doesn't seem to want to, and the only chap he's ever civil to is Bunter—a chap that nobody else will touch with a ten-foot pole!"

"Beast!"

"The queerfulness is terrific!" remarked Hurree Jamset Ram Singh. "But the esteemed Wilmot is preposterously queer in many ways."

"Not such a worm as he makes out, though," said Bob. "He won't have Hacker butting in and making a beak's favourite of him."

"Hacker's a tactless ass!" remarked Nugent. "I suppose he ought to be attached to the chap, being his uncle, but he ought to know that a fellow's better left alone to find his own level."

"He can't know a lot about him," said Bob. "Hobby told us that he said Wilmot was a great gun at footer, at his last school. Well, the man can't play for toffee, or cakes!"

"He, he, he!" came from Billy Bunter. "Lot you know about it!"

"Perhaps you know more about footer than I do, you fat, frowsting, frowsy foozler?" hooted Bob, glaring at the Owl of the Remove across the table.

"Perhaps I do!" grinned Bunter. "I know that Wilmot could jolly well play your head off, if he liked."

"And how do you know that, Bunter?" asked Wharton.

"That's telling!" grinned Bunter.

Bunter's conversation, as a rule, did not get very attentive hearers. But now all the juniors at the tea-table in Study No. 1 looked very attentively at William George Bunter.

Nobody in the Remove knew anything about Wilmot, except that he had been to school before he came to Greyfriars. He never mentioned the name of his former school; but that caused no remark, for he never mentioned anything in connection with himself. Hardly ever, in fact, spoke at all, unless he was spoken to first, and his sulky face did not encourage fellows to press conversation on him.

But some of the fellows had an impression that Bunter knew something about him, though how, they could not guess.

It was singular that a fellow who was not only unfriendly, but actually uncivil, should be civil to Bunter, and Bunter alone, in all the Form.

But that was the curious state of affairs, and during Eric Wilmot's first few days in the school Bunter had dropped in to tea with him, in Study No. 1, as regularly as clockwork.

Which Wharton and Nugent suspected to be the chief reason why the new man had taken to teaing in Hall. Though why he should tolerate Bunter, if he did not want to, was rather a mystery.

"Look here, you fat ass!" said Harry abruptly. "When Wilmot first came here you told a lot of fellows you knew him."

"So I did," said Bunter. "I hope you don't doubt my word, Wharton!"

"You said afterwards that you didn't know him—that he was quite another chap."

"Oh! Yes; so he was!"

"So you knew him, and didn't know him, both! Is that it?" asked Bob, staring at the fat Owl.

"Yes, that's it. I mean, no, that's not it. What I mean is, if you fellows think you're going to pump me about Wilmot you can have another guess," said Bunter. "I'm not letting anything out."

"We don't want to hear anything about the fellow," said Wharton, with a curl of the lip. "Whatever it is, you can keep it to yourself."

"I'm going to," said Bunter. "You see, I told Wilmot I would, and I'm a fellow of my word. Not that there's anything, you know! Absolutely nothing at all! I say, is there any cake?"

"No."

"Pretty measly spread! Wilmot would have stood something better than this if you fellows hadn't edged him out of the study with your bad manners. I think you might be decent to a friend of mine, after all I've done for you. Wilmot always had a cake when I came."

"So will we, when we want you to keep secrets for us!" said Wharton sarcastically.

"Oh, really, Wharton——"

"Well, whatever Bunter knows about the chap, he can't know that he's a footballer!" said Bob. "Look at the way he fooled about yesterday! Of all the fumbling, foozling duds I ever saw, he——"

"He, he, he!"

"Did you ever see him play footer, you cackling fathead?" roared Bob.

"Yes, I jolly well did!" retorted Bunter, "and I saw him score goals, one after another. And I'd like to see any of you do it!"

"What was he playing? An infants' school?" asked Bob.

"No, he wasn't. He was playing——" Bunter broke off suddenly.

"Well, who?"

"Oh, nobody!" said Bunter.

That answer was so surprising that it caused the Famous Five to concentrate stares on the fat Owl again.

"Is that podgy ass potty?" asked Johnny Bull.

"I can jolly well tell you he was playing men who've beaten you more than once!" yapped Bunter.

"Men who've beaten us!" repeated Wharton blankly. "Well, every team we play has won sometimes, of course!"

"Not often," grinned Bob, "but sometimes."

"Do you mean that you've seen him playing a team that plays the Remove?" exclaimed Wharton. "Where and when?"

"That's telling!" chuckled Bunter.

"And why can't you tell us, fathead?" demanded Wharton. "If he was playing any team that we meet he must have been playing for some school. Is there any secret about that, you blithering ass?"

"Yes, rather! I mean, no," amended Bunter. "I know nothing whatever about the chap, as I've told you. If you think I knew him the day he came here, and that he asked me to keep it dark, you're simply mistaken. I've never seen him before, and never seen him play football, especially at any school anywhere near Greyfriars. I say, if there isn't any cake I may as well go—I mean. I want to go to see what's become of old Wilmot."

Bunter rolled to the door.

"All the same," he added, before he went, "he's a topping footballer, and he could play your silly heads off if he jolly well liked. You should have seen him bagging those goals!"

With that, the fat Owl of the Remove rolled away. He left the Famous Five in blank astonishment. Evidently, Bunter did know something about Wilmot, and what he knew appeared to be to the fellow's credit. Yet it seemed that Wilmot had made him keep what he knew a secret. It was all very mysterious.

THE FOURTH CHAPTER.

Smithy Off The Deep End!

HERBERT VERNON-SMITH came into his study—No. 4—in the Remove, and slammed the door, with a slam that woke every echo of the Remove passage.

Tom Redwing, who was jamming the kettle on the fire in the grate, jumped, and uttered an exclamation as a spurt of water from the spout went up his sleeve. He stared round at Smithy.

"What the dickens——"

He left it at that. The black look on the Bounder's face showed that he was in one of his savage tempers—as, indeed, that angry slam of the door indicated. Tom mopped his sleeve with his handkerchief, in silence. The Bounder gave him an angry stare. When Smithy was out of temper he was liable to quarrel with anyone, friend or foe.

"I'm not standin' it!" he growled.

"Anything up?" asked Tom mildly.

THE MAGNET LIBRARY.—No. 1,458.

"You know what's up, as well as I do!"

Tom made no reply to that. Chumming with the Bounder was a matter that required patience.

Smithy waited for him to speak, with the obvious intention of taking whatever he said as an offence. As Redwing said nothing, the Bounder went on:

"I've just seen Wharton about the footer."

"Yes?" said Tom.

"He's going over the men for the Rookwood match. I'm left out."

"Yes," said Tom again.

"Nothing to say?" jeered the Bounder. "I suppose you're taking the side of that cheeky cad?"

"I shouldn't call Wharton names like that, Smithy," said Tom gravely. "And I'm taking his side no more than you are yourself."

"What do you mean by that, you fool?"

"I mean what I say, Smithy. You're off colour this term. You've played rotten football every time, and if you were skipper you wouldn't play a dud against Rookwood."

"So I'm a dud?"

"Just at present—yes," said Tom. "You're the best man in the team, as a rule—ahead of Wharton himself, in my opinion. But you're badly off your form now, and it's partly your own fault. What's the good of pretending you don't know it? You know it better than I do!"

Vernon-Smith gave his chum a glare and tramped restlessly about the study, his hands driven into his trousers pockets. He did know that he was badly off his form that term, and he did know that it was partly his own fault. But that made his exclusion from the Remove no more palatable to him.

"It's not as if the fellow had a big basket to pick from!" he snarled. "I own up that I'm not much class at the moment. But who's he got to stick in my place? That milksop, Nugent——"

"Nugent's not a milksop. I wish you had some of his good temper and his good nature!" said Tom. "He's a good man at the game. Nothing like your class when you're good, but ever so much better than you are now."

"Rubbish!"

"If you can't see that, Smithy——"

"Well, I can't!"

"There's none so blind as those that won't see!" said Tom. "Everybody else in the Remove can see it."

"Don't talk rot!"

"Well, I'd better not talk at all! Let's have tea!"

"Hang tea!"

Smithy, evidently, was not in a reasonable mood. He was sore and savage, and some barbed sympathy from Skinner had made him feel worse.

"Look at the rotten game Nugent played the other day!" he resumed. "The Remove were licked by Hobby and his crew of the Shell. It couldn't have been worse if I'd played."

"It wouldn't have been better!"

"Wharton's up against me this term!" said the Bounder. "It's happened before, and now it's happening again. After we were all so jolly friendly in the Christmas holidays he's started the old trouble over again."

"Bosh!"

"You know it's so!" snarled the Bounder.

"I know it isn't! Wharton's been as disappointed as you yourself by your rotten form this term. It's a blow to him."

"He's looking out for a chance to score over me. I know he was thinking

THE MAGNET LIBRARY.—No. 1,458.

of that new man, Wilmot, to stick in my place. He can't get away with that, as the fellow's turned out such an absolute dud. But a lot of fellows know he was thinking of it."

"Quite naturally, too! Hobson of the Shell said that the chap was a tremendous footballer—he had it from Hacker, and Hacker ought to know whether his nephew can play Soccer or not. It's turned out that he can't—but Wharton thought he could, till he saw him play."

"Oh, you've got an answer to everything, of course!" sneered the Bounder.

"Wharton's right and I'm wrong—speech may be taken as read! Don't let's argue about it, or I shall be punching your head next! Let's have tea."

Smithy flung open the cupboard door with a crash. Then he gave an angry yelp:

"Where's the cake?"

"Isn't it there?"

"No, it isn't! That fat freak Bunter again, I suppose! By gum, I'll teach that frowsy frump a lesson about grub-raiding in my study!"

Tom glanced into the study cupboard. There had been a handsome cake among the other supplies for tea—Smithy's study was always well supplied. It was no longer to be seen.

Smithy, with gleaming eyes, made for the door. In his present mood he needed only a pretext for "rowing" with somebody. Now he had one—and quite a good one.

"Hold on, Smithy!" said Tom hastily. "There's no proof——"

"I don't want any! Is there any man in the Remove who pinches a fellow's tuck except Bunter?"

"Well, no; but——"

"Oh, shut up!"

Vernon-Smith tramped out of the study, and the door closed with another slam that rang along the Remove passage. He tramped along to Study No. 7, and stared into that study. Peter Todd and Tom Dutton were at tea there, but Billy Bunter, the third member of the study was not visible.

"Where's Bunter?" snapped the Bounder.

"Not knowing, can't say!" answered Peter affably. "If you want to catch Bunter——"

"Well, I do!"

"Make a noise like a jam tart!" suggested Peter. "That will fetch him!"

"You silly idiot!"

"Thanks! Same to you, and many of them!"

"Do you know where Bunter is, Dutton?" roared Vernon-Smith. It was necessary to put on a little steam in speaking to Dutton, who was deaf.

Dutton looked up.

"Eh?" he said. "Did you speak to me?"

"Yes, I did, you deaf dummy! Where's Bunter?"

"Grunter yourself!" retorted Dutton.

"Who's grunting?"

"Ha, ha, ha!" roared Toddy.

"You deaf dunderhead!" hooted Smithy. "Do you know where Bunter is? Have you seen that fat owl?"

"Well, the way Bunter grunts is rather foul, I dare say; but if you're making out that I grunt like Bunter I——"

Slam!

Another terrific slam rang along the passage. Questioning Dutton was rather too slow a process for Smithy in his present mood. He slammed the door and departed.

"Seen Bunter?" he yapped, as he passed Study No. 1, where the Famous Five were talking in the doorway after tea.

The Famous Five were discussing what was, just then, a rather burning question in the Remove—making up the eleven for the match with Rookwood School. Smithy, on his way to his study, had stopped to ask the captain of the Remove whether his name was going up. He had received a brief reply in the negative.

So none of the juniors was surprised to see him in the worst of tempers at the present moment. But they were rather surprised to see that the object of his wrath was Bunter. Billy Bunter had nothing to do with football.

"Can't you answer?" snapped the Bounder, without having given any of the five time to speak.

"Well, a fellow might try if you'd give him time to open his mouth, Smithy!" said Bob Cherry cheerfully. "We've seen Bunter—too much of him, in fact!"

"The too-muchfulness was terrific!" remarked Hurree Jamset Ram Singh, with a nod of his dusky head.

"Where did you see him?" snarled the Bounder.

"In this study!" answered Wharton.

Vernon-Smith shoved roughly through the Co. and tramped into Study No. 1.

Johnny Bull gave a growl.

"Better manners, please!" he said.

"He's not here!" snarled the Bounder, after one glare round the study. "What do you mean by saying he was here, Wharton?"

"I meant exactly what I said!" answered the captain of the Remove coolly.

"He's not here."

"Naturally, as it's nearly half an hour since he tea'd with us."

Vernon-Smith breathed hard and tramped out into the passage again. The Famous Five regarded him with cool equanimity. The Bounder's fierce temper had no terrors for those cheery youths.

"Do you know where he is now?" hissed Smithy.

"He said he was going to look for Wilmot! That's the latest news of W. G. B.," said Bob affably. "Further details may be found in the Stop Press columns of our later editions——"

"You silly idiot!"

"What I like about Smithy," said Bob to his friends, "is the polished courtesy of his manners! Such graceful politeness——"

"Ha, ha, ha!"

Herbert Vernon-Smith tramped away to the Remove staircase, leaving the Famous Five laughing.

THE FIFTH CHAPTER.

Backing Up Bunter!

"WILMOT, old chap!"

Billy Bunter had found his "pal."

Eric Wilmot was in the Rag. Some other fellows were there after tea, but Wilmot was not with them. He stood looking out of the window into the quad. In the quadrangle his uncle, Hacker, could be seen in conversation with his Form-master, Quelch. Wilmot's eyes were on them—perhaps he was wondering whether he was the subject of the talk between the two masters. A dark and gloomy frown was on his handsome face.

Nobody else in the room was near him, or taking any notice of him. The new fellow was so sulky and unsociable that the Removites had very soon fallen into the way of leaving him to himself.

He seemed to ask nothing better. And he looked far from pleased when Bunter rolled up and joined him at the window.

Billy Bunter was busy making toast, when Frank Nugent dished up the poached eggs. "Good !" said the fat junior, blinking at the dish. "But aren't you fellows having poached eggs ? " "We are," said Harry Wharton grimly. "Five of us are having one each. Shut up ! " "Oh crikey ! " ejaculated Bunter.

He compressed his lips as he glanced round at the fat Owl.

"I've been looking for you, old fellow !" said Bunter with fat affability.

"Oh !"

"Did you tea in Hall?"

"Yes."

"I was going to ask you to tea in my study."

"Thanks."

The new fellow's manner was so exceedingly dry that even Bunter could not imagine that he was feeling friendly or cordial.

But the fat Owl did not seem to mind. Anything short of a kick was good enough for Bunter.

"Why don't you tea in your own study, old chap?" he asked.

"I don't care to."

"Why not?"

No answer.

"You don't pull with the fellows there," said Bunter. "But I'd always come, old bean ! You could always have my company."

Wilmot looked from the window again. Even Bunter felt a little damped. He did not need his big spectacles to enable him to see that the new fellow wanted to be left alone.

"I dropped in, but you weren't there !" went on Bunter. "The fellows were talking about you."

Wilmot reddened slightly, but did not speak.

"I never let anything out," added Bunter reassuringly. "You rely on me, old chap ! I said I wouldn't, and I won't."

Wilmot breathed hard. He had his own reasons for desiring Bunter to be silent about what he knew. But it was sheer torture to him to be under any sort of obligation to a fellow like Bunter. An obligation of any sort was

irksome to him—with Bunter, it was more than irksome.

"They think you can't play footer !" went on Bunter, with a grin. "I told them you could play their heads off, if you liked. He, he, he !"

"Oh, rot !"

"It isn't rot, old chap ! You could ! I've seen you play, haven't I ?" said Bunter. "That day at St. Jude's, when you played in the team from Topham."

Wilmot cast a hasty glance round, the flush mounting in his cheeks. But no one was near enough to hear.

"Don't talk about that, Bunter !" he muttered.

"Oh, that's all right—I'm not letting anything out," said the fat Owl. "I say, though, you're a bit of an ass, Wilmot, if you don't mind a friend saying so. Wharton would jump at getting you into the eleven if he knew how you play Soccer. Lots of fellows would be glad."

"Very likely."

"Well, why don't you ?"

"That's my business."

"Well, don't be shirty, old chap !" said Bunter. "I don't see why you shouldn't play for the Form, when every other chap would jump at the chance. Wharton would make you, if he knew !"

"Oh, rot !"

"He came jolly near knowing, too !" chuckled Bunter. "Did I ever tell you how I came to be at St. Jude's the day you played there for Topham ?"

"I don't want to know."

"Oh, I'll tell you, old chap ! You see, Wharton and his crowd were going over to see the match on bikes. I started later, and took a taxi. That ass, Cherry, was held up by a puncture, and they never got to St. Jude's at all. He, he, he ! But for that, they'd all have seen you there."

"Oh !" gasped Wilmot.

"Of course, I never knew, then, that you were old Hacker's nephew—never knew Hacker had a nephew at all. I can tell you, I was surprised, the day you came, and I saw you. You've never told me why you left Topham and came here."

Wilmot's handsome face crimsoned, and he turned it away from Bunter.

"Nor why you don't want the fellows to know you were at Topham," pursued Bunter. "Why don't you, old chap ?"

No answer.

"I mean, a chap who's played footer for his school the way you did, would generally swank about it a bit," said Bunter. "I can't see any reason for keeping it dark. I shouldn't."

Wilmot did not speak. It was quite a one-sided conversation. But Billy Bunter did not mind that. He was always prepared to take on more than his fair share of the talking.

"You've never told me what happened that day at St. Jude's, either," he remarked.

Wilmot started violently.

"What do you mean?" he breathed.

"Well, I know something happened," argued Bunter. "You got no end of cheers, the way you played in the match; and afterwards, you came away by yourself, looking awfully sick. Hardly knew you for the same chap, you looked so different. Did you have a row with your friends after the game?"

Bunter paused for a reply, but he did not get one. He rattled on cheerfully.

"And then you suddenly left Topham. You were a Topham chap one week, and a Greyfriars chap the next. It's rather unusual, you know. I mean, you must have gone back to Topham for the new term, or you wouldn't have been playing for them. Then, in the second week of the term you leave, and go to another school. Never knew anything like that before."

Wilmot looked at Bunter searchingly. But there was no suspicion—only fatuous curiosity—in the Owl's podgy face.

Bunter was puzzled, and, as usual, inquisitive. But it had not crossed his fat mind that Wilmot might have had to leave his school for reasons he would not care, or dare, to make known at his new school.

After that searching stare, Eric Wilmot turned his glum gaze on the window again. Friendliness f r o m Bunter was little short of torture to him; but he was glad, at least, that the fellow who knew about him was the most obtuse ass at Greyfriars.

"Still, I'm glad you came here, old top!" went on Bunter. "I like you, you know! Still, I wish you'd tea in your study, as you did at first. I rather miss you there, old chap."

The door of the Rag was flung roughly open, and three or four fellows looked round as the Bounder tramped in.

Some of them grinned.

Displays of temper were not considered the thing at Greyfriars. A fellow who had a jolt was expected to bite on the bullet, as it were, and keep smiling. Smithy was a fellow to do things that were "not done"—which was one reason why he had been given his nickname. Plainly, he was in a very bad temper now; and nobody doubted that it was because his name was missing from the football list for the match at Rookwood.

"Bunter here?" he rapped out.

"I believe so," drawled Skinner. "What's jolly old Bunter done?"

"Bunter didn't drop you out of the eleven, Smithy!" remarked Hazeldene. And the fellows round the fire laughed.

Smithy gave Hazel an evil look. Then, staring round, he spotted Bunter at the window with Wilmot, and strode across to him.

Bunter was blinking round through his big spectacles. He seemed rather alarmed by the sight of the Bounder, in a towering temper. No doubt he had his reasons. As Smithy strode at him, with obviously hostile intentions, the fat Owl dodged round Eric Wilmot.

"I say, Smithy, you keep off!" he exclaimed. "I never had it!"

"You never had what?" hissed Smithy.

"Oh! Nothing! I haven't been in your study at all! I say—— Yaroooh!" roared Bunter, as the angry Bounder grabbed him. "Ow! Leggo! If you kick me, you beast, I'll—— Yoo-hoop! I say, draggimoff! Rescue! I say, Wilmot, back me up! I say, pull him off!"

Eric Wilmot stared at the scene. The other fellows in the Rag were laughing. Bunter yelled wildly in the Bounder's angry grasp. Wilmot hesitated a moment, then he stepped towards the two, and laid a hand on Smithy's arm.

"Chuck that!" he said quietly.

In sheer surprise, Vernon-Smith stared at him. In the week or so that Eric Wilmot had been at Greyfriars Smithy had hardly exchanged a dozen words with him. He had nothing to do with him, and wanted none. He looked on him as a sulky ass, and let it go at that. He was taken quite by surprise by the new fellow barging in like this.

THE MAGNET LIBRARY.—No. 1,458.

"You cheeky ass!" he panted. "Take your paw off my arm!"

"Well, let Bunter alone!"

"I'll please myself about that! If you want to know, the fat rotter's pinched a cake from my study, and I'm going to boot him for it!"

"I haven't!" yelled Bunter. "Leggo! Make him leggo, Wilmot!"

Vernon-Smith jerked his arm away from Wilmot, and pushed the new junior roughly back. Then, grasping Bunter with both hands, he spun him round, preparatory to booting him. Bunter yelled in dire anticipation.

But the boot did not land. Wilmot, with a flash in his eyes, grasped the Bounder by the shoulders and dragged him back. Smithy, already delivering the kick, had a foot in the air; and, standing on one leg, he overbalanced as he was dragged back. He sat down on the floor, with a gasping howl and a heavy bump.

Bunter jerked away, spluttering.

Smithy sat panting. Wilmot stood looking at him. And from the group of juniors at the fire came a loud laugh.

"Ha, ha, ha!"

THE SIXTH CHAPTER.

A Row in the Rag!

HARRY WHARTON & CO. came into the Rag. They had, in point of fact, followed the Bounder down, with the idea—quite well founded—that the fat and fatuous Owl of the Remove might require some protection if Smithy found him. That Bunter had asked for a booting was very probable; but Smithy looked in a mood to exceed the limit.

They stared as they came in—at the sight of Vernon-Smith sitting on the floor, gasping, and the other fellows in the room laughing. As they stared, Smithy leaped to his feet, rather like a jack-in-the-box, and hurled himself at Eric Wilmot.

"Hallo, hallo, hallo!" ejaculated Bob Cherry. "What——"

"Hold on, Smithy!" exclaimed Wharton hastily.

Smithy neither heeded nor even heard. He was attacking Wilmot with right and left, his eyes blazing with fury; and the new fellow was backing away, with his hands up in defence.

He backed—but it was clearly not from fear of anything that the Bounder could do, for his face was perfectly calm, and a faint smile of contemptuous amusement flickered on it. As plainly as looks could speak, the new junior was expressing his disdain for a fellow who could not keep his temper.

It was clear, too, that he was a good boxer. He had to give ground before the fierce attack, but his guard was perfect, and not one of the Bounder's furious blows reached his cool, disdainful face.

Wharton ran hastily between them.

"Hold on, Smithy!" he repeated.

"Stand aside, you fool!" panted the Bounder. "I'll knock you spinning if you meddle here!"

Wilmot dropped his hands as the captain of the Remove interposed. The Bounder, mad with rage, struck at Wharton.

Harry knocked the blow aside, and gave Smithy a push on the chest that sent him back. He would have rebounded in a second, but the whole Co. pushed between him and his adversary.

"Easy does it, old bean!" said Bob Cherry soothingly.

"Will you get out of the way?"

shrieked the Bounder. "I'll knock you out of it if you don't!"

"Go it!" grunted Johnny Bull. "If you can handle five fellows at once, Smithy, I'll be interested to see you do it!"

"The interest will be terrific, my esteemed and absurd Smithy!" grinned the Nabob of Bhanipur.

Smithy stood panting. He was in a mood to hurl himself at the Famous Five, hitting out right and left. Still, that would have effected no purpose, and it was Wilmot he wanted to handle.

"What are you meddling for, you meddlin' fools?" he panted. "Have you taken that cad under your wing? Has he asked you to protect him?"

"I don't see why you fellows are barging in," said Wilmot in a cool, drawling voice. "Why not let the fellow get on with it? I suppose you're not under the delusion that I need any protection?"

"You can hold your cheeky tongue!" snapped Wharton. "I dare say you've asked for a thrashing; you've asked for it in my study a dozen times! But we do things according to rule here. Bare knuckles are barred."

"The barfulness is preposterous, my worthy, sulky Wilmot."

Wilmot shrugged his shoulders.

"If you're going to scrap with the fellow, Smithy——"

"I am!" snarled Smithy.

"Then put the gloves on! Neither of you wants to turn up in Form to-morrow looking like a battered prizefighter, I suppose?"

"I don't care!"

"Nor I!" said Wilmot.

"Well, whether you care or not, you'll toe the line here!" said the captain of the Remove sharply. "I don't know where you've come from, Wilmot, but it was clearly a school where cheeky cads weren't booted enough! You'll put on the gloves, or you'll go over that table and take six with a fives bat!"

"Do you happen to be a prefect, or have they made you headmaster by any chance?" asked Wilmot.

"I happen to be captain of the Form, and that's enough for you! I'm not stopping Smithy; I hope he'll give you the thrashing of your life for your cheek!" said Wharton savagely. "Get the gloves out, Franky!"

Vernon-Smith cooled down a little. He realised that the sympathy of the Famous Five was on his side. They did not know what the quarrel was about as yet; but the disdainful smile on Wilmot's handsome face irritated them almost as much as it enraged the Bounder. Wharton was strongly tempted to wipe it off with a smack.

Nugent brought the gloves, and Skinner hastily closed the door of the Rag. Masters or prefects were not wanted to look in just then. Smithy threw off his jacket and put on the gloves, with a black and bitter face.

"Keep cool, Smithy!" said Harry in a low voice. "That chap is no dud; and if you lose your temper, you're asking for it!"

Vernon-Smith gave a curt nod.

"But what's the row about?" asked Bob Cherry.

"That cheeky rotter laid hands on me!" said the Bounder, between his teeth.

"I say, you fellows——"

"Shut up, Bunter!"

"I say, my pal Wilmot stopped that beast pitching into me!" exclaimed Billy Bunter indignantly. "And if Wilmot doesn't lick him, I jolly well will, so there!"

"Oh!" exclaimed Harry Wharton, rather taken aback. "Is that it? Smithy, you hot-headed ass——"

"Oh, shut up!" snapped the Bounder. "Is that cad ready? I'm not waiting long!"

"Ready when you are!" drawled Wilmot.

Something of the sulky sullenness was gone from the new fellow's face now, and he looked quite keen. The excitement of a row and a scrap seemed to have roused him from his gloomy mood.

"Better take your jacket off," said Bob.

"Not worth the trouble!"

Bob compressed his lips. If this fellow—a nobody from nowhere, as it were—fancied that he could beat one of the heftiest fighting men in the Remove without an effort, Bob could not help hoping that he would find out that he had made a mistake.

"Swank!" grunted Johnny Bull.

Wilmot's lip curled, but he gave no other sign of having heard that remark.

Wharton was looking worried. Having come down to the Rag himself to see that the angry Bounder did not handle Bunter too severely, he found that the new man had forestalled him. This row was on because Wilmot had intervened to protect Bunter—as Wharton had intended to do. It was disconcerting and exasperating to find that a fellow he disliked was in the right.

"Look here, Smithy, you'd better wash this out!" said Harry abruptly. "If you were pitching into Bunter——"

"No bizney of yours!"

"I came down to stop you!" snapped Wharton.

"If you had, you'd have had a scrap on your hands instead of that new tick!" retorted the Bounder.

"You cheeky ass——"

"You've jawed enough! Get out of the way!"

"Oh, go ahead!" exclaimed Wharton angrily. "You're a pair of ill-tempered rotters, and it may do you good to hammer one another!"

"Hear, hear!" grinned Bob. "Six of one and half a dozen of the other! Let them rip, and be blowed to them both!"

"You keep time, Mauly."

"Pleased!" drawled Lord Mauleverer, slowly uncoiling his lazy form from an armchair. "Ready? Shakin' hands? I gather not! Time!"

The word was hardly uttered before the Bounder was springing forward hitting out. Eric Wilmot's hands flashed up, and he met the attack coolly and steadily. His handsome face was keen and alert; his dark eyes gleaming. He gave ground, backing before the fierce attack. But suddenly he stopped, side-stepping a fierce rush, and closed in, hitting out. Right and left crashed on the Bounder, almost lifting him from the floor, and Vernon-Smith went sprawling helplessly and crashed.

"Man down!" said Hazel, with a whistle.

"He, he, he!" came from Billy Bunter. "I say, you fellows, Smithy's done! He, he, he!"

"Shut up, you fat Owl!" growled Johnny Bull.

"He, he, he!"

Bob Cherry picked the Bounder up. Lord Mauleverer called "Time!" and Smithy sank, almost dazedly, on a chair. Wilmot, looking very handsome with a flush in his cheeks and as disdainful as ever, stood and waited.

THE SEVENTH CHAPTER.
Grateful Bunter!

BILLY BUNTER grinned, rejoicing in the victory of his champion.

Bunter had no doubt that the Bounder was "done." But Bunter, as usual, was an ass; the Bounder was not done—he was very far from done. He was hard hit, but hard hitting only roused his fierce and desperate temper. Smithy was the man to fight till he fell, and he was very far from that as yet.

When Lord Mauleverer called "Time!" again, the Bounder leaped up actively. He was a little dizzy, but as determined as ever—or more so. A breathless circle of juniors watched the second round.

It was not uncommon for the Bounder's unreliable temper to lead him into a row, and he always gave a good account of himself. Every man in the Remove knew what a tough nut he was to crack. Of Wilmot nothing was known, except that he was a sulky ass and a dud at footer. But Eric Wilmot was getting special attention now. Whether he could play football or not, it was clear that he could box, and that he was no funk. But nobody except Bunter hoped that he would get the upper hand. His disdainful look put many backs up as well as Wharton's.

Smithy did better in the second round, to the general satisfaction. He kept his temper better in control, which helped him, and he understood now that he was dealing with a fellow up to his weight, which was another help. There were some lively exchanges in that round, and at the end of it Wilmot's handsome, well-shaped nose was red and rather raw, and did not look so handsome. Even with the gloves on, hard punches did damage, and it was lucky for both that they had not been allowed to scrap with bare knuckles.

"Time!"

There was another minute's rest. In that interval Wilmot threw off his jacket. No doubt he, like the Bounder, realised by that time that he was not handling an easy proposition.

Third round was hard and fast. Punishment was given and taken, and all the Remove knew that Smithy was the man to take punishment without turning a hair. But Wilmot seemed able to take it as equably. One of his eyes was winking after that round, and his nose looked less handsome than ever.

In the fourth round, however, fortune visibly swayed in favour of the new fellow. Vernon-Smith, attacking hotly, received a jolt on the jaw that spun him over, and he landed with a heavy bump.

Lord Mauleverer glanced at him, as he lay, and began to count.

"One—two—three——"

Smithy, dazed and dizzy, made a frantic attempt to rise. But he dropped back on his elbow.

"Four—five—six——"

The Bounder got on his knees.

"Seven—eight——"

"Why not chuck it?" broke in Wilmot's cool voice. "I'm satisfied, if you are, Smith—if that's your name! Let's call it a day!"

Harry Wharton gave the new fellow a curious look. He knew quite well that Wilmot made that suggestion because he had the upper hand, and was willing to let the Bounder off the humiliation of a defeat. It showed a generous impulse in the fellow who was regarded as a sullen, sulky ass in the Remove.

"You're interruptin' me, Wilmot!" said Lord Mauleverer. "Eight—nine——"

Vernon-Smith scrambled up somehow.

"Come on!" he breathed.

He knew that he would have been counted out, but for Wilmot's interruption. He knew that the fellow was willing to spare him—and both circumstances added to his bitterness.

He had called the Bounder "Smith." Possibly, knowing and caring so little about fellows in his Form, he did not know that Smithy's name was Vernon-Smith. But to the Bounder it seemed one more sample of his insolence—in keeping with the disdainful smile on his face. In a white fury, the Bounder scrambled at him, attacking savagely.

Wilmot stalled him off. Every fellow there saw that he could have knocked Smithy out, for the dizzy Bounder could hardly keep his legs. But he contented himself with a lazy defence, till Mauly called time again.

Redwing came quietly into the Rag. By that time news that something was "on" was spreading, and the door had

(*Continued on next page.*)

opened and shut several times. Tom Redwing hurried at once to his chum.

"Smithy!" he muttered.

The Bounder sat gasping.

"I'll beat that cur yet!" he muttered hoarsely.

Redwing fanned his blazing face. Lord Mauleverer looked at his watch.

"Time!"

The effort the Bounder made to toe the line was visible to all eyes. But he made it and stood up to his adversary.

"You won't call it a draw?" asked Wilmot.

"Shut up, you cad!" hissed the Bounder.

And he followed up the words with a blow.

That blow was easily warded. The Bounder strove hard to get through his enemy's defence, but in vain. Then, as he slowed down, almost exhausted, Wilmot came on, his hands flashing like lightning, so swift were his blows.

Thud, thud, thud!

The gloves came on the hapless Bounder, and he went headlong.

"Time!"

Tom helped his chum to a chair. The Bounder fell on it. One of his eyes was closed; the other blinked dizzily. It was plain to all now that the Bounder was beaten—plain to all, but Smithy!

When Mauly called time again, he dragged himself up.

Redwing caught hold of his arm.

"You can't go on, Smithy!" he whispered.

"Shut up, you fool!"

Smithy tottered into the ring.

"Smithy, old man!" exclaimed Harry Wharton anxiously.

The Bounder did not heed. Almost blindly he barged towards the cool, steady, Wilmot, punching. Wilmot did not punch in return. He put out a hand and pushed the Bounder, and Smithy sat down on the floor with a bump.

There was a chortle from Billy Bunter, and some of the other fellows grinned.

Redwing helped his chum out of the ring. Even the Bounder realised now that he would be only making himself ridiculous by going on. He sat and panted for breath.

Wilmot put on his jacket. He did not glance at the sea of faces round him. Not a fellow there, except Bunter, was glad to see him win. But it was clear that he cared nothing for what the Remove thought or felt. He walked away quite steadily to the door, and went out of the Rag.

"I say, you fellows, Smithy's whopped!" grinned Billy Bunter. "I say—— Yaroooh! Leave off kicking me, you beast!"

Instead of leaving off, Bob Cherry continued

Billy Bunter cut for the door and scooted out of the Rag.

Eric Wilmot had gone up to the Remove passage. Under the tap at the end of that passage he bathed his face. He looked in the glass, and shrugged his shoulders at the sight of the bruises that marred his good looks. He had won the scrap; but he bore a good many signs of it—signs that were not likely to fade out for some time.

He went back down the passage to Study No. 1. Wharton and Nugent were still downstairs, so he expected to find his study empty. But it was not empty. Billy Bunter was there—and, to Wilmot's surprise, a large cake lay

on the study table. Bunter had already started on it.

Bunter grinned at him affably.

"Have some, old chap?" he said.

Wilmot shook his head.

"I say it's a jolly good cake! Smithy always has jolly good cakes!" said the fat Owl, with his mouth full.

Wilmot started.

"Who—what?" he exclaimed.

"Not that this is Smithy's cake, of course," said Bunter hastily. "I got this cake from Bunter Court—it came to-day. Have some?"

Wilmot looked at him.

"Suspicious beast, you know, making out that a fellow snaffled his cake!" said Bunter. "As if I'd touch a fellow's tuck! I'm above it, I hope! I say, old chap, have some! I've brought it here to whack out with you, because you stood by me, you know! Smithy can't make a fuss about it now—now you've whopped him! He, he, he!"

"Smithy!" repeated Wilmot.

"Not that it's his cake, you know! I know nothing whatever about his cake—don't believe he had one! Just his temper, you know, at being left out of the football! Just like him to fancy that a fellow snaffled his cake and hid it in the box-room till he stopped looking for it! It's all right now that you've whopped him, though! I'd like to see him kick up a fuss after that whopping! He, he, he!"

"You fat rascal!" roared Wilmot.

"Eh?"

"Get out!"

"What?"

Wilmot grabbed the fat Owl by the collar with one hand, and picked up the cake with the other. With a swing of his arm he twirled the Owl of the Remove through the doorway into the passage. As Bunter staggered there, spluttering, he hurled the cake after him.

"Whoop!" roared Bunter.

The cake smote him on the back of the head, broke into fragments, and dropped round him in a shower.

"Wow!" roared Bunter. "I say—Beast! Wow! Catch me whacking out a cake with you again! Yoop!"

Slam!

The door of Study No. 1 closed with a slam, and Billy Bunter was left, spluttering with wrath and indignation, in the midst of a sea of scattered fragments of cake!

THE EIGHTH CHAPTER.

Hacker Again!

"MR. QUELCH!"

The master of the Shell snapped out the name as if he had bitten it off. Prep was going on when Mr. Hacker presented himself in the Remove-master's study.

Quelch, sitting at his table, busy with a pile of papers, looked up, raised his eyebrows slightly at the expression on Hacker's face, and rose to his feet.

"Pray come in, Mr. Hacker," he said, with formal politeness.

Hacker whisked in.

"My nephew, sir——" he barked.

Mr. Quelch's face hardened. Hacker's nephew had been a week in his Form. In that space of time Mr. Quelch had had enough of Hacker's nephew—and enough of Hacker!

"Is anything the matter?" he asked, with an acidity equal to Hacker's own.

"Most certainly, sir, something is the matter. I caught sight of my nephew

a few minutes ago—I believe he was trying to avoid my observation, but I saw him distinctly—on the staircase. His face, sir, is battered and bruised——"

"Indeed!"

"Yesterday, sir, I found him struggling with a mob of boys of your Form—Wharton and his friends. To-day I see him battered and bruised. It appears to me, sir, that Eric is receiving ill-usage in your Form—a matter, sir, for your attention as his Form-master!"

"Undoubtedly," said Mr. Quelch. "If any boy in my Form is receiving ill-usage, I am not likely to overlook the fact. I have not seen Wilmot since class——"

"If you saw him, sir——"

"I shall certainly send for him, and see him. But I must remark, Mr. Hacker, that if Wilmot has found trouble in my Form, the fault is very probably his own. I have observed the boy very carefully, sir, since he has been here—and a more sulky, sullen, and evil-tempered boy I have never seen!"

Mr. Hacker snorted.

"At Topham, sir, my nephew was popular. He had a host of friends! He was the most popular boy in the school!" he barked. "There never was a boy more generally liked. He had many friends, and no enemies, at Topham!"

"It is a pity he did not remain there, in that case," said Mr. Quelch dryly. "For certainly he has made no friends here—neither, it appears to me, does he desire to do so. So far as I have observed, he keeps entirely to himself, and repulses any friendly advances!"

"You are aware, Mr. Quelch, that he would have remained at Topham had it been possible. But the terrible misunderstanding that arose in connection with the incident at St. Jude's School on the occasion of a football match there——"

"Very terrible—if it was a misunderstanding!" said Mr. Quelch, with intensifying dryness of manner.

"Sir! You do not hint——"

"I hint nothing, Mr. Hacker! I say plainly that the judgment of the headmaster of Topham appears to me to be a sound one. After what occurred at St. Jude's, he refused to allow Wilmot to remain at Topham. I fail to see that he could have come to any other decision."

"You are prejudiced against the boy——"

"Naturally, considering the circumstances in which he came here. Dr. Locke acceded to your request, and asked me to give the boy a chance in my Form. I have done so, and intend to continue doing so. But there is no doubt, sir, that the boy has something on his mind—which does not look as if his former headmaster made a mistake!"

"His misfortune at Topham, no doubt, is on his mind. That he has any guilt on his conscience, I do not and cannot believe."

"I trust that your faith in him may be justified, sir. At all events, he will have every opportunity of making good here. He will have fair play, and will be judged by his conduct!"

"He is not getting fair play, sir! It appears to me that your Form have made a set against him—he is ill-used and——"

"If so, he has not failed to give provocation by his sullen and offensive manners!" retorted Mr. Quelch. "But

Vernon-Smith spun Bunter round, preparatory to booting him. Wilmot, with a flash in his eyes, grasped the Bounder by the shoulders, and dragged him back. Smithy, already delivering the kick, had a foot in the air ; and, standing on one leg, he over-balanced as he was dragged back. "Yaroooh !" he gasped.

I will assuredly inquire into this matter. I will send for him !"

Mr. Quelch rang for Trotter.

That chubby youth was dispatched to summon Wilmot from prep to his Form-master's study.

Mr. Hacker stood with a frowning brow while he waited. Mr. Quelch was frowning also. Both masters were intensely annoyed.

In a few minutes, Wilmot entered the study.

He gave a slight start at the sight of his uncle there, and compressed his lips. Wilmot owed much to Mr. Hacker, and no doubt he was grateful. But that tactless gentleman's fussy interventions were a torment to him.

"You sent for me, sir !" he said to his Form-master.

"Look at him, sir !" said Mr. Hacker, before the Remove master could speak.

Mr. Quelch was looking. He was looking at a swollen nose, a bruised cheek, and a discoloured eye. Evidently Wilmot had been in the wars.

"You have been fighting, Wilmot ?" said Mr. Quelch severely.

"Yes, sir !" answered Wilmot quietly.

"With whom ?"

"A Remove fellow, sir !"

"His name ?"

Wilmot was silent.

"Answer your Form-master at once, Eric !" barked Mr. Hacker. "Tell him, immediately, the name of the boy who ill-used you in this manner !"

Wilmot breathed hard.

"I have not been ill-used, sir !" he answered. "I quarrelled with a fellow, and had a scrap with him—he is more knocked about than I am. And it was my fault from beginning to end !"

"Nonsense !" barked Mr. Hacker.

"It is the truth, sir !"

Mr. Quelch gazed very curiously at that new member of his Form. Wilmot's

statement took him rather by surprise.

"You were not in this constant trouble at your former school, Eric !" said Mr. Hacker. "You were never in trouble for fighting there !"

"I had a fight with Crawley once, sir—a fellow in my Form there !"

"I will not allow you to take the blame on yourself, Eric, from a mistaken sense of chivalry. Your Form-master is prepared to give you protection——"

Wilmot crimsoned.

"I am not in need of it, sir !"

"Nonsense !"

"Really, Mr. Hacker, the boy's word must be taken !" exclaimed Mr. Quelch sharply. "He admits that he was to blame. However, I will inquire. Wilmot, I command you to tell me the name of the Remove boy with whom you have been fighting !"

Wilmot's lips set obstinately.

Mr. Quelch's eyes began to gleam. But Hacker weighed in again—he could not keep silent.

"You foolish boy, answer your Form-master ! In any case, Mr. Quelch will see the boy in question in the morning, and see for himself !"

Wilmot realised that that was true. The moment Mr. Quelch's eyes fell on the Bounder, he would know.

"Vernon-Smith, sir !" he said.

"A quarrelsome boy," said Mr. Hacker. "I have noticed him—a boy with a far from excellent reputation."

"That, sir, is not the affair of the master of another Form !" said Mr. Quelch acidly. "I will send for Vernon-Smith !"

Trotter was dispatched again.

Wilmot stood crimson with discomfort. Mr. Quelch, understanding the boy's feelings much more accurately than Hacker did, could not help pitying him. But there was no help for it.

On Hacker's complaint, the matter had to be gone into; and they waited for Vernon-Smith to arrive. And it was like the Bounder to keep them waiting.

THE NINTH CHAPTER.

Just Like Smithy !

HERBERT VERNON-SMITH was seated in the armchair in his study. Redwing was at prep—but the Bounder gave prep no attention. He was not, in fact, in a state to do so. He sprawled in the armchair, tired out, badly damaged, bitterly humiliated, and in the worst temper ever.

He was angry with everything and everybody—himself included. He reflected bitterly that had he kept cooler —had he only kept his passionate temper in better control—the fight in the Rag might have ended differently.

He was a match for the rotter—more than a match for him—he was convinced of that. And he had thrown away his chances—he had never had a real chance after that crashing knock-out in the first round—and he had practically made Wilmot a present of that. So the Bounder told himself, with bitter regret that came too late. It was no use telling anybody else; a fellow who was licked was a fellow who was licked; and "ifs and ahs " would only make fellows smile. The Bounder had been defeated—beaten to the wide —and he had to chew on it, and he found the flavour very bitter !

Redwing attempted no consolation. It was useless, and would only have drawn savage words from his chum. He worked in silence, while the Bounder

(Continued on page 16.)

ST. SAM'S in the STRATTERSPHERE

First Spasm of a Staggering New Serial by DICKY NUGENT

GREYFRIAR[S]

No. 173.   EDITED BY HAR[RY]

Mr. I. Jolliwell Lickham, master of the Fourth Form at St. Sam's, burst into the Head's study, waving a newspaper in his hand.

"Sir!" he gasped. "Here's the very chance you've been looking for! You know you were telling me this morning you'd do almost anything for munny?"

Doctor Birchemall nodded.

"I reckerlect it, Lickham."

"Well, sir," said Mr. Lickham eggsitedly, "have a look at this newspaper offer. It's the chance of a lifetime for you, sir. Breefly, what it amounts to is this: The 'Daily Shreek' is offering a thousand pounds to anyone who is willing to be shot——"

"WHAT?" yelled the Head.

"A thowsand pounds, sir, to anyone who is willing to be shot——"

"SHOT?" hooted the Head.

"Yes, sir!" larfed Mr. Lickham. "But not shot in the way you're thinking of. The munny is to go to the person who is willing to be SHOT TO THE MOON!"

"Oh! Well, that's different!" growled the Head. "Why didn't you say so at first, fathead?"

"Here's the paper, sir," rattled on Mr. Lickham, eagerly. "Seeing's beleeving—and you can read it for yourself, if you like!"

Doctor Birchemall took the paper from his subordinit and glanced through the paragraph Mr. Lickham had been reading. This is what he read:

"£1,000 Reward!

"Professor Potty's marvellous steel cylinder, speshally built to travel through the strattersphere, is unable to start on its proposed jerney to the moon becawse volunteers are lacking. In order to overcome this difficulty, the 'Daily Shreek' has plezzure in offering the Sum of One Thowsand Pounds spot cash to each person who is willing to make the trip. The cylinder will be shot into space as soon as seven volunteers have been found. The rewards will be paid immejately the jerney to the moon and back has been completed. APPLY EARLY AND AVOID THE RUSH!"

The Head's eyes were gleeming, as he handed Mr. Lickham back his paper.

"My hat! It's a grate offer, and no mistake!" he mermered. "Of corse, there's a **certain** amount of risk. It's quite possibul they'll fire the thing in the wrong direction and miss the moon altogether — which mite make it awkward for getting back!"

"Oh, I wouldn't worry about that, if I were you, sir," said Mr. Lickham, who, on the quiet, was rather looking forward to a rest from Doctor Birchemall. "They're bound to supply you with plenty of tuck—and even if you don't hit the moon, you're sure to hit something, sooner or later!"

"Trew enuff!" said the Head, thumping his desk as he rose to his feet. "You have decided me! We'll go!"

Mr. Lickham jumped.

"WE?" he gasped.

"Why, of corse!" grinned Doctor Birchemall. "You didn't think I'd be such a cadd as to leave you behind, Lickham, did you? You'll come with me. Better still, why shouldn't we make it a hundred-per-cent St. Sam's party?"

"But I can't come, sir!" howled Mr. Lickham. "Only yesterday the doctor warned me against travelling long distances. If he knows I'm going up to the moon, he'll go up in the air about it!"

"Nonsense, Lickham!" larfed the Head. "You'll find it just as easy as travelling in the bus to Muggleton. You're coming, and that's that! Now for the other five! I'll summon a General Assembly and ask for volunteers, I think."

Ignoring Mr. Lickham's plaintive pleas to be left out, Doctor Birchemall rang the bell for Binding, the page. And five minnits later the assembulled skool heard with serprize that the Head and Mr. Lickham were contemplating a trip to the moon and wished for five volunteers to go with them.

By the time the Head had finished eggsplaining matters, most of the fellows had made up their minds not to have anything to do with the skeem. It wasn't a very inviting prospect to have to stick inside a steel rocket with nothing but space to jump into when you got tired of Doctor Birchemall. That was the way most of them looked at it.

The result was that when the Head came to the point and asked for volunteers, the only response came from the four most adventcherous juniors at St. Sam's—Jolly and Merry and Bright and Fearless!

"What! Only four?" cride the Head. "Bless my sole! I eggspected a hundred offers, at the very least! Anyway, you four boys can consider yourselves signed on. Now we want another one. Barrell!"

"Ye-e-es, sir!" gasped Tubby Barrell, of the Fourth.

"You have the reputation of being a good cook, I beleeve, and we shall need someone to do the cooking. I nomminate you as the fifth volunteer!"

"Ow! But look here, sir——"

Doctor Birchemall's hand strayed towards his birch.

"You are not, I trust, thinking of raising any objections to being a volunteer, Barrell?" he asked, icily.

"Nunno, sir!" said Tubby, hastily. "I shall be delited to come, sir!"

"Good! Then that completes our gallant little band!" cride the Head. "All that now remains is for me to ring up the 'Daily Shreek' and tell them that we're ready! The skool is dismissed!"

And the Head took a flying leap over his desk and galloped away to the nearest tellyphone. He was soon talking to the editor of the "Daily Shreek." Forchunitly—or unforchunitly, from the point of view of Mr. Lickham and Tubby Barrell—his application turned out to be the first they had receeved, and it wasn't long before all St. Sam's knew that Doctor Birchemall and his volunteers were definitely booked to take a trip to the moon!

Natcherally, there was grate eggsitement about the eggscursion. St. Sam's fellows were not shot into the strattersphere every day of the week, and Jolly and Merry and Bright and Fearless and Barrell found themselves in the limelight with a vengenz as the time for leaving drew near!

There was plenty to do before the grate moment arrived. Clean collars and changes of clothing and tuck hampers had to be packed and flying visits paid to their various homes. None of the boys' parents raised the slitest objection to their being shot to the moon, so long as they promised to keep out of mischeef, and to this they all reddily agreed.

Everything was ready at last, and, one cold and frosty evening, Doctor Birchemall led his volunteers out of the Skool House and marched them down to the playing-fields, where a huge steel

STAND BACK, EVERYBODY!

rocket was waiting for them. Professor Potty, the famus inventor, who was there to see that everything went off all right, called for three cheers for the eggsplorers, and they were given with a will. Then, after final handshakes all round, they marched into the rocket and closed the door.

"Stand back, every[one]!" cride Professor [Potty]; through a megaphe[...] the crowd stepped [...]

A minnit later, [...] fessor struck a ma[tch] lit the fuse of a tre[mendous] cannon-cracker at [...] at the rear of the gr[eat] rocket.

BOOM!

There was a blind[ing] and a deffening [...] flame—and when th[e smoke] had cleared away [...] spectators had picke[d them]selves up again, [Professor] Potty's rocket was [a] dot in the sky. [...] soon after that, it v[anished] from site altogether.

The St. Sam's egg[splorers] were in the stratte[rsphere.] While the rest of th[e crowd] returned to prep [and the] Skool House, the [five] absentees were [whirling] through space i[n the] direction of the m[oon.]

What will happe[n if they] duly reach their ob[jective?] More important sti[ll, what] will happen if they [don't?]

Only the future c[an tell.]

(Look out for the [next] instalment of this [thrilling] and amusing seri[al next] week!)

BORN FOR TH[E ...]

We are told tha[t ...] Dabney, of the [Remove or] Fourth, leaves Gre[yfriars ...] he intends to beco[me an] estate agent and sp[ends his] days letting houses.

He won't need to [adver]tise. People will kn[ow that] he is as soon as as [he has] that "vacant" loo[k on his] face!

WANTED [...]

Two gallons of dis[...] 100 doorsteps, and [a ...] quantity of car[...] They've run short of [...] for TEA IN HALL [...]

WOULD YOU BELIEVE IT?

Harry Wharton is hoping for an opportunity of demonstrating his remarkable skill as a skater this winter. On the frozen Sark he is a master of dazzling turns and glides. Bunter's attempt to imitate him ended at the first "turn"—which brought down the house—and Bunter!

S. Q. I. Field is very proud of his Australian origin, and gave Removites an interesting lecture on Australian Railways in the Rag. "Squiff" says we may hold the speed-record in England, but Australian locomotives are of "record" size. Squiff proved it with photographs.

One week when the "cop[y]" for the "Greyfriars Heral[d]" was unavoidably late, it [was] produced at simply breakn[eck] speed—the Editorial staff, [led] by Harry Wharton, establish[ed] a record! Bull nearly br[oke] his neck rushing to and fr[om] the printer's with the "cop[y]"

HERALD

January 25th, 1936.

ALONZO TODD A SUPER-MAN?

Asks BOB CHERRY

[A]lonzo Todd a [ma]n? Everybody [at Greyfriars]emove is asking [the que]stion, and you'd [be ask]ing it, too, dear [reader i]f you'd seen what [happene]d in the Rag the [other] ening?

[We] were having a [little] concert, and one [of the tu]rns was Bolsover [major w]ho, with typical [modesty], called himself [on the] programme "The Strongest School[boy." I]t was Bolsy's [turn th]at caused it to —

[Bolsy's] speciality was [weightl]ifting, and I must [say he] gave a nifty [turn, and won himself [a lot o]f applause. Every[body a]dmired also the [dumb-bells] he had with him on [the stag]e—particularly a [couple] of those whacking [great du]mbbells weighing [I don't k]now each that you [see the] "strong man" [lift at] the music halls.

[Bolsy, it seemed, had [picked t]hese at a sale [of theat]rical junk in [—] during the Christ-[mas.]

[Each] of these hefty-[weight] articles was so [heavy t]hat it took four [men to] carry it on to the [stage— Skinner, Snoop, [Stott, an]d Desmond. We [all th]ought it would [be too m]uch for Bolsover, [and it c]ertainly did prove [too muc]h for him. He [strained] several minutes [on th]e knee, puffing [and pan]ting and snorting [and gas]ping, before he [could bu]dge it. He got

it above his head eventually, and everybody cheered.

It was just then that Alonzo Todd took a hand in the game.

"My dear Bolsover, I feel it my duty to warn you of the dangers to which you are exposing yourself!" he burbled. "Are you not aware that the lifting of such inordinately weighty articles is likely to have a detrimental effect on your physical health?"

"You mind your own business, Todd!" said Bolsover, scowling.

"But it *is* my business to save a schoolfellow from overstrain which may possibly even bring about internal injury!" cried 'Lonzy. "If you insist on proceeding with this performance, my dear Bolsover——"

"Of course I'm going on with it!" roared Bolsover.

"Then I shall insist on helping you—thus ensuring that you do not lift too much at a time! Pray do not attempt to dissuade me, my dear fellow. It is a pleasure, I assure you!"

So saying, 'Lonzy climbed on to the stage. Bolsover gave a roar. "Look here, you dummy, if you don't clear off, I'll——"

But Alonzo was already helping him, whether Bolsy liked it or not! His bony fingers closed round the bar of the

weight. There was a brief struggle between the two, which ended in Bolsover slipping down on to the stage.

And then Alonzo Todd was left standing in the middle of the stage—with Bolsy's heaviest weight held over his head as easily as if it had been a feather!

There was a yell from the audience.

"What the merry dickens——"

"Are we seeing things?"

"Look at 'Lonzy—and it took four men to bring it on to the stage."

There was a regular uproar for a few minutes, I can tell you! We could hardly believe our eyes. But Alonzo soon showed us that it was no fluke by lifting other weights from Bolsy's stock-in-trade with equal ease! Then Bolsy got up again and put a stop to it by asking who's show it was, anyway, Alonzo Todd's or his? And the World's Strongest Schoolboy act ended in confusion!

STAGGERING SECRET of MAULY'S MARATHON

By SIR JIMMY VIVIAN

Chaps who thought last Wednesday's Junior Paper Chase was going to be easy because Mauly was the hare, had the shock of their life. Instead of being caught in the first half-mile, as everybody thought, Mauly showed the "hounds" a clean pair of heels and wasn't seen again till they got back to Greyfriars.

Now this is about the most surprising thing anyone could possibly have expected from the Languid Lord. The most energetic thing I'd seen him do up till Wednesday this term was when the study clock stopped and he walked down to Big Hall to see if it was time for bed! Apart from that, he has scarcely moved, except when compelled!

But there was no getting away from his paperchase performance. The moment Wingate gave him the signal to start, he bounded away like a giddy greyhound, and he was out of sight round the bend of Friardale Lane before we could say "Jack Robinson!"

Of course, everybody said he couldn't keep it up. But when it came to catching him, there wasn't a man who could get near him—and all the cracks, including Cherry, Russell, and Vernon-Smith, were putting their best feet forward, too!

So the crowd that waited at the gates in the expectation of seeing Mauly being carried back in a state of collapse had the amazing experience of seeing him return five minutes before anyone else, looking as fresh as a daisy! They haven't got over the shock of it yet in Lower School circles!

———

And that's why everyone has been asking if Alonzo Todd is a superman!

Now for the explanation.

The fact is, Mauly didn't go over the course at all.

If we'd been able to see what happened round the bend of the lane, we'd have seen Mauly dash into a wayside cotttage and hand over his bag of "scent" to a tall young fellow he found inside. The tall young fellow, who was already dressed in running clobber, went off like greased lightning. His name was Bill Coverleigh, and he happens to be a local professional long-distance runner with an international reputation!

About two hours later, Bill Coverleigh returned to the cottage and Mauly came out. And, on the strength of a good long sleep, Mauly felt sufficiently energetic to finish the course at quite a respectable trot.

So now you know!

In authorising me to tell you what actually happened, Mauly says he's awfully sorry, begad, that he had to pull wool over any man's eyes, but, dash it all, by insisting on making him the hare, you left him no option. How the dooce, dear men, could a chappie get in his forty winks while he was being pursued across great open spaces by a howling mob of fearfully energetic citizens?

I suppose, after getting such a handsome apology, we shall simply have to forgive him!

ENTIRELY DIFFERENT!

Coker felt awfully bucked the other day when he thought he heard Gosling call him a Titan.

Perhaps he won't be so happy when we tell him the sad truth. Gosling was referring to the small size of the tip Coker had given him for carrying a trunk up to his study. What he actually called Coker was not a Titan, but a "TIGHT 'UN"!

———

As a matter of fact, the answer is that he *isn't*. If you trot along to Bolsover's study and examine those weights of his, you'll soon know why. I've had a good look at them myself and I know!

They aren't made of iron at all, you see. They're fake weights, just made of cardboard—and Bolsy and his pals were just having us all on a bit of string!

HIRE A MODEL!

For half-a-crown I supply a life-sized model of yourself to leave in bed when you go out at night. Beats the beaks every time! — FISHER T. FISH, Study No. 14, Remove.

GREYFRIARS FACTS WHILE YOU WAIT!

[... skating] in the snow, which [en]dly at Greyfriars, [Re]move and Shell [r]esulted in a win [gi]ve by two pulls to [Brown] & Co. couldn't [ge]t slipping—as Bob [sa]y they didn't look [grubb]y" enough!

A 60 m.p.h. gale upset the football match between Remove and Upper Fourth—the wind "blowing" a goal for Temple & Co. following a clearance by one of their full-backs. When the Remove got the wind behind them, however, they quickly piled on a round dozen.

Johnny Bull is very keen on "hot" trumpeting, and drove his study-mates down to the junior common-room when he insisted on practising in the study. When Loder came up with a cane, however, Johnny was forced to flee from the study, "trumpeting" in quite a different way!

The OUTSIDER! By FRANK RICHARDS

(Continued from page 13.)

sat and scowled, and occasionally gave an involuntary gasp.

Then came a tap at the door, and Trotter's chubby face looked in.

"Master Vernon-Smith!"

"Oh, get out!" snarled Smithy.

Trotter gave quite a jump at the sight of the Bounder's face. Scrapping was not exactly uncommon in the Greyfriars Remove. But it was seldom—very seldom indeed—that any fellow was seen with so highly decorated a visage as the Bounder's at that moment.

"Mr. Quelch, sir——" gasped Trotter.

"Bother Mr. Quelch!"

"He says, sir——"

"I don't want to hear what the old ass says!"

"But, sir——"

"Oh, shut up!"

Trotter looked nonplussed. He had to deliver a master's message; and now that he saw the Bounder, he could guess why the message had been sent. Trotter compassioned a fellow, sent for by his Form-master in such circumstances. He was rather glad that he was not a Greyfriars man himself, with such interviews to go through. He stood in the doorway, staring at the Bounder—who turned his back on him and stared at the study fire.

"Smithy, don't be an ass!" said Redwing. "If Quelch has sent for you, you've got to go!"

"Rot!"

"What did Mr. Quelch say, Trotter?" asked Tom.

"I don't want to hear what he said!" snarled the Bounder.

"Well, I do. Weigh in, Trotter!"

"He said that Master Vernon-Smith was to go to his study at once, sir!" said Trotter, getting his message delivered in that oblique manner.

"Tell him he can go and eat coke!" snarled the Bounder.

Trotter grinned. He was not likely to tell Mr. Quelch that!

"I say, sir, the other young gentleman's there," said Trotter, by way of comfort. "If you've been fighting with Master Wilmot, sir, he's getting it, too!"

"Oh, Wilmot's there, is he?" said the Bounder, looking round.

"Yessir! I think I'd go, sir, if I was you," said Trotter. "Mr. Quelch is looking very ratty, sir, and so is Mr. 'Acker."

"Hacker! Is Hacker there?"

"Yessir!"

"What the thump is Hacker there for?"

Trotter grinned again.

"He didn't tell me, sir. But he's looking very bad-tempered, sir, like Mr. Quelch! Hadn't you better go, sir?"

Trotter was really kindly concerned for the angry, obstinate fellow in the armchair. He had had many liberal tips from the wealthy Bounder. Smithy

nad to go, that was certain; he was, in fact, only blowing off steam. But delays were dangerous in dealing with a master like Henry Samuel Quelch.

"It's about the scrap, Smithy," said Redwing. "You and Wilmot will both get into a row for getting your faces marked like that. It's no worse for you than for Wilmot."

"Isn't it?" said the Bounder, with a sneer. "It seems that Hacker's there. Looking after his dear little Eric. Has that cur been sneaking to his uncle?"

"I don't think he's that sort."

"Don't you?" jeered Smithy. "What is his precious uncle doing there, then?"

"Barged in, I dare say. He's always making Wilmot look a fool by barging in. Look here, Smithy, cut off, like a sensible chap!"

"I'd go, sir," said Trotter quite anxiously; and receiving only a scowl in acknowledgment of that well-meant advice, he departed, leaving the wilful Bounder to his own devices.

Vernon-Smith rose slowly from the armchair. He had to go, and he knew it, but it pleased him to take his time about it. But he left the study at last, and went down the passage, several minutes after Trotter had gone.

Even then he did not head direct for Masters' studies. He kicked open the door of No. 1 in the Remove, and scowled in.

Wharton and Nugent looked up from prep.

"Dear little Eric's gone?" sneered the Bounder.

"Wilmot! Trotter came up for him," answered Wharton. "I suppose Quelch has heard of the scrap. You sent for?"

"Oh, yes! Trotter came up for me, too, a few minutes ago."

"If it's a few minutes ago, Smithy, hadn't you better get a move on?" asked Nugent. "Quelch doesn't like being kept waiting."

"Quelch can go and eat coke! Besides, he's got Hacker's company to entertain him!" said the Bounder sardonically. "They're pow-wowing over sweet little Eric getting his beautiful nose punched. I forgot that he was a beak's relation when I went for him."

"Oh, rot!" said Wharton uneasily. "Wilmot wouldn't take any advantage of that. He's an ill-tempered brute, but——"

"What's his uncle doing there, then?"

"I don't suppose he's there at all. Rubbish!"

"I had it from Trotter."

"Oh!" said Harry, rather taken aback. "Well, Quelch isn't the man to let another beak butt in in affairs of his Form. The more Hacker barges in, the better it will be for you."

"Somethin' in that!" said the Bounder, with a grin. "I'll make the most of that. Thanks for the tip."

"I didn't mean——"

"I do!"

And there was a grin on the Bounder's bruised, discoloured face as he went at last down the Remove staircase.

He arrived at long last at his Form-master's study. By that time the atmosphere in that study was quite electric. Quelch did not like being kept waiting —especially with another beak present to see him carelessly treated by a boy in his Form. Hacker was fuming, and Wilmot was standing almost overwhelmed with discomfort and humiliation. Mr. Quelch's gimlet eyes fairly glittered at the Bounder as he came in.

"Vernon-Smith! Why did you not come at once when you were sent for?" rumbled Mr. Quelch. "You have wasted my time."

"You have wasted my time also, Vernon-Smith!" barked Mr. Hacker.

Hacker's intervention saved Smithy from having to answer his Form-master. It was easier to answer Hacker.

"Did you want to see me, sir?" he asked. "I had no idea that I was sent for by any Form-master but my own, or I should certainly not have left my preparation."

"What? You are insolent, Vernon-Smith!"

"I hope not, sir," said the Bounder meekly. "I have always understood, sir, that a fellow here is under his own Form-master's orders, and nobody else's except the Head's. If I am mistaken, my Form-master will set me right."

"You impertinent——"

"Mr. Hacker, will you allow me to speak in dealing with this boy of my Form?" exclaimed Mr. Quelch, in great exasperation.

"That insolent boy, sir——"

"That boy, sir, is perfectly correct in his statement. It was, however, that sent for you, Vernon-Smith. I regret to have interrupted your preparation, and I shall make allowance for it in class to-morrow. It appears, Vernon-Smith, that you have been fighting with Wilmot."

"I'm awfully sorry, sir," said the Bounder, with the same meekness. "I quite forgot that Wilmot was Mr. Hacker's nephew. I will remember another time that Mr. Hacker's nephew must not be touched."

Wilmot winced.

"The fact that Wilmot is Mr. Hacker's nephew has nothing whatever to do with the matter, Vernon-Smith!" snapped the Remove master.

"Oh, sir, I thought it had, from Mr. Hacker being here, waiting for me. I suppose he was waiting for me, as he said I had wasted his time."

Mr. Quelch bit his lip with vexation.

"Vernon-Smith," exclaimed Mr. Hacker, "you——"

"Sorry to interrupt you, sir," said the Bounder, with cool impudence, "but I am answerable to Mr. Quelch, sir, not to you. You have no right to speak to me on the subject, sir."

"What?" stuttered Mr. Hacker, gasping. "You impertinent young rascal, I——"

"I don't think it impertinent, sir, to point out that I am under the authority of my own Form-master, and no other."

"Mr. Quelch, I—I——"

"Mr. Hacker, will you, or will you not, leave this matter in my hands?" exclaimed Mr. Quelch with the greatest acerbity. "Both these boys, sir, belong to my Form, and unless I am left to deal with them, I will dismiss them, sir, and leave the matter where it is."

"Mr. Quelch, I have a right to insist upon justice being done. That insolent young knave, sir——"

"Are you applying that expression, sir, to a boy of my Form, who has made no statement that is not absolutely well-founded and exact?"

"If you uphold this boy in his audacious insolence, sir——"

"I uphold this boy, sir, or any boy in the Remove, in obeying my commands, sir, and those of no other person but his headmaster. Indeed, I forbid him to reply to any remarks you may address to him, sir!" exclaimed Mr. Quelch.

"If you take that view, Mr. Quelch——"

"Most certainly I take that view, sir!"

"Then," exclaimed Mr. Hacker, "I am bound to say, with the very strongest emphasis——"

"What you have to say with such

emphasis, sir, had better be said in private!" snapped Mr. Quelch. "Vernon-Smith! Wilmot! Each of you will take two hundred lines for appearing in so disgraceful a state. Both of you leave my study instantly."

"Mr. Quelch——"

"Mr. Hacker——"

"I insist, sir——"

"It is quite futile to insist, sir, upon overstepping the line of another master's authority."

Wilmot, with burning face, the Bounder with a suppressed grin, left the study. The door closed on the two deeply annoyed and angry Form-masters. Their voices went on after the juniors had left—argument waxing warm.

"You haven't done yourself a lot of good by greasing to a beak," said Vernon-Smith in the passage, with a scornful laugh.

"You know I did not!" panted Wilmot.

"I know you did!"

Wilmot gave him a black look, and the Bounder walked away, and lounged up to the Remove studies. He looked in at the door of Study No. 1 again, with a grin on his discoloured face.

"It worked!" he remarked.

Wharton looked at him rather grimly.

"What rotten trick have you been up to now?" he asked gruffly.

"Taking your tip, old bean! It worked!" chuckled the Bounder, and he went on to his own study—in quite a good humour now, in spite of his defeat and his damages.

THE TENTH CHAPTER.

What Did Bunter Know?

BILLY BUNTER gave Wilmot a stern blink in the Remove dormitory that night.

Billy Bunter was shirty.

He was so shirty that he had very nearly made up his fat mind to throw the fellow over, and have done with him.

Like the prophet of old, W. G. Bunter was very angry, and felt that he did well to be angry.

He had been friendly with that new tick. He had kept his secret for him, though without having the faintest idea that it was a secret, and why it was to be kept. That alone was a considerable thing, for it was not easy for Billy Bunter to keep anything he knew to himself.

Besides that, he had talked to the chap—when hardly anybody else did. Wilmot, certainly, had never shown any sign of enjoying the delights of his conversation. Still, he had done it—indeed, extensively.

Neither had Wilmot seemed to realise properly what an inestimable boon Bunter's friendship was. In fact, the friendship had been all on Bunter's side. The new fellow had tolerated him —barely.

The bare toleration had grown barer and barer. Wilmot had never said no when Bunter had asked himself to tea in his study. But he had taken to teaing in Hall! He never actually walked away from Bunter when the fat and fatuous Owl joined him. But he always got away as soon as he could, and never, on a single occasion, sought Bunter out. He never refused to answer Bunter when he gabbled, but his answers were always as curt as he could make them, and he never volunteered a remark. Really, it was uphill work being friendly with such a fellow, and now that tea in the study seemed to be a thing of the past, it was hardly worth while keeping it on, for the sake of an occasional loan of a bob or two! And now, after all Bunter's patient friendliness, Wilmot had heaved him out of his study, and heaved a cake at his head!

A bang on the head from a cake was disagreeable. Worse than that, the cake had been wasted! Even Bunter had not felt disposed to gather up the fragments from the floor of the Remove passage.

Altogether, Bunter considered that it was too jolly thick, and he was shirty, and he blinked at Wilmot in the dorm with a stern and accusing blink, designed to let the fellow see that he was shirty.

Bunter was a peaceable fellow. He was willing to come round. Wilmot had only to make the advances.

But he didn't. So far from appearing to feel the loss of Bunter's friendship, he seemed to have forgotten Bunter's existence.

He did not even observe Bunter's accusing blink. He did not observe Bunter at all.

It was just as if he regarded Bunter as a fellow who did not matter, and the episode of the cake, as an episode of a trifling nature, to be lightly forgotten!

Which added to Bunter's resentful indignation!

If the fellow supposed that W. G. Bunter could be treated like that, the fellow was making a mistake. Bunter, after all, knew what he knew, so to speak! He did not know why Wilmot wanted to keep Topham dark—but he knew that Wilmot jolly well did!

A smile, a nod, or a cheery word would have been enough for Bunter. But he was utterly ignored. Wilmot, indeed, seemed plunged into even a blacker mood of sulks than was his wont—doubtless the result of that painful interview in Quelch's study. In the dorm he took no heed of anyone, least of all, William George Bunter. And Bunter, knowing what he knew, determined to let the fellow see what he would see!

Wingate put lights out in the Remove dormitory, and left the Form to repose. There was the usual buzz of talk from bed to bed that followed lights out, the coming game with Rookwood being the

(Continued on next page.)

chief topic. Football matches were taken seriously in the Greyfriars Remove; and football matters were rather at sixes and sevens now, with the Bounder out of the team, and cutting up rusty about it.

"I say, you fellows, talking about football——" said Bunter.

"Don't you talk about football, old fat bean!" said Bob Cherry. "Talk about jam tarts and cream puffs, old porpoise. Keep to subjects you understand!"

"Oh, really, Cherry!"

"Better still, shut up!" suggested Johnny Bull.

"Yah! Lot you know about footer!" said Bunter. "You should have seen those Topham men playing at St. Jude's a week or two ago."

In the dark Bunter could not, of course, see Wilmot, but he knew perfectly well that the mention of Topham gave him a jolt. It was Bunter's kind intention to give him a jolt, in return for heaving Smithy's cake at his head!

A fellow who did not value Bunter's friendship couldn't jolly well expect Bunter to keep rotten secrets for him! That was how the fat Owl looked at it.

Not that he was going to let it out. He was only going to give Wilmot the uneasy impression that it was coming out, just to show the cheeky fellow where he got off, as it were!

"Oh, blow Topham!" said Bob. "We don't play Topham!"

"Lucky for you, you don't!" jeered Bunter. "Take some of the swank out of you if you did!"

"Fathead!"

"I saw them walking all over St. Jude's. There was one chap bagged four goals in the game."

"Well, if that's true, he was a good man, for St. Jude's can play Soccer," said Harry Wharton. "But I'll believe that when I see it."

"I saw it!" hooted Bunter.

"Perhaps you saw double, with those specs of yours," suggested Skinner.

"Ha, ha, ha!"

"What's Topham, anyway?" asked Bob. "I've never heard of the show, except through St. Jude's having a fixture with them."

"In Surrey, I believe," said Nugent, "but I've never heard much about them."

"Only Bunter knows what wonderful men they are!" said Johnny Bull sarcastically. "And Bunter knows such a thumping lot about footer! Sort of authority on the game."

"I fancy I know more about it than you do, Bull——"

"What a fertile fancy!" chuckled Bob. "What's the difference between a goalkeeper and a goalpost, Bunter? See if you can answer that."

"Too deep for Bunter," said Squiff.

"Ha, ha, ha!"

"You can cackle," said Bunter, "but that Topham chap I saw bagging goals at St. Jude's was a regular corker. As good as I am myself, at my very best."

"Ha, ha, ha!" came a yell from the whole row of beds.

Even Lord Mauleverer opened his eyes to chortle at that remark.

"Must be a regular International!" chuckled Bob. "If he plays in Bunter's style he ought to be selected for the Colney Hatch eleven."

"We must try to fix up a game with Topham, if they're such hot stuff!" said Harry Wharton, laughing.

"Oh, they'd beat you!" said Bunter disdainfully. "Not that the chap I was

THE MAGNET LIBRARY.—No. 1,458.

mentioning would be playing for them now. He's left Topham."

"They must be weeping over the loss, if he was a footballer like you, old fat man."

"Ha, ha, ha!"

"How do you know he's left Topham? How do you know anything about him at all, you fat gasbag?" asked Hazeldene.

"Well, I jolly well do!" said Bunter.

"You jolly well don't! You don't know anybody at Topham, wherever that may be."

"Perhaps I do, and perhaps I don't," said Bunter mysteriously. "That's telling. I can tell you I know that man jolly well that scored the goals."

"What's his name?" asked Squiff.

"Let's see! I—I forget! I dare say Wilmot knows. Wilmot knows fellows at Topham, don't you, Wilmot?"

"Shut up, you fat fool!" came a voice from Wilmot's bed.

"Oh, really, Wilmot——"

"Well, nobody here wants to hear what Wilmot knows or doesn't know," said Johnny Bull dryly. "You've talked enough, Bunter; go to sleep!"

"Yah!"

However, Billy Bunter let it go at that, and closed his little round eyes and went to sleep.

Further conversation in the Remove dormitory went on to the accompaniment of Bunter's snore. Bunter went to sleep, satisfied that he had let that cheeky tick, Wilmot, know where he got off!

He was not aware that long after slumber had descended on the dormitory the new fellow lay awake, unresting, his eyes sleeplessly on the starlit windows.

Mr. Hacker had done a big thing for his nephew when, after his disaster at Topham, he had obtained for him admission at Greyfriars. But the unhappy fellow wished, from the bottom of his heart, that Mr. Hacker had not done it.

At his old school the finger of scorn had been pointed at him. Even in the darkness his cheeks flushed hotly at the remembrance of the fellows' looks the day he had left Topham School. And if the story came out at Greyfriars, and cold indifference was changed into open contempt and scorn—and it might all come out, if Bunter gave the clue!

Billy Bunter had intended to let the fellow learn where he "got off," but the obtuse Owl was far from guessing how hard he had hit!

THE ELEVENTH CHAPTER.
Hands Off !

THE Bounder grinned.

It was the following morning, in break. Smithy's eyes were on his Form-master, and on the master of the Shell.

Both those gentlemen were taking a little walk in the quad, in the keen, frosty air. Coming along from different directions, they looked like meeting on the path, near the fountain. Each of them, sighting the other, paused for a jerky moment, and then moved on more slowly.

Which made the Bounder grin.

Excessively annoyed words had passed between the two masters in Mr. Quelch's study the previous evening.

Hacker felt that his nephew was not getting justice from Quelch. Quelch considered that Hacker was fussily interfering in affairs of his Form. Smithy had done his best to add fuel to the fire—with some success. The two masters—temporarily—were not on speaking terms.

It was, of course, impossible for one member of the staff to "cut" another member. Such a happening could have caused too much comment in the school. At the same time, they did not want to speak, or to acknowledge one another's existence.

So it was rather awkward, meeting face to face, and it amused the malicious Bounder.

He watched them with interest. So did Eric Wilmot who, alone as usual, was loafing by the House steps with his hands in his pockets. But where the Bounder found amusement, Wilmot seemed to find worry and distress.

More and more slowly the two masters marched on, approaching one another nearer and nearer. And the amused Bounder wondered whether they would pass one another with an icy stare, or a pretence of not seeing one another.

Quelch settled the difficulty by halting, taking a letter from his pocket, and becoming deeply interested in the same.

While his eyes were fixed on that letter, Hacker passed him.

Hacker having passed, Quelch ceased to be interested in that letter, returned it to his pocket, and resumed his walk.

Smithy chuckled, greatly entertained by that little comedy. Then he glanced round at Wilmot's dark, clouded face.

"Amusin', ain't it?" grinned Smithy.

Wilmot did not seem to think so. He gave the Bounder a black look.

"Your own doing!" said Smithy. "And I can tell you it won't buy you anything. Greasing to a beak doesn't pay here."

Wilmot gave him a disdainful stare, but no other reply.

"Even if the beak's a chap's relation," sneered the Bounder. "Quelch isn't the man to stand for it. He's the man to put Hacker right in his place—as I dare say you've found out by this time."

"You really think that I dragged my uncle into our row yesterday?" asked Wilmot quietly.

"I don't think—I know!" answered the Bounder coolly. "And you know you did!"

"You may think as you please!" said Wilmot contemptuously. "I shouldn't like to have a rotten, suspicious mind like yours."

He walked away before the Bounder could answer, leaving Vernon-Smith biting his lip.

Skinner came out of the House and glanced round.

"Seen that new tick, Smithy?" he asked.

"Bother the new tick!" grunted Smithy.

"I've got something for him."

Skinner sighted Wilmot's receding form, and cut after him.

The Bounder watched him curiously. Skinner appeared to have some joke on. He ran after Wilmot, stumbled just as he reached him, and caught hold of him for support.

Wilmot glanced round, annoyed.

"Oh, sorry!" gasped Skinner. "My foot slipped."

He let go and stepped back. Wilmot, without a word, walked on, and the Bounder burst into a chuckle as he saw the trick that Skinner had played. In the moment or two that he had been holding on to Wilmot, Skinner had stuck a card on his back, hooking it there with a fish-hook. It was not a very large card—not large enough for Wilmot to discover it there himself. But it was large enough to be seen

Side-stepping a fierce rush, Wilmot closed in, hitting out. Right and left crashed on Vernon-Smith, almost lifting him from the floor ; and the Bounder went sprawling helplessly and crashed. " Man down ! " cried Hazeldene. " He, he, he ! " cackled Bunter. " I say, you fellows, Smithy's done ! He, he, he ! "

from a distance, and it was written on in big capital letters:

" HANDS OFF !
MUSTN'T PUNCH ERIC !
BEWARE OF MR. HACKER !"

"Ha, ha, ha !" yelled the Bounder.

"Hallo, hallo, hallo ! What's the jolly old joke, Smithy ?" called out Bob Cherry.

"Seen the latest notice ?" grinned Smithy.

"On the board ?"

"No ; on the new tick."

"Wha-a-t ?"

Bob stared round; then, catching sight of the card on Wilmot's back, he roared :

"Ha, ha, ha !"

"Who on earth has done that ?" exclaimed Harry Wharton.

"Somebody who doesn't like a fellow greasing up to beaks," said the Bounder, laughing. "It will be a tip to the cad not to carry tales to his uncle."

"I don't believe he does," said the captain of the Remove, frowning. "In fact, I'm pretty sure he doesn't."

"You love him in your study—what ?" sneered the Bounder.

"No fear ! I'd be glad to make any other study a present of him. But he's no sneak, Smithy," said Wharton, shaking his head. "An ill-tempered brute, if you like ! Never saw a sulkier brute, but——"

"Rats !"

"Ha, ha, ha !" came a yell across the quad.

Many eyes were on that placard hooked to the back of Wilmot's jacket.

"I say, you fellows !" squeaked Billy Bunter. "Look ! He, he, he !"

"Ha, ha, ha !"

"Mustn't punch Eric," chuckled Peter Todd. "Dear little Eric !"

"Sweet little Eric !" chortled Bolsover major.

"Beware of Mr. Hacker !" howled Snoop. "Ha, ha, ha !"

"I guess that the bee's knee," sniggered Fisher T. Fish.

"Ha, ha, ha !"

Wilmot heard the loud laughter from many directions, but it did not occur to him to connect it with himself.

He walked on slowly, his hands driven deep into his pockets, his face wearing the usual sulky expression that had earned him the aversion of the whole Form.

The Remove fellows were not likely to guess that it was the memory of a day of shame and humiliation, the breaking of all his boyish hopes that made Eric Wilmot what he appeared to be. He seemed to them a sulky, disdainful, unsociable outsider, and they regarded him accordingly. And it was widely rumoured in the Form now that he "greased" to a beak, which added contempt to aversion.

Billy Bunter's fat face was suffused with grins. Had the fat Owl still been on friendly terms with Wilmot, he might have tipped him that he was being "guyed" before all the school. But Wilmot could not expect friendly tips from a fellow after heaving a cake at his head.

"He, he, he !" cackled Bunter. "I say, you fellows ! He, he, he !"

Some of the fellows, like Wharton, thought that it was rather too bad. But they could not help laughing.

Wilmot's unconsciousness of the card on his back, his total obliviousness of the fact that he was the object of the roars of laughter, added to the absurdity of the situation.

He walked on, his head held high as usual, his look giving its usual impression of sulky pride. Howls of merriment followed him as he went.

Coker and Potter and Greene of the Fifth were talking in a group when Wilmot passed them. They stared round, wondering what was the cause of that outburst of hilarity. When Wilmot had passed, they saw. Coker burst into a roar.

"Ha, ha, ha ! Look at that, you men ! Is that the kid who's Hacker's nephew ? Look ! Ha, ha, ha !"

Wilmot heard Coker's words and looked round at him. Potter and Greene were grinning, and Coker roaring.

The new junior gave them an angry, disdainful stare. But he walked on again. His ears were burning. It dawned on him now that he was the cause of the merry outbreak in the quad, though he could not guess why.

The bell rang for third school, and the fellows trooped away to the Form-rooms. With the Remove went Wilmot, still unconscious of the card on his back, but only too keenly conscious that he was the object of general amusement and mockery. His handsome face was flushed, his lips set. The Removites were almost in hysterics at the idea of Wilmot going into the Form-room, under Quelch's eyes, with that card on his back. That, evidently, he was going to do.

"Look here ! Enough's as good as a feast !" said Bob Cherry. "I say, Wilmot——"

"Shut up !" snapped the Bounder.

"Rats to you !" answered Bob cheerfully. "Here, Wilmot, I say——"

He broke off as Wilmot, giving him a cold stare, walked on to the Form room door. Bob coloured. His intended warning remained unuttered.

Mr. Quelch came up, and let his Form into the Remove-room. Quelch could see the unusual hilarity among the Removites, but he could not see the cause, which was behind Wilmot's back. He frowned. Quelch did not approve of too much in the way of hilarity, especially in Form.

It was not till all the Remove had gone in that the Remove master spotted the card on the back of the new junior.

He stared at it, and almost jumped.

"Wilmot!" he stuttered.

Wilmot looked round at him.

"Come here, Wilmot!"

"Yes, sir."

"What are you doing with that absurd card stuck on your jacket?" exclaimed Mr. Quelch.

"A card—on my jacket!" repeated Wilmot blankly.

"I suppose you were unaware of it!" snapped Mr. Quelch. "Come here; I will remove it. Ridiculous!"

He unhooked the card. Wilmot glanced at it and crimsoned. He understood the whole thing now.

He stood rooted to the Form-room floor, staring at the card. His eyes flashed round at Herbert Vernon-Smith.

"You rotter!" he shouted. "You did that!"

"Wilmot, if you dare to use such expressions in the Form-room I shall cane you!" exclaimed Mr. Quelch. "Vernon-Smith, did you pin this card to Wilmot's back?"

"No, sir."

"Someone in this Form must have done so, I presume," said Mr. Quelch, frowning. "If such a thing should occur again I shall detain the whole Form for a half-holiday. Now be silent! You may go to your place, Wilmot."

Wilmot went to his place with burning cheeks. Mr. Quelch tore the card across and threw the fragments into his wastepaper-basket. Skinner sighed. Quelch had "put paid" to his little joke; it was not worth a half-holiday's detention to repeat the performance. Still, one performance had been quite a success, judging by the hilarity in the Remove and the crimson discomfort of the victim.

When the Remove went out after third school Hazeldene pushed by Wilmot in the passage, and Skinner gave a yell of warning.

"Look out, Hazel!"

Hazel stared round.

"What——" he began.

"Mustn't touch Eric!"

"Eh? Oh! Ha, ha, ha!"

"Beware of Hacker!" chortled Bolsover major.

"Ha, ha, ha!"

The whole crowd of fellows, entering into the joke, walked round Wilmot with ostentatious care, avoiding contact. The new fellow went out into the quad with a burning face.

THE TWELFTH CHAPTER.
Talking About Topham!

"TALKING about Topham——" remarked Billy Bunter.

Nobody was talking about Topham—or thinking about Topham. Bunter was dragging the subject up by the heels, as it were.

It was nearly tea-time, and a number of fellows were in the tuckshop, when Wilmot came in.

Wilmot had ceased to "tea" in Study No. 1—whether from a dislike of his study-mates, or from a fear of Bunter dropping in, or both. But fellows who "tea'd" in Hall were allowed to take in any reasonable quantity of comestibles to eke out the school fare, which the juniors generally described as "doorsteps and dishwater." Wilmot had come into the school shop for some supplies of that sort, and found plenty of fellows there on the same errand.

It was for Wilmot's benefit that Bunter dragged up Topham. As the fellow had made no advances towards reconciliation, it seemed to the fat Owl that he had not yet learned where he "got off." Bunter was the fellow to show him.

"Who's talking about Topham, fathead?" said Bob Cherry. Bob was engaged in the careful expenditure of a half-crown.

"I am!" answered Bunter.

"Well, don't! We're fed-up on Topham, old fat bean!"

"But, I say, talking about Topham——" persisted Bunter.

Wilmot stood at Mrs. Mimble's counter, waiting his turn to be served, with an expressionless face. No doubt he understood the object of the fat and fatuous Owl; but to appear to ask any favour of a fellow like Bunter was more than his pride could stoop to.

Bunter was far from realising that he was a proper object for contempt. He was, in his own estimation, a very admirable fellow indeed—one of the very best!

"Here, look out, you men!" called out Skinner. "Make room for Eric! You'll have Hacker on your trail!"

Some of the fellows laughed.

"Skinner, old man, that's getting a bit stale," said Harry Wharton. "Dig up a new one, old scout."

"I say, you fellows, talking about Topham——"

"What is that fat ass gabbling about Topham for?" asked Bob in wonder. "He seems to have only one record lately—and that's Topham. Can't you jaw about something else, Bunter?"

"Better still, don't jaw at all!" suggested Wharton.

"The jawfulness is truly terrific," remarked Hurree Jamset Ram Singh.

"Wilmot knows fellows at Topham," said Bunter. "Don't you, Wilmot?"

Wilmot did not seem to hear.

He was selecting one or two things to take away and losing no time. Bunter blinked at him through his big spectacles, with a fat grin.

Bunter's friendship was, so to speak, on offer. It was Wilmot's if he chose to accept the inestimable boon.

If he didn't, he couldn't expect Bunter to be pally.

Bunter did not realise that he was tormenting the new junior. He had not the remotest idea that the mere mention of Topham cut Wilmot like a lash.

The barest possibility of his disgrace at Topham becoming known at Greyfriars made the new junior quiver. It was, indeed, partly for that reason that he had wrapped himself in a defensive armour of sulky pride. If the truth came out there would be no friend to turn him down, as he had made no friends. It was better to be a disliked outsider than to face the possibility of fresh humiliations. So it seemed, at least, to the boy whose little world had fallen in ruins round him so short a time ago.

"I say, you fellows, Wilmot knows the name of that Topham chap who scored the goals at St. Jude's!" declared Bunter

Nobody wanted to speak to Wilmot; but that declaration from Bunter drew a little attention.

Harry Wharton & Co. had narrowly missed seeing that football match at St. Jude's. If a Topham man really had scored four goals against men like Lunn and his team it was a matter of considerable interest to the Remove footballers.

"Is that so?" said Harry. "I don't know anything about Topham, but I'd like to hear of a chap who could bag four goals against Lunn's crowd. Sounds steep."

"Well, I saw him do it," said Bunter.

"But Wilmot didn't, I suppose," said the captain of the Remove. "Wilmot wasn't at St. Jude's that day, was he?"

Bunter chuckled.

"Perhaps he was!" he answered.

Eric Wilmot felt a chill at his heart. It was all coming out now!

"Oh, was he?" said Harry, quite interested, and little dreaming of the

facts. "Did you see that game, Wilmot?"

Wilmot did not answer.

His heart was like ice. It was at St. Jude's, after the match, that the disaster had happened—the incident that had blackened the very sunshine for him. Bunter had not the faintest idea of it; nobody at Greyfriars had, so far. He could not speak.

His silence puzzled the captain of the Remove. A sulky temper was all very well, but surely a fellow could answer a civil question.

"I spoke to you, Wilmot," said Wharton, his colour rising a little.

"Well, don't!" snapped Wilmot.

He did not want to make that answer, but it was the only answer he could make—unless he answered the question.

"By gum!" said Harry Wharton, with a deep breath. He clenched his hands, but he unclenched them again. "You sulky, disagreeable rotter, I've a jolly good mind—— Let's get out of this, you men; that fellow makes me feel ill."

He left the school shop with his friends.

"Well, that's the limit!" said Skinner. "Fancy the new tick having the neck to snub his Lofty Magnificence Wharton!" Skinner grinned. He rather enjoyed seeing the captain of the Form taken down a peg.

"Cheeky cad!" grunted Bolsover major. "I'd have punched his cheeky face if I'd been Wharton!"

"I say, you fellows——"

"Too tough for Wharton to punch!" grinned Skinner. "He doesn't want to punch a man who could lick Smithy!"

Wilmot looked round at him.

"That's a lie, Skinner," he said very distinctly, "and you know it!"

Skinner stared at him, quite taken aback. Wilmot turned contemptuously away from him—having made one more enemy! He began to collect his purchases.

"I say, you fellows, you ask Wilmot; he knows the name of that Topham man who beat St. Jude's——" Bunter was going on.

"Oh, shut up, Bunter!" growled Squiff. "Nobody wants to speak to that sulky brute!"

"Well, let's see, I fancy I could remember the name if I tried," said Bunter. "Let's see, was it Wilson, or Wilkins, or——"

"Carry some of these things in for me, will you, Bunter?" asked Wilmot. "I suppose you're coming in to tea."

Billy Bunter beamed. Friendship, evidently, was on its old footing. The Topham stunt had worked.

"Yes, rather, old chap!" grinned Bunter.

"But what's that name you were going to tell us?" asked Squiff.

"I forget."

"You fat chump!"

Bunter carried Wilmot's purchases out of the shop, and walked across to the House with the new junior.

Wilmot had come round! He had put his pride in his pocket—he had had to! Bunter grinned cheerfully as he trotted by the side of the new junior. He did not know how near Wilmot was to booting him across the quad!

At the tea-table in Hall, Bunter sat down by the side of the glum-faced junior, and helped him to dispose of the supplies from the tuckshop. Bunter had even more than the lion's share that he had marked out for his own. Eric Wilmot ate little, and that hastily, and got away. But Bunter did not mind. he was left to finish the supplies, which he duly did to the last crumb.

THE THIRTEENTH CHAPTER.
Called Over The Coals!

"WHARTON!"

"Hallo, Hobby!"

"Hacker wants you!"

Harry Wharton stared at Hobson of the Shell.

"Hacker wants me?" he repeated. "What the thump does your beak want a Remove man for?"

"Blessed if I know!" answered Hobby. "But he told me to tell you! Perhaps it's something about that darling nephew of his! Haven't you tucked him up nicely in your dorm of a night? Or have you forgotten his hot-water bottle?"

Hobby was sarcastic!

"Something serious like that, I fancy, from Hacker's look!" went on Hobby, still sarcastic. "I hear that Hacker butts in every other day to see that jolly old Eric isn't badly treated. He got Smithy, of your Form, into a row for punching him, I hear."

Wharton knitted his brows. Whether Eric Wilmot "greased to a beak" or not, Mr. Hacker certainly seemed bent on making it look as if he did! The captain of the Remove most certainly did not want to see Hacker on that subject. Since that talk in the school shop, a day or two ago, his feelings towards Wilmot had been less amicable than ever. He liked neither Wilmot nor his uncle, and wanted to have nothing to do with either.

"Your beak and my beak hardly speak now, I hear," went on Hobson. "Dear Eric seems to have set them by the ears! And the worst of it is, I never see the chap without wanting to punch his cheeky head, and I can't do it, because it means a row with Hacker! Rotten, ain't it?"

Hobby of the Shell walked on, and Wharton slowly made his way to the House.

Vernon-Smith met him as he was going in.

"Thinking it out?" he asked.

"Eh! What?" asked Harry.

"I mean, we're pretty close on the Rookwood date now," said the Bounder. "If you're going to do the decent thing, instead of giving a good man's place to Nugent because he's your chum——"

"Oh, don't talk rot!" interrupted Wharton angrily. "You're out of the team for Rookwood, because you're off your form, and I've got a strong suspicion, too, that you're off your form chiefly because you've been losing sleep through breaking bounds after lights-out, and smoking filthy cigarettes! If

that's the case, you've let us down, and the less you say about it, the better!"

"You're not goin' to play me, then?" sneered the Bounder.

"Not unless you show a big change before the date!"

"That's not what you were wrinkling your face about, then?"

"Was I? No; I've got to go to see Hacker, and I don't want to, but I suppose I must!" grunted the captain of the Remove.

"You've got to go to see Hacker!" repeated Smithy.

"He's just sent Hobby to tell me."

"Don't go!"

"I must, fathead!"

"You needn't! I told Hacker to his face the other day that I wouldn't come at his orders, and Quelch stood by me, too!"

"I'm not so keen on making mischief as you are, Smithy!" answered Wharton dryly, and he passed the Bounder, and went into the House.

He went very slowly to Masters' studies.

Hacker could only want to see him about his nephew in the Remove; he could think of no other reason. Had the fellow been carrying complaints to his uncle, as the Bounder believed? It looked like it, but Wharton could not quite think so.

But he was almost tempted to act on the Bounder's advice, and decline to obey the summons. Hacker had no right to send for one of Quelch's boys—it was some more of his fussy interference!

However, he continued on his way, and tapped at Hacker's door. He was not surprised to find the master of the Shell with a frown on his acid face.

"You sent for me, sir?" said Harry respectfully.

"Yes, Wharton! I sent for you!" said Mr. Hacker. "I desire to see you on the subject of my nephew in your Form."

Wharton did not reply that he had guessed that one! But that was the thought in his mind.

"You are, I understand, football captain in your Form," said Mr. Hacker.

"Yes, sir," said Harry, in utter wonder. It had never occurred to him that Hacker intended to speak about footer. Hacker was well known to take little or no interest in the game. Seldom or never did he roll down to see his Form play, as other masters did.

"Quite so," said Mr. Hacker. "So I understood! That is why I require an explanation from you, Wharton."

"I don't understand you, sir," said the bewildered junior.

"My nephew, Eric—I should say, Wilmot—was considered the finest junior footballer at his last school!" said Mr. Hacker. "Yet I find that he is entirely left out of your Form games. Why is this?"

Wharton could only stare blankly.

Apparently Hacker had been looking into Remove football matters—entirely on his nephew's account, that was certain.

He had learned that Wilmot was taking no part in the Form games. He had not, evidently, learned that that was Wilmot's own fault. Certainly he was not aware that, so far from desiring to play footer, Wilmot had tried to get out of even compulsory practice—which no fellow was allowed to do.

Hacker did not know that, on the occasion when he had come on the Famous Five hooking Wilmot downstairs, they had been getting him down to the changing-room by main force.

Since that date, the new junior had turned up on compulsory occasions—but only on those occasions, and had always got away as soon as he could, and never shown anything like quality. Of all this Hacker, obviously, was unaware.

Wharton said nothing. He did not want to tell Hacker that his nephew was a dud and a frowsting slacker. And really, there was nothing else to tell him.

"You will explain this, Wharton," said Mr. Hacker, after having paused, like Brutus, for a reply, and received none, like Brutus. "I am aware that you are not on friendly terms with Eric—hem!—my nephew. I trust that this unfriendly personal feeling has not led you to disregard the just claims of a boy in your Form."

"Not at all, sir!"

"I believe," said Mr. Hacker, "that a —hem!—a fixture—a regular match— with another school, is at hand——"

"The Rookwood match—yes, sir."

"Is my nephew selected to play in that match?"

Wharton almost laughed.

"No, sir," he answered.

"Why not?" demanded Mr. Hacker.

"I'd rather not talk about Wilmot, if you don't mind, sir!" said Harry.

He was incapable of the Bounder's impudence; but he felt strongly tempted to speak, just then, in Smithy's style.

"I have sent for you to talk about him, Wharton!" answered Mr. Hacker. "I should have placed the matter before your Form-master; but, for various reasons, I prefer not to discuss the matter with Mr. Quelch."

Wharton was able to guess those reasons!

"You, as football captain, are responsible in the matter," continued Mr. Hacker. "Therefore, I am addressing you, Wharton! I desire—in fact, I require—to know why my nephew, certainly as good a footballer as any boy in the Lower Fourth Form, is excluded from the matches."

"But, sir——"

"I will not allow injustice to be done to my nephew!" said Mr. Hacker. "I desire you to understand that very clearly, Wharton!"

"Nobody wants to do him injustice, that I know of, sir!" answered Harry, wondering what Wilmot would have felt like, could he have overheard that extraordinary conversation.

"I am glad to hear that, Wharton! Then, answer my question! For what reason is Eric—I mean, my nephew—excluded from the Form games?"

"Have you ever seen him play footer, sir?" asked Harry.

"Certainly I have! I am not speaking without knowledge!" snapped Mr. Hacker. "On several occasions I visited his last school, and saw him play in matches there. It was agreed by all that he was the best junior footballer at—at—at the school."

"I can't imagine what sort of footer they played there, then, sir! I'd as soon put Bunter in my team, as Wilmot."

"What? What do you mean, Wharton?"

"Only what I say, sir! I don't want to talk about Wilmot—but as you force me to speak, I must tell you that he can't play Soccer for toffee, and doesn't seem to want to, either."

"He cannot play Soccer!" repeated Mr. Hacker.

"If he can, he's shown no sign of it here," said Harry.

"Nonsense!"

Wharton made no answer to that.

"If you are so ignorant of the game, Wharton, that you do not know a first-class footballer when you see one, it is amazing that you should be captain of football in your Form."

"It would be rather amazing, sir, I admit! But I'm supposed, in the Remove, to know a little bit about the game."

"It is either ignorance or prejudice, I repeat. Eric—Wilmot—was the acknowledged best player of the game at his last school."

"May I ask what school it was, sir?" asked Harry. He was really interested to know at what school a foozling dud like Wilmot was considered the best junior footballer.

"That—that is immaterial," said Mr. Hacker hastily. "You are not here to ask questions, Wharton, but to answer them."

Wharton was trying hard to avoid following the Bounder's example. It was bad form to "cheek" a master; and he had a keener sense of the fitness of things than Smithy ever had. But he was getting near the limit of his patience now.

"May I point out, sir, that you have no right to question me, especially about football matters," he said, as respectfully as the nature of the remark allowed. "I am responsible to Wingate, the captain of the school, and after him to Mr. Lascelles, the games-master. Neither of them would let me carry on if I failed to spot a first-class man for the game. Both of them keep an eye on Remove football."

Mr. Hacker appeared a little struck by that remark. He was silent for several moments. But he came back to the point after those few moments, just as if the captain of the Remove had not spoken at all.

"Why is my nephew excluded from the team that is to meet Rookwood, Wharton?"

"Do you really want me to tell you, sir?"

"Certainly I do!"

"Very well. It's because he's a dud at the game, and a slacker, too, and no good! I'll play him as soon as we fix up matches at hopscotch, or marbles; but so long as it's Soccer, he's out, and stays out!"

The master of the Shell blinked at Wharton. He was getting plain English now—very plain indeed, with no trimmings. He did not seem to like it, now he had got it.

His acid face was suffused with red. "Wharton," he gasped, "you are disrespectful!"

"You've forced me to speak plainly, sir. If it's disrespectful, I can't help it. I don't want to talk about Wilmot at all. But you've asked me, and I've told you."

"You are speaking falsely, Wharton!" barked Mr. Hacker.

Wharton gave him one look, and walked to the door. The master of the Shell stared after him.

"Stop!" he barked. "I have not told you to go, Wharton! Remain here till I have finished! I order you——"

Without answering, and without turning his head, Wharton walked out of the study, and shut the door after him. He had had enough of Hacker. Quite unintentionally, and against his will, he had, after all, followed the Bounder's example in dealing with that gentleman —only rather more so!

He went down the passage with flushed face. Mr. Hacker was left staring at the shut door.

THE FOURTEENTH CHAPTER.

Wilmot To Play!

WINGATE coughed.

Harry Wharton and Frank Nugent smiled.

They were in Study No. 1 in the Remove, when the captain of Greyfriars dropped in. A visit from so great a man as the captain of the school was, of course, a distinguished occasion, and as Wingate did not bring his ash-plant with him, there was no cause for alarm.

Apparently, the Greyfriars captain had dropped in to say something. But it appeared, also, that he had some difficulty in saying it. Having made a few desultory remarks on the subject of football, Wingate coughed—and coughed again. Whereat the juniors smiled. It was rather unusual to see old Wingate hesitating, especially in dealing with Lower boys. Generally he came very directly to the point.

"That new kid's not here?" remarked Wingate at last.

"Wilmot? No—he doesn't trouble the study much," said Harry.

"You don't pull with him?"

"Not a lot!"

"Well, look here!" said Wingate. "I was going to speak to you about him, Wharton, as captain of your Form."

Nugent took the hint and left the study.

Wingate waited till the door closed on him. Wharton waited, too—with a rather grim expression coming over his face.

He had a feeling of being fed-up with Wilmot—fed-up to the back teeth. He had heard enough about him from Hacker. If more was coming, from Wingate, it was getting beyond tolerating.

Wingate gave another cough. He leaned his broad shoulders on the mantelpiece, and looked at Wharton's set face.

"What's the kid's footer like?" he asked.

"Rotten!" answered Harry briefly.

"Keen?"

"About as keen as Bunter."

Wingate laughed.

"Hacker seems to think differently," he said.

"I suppose I mustn't tell a prefect that a Form-master is an ass!" said Wharton. "But may I say that Hacker doesn't know what he is talking about?"

"Well, the old bean isn't a whale on games," admitted the Greyfriars captain. "But he must know a bit. I've noticed that kid—he seems a sulky little beast. But he's got the build of a good forward."

"Oh, he's fit enough, if he cared for the game!"

"And he doesn't?"

"He seems to loathe it."

"That's dashed queer!" said Wingate thoughtfully. "Hacker may be mistaken about his form, but he can't be mistaken about the kid having played for his last school. That's a matter of fact, not of opinion."

"Some school!" said Wharton, with a curl of the lip. "Nugent minor wouldn't play him for the Second Form here."

"Still, he must have been fairly keen at his last school, and must have been able to play a game of sorts. Hacker thinks he was a tremendous games man!"

"Hacker's a—what I mustn't call him to a prefect."

"Well, look here!" said Wingate. "Hacker has been talking to me——"

"I guessed that one!"

" Why is my nephew excluded from the team that is to meet Rookwood ?" asked Mr. Hacker acidly. "Do you really want me to tell you, sir ? " asked Wharton. "Certainly I do ! " " Very well ; it's because he's a dud at the game. I'll play him, as soon as we fix up matches at hop-scotch or marbles. So long as it's Soccer, Wilmot's out, and stays out ! " The master of the Shell fairly blinked at the junior captain.

"He's frightfully in earnest about it—he seems to think that the kid isn't getting a fair show !"

"He's doing the kid no good by barging in."

"Taken as read," said Wingate. "But, look here ! Hacker's very keen about it, and he talked to me for a solid half-hour. I don't want that over again, if I can help it. He's asked me to step in, as head of the games."

"As head of the games, you can tell him that his nephew is in good form to play a girls' school at croquet; but is no good for Soccer."

"Thanks ! I don't want to see Hacker blow up like a bomb ! Look here ! What about giving him a chance in a match ?"

Wharton's eyes gleamed.

"I'll resign the Form captaincy, if you like," he said. "So long as I'm skipper, he plays in no Remove matches."

"Don't get your back up, kid !" said Wingate soothingly. "I'm not speaking of the Rookwood game, or St. Jim's, or St. Jude's. You're playing a Form match on Saturday—Temple's lot in the Fourth."

"Oh !" Wharton laughed scoffingly. "Anybody can play those foozlers. I've played Bunter against the Fourth ! I wouldn't mind playing Wilmot."

"Well, then, a Form match is a match," said Wingate. "If you have to carry a passenger, it will be all the harder practice for you, see ? It's only the same as playing a man short."

"Just the same, so long as Wilmot doesn't get in the way. If he does, he will get barged out of it fast enough."

"Well, look here ! I'd like to satisfy Hacker, if possible, that his blessed Eric isn't being boycotted," said Wingate.

"And the fact is, Wharton, I've had an eye on that sulky young tick, and I believe he could play if he liked. It looks to me as if he never wanted to come here, and has his back up with things generally. Football may help to pull him round. Mind, I'm not giving you any orders—I'm asking you to oblige me by giving him a chance in a Form match."

Harry Wharton laughed.

"Invitations from royalty amount to commands, don't they ?" he said. "I'll do it if you like, Wingate. Can't see any sense in it. But it's a go !"

"Done, then !" said Wingate, and, with a friendly nod to the junior, he went out of the study.

It was not pleasant for Wharton. It was not Wingate's authority, but the fact that he admired and respected the captain of Greyfriars, that caused him to concede the point. It was true that a "dud" in the team that played Temple & Co. of the Fourth did not spell danger. But Wharton wanted to have nothing to do with the sulky new fellow, and he had a feeling of having been overruled in his own province.

However, he made up his mind to it with the best grace possible.

Nugent came back to the study and found his chum pencilling a footer list. He glanced at it and whistled.

"Wilmot !" he ejaculated.

"He won't do any harm, playing the Fourth," said Harry.

"But will he play ?"

Wharton started.

"Will he play ?" he repeated.

That had not occurred to him. A fellow picked out to play had to play—generally jumped at it. Wharton felt a gust of anger surge over him.

He had had a "jaw" from Hacker,

and another "jaw" from Wingate, and, against his own will, had put Wilmot down to play. Yet it was quite on the cards that the sullen, obstinate fellow, instead of jumping at the chance, and regarding it as a boon and a blessing, might reject it—coolly and contemptuously. He was no party, Wharton felt sure, to Hacker's meddling; probably did not know that Hacker had barged in at all. If he refused——

"He doesn't seem to care for footer," said Nugent, "and he seems as obstinate as a mule. I rather think he may decline."

Wharton set his lips.

"Let him !" he said. "I've had enough worry over that sulky tick ! I'd as soon play Bunter, so far as Soccer goes. I've told Wingate that he's going to play on Saturday—and he's going to play ! If he refuses——"

"Well, he might——"

"He might !" agreed the captain of the Remove, with gleaming eyes. "Let him, and we'll see whether I shall have better luck than Smithy in giving him the hiding he's been asking for ever since he came here !"

"But, old fellow——"

"Don't let's talk about him any more, or I shall punch his head when he comes up to prep !"

Nugent changed the subject at once. When Wilmot came up to his study to prep, there was the usual silence there to greet him.

In any other circumstances, Wharton would have mentioned the matter at once—knowing that the news would be welcome to any fellow. But he said no word to Wilmot. He would know, when he saw his name in the list put up for the Form match—and that was good enough. He could like it, or lump it, and make the best of it—or the worst!

THE FIFTEENTH CHAPTER.

Bitter Blood!

"THAT tick!"

"That sulky ass!"

"What rot!"

"That dud!"

"Wilmot!" said Vernon-Smith, with a scoffing laugh. "Well, that's the limit —the jolly old limit!"

It was Friday evening, after prep, and the list was up in the Rag. It was not a matter of deep interest in the Remove, for the match with Temple & Co. of the Fourth was little more than a walk-over for the strenuous footballers of the Remove. Still, fellows looked to see if their names were in. Smithy's name was there— which he took as no compliment. But the name that drew general attention was that of E. Wilmot.

"So Wharton's resigned the captaincy!" said Smithy, with a jeering grin.

"Has he?" exclaimed Hazel.

"Looks like it! Can't be two captains in one team—and Hacker has become skipper, judging from this."

At which there was a loud laugh.

"Think Hacker worked this?" asked Skinner.

"I don't think—I know! Wharton wouldn't touch the fellow with a punt-pole if he could help it! He's not put in because he can play footer, I suppose —as he can't! He doesn't even want to! Remove footer is being run from the Shell beak's study now."

And there was a growl from some of the fellows. Wharton had said nothing; but the thing was clear enough.

"I say, you fellows——"

"Oh, shut up, Bunter!"

Billy Bunter was blinking at the list through his big spectacles. He was not hoping to see his name there. He was dreading to see it there! Luckily, his dread proved unfounded. Wharton had sometimes put the fat Owl into a game where he could do no damage; but this time, at least, he had not repeated what W. G. Bunter regarded as a scurvy trick!

Still, Bunter was interested in the list. He knew, if nobody else did, that Eric Wilmot, late of Topham, was a first-class footballer—if he chose! Few, if any, in the Remove, were his equals in that line, judging by what the Owl had seen at St. Jude's.

"I say, has Wharton found out what a topper he is?" asked Bunter. "I say, he will walk all over the Fourth!"

"Shut up, you silly ass!" hooted the Bounder.

Bunter's opinions on Soccer were not wanted. Generally they were not very valuable.

"Well, you see," said Bunter, "that chap can play your head off, if he likes, Smithy! He's as good at footer as at boxing!"

Smithy did not answer in words. He let out a foot, and the fat Owl departed with a yell.

"Here come his Nibs!" murmured Hazel.

Wilmot came into the Rag.

Every eye was turned on him—not with a friendly look. He could see that something unusual was on, though he did not yet know what it was.

"Gratters, Wilmot!" called out the Bounder sardonically.

Wilmot gave him an icy glance.

"Your name's up!" called out Skinner.

To his surprise, he could see that the new fellow was unaware of it. Most of the fellows were taking it for granted that that name, in the football list, was the outcome of "greasing" to a beak!

"My name?" repeated Wilmot, in astonishment. "What do you mean?"

"Didn't you know?" sneered the Bounder.

Without replying, Wilmot came over to the group, and glanced at the paper. His brow darkened.

He said nothing, but walked out of the Rag. The juniors stared after him and exchanged curious glances. Even the Bounder was puzzled.

"He doesn't seem fearfully bucked!" remarked Hazel.

"He must have wangled it with his uncle!" snapped the Bounder. "Wharton never wanted to put him in."

"That's a cert!" agreed Peter Todd. "But—well, if he's pleased, he doesn't look it! After all, he doesn't care for Soccer."

It was quite a puzzle to the Removites. Heedless of what they said or thought, Wilmot went up to the Remove passage. He found Harry Wharton & Co on the landing, chatting there before they came down to the Rag after prep. He went up directly to the captain of the Remove.

Wharton looked at him, and his face set.

"I've just seen a football notice downstairs!" said Wilmot.

"Well?"

"My name's in it."

"Well?"

The Co. stood silent. Trouble, it was clear, was at hand.

"I'm new here," said Wilmot, in quiet, icy tones. "I quite understand that games practice is compulsory, and that I made a fool of myself last week when I refused to turn up. I've turned up since on compulsory dates. I'm asking for information now."

"Well?"

"Is to-morrow a compulsory date?"

"No."

"A fellow is not bound, by any rule, to play in a match if he doesn't care to?"

Wharton paused a moment before replying.

"A fellow is generally glad to play in a match!" he said at last.

"I haven't asked you that!" Wilmot pointed out. "I asked you whether there is a rule, enforced by the school authorities, to make a fellow play in a match on a date when games practice isn't compulsory?"

"No!" said Wharton, with a deep breath.

"You frowsy slacker——" began Johnny Bull, in a deep voice.

But Johnny stopped at that. It was a matter for the captain of the Form to deal with. Moreover, Johnny realised, even as he spoke, that whatever was the matter with Eric Wilmot, he was not a frowsy slacker! He did not, at all events, look the part!

"Then I'm not bound to play?" asked Wilmot, in the same icy tones, and taking no more notice of Johnny Bull than of the old oak banisters.

Wharton paused again before replying.

"I only want to know!" added Wilmot, with a faint touch of sarcasm.

"I'll tell you!" said Harry quietly. "If a man's picked out to play, he plays. Generally he's glad to. If he's sick, he can say so. If he isn't, he plays. If he's too slack to want to

play, he's generally ashamed to own up to it. If he's a footer funk, it's hard luck—but he can get over that better by doing his best, than by slouching about with his hands in his pockets."

"All that's frightfully interesting," said Wilmot. "But you're not answering my question." He seemed quite unmoved by the contempt in the look and tone of his Form captain. "I gather that I'm not bound to play if I don't choose?"

"No!" said Harry at last.

"Thanks! Will you take my name out of the list, then?"

"No!" said Wharton again.

Wilmot knitted his eyebrows.

"What's the good of leaving it in when I shan't be playing?" he asked.

"You will be playing."

"Haven't you just said that I have a right to stand out?"

"Quite! But it's never been heard of before in the Remove for a man to refuse to play when called on. Even Bunter——"

"I'm not asking for lessons in the manners and customs of the Lower Fourth Form at this school! Thanks all the same!"

"You'd better hear me!" said Wharton, keeping his temper with great difficulty. "It's never been heard of before, as I've said, and you're not here to make history. It's not going to be heard of now! You're going to turn up to-morrow with the Form team to play the Fourth!"

"I'm going to do nothing of the sort!"

There was a pause. Wilmot made a movement to go.

"Hold on!" said Harry quietly. "We'd better have this clear! You're not wanted in the team—you know that! You're not wanted at Greyfriars, if you come to that! You've made every man in the Form dislike you, with your rotten sulky temper! You're a dud at footer, a slacker, and a sullen toad! Nobody wants you! But I've practically had orders from the head of the games to play you, and you're going to play!"

"I don't see why Wingate should butt in."

"None so blind as those who won't see!" said Harry scornfully.

Wilmot looked at him, evidently puzzled; then, as he comprehended, a crimson flush came over his face.

"Do you mean that my uncle——"

"Didn't you know?"

"I did not!"

"Well, you know now! And I'm not going to be called over the coals by Wingate and jawed again by your precious uncle because you're too sulky and slack to do what any decent fellow would be glad to do. You're going to play football to-morrow!"

Wilmot stood silent for a moment. The crimson faded out of his handsome face, leaving him pale.

"I'm sorry!" he said at length. "I never knew——" he paused. "Mr. Hacker means well, of course——" He paused again. "But if I wanted to play, I'd refuse a place in the team on those terms. If you mean that you've been ragged into playing me, I wouldn't be found dead in your eleven!"

"Very right and proper, I've no doubt," said the captain of the Remove. "But that doesn't let me out! You're playing to-morrow! That's settled!"

"Never!" said Wilmot forcibly.

"Never's a long word," said Harry. "I can't take you by the neck, and make you play in a match, as we were doing to make you turn up at games practice the day your uncle barged in. But if you don't turn up——"

"I shall not turn up!"

"You've licked Smithy," said Wharton. "I fancy he might have had better luck if he'd kept cool. I shall keep cool, I hope. At any rate, I'm going to do my best to give you the thrashing you're asking for! If you're not on Little Side for the game to-morrow, I will look into the study for for you afterwards, and shall expect to find you there!"

Wilmot shrugged his shoulders.

"You'll find me if you want me," he said. "I'll make a point of it!"

He turned and walked away.

He left deep silence behind him. Harry Wharton's face was almost pale with intense anger. The Co. exchanged uncomfortable looks.

"After all, the chap's right in a way," said Bob slowly at last. "No decent fellow would want to be bunged into a team by favouritism."

"That's so, Harry," said Nugent hesitatingly.

Harry Wharton nodded.

THE SIXTEENTH CHAPTER.

Under The Shadow!

ERIC WILMOT'S name remained in the Remove football list.

The next morning Wingate of the Sixth saw it there, and gave a satisfied nod. Fussy Mr. Hacker, seldom known to take any interest in games, took the trouble to give that list a glance, no doubt having heard from Wingate what he might expect to see there. He, too, gave a satisfied nod.

Wingate was satisfied, and Hacker was satisfied, but there was little satisfaction elsewhere.

Wharton said nothing, and Wilmot said nothing, and most of the Remove remained in the belief that Wilmot was playing, and in the belief that his uncle, the Shell beak, had wangled it. If Wilmot had been unpopular before, he was doubly and trebly unpopular now. Wharton, too, came in for some severe criticism for having allowed himself to be dictated to in such a matter.

Meanwhile, with all the Remove irritated because Wilmot was going to play, the captain of that Form was still more deeply and intensely irritated because he wasn't—which was a very unusual and peculiar state of affairs.

When the footballers went to the changing-room in the afternoon, Eric Wilmot did not go with them. Wharton noticed his absence, with a bitter compression of the lips.

Bob Cherry, always anxious to pour oil on the troubled waters, scuttled out to look for the fellow. It was incomprehensible to Bob's honest mind that a fellow who had a chance of playing football should prefer to loaf about in the sulks.

"Seen Wilmot, Bunter?" he called out.

"He's gone to Quelch's study," answered the fat Owl.

"Oh blow!"

Bob went along to Masters' Passage, to wait for Wilmot when he came away from Quelch. He waited at the corner impatiently, hoping that the fellow would not be long with the Remove beak.

As a matter of fact, he was not long. But Bob little guessed why he had been called in by the Remove beak.

Mr. Quelch, in his study, was handing him a letter.

"This letter has come for you, Wilmot," said the Remove master coldly. "It was not placed in the rack as usual, because——" He paused. "I understand from Mr. Hacker that, for—

h'm—certain reasons, the name of your former school has not been mentioned here!"

"That is so, sir!" answered Wilmot, in a low voice, his eyes on the floor.

"It would therefore have been judicious," said Mr. Quelch, "to hold no correspondence with your former friends at Topham, Wilmot!"

"I have had none, sir! Nobody there knows that I came to Greyfriars."

Mr. Quelch tapped the letter.

"This does not look like it," he said curtly. "The postmark on that envelope is Topham!"

Wilmot started violently.

He looked at the letter. Evidently he recognised the handwriting of the address—a thin, spidery hand.

"Crawley!" he muttered.

"It would have been wiser to tell no one, Wilmot."

"I told no one, sir! But that fellow Crawley knew I had an uncle a master here, so I suppose he guessed——"

"It is very unfortunate," said Mr. Quelch. "The postmark would probably have been noticed had the letter been placed in the rack as usual. However, there is no harm done. You may take the letter, Wilmot."

Wilmot left the study with the letter in his hand, and an overwhelmed expression on his face. He did not see Bob Cherry waiting at the corner till Bob caught him by the arm.

"Time, old man!" said Bob amicably. "Come along, and——"

Wilmot wrenched his arm away.

"What do you mean? Let me alone!"

"Time to change for footer, old bean," said Bob soothingly. "Hadn't you better——"

"Leave me alone, you fool!"

Wilmot tramped past him and went up to his study in the Remove, the letter still in his hand. Bob stared after him. He refrained from following him and banging his head on the banisters, as he was strongly tempted to do. There was something more than sulks in the fellow's look—he looked like a fellow knocked out by an unexpected blow.

Bob went quietly back to the changing-room.

"Isn't our dear Eric turnin' up, after all?" called out the Bounder. "Has the dear boy changed his mind?"

"Are we going to wait for him?" sneered Hazel.

"No!" said Wharton, with a deep breath.

"You'll want another man," said Bolsover major. He was keen enough.

"Yes; you get changed, Bolsover."

"Like a bird!"

The Remove team went down to the field without Eric Wilmot. There was a good deal of curiosity on the subject; the Bounder was quite perplexed. So far as Smithy could see, the fellow had "wangled" this by greasing to a beak, and then, at the last moment, turned it down. Anyhow, Wilmot was not there; and the Form match was played without him.

Temple, Dabney & Co., of the Fourth, went through their usual grilling at the hands of the Remove. Vernon-Smith played a hard game, in the hope of convincing the captain of the Remove that he really was the man for the Rookwood match when it came along. But he was sadly off his form, and did not succeed in convincing even himself.

But Temple & Co. were handsomely beaten by three to nil, all the same. After the match, in the changing-room, there was a good deal of talk about

Wilmot, and his peculiar and unexpected proceedings. Wharton did not join in it.

Having changed very quickly, he left before the other fellows. Frank Nugent, with his head poking out of a shirt half-on, stopped him at the door.

"Harry, old chap——" he muttered.

Wharton looked at him grimly.

"Well?" he said.

"It's not worth while——" said Nugent uneasily.

"I don't agree!"

Harry Wharton walked away with that. He was in almost a white heat with intense anger. He had told Wilmot what to expect if he did not turn up for the match; and the fellow had not turned up. Now he was going to take the consequences.

Quietly, but with a grim set face, he went up to the Remove passage. He had no doubt that he would find Wilmot in the study. Whatever the fellow was, he was not a funk. He had said that he would be there, and Wharton had no doubt of finding him there.

The door of Study No. 1 in the Remove was half-open. There was no sound from the study.

Wharton glanced in.

His lips came hard together. If the fellow was not there—— The next moment he saw that Wilmot was there; though so silent and still that anyone might have supposed that the study was unoccupied.

If he had heard Wharton's footsteps, he did not stir. But it was clear that he had not heard them.

He was sitting in the window-seat, with the glimmer of the winter sun on his head. But his face could not be seen—it was buried in his hands, his elbows resting on his knees.

Wharton stared at him.

This was not the sulky, defiant, insolent fellow he had expected to see. It was a fellow limp, overwhelmed, crushed. Clearly, he did not know that Wharton was there. He was unconscious of everything but the black trouble that weighed him down.

Wharton did not speak. He could only stare. Insensibly, his anger faded away. What was the matter with the fellow to crush him like this? A letter lay on the floor at his feet. It looked as if it had been savagely crumpled before it was dropped.

Wilmot sat there, with hidden face, like a figure of stone. Then Wharton saw him stir, and he stepped back quickly out of the study. He disliked the fellow intensely, but he wanted to spare him the humiliation of having been seen thus.

He heard Wilmot's voice in a low broken tone as he stepped back.

"What am I going to do? Oh, what—what am I going to do now?"

Harry Wharton went quietly down the passage to the stairs. His anger was gone—utterly gone—at the sight of that vision of misery and despair. Quietly, the captain of the Remove went down the stairs.

. . . . . .

Harry Wharton's chums were surprised and relieved to find that the expected "row" had not come off. But he did not tell them why.

THE END.

(The next story in this grand series featuring Eric Wilmot is entitled: "THE FORM-MASTER'S FAVOURITE!" Look out for it in next Saturday's bumper issue of the MAGNET, chums!)

THE MAGNET LIBRARY.—No. 1,458.

DAN of the DOGGER BANK!

By DAVID GOODWIN.

Some Sea Trip!

KENNETH GRAHAM, son of a millionaire shipowner, is rescued off the Dogger Bank by the crew of the fishing trawler, Grey Seal.

His past life a blank, he is given the name of "Dogger Dan," and signed on as fifth hand under Skipper Atheling, Finn Macoul. Wat Griffiths, and Buck Atheling.

Aware of his nephew's fate, and knowing that he will be heir to the shipowner's money when his brother dies, Dudley Graham engages Jake Rebow and his cut-throats of the Black Squadron to get Kenneth out of the way for ever.

Following a fruitless attempt on their lives by Rebow's confederates, Dan and Buck Atheling are wrecked on Baltrum Island, the only occupant of which is a wealthy old Dutchman named Jan Osterling, who is later brutally attacked by two of the Squadron's men and left to die.

Before breathing his last, Jan asks the boys to hand over his savings to his nephew Max, in return for which he hands them a chart, disclosing the whereabouts of a hidden treasure worth £5,000, to be divided between them.

Dan and Buck eventually rejoin the Grey Seal, but fail to interest Skipper Atheling in the matter of the treasure.

Later, while out fishing in the ship's boat, the two chums try to bag a whale. Misfortune befalls them, however, for the whale gets away, towing the boat and its occupants along in its wake like a torpedo-boat on steaming trial.

They rushed along without a pause, tearing over the sea in a white lather of foam, the wind whistling in their ears.

Dan cast a glance over his shoulder. "The Seal's nearly out of sight!" he said. "What's to be done?"

"Can't do anything," gasped Buck, "except wait till the whale exhausts himself an' dies! He's wounded deep. If you got into the bows to cut the line the boat'd go down head-first."

"Wish he'd tow us to Baltrum!" said Dan, giddy with the sense of speed. Then suddenly his voice changed. "He's stopping! He's done for!"

"Ay, he's in his flurry!" cried Dick. "Now look out for squalls!"

The whale slowed down, stopped, and began to lash the water in its death-agony. The harpoon had taken strong effect. The impetus of the boat had drove her right alongside.

A practised whaling-crew, in a proper boat, would have known how to deal with the situation. But with the two chums it was different. Before they could run out the oars, they were in the centre of danger.

Flap—whack! went the huge tail, with a force that would have knocked down a cottage. It struck the boat with a splintering crash, breaking it nearly in half, and flinging the boys into the water. Dan and Buck were fortunate not to be killed outright by the blow, which just missed them.

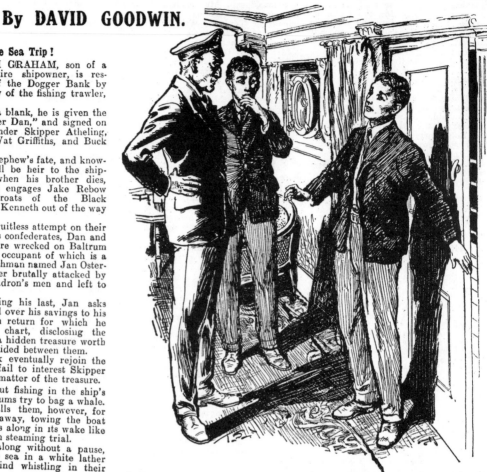

As Dan's eyes met those of the yacht-owner, the big man started violently. "Uncle Dudley!" gasped Dan, catching his breath.

Desperately they struck out away from the furious turmoil. The water was red with blood and tainted as though with musk. Presently the struggles ceased, and the whale, dying, sank to the sea-bottom.

"If we'd only known!" groaned Buck an hour later.

The sun was going down, and the air grew chill, and the water chillier still. The boys were clinging to the wrecked boat—as much of it as floated—and there was no sign of help. The Grey Seal was nowhere to be seen.

"If we'd known, we could ha' avoided this. I've heard some o' these brutes sink when they're killed."

"It looks as if he's done his best to kill us," said Dan, trying to still his chattering teeth. "Not a vessel in sight, and no food or drink. Can't hold out till morning like this. The water's deathly cold. I'm numb to the bone already."

"Same here," said Buck. "Better ha' let the beast alone."

Hour after hour the boys drifted on, not knowing which moment would be their last. Their numbed arms only clung to the boat mechanically. Soon they knew the end must come.

Towards morning, when he had given up hope and could hold on no longer, Dan raised despairing eyes, and saw the triangle of lights of a steamer coming towards them, bow on.

"Wake up, old boy!" he said hoarsely in Buck's ear. "Here's a vessel coming along!"

Buck was already nearly in the grip of the fatal lethargy of cold and exhaustion, when the new hope roused him.

"A steamer comin' right at us! Save your breath, an' get ready to shout as soon as she's near enough!"

The vessel came on, the throb of her engines beating steadily in the silence of the night. It seemed as though she would run the boys down.

Then, as she approached, a hoarse, angry cry rang out—a wild laugh, as of a man crazed by drink or madness.

She steamed along steadily, and showed herself as a low, black vessel of shapely lines.

"A queer ship, that!" muttered Buck. "Why, she's a yacht! Let's shout, Dan —both together!"

"Ahoy! Ahoy! Ahoy!"

The yacht glided past, taking no heed.

Printed in Great Britain and published every Saturday by the Proprietors, The Amalgamated Press, Ltd., The Fleetway House, Farringdon Street, London. E.C.4. Advertisement offices : The Fleetway House, Farringdon Street, London, E.C.4. Registered for transmission by Canadian Magazine Post. Subscription rates : Inland and Abroad, 11s. per annum; 5s. 6d. for six months. Sole Agents for Australia and New Zealand : Messrs. Gordon & Gotch, Ltd., and for South Africa : Central News Agency, Ltd.—Saturday, January 25th, 1936.

Despairingly the boys shouted. A man looked over the side, listened, and spoke. Still the yacht went on.

"If she passes," groaned Dan, "we haven't another half-hour to live!"

There was a noise of quarrelling upon the vessel's bridge, and again the wild, drunken laugh sounded from somewhere in the heart of her. Then followed the sound of a blow and a sharp, double ring in the engine-room. The vessel slowed down.

The moonbeams played upon her stern, showing in raised golden letters the name—Ercildoune. Over the waters sounded the screech of davit-blocks, as a boat was lowered away.

A prayer of thankfulness rose to the lips of the boys. Then Buck, staring at the strange craft, uttered a startled exclamation.

"Dan—Dan!" he cried. "It's the black steam yacht—the one that ran us down on the Dogger!"

A Shock For Two !

"HAUL 'em aboard, you fox-eyed dago, or I'll lay you out! Ah, you drop 'em back, an' see what happens!"

Buck and Dan, dripping, sore, and exhausted, were helped out of the quarter-boat on to the deck of the steam-yacht.

A dark-brown, Southern-looking sailor was their helper, and he looked as though he did not like his job. But the savage voice of the English mate by the rail warned him, as above, and the man obeyed.

Buck thought it a rather rum order to give. Why should the Portuguese want to drop them back again?

But he was too exhausted to think it out.

"Welcome aboard, my lads!" said the mate, a strong-faced, tough-looking man, in smart yacht uniform. "Glad to ha' pulled you out of it, though it's a pity you ain't chanced on a better vessel."

"Get to your stations, there! you yellow scum, there! Steward, take these lads below. Give 'em hot cocoa an' grub, an' rig 'em out in dry clothes. Come up to the bridge when it's done, young 'uns. It's my watch. Jack Ward's my name, an' mate's my rating."

The steward was a foreigner like the crew; the boys could get nothing out of him.

"This is a rum go!" said Buck. "Crew are all dagoes; but I'll bet my last bob that this is the craft that ran us down off the Little Bank, when you fell overboard through the old Seal's broken rail!"

"Sure you didn't make a mistake?" put in Dan dubiously.

They went up the bridge ladder, and the mate greeted them cheerily.

"Feel better, young 'uns?" he asked kindly. "Now let's hear how you come adrift on half a boat."

"Hadn't we better pay our respects to the owner, Mr. Mate?" asked Buck.

"If you'll take my tip, you'll do nothing o' the kind, my lad," answered the mate. "However, he's below in the saloon or his smokin'-room, an' you can go if you like."

"One of us ought to thank him," said Dan. "You're the eldest, Buck. If he hadn't owned a yacht, we should be food for fish by this time."

Buck went off rather reluctantly, and Dan, standing by the mate, and looking out over the starlit sea, told the tale of his late disaster with the whale.

"If I were a landsman," said the mate, "I should call you a blessed liar; but I've known queerer things happen at sea."

"You're right," said Dan. "I've got one in my mind at the present moment, and it's worrying me."

"What may that be?" said the mate.

"Well, don't be offended, but did you ever—er—that is to say, did this vessel ever—"

"Spill it out, my lad!" said the mate inelegantly, as Dan paused.

"Did this craft happen to run down a fishing-smack about three weeks ago on the Little Bank?"

The mate turned and bent a searching look upon Dan.

"What d'you mean?" he asked.

"I was on the smack," said Dan,

The instant he had spoken a doubt assailed him.

There was a moment's silence.

"Sure she did!" said the mate.

"Ah!" returned Dan. "An' p'r'aps you'll tell me why she didn't stand by afterwards?"

"If you want to know, I reckon it was because she didn't want to."

"Well," said Dan, "I know it isn't much good talking of these little blunders after they've happened. I s'pose you know the smack's name?"

"I know nothin' about her," said the mate. "It was my watch below. But as for tellin' you about it, my lad," he continued fiercely, "I don't care who knows. It's likely, as far as I can see, that you'll be the only soul outside this

---

---

ship's company I'll get the chance to tell!"

He raised his voice, and his tones were sharp with anger.

"I'll tell you another thing, my lad—you're better off on this ship than if you'd been left in the water, but not much! She's a dud ship; I wish I was off her!

"If I hadn't hazed those dagoes so they daren't call their souls their own, you wouldn't ha' been picked up at all. They only did it because they knew I'd ha' rammed the boat an' sent 'em to Davy if they'd refused! An' if it had been the captain's watch, neither he nor they would have seen or heard you, though you might ha' yelled loud enough to split a steam-whistle.

"This craft don't care to have outsiders aboard. But there's one outsider on her, an' he's outside the whole bunch. D'you know who that is?"

"Apparently it's you!" said Dan.

"Right! And I wish I was farther outside yet. D'ye hear that?"

From the interior of the vessel rang the wild, uncanny yell that had startled Dan when he was in the water.

"That's the skipper," said the mate scornfully, "nursin' the jimjams an' a bottle o' brandy. D'ye see?"

"But does the owner allow that?"

"He's got to allow it, my son. An' that'll show you what sort of a man he is. The owner is, by nature, the last man alive to take sauce from any livin' soul; but the skipper knows too much. So do the crew.

"They're all staunch by the owner, for they're a dirty lot, an' they'll stick by any blackguard who pays. This here yacht's been at sea a month. What her game is I'm just findin' out. She's thick with the worst nest o' toughs on the Northern Sea."

"You mean Rebow's lot?" said Dan.

"That's it, my lad. They're hand in glove with 'em, but only on one job. I'll tell you what—there's someone wants puttin' out o' the way. It's my belief he was on that smack o' yours, whoever he be, an' next time this craft meets his craft, he'll go to the bottom with her!"

"Ah!" said Dan.

"I asks for my discharge before I was aboard here a week. They tells me she ain't bound for a port yet; I've got to stay.

"Says I: 'Put me on the first craft we meet, an' I'm content. I ain't going to deal with a craft that has any truck with the Black Fleet.' They tries to rope me in with themselves, an' offers ten quid a week an' one hundred pounds bonus.

"The skipper puts it to me, an' if you'll look at him you'll see four of his front teeth are unshipped. That's all the answer he got. Seein' I wouldn't come round, they've tried to out me and stop my mouth. But, mark you, when it's my watch, I make this mob o' dagoes skip like goats if I as much as wink an eyelid!"

Dan's brain was in a whirl. Why this costly, luxurious steamer should concern herself with the sinking of the Grey Seal; why the owner, plainly a man of some wealth, should deal with the Black Fleet Squadron, puzzled him.

Meanwhile, Buck, who was seeking the owner below, was at first unsuccessful. As he was passing a smoking-lounge a tall, hook-nosed, bronze-skinned man stepped out and stared at him angrily.

"You the owner, sir?" asked Buck.

"Who the blazes are you?" said the tall man.

"Your craft has just picked me an' my mate up, an' we want to thank you. Buck Atheling's my name, o' the Grey Seal."

The big man suppressed a start, and his tone changed. A queer light shone in his eyes. He looked at Buck and smiled.

"Did she, by Jove!" he exclaimed. "I'm glad we had the chance of saving you. Come in and tell me all about it!"

The tall man led the way into the luxurious smoking-lounge, where he motioned the boy to a seat, and took one himself. His dark eyes roved over Buck restlessly.

"We were upset in the long-boat, sir," began Buck, preferring to say nothing of the escapade with the whale, "an' we'd been in the water a couple of hours when you picked us up. We've seen your craft before, I think."

"Seen me before? Where?"

"Not you, sir—the craft," said Buck. He did not want to open the subject now that he owed a debt of gratitude to the yacht; but he saw the owner meant to hear more. "The fact is, we—we thought this was the same vessel that ran into our trawler three weeks back on the Dogger."

"Impossible, my lad!" said the big man. "The yacht and I were at Weymouth at that time. We only came up-Channel two days ago."

"I must be mistaken, then," said Buck; and his face cleared.

The man's tones carried conviction,

and it did not occur to Buck to doubt him.

"Sorry, sir!" he said apologetically. He looked round at the tasteful and comfortable appointments of the lounge-cabin.

"You're fond of the sea, I suppose?" he continued simply. "Must be fine for anybody who can afford to just cruise about and enjoy it."

"You are right, my lad," said his host, with a pleasant smile. "I love the sea, and I live on my craft. I make it my business to know as much about the wide and narrow waters as an amateur can. But I often envy you fishers, who know the real job, and who fall in with all kinds of adventures. I am always searching for adventures—a derelict, treasure-spot. I believe even a shipwreck would delight me. But they never come my way."

"You mightn't like them if they did, sir," said Buck, grinning.

An inspiration shot through him. Here they were on a smart vessel, whose owner did not mind where he went, who loved an adventure, and who was plainly a rich man, and could, therefore, be trusted not to play false in a matter of money. Jan Osterling's treasure still lay buried on Baltrum Island, and the memory of it, and Atheling's unbelief in it, lived in Buck's brain night and day and tormented him. Here was too good a chance to miss.

"You are looking for an adventure, sir," said Buck. "I might put one in your way, and one with money in it, too. Will you help me and my mate? We'll go shares, if you like?"

"That sounds exciting," exclaimed the yacht-owner, with a laugh. "Tell me all about it."

Leaving out the details, but omitting nothing that was essential, Buck told the story of Jan Osterling's gold.

The yacht-owner was inclined to laugh at first; but Buck's earnest tones convinced him. And part of the tale he already knew.

"That's an interesting story," he said slowly. "Have you the chart you spoke of, showing the bearings of the treasure?"

"My mate has it, sir," said Buck. "I'll have a word with him."

A few moments later Dan, standing on the bridge, felt Buck's hand on his shoulder.

The younger boy's head was whirling with the thoughts that the mate's story had awakened in him. New ideas formed themselves, old ones returned, and as his brain cleared Dan felt a kind of click in his brain-pan, as though a

spring had suddenly uncoiled there. His emotions made him feel almost physically sick.

The memory of Dogger Dan was returning.

"Let me have Jan Osterling's plan, old boy," said Buck. "The owner of this hooker is going to help us find the treasure."

Buck's voice sounded faint and far away to Dan's ear. He was deep in other thoughts.

Mechanically, not knowing what he was doing, he drew the little parchment chart from his breast-pocket and handed it to Buck, who started at once for the cabin.

Before he had vanished down the companion Dan turned and walked slowly after him.

"Here's the chart, sir," said Buck, entering the lounge cabin and showing the plan to his host.

The yacht-owner took it and examined it closely. His face gave no sign of emotion.

"Looks all right, unless it's a fake," he said at last, returning it as Buck held out his hand. "We'll go to Baltrum and investigate. By the way, who is the companion you spoke of? Bring him in here, I'd like to see him."

"He's here now, sir," said Buck, as a footstep sounded outside.

The door opened, and Dan entered. As his eyes met those of the yacht-owner the big man started violently, and in his eyes dawned a gleam of fierce satisfaction, which was suppressed an instant later.

Dan stopped suddenly, and caught his breath.

"Uncle Dudley!" he gasped.

Dead silence followed Dan's exclamation. Buck stood staring from one to the other, amazed.

"Pardon me," said Dudley Graham, with perfect composure, "but I fail to understand you!"

"Do you mean to say," said Dan slowly, "that you are not my Uncle Dudley? Either I'm mad or you are!"

Dudley turned to Buck with a pitying air.

"Is your companion right in the head?" he asked.

"Well, I—I—we——" Buck stammered, hardly knowing what to say.

He had a strong suspicion that the bee in Dan's bonnet was beginning to buzz again.

"Quite so! Quite so!" said the yacht-owner sympathetically. "A sad case! And whom do you imagine yourself to be, my poor lad?" he continued, turning to Dan again.

"I'm Kenneth Graham, son of Donald

Graham, the ship-builder, of Greenock."

Buck looked at his chum in amazement.

"What's your opinion?" said Dudley, addressing Buck. "Do you know him by that name?"

"We call him Dogger Dan on the old Seal," said Buck, bewildered. "But it may be true, for all I know," he continued, shooting a keen glance at the yacht-owner. "We picked him up at sea. He had a crack on the head, and didn't know his name. But if Dan says so I believe him. Son o' Donald Graham! Gosh!"

"You will perhaps allow me to know my own brother's son," said Dudley calmly. "This lad is certainly not he. He has been injured in the head, you say, and lost his memory. The delusion has taken shape!"

Dan said nothing, but kept his eyes fixed on the bronzed man who denied his relationship in such a quiet, polished voice.

"However," said Dudley, with a smile, "let us say no more about that. What you both need most is a good meal, I imagine. Come to the saloon in a quarter of an hour's time, and we will do what we can for you."

The boys left the lounge.

The moment he was outside Dan darted up to the bridge. The mate was still in charge.

"Ward," said Dan anxiously, "will you do something for me?"

"Ay," said the mate—"and welcome! You and that other kid are the only white folk on the ship! What d'ye want?"

"Can you send a radio message for me?" asked Dan.

"Sorry, I can't!" The mate shook his head. "We've got aerials and a receiver, o' course; we can receive messages. But we ain't got any transmitting plant; I dunno why. This is a silent ship; she can listen, but she don't talk."

"Well, can you signal the first passing ship that's got radio and tell her to broadcast a wireless message?"

"Ay, I can do that, of course. It won't be easy, with this crew o' monkeys puttin' their oar into everything—but I'll do it! What's the message?"

"To Donald Graham, Yacht Valhalla —or wherever he may be. Tell him that his son, Kenneth Graham, is alive and is on Dudley's yacht, Ercildoune! And give our position and reckoning—as near as you can."

(Boys, whatever you do, don't fail to read next week's gripping chapters of this popular sea-adventure story—you'll vote 'em great!)

The Magnet 2ᴰ

COME INTO the OFFICE, BOYS ~ AND GIRLS !

Your Editor is always pleased to hear from his readers. Write to him : Editor of the "Magnet," The Amalgamated Press, Ltd., Fleetway House, Farringdon Street, London, E.C.4. A stamped, addressed envelope will ensure a reply.

WELL, chums, I can imagine how anxious you all are to read this week's chat. For did I not tell you last week that I had something up my sleeve—something that would make you sit up and take notice ? I will, therefore, proceed to let the cat out of the bag.

FREE GIFTS ARE COMING YOUR WAY !

How's that for a jolly surprise ? Naturally enough, you all want to know what form these FREE GIFTS take, so I guess I'll spill the beans, as our old friend Fisher T. Fish would say. A fortnight from now—in the MAGNET dated February 15th—every reader will receive ABSOLUTELY FREE a pair of

MAGIC SPECTACLES,

together with the first of a set of

PICTURES THAT COME TO LIFE !

The wonderful spectacles—a first-rate scientific novelty in themselves—cause the specially printed photographs, which are presented with them, to spring to life in the most amazing way. Further pictures, of a diversity of interesting subjects, will be presented to readers from week to week, and the whole set, together with the "magic" spectacles, will make up a most fascinating and intriguing gift, which will keep you and your friends amused for hours.

This is the most novel and interesting gift that has ever been presented with any boys' paper, so that it is up to you, chums, to tell your newsagent to reserve a copy of the MAGNET for you every week in order that you may make sure of getting

THESE SCIENTIFIC FREE GIFTS

and the complete set of Special Pictures. Seeing is believing, chums, so don't wait to hear what other boys and girls have to say about these marvellous FREE GIFTS—be one of the first to get them by placing a regular order for the MAGNET at the very earliest opportunity.

In conjunction with this greatest-ever free gift scheme I am arranging

AN EXTRA-SPECIAL PROGRAMME

of stories. Frank Richards is turning in a grand new series of Greyfriars yarns, in which a conspicuous part is played by a character so many of you have been wanting to meet again—Jim Valentine, who was more commonly known as "Dick, the Penman." You remember him, don't you ? Jim Valentine was a character that will for ever remain in the minds of MAGNET readers. I know you will all be glad to renew your acquaintance with him in one of the finest and most exciting series of stories Frank Richards has ever penned. Now for the next special treat. George E. Rochester, who has written so many masterpieces for us, is contributing a tip-top tale of adventure on land, sea and in the air, with an

THE MAGNET LIBRARY.—No. 1,459.

entirely original plot. These together with our other features will make a strong programme, what ? Make a note of the date so that you don't forget—February 15th issue, which, incidentally, will be on sale FRIDAY, February 7th, 1936.

I'VE received rather a poser from Charles Goom, one of my Berkshire readers, this week. He wants to know which are

THE BIGGEST AIRWAYS IN THE WORLD !

That's rather a peculiar question, because I am not quite sure what he means by "Airways." But he will probably learn what he wants to know from the following particulars :

The largest land plane in the world is the Soviet plane called the "Maxim Gorky." It carries 40 passengers, and has a crew of 23. It is fitted with a printing plant, a "movie" projector, and loudspeakers, and is used for carrying out educational work in out-of-the-way parts of Russia.

The longest air race in the world will be that which is being organised in America at the present moment. The course will be about 20,000 miles in length, and is called the "Around the Americas" course. From New York the aviators must fly round the east coast of the United States to Christobal. Then they must go around the east coast of South America as far as Buenos Aires, across the Andes to Santiago, and back via the west coasts of South, Central and North America, via Mexico City, San Francisco and Chicago.

It remains to be seen which will become the longest airway passenger route. At the time of writing, various countries are entering into competition with each other to provide transatlantic airway routes. The Graf Zeppelin now holds the record for the longest passenger route. But the big air companies of other countries are amalgamating their resources, and in a short while we are likely to see vast strides in the airways of the world.

SOME very strange things happen in this weird old world of ours. Here is a further selection of these curiosities which I have collected for you. Do you know that

ANTS CAN KILL ELEPHANTS ?

Driver ants swarm in the African jungles, and do not hesitate to attack even elephants ! The ants travel in armies comprising hundreds of thousands, and the elephant is so bulky that it cannot fight against such small enemies. If the elephant can gain the safety of deep water it can escape. If not fortunate enough, it is doomed. The ants make for the elephant's trunk, and drive the beast almost mad with pain. Hundreds of thousands more ants cover its body, and their numbers are so great that they can tear aside even the toughest parts of its hide. It is estimated that an army of driver ants can eat the whole of an

elephant, except the skeleton, in three days !

Here is another interesting paragraph concerning

THE GHOST CITY OF INDIA !

It is the city of Fatehpur Sikri, and was constructed by a famous Mogul emperor in 1569. It is built of marble and sandstone, contains a magnificent emperor's palace, an arch of victory, and extensive soldiers' quarters and stables. Altogether, it is seven miles in circumference, and yet, fifty years after it was built, it was abandoned, and no one has lived there since. Furthermore, although there are many legends about this ghost city, its true history cannot be traced. It is said that the reason for its abandonment was because the water supply was impure. Anyway, for well over three hundred years this strange city of ghosts has been deserted.

THINGS YOU'D HARDLY BELIEVE

have always been popular with my readers, so here are some more strange, but certainly interesting, facts :

A Whale with Two Heads was once caught off South Georgia, a British whaling station in the South Atlantic.

A Man who Ate his Boots ! On the outbreak of the Russia-Japanese war a Moscow merchant bet that he would eat his boots if the Japanese were not beaten. He lost his bet—had his boots cooked—and kept his word by eating them !

A Man with a Billion Pounds is Richer than a Man with Seven Billion Dollars ! A billion in Britain is a million million. In America a billion is only a thousand millions !

A Fish that has Four Eyes ! The Anableps, a South American fish, possesses two pairs of eyes. One pair are nearsighted for use under water. The upper pair are long-sighted, and enable the fish to see insects when swimming with its head only partly submerged.

A Cavern Illuminated by Insects ! Glow-worm Grotto, in the Waitomo Caves, New Zealand, is the haunt of millions of tiny glow-worms. The glowworms provide all the natural light to illuminate the cave.

Men Buried within Growing Trees ! In Borneo certain tribes cut out graves from huge trees, bury their chiefs inside, and then seal up the trees !

I guess the above paragraphs will give you something to think about, chums. And now I know what you are thinking about at the moment, and that is : "What has the MAGNET in store for next week ?"

Something good, you may be sure. Your Editor, his staff, his authors and artists have been busier than ever lately, and we have something specially good in store for you next week. First of all there is

"THE REMOVE'S RECRUIT !" By Frank Richards,

the final yarn in our present series, featuring Eric Wilmot. Up till now Wilmot has seemed a queer sort of fellow, but in this grand story he "pulls his socks up" with a vengeance ! Like all Frank Richards' stories, this yarn is calculated to keep you enthralled from the first chapter to the last. There are lots of thrills in store for you, and lots of humour, too. Our serial, as mentioned earlier on, closes down with next week's chapters, but there's no scarcity of thrills, believe me. The smaller features follow as usual. A final word—place a standing order with your newsagent for the MAGNET right away !

Don't forget the Great Free Gift Programme for the week after next !

YOUR EDITOR.

The FORM-MASTER'S FAVOURITE!

By FRANK RICHARDS

Harry Wharton & Co., of the Greyfriars Remove, are only too pleased to welcome new boys into the fold. But a sulky, sullen and discontented fellow like Eric Wilmot—dubbed the Form-master's favourite—is a horse of a different colour !

THE FIRST CHAPTER.

A Rag in the Remove !

"HENRY'S late !" remarked Bob Cherry.

There was a chuckle in the Remove Form Room at Greyfriars.

The Remove had come in for third school at the sound of the bell, but Mr. Quelch, instead of being punctually on the spot, as usual, was not to be seen.

Mr. Quelch rejoiced in the given names of Henry Samuel; but what he would have thought, had he heard a member of his Form speak of him as "Henry," was unimaginable.

What he would have done was more easily to be guessed! So it was rather fortunate for Bob that "Henry" was out of hearing.

"I say, you fellows, the old bean's talking to Hacker!" said Billy Bunter. "Hacker stopped him at the end of the passage."

"Good old Hacker!" remarked Johnny Bull. "I don't like Hacker's jaw myself, but let's hope that Quelch does."

"Let us hope that the jawfulness will be terrific!" agreed Hurree Jamset Ram Singh.

The Remove were by no means unwilling to wait for Quelch. Third lesson that morning dealt with Latin prose. Hardly a man in the Remove was eager to get on with Latin prose. Quelch was welcome to "jaw" with Mr. Hacker, the master of the Shell, as long as he liked—or longer.

Vernon-Smith glanced out of the doorway.

In the distance he had a glimpse of the two masters—Mr. Hacker talking, Mr. Quelch revealing distinct signs of impatience.

The Bounder grinned as he turned back into the Form-room.

"All serene !" he said. "Hacker's got him ! More power to his elbow—I mean, to his jawbone !"

"Ha, ha, ha !"

The Removites were not without resources to fill up the time of waiting.

A model Form, of course, would have sorted out their books and concentrated on study, absorbing knowledge so far as that could be done without the assistance of their "beak."

But the Remove were not a model Form !

Only Mark Linley, who was a bit of a swot, opened a school book—and Bolsover major promptly jerked it away and spun it across the Form-room. Smithy, coming back from the door, met it in transit, and neatly passed it with a prompt foot; and three or four fellows immediately rushed after it.

"On the ball !" chirruped Bob Cherry.

"Hold on !" exclaimed Harry Wharton. Head boy of the Remove was supposed to keep some sort of order in the absence of the beak.

"Rats !" retorted the Bounder.

"Quelch may blow in any minute, you ass !"

"Oh, Quelch is safe enough," said Skinner, with a snigger. "If Hacker's got him on the subject of his dear little Eric he won't let him off in a hurry."

At which there was a loud laugh in the Remove.

Eric Wilmot, the new fellow in that Form, was sitting quietly at his desk. He did not look up, but his handsome face flushed. The fact that he was Mr. Hacker's nephew did not make things easier for the new junior.

It made them harder. For there was little doubt that Skinner was right. Fussy Mr. Hacker was just the man to stop Quelch on his way to take his class to talk to him on that very subject.

"Oh, shut up, Skinner !" said Frank Nugent, always good-natured. He did not like the new fellow—nobody in the Remove did; but he could feel for him on the subject of his fussy relative on the staff.

"My dear chap," said Skinner, "somebody chucked a snowball at Wilmot—I mean, Eric—in the quad in break. Think Hacker didn't spot it? Doesn't he spot everything that happens to Eric?"

There was another laugh, and Wilmot's ears burned.

"Bet you," continued Skinner, "Hacker's got Quelch on that very subject now. Bet you he's asking Quelch to hold an inquiry !"

"Ha, ha, ha !"

"Mustn't touch Eric !" said Skinner, shaking his head. "Fellows may look, but they mustn't touch !"

Wilmot glanced round at Skinner.

"Shut up, Skinner !" he said.

He spoke very quietly. But his cold, steady look daunted Skinner, who remembered—in time—that this fellow had beaten the Bounder in a scrap.

Skinner, with an uneasy snigger, shut up and turned away.

Whiz !

THE MAGNET LIBRARY.—No. 1,459.

Mark Linley's Latin grammar was leading the life of a Soccer ball. It came back to Vernon-Smith, who kicked it again, landing it full and fair in the handsome face of Eric Wilmot.

"Goal!" chortled the Bounder.

"Ha, ha, ha!"

"Well kicked!"

Wilmot leaped to his feet.

He rushed out of the desks, straight at the Bounder. Before Herbert Vernon-Smith knew what was happening the new fellow had grasped him, whirled him over, and was banging his head on Mr. Quelch's desk.

"Oh, my hat!"

"Look out!"

"Stop that, Wilmot!" shouted Harry Wharton.

"Wildcat!" said Skinner.

The Bounder yelled with rage and struggled wildly. But Wilmot, in that passionate outbreak of temper, seemed to have the strength of two or three fellows.

The Bounder, tough as he was, crumpled up in his angry grasp. His hapless head banged against Quelch's desk.

Tom Redwing ran forward, to drag the angry fellow away from his chum. Wilmot released one hand and shoved him back—with a shove that made Redwing stagger. Then he banged Smithy's head again.

"I say, you fellows!" squeaked Billy Bunter. His big spectacles were turned on an angular figure that had appeared in the doorway. Mr. Quelch had got away from Hacker sooner than Skinner had predicted.

But nobody else noticed Mr. Quelch's arrival. All eyes were fixed on the Bounder struggling helplessly in the grasp of Eric Wilmot.

Bang!

His head smote again.

Mr. Quelch gazed as if transfixed for a moment. Then he strode into the Form-room, his eyes glittering.

"Wilmot," he thundered, "how dare you! Release Vernon-Smith at once! How dare you, Wilmot!"

THE SECOND CHAPTER.

Wrathy!

"QUELCH!"

"Oh crumbs!"

There was a rush of the juniors to their places.

Almost in the twinkling of an eye the Removites were at their desks. Only two remained out of place—Smithy and Wilmot.

At the Form-master's voice Eric Wilmot released the Bounder instantly and turned a crimson face towards Mr. Quelch.

Vernon-Smith sprawled, panting, on the floor.

A few seconds ago the Remove-room had been full of sound. Now a pin might have been heard to drop there. For a moment or two the silence was almost awful!

Then Mr. Quelch spoke again.

"Vernon-Smith, go to your place!"

The Bounder scrambled up. He was red with rage. Even his Form-master's presence barely restrained him from hurling himself at the fellow who had handled him. But he choked back his fury and tramped away in silence to his desk.

Wilmot remained facing the Remove master. Evidently it was upon his head that the vials of wrath were to be poured.

Mr. Quelch's expressive face was set with anger.

He had reasons for not desiring Wilmot in his Form at all. He had been bothered to the limit of patience by Mr. Hacker's fussy concern for his relative in the Remove. Only a minute ago he had been exchanging sharp words with the master of the Shell on that very topic. For it was true as Skinner guessed, that Hacker, from his study window, had seen his nephew's cap knocked off by a snowball in the quad, and with his usual tactlessness Hacker had taken that trifling incident up. Quelch had been driven to tell Hacker that his nephew had not come to Greyfriars to be dry-nursed—a remark which sent Mr. Hacker back to his own Form-room in a highly offended frame of mind. Equally annoyed, Quelch had come along to the Remove-room—to behold Hacker's nephew in the act of banging another fellow's head on his own particular desk!

Hacker seemed to be under the delusion that his nephew required to be protected in a rough-and-ready Form like the Remove. Really this did not look like it.

"How dare you, Wilmot!" repeated Mr. Quelch. "How dare you handle another boy in that ruffianly manner!"

"Sorry, sir!" muttered Wilmot. He realised that his angry temper had carried him too far.

"Only last week," said Mr. Quelch, "you were fighting with Vernon-Smith, and I received a complaint on the subject." He did not add that the complaint had come from Hacker, but all the Remove knew.

Wilmot's face, already crimson, burned.

"I never complained, sir——" he muttered.

"You had little reason to do so, I think, as I find you handling the same boy like a ruffianly bully!" snapped Mr. Quelch.

The Bounder gritted his teeth.

The knocking of his head on Quelch's desk had not been pleasant, but Smithy would rather have had it knocked off than have been supposed to be in need of protection from his Form-master. He jumped to his feet.

"If you please, sir——"

"You may be silent, Vernon-Smith, and——"

"I started the row, sir——"

"You will take a hundred lines, Vernon-Smith, and be silent."

"That fellow can't handle me!" said the Bounder savagely. "If he hadn't taken me by surprise——"

"If you speak another word, Vernon-Smith, I shall give you a detention for the half-holiday this afternoon."

The Bounder sat down again in savage silence. He did not want a detention. There was football that afternoon in the Remove.

"Wilmot!" Mr. Quelch fixed his gimlet-eyes on the new junior again. "You have been more trouble to me than any other boy in the Form since you came here. You appear to have made yourself generally disliked by a sullen, sulky—I may say, evil temper. You will have to learn, Wilmot, to restrain that temper—in the Form-room, at least."

Wilmot did not answer. He stood silent, with the sulky expression that seemed habitual to his face settling there darkly.

"I shall punish you for this outbreak," went on Mr. Quelch, "by a half-holiday's detention. You will be detained this afternoon, Wilmot, from two o'clock till tea-time. Now go to your place."

Wilmot gave a start.

"Detained this afternoon, sir!" he repeated.

"Yes. Go to your place at once."

"But, sir——" stammered Wilmot.

He seemed quite taken aback by that sentence. Really it was not a severe one, in the circumstances. Most of the fellows had expected Quelch to order him to bend over and take six.

Neither was the loss of a half-holiday such a blow to Wilmot as it would have been to most fellows. He was not in the football, and he did not want to be. He had not made a single friend in the Form—unless Billy Bunter was to be counted as one—so he could have fixed up nothing in another fellow's company for that half-holiday. Indeed, he generally spent his half-holidays in solitary rambles.

But he seemed quite overwhelmed. Mr. Quelch, noticing it, paused. He was a severe gentleman, and at the moment he was very angry, but in matters of the Form games he was a very considerate master.

"Wharton!" he rapped.

"Yes, sir!" answered the captain of the Remove.

"Is there a football match this afternoon?"

"Yes, sir—a pick-up game."

"Is Wilmot playing in it?"

"Oh, no!" answered Harry, suppressing a smile. Some of the Removites grinned. Wilmot turned up unwillingly for games practice when that was compulsory, on other occasions he was never seen near Little Side. That added to his unpopularity in the Remove—if it needed adding to.

"Very good!" said Mr. Quelch. "Go to your place, Wilmot."

"But, sir——"

"If you say another word, Wilmot, I shall cane you!"

Wilmot turned and went to his place. His handsome face was darker than before.

Some of the fellows looked at him curiously. Why a fellow should seem so overwhelmed by a sentence of detention when, as a rule, he had nothing to do on a half-holiday was rather a puzzle, but it was plain that Wilmot was troubled and dismayed by that sentence.

The Remove were particularly good during that lesson. There was a glint in Quelch's gimlet-eye—and nobody wanted to catch that eye. Even Billy Bunter contrived to give a little attention; even Lord Mauleverer tried hard to take a little interest in Latin syntax. But Wilmot was letting his thoughts wander, and two or three times Quelch called him sharply to order, and every time he spoke to the new junior there seemed to be a more acid edge to Quelch's tongue.

When the Form were dismissed Wilmot lingered after the others. Mr. Quelch, busy with papers at his high desk, glanced at him icily.

Doubtless the new junior had lingered with some idea of making an appeal to be let off that afternoon, but that icy stare from Quelch discouraged him. It would have been futile, and he knew it.

Slowly he followed the other fellows from the Form-room.

They were going out into the keen, frosty air of the quadrangle. Nobody had a word to say to Wilmot. Fellows who had been disposed to be friendly—or, at least, civil—had given him up as a bad job. Only Bunter was hanging about for him—which did not seem to gratify the new fellow as he came along. The fat Owl gave him a cheery, fat grin.

"Oh, here you are, old chap!" said Bunter. "I say, tough luck getting detention this afternoon—what?"

Wilmot, with the curtest of nods, walked on. Bunter rolled by his side.

"Not that it will hurt you much, of course," went on Bunter. "You never have anything to do on a half-holiday, do you?"

No answer from Wilmot. He quickened his pace a little; so did Bunter.

"No friends or anything," went on Bunter. "Except me, of course. I stick to you, don't I, old chap?"

There was no doubt that Bunter did. But Wilmot's look did not indicate that it afforded him any pleasure. He walked a little faster. So did Bunter.

"But I was going to tell you something, old fellow," added Bunter. "I say, what do you think?"

Wilmot did not state what he thought.

"Guess!" said Bunter.

Wilmot did not guess.

THE THIRD CHAPTER.
Proof Positive.

HERBERT VERNON-SMITH burst into a loud laugh.

There was nothing, so far as the other fellows could see, to amuse the Bounder, and they looked at him in surprise.

The Famous Five of the Remove were talking in a group with Peter Todd, Tom Brown, Squiff, and two or three other Removites. The topic was Soccer —an interesting one to the Removites. Vernon-Smith was standing with them, his hands in his pockets, and a scowl on his face, not joining in the talk. Smithy, once a pillar of strength in the Remove Eleven, was hopelessly off his form this term, and had almost ceased to count in Remove football—a position that was a constant irritant to

shop. Temple of the Fourth was brushing a speck of dust from an immaculate sleeve. These things—and others—were to be seen in the quad, but there was nothing of a specially comic nature.

"That new tick!" said the Bounder.

"Can't see him," said Bob. "What about him, anyhow?"

"Look at Hacker's window!"

The juniors were standing not far from the windows of Masters' Studies. Many of those windows were open, to admit the bright, frosty sunshine of the winter morning.

Hacker's was open, and the interior of the study could be seen if anyone was interested therein. Nobody was—till what was passing there caught the Bounder's eye, and he drew the attention of the other fellows to it.

Mr. Hacker was in his study. Stand-

Vernon-Smith, tough as he was, crumpled up in Wilmot's angry grasp. His hapless head banged against Quelch's desk. "I say, you fellows!" squeaked Billy Bunter. His big spectacles had turned on an angular figure that had appeared in the doorway. It was that of Mr. Quelch, the master of the Remove!

"Well, I'll tell you," said the fat Owl. "Mrs. Mimble's got in a fresh lot of meringues! I had one in break, and I can tell you they're spiffing! I say, there'll be a rush on them when the fellows know! Come on!"

Wilmot did not come on.

He cut off.

"I say, Wilmot!" shouted Bunter.

Wilmot disappeared.

"Beast!"

Billy Bunter went to the tuckshop alone; but, owing to a lack of cash, or of a friend with cash, he was only able to feast his eyes, instead of his fat interior—which was very annoying to the Owl of the Remove, and made him feel strongly tempted to tell Wilmot what he thought of him. Still, there was tea-time to be considered; so, on second thoughts—proverbially the best—Bunter kept to himself what he thought of the sulky new fellow.

the Bounder's arrogant temper. His sudden harsh, sardonic laugh broke on the cheery chat.

"What's the joke, fathead?" asked Bob Cherry.

"Look round and see!" grinned the Bounder.

Bob and the other fellows looked round. There were plenty of fellows and some masters to be seen in the quad. Prout, master of the Fifth, was walking there, stately and portly, with Monsieur Charpentier, little and dapper. Wingate of the Sixth could be seen with Gwynne of that Form. Coker of the Fifth was talking to Potter and Greene, apparently laying down the law in his usual style. Nugent minor of the Second was scraping some remnant of snow from a corner, no doubt with hostile intentions towards some other fag. Billy Bunter was blinking in at the window of the school

ing before him was his nephew in the Remove—Eric Wilmot.

All eyes fixed on that little scene.

The Bounder laughed again—a sardonic laugh.

"Caught in the act!" he chuckled.

"Oh!" said Harry Wharton, rather blankly.

"The sneaking tick!" grunted Johnny Bull.

"Rotten worm!" said Squiff.

"The rottenness of the esteemed worm is terrific!" declared Hurree Jamset Ram Singh.

Harry Wharton, gazing at Hacker's window, frowned. Wharton was on the worst of terms with the new junior—all the more, perhaps, because Wilmot had been placed in Study No. 1 in the Remove, with him and Nugent, and so he had more than a fair share of the fellow's sulky looks. But Wharton had

THE MAGNET LIBRARY.—No. 1,459.

never believed that Wilmot "greased" up to his uncle, the beak

The Bounder was sure of it. But, as Smithy had had a row with him, and had been licked in a scrap, he was probably prejudiced on the subject.

It was known all over the Remove that Hacker "fussed," and that he had bothered Quelch about "Eric." Many fellows took the Bounder's view that Wilmot made the most of his relationship with a Form-master. But Wharton had inclined to the view that Wilmot thoroughly disliked Hacker's well-meant but tactless interventions on his behalf. He did not believe for a moment that the new fellow carried complaints to his uncle.

So it was a little startling to see him at the present moment in Hacker's study, deep in talk with Hacker. Remove fellows, of course, had nothing to do with the master of the Shell, and had no business in his study.

Wharton compressed his lips. He had refused to take the Bounder's view, and had, indeed, told Smithy that it was all rot, and malicious rot! Now he did not know what to say.

"What about it now?" grinned the Bounder. "I bet I can make a guess at what he's telling dear nunky."

"Oh, rubbish!" said Bob uneasily. "After all, the man's his uncle. Why shouldn't he drop into his study and speak to him?"

"Yes, that's it," said Harry, relieved by the suggestion. "I dare say Hacker makes him come in and jaw, too."

"Quite likely," agreed Nugent.

"The chap would show a little more sense in keeping away from Hacker's study, knowing what all the fellows think!" remarked Peter Todd dryly.

"Well, he doesn't care much what fellows think," said Bob.

· "Then he jolly well ought to!"

"The oughtfulness is terrific!"

Vernon-Smith sneered unpleasantly.

"You don't think that cad is greasing up to Hacker at this very minute," he asked, "telling him tales of woe?"

"I don't see any reason to suppose so!" said Harry Wharton curtly. "I don't like the chap any more than you do, but I don't see calling him a greasy sneak without any proof."

"And you can't guess what he's telling Hacker?"

"No; and I don't want to!"

"Well, I can guess. He's complaining to Hacker about Quelch detaining him for the afternoon, and asking dear uncle to barge in."

"Oh, rot!"

"Shouldn't wonder!" said Todd. "He seemed knocked all of a heap by getting that detention, though goodness knows why; he doesn't have a fearful lot to do on a half-holiday."

"He will miss Bunter's company," suggested Squiff.

"Ha, ha, ha!"

"Hallo! There he goes!" said the Bounder, his eyes on Hacker's window. "The dear boy's told his tale of woe! What's the betting that we don't see Hacker hike along to Quelch's study?"

"Rubbish!" said Wharton. "Look here, Smithy, chuck it! Fellows aren't supposed to stare in at beaks' windows, and——"

"Hacker's going!"

"Oh!"

Mr. Hacker was seen to leave his study almost immediately after Wilmot. The Bounder chuckled explosively. It was a sheer relish to him to see this apparent proof of what he had always said of the new fellow.

"Come along, you men!" grinned Smithy. "Quelch's window is open, by

good luck! Let's see Hacker barge in!"

"I'm not moving!" said Wharton curtly.

"Please yourself!"

The Bounder changed his position, so that he could look into Mr. Quelch's study instead of Mr. Hacker's. He had no doubt that Hacker, having listened to a tale of complaint from Eric Wilmot, was going to see Wilmot's Form-master about it. And he was very keen indeed to prove it.

Wharton, frowning, remained where he was. Whether the Bounder was right or wrong, Wharton had no intention of peering in at windows to find out. But some of the fellows went with Smithy.

They were rewarded by the sight of Hacker entering Mr. Quelch's study. They saw Mr. Quelch lay down his pen and rise to his feet, with a cold, grim expression on his severe face. That expression might have warned Hacker that he did not want to hear anything about Wilmot, if the master of the Shell had been able to take a hint.

"What did I tell you?" whispered the Bounder.

"Looks like a catch!" admitted Bob Cherry. "Blessed if I really believed that Wilmot was such a greaser!"

"I've said so often enough."

"You'd say anything of a fellow who punched your nose, old bean!" said Bob cheerfully. "But I must say it looks as if you were right."

The juniors were too distant to hear what was said in Quelch's study. But they saw Quelch's face darken, and a flush come into Mr. Hacker's face. It was quite plain that the conversation was not of a friendly or agreeable nature.

Mr. Quelch was indeed the very last master at Greyfriars to allow another beak to interfere in matters pertaining to his Form. It was much to his credit that he treated Wilmot with strict justice, in spite of his uncle's fussy interventions.

Vernon-Smith left the other fellows and cut towards the House. Nobody followed him. The Bounder, little scrupulous in matters where his personal dislikes were concerned, intended to know for certain what the discussion was about in the Remove master's study.

It was easy enough. Having reached the House, he walked along under the windows of Masters' Studies. Those windows were high up from the ground; Quelch's window-sill was above the Bounder's head. He was able to walk past without being observed from within. Under the window he stopped.

"Rotten trick!" grunted Bob Cherry; and he went back to rejoin Wharton. And most of the fellows agreed.

The Bounder did not care. He had a deep and bitter grudge against Wilmot, and he was determined to have proof that the fellow was, as he called him, a greaser. As he stopped under the window, he had immediate proof, at least, that Hacker had called to see Quelch about his nephew's detention. Quelch's voice, raised a little in sharp tones, floated from the window.

"I must speak plainly, Mr. Hacker! I decline—I absolutely decline—to permit interference by another member of Dr. Locke's staff in matters of my Form! The fact that Wilmot is your nephew is immaterial!"

"Quite so, sir. But——"

"It would be for the boy's benefit, sir, to leave him to find his place without this constant mollycoddling!"

"Mr. Quelch!"

"You force me to speak plainly, sir! I do not believe that the boy desires your intervention. I believe that it causes him pain and humiliation."

"In the present matter——"

"The present matter, sir, differs from no other matter! Wilmot has been given a detention for disorderly conduct in the Form-room! The matter, sir, ends there!"

"It cannot end there, Mr. Quelch, on this particular occasion! I will explain to you——"

"I desire to hear no explanation! I refuse—I absolutely refuse—to reconsider the matter!"

"My nephew——"

"Your nephew, sir, is at Greyfriars on precisely the same footing as any other boy in the Lower Fourth Form! I should consider it a dereliction of my duty, sir, to treat him otherwise!"

"No doubt. But on this especial afternoon my nephew is very——"

"Am I to understand that Wilmot has asked you to speak to me on this subject?" exclaimed Mr. Quelch.

"He has certainly requested me in this particular instance——"

"Enough, sir!" Quelch's voice was rising. "A boy of my Form has requested the master of another Form to

Something New!

intervene between him and his Form-master! In all my experience as a schoolmaster, I have never heard of such a thing!"

"If you will hear me——"

"I will not hear you, sir! I will not hear one word! I request you, sir, to leave my study!" exclaimed Mr. Quelch, his voice fairly thrilling with indignation.

"One word, sir——"

"Not one word! Not one syllable! Nothing, sir, will induce me to rescind Wilmot's detention! If the Head himself made the request, sir, I would rather resign my position here than accede!"

"Mr. Quelch——"

"I will not hear you, sir! If you will not leave this study, I will leave it myself!" hooted Mr. Quelch.

That appeared to be enough, even for Hacker! Vernon-Smith, under the window, heard the study door close.

"Upon my word!" he heard Mr. Quelch exclaim. "Upon my word! Unheard-of! In all my career as a schoolmaster! Upon my word!"

The Bounder strolled away grinning. Before the dinner-bell rang, all the Remove had heard an interesting account of that conversation in Henry Samuel Quelch's study.

When Wilmot sat down, he could not fail to see the mocking grins, and hear the derisive whispers of the Remove fellows. And fellows who were not grinning were looking scornful and contemptuous. He glanced at Wharton, and the contempt he read in the face of the captain of the Remove brought a flush to his cheeks. "Greasing" to a beak was a dire offence in the eyes of all Greyfriars, and the fact that the hapless new fellow was incapable of such a mean action was not likely to be recognised in the face of what looked like proof positive.

THE FOURTH CHAPTER.
Just Like Smithy!

HERBERT VERNON-SMITH came out of the House after dinner and sauntered in the quad, with his hands in his pockets and a wrinkle of thought in his brow.

It was a cold, clear afternoon, with a nip of frost in the air, and most of the Remove were thinking of footer with cheery anticipation.

Other thoughts, however, were in the Bounder's mind, and his chum, Redwing, joining him in the quad, could guess those thoughts, from the expression on his face. As they walked together, Smithy gave him a sidelong look or two, and Redwing broke the silence abruptly.

"Don't be a fool, Smithy!"

"Thought-reader?" grinned Smithy.

"The Rookwood date's not far off now. You've still got a chance of pulling up, and Wharton would jump at playing you, if you were anything like your old form."

"He's picked out Nugent for my place."

"Only as a makeshift, you know that."

"Think he'd turn his best pal down again if I pulled up in time for the Rookwood date?" sneered the Bounder.

"You know he would! Nugent himself would gladly stand out to make room for you, if you were worth the place."

"Well, according to Wharton, I'm not. And I don't see mucking about for an afternoon in a rotten pick-up, if nothing's coming of it," said the Bounder sullenly. "It's not as if it were a match—even a Form match. Mucking about in the mud for nothing——"

The Bounder was arguing with his own conscience, rather than with his chum. He wanted to get out of gates that afternoon on an excursion with Pon & Co., of Highcliffe. And he had the grace to be rather ashamed of himself.

Tom Redwing knitted his brows. When that kink of blackguardism was uppermost in the Bounder, Tom liked him least, and found it most difficult to keep patient with him.

"You've made an exhibition of yourself with your rotten temper, because you've been dropped out of the eleven," he said hotly. "That was really the cause of your scrap with Wilmot the other day. You were hunting for trouble. There's time before Rookwood for you to pull up, if you take care, and stick hard to practice. And you're going to let it slip——"

"I'm not going to waste time if I'm out of the eleven. I'll put it plain to Wharton. If he wants me for Rook-

See page 2.

wood, I'll stay in to-day and collect mud with the Remove. If not——"

Without finishing that remark, Vernon-Smith left his chum and cut across the quad, spotting the captain of the Remove in the distance. Harry Wharton greeted him with a cheery smile and nod.

"Kick off soon after two, Smithy," he said. "Ripping day for a game, what?"

"Um! Yes!" The Bounder coloured a little, thinking of what he was going to say, and noting Wharton's unsuspiciousness. "But——"

"I was just thinking out the sides," went on Wharton. "Look here, Smithy, do try to pull yourself together a bit! There's still time, if you really put your beef into it. I don't want to barge into your personal affairs and give you sermons—but have a little sense! Cigarettes in the study are no good for a footballer! Nugent's keen and willing, and, of course, I'd be keen to play him, but we want you to help us beat Rookwood."

Smithy stood silent. As a salve to his conscience he had been trying to believe that the captain of the Remove was glad to edge him out of the team to make room for his own chum. He could hardly affect to believe anything of that kind now.

"Who said I smoke in the study?" he said, at last, sullenly. "Has Redwing been——"

"Don't be an ass, old chap!" answered Wharton. "Redwing isn't likely to talk about what you do. Nobody's said so—but a fellow has eyes! Last term you were as good a man as we ever had in the team! This term you're rotten!"

"Thanks!" sneered the Bounder.

"There's no other word for it," said Harry. "Even against the Fourth, the other day, you put up a rotten show. I know that a man is often off colour by no fault of his own—it might happen to any chap—it does, in fact, sooner or later, to everyone. But it's gone so very far in your case—and so I can't help thinking——"

"You mean that I'm not good enough for the Rookwood game?"

"None at all, as you are at present! I'd as soon play Skinner or Snoop."

"Why not say Bunter?"

"Well, it's not so bad as that, but I'd very nearly as soon play Bunter as you in your present shape, Smithy! But if you'd only manage to get back some of your real form——"

"If I keep slogging at practice, till I get as stale as a railway bun, I may have a remote chance of getting into the eleven again! Is that it?"

Wharton gave him a quick look. He knew the Bounder—and he knew the signs. Smithy was looking for trouble! Why, Wharton could not guess for the moment.

"That's not good enough!" said Vernon-Smith curtly. "Tell me I'm wanted for Rookwood and I'll slog and slog. But I'm not a man to be picked up one minute and chucked over the next. If I'm not in the eleven, I don't see slogging in the mud for nothing."

"Are you following Wilmot's lead, and claiming the right to slack except on compulsory days?" asked Wharton contemptuously.

"Give a man a plain answer! Am I wanted for Rookwood?"

"Not on your present form."

"Then you can leave me out of the pick-up to-day!"

"Let's have this plain," said Harry quietly, but with a glint in his eyes. "You can't pull the wool over my eyes, Smithy. I know you too well. Have you got something on for this afternoon, and are you trying to find an excuse for cutting the pick-up for that reason?"

"I can do as I like, I think, without finding excuses. Leave me out of the eleven, and you can leave me out of your dashed pick-ups! That's that!"

"You're left out of both, then!" said Wharton curtly. "I suppose it's no good telling you you ought to be ashamed of yourself! You know that! Don't talk to me any more—you make me ill."

The Bounder swung away sullenly. Wharton, who had been looking very bright and cheery, had a clouded face as he walked on.

He had had a strong suspicion that the Bounder's loss of form was due to a revival of old blackguardly manners and customs. More than once, that term, he had fancied that Smithy's bed was empty in the Remove dormitory after lights out, which meant a resumption of his old reckless escapades. Late hours and smokes fully accounted for the Bounder crocking up so hopelessly at football.

In such circumstances, it was sheer impudence for a fellow to kick up a fuss about being dropped out of the team. But the Bounder had not only kicked up a fuss—he had displayed his angry temper to all the Remove.

Wharton had been hoping that Smithy would pull up, and pull round, in time for the match with Rookwood School. He wanted his very best men to meet Jimmy Silver & Co., of Rookwood. He realised now that there was no hope of that—and the Bounder was definitely marked off, in his mind.

The sight of Eric Wilmot in the quad, going down to the gates, brought another frown to his brow.

Wilmot had the build, and the look, of a good man at the game; he could have been a good footballer if he chose. According to his uncle, Hacker, he had played for his former school, and had been a great man at games there. At Greyfriars he seemed nothing but a slacker and a dud. But he might have been just the man his Form captain needed—if he had liked. Wharton disliked him—nobody could help disliking so sulky and sullen and discontented a fellow. But he would have welcomed him into the fold with open arms, if he had shown anything like keenness—which he never did.

But he wondered sometimes whether the fellow's fumbling at footer was genuine, or part and parcel of his sullenness. Everybody knew that he had not wanted to come to Greyfriars, and that he seemed bent on making the worst, instead of the best, of what could not be helped. He had wanted, it seemed, to stay at his old school, wherever that was, and why he hadn't was rather a mystery to Wharton. He could not help entertaining a suspicion that Wilmot had had no choice about leaving.

But, looking at him now, a new idea came into Wharton's mind. The Bounder had let him down, and that was that. If there was anything in Wilmot—if the fellow would throw over his sulky sullenness and try and

THE MAGNET LIBRARY.—No. 1,459.

show what he could do—— It was rather like catching at a straw. Then, as he stood looking at the fellow and thinking it over, Wharton remembered that Wilmot was under detention that afternoon—and he was going down to the gates with the evident intention of going out.

Wharton cut after him.

"Hold on, Wilmot!" he called out.

The new junior looked round.

"What do you want?" he snapped.

"Forgotten detention?"

"No bizney of yours!" said Wilmot, and he swung on.

Harry Wharton's momentary idea of speaking civilly to the fellow and asking him to play in the pick-up vanished at once. It was replaced by an impulse to punch his head.

Wilmot walked quickly to the gates. As he did so, Gosling came out of his lodge and stepped in his way.

"Sorry, sir—Mr. Quelch's horders!" said Gosling.

Wilmot gave him a fierce, angry look.

"What the dickens do you mean?" he exclaimed. "Let me pass at once!"

Gosling shook his gnarled head. Evidently Mr. Quelch had spoken to the school porter on the subject. That had been the outcome of Mr. Hacker's interference.

"You're in detention, sir," said Gosling. "You can't go out of gates, sir!"

"Let me pass! You can report me if you like!"

Another shake of Gosling's head.

"Mr. Quelch's horders, sir, you're not to go out!" he answered.

Wilmot looked for a moment as if he would shove the old porter aside by main force and go. But he thought better of that, turned, and walked back.

Harry Wharton called to him in passing.

"Look here, Wilmot——"

Without even a glance at him, Wilmot walked on. The Bounder, coming down to the gates, looked at one and then at the other and laughed. Wharton was left undecided whether to punch Smithy's head or Wilmot's. Fortunately, both were out of his reach before he decided.

THE FIFTH CHAPTER.

Bunter Keeps It Dark!

"SEEN Bunter?"

"Bunter!" repeated Bob Cherry. "That frowsy frump! I want to speak to him!"

"Don't say you're rolling that barrel into the pick-up, old man!" said Bob, in astonishment.

Harry Wharton laughed.

"No, ass! But I've been thinking about Wilmot!"

"That dud?" said Bob, still astonished.

"Is he a dud?" said Harry.

"Is he anything else? What the dickens are you getting at?" demanded Bob. "Dud, and slacker, and worm generally! Is this second childhood, or what?"

"I can't make up my mind about that chap, Bob!" said Harry Wharton. "You know what Hobby of the Shell told us before he came—Hacker told him Wilmot had been a great games man at his last school, and would make a figure in the footer here. I thought of him for the Remove Eleven then, before I even saw him. But after-wards——"

"When he turned out a sulky toad, and a slacker, and a dud——"

"Sulky toad, certainly," said Harry. "But—Hacker must know whether he played for his last school or not, and he says he did. He made a silly fuss about the fellow being left out of the Form games, and jawed to Wingate, and I agreed to put him in a Form match last Saturday."

"And he never turned up!"

"I know. But—I've wondered a bit whether it's only his sulky temper, and whether Hacker may be right about him. After all, he's his uncle, and ought to know."

"Fat lot Hacker knows about Soccer."

"Next to nothing. But he said that he had seen Wilmot play for his last school."

"Some school—if that fumbling foozler played for it!" grunted Bob. "What school was it?"

"Hacker never said. But they must have been able to play some sort of game there. The fellow seems such a sulky brute that I've wondered whether his foozling on the footer ground is only rotten sullenness!"

"Why?"

"Well, he seems to want to keep to himself and have nothing to do with the Form or any of its giddy works!"

"Then let him!"

"If he's a good man, we want him."

"He isn't good—he's rotten bad!"

"I'm not feeling sure of that! Bunter knows something about the fellow. He's talked of having seen him play footer, and play a great game!"

"Bunter's always talking rot!"

"I know. But he does know something of the fellow. He's the only chap Wilmot ever speaks to here of his own accord," said Harry. "Bunter's always spinning idiotic yarns. But that's a very queer yarn to come into his silly head if there's nothing in it! I've been thinking of asking Bunter about it, and getting the truth out of him."

"There isn't any in him!"

"Well, let's try," said Harry. "Where is the fat slug now?"

"The tuckshop would be a safe guess."

"Come on, then!"

It was quite a safe guess. Billy Bunter was discovered gazing at the window of Mrs. Mimble's establishment, in the corner behind the elms. His little round eyes had a mournful look behind his big round spectacles. Like a podgy Peri at the gate of Paradise, Bunter was gazing at the good things beyond his reach.

But he blinked round hopelessly as Wharton and Bob came up.

"I say, you fellows, what do you think's happened?" asked Bunter. "I say, my postal order hasn't come! I was expecting it this morning!"

"Not really?" asked Bob sarcastically.

"Yes, really, old chap! It's rather surprising that it hasn't come!"

"It would be more surprising if it had!"

"Oh, really, Cherry——"

"I've been looking for you, Bunter," said Harry.

"Oh, good!" said Bunter, brightening. "Is it a feed? I'm on, old fellow!"

"So likely to be a feed just before football!" said Bob.

Bunter's fat face fell again. It was not very long since dinner—but Billy Bunter was ready for a feed. In such matters his motto was the old Scottish one: "Ready, ay, ready!"

"If you happen to have half-a-crown you don't want, Wilmot——" said Bunter. "You fat ass!" snapped Wilmot. "I want to know whether Quelch has gone out of gates. I——" The detained junior broke off, as Bunter gave a sudden jump, and bolted. Wilmot, looking round, sighted Mr. Quelch approaching.

But he realised that these silly asses were not likely to stuff jam tarts and cream puffs just before footer. Bunter would have swapped the English Cup for a jam tart. But he realised sadly that these benighted duffers had quite different ideas.

"Well, look here," he said. "If you can lend a chap a bob till that postal order comes——"

"You were talking about Wilmot the other day——" began Harry.

"I can't borrow anything of Wilmot now," said Bunter peevishly. "He's in detention, the silly ass! Can't go to the Form-room——"

"For the love of Mike, leave off thinking of food for a minute or two!" exclaimed Wharton impatiently. "Look here, you were saying that you saw Wilmot playing footer."

"Eh? So I did!"

"You said you saw him bag goals against a good team."

"What about it?"

"Well, was it true?"

"Oh, really, Wharton! Don't I always tell the truth?"

"Oh scissors!"

"If you doubt my word, Harry Wharton——" began Bunter, with a great deal of dignity.

"Look here, you fat ass, try to tell the truth for once, anyhow! If you saw Wilmot play football, it must have been before he came to Greyfriars—he's only foozled at it here! When was it?"

"In the week before he came."

"And where?"

Billy Bunter did not answer that question. To the surprise of the chums of the Remove, he grinned, and favoured them with a fat wink.

"That's telling!" he remarked.

"Well, I want you to tell me, fathead!"

"You can't pump me!" explained Bunter. "Wilmot's a friend of mine, and I'm not saying anything about him!"

"You howling ass, you can say where he played football, I suppose?"

"I can't—and won't!"

"Why not?"

"Well, you see," said Bunter cautiously, "if you knew that, you'd know the lot."

"The lot?" repeated Harry blankly. "And what's the 'lot'?"

"Oh! Nothing."

"Nothing?" ejaculated Bob.

"Nothing at all, old chap! I say, about lending me a bob——"

"It must have been somewhere near Greyfriars, if you saw it at all," said Harry Wharton. "So far as I know, the only outside match you've seen this term, was the game at St. Jude's, when they played Topham. We were prevented from seeing that game, as we intended—but you saw it——"

"No, I didn't!" contradicted Bunter promptly.

"You blithering idiot!" roared Bob. "You've told us a dozen times that you did!"

"Well, that—that was only a—a figure of speech, old chap! What I really meant was, that I didn't!"

"Oh crumbs!"

"I never went there after all," said Bunter. "Catch me standing about in the cold, watching a silly footer match! Besides, I only went because you fellows said you would be there, and there would be tea afterwards at the Pagoda in Lantham, or somewhere. You let me

down, as you never turned up——"

"Then you were there?"

"Oh! No! I—I wasn't there!"

"You benighted owl——"

"Oh, really, Wharton——"

"You blithering bletherer——"

"Beast!"

Getting the truth out of Bunter seemed rather uphill work.

"Now, look here, you frabjous ass," said Harry, "I've got an idea that that man Wilmot can play Soccer, if he likes, as his uncle makes out. If it's true that you've seen him play a good game——"

"I'm not accustomed to having my word doubted, Wharton," said Billy Bunter loftily. "I can jolly well tell you, that Wilmot could play your heads off, if he liked. Blessed if I know why he doesn't play here, when he's such a topper! Sulks, I suppose. He could, if he liked."

"You saw him bag goals?"

"Lots."

"Where?" roared Wharton.

Bunter winked again.

"That's telling!" he grinned.

"What team was he playing for?"

"That's telling, too!"

"Oh, kick him!" growled Bob.

"Here, you keep off, you beast——"

Bunter jumped back.

"There's some sort of a secret between Bunter and that new tick," said the captain of the Remove. "That can be the only reason why he stands the fat freak. But——"

"You cheeky beast!"

"But Wilmot can't want him to keep it dark about a football match! Why should he?"

"That's all you know!" grinned Bunter.

THE MAGNET LIBRARY.—No. 1,459.

"Does he, then?"

"Oh! No! Nothing of the sort!"

"We were going to play footer this afternoon," said Bob Cherry. "We'd better put it off till Saturday, at this rate—if it's got to wait till you get some truth out of Bunter. I told you there wasn't any in him."

"Oh, really, Cherry——"

Harry Wharton looked fixedly at Bunter. The endless and complicated prevarications of the fat Owl showed one thing—that he had a secret to keep, concerning Wilmot. If Bunter really had seen Wilmot play a great game of Soccer it was incomprehensible that the fellow should want him to keep it dark. But Wharton was growing more certain that Bunter had.

"Will you tell me the truth, you fat idiot?" said Harry at last. "Can't you understand that I've got good reasons for wanting to know whether Wilmot can play Soccer or not?"

"I've told you he can—better than you can," said Bunter. "He could play your head off, and not half try. I've seen him!"

"Where?" hooted Wharton.

"I mean, I haven't seen him——" amended Bunter hastily.

"What?"

"The fact is, I know nothing at all about the chap, and he never asked me to keep it dark, the day he came!" declared Bunter. "Besides, I promised him I wouldn't let it out, and I'm a fellow of my word, I hope. Not that there's anything to let out, you know—I don't mean that! Nothing at all—absolutely nothing."

It was not perhaps surprising that Wharton, by that time, gave up the idea of getting the truth out of Bunter. If there was any in him, the extraction was too long and difficult a process.

He grabbed the fat Owl by the collar instead.

"Here, I say, leggo!" howled Bunter. Squash!

Bunter's bullet head was pressed firmly against the school shop window, fairly squashing his nose against the glass.

"Yoop! Leggo! Wow!" yelled Bunter, struggling wildly.

Squash!

"Yarooooh!"

Bump!

Bunter sat down, hard.

He roared, and Wharton and Bob walked away, and left him to roar. The difficult task was given up; if there was any truth in Bunter, it remained there.

THE SIXTH CHAPTER.

Caged!

ERIC WILMOT'S handsome face—marred by a sullen scowl—was framed in the Form-room window. He stood looking out into the quad, bright in the winter sunshine.

Mr. Quelch, with a grim unbending visage, had marched him in to detention at the appointed hour. He had set him a task to keep him occupied till five o'clock. Wilmot had not touched it, or looked at it.

It was the first time, since he had been at Greyfriars, that he had had anything particular to do on a half-holiday. But now it seemed to be very particular indeed.

Quite contrary to what the Remove fellows believed to be his custom, he had gone to the length of asking his uncle, the master of the Shell, to intercede for him.

It had failed; as he realised now that it had been bound to fail. Mr. Hacker's fussy interferences, time and again, had fed Quelch up, and he was adamant—ready, as it were, to fly off the handle, at a mere hint of intervention from Wilmot's uncle.

Toadying to a master—which the Greyfriars fellows called "greasing to a beak"—was not one of the new fellow's failings. But he had given the Remove what looked like proof positive that it was.

That occasion was the single occasion on which he had asked Hacker to intervene. The Removites believed that it was the only occasion on which he had been spotted doing so.

But Wilmot was not worrying now about what the Remove fellows thought. He cared little—and he had more weighty matters on his mind. He was going out that afternoon—from his own point of view, he had to go!

The question was, how? Breaking detention was not an easy matter—and it was a very serious matter. It was quite on the cards that he might be expelled for it; for, after what had already happened, it would be taken as an utterly reckless and insolent act of defiance.

Some Remove fellows came along and glanced at the handsome, sulky face staring from the window. Skinner winked at his friends, Snoop and Stott.

"Nunky couldn't wangle it after all!" he remarked. "Poor little Eric! Detained by a nasty Form-master after taking the trouble to tell tales to nunky!"

"Ha, ha, ha!" roared Snoop and Stott.

Wilmot stepped from the window. Skinner & Co. passed on, chuckling.

When they were gone he looked out again. A fat figure came rolling from the direction of the tuckshop.

Billy Bunter blinked up, through his big spectacles, and gave Wilmot a cheery grin.

"Oh, there you are, old chap!" he said. "I say, Wilmot——"

"Has Quelch gone out?" asked Wilmot.

"Eh? I don't know——"

"He often goes out for a walk on a half-holiday," said Wilmot. "Look here, Bunter, find out if Quelch has gone out, will you?"

Billy Bunter had constituted himself Wilmot's pal in the Remove—with so little encouragement from Wilmot that any fellow but Bunter would have given it up as a bad job. This was the first time that his "pal" had asked anything of him, so Bunter might have been expected to jump at the chance of being pally. But he did not jump.

Bunter might, or might not, have sympathised with the fellow under detention. But his chief concern, as usual, was for his fat self.

"I say, old chap, don't you think of cutting!" he advised. "Quelch would be frightfully ratty. I say, never mind Quelch! If you happen to have half-a-crown you don't want——"

"Look here, Bunter——"

"What I mean is, I'm short of tin this afternoon," explained Bunter. "I've been disappointed about a postal order."

"You fat ass!"

"Oh, really, Wilmot——"

"I want to know whether Quelch has gone out of gates? I——"

Eric Wilmot broke off as Bunter gave a sudden jump and bolted, forgetful even of the half-crown he had desired to borrow.

Wilmot looked round, and sighted a tall, angular form coming round the

corner of the building. Instantly he stepped back from the window.

He no longer needed to inquire whether Quelch had gone out that afternoon. Obviously he hadn't, for there he was taking a walk by the Form-room windows.

With a black brow Wilmot dropped on his form. But he did not look at the task on the desk before him.

He was not going to touch that. He was going out—he had to go—Quelch, or no Quelch. But if the Remove-master saw him——

He waited about five minutes—long and impatient minutes—and then returned to the window. Mr. Quelch had passed on, and disappeared.

Plenty of fellows were to be seen in the quad. There were so many Remove men about that it was clear that the pick-up game had not yet started. In the distance some Sixth Form men could be seen. He recognised Wingate and Gwynne and Sykes. They were not looking towards him—probably would not notice him if he dropped from the Form-room window. But one of them was fairly certain to spot him, if he cut, before he could get away.

Did the prefects know he was under detention? More likely than not. Quelch had spoken to the school porter, which looked as if he had a suspicion that the detained junior might "cut."

Wilmot gritted his teeth.

It was useless to clamber out, only to be taken by the collar by a big Sixth Form man, and marched in again to punishment. For the punishment he cared nothing; but it would defeat the end in view.

He saw Harry Wharton coming along the path by the windows. He was alone; his friends not with him as usual. Once more Wilmot stepped back from the open window; he did not want the head boy of the Form to see him there, and guess his intention.

To his surprise, his name was called. It was called from outside in rather cautious tones; but he heard, and he recognised Wharton's voice. In sheer surprise, he put his head out of the window.

Wharton gave him a smile.

"You heard me?" he asked. "I couldn't shout. Mustn't speak to a man in detention, you know, if the beaks knew."

"You don't want to speak to me, I suppose?"

"I shouldn't have called you if I didn't," said Wharton dryly. "You're not too fearfully keen on a detention task to be able to spare a minute—what?"

"No. What do you want?"

"We're playing in a pick-up this afternoon, as you know. Like to play?"

Wilmot stared.

"No," he answered curtly.

"I expected that," nodded Wharton. "That's your usual pleasant and chatty style, isn't it?"

"If you've got anything to say——"

"I have. I've been thinking it over, and I fancy there may be something in what Hacker has said about your being a footballer. Bunter seems to know something about it, though he tells so many idiotic lies that there's no making head or tail of what he says. But he knows——"

Wilmot changed colour.

"Bunter!" he breathed. "What has Bunter told you?"

Wharton could see, but affected not to see, that there was alarm in Wilmot's face. He was smitten by a sudden fear that the loquacious Owl had let out his secret, whatever it was.

"Only what he's said before, more than once—that he's seen you play Soccer and bag goals——"

"Oh!" said Wilmot, with undisguised relief. "I—I see."

He had dreaded, for a moment, that Bunter had told of having seen him play at St. Jude's in the Topham team. Had that become known, it would have become known that his former school was Topham, which he had had to leave, in circumstances which he trembled to think of letting Greyfriars learn.

"To come to the point," went on Harry. "I believe there's something in it. You've mucked about like an ass on the football field here, but I'm wondering whether you could play a good game if you liked. If it was only rotten, silly sulks, why not chuck it, and be a sensible chap?"

"Is that what you came here to say to me?"

"And some more," said Harry, determined not to notice the unpleasantness of the fellow's manner. "We've got room in the team for a man, if you're anything within miles of what your Uncle Hacker thinks you are. Most fellows would jump at the chance of playing Rookwood."

"I shouldn't."

"Well, why not?"

"I don't choose to play footer here. And you don't want a man, I suppose, who's generally found guilty of greasing to the beak?" said Wilmot, with bitter sarcasm.

"That's got nothing to do with footer. I never believed it of you till this morning, when it was made pretty clear. But——"

"Well, what?" snapped Wilmot impatiently.

"You seemed knocked over at being detained this afternoon. You've asked your uncle to butt in and get you off. If that means that you're getting a bit more keen——"

"Keen—on what?"

"Footer, of course," said Harry. "There's nothing else going on to-day that I know of. If you want to play footer, I'm offering you a chance in the pick-up. If you don't, I can't imagine why you care whether you're detained or not. You might as well be in the Form-room as slouching about scowling."

Wilmot stared at him. Wharton, of course, knew nothing of his having an urgent engagement out of gates that afternoon. He had never had one before, so it was not easy to guess. With football filling his own thoughts, the captain of the Remove had drawn his own conclusions—quite erroneous ones, as it happened.

"If that's it," went on Harry, while Wilmot stared at him in silence, "I can help you out, I think. A man's let me down this afternoon, and I shall have to play another man in the side. You see, though it's only a pick-up game, we're playing a full team a side. Well, if I put it to Quelch that you're wanted in a game, ten-to-one he will let you off detention. There's one good thing about Quelch—he never crabs a game."

Wilmot gave a sudden start, and his eyes lightened.

"You could get me off detention?"

"I think so, by putting it nicely and tactfully to Quelch." Wharton smiled. "I'd jolly well do my best, anyhow. The fact is, Quelch is fed-up with your sulks, like everybody else, and I know he would be jolly glad to see you joining in a game with the Form of your own accord. I believe I could work it."

"I'd be jolly glad!" exclaimed Wilmot breathlessly.

"It's a go, then," said Harry. "I'll try it on."

And, feeling for the first time something like cordiality towards the new junior, the captain of the Remove walked away, and went into the House. He took it for granted that it was to play in the pick-up that Wilmot was to get out of detention. He did not guess the thoughts in the new fellow's mind as Wilmot watched him go.

THE SEVENTH CHAPTER.
Wharton Has His Way!

"YOU silly ass!"

"You chump!"

"The chumpfulness is terrific!"

"Wash it out, Wharton!"

Harry Wharton smiled. The other Remove footballers, it was clear, were not much taken with the idea. They had gathered in the changing-room to get ready for the pick-up. And there was a good deal of discussion going on about the Bounder's absence when Wharton looked in.

Nearly all the Remove were there. The Lower Fourth was a numerous Form, but, barring a few hopeless slackers, like Bunter and Skinner and a few others, all the Form was wanted to make up two elevens. Even Lord Mauleverer had turned up, though it was true that Bob Cherry had solemnly promised him to stick his noble head in the coal-locker in Study No. 12 if he didn't. His lazy lordship, choosing the lesser of two evils, decided on Soccer.

Nearly all the Remove were present, and nearly all the Remove told their skipper what they thought of him and his intellect in entertaining the idea of playing a dud, a slacker, and a sulky tick, even in a pick-up game.

"That slacker," said Bolsover major.

On the present occasion Percy Bolsover had a chance of showing what he could do at back. He was, at all events, keen.

"That dud!" said Hazeldene.

"That greaser!" said Peter Todd.

"That toady!" grunted Johnny Bull.

"He's in detention, too!" said Squiff.

"Leave him there!" said Tom Brown.

"You're an ass, Wharton!"

"And a fathead!"

"And a footling duffer!"

"Thanks all round!" said the captain of the Remove imperturbably. "I've mentioned this to you men before speaking to Quelch, because I want you to be civil to the chap when he joins up."

"Is he ever civil to anybody?" inquired Ogilvy.

"Not often!" agreed Wharton. "But you're not going to take his manners as a model, are you, Oggy?"

"Well, no, ass! But——"

"I've an idea that the man can play Soccer if he chooses," remarked Wharton.

"What an idiotic idea!" remarked Russell.

"The idiocy is terrific, my esteemed Wharton!" remarked Hurree Jamset Ram Singh, shaking his dusky head.

"Bunter says——"

"Ye gods!" groaned Johnny Bull. "Are you going to take tips on Soccer from Bunter?"

"Have you asked Mrs. Kebble what she thinks?" inquired Ogilvy, with intense sarcasm. "Or Mrs. Kebble's cat?"

"Ha, ha, ha!"

"My dear men, be reasonable!" said Wharton. "If I'm making a mistake——"

"No 'if' about it!"

"You are!"

"Well, if I am, it's only a pick-up practice game, and no harm done. Just make the chap feel that he's welcome on his field, and don't take any notice of his sulky looks. Give him a chance—see?"

"Oh, that's all right!" said Frank Nugent. "Nobody wants him, I suppose —but nobody's going to be unpleasant to him."

"If he gets in my light——" said Bolsover major.

"Or in mine——" said Peter Todd.

"Gentlemen, chaps, and sportsmen," said Bob Cherry. "Wharton's a silly ass, as we are all agreed——"

"Hear, hear!"

"But let him rip, and don't make it hard for that tick if he's really showing some sign of decency at last. If he's really keen on footer for once, it shows that he isn't the utter worm he makes out that he is——"

"Ha, ha, ha!"

"And it's quite true that he looked fearfully sick when Quelch gave him detention, so Wharton may be right——"

"Just a bare possible chance?" suggested Wharton sarcastically. "Well, I'll hike along and speak to Quelch."

Leaving the changing-room in a buzz, the captain of the Remove went along to Masters' Studies.

He gave a discreet tap at Mr. Quelch's door. He had seen the Remove master go in, after a walk in the quad, and hoped that that walk after lunch had had a soothing effect on him. But the bark that came as he tapped at the door did not sound very encouraging.

(Continued on next page.)

"Come in!"

Wharton entered.

Mr. Quelch's face was grimly set, his eyes glinting. But his expression changed at the sight of his head boy.

Wharton guessed—correctly—that his Form-master had fancied that it was Hacker again. That Gorgon-like look had been turned on for the master of the Shell. Quelch changed it into a frosty smile for Wharton.

"Oh! Wharton!" he said. "Pray come in, Wharton! Are you not playing football this afternoon?"

"Just going to, sir," said Harry. "But there's a man who was going to play, who can't turn up, and——" He broke off.

It was true that Smithy had let him down; but that was not the only, or the chief, reason why he wanted Wilmot.

"Well?" said Mr. Quelch, a little puzzled.

"I was going to ask you, sir, whether you could possibly let Wilmot off to play football?" said Harry, taking the plunge.

Mr. Quelch's face hardened.

"I asked you in the Form-room, Wharton, whether Wilmot was in a match to-day, and you replied that he was not. What do you mean?"

"He wasn't, sir, then," explained Harry. "But I'm a man short, and I'd like him in the team. But that's not the only reason. I know you noticed, sir, that he seemed very sick at being detained; and that put a new idea into my head. He's never been keen on football before. If he's getting keen, it seems rather hard for him to have to cut the game." Wharton coloured a little. "I'm speaking now, sir, as head boy, as well as football captain. I know you don't like the way Wilmot has been going on since he came here——"

"I certainly do not!" said Mr. Quelch dryly.

"If he got into the football, and it led to his becoming a little more friendly with the other fellows, it would be a good thing for him, sir."

Mr. Quelch sat silent, thinking.

It was true, as his head boy knew very well, that he was concerned about the sulky, reserved fellow, who seemed to have chosen to be an outcast in his Form.

"You feel friendly towards this boy, Wharton?" he asked abruptly.

"Well, no, sir!" said Harry frankly. "I don't like him. But I hate to see any fellow shut up in himself like an oyster. It can't be good for any chap."

"That is certainly correct," said Mr. Quelch; "though in Wilmot's case there may be reasons——" He broke off sharply. "Undoubtedly, Wharton, it would be for this boy's benefit to take a share in the life of the Form. I had no idea whatever that he was thinking of football when he looked so dismayed this morning. I put the question to you. But if that is the actual fact——"

"I've spoken to him, sir, and he seems very keen." Wharton did not add that he had spoken to Wilmot after he had gone in to detention. That was a detail it was more tactful not to mention.

Mr. Quelch was silent again.

"Very well, Wharton," he said, at length. "On the understanding that Wilmot is to play football with his Form, I will excuse him from detention. You may tell him so, from me."

"Oh, thank you, sir!" said Wharton gratefully, and he left the Form-master's study with a light step and a cheery face.

Mr. Quelch was left looking very thoughtful.

Harry Wharton lost no time in getting to the Form-room. He found Eric Wilmot waiting impatiently.

"All serene!" said Harry, smiling in at the open door. "You're let off, to play in the pick-up, Wilmot. Official, from Quelch!"

"Oh!" gasped Wilmot.

"Chuck your books away, old bean, and come along to the changing-room," said Harry. "I'll wait for you."

"Don't wait!" said Wilmot hastily.

"Well, come along as quick as you can! It's jolly near time we got down to the field."

Wharton left Wilmot and hurried back to the changing-room. The new boy left the Form-room more slowly, giving him time to get out of sight. But it was not in the direction of the changing-room that he went.

THE EIGHTH CHAPTER.

An Old Acquaintance!

"WILMOT!"

Wingate of the Sixth rapped out the name.

Eric Wilmot stopped. The Sixth Form man came up to him with a frowning brow.

"You're under detention, Wilmot!" he said sternly. "Your Form-master spoke to me about it. What are you doing out of the House?"

"I'm let off!" muttered Wilmot.

Wingate eyed him doubtfully and suspiciously. From Mr. Quelch's manner when he had mentioned the subject, the Greyfriars captain considered it very unlikely indeed that that statement was correct.

Had Wilmot been with the Remove footballers, the matter would have been easy to settle—a word from Wharton would have been enough. But he was not with the footballers when the prefect spotted and stopped him. The Remove footballers were in the changing-room—expecting to see Wilmot there! They were not likely to see him.

Wilmot breathed hard.

"Quelch sent Wharton to tell me, Wingate!" he muttered. "I suppose you can take my word for it."

"I'd rather take Quelch's!" said Wingate dryly. "Come along! I can speak to him at his window."

Wilmot hesitated a moment. He had a chance—an unlooked-for chance—to keep his mysterious appointment out of gates. He was already a little late, and dreaded to be too late—with consequences of which he dared hardly think. But it was futile to attempt to bolt under Wingate's eye, and he went back to the House with the Greyfriars captain.

That walk of a few minutes was a sheer agony to him. Every moment he dreaded to see Wharton looking for him. Wharton had got him off detention to play in the pick-up, and never dreamed of double-dealing on his part. But if he found him going out of gates——

But Wharton was not to be seen, and they stopped at the open window of Mr. Quelch's study. The Remove-master glanced round at Wingate there. He did not see Wilmot, whose head was below the level of the high sill.

"Excuse me one moment, sir!" said Wingate. "Wilmot tells me that he is let off detention—am I to take his word?"

"Yes, that is correct, Wingate," answered the Remove-master.

"Very well, sir!"

Wingate stepped away from the

window. He gave Wilmot a nod and a smile.

"You can cut!" he said.

Wilmot was only too glad to cut. He fairly ran. A fat squeak floated to his ears as he headed for the gates again.

"I say, Wilmot——"

Deaf to the voice of Billy Bunter, he hurried on.

Like a lion from his lair, William Gosling hopped out of his lodge.

"Now, Master Wilmot!" said Gosling. "This 'ere is the second time, and I'll report yer! Wot I says is this 'ere——"

"Let me pass, you old fool!" almost hissed Wilmot. "My Form-master's let me off detention!"

"He ain't told me so!" grunted Gosling. "And if you was allowed out of gates, Mr. Quelch would 'ave sent me word."

Wilmot panted. It was another obstacle in his path. He was not, in fact, free to go out of gates; Quelch supposed that he was with the footballers.

Arguing the matter with Gosling meant further loss of time. He turned round and walked back, leaving the old porter grunting and eyeing him very suspiciously.

"I say, Wilmot old chap——" squeaked Bunter.

Wilmot hurried on. Bunter rolled in pursuit and followed him into the old cloisters.

"I say!" yelled Bunter, puffing and blowing. "I say, old fellow, don't you cut detention, old chap! You'll get into a fearful row! I say, lend me a bob before you go! Beast!"

Bunter was still at a distance, when, with the aid of his big spectacles, he spotted Wilmot clambering over an ivied wall.

Heedless of Bunter's squeak, Wilmot dropped on the outside, and cut away at a rapid run.

In a couple of minutes he was on the Courtfield road, and going at a steady trot, heading for the town across the common.

He was clear of Greyfriars now. The miserable trick he had played on the captain of the Remove caused him some compunction. He had not said that he would play football; Wharton had taken that for granted.

Only on that plea was it possible to get off detention; and Wharton had practically been led to giving his word that he was in the pick-up game.

If this was not double-dealing, it was perilously like it. Still, he had not actually said that he would play, and he drew what comfort he could from that.

A bunch of fellows, on the Courtfield road, stared at Wilmot as he passed. He recognised Herbert Vernon-Smith, but did not know his companions—he had never seen Ponsonby and Gadsby and Vavasour, of Highcliffe School, before. The Bounder stared and burst into a mocking laugh.

"Great pip! Did Hacker get you off, after all, Wilmot?" he called out.

Wilmot made no answer; he ran on, leaving Smithy and his Highcliffe friends staring after him. They were far out of sight, when he sighted another fellow on the road, strolling along from the direction of the town.

That fellow, a rather weedy-looking specimen, with narrow features, and sly, sharp eyes—waved his hand at the sight of Wilmot. The Greyfriars junior slowed down.

"Coming along, after all?" asked the weedy fellow, with a grin, as they met.

" Is Wilmot not here, Wharton ? " asked Mr. Quelch, very quietly. " No, sir ! " answered the junior skipper. " Am I to understand that you have deliberately deluded me ? " continued the Form-master. " I hope not, sir ! " said Wharton, with burning cheeks. " I expected Wilmot to turn up, or I shouldn't have begged him off detention ! "

" Yes," muttered Wilmot. " Can't you see, Crawley ? "

Crawley nodded and grinned.

" I thought I'd walk part of the way and meet you ! " he drawled.

" You mean that you were coming on to Greyfriars, if I didn't meet you in Courtfield, as you said in your letter that you would ! " said Wilmot, in a low, bitter voice.

" You're not pleased to see a Topham man again ? " asked Crawley.

" You know I'm not ! "

" I don't see why you shouldn't be ! Especially me ! "

" Especially you ! " muttered Wilmot. " I never could stand you at Topham ! We've never been friends. I always barred you—as every decent chap at Topham did ! "

" I'm the only Topham man willing to speak to you, all the same—any other fellow there would cut you dead as a doornail, after what you've done ! " said Crawley, with a sneer.

" I've done—nothing ! " said Wilmot, between his teeth. " And I believe you know it, Crawley ! "

" Nothing ! That day at St. Jude's—— "

" Nothing ! " repeated Wilmot. " And you know it ! "

Crawley stared at him.

" How should I know it ? " he demanded. " I was there to see the match, but I never saw what you did, or didn't do, after the match—— "

" You know it ! You're a rotter, Crawley, as I've told you often enough at Topham, but if you believed that I had picked a pocket in a dressing-room, you wouldn't speak to me again—not even you ! " said Wilmot, with intense bitterness.

The weedy Topham fellow stood look-ing at him. A slight flush of colour came into his sallow face.

" You wouldn't speak to a chap after such a thing ? " he asked.

" I ! No ! I'd not touch a thief with a barge-pole ! " said Wilmot forcibly. " I'd boot him if he dared speak to me ! "

Crawley laughed uneasily.

" Lucky for you I'm not so particular ! " he remarked.

" You don't believe it—you can't ! I don't see the luck, anyway ! I barred you at Topham—and I don't want to see you now ! You know I don't ! I never told you I was at Greyfriars—you guessed, because you knew I had an uncle a master there ! "

" You wouldn't have known even that if you'd minded your own business ! Other fellows had seen my uncle, when he came to Topham, without nosing out that he was a schoolmaster ! You never could mind your own business ! What have you come here for ? "

" Shall we walk on to the school ? " drawled Crawley.

" No ! " answered Wilmot fiercely.

" Let's walk back into the town, then—there's a rather decent teashop near the station—— "

Wilmot nodded curtly, and they walked on together to Courtfield.

THE NINTH CHAPTER.
Fooled !

HARRY WHARTON was looking pleased. He was the only fellow among the Remove footballers who was.

Every other fellow thought —and said—that it was a rotten idea to put Wilmot in the game ! Only that day it had been proved con-clusively—at least, to the satisfaction of the Remove—that the Bounder's accusa-tion was true—Wilmot " greased to a beak."

Unless the fellow was pretending—for no imaginable reason—he couldn't play Soccer, and didn't want to ! All he wanted, apparently, was to sulk and make himself disagreeable.

If he had agreed to play it was only to get out of detention—and he would fumble and foozle, as usual, and get away the minute he could !

That being the general view, Whar-ton could not expect much enthusiasm over his new recruit !

Nevertheless, a conviction was grow-ing in Wharton's mind that there was more in the sulky new fellow than met the eye.

He suspected that he had had some trouble at his last school ; which ex-plained, if it did not excuse, his sullen-ness of temper. From the confusion of Bunter's prevarications, one fact seemed to emerge—that the fat Owl had, some-where or other, seen Wilmot play foot-ball and capture goals. And Hacker declared that he had played for his former school—and Hacker must know.

It was, at least, worth while to try the fellow out.

And if it did prove that he could play, that he was a good man for the eleven, it would be a good thing for Wilmot, a good thing for the team, and a good thing all round.

So Harry Wharton was pleased—though he had the pleasure all to him-self. He was only anxious that the fellows should be civil to Wilmot when he came in—rather a doubtful matter,

(Continued on page 16.)

DROPPING IN ON MARS!

Instalment No. 2 of Dicky Nugent's Amazing Serial: "St. Sam's in the Strattersphere!"

GREYFRIA

No. 174.   EDITED BY

"Lumme!"

It was Mr. I. Jolliwell Lickham, of the St. Sam's Fourth, who made that eggsclamation. He had been sitting in an armchair seat in Professor Potty's steel rocket, reading the newspaper he had brought with him to while away the jerney to the moon, when something made him sit bolt upright with a sudden startled gasp.

"Lumme!" he repeated.

"Lickham! Lickham! How many more times am I to tell you not to use common eggspressions like Lumme!'?" cride Doctor Birchemall weerily. "Let us keep to civilised standards, Lickham, even though we happen to be a cupple of thowsand miles off the earth! If you want to eggspress serprize, say 'Grate pip!' or 'Oh, my giddy aunt!'—not 'Lumme!' What's the trubble, anyway?"

"Trubble enuff, sir, I can give you my word!" wimpered Mr. Lickham. "I've just remembered that the new moon's only two days old! Do you realise what that means, sir? It means that there will hardly be enuff of it for us to see—let alone land on!"

Doctor Birchemall wissled.

"Few! I never thought of that!" he gasped. "Lemme see!"

He darted across to the winder of Professor Potty's rocket, where Jolly and Merry and Bright and Fearless and Barrell of the Fourth were gazing out into the strattersphere. One glance was suffishant. It was only a crescent moon, and a jolly thin crescent moon at that! The Head gave a snort of disgust.

Jack Jolly & Co. looked round.

"Hallo, hallo, sir!" cride Jack Jolly. "What's up?"

"We are—and I jolly well wish we'd stayed down, now!" growled the Head. "It's a new moon, boys! There's hardly anything of it!"

"Oh, grate pip!"

"Half a minnit, sir!" broke in Frank Fearless. "Haven't you always taught us at St. Sam's that the moon is always there, even when there's only a slice of it showing?"

"Probably I have," said the Head, with a rye grin. "But it's one thing to beleeve that while you're in a class-room at St. Sam's, and quite another to beleeve it when you're actually on your way to the moon!"

"Oh, crums! What's going to happen, then, sir, if we don't land on the moon?"

"Presumably we shall go careering on in a straight line till we hit something—and then we shall see stars!" said the Head, with a roguish twinkle in his eyes.

"Ha, ha, ha!"

A howl of terror from Mr. Lickham interrupted the juniors' laughter.

"Yaroooooo! I want to go back! Let's man the lifeboats!"

"Unforchunitly, my dear Lickham, we omitted to bring any! However, we can throw you out, if you like, and see what happens to you!"

"Wooooop! Leggo, bust you!" shreeked Mr. Lickham, as the Head joakingly reached forward. "I'm not going floating about in the strattersphere without visible means of support, to please you or anyone else! I won't stand——"

"Then sit down, old bean!" grinned the Head, putting the Fourth Form master gently but firmly back into his seat. "And talking about visible means of support reminds me—we haven't had supper yet! Barrell!"

"Ye-es, sir!" stammered Tubby Barrell, who was wobbling like a jelly with fright.

"Just grill a few sossidges and make some coffy, will you? Then we'll all sit down and have supper."

"Yes, sir," said Tubby, brightening up. "But I'm afraid we'll have to have the coffy black. We've run right out of milk."

The Head frowned for a moment. Then he crossed over to the winder and chuckled.

"Bless my sole! It couldn't have happened at a better time!" he eggsclaimed. "Give me a jug, somebody!"

Tubby Barrell handed Doctor Birchemall a jug, and the Head cawtiously opened the winder and held the jug out into space. When he drew it back a moment later the juniors were serprized to see that it was full of milk!

"What the thump——" they ejaculated.

"Serprized, boys, eh?" larfed the Head, as he deposited the jug on the table. "There's no need to be, though, really, you know. As it happens, you see, we are at present passing through the Milky Way. So the obvious thing to do, as we had run short of milk, was to dip the jug and help ourselves!"

"Grate pip!"

"Now get on with those sosses, Barrell!" ordered Doctor Birchemall.

Everybody cheered up wunderfully under the warming inflewance of supper, and by the time the last crum had vannished, even Mr. Lickham was looking quite happy. But the Head soon reminded him of his trubbles again, when he spoke to Tubby.

"Why, Barrell," the Head said, "you look a new man after your feed. Your fizz is beaming like a full moon!"

"Groooo!" groaned Mr. Lickham. "That reminds me again that there's only a new moon at present! Let's have a look and see if we're near it by this time!"

He led the way to the winder. When he looked out, a hollow moan escaped his lips.

"I knew it!" he cride. "We're not going to land on the moon at all! We're just passing through it!"

"Oh, my hat!"

Doctor Birchemall and the boys could see for themselves that what Mr. Lickham had said was only too trew. In spite of what the text-books at St. Sam's said about it, the crescent moon was only a crescent, and nothing more—and there wasn't the slitest hoap of landing on it!

"That shows how much reliance you can place in dashed astronomers!" remarked the Head bitterly, as they saw the moon gradually reseeding from them. "I'll jolly well tell 'em what I think of 'em when we get back."

"'When'!" groaned Mr. Lickham. "You mean 'if,' don't you, sir?"

"Well, anyway, even if it comes to the worst, I eggspect we shall land on one of the hevvenly bodies

sooner or later," said the Head hoapfully. "So it may not be so bad, Lickham, after all!"

"That's all very well, sir, but you have to remember that Professor Potty's rocket was only desined for coming back from the moon," groaned Mr. Lickham. "What's

going to happen to us on a hevvenly which we can't

"In that case, the only thing be to stay there the Head. "I we shall find amuse us. After be rather fun, a new planet fo of our lives, wo

"No, it won't Mr. Lickham. imagine I want the rest of my d round a blessed s made a jolly bi I can tell you!

"Land ho!" Frank Fearless moment, happily ing an argewm looked like deve rather heated lin

All eyes wer out of the win and there was a interest from t cherers as they they were appr big planet.

"Bless my so claimed Doctor B "That's Mars!"

"Isn't that t that's supposed habited, sir? Merry.

The Head nod

"Quite right, is said that th which you can s marked across t are canals. We see whether that water or not."

"My hat!" Lickham. "We' towards it at a a speed now! we're being dra on to the surfi planet by magnet sir?"

"Eggsactly.

(Continued at next colum

WOULD YOU BELIEVE IT?

Mr. Prout looked very proud when he returned from a shooting expedition, having brought down a hare. Skinner, who watched the feat, spread the story that "Prouty" had, in reality, been aiming at a pheasant. When he heard it, Mr. Prout's ears burned. Why? That was the "burning" question!

Parts of Greyfriars are very old, having been built by the monks themselves in the twelfth century. It is said that the ghost of the last abbot still walks in the cloisters—and it is a fact that nervous fags won't go near the spot after dark! Bunter refuses to go "cloister"!! it, either!

Though Loder and Walke Sixth are "pals," there is lost between them. When lost money gambling Cross Keys, Loder should have been more When Loder backed a Walker chuckled. A "sportsmen"—quite di Wingate!

HE TRUTH ABOUT e HOODED HORROR

By TOM BROWN

n't worry any more t the Hooded Horror e School House, you ! I've tracked it to its nd found out all about nd you can take my , for it, there's nothing scared of !

needed a bit of nerve ollow it up, I don't admitting ! As those ve seen it know, it's a y weird sight in a y dusk.

ere's a hood over its and a wrap round its h. A long, nondescript ent hangs over its and flaps around its It shuffles along with ook-like step—down Remove stairs, through Hall, then out into the owy quad. Smoke can en coming away from thin wisps at times !

t I overcame my fears followed it. I wanted d out its secret.

ter leaving the School e, it went for a walk round the quad and through the Cloisters. Then it came back to the House, glided up the stairs again, and returned to the Re-move passage. And, believe it or not, it finished up by turn-ing into Study No. 7 !

I plucked up courage and followed it in before it could shut the door ! Then it threw back its hood and revealed to my astonished gaze the classic features of dear old Alonzo Todd !

"What the merry dickens——" I gasped.

"Good-evening, my dear Brown !" beamed 'Lonzy.

"What's the idea of the disguise ?" I asked in amazement.

"Disguise, my dear Brown ? I assure you I had no intention of dis-guising myself ! Are you referring, perchance, to my unorthodox habiliments ?"

"Just that !" I nodded. "What's the idea of 'em, 'Lonzy ?"

Alonzo Todd beamed.

"I can easily explain that, my dear Brown, and I hasten with pleasure to do so. You see, I am at present suffering from a form of dyspepsia which requires that I should take a walk after tea each day."

"Well ?"

"But the doctor has forbidden me, on account of a cold from which I am also suffering, to go out of doors after dark unless I am well wrapped up !"

ntinued from previous column.)

s one of grate gravity," the Head. "Strap on crash helmets and air-oned suits, lads ! It be long now before and !"

hat is going to happen r old pals now ? For nswer, read the full-of-s instalment of " St. s in the Strattersphere " he next issue of the ald.")

"Well ?"

"That being the case," smiled 'Lonzy, "I have gone to some pains to wrap myself up well before I take a walk ! That is all !"

"M-m-my hat ! But the smoke that was coming from you ?" I asked faintly.

"That, my dear Brown, was from my home-made winter-warmer," explained 'Lonzy. "Here it is !"

"Grooooogh ! Ouch ! Keepitaway !" I yelled, as Alonzo Todd put in front of my nose an old cocoa tin full of burning rags.

"If there is any more information I can give you——" said 'Lonzy.

"Thanks. But I've just remembered an important appointment !" I gasped, holding a handkerchief to my nose as the smell of 'Lonzy's winter-warmer spread itself over the study.

And off I hopped, with the firm intention of leaving 'Lonzy severely alone till the weather gets warmer and the need for cocoa tins filled with burning rags has passed !

COKER SHOULD WEAR A LABEL!

Declares BOB CHERRY

I've always said that Coker is a menace to himself as well as to the general public, and what happened this week proves it beyond all doubt.

It was Sam's escape from captivity that did it. Sam is a gorilla, and one of the stars of Barley & Bainham's circus, which has been pitched on Courtfield Common all the week. When the news went forth that Sam had escaped, there was a bit of a panic in the district, believe me !

They said the tricks that Sam did in the ring would be nothing compared with the tricks he'd get up to with the first human being he had in his clutches. So everybody was jolly anxious to see Sam safely under lock and key again, and armed searchers started scouring the countryside to see if they could find him.

Mr. Prout headed one party from Greyfriars. Mr. Prout carried his celebrated Winchester repeater, and the seniors with him were armed with rifles belonging to the school cadet corps.

Coker headed another party—consisting of himself only ! Even Potter and Greene weren't risking an afternoon with Coker while he was carrying a loaded rifle !

Mr. Prout's party spent about two hours before they got on the track of anything, but at the end of that time their patience was rewarded, and they discovered unmistakable signs that a big biped had been treading down the undergrowth and crashing through the bushes in Friardale Woods. Of course, they followed the trail without waste of time.

It wasn't long before they caught up with their quarry. There he was, crouching behind a tree, just as though he was waiting to fall on some victim and rend him limb from limb ! Mr. Prout made a sign for silence.

"Quiet, boys !" he said, as he raised his rifle. "The creature is obviously in wait for somebody. There is no alternative but to kill him."

"Kill him ?"

"Yes, leave it to me ! "

The seniors nodded and examined their own guns —just in case Prout missed.

"Ugly-looking brute, what ?" Blundell murmured.

"What-ho ! Something uncannily human about him, though," said Tomlinson major. "Reminds me of someone I know—can't quite think who."

Potter screwed his eyes up and examined the beast more closely. Then he jumped.

"Half a minute, sir——"

"Please do not talk, Potter, while I am taking aim !" grunted Mr. Prout.

"Yes, but half a minute, sir ! Are you sure it's the gorilla ?"

Mr. Prout lowered his gun and examined his target again.

"Why, undoubtedly it is !" he boomed. "The figure and the physiognomy are most certainly those of a gorilla, Potter. What do you imagine it to be ?" Potter hesitated.

"I'm not sure, of course, sir. It's very much like a gorilla, I know. But it looks a lot like Coker, too !"

"Oh !" gasped Mr. Prout. "Surely it cannot be——"

"Let's go a little closer and see," suggested Blundell.

The entire party moved forward, and sure enough when they examined the crouching figure closely they found that it was none other than Coker !

Needless to say, the thought that he had almost shot one of his own pupils gave Mr. Prout quite a shock. He returned to Grey-friars without troubling any more about Sam—which was just as well, since it after-wards turned out that circus hands had trapped the missing animal earlier in the afternoon !

Well, that's all, lads. But it does give you an idea of the danger Coker's continually running, doesn't it ? To me, it seems idiotic that he should go about like an ordinary human being when he's in such dire danger all the time of being mistaken for an escap-ing gorilla. He's a giddy danger to the public and a danger to himself !

Why shouldn't he be made to wear a label ? Either that or a mask !

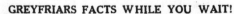

GREYFRIARS FACTS WHILE YOU WAIT!

ecope presented to him by so fascinated Alonzo he was late for class. ed as to why he had for-was time for the study of life. 'Lonzy said he had dying minute life in a water from a pond ! Mr. s still "pond "-ering his reply !

Removites were keenly interested when Lord Conway, brother of Arthur Augustus D'Arcy, of St. Jim's, flew over in his new mono-spar speed plane. Conway dropped a message " hot " from Tom Merry at St. Jim's—an invi-tation to a footer fixture. Harry Wharton & Co. went " up in the air " with excitement !

Billy Bunter says better menus are needed at Greyfriars. Bunter's idea is to turn the dining-hall into a non-stop snack counter, catering day and night ! Peter Todd says Bunter would like to live at the meal table. His sole supporter in his " campaign " is his equally greedy young brother, Sammy !

(Continued from page 13.)

as Wilmot had made a good many enemies and no friends. Still, if he was going to try to do the decent thing, plenty of the Removites were ready to give him a chance.

Certainly, if he dropped his sulks, and played up like other fellows, it would make a big difference in his favour.

The juniors changed, and were ready. But Wilmot had not come in. Harry Wharton glanced at the door a good many times.

He expected Wilmot to follow him to the changing-room almost at his heels, and could not understand the delay.

"I suppose he's coming?" said Bob Cherry at last.

"Of course he's coming, fathead!" said Wharton, rather tartly.

"Well, old bean, he hasn't come!"

"I know that, ass! He's coming, though!"

But Wilmot did not come. Wharton went to the door and looked out. Wilmot was not in sight. Looking round, he saw Ogilvy wink at Bob, who laughed.

"He's coming!" said Harry, with all the more positiveness, because a slight doubt was dawning in his own mind.

"See him coming?" asked Bob.

"No!"

"He's taking his time!"

"Well, he'll come!"

"Let's all sit round and wait for him, shall we?" asked Bolsover major. "In about an hour or so, Wharton will begin to see that the chap was only pulling his leg."

"What do you mean, you silly ass?" asked Wharton gruffly.

"I mean what I say!" retorted Bolsover. "The tick's not coming at all! You got him out of detention with that yarn to Quelch, and he let you do it—but he loathes football, and he won't play if he can help it."

"Looks like it!" said Squiff.

"The lookfulness is terrific!"

"Well, I must say it does look like it," said Bob Cherry. "You've had your leg pulled, old fellow."

Wharton stood silent. A gust of anger swept through him. It did look like it—he could not doubt that now. Never a suspicion had crossed his mind. But why did not Wilmot arrive?

"I don't believe it!" he said slowly. "I can't! No fellow could be such a rotter—making me go to Quelch, and practically tell him lies. He couldn't put me in such a position. No fellow would!"

"No decent fellow!" said Nugent.

"A fellow who greases to a beak will do anything!" said Hazeldene. "He just wanted to get out of detention, that's all!"

"He was let out to play football—no other reason! If he doesn't play, he will have to get back to it!"

THE MAGNET LIBRARY.—No. 1,459.

"Bet he's out of gates by this time!" said Hazel.

Wharton's eyes gleamed.

"Rot! He wouldn't—he couldn't! If he has—— But he hasn't! Perhaps old Hacker has nobbled him—he's always working at his chin. Look here! You men get down to the ground, and I'll have a look round for Wilmot. I'll bring him along with me."

"I don't think!" grunted Johnny Bull.

"Oh, rubbish!"

Some of the fellows were grinning as they went, some frowning. Every fellow there believed, by this time, that Wilmot had pulled Wharton's leg, to get out of detention, and had no idea whatever of taking part in the pick-up.

Wharton could not, and would not, believe it; but the conviction was growing at the back of his mind.

He threw on his coat, and went to look for Wilmot. He ran to the Form-room first; but, as he expected, the fellow was gone. Then he went out into the quad, and looked about him.

Wilmot was not to be seen. But Mr. Hacker was to be seen at his study window, and Wharton stopped there to speak to him. Hacker might know what had become of his nephew.

"Can you tell me where Wilmot is, sir?" asked Harry.

The master of the Shell raised his eyebrows.

"I understood, Wharton, that my nephew had been detained by his Form-master!" he answered stiffly.

Evidently Hacker knew nothing. He supposed that Wilmot was still in detention. Wharton went on his way, to look farther.

"I say, old chap, ain't you playing football?" Billy Bunter, coming back from the Cloisters, blinked at him through his big spectacles. "I say, Harry, old man, if you've got a bob you don't want——"

"Seen Wilmot?" asked Harry.

Bunter grinned.

"Yes, rather! I say, he'll get into an awful row with Quelch! He's cut!"

"He was let off!" said Harry.

"Was he? Smithy said he heard Hacker asking old Quelch, and the old bean bit him, and refused. If he was let off, what did he want to climb out over the Cloister wall for?" asked Bunter.

"Has he gone out?"

"Yes."

Bunter blinked at Wharton, astonished by the expression that came over his face.

"You're sure?" breathed Wharton.

"Yes. I called to him, but he wouldn't stop!" said Bunter. "I thought he was breaking out of detention—cutting off like that, and getting away over the wall. But if he was let off, why shouldn't he go out, if he likes?"

Wharton did not answer that question. There was no doubt about it now; he had been made a fool of. The fellow had simply taken advantage of his unsuspiciousness, to make use of his. The passionate anger in his face startled Billy Bunter.

"I say, old chap, what are you getting shirty about?" asked the mystified Owl. "A chap can go out on a half-holiday if he likes, can't he?"

Wharton did not speak. He was trying to think it out. He had begged Wilmot off, with Quelch, to play football. Not for any other reason would he have done so, or dreamed of doing so; nor, indeed, could he have done so. Mr. Quelch, in that belief, had made a great concession. Wharton, quite unin-

tentionally, had deceived him. What was Quelch going to think, if he found out?

Wharton's anger at the knowledge that he had been tricked, was so intense that he could hardly have spoken. He had been deceived; he had deceived his Form-master in turn, and all the fellows were laughing at his simplicity at being taken in. Yet he could not blame himself.

The fellow had been feverishly keen to get out of detention, and for what reason? A solitary ramble on his own could not have been a very great attraction. He could hardly be supposed to have any important business to attend to that afternoon. Had he done this out of sheer, sulky malice? It looked like it.

Turning away from the astonished Owl, Wharton strode down to Little Side. The Remove men were waiting for him there, and they grinned at one another when they saw him come alone. Not a man expected to see Wilmot coming with him. They would have been surprised had Wilmot appeared.

"Found him?" jeered Bolsover major.

"No!"

Wharton's look did not encourage jesting on the subject. Even Bolsover, after a glance at his set face, let the subject drop.

Wilmot was dismissed from discussion, if not from mind; and the juniors settled down to the pick-up game. But the captain of the Remove, for once, gave less thought to the game, on the football field, than to other matters. The outcast of the Remove had made a fool of him, and got away with it—but there was a reckoning in store.

THE TENTH CHAPTER.

Where Is Wilmot?

MR. QUELCH laid down his pen, rose from his table, and stood at his study window, looking out into the frosty sunshine. He had a glimpse, in the distance, of youthful figures in active motion.

Quelch smiled genially. He was in a genial mood. The new boy in his Form, with his sullen, reserved ways, had been a trouble on his mind; all the more, because he knew why Wilmot had had to leave Topham, and could hardly approve of the boy being admitted to Greyfriars.

It was possible, of course, that Mr. Hacker's belief in his nephew was well-founded; that some terrible mistake had been made. The kind old Head, though probably with many misgivings, had acceded to Hacker's earnest entreaty to give the boy a new chance. Naturally, he had told Mr. Quelch the circumstances, as Wilmot was placed in Quelch's Form, and requested the Remove master to observe him somewhat particularly. Quelch had done so—and what he had observed had dissatisfied him more and more.

The boy's sulky gloom might be the result of a wounded spirit, suffering under unjust suspicion and condemnation. It might be the result of a guilty conscience. Mr. Quelch tried to keep an open mind on the subject.

It was, at all events, a relief to him, if the boy was changing his sullen, sulky ways, and trying to make the best instead of the worst of things. If he was guiltless, he was to be pitied. If he was guilty, he had had a lesson to last a lifetime. It was up to him to pull himself together, and live in the present and the future, instead of brooding on the dismal past. It looked now as if he was doing so—and Quelch was relieved and pleased.

In that unaccustomed, genial mood, Mr. Quelch left his study, and the House, and walked down to Little Side to give the footballers a few minutes of his valuable time. He often looked on at Remove matches—quite unlike Hacker, who seemed hardly to know that the Shell played Soccer at all. Now he expected to see Wilmot, no longer a sullen outcast, joining in a cheery game, and making a new start, after the thoroughly bad start he had made.

Looking at the active figures on the field, Quelch tried to pick out Wilmot—and failed!

There was some mud about, and some faces were spattered with the same. But after a few minutes' observation, it dawned upon Mr. Quelch that Eric Wilmot was not on the field at all.

He was puzzled at first. It was not likely to occur to him in a hurry that his head boy had deceived him with a lying tale to get a fellow off detention—especially a fellow who was no friend of his.

A player might have had a knock, and gone off. In a pick-up, he might have been replaced by another man; it was only a practice game, with all Removites playing. But Wilmot was not to be seen anywhere about, and Mr. Quelch gradually grew doubtful.

He was not the man to interrupt a game. Hobson of the Shell was referee in the pick-up, and Mr. Quelch waited till Hobby blew the whistle for half-time. Then he called to Wharton.

As the Remove master had been on the spot more than ten minutes, by then all the fellows knew, of course, that he was there. Wharton's feelings, when he saw him, may be better imagined than described.

When Mr. Quelch called him, at half-time, the captain of the Remove came over to his Form-master, rather wishing that the football field would open and swallow him up.

The other fellows exchanged glances.

"Wharton's for it!" murmured Hazel.

"Well, he's asked for it!" remarked Bolsover major. "He let that tick take him in—or was he taken in? Must have been a fool, if he was."

"Of course he was, fathead!" growled Bob.

"Well, Quelch may believe he was!" jeered Bolsover. "More likely to think Wharton was pulling his leg to get the fellow off."

Wharton stopped before his Form-master. He knew what was coming.

"Is not Wilmot here, Wharton?" asked Mr. Quelch very quietly.

"No, sir!"

"Where is he?"

"I don't know."

Quelch's eyebrows rose expressively.

"You do not know, Wharton!" he repeated, in a rising tone that reached the ears of the other footballers. "Has he been here at all?"

"No, sir!"

"He has not played in the game?"

"No!"

"And you do not know where he is?"

"A fellow told me he had gone out. I don't know anything more than that."

There was a moment of tense silence.

"Am I to understand, Wharton, that you have deliberately deluded me?" asked Mr. Quelch very quietly.

"I hope not, sir!" said Harry, with burning cheeks. "I acted in good faith. I thought he was coming here to play in the pick-up, or I shouldn't have spoken to you about him."

"Did he say so?"

"Yes—no!" Wharton tried to remember what Wilmot had said at the Form-room window. Bitterly and intensely angry as he was, he wanted to be fair to the fellow. "He said he'd be jolly glad, I remember! I thought, of course, that he meant about the football."

"I understand!"

There was another silence.

"I—I seem to have been mistaken, sir!" said Harry, red as a beetroot. "I'm bound to say that Wilmot never said he would play—never said he wanted to—I took it all for granted! I—I thought he understood that it was only on account of the football that I could beg him off. But he may not have understood—he's new here, and so——"

"Quite!" said Mr. Quelch grimly. "I will not interrupt your game, Wharton—and please do not think that I blame you for having been, as I fear, deceived by an unscrupulous boy. I would rather see any boy in my Form trustful than suspicious. It is possible, as you say, that there was a misunderstanding on both sides, the boy being new here——"

"Yes, sir, that's quite possible," said Wharton eagerly. His own private intention was to make Wilmot sorry for that deception; but he had a schoolboy's natural repugnance to giving a fellow away to a "beak." "I—I was so full of it myself, sir, that I never really gave him a chance to speak. I can see now that I was taking a lot for granted——"

"Quite so, Wharton."

Mr. Quelch gave his head boy a kind nod and walked away. Harry Wharton went back to the footballers.

"You're in luck, old man," said Bob Cherry. "Some beaks——"

"Quelch knows that Wharton wouldn't deceive him," said Redwing.

"Yes," said Harry, with a deep breath. "He knows I'm not a rotter, so he must think I'm a fool. It's one or the other."

"Well, you were a bit of an ass, to be taken in like that," said Hazel.

"I know that!"

"More than a bit!" said Bolsover major. "A silly fathead, if you ask me!"

"Nobody asked you!" snapped Wharton.

"Well, I think——"

"No, you don't!" said Bob Cherry. "You can't do it, old man, with a head-piece like yours. If you could think, you'd think of some dodge for playing back less like a mad elephant."

Hobson of the Shell weighed in.

"Is this a football match, or a conversazione?" he asked. "Don't mind me—I only want to know."

And the second half started.

The pick-up was played out to a finish, and the Remove fellows went back to the changing-room. There the one topic

(Continued on next page.)

GREYFRIARS INTERVIEWS

English, Irish, Scotch and Welsh—they all come under the eagle eye and pen of the Greyfriars Rhymester. This week our long-haired poet selects

DAVID MORGAN,

the Welsh junior of the Remove.

(1)
David Morgan comes from Wales,
  Yes, that's his nationality !
The land of bards and fairy tales,
  The gallant Principality !
The men of Harlech marching still
  Through mountain mists and mystery
Have set their seal on every hill
  And left a book of history.

(2)
And from this land of harp and drum
  Has come our own Welsh warrior,
His country's name, now he has come,
  Is not a whit the sorrier,
For he's a credit to the land
  That I have praised so wordily,
And for his country he will stand
  To guard her honour sturdily.

(3)
He isn't often to the fore
  In any Greyfriars chronicle,
He's not a fathead, not a bore,
  And doesn't wear a monocle !
The hero's line is not his style,
  And yet it's undeniable
That he adorns the rank and file,
  So steady and reliable.

(4)
I called to see him yesterday,
  He greeted me with brevity,
His voice and features, sad to say,
  Contained no trace of levity !
"Sit down," he said. "Don't interfere !"
And if you'd seen the business
That occupied him, you would fear
  His brain had turned to dizziness !

(5)
A china basin stood in view,
  And in its near vicinity,
Were cinders, ink and liquid glue,
  A really horrid trinity !
I watched the silly fathead mix
  These odorous ingredients.
"My word," I said. "Of all the tricks!
  That's downright disobedience !"

(6)
It was ! Upon his study door
  He perched the basin fragilely,
While I moved back along the floor,
  And moved, I tell you, agilely !
I asked him : "Why the booby-trap ?"
  And Morgan started yammering ;
"For Coker of the Fifth, old chap !
  He promised me a hammering !"

(7)

"And what do you want, anyway ?"
  He asked, and I with merriment
Decided that the chance would pay
  To try a small experiment.
"You're wanted on the phone, old scout !"
I told him, and no sooner, all
His plans forgot, he hurried out !
  Well, that was Morgan's funeral !

was Eric Wilmot—and what was going to happen to him.

Harry Wharton did not join in the talk. He was too deeply incensed to talk about it. But he was very anxious—more anxious than the other fellows—for Wilmot to return.

THE ELEVENTH CHAPTER.

Called To Account!

MR. PROUT, master of the Fifth, took roll-call in Hall that evening.

When Prout's fruity voice called "Wilmot," a quiet "adsum" came from the ranks of the Remove.

Eric Wilmot was there in his place; his manner as quiet and self-possessed, with a touch of disdain, as usual, seemingly unconscious of the fact that he was the object of general attention in his Form. He could hardly have been unaware of it; but his face, at all events, expressed nothing.

Harry Wharton had given him one look when he came in; that was all. He noticed that Wilmot coloured for a moment under his glance; the fellow had the grace to be a little ashamed of his trickery.

For the moment, however, the captain of the Remove took no further notice of him. He was going to deal with him after Hall; but, as it happened, Mr. Quelch came first!

When roll was ended the Remove master curtly told Wilmot to follow him to his study, and the new junior disappeared at the heels of Henry Samuel Quelch. Some of the Removites noticed that Mr. Hacker had his eye on both of them as they went; and there were smiles and winks—Hacker, evidently, was concerned about his precious Eric! He certainly had cause on this occasion.

Mr. Quelch did not address the delinquent till they were in his study, where Wilmot stood before him with the same steady, calm face he had shown in Hall. Possibly the junior did not know what was coming to him.

Nobody in the Remove had said a word to him so far, so he could not have known that Quelch had gone down to the pick-up, and missed him. Possibly, he was wondering what Quelch had called him in for. He was soon enlightened, in that case.

"You have been out of gates, Wilmot!" said the Remove master.

"Yes, sir!"

"Where have you been?"

"To Courtfield."

"And what did you do in Courtfield?"

"I had tea at the bunshop there."

Quelch gave Wilmot a searching look. Perhaps a suspicion had been in his mind that the new fellow had had some business out of gates of a questionable kind that afternoon. But, with all his faults, Wilmot had never given any sign of being a reckless scapegrace like Vernon-Smith, or a dingy black sheep like Skinner.

"You were in detention this afternoon, Wilmot!" went on the Remove master, after that searching look.

"I understood from Wharton that I was let off, sir."

"That is correct, Wilmot! You were released from detention to play in a football match, at your Form captain's request. For no other reason should I have thought, for one moment, of excusing you. I think you were aware of that."

Wilmot was silent.

His face was dark and bitter. The thought was in his mind that Wharton,

in his resentment of the trick that had been played on him, had reported his trickery to the Remove master. It was quite easy for Mr. Quelch to read that thought in his face, and his own brow darkened.

"I went down to the football ground, Wilmot, and missed you," said Mr. Quelch, with icy coldness.

"Oh!" muttered Wilmot, flushing.

"Wharton believed that you were eager to join in the game—for that reason he begged you off detention, and for that reason I acceded. There is a remote possibility that you misunderstood one another. I require a plain and truthful answer from you, Wilmot! Did you suppose, for one moment, that you were released from detention to do as you pleased—that you were free to go out of gates like any other boy on a half-holiday?"

Wilmot hesitated a moment.

"No, sir!" he admitted.

"You knew that you were released for one reason and one reason alone—your Form captain's request that you should be allowed to play football?"

"Yes!"

"I am glad you are frank, at all events!" said Mr. Quelch. "It follows, then, that you took advantage of Wharton's faith in you to deceive him, and cause him to deceive me, on this subject?"

"I never said I would play in the pick-up, sir."

"You allowed your Form captain to believe so?"

"Well, yes."

"You knew that otherwise he could not have ventured to ask me to release you?"

"Yes," said Wilmot, in a low voice.

"Do you not consider that an unworthy deception, Wilmot?"

"Yes," breathed Wilmot.

"I am glad you can see it. I judge by your look that you are ashamed of having been guilty of such a wretched and contemptible subterfuge."

"Yes," muttered Wilmot again, his face scarlet.

"Very well!" said Mr. Quelch. "If you had answered me untruthfully, Wilmot, I should have taken you to Dr. Locke and requested him to send you away from Greyfriars. As you have admitted your fault without any attempt at prevarication, I shall not do so."

"Thank you, sir!"

"I shall, however, report your action to your headmaster, and you will receive a public flogging!" said Mr. Quelch. "You may now go."

Wilmot went in silence.

As he came out of Masters' Passage he found a number of Remove fellows waiting for him at the corner.

He would have passed them, but two of them stepped towards him and took his arms—Bob Cherry and Johnny Bull.

"This way!" said Bob.

Wilmot resisted angrily.

"Let me alone!" he snapped.

"You're wanted in the Rag!" said Harry Wharton.

"I'm not coming!"

"I think you are. Take him along!"

"'Ware beaks!" said Peter Todd. "If Hacker's about——"

"Bother Hacker!"

Wilmot was resisting, but he ceased suddenly to do so, and went quietly with the Removites. They walked him into the Rag, and the door was shut.

Nearly all the Remove were there.

"Oh, you've got him!" grinned Bolsover major.

"Here he is!" answered Bob.

"Didn't he howl for Hacker?" jeered Bolsover.

"No."

Wilmot's arms were released when he was safe in the Rag. He put his hands in his pockets and faced the grim-looking Removites.

"Well, what do you want?" he asked calmly. "Not my company, I suppose?"

"Hardly!" said Bob Cherry.

"Nobody's likely to want your company, I think," said the captain of the Remove contemptuously. "If I fancied, for a minute, this afternoon, that you might possibly act like a decent fellow, I've found out my mistake."

Wilmot winced.

"I owe you an apology," he said, in a low voice. "I know I took you in, and I'm sorry for that. But——"

"But what?"

"Oh, nothing," said Wilmot wearily. "Go ahead, whatever you want! If it's a ragging, I can stand it."

"It's not a ragging," said Harry. "You made a fool of me, and might have landed me into a fearful row with Quelch. I suppose you expected to be called to account for it."

"I dare say I should have, if I'd thought about it!"

"And you didn't?"

"No, I've other things to think of." Wharton breathed hard.

"Well, you'd better think about it now," he said. "First of all, though, I want to know what Quelch is going to do."

"Better ask him."

"I'm asking you. If you're getting toco from Quelch you won't want any more from me."

"Oh, I don't mind!" said Wilmot, with cool disdain. "I've no doubt you're a very terrifying fellow, but I'm not feeling all in a tremble. I almost fancy I could survive your wrath."

"He, he, he!" from Billy Bunter.

That cackle was followed by a loud howl as somebody kicked Bunter.

"Quelch would have known nothing about it if I could have helped it," said Harry. "But he found out, and he's bound to do something. He's told you, I suppose, as he called you into his study? Cough it up!"

Wilmot shrugged his shoulders.

"Head's flogging!" he said briefly.

Harry Wharton paused. His knuckles were almost itching to land on the cool, disdainful face of the fellow who had made him look like a fool to all the Form, but he restrained himself.

"Very well," he said, "if you're getting that we'll call it a day. You've asked for it, and it serves you jolly well right."

"I know that. But don't let me off if you don't feel disposed," said Wilmot coolly. "I licked that fellow Smith the other day, after he started in to mop up the school with me. I think I could put up some sort of a feeble show, even against your high mightiness."

"Oh, punch his head!" growled Johnny Bull.

"The punchfulness is the proper caper!" remarked Hurree Jamset Ram Singh.

"Rot!" interposed Frank Nugent hastily. "What does the fellow's check matter? If he's getting a flogging from the Beak, leave him alone."

"I'm going to," said Wharton, with a deep breath. "He's not a fellow I'm anxious to touch, anyhow."

"He won't get that flogging!" said Vernon-Smith.

"Why won't he, fathead?"

"Because he will grease up to Hacker, and Hacker will get him off," sneered the Bounder.

"Oh!" exclaimed Wharton.

" You've got to listen to me, Wharton," said Wilmot. Wharton struck his hand aside. " Keep away from me, you cur ! "
he snapped. " Don't talk to me ! " Smack ! With a sudden movement, Wilmot struck the captain of the Remove across
the face with his open hand. The smack rang through the Rag almost like a pistol-shot.

Wilmot turned fiercely on the Bounder.

"That's a lie!" he said, between his teeth. "And if I've treated Wharton badly to-day, as I admit, I haven't treated him so rottenly as you have. He would never have asked me to play in the pick-up, or thought of me for football at all, if you hadn't let him down—and you did it because you're a disgraceful blackguard, who ought to be kicked out of the school."

"Oh, gum!" said Ogilvy. "Wilmot hasn't been here long, but he's got to know you pretty well, Smithy!"

"Ha, ha, ha!"

The Bounder, with a flaming face, made a stride towards Wilmot.

Tom Redwing caught him by the arm and pulled him back, and Wharton interposed.

"Hands off, Smithy!" he snapped.

"You heard what he said!" yelled the Bounder furiously.

"Yes, and it was true, every word of it. If you don't like it, you can lump it! If Wilmot gets off that flogging, through Hacker, he will have a fight on his hands—with me. You've acted worse than he has, and you ought to be jolly well booted!"

"Hear, hear!" said Bob Cherry.

"You can cut, Wilmot!" added Wharton scornfully. "I don't know whether Hacker will get you off——"

"Nothing of the kind. I——"

"Well, if he does you can get ready for a scrap, that's all! Now cut as soon as you like—and the sooner the better!"

Hisses followed Wilmot as he left the Rag without another word. Dislike and contempt were in almost every face, and he did not seem to care. Perhaps the thought was in his mind of how much worse it would have been had the Greyfriars fellows known more—had

they known what Crawley of the Fourth Form at Topham could have told them!

THE TWELFTH CHAPTER.

Washed Out !

"NOT to-day!" sneered Smithy. "Nor any day!" jeered Skinner.

It looked as if Smithy was right in his declaration.

It was the following day, and nothing more had been heard of the sentence passed on Eric Wilmot.

That Quelch had his back up, and would report him for a flogging, nobody doubted. He had asked for it, and he would get it, if it was left in Quelch's hands. But nobody doubted, either, that the master of the Shell would barge in and do his best with the Head.

So, in the minds of the juniors, the matter was uncertain. A fellow "up" for a flogging was never left long in suspense. If it was coming off, it would come off in the morning.

But it did not come off in the morning. Neither had it come off in the afternoon.

Many eyes, turned on Mr. Quelch's face in the Form-room, read grimness there, but nothing else. He took no special notice of Wilmot. And when classes were over for the day and nothing had happened there could be no further doubt that Hacker had butted in—and with success.

Nobody, certainly, wanted a fellow flogged. Even an outcast like Wilmot would have received some sympathy had he been called on to suffer under the Head's birch before a sea of eyes in the Hall. But for a fellow to get off a flogging, or anything else, by "greas-

ing to a beak" was the limit. Favouritism, always unpopular, was more than ever unpopular, in Wilmot's case.

After school that day, when Mr. Quelch finally dismissed the Remove, some of the fellows wondered whether he was going to make any reference to the subject.

As he did not, no one could doubt further that the affair was at an end—that Wilmot was let off, and the matter dropped. Hence the Bounder's sneering remark and Skinner's jeer as the juniors went out.

Eric Wilmot paused on his way to the door. He was more surprised than the other fellows by his escape. He knew, of course, to what the other fellows attributed it, and the Remove would have been astonished to learn how little satisfaction his escape gave him.

He hesitated a few moments at the doorway, and then went back into the room and stopped at Mr. Quelch's desk. Mr. Quelch, busy with papers there, glanced up at him with an icy glance.

"What do you want, Wilmot?" he asked.

"You told me yesterday, sir, that I was to be reported to the headmaster for a flogging," said Wilmot in a low, even tone. "I have heard nothing further about it, sir."

"I imagined you were aware that your sentence was rescinded, Wilmot," answered Mr. Quelch, with great dryness of manner. "Has not Mr. Hacker told you so?"

Wilmot crimsoned.

"I have not seen Mr. Hacker to-day, sir."

He did not add that he had carefully avoided seeing the master of the Shell. Indifferent as he seemed to the opinion of his Form, he could not have liked being condemned by all the Remove as a toady.

"Indeed !" said Mr Quelch, with a touch of irony. "I was not aware of that, Wilmot, or I would have spoken to you. The sentence is rescinded. You may go."

Wilmot did not go.

"May I ask why it is rescinded, sir ?" he said quietly. "I have no right to be treated differently from any other fellow."

"That is true, Wilmot. But——"

"If my uncle, sir "—Wilmot's cheeks burned—"if my uncle has interfered, sir, I hope you will believe that I never asked him to do so, or wished him to do so. I do not want to be flogged, of course ; but I would rather be flogged a dozen times than—than——" He stammered, and went on again : "If my uncle spoke to the headmaster, sir——"

"Your uncle spoke to me, Wilmot. He made an explanation that caused me to decide not to report the matter to Dr. Locke. The Head has therefore not been acquainted with the matter at all."

"Oh !" gasped Wilmot.

"Your conduct," said Mr. Quelch icily, "was inexcusable. But, in view of what Mr. Hacker has said, I am compelled to make allowances. Had I been aware of the circumstances at the time, I should have given you leave out of gates yesterday afternoon."

"Oh !" repeated Wilmot.

"If you had told me your reason, I should have understood," went on Mr. Quelch. "The whole situation is unusual, disagreeable—indeed, almost intolerable ! But I understand your difficulty. From what Mr. Hacker says, it seems that a boy belonging to your former school was so thoughtless and inconsiderate as to pay you a visit yesterday——"

"That was why I asked my uncle to speak to you, sir. I have never asked him before——"

"Possibly—possibly ! Certainly, in the very peculiar circumstances, it would be injudicious for a Topham boy to come here," said Mr. Quelch. "I fail to see why you could not have written to him to tell him not to come.

Still, as it appears that he arranged to meet you in Courtfield, and said that he would come on to Greyfriars if he did not see you there, I should certainly have given you leave to go out, had you explained."

"I did not know that, sir."

"But such a thing had better not occur again," said Mr. Quelch. "If you have friends at your former school who desire to keep up your acquaintance, in spite of what has happened, it would be wiser to warn them to leave you alone here, Wilmot. If the facts become known in this school, I scarcely see how you can remain here !"

"I never wanted to come here, sir !"

"That was not for you to decide, Wilmot. You have been given a chance that you had no right to expect, and you should be grateful. You may go."

Wilmot opened his lips, closed them again, and left the Form-room in silence. He understood now why the flogging was washed out. Hacker had not gone to the Head and begged him off, as the Remove believed ; he had explained the boy's strange position to Quelch. A dozen floggings would not have hurt and humiliated his proud spirit so much.

Neither was it an explanation that could be given to the school. The Greyfriars fellows had to be left in the belief that it was favouritism.

After tea Wilmot went into the Rag. Harry Wharton & Co. were there with other fellows of the Remove, and the new junior went directly up to Wharton.

The captain of the Remove eyed him with cool contempt as he came up. Wilmot spoke quietly and calmly.

"I've heard that the flogging is washed out, Wharton."

"Nobody needs telling that !" answered Harry, with a curl of the lip.

"Gratters !" said Johnny Bull sarcastically.

"The gratterfulness is terrific, my esteemed greasy Wilmot !" murmured the Nabob of Bhanipur.

Wilmot took no notice of the Co. His eyes were fixed on Wharton's scornful face.

"You told me yesterday that you were going to call me to account if the

flogging did not come off," he said.

"Well, here I am !"

Harry Wharton laughed.

"Oh, that's washed out, too !" he answered. "You see, you've got a friend at court. Much good may it do you !"

"I don't understand you."

"I fancy you understand pretty well."

"You can't mean that my uncle has spoken to you—or that you'd take any notice if he did !"

"Hardly !" said the captain of the Remove. "I'd like Hacker to barge in. I'd be glad of the chance of telling him to mind his own business !"

"Then what do you mean ?"

"I mean, if you want to know—and if you don't know already—that Quelch sent for me to-day, and asked me to let the whole matter drop !" snapped Wharton. "I dare say he guessed that something would be on. Anyhow, he asked me to let it drop, and I said I would, so that's that !"

Wilmot stood silent. Wharton turned away from him, with open contempt. There was a laugh from some of the fellows in the Rag.

"Dear Eric mustn't be touched !" said the Bounder. "It's getting pretty thick, isn't it ?"

"Wharton !" said Wilmot.

The captain of the Remove did not seem to hear.

"Wharton !"

Wharton's back remained turned to him. He stepped forward, and laid his hand on Wharton's shoulder.

"You've got to listen to me," he said.

Wharton struck his hand off.

"Keep away from me, you cur !" he said. "Don't talk to me !"

"You've told Quelch you'd let the matter drop," said Wilmot. "That's your affair. I haven't said that I would let it drop."

"You !" snapped Wharton "I suppose you're pretty keen to let it drop, as you seem to have wangled it with your uncle !"

"I've done nothing of the kind !"

"Oh rot !"

"You fellows can think what you like—I don't care much !" said Wilmot disdainfully "All the same, I'm going to prove that I had nothing to do with getting the matter dropped—so far as you are concerned, at least, Wharton !"

"And how are you going to do that ?" asked Harry contemptuously.

"Like this !"

Smack !

With a sudden movement, Wilmot struck the captain of the Remove across the face with his open hand. The smack rang through the Rag almost like a pistol-shot.

Wharton staggered.

The next moment he was leaping at Wilmot, and the next they were fighting furiously.

THE THIRTEENTH CHAPTER.

Hammer and Tongs !

"A FIGHT !"

"Shut the door !"

"I say, you fellows——"

"Shut that door ! Wingate's in the passage !"

The door of the Rag slammed. Three or four fellows lined up with their backs to it, so that it could not be easily opened from without.

Wingate, or any other prefect, was not wanted in the Rag just then. With eager, excited faces, the juniors gathered round the combat.

Lord Mauleverer sat upright in the armchair in which he was gracefully taking his ease.

"What about the gloves, you men?" he asked.

But Mauly was not heeded.

The Bounder grinned at Redwing.

"Wharton barged in and insisted on the gloves when I had my scrap with that cad!" he remarked. "He seems to have forgotten that!"

"No wonder," said Tom. "I hope he'll knock the cad into a cocked hat!"

"More power to his giddy elbow!" chuckled Smithy. "The brute's asked for it, and no mistake! Blessed if I can make that worm Wilmot out, though. He can't have sneaked to the beaks for protection, and then walked in and asked for it like this!"

"I suppose he wants to make that clear," said Tom.

"Well, he's making it clear—but it's going to cost him a record hiding!" said Vernon-Smith. "I could have handled him that time if I'd had sense enough to keep my temper. Wharton can handle him!"

"They ought to have the gloves on!" muttered Nugent uneasily.

"No good chipping in now," said Bob Cherry.

That was plain enough. Not only were there no gloves, but there were no rounds in that fierce fight.

Harry Wharton's temper was at boiling-point. He had been badly and unscrupulously treated, and he had let the matter drop, at his Form-master's request. That smack in the face before a crowd of fellows had been the result. For the moment, the captain of the Remove was conscious of nothing but a fierce desire to give the fellow what he had asked for.

But angry as he was, he kept a cool head, so far as the scrapping was concerned. He was not going to ask for a licking, throwing away his chances in sheer hot-headed rage and excitement as the Bounder had done.

Wilmot, on his side, was equally bitter and determined. He had been sorry for his trickery of the previous day and ashamed of it. He had only been guilty of it under the pressure of what seemed to him unavoidable necessity. But contempt was hard to bear.

He was proving, at all events, that he had not sought protection from the consequences of his action.

Nobody could suppose that now.

But he was proving it at a cost, as the Bounder had sardonically remarked. Whether he was a match for Wharton or not in other circumstances, he was no match for him now.

For three or four minutes the fight went on, hot and strong, with such punishment given and taken as was seldom seen in a schoolboy scrap. Then Wilmot went with a crash to the floor.

Wharton stood panting.

"Man down!" grinned the Bounder.

"Good egg!" gasped Bob Cherry.

Wilmot lay on his back, gasping for breath, dazed and dizzy. Nobody approached him, till Billy Bunter rolled forward.

Friendly attentions from the fat Owl, however, did not seem very welcome to the outcast of the Remove.

He pushed Bunter's fat paw aside and staggered to his feet. He stood unsteadily, almost rocking on his legs.

"Shove the gloves on!" said Nugent, taking advantage of the pause. "You can't go on with the knuckles!"

But before he had finished speaking, Wilmot had recovered a little and was springing forward again.

Harry Wharton met him with left and right.

"By gum! Some scrap!" said the

Bounder, with glistening eyes, as he watched. "It's Wharton's fight! But I'll say this for that rotter—he's got pluck!"

The door-handle turned. Someone was trying to get into the room. The fellows at the door braced their shoulders against it.

The door was angrily pushed.

"Let me in at once!" came the sharp voice of Wingate of the Sixth.

"We can't hear that!" murmured Squiff. "Stick it!"

And the shoulders remained braced at the door, and the captain of Greyfriars pushed, in vain, at the outer side. Meanwhile, the fight went on, hard and fast and furious.

"Will you open this door, you young sweeps?" came the Greyfriars captain's angry roar.

The fellows inside still turned a deaf ear. Wingate's voice was heard calling:

"Here—Gwynne—Sykes—Blundell—lend me a hand here!"

There was a mighty heave at the door. Under the hefty shove of three

or four big seniors it flew open, and the juniors inside went scattering and stumbling.

Wingate of the Sixth strode in with a frowning brow. He stared in surprise and wrath at the fight.

"Stop that!" he roared.

Neither of the combatants heeded if they heard. Fierce blows were still being exchanged when Wingate strode at them, grasped them by their collars, and fairly wrenched them apart.

Wharton staggered in one direction, and brought up against Bob Cherry, who extended a helping hand and caught him. Wilmot staggered in another—but there was no helping hand for him, and he stumbled over and fell. He picked himself up again, panting.

"You young rascals!" said Wingate. "Fighting—with bare knuckles! You know better than this, Wharton! Is that the sort of example you set, as head boy, in the Remove?"

Wharton gasped for breath.

"Will you let us finish with the gloves on, Wingate?"

"No, I won't, you young hooligan! You've done damage enough—and so has Wilmot—from the look of both of you! I'd give you six each, only you'll get something more from Quelch when he sees your faces!"

"Oh, Wilmot won't get anything!" said the Bounder, laughing. "Wilmot's got a friend at court!"

"Take a hundred lines for cheek, Vernon-Smith! Say anything of that kind again, and I'll give you a lick with this ash!"

"I'm mum!" said Smithy. "I won't say another word till I get a relation on the staff!"

"Ha, ha, ha!"

The next moment the Bounder yelled, as Wingate made good his word—a hefty lick of the prefect's ashplant making Smithy almost hop.

"Any more, and I'll give you six!" snapped Wingate. And the Bounder wisely said no more.

"Now, Wharton and Wilmot, go and bathe your faces. And mind, no more of this!" said Wingate sternly. "If I find you scrapping again, I'll take you both to the Head! Mind, I mean that. Get out of this, both of you!"

Frowning, the Greyfriars captain shepherded both the damaged juniors out of the Rag. The fight had not come to an end—though there was little doubt how it would have ended had not Wingate intervened.

"Bit of luck for that worm Wingate barging in!" Bob Cherry remarked.

"He has a lot of that kind of luck," said the Bounder sarcastically. "How did Wingate happen to be on the spot? We've had plenty of scraps here without a prefect butting in. Of course, he was tipped to keep an eye on dear little Eric!"

"Hacker!" grinned Skinner.

"Of course!"

As a matter of fact, Mr. Quelch, foreseeing probable trouble in his Form, had asked Wingate to keep an eye on the Rag. But the fellows there had no doubt that the Bounder was right.

THE FOURTEENTH CHAPTER.
Puzzle—Find Eric!

"WHERE'S Eric?"

"Locked in Gosling's woodshed."

Mr. Hacker started violently.

Walking in the quadrangle, the master of the Shell came within earshot of Vernon-Smith and Skinner—talking together, with grinning faces.

They did not seem to see him, and certainly they did not lower their voices as he came by. He heard both question and answer quite plainly.

It was Skinner who asked the question—the Bounder who answered it. Both of them chuckled.

Mr. Hacker turned towards the two juniors, and strode up to them.

"Vernon-Smith! Skinner!" he rapped.

Smithy and Skinner spun round.

"Oh!" gasped Skinner.

"Yes, sir!" said the Bounder.

"I heard what you said!" thundered the master of the Shell.

"Did you, sir?" said the Bounder coolly. "Well, we're allowed to talk in the quad, sir!"

"What?" exclaimed Mr. Hacker. "I heard you say that you locked my nephew in the wood-shed, Vernon-Smith!"

"I never mentioned your nephew, sir! I wouldn't touch him with a barge-pole if I could help it!"

"How dare you utter such impudent falsehoods, Vernon-Smith? You were certainly speaking of my nephew! Is there a single other boy at Greyfriars whose name is Eric?"

"Not that I know of, sir!"

"Then what is the use of such a falsehood, Vernon-Smith! I shall report this to your Form-master! But first, give me the key of the shed, so that Eric—my nephew—can be released first."

"I haven't the key, sir!"

"Have you returned it to Gosling?"

"No, sir!"

"Then what have you done with it?"

"I haven't had it."

Mr. Hacker fairly gasped with wrath. After what he had heard, he was not likely to believe that statement.

"Vernon-Smith, I command you to hand me that key instantly!"

"I can't give you what I've not got, sir," said the Bounder. "And I tell you again—that I've not touched your nephew! He's not a nice chap to touch!"

"I think he's gone out of gates, sir," said Skinner blandly. "I rather think I saw him go out after dinner."

"Skinner, you are as untruthful as Vernon-Smith! I heard you ask Vernon-Smith where Eric was, and he answered that my nephew was locked in the woodshed. How dare you utter such palpable falsehoods?"

"I don't think Mr. Quelch would like fellows of his Form to be called liars, sir," said Skinner.

"Silence, Skinner! Once more, Vernon-Smith, I order you to hand me the key to release my nephew, otherwise, I shall take you immediately to your Form-master, who will compel you to do so."

"I've said I haven't the key."

"That is enough! Come with me!"

Mr. Hacker dropped his hand on the Bounder's shoulder, and hooked him away towards the House.

Vernon-Smith winked at Skinner as he went. Skinner was left grinning. Dozens of fellows stared at the Bounder as he was led away.

"I say, you fellows!" squeaked Billy Bunter. "I say, Smithy's in a row again! Hacker's got him!"

"What the dickens is the row now?" asked Harry Wharton.

But his friends shook their heads. Nobody knew what the row was.

But everybody was curious to know, and a crowd gathered and followed the master of the Shell and Vernon-Smith.

"Here, Wharton!" called out Smithy.

"Yes," answered Harry, coming towards him.

Football difficulties had caused rather a strain between the captain of the Remove, and that wilful and reckless member of the Form. But every Remove man was up against meddling by the master of the Shell.

"Do not speak to this boy, Wharton!" snapped Mr. Hacker. "I have no time to delay! Come with me, Vernon-Smith!"

"You're head boy of the Remove, Wharton," said the Bounder coolly. "Will you tell me officially whether I'm bound to let myself be walked off by a beak who isn't my Form-master? I suppose you know."

"You'd better go, anyhow," said Harry.

He had to follow on to answer the Bounder, as Hacker was marching him on without a pause.

"You don't think I'm entitled to knock Hacker's paw off my shoulder?" asked the Bounder.

"Ha, ha, ha!" yelled the juniors, within hearing.

Smithy, of course, was only asking that question to "cheek" Hacker.

"Don't be an ass!" said Harry Wharton.

"Well, I only want to know," said the Bounder. "You know what a stickler I am for law and order, and all that."

"Ha, ha, ha!"

"Silence, Vernon-Smith!" hooted Mr. Hacker. "How dare you be so insolent! I order you to be silent!"

"I take orders from my Form-master, sir, and from no other!"

THE MAGNET LIBRARY.—No. 1,459.

answered the Bounder, with cool impertinence.

Mr. Hacker came very near boxing his ears at that. But he refrained. Possibly he suspected that Smithy would have liked nothing better, not, of course, the actual smite, but the row with Quelch that would indubitably have followed had Hacker boxed Remove ears.

"Hallo, hallo, hallo! Here's Quelch!" exclaimed Bob Cherry.

Mr. Quelch appeared from the doorway. No doubt he had spotted the excitement in the quad from his study window.

Quelch was always calm. But it was a dangerous calmness now as he came quickly to meet Hacker and the Bounder.

"What does this mean, please?" he asked, in a voice that would have made a refrigerator seem warm and genial. "Mr. Hacker, will you have the kindness to release this boy of my Form?"

"I was bringing this boy of your Form to you, sir," hooted Hacker.

"I am assured that the boy would have followed you, sir, without being practically dragged across the quadrangle."

"Certainly, sir!" said Vernon-Smith, with respectful meekness.

Smithy was not always meek and respectful, even to his own beak. But it suited him now to be both.

Mr. Hacker dropped his hand from the Bounder's shoulder. More and more fellows gathered round—not only Remove, but Fourth and Shell, and seniors and fags. The scene was getting a very numerous audience.

"Now, Mr. Hacker, if you will kindly acquaint me with——"

"My nepher, sir," spluttered Hacker.

"Upon my word, sir!" exclaimed Mr. Quelch. "Wilmot again! Vernon-Smith, have you been quarrelling with Wilmot?"

"No, sir. I'm very careful indeed not to quarrel with Wilmot, sir," said the Bounder meekly. "I know Mr. Hacker doesn't like it, sir."

"This boy has locked my nephew in the woodshed, and refuses—insolently refuses—to hand me the key to release him!" almost shouted Mr. Hacker.

"If you have played such a foolish prank, Vernon-Smith——"

"I haven't, sir!"

"Have you locked Wilmot in the woodshed?"

"No, sir!"

"Is he there at all?"

"I don't know where he is, sir."

"You see, Mr. Hacker——"

"I see, sir, that this boy, Vernon-Smith, has no scruple in uttering the most unscrupulous falsehoods!" gasped Mr. Hacker. "He has locked my nephew in the woodshed, and I demand the key!"

"For what reason, Mr. Hacker, do you suppose that Vernon-Smith has done anything of the kind?" exclaimed the Remove-master.

"Because, sir, I heard him say so with his own lips," snorted Mr. Hacker. "He was telling another Remove boy what he had done when I passed him a few minutes ago."

"If you are sure of that, sir——"

"I can believe my own ears, sir. I demand that the key be given to me at once! I will not allow such malicious pranks to be played on my nephew, sir."

"If you have the key, Vernon-Smith, I——"

"I haven't, sir!"

Mr. Quelch gave him a searching look. He knew the unpopularity of Wilmot in his Form, and he knew that

Vernon-Smith was the fellow to play that jape, or any other. And Hacker's statement was positive.

"We had better proceed to Gosling's shed, Mr. Hacker!" he said curtly. "I can scarcely believe that Vernon-Smith would venture to speak to me untruthfully; but it is easy to ascertain."

"Very well, sir!" snorted Mr. Hacker.

"Follow me, Vernon-Smith!"

"Certainly, sir!"

Mr. Hacker whisked away, and Mr. Quelch whisked with him. Hacker's face was red with wrath; Quelch's set with grim vexation. He was more than tired of Hacker's fussy concern for that member of his Form; but he had no choice about taking up this matter.

He had told Vernon-Smith to follow him; but he had not told the rest of the Remove. However, they followed. Quite an army marched away after the two masters.

The sight of such a procession naturally drew the general attention. More and more fellows joined up. Dozens of voices inquired what was on. The news spread that Wilmot had been locked in Gosling's woodshed by the Bounder, and that Hacker was barging in again. Most of the fellows were laughing.

Any jape on the most unpopular fellow in the Remove was likely to be generally approved. But nobody envied the Bounder if Hacker's nephew really was discovered locked up among Gosling's faggots. The more Quelch was fed-up with Hacker and his nephew, the more certain he was to come down hard and heavy on any fellow who set Hacker going.

"Smithy's asking for it this time," remarked Bob Cherry. "Must have been a fool to let Hacker hear him."

Harry Wharton laughed.

"Whatever Smithy is, he isn't a fool!" he said. "I fancy he never let Hacker hear anything he didn't want him to hear."

"Oh, my hat! Do you think he's pulling Hacker's leg, somehow?"

"I shouldn't wonder."

The army arrived at the woodshed Mr. Quelch tried the door, and found it locked. There was nothing unusual about that. Gosling kept that shed locked, except when he forgot to do so. There was a window, but it was fastened. Mr. Quelch rapped sharply on the door.

"Wilmot—are you here, Wilmot?"

There was no reply from within.

The woodshed appeared to be untenanted. Mr. Quelch turned impatiently to the master of the Shell.

"No one is here, Mr. Hacker. Evidently you must have misunderstood whatever it was you heard this boy say."

"I did not misunderstand, sir! Vernon-Smith, do you dare to deny that you said to another Remove boy, in my hearing, that my nephew was locked in Gosling's woodshed?"

"Certainly I deny that, sir!" said the Bounder.

"You—you—you deny it?" gasped Mr. Hacker, hardly able to believe his ears. He knew what he had heard Smithy say to Skinner.

"Yes, I deny having spoken about your nephew at all, sir."

Mr. Hacker almost gurgled.

"Mr. Quelch! This boy's impudence and untruthfulness pass all bounds! I repeat that I distinctly heard him——"

"Wilmot cannot be here, sir, or he would answer me!" said Mr. Quelch, and he rapped on the locked door again.

Under the hefty shove of three or four big seniors, the door of the Rag flew open, and the juniors inside went scattering and stumbling. Wingate strode in, with a frowning brow. "Stop that!" he roared. Neither Wharton nor Wilmot heeded, if they heard. They were fighting furiously.

"Wilmot! Are you there? Are you there, Wilmot?"

"Wrong number!" murmured Skinner, and there was a chortle.

"Silence! Mr. Hacker, it is clear that your nephew is not there——"

"I am not assured of that, sir! He is possibly prevented from answering. That Vernon-Smith locked him in this shed, I know, on Vernon-Smith's own statement. He has the key on him——"

"Have you the key, Vernon-Smith?"

"No, sir."

"Wharton! Please go to Gosling's lodge and request him to step here, bringing with him the key of the woodshed."

"Certainly, sir!"

Harry Wharton cut off. The rest of the fellows remained, with the two masters, outside the door of the woodshed. Mr. Hacker had a mental picture of his nephew, with a duster stuffed in his mouth, perhaps tied to Gosling's bench in the woodshed. That so far as Mr. Hacker could see, was the only way of accounting for his silence—as he was absolutely convinced that Eric was in the shed. Mr. Quelch suspected nothing of the sort. All Mr. Quelch suspected was, that Hacker was a fussy old donkey.

However, they waited, till Gosling arrived, grunting, with the key of the woodshed in his horny hand.

THE FIFTEENTH CHAPTER.

"Eric, or Little by Little!"

"UNLOCK this shed, please, Gosling!" rapped Mr. Quelch.

"Yessir!" grunted Gosling. Gosling did not know what was the matter. He was surprised, and not pleased, by the sight of a numerous crowd gathered round his woodshed. He could not begin to imagine why two members of Dr. Locke's staff were interested in the interior of that building. Privately, he thought it a cheek on their part.

Gosling never butted into a master's study—so why should a master butt into Gosling's woodshed? Not being in a position to say what he thought, Gosling grunted expressively, and fumbled slowly with the big iron key.

"Lose no time, Gosling!" snapped Mr. Hacker. "My nephew has been locked in that shed! I am here to release him."

Gosling blinked round at the master of the Shell.

"There ain't nobody in this 'ere shed, sir!" he grunted.

"I have told you that my nephew is there! Lose no time!"

"'Ow'd he get in, then, sir?" demanded Gosling. "The winder's shut! Mr. Quelch, sir, if that young limb's playing tricks in my woodshed, sir——"

"He has been locked in by another boy!" snapped Mr. Hacker. "You are very much to blame, Gosling, for allowing the key to go out of your hands."

"Wot I says, is this 'ere, sir——"

"You have allowed this boy, Vernon-Smith, to take your key——"

"I ain't, sir!"

"Has the key been out of your hands to-day, Gosling?" asked Mr. Quelch.

"'Course it has, sir!" answered Gosling.

"I knew it!" exclaimed Mr. Hacker. "You say that Vernon-Smith has not had it, but you admit that it has been out of your hands. Where has it been, while it was out of your hands?"

"In my trousis pocket," answered Gosling.

"Wha-a-at!"

"Ha, ha, ha!" shrieked the whole audience. Even Mr. Quelch smiled.

"In—in—in your trousers pocket!" gasped Mr. Hacker. "Nonsense! Absurd! Open that door at once, Gosling! You are wasting time with your foolishness!"

Gosling, with an emphatic grunt, fumbled with the key. He was in no hurry to oblige a gentleman who described his remarks as foolishness.

However, the door was thrown open at last.

Pushing Gosling aside, Mr. Hacker rushed in. Mr. Quelch followed him. Fellows packed themselves round the door to stare in after them.

Mr. Hacker's mental picture of Eric, with a duster in his mouth to keep him from calling for help, did not materialise.

The woodshed was empty—save for its customary contents.

There were logs, there were faggots; there was Gosling's bench with some tools lying on it—there were other such things, but there was no human inhabitant.

One thing, perhaps, was a little unusual. A book lay on the bench. Gosling was no reader of books, and, had he been, he would not have been likely to select a volume that looked like a schoolboy's prize book, as that volume did. But no one, for the moment, noticed that trifle.

Mr. Hacker stared round the interior of the shed. Staring at logs and faggots, however, could not turn them into what he sought.

Even Hacker had to admit that Wilmot was not there.

"Well, sir, are you satisfied now?" asked Mr. Quelch tartly.

"No, sir!" said Mr. Hacker, with bitter wrath. "I am not satisfied! I am very far from satisfied! Gosling!"

"Yessir!" grunted Gosling, as disrespectfully as he dared.

"Has my nephew been in this woodshed at all?"

"Not as I knows of. I'd report him to Mr. Quelch, if he come messing round my woodshed."

"Has Vernon-Smith been here?"

"Yessir."

"Oh! He has been here! And why was he here, and when?" demanded Mr. Hacker, with a lingering hope that he was on the trail of something.

"Master Vernon-Smith looked in when I was 'ere after dinner, sir," grunted Gosling. "He give me a book!"

"A—a—a book?"

"Yessir! He says, says he, an aunt give him that there book at Christmas, and he don't want it, he says, and he says, says he, p'r'aps I could get a bob for it, he says, and I says, leave it 'ere, I says, and thank you kindly, I says."

Mr. Hacker snorted. It was very probable that Smithy would dispose thus of a volume given him by a kind aunt at Christmas—especially if it was a volume of an improving nature. But Hacker did not want to hear about it.

"Really, Mr. Hacker——" said the Remove-master.

He was more conscious than the angry master of the Shell, of the array of grinning faces in the doorway.

"Mr. Quelch! My nephew is not here!" exclaimed Mr. Hacker. "Either he has been here and is now gone, or——"

"Does anyone know where Wilmot is?" asked Mr. Quelch, with a glance at the army outside.

"He went out of gates after dinner, sir!" answered Skinner. "I told Mr. Hacker so when he asked us——"

"Really, Mr. Hacker, if Skinner told you——"

"I did not believe Skinner's statement, sir, in view of what I heard Vernon-Smith say. I regarded it, sir, as a palpable attempt to deceive me."

"But Wilmot's really gone out, sir!" cut in Hazeldene. "I saw him go out after dinner."

"So did I," added another voice.

"There appears to be no doubt of it, Mr. Hacker——"

"No, sir!" said Mr. Hacker bitterly. "I see that now, sir. I am driven to the conclusion that it was not, as I supposed, by chance, that I overheard Vernon-Smith make his statement in the quadrangle. I believe now, sir, that he saw me coming, and affected not to do so, and spoke in my hearing, sir, to mislead me——"

"Pulling the old bean's leg!" said a voice from the back of the crowd.

"Ha, ha, ha!"

"Silence!" exclaimed Mr. Quelch. "If the matter is as you suppose, sir, Vernon-Smith will certainly be punished for having played such—such an inconsiderate prank. Vernon-Smith!"

"Yes, sir!"

"I demand to know exactly what you said, which Mr. Hacker appears to have misunderstood——"

"I did not misunderstand, Mr. Quelch. There was no question of misunderstanding a plain statement——"

"Did you state, in Mr. Hacker's hearing, that you had locked Wilmot in this woodshed, Vernon-Smith?"

"No, sir; I never mentioned Wilmot."

"Is my word to be taken, sir, or the word of that unscrupulous boy?" almost shrieked Mr. Hacker.

"Your word, certainly, is to be taken, sir!" said Mr. Quelch. "But it is clear that some misunderstanding has arisen. It was Skinner, I think, to whom Vernon-Smith was speaking. Skinner!"

"Yes, sir!"

"What did Vernon-Smith say about Mr. Hacker's nephew?"

"Nothing, sir! He never mentioned Mr. Hacker's nephew."

"Take care what you say, Skinner! Vernon-Smith must have used a name in speaking of anyone. Did he use Wilmot's name?"

"No, sir!"

"You are sure, Mr. Hacker, that you heard Vernon-Smith utter the name of Wilmot?"

"He uttered the name of Eric, sir! There is no other boy at Greyfriars named Eric, so far as my knowledge extends."

"Or mine!" said Mr. Quelch. "Now answer me carefully, Vernon-Smith! If you used the name of Eric, you were obviously alluding to Mr. Hacker's nephew. Do you deny that you uttered that name?"

"Oh, no, sir!" said Vernon-Smith, "I spoke the name of Eric, sir! So far as I remember, Skinner asked me where Eric was, and I said, locked in the woodshed."

"That is so, sir!" said Skinner.

Mr. Quelch gazed at them. Hacker glared at them. The army outside, cramming the doorway, gazed. So far as anyone could see, the Bounder was admitting the whole charge. But he seemed quite cool and cheerful.

"You said, in Mr. Hacker's hearing, that Eric was locked in the woodshed," repeated Mr. Quelch.

"It's not my fault that Mr. Hacker heard me, sir! I couldn't know that he was listening behind my back."

"Oh, crumbs!" breathed Bob Cherry.

Mr. Hacker gurgled.

"Mr. Hacker overheard you by chance, as you are well aware, Vernon-Smith," said Mr. Quelch, sternly. "You can have made such a false statement only to mislead him——"

"It was not a false statement, sir!"

"Not!" exclaimed Mr. Quelch.

"Certainly not, sir! Mr. Hacker's nephew isn't the only Eric in the world."

"There is no other boy at Greyfriars of that name, Vernon-Smith."

"I know, sir! The chap I was speaking of to Skinner wasn't a Greyfriars man."

"Not a Greyfriars man! You are not pretending, Vernon-Smith, that you locked a boy belonging to some other school in this woodshed."

"Not at all, sir! I never said I locked him in. I said Eric was locked in the woodshed. It was Gosling who locked the door. I tried to explain to Mr. Hacker, sir, that I wasn't speaking of Wilmot, but he wouldn't take any notice!" said the Bounder, meekly. "You see, sir, Skinner knew that I'd been given a copy of Eric at Christmas——"

"A—a—a copy of Eric!"

"Yes, sir, a very well-known book, often given as a present to good boys like me, sir. It's called 'Eric, or Little by Little'——"

"Eric, or Little by Little!" repeated Mr. Quelch, like a man in a dream.

"Yes, sir! There it is, on the bench."

Mr. Quelch turned an almost dazed eye on the volume lying on the bench, which the Bounder had received from a kind aunt at Christmas, and which he had turned over, unread, to Gosling.

In gilt letters on the cover, was the title: "Eric, or Little by Little."

Mr. Quelch, of course, had heard of that celebrated and eminent work. He

had, indeed, had a copy of it presented to him in his far-off boyhood, which he could remember that he had, like Smithy, omitted to read.

Quelch gazed at "Eric, or Little by Little," Mr. Hacker gazed at it. They seemed bereft of speech.

"Skinner thought he'd like to look at it, sir, knowing I had it," said the Bounder, meekly. "He asked me where it was, and I said it was locked in the woodshed! You see, sir, I'd already given it to Gosling, as I didn't want it."

"Oh!" gasped Mr. Quelch.

"Oh!" gasped Mr. Hacker.

"I was quite surprised, sir, when Mr. Hacker thought I was speaking of Wilmot," said the Bounder. "I told him I wasn't—so did Skinner! We both told him we'd locked nobody in the woodshed. He wouldn't listen, sir."

The cram at the doorway gazed at Smithy.

They knew that the Bounder had a nerve; but they had never suspected him of nerve to this extent.

Every fellow there knew that he had worked the whole thing—first giving the book to Gosling, then fixing up a conversation for Mr. Hacker to overhear—knowing that that fussy and hasty gentleman would fall blindly into the trap. Mr. Quelch probably, suspected as much.

Nevertheless, the Bounder was not to be blamed. The whole fault was Hacker's. He had overheard words spoken among juniors, had misunderstood them, and refused to listen to denials and explanations. He had made a complete and egregious fool of himself—a fact of which he was, by this time, well aware!

Hacker's face was like unto a newly boiled beetroot in hue. He could not even be sure that the Bounder had tricked him. Smithy and Skinner had been—ostensibly, at least—speaking of the book that lay on Gosling's bench. It was difficult to prove otherwise. They had told him that they were not speaking of his nephew—they could do no more than that!

Without another word, Mr. Hacker strode out of the woodshed, shoved his way through a grinning crowd, and disappeared.

"Vernon-Smith!" said Mr. Quelch.

"Yes, sir!" said the meek and respectful Bounder.

Mr. Quelch paused. What was he to say? How could he blame either Smithy or Skinner, because their harmless words had been overheard by a fussy and suspicious man who had misunderstood them?

The whole thing was utterly ridiculous. Mr. Quelch wisely decided to leave it where it was, and he hurried away after Mr. Hacker. Gosling, grunting, locked his woodshed again. Fellows who had tried to suppress their merriment, in the presence of Mr. Quelch, let it go when he departed. As he hurried back to the House, the Remove master heard a hilarious roar behind him.

"Ha, ha, ha!"

"That ass, Hacker——"

"Ha, ha, ha!"

"That old donkey, Hacker——"

"Ha, ha, ha! Eric, or Little by Little! Ha, ha, ha!"

"Fancy Hacker making such a silly mistake!" said the Bounder. "Thinking a chap was speaking about his precious nephew, when he was only speaking about a book—a well-known book, too!"

"Ha, ha, ha!"

"You didn't mean him to make that mistake?" chuckled Bob Cherry.

"My dear chap, am I the man to pull a beak's leg?"

(Continued on page 28.)

DAN of the DOGGER BANK!

By DAVID GOODWIN.

The Groping Hand !

KENNETH GRAHAM, son of a millionaire shipowner, is rescued off the Dogger Bank by the crew of the fishing trawler, Grey Seal.

His past life a blank, he is given the name of "Dogger Dan," and signed on as fifth hand under Skipper Atheling, Finn Macoul, Wat Griffiths, and Buck Atheling.

Aware of his nephew's fate, and knowing that he will be heir to the shipowner's money when his brother dies, Dudley Graham engages Jake Rebow and his cutthroats of the Black Squadron to get Kenneth out of the way for ever.

Following a series of thrilling encounters with Rebow's confederates, Dan and Buck Atheling are wrecked on Baltrum Island, where they meet a wealthy old Dutchman named Jan Osterling, who is later brutally attacked by the squadron men and left to die.

Before breathing his last, Jan asks the boys to hand over his savings to his nephew Max, in return for which he hands them a chart disclosing the whereabouts of a hidden treasure worth £5,000, to be divided between them.

Dan and Buck rejoin the Grey Seal, after which they go out fishing in the ship's boat. The craft is overturned, however, and the boys are picked up by a passing yacht, the owner of which is none other than Dudley Graham.

Dan's memory returns as the result of meeting his uncle, but Dudley denies relationship.

Making friends with Jack Ward, the mate, Dan tells the story of his adventures, and then asks the man to signal to the first passing ship, telling her to broadcast a message to Donald Graham, telling of his son's whereabouts.

"Whew !" whistled Jack Ward. He stared at Dan in amazement. "You ain't pulling my leg? Is this straight?"

"Straight as the mast! I'm Kenneth Graham! And it'll be the best day's work you ever did in your life."

"Never mind that, lad," returned the mate gleefully. "I'm with you! I see the game. It's you Dudley Graham's after. He's got you set here. Watch yourself below, lad, an' I'll watch you on deck. There's one more thing, too. If he can't make away with you—an' he won't do it openly, for he'll not give the crew the chance to hang a murder charge over his head for the rest of his life—he'll soon have you out o' these waters. Have you any notion where he might go?"

Dan thought for a moment, and an idea flashed into his head.

"Baltrum Island, and within three days' time !" he answered. "Add that to your signal."

"The first vessel that passes after daybreak shall have it !" said Ward.

And, after a quick hand-grip, Dan and the mate parted.

Buck was at the foot of the ladder.

"Tell me, Dan," he said anxiously, "is all this true ?"

"Every word of it," said Dan. "And Dudley Graham, who makes out that he does not know me, will take the first chance he gets of putting me out of the way. Now you have the key to all we've gone through—and all the rest of it !"

As the blade buried itself in the Japanese rug, Dan grasped the wrist with all his force and clung to it !

Dan also told Buck what he had arranged with Jack Ward.

"Good work !" said Buck. "You've got the machinery moving, an' if it works, should anything happen to you here, Dudley Graham will pay the bill. Now, come and see him. Don't let on, but just lie an' watch !"

"Ship's fare, my lads," said Dudley pleasantly, as the boys entered the dining-saloon and sat down to a table laid with gleaming silver and crystal, "or yacht's fare, if you like to call it that."

"That's nearer the mark, sir," said Buck, as a dainty first course was set before them—"at least, it ain't what we call ship's fare on the old Seal."

Dudley motioned the steward to withdraw, and the trio dined in private.

Dudley made himself agreeable, and towards the end of the meal, as Dan filled his glass with mild claret—for he had refused to tackle anything stronger —Dudley drank to his health.

"Here's to a successful voyage to Baltrum !" he said. "Cheer-oh, lads !"

And the meal continued.

"By the way," said Dudley, before they rose, "would you allow me to look at that chart of yours again?"

Dan unconsciously passed his hand to his breast pocket, as though to take out Jan Osterling's plan, which Buck had returned to him.

He stopped, however, in time, but not before Dudley noted the movement.

"I'd better make you a copy of it," said Dan, buttoning up his coat, "then we shall both know a bit more about it."

He had not the slightest intention of doing anything of the sort, neither did he mean to let Dudley finger the chart again. He realised full well that it was too complicated for any to keep its bearings accurately in memory.

Dudley smiled.

"I expect you're pretty tired after your experiences," he said, "so I won't keep you up. The steward will show you to your state-rooms. Breakfast whenever you like. Good-night !"

The steward conducted the boys to two different rooms.

As soon as Buck had inspected his quarters he joined Dan again.

"Is this yours?" he said, looking round the cabin. "Ah! Next to the owner's room." He lowered his voice. "Let's have a look at your bunk."

The sleeping-berth was a recess in the wall, and by one side hung half a dozen hooks for clothes.

"This berth must jut into the next room," said Buck. "Yes, there's a cupboard beneath it on the other side of the wall. Queer arrangement! Those hooks are the only ones in the room. Well, you just hang your clothes on them. Don't do anything silly!"

"Not if I can help it," said Dan.

"An' there's one thing more, old son," said Buck in a low voice—"don't turn in! Sit up for a spell an' watch. I'm goin' to. If there's anything wrong, shout, an' I'll be with you in two shakes!"

He departed quietly, and closed the door. For quite half an hour Dan stood by the candle-lamp thinking. After a while he withdrew the plan from his pocket, tore the blank half-sheet of parchment off, and with pen and ink, began copying old Jan's chart carefully.

It took him some time, after which he put out the candle, undressed in the dark, and hung his clothes neatly on the pegs by the bunk. A suit of clean pyjamas lay in the berth, and he put them on.

The lamps, still burning in the alleyway outside—for a ship's passage lights are never put out at night—shed a dim light through the cabin. When Dan's eyes got used to the gloom he found he could see pretty well.

He did not get into the berth, but merely disarranged the bedclothes. Then he took a seat on a chair on the opposite side of the little sleeping-room, holding himself ready.

Tired as he was, he fought with his drowsiness, and did not allow sleep to overcome him. But it was a hard struggle. Hour after hour seemed to crawl by.

Dan was nodding, when a faint, tiny scratching sound set all his senses on the alert.

He fixed his eyes keenly on the spot whence it came.

Suddenly a small square of a panel by the side of the bed opened like a trapdoor, and slowly but gently a long, brown hand slid through it and groped around, feeling softly about the clothes that Dan had hung on the hooks.

The hand stopped at the pilot-cloth jacket, and deftly ran over it till it reached the inner breast pocket, into which it groped.

Dan watched as though fascinated. His nerves were strung to breaking-pitch, and all his muscles were tense.

The long, brown hand rose slowly from the pocket, drawing out, tightly held between its first and second fingers, the yellow parchment on which was the secret of Jan Osterling's treasure.

Signalling The News!

THE parchment trembled a little between the two fingers that held it, as it was drawn clear of the coat-pocket.

Dan watched the hand as if fascinated, as it felt round about the little trapdoor in the panelling of the cabin. The fingers deftly laid over the flap of the hanging coat again, and left it just as it had been.

"Just as I thought!" mused Dan. "Buck was right. I'd no idea there was an opening just there, though. I must have a good look at it later on."

The hand began to withdraw slowly and noiselessly with its booty, but Dan made no sign. He watched the precious parchment disappearing, without moving a muscle. A curious smile played about the corners of his mouth, but he made no effort to rescue the chart that held the secret of Jan Osterling's treasure.

The hand vanished, and the little trapdoor closed without a sound.

Dan bestowed on it one solemn wink. Then, thoroughly worn out, he surrendered himself to the charms of sleep, and dozed off lightly where he sat.

For some hours he remained thus, opening his eyes only when the first streak of dawn began to struggle through the porthole. Then, seeing that the open day had come to banish all deeds of darkness, he climbed confidently into his bunk, and was soon sleeping peacefully.

It was nearly ten o'clock when he rose and dressed. As he opened the door he met Buck about to enter. At the same moment Dudley Graham came up the alleyway and bore down on the two boys.

"Breakfast is just ready, lads!" he said. "Come along!"

Dudley Graham led them into the dining-saloon, and the three seated themselves. The boys were civil, but cool, and Dudley wore an air of joviality.

There was a gleam of triumph in his dark eyes which he could hardly suppress, and Dan, watching him carefully, sized up his feelings pretty accurately. Dudley was plainly pleased with himself at having secured the treasure-chart.

"I'm not quite certain where we shall make for to-day," he said, "but I think the sooner we get to Baltrum, and look into the business of this treasure of yours, the better!"

"Right-ho!" said Dan quietly. "Hope we shall find it when we get there! Might take a bit of doing, sir!"

"Oh, your chart ought to make that simple enough, if the gold really exists. By the way, did you lock your state-room door last night?"

"No," returned Dan, "I didn't. Why?"

"I ought to have warned you to," said Dudley. "There's a thief somewhere on this vessel. I've lost several things out of my pockets while my clothes have been hanging up at night. But although I've done my best to find who the thief is, I have not been successful."

"I think I could lay my hands on him pretty easy!" thought Dan.

But he contented himself with remarking that he would lock his door another night.

When breakfast was over Dudley withdrew, and the boys went up on deck.

Buck drew a long breath.

"It's like sitting and smoking in a barrel of gunpowder to take one's meals with that fellow and listen to his talk," he said. "He's beastly pleased with himself this morning, somehow. I wonder why."

"You wouldn't wonder if you'd been in my room last night," said Dan.

And he told Buck all that happened in the state-room.

"What!" said Buck, aghast. "He got the chart, then?"

"Yes," said Dan. "He did that!"

"Couldn't you do anything to stop him, you young chump?"

"I didn't try. It wasn't my chart he got. It was a copy that I'd made. There was a pen and ink in the room, and I tore the blank half-sheet of parchment off the plan and made a pretty good imitation of the real thing. He didn't spot the difference, or he wouldn't have been so pleased this morning. If he follows the fake plan, he'll be digging holes for the treasure on the other side of the island."

"Good!" exclaimed Buck, with a chuckle. "O.K., Dan! Here's the mate. They're changing the watch."

"'Mornin', lads—'mornin'!" said Jack Ward. "They ain't cut your throats yet, then?" he added cheerfully. "No. they ain't done it, 'cos they don't dare! Dudley don't want no evidence! But if you smell trouble, shout for me. I'll come and drill holes in anyone as offers to touch ye!"

He hitched his right side coat-pocket as he spoke. The outline of something heavy and hard showed in it.

"But ain't that a steamer we're raisin' on the weather bow?" he continued, staring out over the sea. "A Hull packet, by her looks. I'll bear away down on her and let her have your signal."

"Thank you, Mr. Ward!" said Dan. "I'll never forget your kindness. And now——"

"And now," put in the mate, "look out for squalls! If Dudley tumbles to the game, there'll be feathers flying! You kids had better go below, out of harm's way."

"Not us," said Dan softly; "we'll stay put!"

With a shrug of the shoulders, the mate fetched the code-book out of the charthouse, and called up a deck-hand to hoist the code-flag. The skipper was below, for he had been sober for some three hours, and was making up for lost time.

Down towards the steamer swept the Ercildoune, and slowed down about two hundred yards from her. The strange vessel was a fast Hamburg packet, bound Englandward.

After a rapid glance at the code-book, the yacht's mate gave his orders to the sulky dago deck-hand, with a couple of kicks, as a warning to get a move on.

Up fluttered the four flags, snapping and cracking in the breeze, as they flew from the gilded vane of the yacht's foremast.

There was a stir aboard the steamer, a pause, and then her answering pennant was run up.

Another signal took the place of the first on the Ercildoune.

"They've got it, lads!" said the mate triumphantly. "Your father'll know what's happened now. That steamer's bound for Hull."

"Hull!" cried Dan. "Buck, my father's yacht lies there—the Valhalla!"

"Valhalla!" exclaimed Buck. "Why, she's a thousand-ton ocean-goer! I've seen her! What about Dudley Graham now?"

"Don't crow too loud, my lads," said the mate grimly. "If ever you leave this craft alive, it'll be a miracle, whatever happens to Dudley. There, the steamer's answerin'. Now to let 'em know where to find you. Baltrum Island, you said. Sure o' that?"

"It's that, or nothing," said Dan. "Make it Baltrum!"

Up went the signal, and the steamer acknowledged it with a flutter of her code pennant.

At that moment Dudley Graham stepped up from the companion-way.

As he did so, the mate turned to the surly signalman.

"Down with that signal, you snuff-coloured sweep!" he roared. "D'ye hear me? And get a move on!"

Dudley's eye ran aloft in a moment. He read the letters of the four flags and cast a glance at the Hull steamer.

Printed in Great Britain and published every Saturday by the Proprietors, The Amalgamated Press, Ltd., The Fleetway House, Farringdon Street, London, E.C.4. Advertisement offices: The Fleetway House, Farringdon Street, London, E.C.4. Registered for transmission by Canadian Magazine Post. Subscription rates: Inland and Abroad, 11s. per annum; 5s. 6d. for six months. Sole Agents for Australia and New Zealand: Messrs. Gordon & Gotch Ltd., and for South Africa: Central News Agency, Ltd.—Saturday, January 25th, 1936.

Then, with a suspicious stare at the mate, he pounced upon the signal-book, and looked up the code message to get its meaning.

After discovering what he wanted, he shut the book with a slam, his eyes blazing, his dark face pale with fury. Then he leapt forward as if he would seize Jack Ward by the throat.

The mate turned coolly, looking his aggressor in the eyes.

"Steady there, mister!" said Ward quietly.

"You dog!" said Dudley, in a low voice. "Would you dare?"

"I'm in charge o' this bridge," said Ward unpleasantly, "and if you're not off it by the ladder in ten seconds, you'll go over the rails instead—with my boot to give you a lift!"

"You insolent blackguard!" raged Dudley. "I'm the owner of this vessel, and I'll go where I choose!"

"Ten seconds, I said!" repeated the mate, lifting his foot. "One—two—three—four—five—six——"

Dudley turned and walked sullenly down the ladder.

"Nine—ten!" concluded the mate. "You only just did it, mister! Better move sharper next time, or you'll be wanting a stretcher to take you below!"

"You ruffian!" cried Dudley. Then, turning to the crew, he roared: "Find the captain, some of you! Don't stand staring like fools!"

After some delay, during which Jack Ward attended coolly to his business, the dago captain came unsteadily along the deck.

"Put that insolent scoundrel in irons for mutiny!" shouted Dudley, pointing to the mate. "And shove him into the empty bunker!"

But the sallow-skinned captain, after taking a good look at Ward, pulled his fuddled wits together, and whispered into the owner's ear, a twinkle of cunning in his ferrety eyes.

Dudley's anger seemed to cool down.

"You're right," he said viciously; "safest, after all. See to it at once!"

With a savage glare at the mate, he went below.

More Treachery!

THE dago skipper, turning unsteadily to Ward, gave him a course to steer that brought the vessel's head right round. Then he slunk below, while the crew gathered in groups, whispering.

"That's the stuff to give 'im, Ward!" said Dan. "You've put the wind up him!"

"I mean to keep my own end up as long as I'm alive to do it!" returned the mate grimly. "I don't know how long it may last, so I'm makin' the most of it!"

"What course was that the skipper gave you?" asked Dan.

"It'll take us pretty near Baltrum," replied Ward. "What we're going there for beats me. You seem to know more about it than I do!"

"I'll tell you," said Dan. "There's five thousand pounds buried there, and Buck here told Dudley about it before he knew who the rascal was."

"Whew!" said the mate.

"You may well whistle!" said Dan. "Dudley pinched the chart showing where it's buried from me last night. He'll get plenty of exercise digging!"

"Five thousand pounds!" murmured the mate. "Is that straight, young 'un?"

"Straight," said Dan. "And you can have your share if you help get clear of this den of thieves. It's ours by right!"

"This cruise looks like panning out better than I thought," commented Jack Ward; "though, at the best, we're more likely to see the sea bottom. Dudley'll be on to it like a wild-cat!"

"We've got a biggish crowd against us," said Buck.

"Shipload o' dagos!" said the mate. "I'd think shame to be put out o' the way by them. It's the Black Fleet I'm thinkin' of. Two o' the hands are spies o' theirs, and Dudley's hand-in-glove wi' 'em."

"But he'll never let the blacks into the game with five thousand pounds to win," said Dan. "He knows he wouldn't get much of it to finger."

"No; he'll use it as a bait to get you into their hands an' a knife into your back!" said the mate. "You know what the Blacks are. They've a thousand pounds to get by putting you out o' the way. Once they get you on that island, you'll mighty soon be food for crabs. What does Dudley care for five thousand pounds when he'll win a couple o' million by putting your light out!"

He broke off suddenly as from the bows of the ship shone the gleam of a match. A moment later a signalling torch shot a series of flashes into the darkness.

"Keep your eye on the steersman!" muttered Ward to the boys, darting down from the bridge. "I'll stop that game!"

Buck stood by the man at the wheel and saw that he kept his course.

In the gloom of the high bows, Dan saw a scuffle and a heaving of dark figures. There was an Italian oath, a yelp of pain, and then somebody went rolling across the fore-deck.

Shortly afterwards an electric torch was flung overboard, and vanished in the dark waters.

Jack Ward stepped back on to the bridge.

"I reckon I cured him of signalling without orders from me!" he remarked. "His nose'll never be what it was again. But I'm afraid the mischief's done."

He peered out over the dark sea, watching anxiously. Far away on the weather quarter two faint, short gleams and one longer one winked in the gloom, mere points of light on the horizon.

"My Sam!" said Dan. "That's the Black Fleet's night signal!"

"That's what it is!" said Ward, while Buck stared gloomily out over the heaving sea. "It's a long way off, though. That rat daren't go below to report, an' you can bet I shan't shift my course. We may lose 'em yet. Are you boys goin' to turn in to-night?"

"Yes," said Buck. "We've got to get some rest, or we shan't be fit for much. Besides, it'll rouse too much suspicion if we don't turn in. Shan't get much sleep, though——"

"You're quite right. Best to turn in. But be mighty careful. Good-night, lads!"

"Look here, Dan," said Buck, as they left the bridge, "that bunk of yours doesn't please me, with its underside opening over Dudley's cabin. Don't you get into it, an' mind you yell for me if anything goes wrong. We'll take the offensive ourselves when it does. We're best at that."

"Rather!" said Dan.

And after dinner—at which Dudley did not join them—they parted, and went to their cabins.

The only thing Dan took off was his jacket. He had an idea that Dudley Graham, having what he wanted, might be tempted to try quick measures under cover of darkness.

The knowledge that in a few hours the news of Kenneth Graham's whereabouts would reach his father, if it had not done so already, would drive him to extremes.

"I'll have to find a substitute to lie in this little bed," said Dan, disarranging the blankets.

He picked up the Japanese rug from the floor, and rolled it up, grinning the while. Then he wrapped a pyjama jacket round it artistically, and placed it under the sheets. It was very dark in the bunk. A sponge, half-covered by the counterpane, did duty for a head, and Dan, drawing back, surveyed his handiwork with pride.

"Wish you luck!" he said to the figure under the clothes. "You're Kenneth Graham, son of the millionaire, an' you're used to a soft bed an' white sheets, so lie there an' take your chance."

Dan turned the light out, and sat waiting patiently. The wash of the seas on the outside of the vessel made a soothing lullaby, and Dan, secure that he had at last nothing to lose, now that he had quitted the dangerous bunk, and had the chart of the treasure inside his vest, felt very sleepy.

Dan had had little rest lately, and very soon drowsiness overcame him, and he dozed into unconsciousness.

He awoke with a slight start. How long he had been asleep he did not know; but a glance at the porthole showed him that dawn was beginning to filter through the blackness of night. It was still dark.

A gentle creaking in the bulkhead, so faint as to be hardly audible, aroused the danger-signal in his brain.

His eyes, trained to the gloom, were fixed on the matchboarding that lined the back of the bunk over the clothes hooks.

Slowly and quietly the trapdoor he had seen the night before opened out.

The well-shaped, muscular brown hand was thrust through, as before. But it was less innocent this time. Its wiry fingers gripped the haft of a long, dull steel knife.

The little finger was turned downwards, and softly as the touch of a woman it traced the outline of the bundle under the clothes, till it stopped over the place where the sleeper's breast should be.

Slowly the hand was raised, higher, and yet a little higher. Then the blade descended like lightning, and buried itself in the Japanese rug.

Springing forward like a panther, Dan grasped the wrist with all his force and clung to it.

"Buck!" he yelled. "Buck!"

(For the concluding chapters of this great adventure yarn, chums, see next Saturday's MAGNET.)

THE FORM-MASTER'S FAVOURITE!

(Continued from page 24.)

"Ha, ha, ha!"

The crowd streamed back to the quad, howling with laughter. Hacker, shut up in his study, heard the sound of hilarity. Only a deaf man could have failed to hear—and he would have had to be very deaf! Perhaps Hacker enjoyed that sound of boyish merriment. But he did not look as if he did!

THE SIXTEENTH CHAPTER.
Too Late!

"**N**O!"

"Look here, Wharton——"

"Oh, get out!"

Eric Wilmot, coming up the Remove passage from the landing, heard that exchange of words, at the doorway of Study No. 1.

Herbert Vernon-Smith was standing in the doorway of the study, with a scowl on his face. Wharton evidently was within. The captain of the Remove, in fact, was seated at the study table, going over the list of men for the Rookwood match, now near at hand. Smithy had interrupted him—and was getting the reception he might have expected from the skipper he had let down.

"Cut it out, Smithy!" came Wharton's voice curtly. "You've let us down once, and you're not having a chance of doing it again."

"I'll stick to games like glue——"

"Unless you happen to have an appointment with Pon & Co. to play billiards somewhere!" said Wharton sarcastically. "Don't talk rot!"

"You've got to make up a team somehow," said the Bounder sullenly. "You're not still thinking of that greasy toad Wilmot, I suppose?"

"Hardly!"

"Nugent's no good for the Rookwood game, and you know it as well as I do!"

"He won't conk out through smoking cigarettes just before the game, anyhow. You might!"

"Oh, go and bag a licking from Rookwood if you like!" snarled the Bounder. "I'll come and watch them score five or six to nil!"

"Do!" said Harry. "It will do you more good than frowsing about with smokes. Anyhow, you're out of the team, and you stay out! Clear off, and leave me to work it out; you've made it harder for me."

"I'm willing——"

"Well, I'm not! For goodness' sake, give a fellow a rest!"

The Bounder, with a black brow, swung away from the study and tramped up the passage, Eric Wilmot glancing after him as he went; then the new junior, in the study doorway, looked in.

Wharton sat at the table, with a wrinkled brow over his football list.

He wanted, if he could, to take a winning team over to Rookwood, and it was a worry on his mind that the best man in the eleven had let him down. The Bounder had failed him, and the brief hope he had entertained that Wilmot might prove to be the right man in the right place had failed him also. It was Nugent or nobody, and, keen as he was to play his best chum, he was afflicted with doubts.

He rose from the table and put the list in his pocket, and as he did so became aware of the new junior in the doorway.

His face hardened. Since the interrupted fight in the Rag the two had not exchanged a word. Wilmot was seldom in the study, and when he was there a freezing silence reigned. The feeling on Wharton's side was aversion and contempt; on Wilmot's it seemed to be disdainful indifference.

But there was a change in Wilmot's look at the moment. He opened his lips to speak, but closed them again uncertainly, and Wharton came towards the door. Wilmot stepped in.

"I'd like to speak a word," he said.

Wharton halted impatiently.

"What do you want? You're barred in this study, and you know it! Get it off your chest if you've got anything to say, and cut it short!"

"I treated you rottenly the other day," muttered Wilmot.

"Has that just occurred to you?"

"No," said Wilmot quietly; "I knew it at the time. But if you'd known how much I wanted to get out of gates that afternoon, I think you might make allowances. I had a particular reason, though I can't tell you what it was——"

"I don't want to know."

"Leave it at that. I had a row with you afterwards, but you needn't worry about that. You had the best of it, and I was very nearly done when Wingate butted in and stopped us——"

"Well?"

Wharton rapped out the curt word impatiently. Wilmot coloured. He had rejected every friendly advance, and he could hardly wonder that the captain of the Remove was fed-up with him, and only wanted to keep shut of him. Now that he seemed to be changing his tactics he met with no encouragement whatever. But he went on quietly:

"I've said I was sorry for that trick I played you——"

"No need to say so again."

"I'd like to make up for it if I could."

"What rot!"

"You don't make it easy for a fellow," said Wilmot. "But, look here, you're in a difficulty over the football."

"Do you take enough interest in the game to have noticed that?" asked the captain of the Remove sarcastically. "Don't tell me you care a brass button about it. I shouldn't believe you."

"From what I hear, Vernon-Smith was your best winger, and he's let you down——"

"What about it?"

"You want a man in his place," said Wilmot. "Any use my offering?"

Wharton stared at him.

"You?"

"Yes. I don't know what Vernon-Smith is like when he's good; he's put up rotten football ever since I've been here. But I think I'm as good as he ever was. I won't ask you to take my word for it, but if you care to put me in a pick-up game I'll let you see for yourself. I never meant to play Soccer here—I was going to chuck that, along with everything else—but it's not long since I was playing, and I was considered pretty good."

Wharton looked at him.

"Then it's true what Bunter says—that he's seen you playing Soccer, and seen you bag goals against a good team?"

"Yes, that's true."

"Then I was on the right track, after all?"

Wilmot smiled faintly.

"Yes," he answered. "I'll prove it if you like. And if you want me I'll fill that place in the team for the Rookwood game."

"And you think I'd trust you?" said the captain of the Remove contemptuously. "I don't know whether you mean what you say, or whether you're pulling my leg again—but I know I wouldn't trust you an inch. You've made use of me once; but once bitten is twice shy! Is that all you've got to say?"

"Yes," said Wilmot in a low voice, "that's all."

"Then I'll clear."

Harry Wharton walked out of the study; Wilmot was left standing with burning cheeks.

THE END.

(The final yarn in this grand series, featuring Eric Wilmot, is entitled: "THE REMOVE'S RECRUIT!" Be sure to read it, chums. And on no account forget February 15th—the date of our BUMPER FREE GIFT ISSUE of the MAGNET. Make sure of your copy by ordering it NOW!)

The Magnet
2D

FREE NEXT WEEK!
MAGIC SPECTACLES

and **SET OF PICTURES** *That Come to Life!*

▼

FREE
IN NEXT WEEK'S *"Magnet"*

The REMOVE'S RECRUIT!

By FRANK RICHARDS

THE FIRST CHAPTER.

Smithy's Rag!

"BAG him!"

Harry Wharton heard that whisper in the dark, and jumped.

He was coming down from his study, and, to his surprise, found that the light was out on the Remove staircase.

He was groping for the switch at the head of the stairs when that whisper reached him from the landing below.

Suppressed as the voice was, he recognised the tones of Herbert Vernon-Smith, the Bounder of Greyfriars.

He stared down over the banisters.

But the well of the staircase was like a pit of blackness. He could see nothing.

But he could hear a sound of suppressed breathing, and a subdued chuckle; then came a sound of scuffling.

Somebody had been collared in the dark.

That somebody, coming up the stairs, had evidently run into an ambush on the middle landing. Smithy and his companions had been waiting in the dark, and they had bagged him as he came.

Evidently it was a "rag."

The sound of scuffling intensified. Judging by it, a good many fellows were mixed up on the landing. Whoever it was that had been "bagged," was putting up a strenuous resistance. It was quite a terrific struggle.

THE MAGNET LIBRARY.—No. 1,460.

"Ow!" came a sudden howl. There was a heavy fall.

"Look out!"

"Hold him!"

"Scrag him!"

"Pin the brute!"

The panting voices floated up in the dark, and Wharton grinned as he heard them. The Bounder & Co. had caught their victim, whoever he was; but he seemed to be giving them a lot of trouble. Wharton wondered whether it was Coker of the Fifth. If this was a rag on Horace Coker, he was quite willing to lend a hand—and it sounded as if one was needed.

"Got him!" came the panting tones of the Bounder.

There was a thudding, and a scuffling and scrambling. Somebody was down, with fellows scrambling over him.

"Where's the duster?"

"Haven't you got it, you ass?"

"Here it is!"

"Stick it in his mouth!"

A gurgle followed.

Harry Wharton ceased to grin. The Bounder was the fellow for wild and reckless rags; but this seemed to the captain of the Remove rather beyond the limit. He leaned over the banisters and called down:

"Draw it mild, Smithy!"

There was a startled exclamation below. Two or three voices exclaimed together:

"Who's that?"

"Is that Wharton?"

The Bounder's voice came with a snap.

"Keep out of this, Wharton! You're

not wanted here! Mind your own bizney!"

"Sounds to me as if I am wanted," answered the captain of the Remove. "A rag's a rag, Smithy; but there's a limit, though you don't seem to know it."

He groped for the switch again, found it, and turned on the light. Then he ran down to the middle landing.

Half a dozen of the Remove were there. A fellow was sprawling on his back, with Bolsover major clapping a hand over a duster stuffed into his mouth. Skinner and Snoop were holding his arms. Vernon-Smith and Stott were grabbing his legs.

But the victim was not, as Wharton had supposed, Coker of the Fifth. He was a junior—no other than Eric Wilmot, the new fellow in the Remove.

Wilmot's handsome face was crimson with exertion, his eyes flashing. He was still striving to resist, though in vain.

"Wilmot!" exclaimed Harry.

The raggers blinked at him in the sudden light. The Bounder gave him an angry glare.

"You fool! What did you put the light on for? The cad will know us now—to tell tales to his dashed Uncle Hacker."

"Let him go!"

"Rats to you!" snarled the Bounder.

"But what on earth's the game?" exclaimed Harry Wharton. "I don't like the fellow any more than you do, Smithy; but there's a limit, as I said. What are you up to, anyhow?"

"I'll tell you!" snapped the Bounder.

"We're going to stick the fellow in his uncle's study, for Hacker to find when he comes back from the Masters' Meeting in Common-room. He greases up to Hacker, and we're jolly well going to show Hacker what we think of a sneak in the Remove!"

"You mad ass!" exclaimed Wharton, aghast.

He understood now why the ambush had been laid in the dark.

It was believed in the Remove that Eric Wilmot "greased," as the juniors described it, to his uncle, who was master of the Shell. Certainly Hacker, who was fussy, had given Mr. Quelch, the master of the Remove, a good deal of worry about that new member of his Form.

If that reckless rag was carried out, obviously it was necessary to keep the identity of the raggers a secret. If Wilmot was able to name them, nobody doubted that he would do so.

For which reason Smithy's companions were now looking very dubious. Wharton, turning on the light, had rather spoiled the scheme.

"Tie up his fins, Skinner!" snapped the Bounder.

Skinner hesitated.

In the dark, which cloaked his identity, Skinner was prepared to back up the Bounder to any extent. But his nerve evaporated in the light.

"Look here! He's seen us now, Smithy!" muttered Skinner.

"I don't care!"

"Well, I do! I don't want to be up for a Head's flogging! The tick will give Hacker our names——"

"Let him!"

"Look here!" muttered Snoop. "The game's up, through that fool Wharton! Better chuck it, Smithy!"

"Much better," said Harry. "Chuck it, for goodness' sake, Smithy! There'll be a fearful row if you start Hacker on to Quelch again about his precious Eric. You don't want a row with Quelch."

"Bless Quelch! Give me that duster, Skinner, if you're in a funk."

The Bounder jerked the duster from Skinner, and dragged Wilmot's wrists together. His comrades might be dubious, and disposed to "chuck it"; but the Bounder was obstinately determined to carry on, regardless of consequences.

Harry Wharton stepped forward, pushed Bolsover aside, and pulled the gag from Wilmot's mouth. The Bounder gave a yell of rage.

"Hands off, you meddling fool!"

"Chuck it!" said Harry decisively. "It's too thick, Smithy! Buck up, Wilmot! I'll lend you a hand out of this!"

Wilmot panted.

"Wait till you're asked! I've not asked you to help me!"

"Oh!" ejaculated Wharton.

The Bounder laughed scoffingly.

"That's the thanks you get from the rotter! Now mind your own business, and leave us alone!"

Wharton set his lips, and stepped back.

"Very well," he said. "If you don't want any help, Wilmot, I won't shove it at you! You've asked for this, anyhow, with your greasing and sneaking——"

"That's a lie!"

Wharton gave him a look, turned, and went up the Remove staircase again. Bolsover major grabbed the gag again, and shoved it back into Eric Wilmot's mouth, in spite of his struggles. The Bounder knotted the other duster round his wrists.

"Now give me a hand with the cad!" he snapped.

"But he knows us now," faltered Skinner. "He will tell Hacker. We shall all be up before the Head."

"You can crawl away if you're funky," said the Bounder scornfully.

Skinner did not need telling twice. He went up the Remove staircase after Wharton, and Snoop, after a moment's hesitation, followed him.

"You fellows got cold feet, too?" sneered the Bounder, with a glare at Stott and Bolsover major.

"Carry on!" said Bolsover stolidly. "The cad will sneak about this, anyhow, so we may as well put it through."

"In for a penny, in for a pound!" said Stott.

With the shadow of the past cast behind him, Eric Wilmot, the new boy in the Greyfriars Remove, turns over a new leaf and comes out strong as a footballer!

"Get him along, then!"

And Eric Wilmot, in the grasp of the three, was walked down the lower stairs.

Stott cut ahead to scout. But he returned with the report that all was clear. The Masters' Meeting was going on in Common-room; Masters' Studies, generally a dangerous quarter for juniors, was quite safe. And Eric Wilmot, still vainly attempting to resist, was bundled along hurriedly to the study of Mr. Hacker, the master of the Shell.

THE SECOND CHAPTER.
Bunter Wants His Pal !

"SHIRTY?" asked Billy Bunter. "Fathead!"

"Well, you look it! You've got a rotten temper, Wharton!"

"Ass!"

"How Nugent can stand it I don't know!" said the fat Owl of the Remove. "How do you stand it, Nugent?"

Frank Nugent did not answer that question. He picked up a Latin dictionary from the study table and took aim. The missile whizzed.

Bunter dodged just in time.

The "dick" crashed on the door of Study No. 1. It dropped to the floor with a thud.

"Beast!" gasped Bunter.

"Inkpot next?" asked Frank Nugent. "If you're not outside in one jump——"

"Look here, a chap can come into a study to see a pal!" hooted Bunter, with wary eyes and spectacles on the look-out for the inkpot. "Where's Wilmot?"

"Don't know, and don't care!"

"Well, a man expects to find a man in his study!" grunted Bunter. "Wharton been rowing with him again? You're always rowing, Wharton."

"Oh, get out, you fat ass!" said the captain of the Remove.

Harry Wharton was not looking exactly "shirty," as Bunter described it. But he was undoubtedly in an annoyed frame of mind when he came back to his study after the encounter on the staircase.

He "barred" Hacker's nephew, and it had been rather against the grain that he had offered to help him out of the hands of the raggers. Wilmot's refusal of his help was neither grateful nor comforting. He wished that he had left the fellow alone in the first place—as he had done after that rebuff.

At the same time, he was rather worried about the Bounder's wild rag. Had such a rag been carried out in secret it would have been reckless enough. But, owing to Wharton, there was no longer any secret about it, and a little common sense would have made Smithy "chuck" it.

If Wilmot gave the raggers away, when inquiry was made, there would be heavy punishments—and Wharton had no doubt that he would. And, though he was not on the best of terms with Smithy just now, he hated the idea of being the cause of the Bounder getting a Head's flogging. Altogether the whole thing was a worry.

"I want to see Wilmot," went on Billy Bunter. "I hardly ever find him in this study. You might be civil to a pal of mine."

"You'd hardly ever find him at all, if he could help it!" grinned Frank Nugent. "You may be Wilmot's pal—but everybody knows exactly how pally he feels to you, you fat fraud."

"Oh, really, Nugent!"

"Go and look for him, and take your face away with you!" grunted the captain of the Remove. "It worries me."

"That's you all over, Wharton—jealous of a chap's good looks——"

"Oh, my hat!"

"The fact is, you fellows," said Bunter confidentially, "I've been disappointed about a postal order——"

"And that's why you want to see Wilmot?" snapped Wharton. "How many bobs and half-crowns have you borrowed from him since he came?"

"I suppose a pal can lend a pal a bob or two, without you barging in, Wharton!" said Billy Bunter warmly. "Wilmot may have lent me a few half-crowns! Well, considering what I've done for him——"

"Well, what have you done for him?"

"Oh, nothing!" said Bunter promptly.

"I don't know anything about the chap, as I've told you a lot of times, and I'm not keeping it dark. He never asked me to, the day he came. Besides, I promised I would, and I'm a fellow of my word, I hope."

Nugent laughed, and Harry Wharton's frowning face broke into a grin. Billy Bunter had his own inimitable way of keeping a secret.

What Bunter could possibly know about the new fellow that Wilmot wanted him to keep dark, was rather a mystery.

But that there was something was revealed by the masterly way Bunter kept the secret, as well as by the fact that Wilmot tolerated the friendship of the fat and fatuous Owl.

Hacker's nephew had made no friends in the Remove, though he had made plenty of enemies. Least of all was he likely to have desired to make friends with Billy Bunter.

He avoided Bunter as much as he could, and when he could not avoid him he tolerated him with ill-concealed impatience. Even Bunter, probably, would have been fed up with a friendship on those lines, but for the fact that he found his pal very useful on occasions—rather frequent occasions—when his celebrated postal order failed to arrive.

The fat Owl blinked indignantly through his big spectacles at two grinning faces.

"I say, you fellows, I must say you're rotten suspicious beasts!" he said, with deep indignation. "Think I'd ask Wilmot to lend me half-crowns because I'm keeping it dark for him about—about——"

"About what?" chuckled Nugent.

"Oh, nothing! What I mean is, it's got nothing to do with it! I oblige a fellow. He obliges me. Think I'm not going to square?" demanded Bunter hotly. "I shall settle up every bob that Wilmot has lent me this term, when my postal order comes."

"Ha, ha, ha!"

"Blessed if I see anything to cackle at! You fellows may not be so particular about such things—I've always been. But the trouble at the present moment," added Bunter, "is this—I was expecting a postal order from a titled relation, and it hasn't come. To tell you the truth, I'm absolutely stony now."

"That's rather unusual!" remarked Frank Nugent.

"Yes, it's rather unusual for me to be stony, old chap——"

"I mean, for you to tell the truth!"

"Beast! Look here, where's Wilmot? I've asked half a dozen fellows, and they don't know. That beast Cherry——"

"Hallo, hallo, hallo!" said Bob Cherry's cheery voice at the door. "Who's a beast, old fat man?"

Bunter spun round.

"Oh! I—I didn't see you, old chap! I wasn't speaking of you, old fellow—I meant that beast Bull——"

"Me?" asked Johnny Bull, appearing in the passage behind Bob.

"Oh crikey! Nunno!" gasped Bunter. "I mean, I was speaking of Inky——"

"My esteemed self?" inquired Hurree Jamset Ram Singh, as his dusky face grinned into the study over Johnny's shoulder.

"Oh lor'! No! I—I meant——"

"Ha, ha, ha!"

"Well, which one did you mean?" chuckled Bob Cherry. "The one you meant is going to biff you on the crumpet! Say which!"

"I—I didn't mean any of you fellows."

I was really speaking of Smithy!" stammered Bunter. "That beast Smithy——"

"Well, Smithy's nowhere about!" said Bob. "Sure you didn't mean that I was a beast, old fat freak?" He lifted his foot.

"No, old fellow!" Bunter dodged hastily. "But I say, you fellows, you might tell me where Wilmot is? It's tea-time——"

"Useful man at tea-time!" grinned Bob. "The chap's a worm, and a tick, and greases to the beaks, and can't play football—but useful at tea-time."

"He could play your head off at footer, and chance it!" retorted Bunter. "I've seen him bagging goals——"

"Gammon! Don't spin that yarn again, Bunter!"

"I tell you I've seen him——"

"And I tell you you haven't. Ring off! Looked in to see if you've settled about the Rookwood team, Wharton, old bean——"

"It's practically settled," said Harry. "Nugent will have to play in Smithy's place, as he's no good, and——"

"And we'll hope for the best!" said Nugent, with a grimace.

"I say, you fellows, if you want my advice——"

"Shut up!" roared the Famous Five, with one voice. Advice from Billy Bunter on the subject of football really was not wanted in Study No. 1.

"Well, I could give you a tip!" declared Bunter. "If you want to beat Rookwood, you couldn't do better than play my pal Wilmot—if he'd play, of course. I'd use my influence with him——"

"Cheese it!"

"Chuck it!"

"Shut up!"

"Yah!" retorted Bunter. He rolled to the door. In the doorway, out of reach, he turned, and gave the Famous Five a scornful blink through his big spectacles. "Fat lot you fellows know about Soccer! Look at the way Cherry falls over his own feet, and Bull barges about like a mad walrus, and the rest of you fumble and foozle! Soccer! Yah! Marbles is your game!"

Having delivered that Parthian shot, Bunter bolted. Really, it was only judicious to get promptly out of reach of the Famous Five, after delivering that devastating opinion of their powers as exponents of the great game of Soccer.

It was rather unfortunate for Bunter that as he bolted out of the study doorway Herbert Vernon-Smith reached it, coming along from the stairs with a grin on his face.

It was unfortunate for Smithy, too!

The grin vanished from his face as Bunter barged into him, sending him spinning. Bunter's weight in a charge was no light matter.

"Oh!" gasped the Bounder.

"Ooooogh!" spluttered Bunter.

The fat junior reeled from the shock. Vernon-Smith went over with a bump. The Famous Five, staring out of the study, roared.

"Ha, ha, ha!"

The Bounder was on his feet in a twinkling. He jumped at Bunter. He was damaged, and he seemed to want to pass the damage on.

"I say—— Ow! Leggo!" howled Bunter. "I say, I never saw you—— Yarooooh! I say, old chap—— Yah, you beast—— Whoop!"

Thump, thump, thump!

"Whoop! I say, old beast—I mean, old chap—— Yarooooh! Leggo! I'll jolly well—— Yarooop! I say, you fellows, draggimoff!" yelled Bunter.

"Ha, ha, ha!"

"There, you fat idiot!" gasped the

Bounder breathlessly. "There, you blithering owl! There, you piffling porker——"

"Ow! Beast! Wow!"

"'Nuff's as good as a feast, Smithy!" gasped Bob Cherry, and he grabbed hold of the angry Bounder, and dragged him off Bunter.

"Hands off, you fool!"

"Cut, Bunter, you fat ass!"

Bunter promptly cut. Vernon-Smith wrenched himself away from Bob Cherry's grasp, with an angry glare at the cheery Bob.

"What have you done with Wilmot, Smithy?" asked Harry Wharton.

The angry scowl faded from the Bounder's face, and the grin returned to it.

"Fixed him up in Hacker's study, ready for the old bean to find!" he answered.

"I hope he'll get away before Hacker gets——"

"He can't, I fancy; he's tied to a chair on Hacker's table."

"Oh crumbs!"

"With Hacker's wastepaper-basket on his head——"

"Oh, my hat!"

"And Hacker's inkpot poured over him——"

"Smithy, you mad ass——"

"Surprise for Hacker when he rolls home after the beaks' pow-wow—what?" grinned the Bounder.

"There'll be a fearful row!"

"I shouldn't wonder!"

The Bounder, grinning, went on up the passage. Harry Wharton & Co. looked at one another in silence Even the Rookwood match was banished from their thoughts by the Bounder's news. That there would be a tremendous "row" was certain! And it was not long in coming!

THE THIRD CHAPTER.

A Shock For Hacker!

"MY dear Quelch——" said Mr. Hacker.

Mr. Quelch compressed his lips a little.

The Masters' Meeting—which Smithy disrespectfully described as the "Beaks' Pow-Wow"—was over, and the various members of the staff leaving the Common-room.

Mr. Prout, master of the Fifth, was still booming—Capper and Wiggins reluctantly lingering to listen to the boom. Mr. Quelch was rather accelerating, as Hacker came out after him; he had a suspicion that Hacker was going to talk, and he did not want any talk from Hacker. He could guess the subject in advance.

However, he slowed, as Hacker called —he could not actually cut the master of the Shell. And they walked along to Masters' Studies together.

"I was going to speak to you, Quelch, about my nephew in your Form!" said Mr. Hacker.

The Remove master suppressed a snort! He had, of course, guessed that one. He made no reply, and Hacker went on:

"You have doubtless observed Eric since he has been here——"

"He has been very much thrust upon my attention, Mr. Hacker!" said the Remove master. "Really, sir——"

"I am, naturally, somewhat concerned about him, as his uncle, sir." said Mr. Hacker stiffly. "The Remove is a somewhat rough and unruly Form——"

"It is my Form, Mr. Hacker!" said Quelch, very distinctly.

"You will not expect me to be satisfied, Mr. Quelch, with my nephew's progress in your Form!" said Mr. Hacker tartly. "At his last school he was universally popular; here, I cannot help noticing that a dead set appears to have been made against him by the other boys——"

"His own fault, sir!" said Mr. Quelch. "A sulky, sullen temper is no recommendation, sir! Wilmot appears to desire to make no friends—it would almost appear that he desires to make enemies."

"No doubt his misfortune at Topham may have affected his outlook a little," conceded Mr. Hacker. "Allowances must be made for that."

"Allowances are made for it by me! They cannot be made by the Remove

"If he has not carried complaints to you, sir——"

"He certainly has not!" exclaimed Mr. Hacker. "On one occasion only he asked me to use my influence with you to excuse him from detention. I told you so. On no other single occasion, sir——"

"Then, sir, your own want of tact has caused that impression in the Remove," said Mr. Quelch grimly. "For there is no doubt that the whole Form believes him guilty of toadying—what they call 'greasing.' If you desire your nephew, sir, to have a less unpleasant time in my Form, I recommend you strongly to leave him entirely to himself, and even to forget that you have a nephew at Greyfriars at all."

"Really, Mr. Quelch——"

retained so complete a faith in the Topham junior who had been expelled in disgrace.

Having switched on the light, the master of the Shell turned towards his table. Then he suddenly stopped, staring transfixed.

He was not alone in the study.

He stared at the strange sight that met his eyes, almost unbelievingly. A junior was seated in a chair on the table. He sat there without moving—for the excellent reason that his legs were tied to the chair. He sat silent—for the equally excellent reason that a duster was stuffed into his mouth. Another duster secured his wrists together.

Hacker did not recognise him for the moment. The handsome face was dis-

Sounds of commotion coming up from below reached Wharton's ears. He switched on the light and raced down the stairs. On the landing below he saw a fellow sprawled on his back. Skinner and Snoop held his arms, and Vernon-Smith and Stott his legs, while Bolsover stuffed a duster into his mouth. The victim was not, as Wharton at first supposed, Coker of the Fifth, but Eric Wilmot, the new boy. "What's the game?" exclaimed Wharton.

boys, who know nothing whatever about it. You do not desire them to know, I presume?"

"My nephew could not remain here if the circumstances were known, as you are very well aware, Mr. Quelch. He was innocent of what was laid to his charge, as I most fully and firmly believe——"

"I trust you are right, sir!" said Mr. Quelch dryly. "Innocent or otherwise, he would be well advised to change his ways here. From your account of him, he was a prominent footballer at Topham; here, he has sulkily refused to take part in the Form games. More than that, sir, there seems to be a general impression in my Form that he is a tale-bearer—what the boys call a sneak, sir! That they cannot be expected to forgive."

"That is certainly unjust and untrue!" exclaimed Mr. Hacker warmly. "Eric is quite incapable——"

"Really, Mr. Hacker——"

"It appears useless to discuss the matter with you, Mr. Quelch!" said the master of the Shell acidly.

"Quite, sir!" said Mr. Quelch. "I fully agree!"

And, leaving Mr. Hacker at his study door, the Remove master walked on to his own study, glad to be done with Hacker and the topic of Hacker's nephew.

Mr. Hacker, frowning, entered his study and switched on the light. Mr. Hacker was very far from realising that he mistook a fussy urge for interference for a strict sense of duty. The fact was plain to Mr. Quelch.

But Hacker certainly had cause to be concerned about his nephew, who had been turned out of his school, and whom Dr. Locke had been extremely doubtful about admitting to Greyfriars.

Hacker's was not a trusting nature, so no doubt it was to his credit that he

figured by streaks of ink, poured over it with a liberal hand; and the waste-paper-basket, inverted on the junior's head, came down to the bridge of his nose. Blindfolded by that extraordinary headgear, the tied junior could not see Hacker.

"Good gracious!" gasped Mr. Hacker, finding his voice. "Who—what—— What—who——"

A mumble came from the gagged junior.

"Who are you?" thundered Mr. Hacker. "What are you doing here? What does this mean?"

Mumble!

Mr. Hacker spotted the gag, and realised that the prisoner of his study could not speak. He grabbed it and jerked it away. Then he knocked the wastepaper-basket off the prisoner's head.

Then, in spite of the smears and streaks of ink, he recognised Wilmot of the Remove.

"Eric!" he stuttered.

Wilmot, his face crimson where it was not black with ink, stared at his uncle. He had wriggled and struggled wildly, since the Bounder & Co. had left him there, but without being able to get loose—Smithy had taken good care of that!

He had hoped, and longed, that when he was found, it would be by anybody but his Uncle Hacker. But that was not likely, in Hacker's study. And it was Hacker who had found him.

"Eric!" repeated Mr. Hacker, almost dizzily.

"I—I say, get me loose, will you?" muttered Wilmot. "It—it's all right, sir! Only a rag—a joke——"

"The—the rascals! The—the ruffians! The Remove boys have done this!" spluttered the master of the Shell.

Wilmot made no answer.

"Tell me who did this, Eric."

No reply.

"Cannot you speak?" gasped Mr. Hacker. "My poor boy!" He did not notice Wilmot wince. "I will release you at once, and report this matter instantly to Quelch! They shall be flogged—expelled——"

Hurriedly the master of the Shell released the hapless fellow. Eric Wilmot almost fell off the table.

"Uncle!" he exclaimed. "Don't——"

Deaf to his nephew's voice, Mr. Hacker rushed—almost bounded—from the study! With his gown streaming behind him, in his haste, he rushed up the passage like a thunderstorm—to acquaint Mr. Quelch, without loss of time, with this latest and greatest outrage by that rough and unruly Form, the Remove!

THE FOURTH CHAPTER.

Unexpected!

WINGATE of the Sixth came up to the Remove passage. Harry Wharton & Co. did not need telling why he had come; neither did the Bounder or his friends.

"Form-room at once!" called out the Greyfriars captain.

Most of the Remove fellows were in their studies, or the passage, after tea. Many of them knew, or guessed, what was on; but most of the Form were in ignorance of the Bounder's wild rag.

"Anything up, Wingate?" called out Peter Todd.

"Yes!" answered Wingate curtly.

"I say, you fellows——"

"Are we all wanted?" asked Hazeldene.

"All the Remove, and at once!" rapped Wingate, and he went down the stairs again. "See that every man goes in, Wharton."

"Yes, Wingate."

"What on earth's the row?" asked Squiff.

The Bounder, in the doorway of Study No 4, laughed.

"Something happened to Eric, perhaps!" he remarked. "Where's dear little Eric? Anybody seen Eric?"

"Isn't he in your study, Wharton?" asked Tom Redwing.

"No!"

"Have you been ragging him, Smithy, you ass?" asked Redwing, with an uneasy look at his chum.

"If you think so, old bean, don't

mention it to Quelch!" said the Bounder, laughing.

"No need—Wilmot will tell his uncle, I suppose," said Redwing, "and Hacker will tell Quelch."

"Silly ass, if you have been ragging that greaser!" said Ogilvy. "But what is the whole Form wanted for? I suppose we haven't all been ragging dear little sweet Eric!"

"Blessed if I know!" said Smithy. "Looks like an inquiry—so Quelch can't have the names yet."

"Then there has been a rag?" asked Toddy.

"Shouldn't wonder."

"Get a move on, you men!" said Harry Wharton. "We're all wanted."

"Wilmot can't have given the names yet!" muttered Skinner. "Of course he will. You were an ass to carry on, Smithy——"

"All that fool Wharton's fault, for turning on the light!" growled Bolsover major. "That tick would never have known us in the dark."

"Sorry!" said the captain of the Remove. "But you should have chucked it——"

"Wish we had!" grunted Bolsover. Now that the hour of reckoning had arrived, Bolsover was not feeling so bold and reckless. "A man might be sacked for it!"

"Couldn't sack five men in a bunch!" said Smithy.

"Five!" repeated Skinner. "Look here, I had nothing to do with sticking the cad in Hacker's study—you know that!"

"Nor I!" mumbled Snoop.

"I'm afraid you backed out too late to dodge the consequences, old beans!" grinned the Bounder. "We're all for it. Bet you Eric will give all the names!"

"Draw it mild, Smithy!" said Lord Mauleverer. "I don't think the fellow's a sneak! Sulky tick, if you like; but——"

"Then you're a silly ass!" snapped the Bounder. "Every man in the Form knows he's a greaser and a sneak, and that's why he's been ragged."

"Is that why?" asked Mauly.

"Yes, ass!"

"Not because he whopped you in a scrap?"

"Ha, ha, ha!"

"Look here, you silly, cheeky idiot——"

"Oh, come on!" exclaimed Harry Wharton. "If we keep Quelch waiting, it won't improve matters."

Some of the Removites were already going down the stairs. The rest followed them. Harry Wharton rooted out other members of the Form from the Rag, and the whole of the Remove marched to their Form-room—with the exception of Eric Wilmot, who was not to be seen.

He was seen, however, as soon as the juniors arrived in the Remove-room.

He was standing there with his uncle, the master of the Shell, and Mr. Quelch. Some of the juniors grinned at the sight of him. His face was still streaked and smeared with ink, his hair tousled like a mop. He had not yet had time to put himself to rights after the rag.

But the expression on Mr. Quelch's face showed that it was no grinning matter. Hacker was almost purple; but the Remove master was pale with anger.

Fed-up as he was with Hacker and his nephew, nothing could have been more unwelcome to Mr. Quelch than

this tremendous rag. It was a rag beyond all bounds—quite outside the limit. And it placed the Remove master in an awkward and painful position. It seemed to justify Hacker's continual complaints that his nephew was ill-used in Quelch's Form.

Mr. Quelch's eyes glittered at his Form, as they stood in silence. It was clear that he was going to take the sternest possible view of this occurrence.

It was not a matter for canings or detentions. It meant floggings from the Head, at least.

Indeed, it was quite possible that it might mean expulsions. Even the hardy and reckless Bounder felt a twinge of uneasiness, as he read the expression on the speaking countenance of Henry Samuel Quelch.

"Boys!" said Mr. Quelch, in a voice that was not loud, but very deep. "An outrage—an unprecedented outrage—has taken place during the Masters' Meeting a short time ago! Every boy who entered Mr. Hacker's study will stand forward!"

Nobody stood forward.

Skinner and Snoop wriggled uneasily, with sickly faces. Having backed out before the actual rag had taken place, they hoped to escape the consequences, or the worst of them, at least. But they were deeply alarmed.

Bolsover major and Stott looked surly. The Bounder was as cool as ice. He had not the slightest doubt that Wilmot was going to give him away. But he had no intention of giving himself away.

There was a brief pause.

"I call upon the boys concerned in this outrage to stand forward!" said Mr. Quelch.

There was no stir in the ranks of the Remove. If Mr. Quelch expected any fellow to own up, he was disappointed.

Mr. Hacker broke in.

"My nephew, sir, can give you the names of the boys who attacked him!" he barked. "It is useless to ask your Form to admit what they have done."

"Please leave this matter in my hands, Mr. Hacker!"

"Very well, sir; but I insist——"

"I shall deal with this matter, sir, in my own Form-room, in my own way!" said Mr. Quelch.

"You will not be able to extract the truth from your Form, sir!" barked Mr. Hacker.

"Mr. Quelch will hear the truth from his Form, or nothing, sir!" said Harry Wharton coolly.

Hacker gave the captain of the Remove a glare.

"Were you concerned in this, Wharton? I think it very probable! Tell me, at once, if you were concerned in this!"

"I shall answer my own Form-master, sir, if he questions me!" retorted Wharton. "I am here at Mr. Quelch's orders——"

"You insolent young rascal——"

"Mr. Hacker, I insist upon your leaving this matter in my hands!" exclaimed Mr. Quelch. "I will not permit you, sir, to question my Form."

"Mr. Quelch——"

"Until you are silent, sir, the matter cannot proceed!" said the Remove master.

Mr. Hacker controlled himself with difficulty.

"Now, my boys," went on Mr. Quelch, "the truth of this matter must be made known. An unprecedented outrage has taken place in a master's study. Wilmot, of this Form, appears to have been taken by violence to Mr. Hacker's study, tied to a chair on the table, gagged with a duster, and smothered with ink!

"It is a matter for the headmaster to deal with, and I hope and trust that Dr. Locke will not consider it necessary to expel any member of the Form. But he is certain to take an extremely serious view of an outrage in a master's study! Once more, I ask the boys concerned in this matter to stand forward!"

There was another pause.

"Very well," said Mr. Quelch at last. "If the boys concerned will not confess, I have no alternative but to ask Wilmot to name them."

There was a sound of hissing in the Remove.

"Silence! Wilmot, give me the names

of the boys who carried you to Mr. Hacker's study."

Wilmot made no answer.

"Speak, Eric!" snapped Mr. Hacker. "Do you not hear your Form-master? What is the matter with the boy? Answer Mr. Quelch at once!"

"I've nothing to say, sir," said Wilmot quietly.

"What do you mean? You know the names of the boys who attacked you!" exclaimed Mr. Hacker.

"Yes, sir."

"Give Mr. Quelch the names at once!"

Wilmot set his lips obstinately, but did not speak. Mr. Hacker stared at him in angry perplexity. Mr. Quelch gave him a very curious look.

"Wilmot, I understand your reluctance to answer," he said. "But this is no ordinary matter. I order you, as your Form-master, to give the names."

"I can't, sir."

"You know the names?"

"Yes, sir."

"Then give them to me at once."

Wilmot did not speak.

"Will you answer, Eric?" thundered Mr. Hacker.

Wilmot drew a deep breath.

"No, sir," he said.

THE FIFTH CHAPTER.

Nothing To Say!

THERE was a deep silence in the Remove Form Room.

Every eye was fixed on Eric Wilmot

Not a man in the Form, except Mauly, had doubted that he would give the names of the raggers—that he would be glad to give them.

His refusal to speak was utterly unexpected.

A fellow who "greased to a beak"— who was believed to carry tales to his uncle's study—was expected to "sneak" as a matter of course. Indeed, a fellow who was no sneak would hardly have been expected to remain silent in face of a direct order from his Form-master.

But Wilmot stood silent.

Skinner and Snoop breathed a little more freely. Was it possible that the fellow was not going to give them away, after all? Bolsover major and Stott looked relieved. As for the Bounder, he was completely puzzled.

A pin might have been heard to drop in the Remove-room for some moments. Mr. Quelch broke the silence.

"Wilmot!"

"Yes, sir?"

"I repeat that this is no ordinary matter—not a matter for schoolboy scruples. I have given you an order!"

"I heard you, sir."

"You will obey me, Wilmot!"

"I can't, sir."

"And why cannot you?" demanded Mr. Quelch, his voice rising.

"I can't give the names, sir."

"Preposterous!" exclaimed Mr. Hacker. "But I think I understand, sir. My nephew expects further ill-usage in your Form, sir, in the event of——"

Wilmot's face flamed.

"Nothing of the kind!" he exclaimed

hotly. "I can take care of myself! I won't give the names——"

"Eric!"

"I won't give the names! I'm not a sneak or an informer! I'll be sacked before I'll give the names!"

"Oh gad!" murmured the Bounder. "What game is that tick playing now?"

"He means it," muttered Redwing.

"Rot!"

"You will certainly be punished, Wilmot, and with great severity, if you refuse to obey an order from your Form-master," said Mr. Quelch grimly.

"Very well, sir; I know that."

"Absurd!" hooted Mr. Hacker. "Eric, speak at once! Your Form-master has told you that this is not a matter for schoolboy scruples. Speak at once!"

"I can't, sir."

"If you refuse to obey your Form-master, Eric, you will not refuse to obey your uncle! I speak as your relative in ordering you to give the names."

Wilmot looked at his uncle. Mr. Hacker, according to his lights, was a good and conscientious man and a kind uncle; it was owing to him that the boy had a chance at Greyfriars after his disaster at Topham. But his goodness and kindness, which were undoubted, were outweighed by an acid and irascible temper and a fussy desire to interfere.

"I'm sorry, sir," said Wilmot steadily, "but you cannot give me orders as my uncle, here. I hope I'm grateful for your many kindnesses to me, sir; but here I am a Greyfriars boy, under nobody's orders but my Form-master's."

The Removites could scarcely believe their ears. Mr. Hacker could hardly believe his.

"Upon my word!" gasped Mr. Hacker. "Do I hear aright? I have been your friend, your protector, and you repay me with this insolence——"

"I hope I am not insolent, sir. But I don't need protection any more than any other fellow in the Remove."

"Upon my word!"

Mr. Quelch suppressed a smile. Hacker was staring at Wilmot, dumbfounded.

"Looks as if the chap isn't such a worm, after all," murmured Bob Cherry.

"The lookfulness is terrific."

"Blessed if I make him out!" muttered Harry Wharton. "Everybody thought——"

"Everybody seems to have been wrong," grinned Bob.

"Silence!" rapped Mr. Quelch, as murmurs reached his ears. "Now, Wilmot, you will listen to me! I command you——"

Wilmot's inky face set stubbornly.

"I've nothing to say, sir."

"Leave this boy to me for the moment, Mr. Quelch," said the master of the Shell, his voice husky with anger. "Eric, give me your attention! You must give me the names of the perpetrators of this outrage, so that they may be dealt with by your headmaster. If you refuse to do so——"

"I do refuse, sir."

"If you refuse, your Form-master will deal with you for disobedience. And I," added Mr. Hacker, his voice trembling with passion—"I will have nothing further to do with you! I will forget that you are my nephew! I will wash my hands of an ungrateful and stubborn boy!"

"Very well, sir."

"What—what did you say?"

"I said, very well, sir."

Mr. Hacker gave him one look, turned, and whisked out of the Remove-room; the door closed after him—hard.

The bang was followed by dead silence.

Mr. Quelch stood looking at Wilmot. As a Form-master he could not pass over the boy's disobedience to a direct order; but in other respects Eric Wilmot had risen very considerably in his estimation—as he had, undoubtedly, in that of the Remove.

"I hardly know what to say to you, Wilmot," said Mr. Quelch at last. "If you refuse to obey me, your Form-master, you know the consequences."

"Yes, sir."

"In such a case I can only report your conduct to your headmaster, with a request that you may be sent away from the school."

"I know, sir."

"Very well. Will you give me the names I require?"

The Remove hung on Wilmot's answer. It came in a voice low but clear.

"No, sir."

"Oh crikey!" squeaked Billy Bunter.

"Silence! Wilmot, I shall consider this matter, and deal with you later. For the present the Form is dismissed."

In amazed silence the Remove filed out of the Form-room. In the passage there was an outbreak of buzzing voices.

"Who'd have thought it?" asked Bob Cherry.

"I did, old bean!" murmured Lord Mauleverer.

"Well, you're an ass, Mauly!"

"Seems to me that Mauly's the only man here who isn't an ass," said Harry Wharton.

"Yaas," agreed Mauly, "that's so."

"I say, you fellows——"

"The chap's a toad," said Harry, "but he's no sneak. And it's all rot about his greasing up to Hacker; he's sent the old bean off in a towering rage. The fellow's all right in his own way."

"He's up to somethin'," said the Bounder.

"Oh, rot!" said Wharton gruffly.

"I tell you——"

"Rubbish! If he'd given you away, you'd have got a Beak's flogging—and very likely the sack! And he's got something coming to him for refusing to obey Quelch's order. You'd better shut up, Smithy!"

The Bounder shrugged his shoulders, and walked away—puzzled, relieved, but still sceptical. But in the Remove generally there was quite a revulsion of feeling.

Mr. Hacker, with the best intentions, had done the worst possible for his nephew since Wilmot had been at Greyfriars. But in bringing about that scene in the Form-room, he had inadvertently done better than he dreamed. Fellows who disliked Wilmot most, for his sulky looks and bitter tongue, felt concerned about him now—wondering what he was going to get from Quelch!

The fellow who had been regarded as a sneak and a "greaser," had proved, beyond question, that he was neither— at a risk to himself that few fellows would have been prepared to run. It was unexpected—it was amazing—and it kept the Remove in a buzz of excited discussion.

THE SIXTH CHAPTER.

Not Pally!

HARRY WHARTON paused—opened his lips—and closed them again. He hesitated.

It was the following day—and a half-holiday at Greyfriars. When the

Mr. Hacker's eyes opened wide at the sight of the junior tied to the chair on his table. "Good gracious!" gasped the Shell master, finding his voice at last, but failing to recognise the junior. "Who—what—what—who——" A mumble came from the gagged junior.

Greyfriars fellows came out after dinner, Wharton sighted Wilmot—going into the quad, alone, as usual.

He was tempted to speak; but the half-sulky, half-disdainful expression on the new junior's face gave him pause, and Wilmot passed on.

Wharton stood looking after him doubtfully.

Then he smiled, as he saw Mr. Hacker.

The master of the Shell, walking in the quad, passed his nephew—but, for the first time since Wilmot had been at Greyfriars, passed him with an unregarding eye.

Wilmot might have been the veriest stranger to Mr. Hacker. Hacker did not even give him a glance.

Evidently Mr. Hacker was still very annoyed about the occurrences of the previous day. Equally evidently, he was sticking to what he had declared in the Remove Form Room. Henceforward, Eric Wilmot was, in his eyes, simply a Remove boy, like any other—no longer the object of his fussy concern.

Making up his mind, Harry Wharton followed the new junior, and overtook him. He tapped him on the arm, and Wilmot glanced round.

"Sorry!" said Harry.

"What about?"

"You can guess! You've put everybody's back up, Wilmot; but it was decent of you to act as you did yesterday. There would have been floggings all round—and very likely the sack for Smithy! A good many fellows would have given them away—considering what they did."

"I shouldn't!"

"We know that—now!" Wharton carefully took no notice of the fellow's curt, dry manner. "Look here,

Wilmot! You've set yourself right with the Form, to a good extent! Why not carry on the good work?"

Wilmot stared at him.

"I don't quite see——"

"Chuck up sulking, and being a sullen ass, and all that!" said Harry. "Look here! We're putting in some games practice this afternoon, and after that, going out on the bikes. Will you join up?"

"No!"

Wharton breathed rather hard.

He had felt that it was up to him to make some advance to bridge the gulf between that peculiar new fellow and the rest of the Form. Wilmot had been misjudged, though it was largely his own fault. But bridging the gulf seemed rather uphill work.

"I can't make you out, Wilmot!" said the captain of the Remove at last. "Do you want to live in a school like this like a sort of Robinson Crusoe?"

Wilmot smiled involuntarily.

"What's the good of it?" went on Wharton. "If you came a mucker at your last school, you don't want to repeat the performance here, I suppose?"

The new junior started violently, and the red rushed into his face.

"Has Bunter——" he stammered. He broke off quickly. "What do you mean? What do you know?"

"Nothing!" answered Harry. "But a blind man could see that you've got something on your mind. It's not natural for a fellow to behave as you do. And everybody in the Remove knows that Bunter knows something or other that you've asked him to keep dark."

"If that's so, it's my own business."

"I know! I'm not inquisitive," said

Harry. "Nobody wants to know anything about your affairs. But a fellow is expected to keep a civil tongue in his head. According to what Hacker's said, you're no end of a footballer, and played for your last school, wherever that was. That ass Bunter spins a yarn about having seen you do terrific stunts at Soccer, and I believe he did, though I'm blessed if I know where he can have seen it. Why not give yourself a chance?"

Wilmot made no reply.

"I shouldn't be speaking to you like this, or at all, but for what happened yesterday," added Wharton frankly. "But——"

"I guessed that one!" said Wilmot, with a curl of the lip. "And I'm not asking to be taken up, by you or any man in the Remove. I only want to keep to myself, and be let alone."

"If that's what you want, you'll get it! But I can't understand a chap chucking footer, if he's good at the game. Will you join up?"

There was a perceptible hesitation before Wilmot replied. But the answer came curtly:

"No—thanks!"

"Well, you're an ass!" said Harry.

"Thanks again!"

"I say, you fellows——"

Billy Bunter rolled up. Harry Wharton walked away. He had had enough of Wilmot, and he did not want any of Billy Bunter.

Wilmot would have walked away also, but the fat Owl caught hold of his sleeve.

"Hold on, old chap!" he said.

Wilmot held on. The look on his face would have discouraged any fellow but

THE MAGNET LIBRARY.—No. 1,460.

Bunter. But William George Bunter was not easily discouraged.

"I say, old chap, it's a topping afternoon for a run out of gates!" said Bunter cheerfully.

"I'm not going out."

"Like a walk down to Courtfield?"

"No!"

"And tea at the bunshop?" said Bunter temptingly. "My treat, you know. I say, Wilmot, I'm rather sorry, but my postal order hasn't come yet. I say, don't walk away while a chap's talking! You've lent me a few small sums since you've been here, old chap, but——"

"Never mind that!" said Wilmot, displaying very visible signs of impatience. As he had no friend in his Form, he might have been expected—at least, by Bunter—to be glad of the fat Owl's friendship. But if he was feeling any gladness, his looks belied him.

"But I do mind!" said Bunter firmly. "I'm rather particular about such things, Wilmot. We are here, you know! It may have been different at Topham!"

Wilmot gave a quick glance round, and Bunter grinned. When the new fellow showed too visible signs of being fed-up with Bunter, the fat Owl had a cheery way of mentioning Topham! It was a hint to Wilmot that a fellow knew what he knew, so to speak.

Why Wilmot wanted to keep his former school dark, was a complete mystery to Bunter. But he knew that Wilmot did, and that was enough for him.

"Shut up, you ass!" muttered Wilmot.

"Oh, really, Wilmot——"

"Oh, buzz off, Bunter!" said the new junior impatiently. "Do give a fellow a rest!"

"If that's what you call pally, Wilmot, I——"

Wilmot set his lips. Billy Bunter was very near, at that moment, to stopping a boot with his tight trousers! Bunter had been very near it many times since he had established himself as Wilmot's "pal." Never had a generous friendship been so lightly prized!

"As I was saying," went on Bunter, with a great deal of dignity, "I've been disappointed about a postal order, so I shan't be able to settle those few trifling sums at present——"

"Never mind, then!"

"I've said that I do mind! But I shall have to let it stand over till next week. Perhaps the week after. Now, what about a walk down to Courtfield?"

"No!"

"We'll take the motor-bus, if you like."

"I don't like!"

"We can get a jolly decent tea at the bunshop!" said Bunter. "My treat, you know! I shall have to ask you to lend me ten bob, that's all!"

The idea of expending ten shillings for the pleasure of watching Bunter feed at the bunshop in Courtfield, did not seem to appeal to the new junior, somehow. He grunted.

"I say, you're not detained, are you?" asked Bunter. "Has Quelch come down on you, old chap? I say, I don't believe he was so ratty with you yesterday as he made out. He doesn't like fellows sneaking. Your uncle's a bit of a blighter, I must say, but——"

"Shut up!" muttered Wilmot.

Mr. Quelch, coming out of the House, glanced at the two juniors. Bunter, having his back to him, and having, of course, no eyes in the back of his head, did not see him. He rattled on:

"I believe Quelch is going to let the matter drop. Most of the fellows think so. He isn't an old toad like Hacker, you know."

"You fat idiot! Shut up!" hissed Wilmot. Mr. Quelch was coming along directly towards them "Quelch——"

Bunter, not seeing Mr. Quelch with the back of his bullet head, did not see any reason for shutting up. Bunter seldom shut up, anyhow.

"Quelch is a crusty old stick!" he went on cheerily. "But Hacker's really the limit, you know! A regular acid drop! Crusty old toad——"

"Bunter!"

"Oh lor'!"

Billy Bunter spun round in alarm. His eyes almost popped through his spectacles at his Form-master.

Mr. Quelch gave him a severe frown.

"Bunter, are you venturing to speak of a gentleman on Dr. Locke's staff in such terms?" exclaimed Mr. Quelch.

"Oh, no, sir!" gasped Bunter. "I wasn't speaking of Mr. Hacker, sir! I —was—was speaking of somebody else of—of the same name, sir——"

"You will take two hundred lines, Bunter——"

"Oh crikey!"

"And go into the House at once and write them!"

"Oh lor'!"

"If the lines are not brought to me by tea-time, Bunter, I shall cane you!"

"Oh crumbs!"

Mr. Quelch walked on. Billy Bunter gave his back a devastating blink.

"Beast!" he gasped, when Quelch was out of hearing. "I say, Wilmot, old chap, you do those lines for me, will you?"

"No!"

"Oh, really, old fellow, you can make your fist like mine! Look here, I'll do the first line, and you can copy the fist—— I say, don't walk off while a chap's talking to you!" roared Bunter. "I say——"

But Wilmot was going, evidently having had enough of Billy Bunter's fascinating company and entrancing conversation. Heedless of Bunter's roar, he accelerated.

"Beast!" hooted Bunter.

And the fat Owl went, indignantly and morosely, into the House to write his lines—or, at least, to squat in the armchair in Study No. 7, and think about doing them.

Wilmot, with a clouded brow, went out of gates for one of the solitary rambles with which he was accustomed to kill time on a half-holiday The new junior had made no friends at his new school, and the alternative was a sulky solitude. But even that was preferable to the valuable friendship of William George Bunter.

———

THE SEVENTH CHAPTER.

A Surprising Discovery!

"HALLO, hallo, hallo!"

"Old Lunn!"

Five cheery cyclists slowed down and jumped off their machines. The Famous Five had been for a spin in the cold, clear, frosty afternoon, and were coming back in a whizzing bunch along the road when they sighted the St. Jude's junior.

Lunn of the Fourth Form at St. Jude's, was standing by the roadside, with a bike upended under a tree, evidently having found trouble with a puncture. He glanced round, and nodded to the Greyfriars fellows.

"Want any help?" asked Bob.

"Thanks, I've finished the dashed thing!" answered Lunn. "Must have picked up a thorn on the footpath! All

right now. I've only got to pump up the brute! Blow it!"

"Rotten luck!" said Bob. "I had a puncture the day we were coming over to see your match at St. Jude's, and we never got there. Bunter told us that you let Topham beat you."

"We won't let you beat us, anyhow, when you come along!" said Lunn. "You can get ready for a walloping!"

"Then Topham did pull it off?" asked Harry. "We were coming over to see the game, but Bob's bike conked out. Bunter went over in a taxi, and it's been a mystery ever since who paid for the taxi."

Lunn chuckled.

"You missed a good game," he said. "Topham aren't up to our weight, really——"

"That's why they won?" asked Johnny Bull.

"Oh, don't be an ass! Topham aren't whales at Soccer," said Lunn. "But they had a wonderful man—a real corker—and he lapped up goals like a cat lapping up milk! You should have seen him!"

"Wish we had!" said Bob. "Should have but for that rotten puncture! Bunter told us something about it; even Bunter noticed it, so the man must have been a regular eye-opener!"

"He was," said the St. Jude's junior. "I'm not likely to forget that chap; it was a queer business."

"His goal-getting?"

"No; what happened afterwards. Can't make it out to this day!" said the St. Jude's junior. "They had some sort of a row in the dressing-room after the game. Fancy that at a football match! You'd have thought they worshipped the ground that chap trod on after the game when he'd piled up the goals. And then afterwards—goodness knows what happened! But he went off by himself, and the team went back to Topham without him——"

Lunn broke off suddenly.

From the footpath, near which the group of schoolboys stood, a schoolboy came into sight, walking along, with a moody face, his hands in his pockets and his eyes on the ground.

Lunn stared at him.

"Well, my hat!" he ejaculated. "Talk of angels, and you hear the rustle of their wings—what?"

Harry Wharton & Co. looked round. It was Eric Wilmot, the new fellow in the Remove, coming down the footpath, returning to the school after his solitary ramble.

He looked up and saw the chums of the Remove. Whether he noticed Lunn or not, they could not tell; but he turned abruptly from the path and went through the wood, evidently desirous of avoiding a meeting.

Bob Cherry grinned.

"Cheery and friendly as ever!" he remarked.

"You know that chap?" asked Lunn, staring after Wilmot as he disappeared among the frosty trunks of Friardale Wood.

"Well, yes, rather!" said Bob. "Do you know him, Lunny?"

"Only met him once, on the football ground," answered Lunn. "But I shan't forget him in a hurry. That's the chap I was speaking of."

"What?"

"Who?"

"That's Wilmot!" exclaimed Wharton.

"Yes; that's his name." The St. Jude's junior nodded. "Can't imagine what a Topham man is doing walking about here; his school must be sixty miles away!"

"His school?" repeated Wharton.

"Yes, Topham——"

"His school's Greyfriars," said Harry.

"Greyfriars?" repeated Lunn. "You don't mean to say he's at your school now?"

"He's a new chap in our Form. He's only been in the Remove two or three weeks," said Bob, in wonder. "Mean to say that he's the chap who piled up goals for Topham?"

"He's the chap all right! Jolly odd that he should leave his school just after the term started and go to another show!" said Lunn, mystified. "My hat, we shall have to pull up our socks when we meet you if you've got that sportsman playing for you!"

"But we haven't," said Harry. "Don't you know a footballer when you see one?" asked the St. Jude's junior "I tell you, that man Wilmot came through us like a knife through cheese! The rest were nowhere! But he walked all over us, and did what he liked with the ball! Four goals off his own boot——"

"He's a dud at footer!" roared Johnny Bull. "He's never touched a ball at Greyfriars except to foozle it!"

"You should have seen him that day at St. Jude's!" grinned Lunn. "Ask

your fat man Bunter! He saw him——" Bob Cherry gave a yell

"Oh, my hat! That's where Bunter saw Wilmot play and pile up goals; we know he saw that match at St. Jude's! What has the blithering idiot kept it dark for?"

"That's it!" said Nugent, with a nod.

"Look here, Lunn," said Harry Wharton, "are you sure it's the same chap?"

"Am I sure he kicked four goals for Topham?" grunted Lunn. "Think I'd forget him after that? Besides, the name's the same—Wilmot! There were a dozen Topham men there that day, and they were all yelling 'Wilmot!' and 'Good old Eric!' at the top of their voices. Of course he's the same chap!"

"Eric!" said Nugent. "His name's Eric all right! That settles it!"

"Hasn't he let on at Greyfriars that he plays footer?" asked Lunn. "He must be pulling your leg—goodness knows why! I'll tell you this—you haven't got a man that could play one half of him, and we haven't, either! I tell you, he's a real corking miracle at Soccer, and I'd give any three of my forwards to have him in my front line! If he's left Topham, we shall beat them when we go over there, that's a comfort!"

"Well, my only hat!" said Bob.

Lunn pulled his bike out into the road, and put a leg over it.

"Must be blowing along," he remarked. "See you chaps again, when we come over to beat you at footer! Leave Wilmot out, for my sake!"

He waved his hand and rode away for St. Jude's. Harry Wharton & Co. stared after him, and then stared at one another. That chance meeting had brought about an astonishing discovery.

"That dud—the man who piled up goals for Topham!" said Bob. "What is his silly game, then, making out that he doesn't care for footer?"

"He's no dud, at any rate, from what Lunn says," said Harry Wharton. "I've

thought before that his foozling at footer was only part and parcel of his sulks—and I'm sure of it now."

"But why?"

"Goodness knows! But one thing's jolly certain," said the captain of the Remove emphatically. "Now we know what Wilmot is like at Soccer, he's the man we want for Rookwood. Sorry, Franky, but——"

"Don't mind me!" said Nugent, with rather a grimace. "I don't make out that I could pile up four goals against St. Jude's."

"Only a jolly good man could!" said Harry. "I can't make Wilmot out; but one thing's a cert—he's going to play for the Form if we have to take him by his ears and make him! Come on!"

And the Famous Five remounted their jiggers and rode home to Greyfriars, greatly surprised by what they had learned from the junior captain of St. Jude's. Why Wilmot had kept it dark, when it was so much to his credit, was a mystery they could not begin to fathom. But it was "dark" no longer, and Harry Wharton's mind was made up—Wilmot was going to play for Greyfriars in the Rookwood match, even if he had, as he put it, to take him by his ears to make him!

THE EIGHTH CHAPTER.

Let Down!

"JUST the chap I want!" said Billy Bunter.

Wilmot compressed his lips.

If he was just the chap Bunter wanted, it was clear that Bunter was not just the chap he wanted!

The new fellow had just come in, a little tired after his long ramble, when Bunter spotted him in the Remove passage.

Wilmot had paused outside his study—No. 1 in the Remove. He did not care for the crowd in the Rag, but the sound of voices from his study told him that Harry Wharton & Co. had got in. Billy Bunter, blinking out of Study No. 7 through his big spectacles, spotted him as he stood hesitating, and bore down on him.

"Come into my study, old chap!" said Bunter.

Wilmot did not move. He did not want company in his own study, but he would have preferred it to Bunter's.

But the fat Owl was not to be denied. He grabbed the new fellow by the arm, and almost dragged him along to Study No. 7.

"Look here——" muttered Wilmot.

"Oh, come in!" urged Bunter. "It's rather particular! In fact, I want you to do me a favour."

Wilmot unwillingly followed him into Study No. 7. Peter Todd and Tom Dutton were teaing out, and they had the study to themselves.

"Well, what is it?" asked Wilmot restively.

"Tea-time——"

"I'm going to tea in Hall——"

"I'll come with you, old chap—lots of time yet. I'll help you carry in a few things, if you're going to do any shopping! But never mind that now—tea can wait a bit."

Wilmot stared at him. He had had a good deal of conversation from Billy Bunter during the past few weeks. But this was the first time that he had heard Bunter suggest letting a meal wait a bit!

"It's my lines!" explained Bunter.

"Lines?" repeated Wilmot.

"You remember Quelch gave me two hundred lines because he heard me talking about your beastly uncle——"

THE MAGNET LIBRARY.—No. 1,460.

"My what?"

"Beastly uncle! Well, I haven't done the lines!" said Bunter. "I was going to—in fact, I started two or three times, but they never got done."

"Better wire in, then, before it's too late!" suggested Wilmot, making a move towards the door.

"Don't go, old chap! It's too late already," explained the fat Owl. "Old Quelch said they were to be handed in by tea-time. Well, it's tea-time now. He may be up after them any minute. If I don't take them to his study pretty quick, he will come up here—and I can tell you he will bring a cane with him. Don't go! I can't take them as they're not done, can I? But I jolly well don't want to be whopped."

Bunter rolled between Wilmot and the door.

Wilmot, it was quite clear, was anxious to go. Bunter was anxious for him to stay.

Without rolling the fat junior out of his way, Wilmot could not depart. So he stayed. But his manner grew more and more restive.

"Look here, cut it short!" he said.

"You're not in a hurry, I suppose—"

"Well, I am."

"Rot!" said Bunter. "You've got no friends—nobody ever speaks to you; you've always got lots of time on your hands. Don't you try to gammon me, Wilmot. I'm your only friend here, and I think you might be a bit grateful, too. I must say that."

"You fat fool!"

"Oh, really, old chap—"

"What do you want? Cut it short, I tell you!"

"I'm telling you as fast as I can, only you keep on interrupting me. A chap can hardly get in a word edge-wise. Look here, there's my lines—you can see how much I've done."

Bunter pointed a fat forefinger at a sheaf of impot paper on the study table.

On the top sheet was written a single line: "Arma virumque cano, Trojae qui primus ab oris—"

That, apparently, was the total contribution Bunter had made, so far, towards the two hundred lines awarded him by Mr. Quelch. Certainly, little time remained for writing the remaining hundred and ninety-nine.

Wilmot glanced at the scrawl, and then stared impatiently at Bunter. He could not in the least make out what the fat Owl wanted.

"Will you tell me what you want and let me get out?" asked Wilmot, breathing hard.

"I'm telling you, ain't I? Look here, you're going to chuck that stack of paper in the fire—"

"What on earth—"

"And explain to Quelch when he comes that you used my lines to light the study fire for tea! See?"

"But the fire's lighted already—"

"Quelch won't know that, ass! If you tell him you lighted it, why shouldn't he believe you, fathead? By careless-ness, you know, you grabbed my lines to light it with. Quelch will see bits of burnt paper in the grate. He won't know they hadn't been written on. See?"

Bunter bestowed a fat wink on the astonished Wilmot. Evidently, Bunter had given a good deal of thought to this brilliant scheme for eluding the wrath—and the cane—of his Form-master. No doubt he had been think-ing out this astute dodge, instead of writing the lines.

But Wilmot did not seem fearfully keen.

"If you want lies told to Quelch, you can tell them yourself!" he suggested.

"That's where you're wrong!" ex-plained Bunter. "If I spun Quelch that yarn, he wouldn't believe me. He's doubted my word before. Do you know what he'd do? He'd whop me for—for what he'd call prevarication, and make me write the lines over again—very likely double 'em! Well, that's not what I want. Quelch wouldn't believe for a minute that I'd written my lines, and they got burned by accident, if I told him."

"Probably not!"

"You see, I need a pal to stand by me in this," said Bunter. "You're a sulky toad, Wilmot, and Quelch doesn't like you—nobody could, really, you know, as I dare say you know as well as I do—but he'd take your word. It's not fair to take one fellow's word and not another's, but I never get fair play. There's no such thing as justice here. I never get justice."

SHIPPING WONDERS OF THE WORLD
A Book for Old and Young

From the very earliest times man's conquest of the sea has exerted an irresistible fascina-tion; every child has longed to sail the Southern seas in search of treasure; in later years we are inevitably stirred by some voyage of heroism and discovery, or by the sight of a gigantic liner in port, a battleship ready for action, or a yacht racing. SHIPPING WONDERS OF THE WORLD, the new Part Work out to-day, costs 7d. a week, and for this low figure you are offered a book of the sea without parallel in living memory, either in completeness, in sheer fascination or in interest.

Vividly and accurately, in simple, telling lan-guage the work relates all that is known of shipping from the time when a boat was fashioned from the bark of a tree until to-day, when a small town of people can be taken with absolute safety and certainty, thousands of miles in a few days.

It would be difficult to praise too highly the gallery of illustrations in the work, of which there are over 2,000 collected from all over the world. In addition to many hundreds of photographs there are superb reproductions of the masterpieces of famous sea-artists, and a great many diagrams and plans.

SHIPPING WONDERS OF THE WORLD is a book of first-rate importance. Part 1, out now, contains an exquisite Free Gift—a picture of R.M.S. Queen Mary—a perfect copy of Frank H. Mason's masterly engraving of the new British super-liner, ready for framing. The completed work can be bound very cheaply into two handsome volumes which will be a constant source of interest, delight and pride. To avoid disappointment it is advisable to place an order with your newsagent when you buy Part 1. There will be a very heavy demand.

"Don't you?" gasped Wilmot.

"You tell Quelch you used my lines by mistake to light the fire."

"Rubbish!"

"And if he asks you whether they were all written, you say, yes, they were. You saw me write them—"

"Oh, my hat!"

"And it will be all right. Quelch is a beast, but he wouldn't give a fellow an impot to write over again, just be-cause of an accident that might happen in any study. You can tell him you sat here with me while I was writing the lines—just as well to make the thing complete, you know. You can't be too careful in dealing with a man like Quelch. He's suspicious."

"Have you finished?"

"Yes; that's the lot. Wait here till Quelch comes. He's sure to come up if I don't go down. But get those papers in the fire to begin with. Leave bits about the fender. Where are you going? I say, Wilmot—"

Bunter grabbed the new junior by the arm as Wilmot pushed him aside.

Wilmot jerked his arm away, and strode to the door.

Billy Bunter blinked after him, his little round eyes gleaming with wrath behind his big round spectacles.

His pal had let him down.

After all the mental exercise Bunter had put in, thinking out that brilliant wheeze, Wilmot, the fellow whose secret he was keeping, wasn't going to play up. Bunter fairly gasped with wrath.

"Look here, you rotter!" he bawled. "I shall get that impot doubled."

"Serve you right!"

"Wha-a-t!"

Bunter jumped after the new junior. He grabbed his arm again as Wilmot was stepping out of the study.

"Look here, you cad!" howled Bunter. "If you think you're going to let me down like this, after all I've done for you, I can jolly well say—— Whooop!"

A forcible shove on his fat chest sent Bunter toppling. He sat down in Study No 7 with a bump that made the furniture dance.

"Oooogh!" gasped Bunter.

Wilmot strode away.

"Ow!" gasped Bunter. "Wow! Ooogh! Beast! Ungrateful rotter! Letting a fellow down! Ow! I say, Wilmot! Beast!"

Wilmot was gone. Bunter was left in happy anticipation of a call from Quelch, without a pal to help him carry through his astute scheme. Really, it was rough luck on the fat Owl, after all his mental efforts in thinking out that scheme. And the fact that it was exactly what he de-served seemed to afford Billy Bunter no comfort whatever.

THE NINTH CHAPTER.
The Secret Out!

"COME in!"

The door of Study No. 1 was wide open as Eric Wil-mot went back towards the stairs. Five smiling juniors emerged from that study, and surrounded him in the passage.

Wilmot, supposing for a moment that it was a rag, clenched his hands. But the next moment he saw that it was no rag.

They surrounded him with cheery smiles, and edged him into the study doorway, evidently with no hostile intentions.

The table was laid for tea in Study No. 1. There was rather a spread. The Famous Five, it seemed, had been busy getting it ready when Wilmot came up, and Billy Bunter had cap-tured him.

"We heard you," explained Whar-ton. "We've been waiting for you to come in."

"I don't see why."

"It's rather a long time since you tea'd in this study," remarked Frank Nugent. "You haven't had your tea?"

"I'm going down to Hall."

"You're not," grinned Bob Cherry.

"Look here!"

"Trot in!" said Johnny Bull.

"I'm going——"

"Not at all; you're coming!" said Harry Wharton.

And Wilmot came. With five fel-lows pushing him into the study, he had not a great deal of choice about it.

Wharton shut the door.

"Here's your chair, Wilmot," said Nugent.

"I'm not teaing here."

"You are!"

"Look here! What's the fool game?" exclaimed Wilmot angrily.

"I'm sorry, sir!" said Wilmot steadily. "But you cannot give me orders as my uncle, here! I hope I'm grateful for your kindnesses to me, sir; but here I am a Greyfriars boy, under nobody's orders but my Form-master's." "Upon my word!" gasped Mr. Hacker. "Do I hear aright? I have been your friend, your protector, and you repay me with this insolence!"

"You don't want me here, any more than I want your company. Is this a rag, or what?"

"Sit down, old bean!"

"Well, I won't!"

"Sit him down!" said Johnny Bull.

Wilmot was twirled to the chair placed ready for him at the table, and sat in it. He rose to his feet at once; and Bob's powerful hands on his shoulders sat him down again.

"Like sosses and ham?" asked Wharton hospitably.

"No!"

"And poached eggs?"

"No!"

"Look here, you sulky toad——" began Johnny Bull.

"Shush!" said Bob chidingly. "None of these painful truths now. Wilmot, old man, you're an honoured guest."

"Don't be a silly ass!"

"We've got something to talk about to you."

"I don't want to hear it."

"You don't like our company?" asked Bob sadly.

"No!"

"Well, if you prefer Bunter's, we'll ask him in. I fancy he would come, if he knew we had sosses and ham and poached eggs."

"Ha, ha, ha!"

"Oh, don't talk rot!" snapped Wilmot. "I don't want to tea here. Can't you leave a fellow alone? Look here! If you don't let me clear, I shall hit out! I'm fed-up with this!"

"By Jove!" said Harry Wharton. "I've never seen Topham, and don't know anybody there. But they must be regular whales on teaching fellows manners."

"The whalefulness must be terrific!" grinned Hurree Jamset Ram Singh.

Wilmot caught his breath.

He was rising from the chair again, with the evident intention of punching his way out of that hospitable study—or, at least, attempting to do so. But at the mention of Topham he dropped back. The angry red faded from his face, leaving it pale and almost haggard.

The change was so startling that the Famous Five stared at him. Since their meeting with Lunn of St. Jude's they knew that Wilmot had been a Topham fellow. But certainly it had never occurred to any of them that the mention of his old school would produce an effect anything like this on Eric Wilmot.

"I say! What's the matter, old scout?" asked Bob uneasily.

Wilmot did not answer.

He sat in his chair as if overwhelmed.

The chums of the Remove exchanged startled glances. Harry Wharton broke a painful silence.

"Look here, Wilmot! We want to speak to you! We want to wash out all that rot of yours, and get you to play up like a sensible chap. I don't know what your game is, but it seems to me absolutely idiotic. But, look here! If you want to go, go, and be blowed to you!"

But Wilmot, now that he was free to go, did not stir. He sat heavily in the chair as if he had lost the power of his limbs.

"So it's out!" he said, in a husky voice.

"Eh? What's out?"

"Didn't you just say——" stammered Wilmot.

"Oh, about Topham! Yes; it's out that you were a Topham man. Why shouldn't it be? Have you been keeping that a secret, as well as your Soccer?"

Wilmot looked at him, mute.

He had been so sulky, so reserved, so uncommunicative, that nobody appeared to have remarked on the fact that he had never mentioned his former school. He had never mentioned anything in connection with himself, so his reserve on that subject excited no special notice.

Certainly his manners and customs had led Wharton to entertain a suspicion that he had been in trouble of some sort at his last school. But the captain of the Remove had not given the matter much thought.

Now, however, all the five could see how matters stood. They had been utterly mystified by the knowledge that Wilmot had asked Bunter to "keep dark" his Soccer exploits at St. Jude's. They understood now. As soon as it was known that he was the goal-getter who had scored so wonderfully at St. Jude's, it would be known that he came from Topham. And that was what he wanted to keep secret.

There was a very uncomfortable silence in the study.

Wilmot broke it.

"So Bunter's told you——"

"Bunter's told us nothing!" answered Harry Wharton. "If that fat freak promised to keep your secret even Bunter wouldn't let it out—though I must say he's got his own weird way of keeping it. But Bunter hasn't told us that you came here from Topham."

"How did you know, then?" muttered Wilmot. "Has Crawley——"

"Crawley! Who's Crawley?"

"Nobody here of that name that I know of," said Bob.

"A Topham chap—a chap who doesn't like me!" muttered Wilmot. "He came over with our team that day at St. Jude's. He knows I'm here! But—he hasn't——"

"Never heard of him!" said Harry.

"Then how——"

"Easy enough," answered Wharton. "I can't imagine why you've been keeping your last school a secret, but you must have been an ass to think you could get away with it."

"Only Bunter knew, through that rotten chance of seeing me play in the match at St. Jude's!" muttered Wilmot.

"But all St. Jude's saw you," answered Harry. "Do you think they'd forget a man who scored four goals against them in a Soccer match?"

Wilmot started.

"Do you know anybody at St. Jude's?" he stammered.

"Do we? We have regular fixtures with St. Jude's—you'd know that if you took any interest at all in our matches."

"Didn't you know?" grunted Johnny Bull.

Wilmot shook his head.

"Why, you ass," said Harry, "St. Jude's are coming over here to play football in a week or two. Any man from there would have recognised you at once if he'd seen you here."

"Oh!" muttered Wilmot.

"It was a St. Jude's man told us who you were," went on the captain of the Remove. "Didn't you see the chap we were talking to when you ran into us this afternoon?"

"I saw somebody with a bike—I never noticed him——"

"He noticed you!" grinned Bob Cherry. "He remembered the man who had piled up goals on the St. Jude's ground, you see!"

"I—I see!"

"That's how we knew!" said Harry. "If you don't want us to mention it we won't! But it's not a thing a fellow can keep dark. Is that why you've let Bunter stick on to you—because he knew?"

"Why else?"

"Well, you're rather a fathead, old chap! Oh!" went on Wharton, light breaking in on his mind. "Is that why you've been such a sulky, unsociable tick—to keep fellows from asking you——"

"So that's it!" said Nugent. "But why——"

Johnny Bull gave a grunt.

"What were you turfed out of Topham for, Wilmot?" he asked very quietly.

Wilmot did not speak.

His face reddened, and paled again. Now that his secret was known its reason was easy enough for anyone to guess. He had kept Topham dark because he dared not let it be known. And he could have had only one reason. There had been a vague suspicion of it in Harry Wharton's mind. It was now a certainty. Wilmot was silent; but the Famous Five knew, as well as if he had told them, that he had been expelled from Topham School.

———

THE TENTH CHAPTER.
What Happened At St. Jude's!

HARRY WHARTON & CO. stood looking in silence at the crushed, shame-faced fellow, almost hunched in his chair. Sosses and poached eggs were getting

cold on the table, but no one noticed them.

The chums of the Remove had intended that spread to be a sort of feast of reconciliation; they had resolved to get Wilmot out of his "sulks," to argue him into acting more reasonably and sensibly, and to rope him into the Form footer.

Now they understood.

That sulky, disdainful temper had been a screen to hide a wretched secret. Partly from the weight of a miserable remembrance on his mind, partly from a fear of questions, the new fellow in the Remove had set himself apart—resolved never to enter upon a friendly or confidential footing with any fellow in his Form.

Only Bunter knew—and by tolerating the fat Owl's fatuous friendship he had kept Bunter silent.

But the whole thing had been in vain! Even while he was keeping all the Remove at armslength, wrapping himself up in solitary disdain and sulky silence, the secret he was keeping might have come out at any moment—was practically certain to come out sooner or later—as, indeed, it had done now.

That chance meeting with Lunn had done it. But any such chance might have happened at any time. It had been almost certain to happen when the St. Jude's team came over to play Greyfriars. There would be a crowd of them—and any one of them would have recognised Wilmot if he had seen him.

He had kept Bunter quiet—he had prevailed on Crawley of Topham not to pay him another visit. And all the while his secret trembled on the edge of the revelation that was inevitable.

He knew it now.

"Well," said Harry Wharton, after a long and painful silence, "I'm sorry, Wilmot; but you can see for yourself that it was bound to come out."

Wilmot nodded.

"I know that—now!" he said in a low, almost inaudible voice.

"You've gone the wrong way to work," said Harry uncomfortably. "Topham's miles from here, in another county. Nobody here knows the place—hardly heard of it! If you'd said out plain that you came from Topham nobody would have fancied——"

"I dared not!" breathed Wilmot.

"I see that—but you were wrong, all the same. Keeping it dark was the way to make fellows curious about it—only, of course, nobody ever thought of asking you anything as you were so dashed sulky. But now——"

"Oh, tell all the Form—tell all the school!" said Wilmot wearily. "Now it's out I shall have to clear!"

"I don't see why!"

"I do!" said Johnny Bull grimly. "We don't want a man here who's been sacked from another school. Fellows aren't sacked for nothing."

Wharton paused.

"Well, we don't know the circumstances," he said. "I've heard of a man being sacked from school for a fool trick of locking his beak in a study."

"If it was a harmless fool trick Wilmot wouldn't have carried on as he's done."

"My esteemed Johnny——" murmured the Nabob of Bhanipur.

"Give a chap a chance!" said the captain of the Remove. "I suppose it means that you were sacked, Wilmot?"

"You know it now."

"Some fool trick like——"

"No!"

"It can't be so jolly bad, or Dr. Locke would never have let you in here," said Wharton uneasily.

"Oh, that's an easy one!" grunted Johnny Bull. "Hacker wangled that!"

"I suppose he did—but Hacker couldn't have wangled it unless the Head believed that the chap ought to have a chance!" said Harry. "The Head wouldn't let a bad character into the school. Hacker believes in the chap, anyhow—he's a fussy old ass, but his opinion's worth something about his own nephew. He must know him pretty well."

"My uncle stood by me," muttered Wilmot. "He got me in here! I wish he hadn't—I never wanted——"

"Well, you're here now!" said Harry. "Will you tell us what it was you did at Topham, Wilmot? It's only fair to us."

"Oh, quite!" said Wilmot bitterly. "I did—nothing!"

"Sacked for nothing?" asked Johnny Bull sarcastically.

"Yes!"

"Oh crikey!"

"I don't expect you to believe me. But that's how it was," muttered Wilmot. "I was believed to have done a thing I'd rather cut off my hand than do—and I'm not blaming my headmaster, either—he couldn't act otherwise than as he did——"

"Hacker doesn't believe you did it?" asked Wharton quietly.

"No! He wouldn't have bunged me in here if he had."

"Well, Hacker's fussy, but he's a keen old bird—not what I should call a trustful man!" said Harry. "Hacker may be right."

"But what the dickens was it happened at Topham?" asked Nugent.

"Not at Topham—it was that day at St. Jude's!" muttered Wilmot wearily. "After the match——"

Bob Cherry whistled.

"Lunn said there was a row among the Topham men after that match!" he exclaimed. "The St. Jude's men don't seem to know what it was about."

"It was kept dark there—but it had to come out at Topham," muttered Wilmot wretchedly. "I—I cleared off by myself—the team went home without me—I got back on my own, and then—then——" He broke off, with a shiver.

"But what——"

"I can't tell you! It's too rotten! You'd believe—— But why shouldn't I? I never did it!" Wilmot lifted his head, the old, proud, disdainful look coming back to his colourless face. "I'll tell you, and you can dashed well think what you like! A chap's notecase was pinched out of his pocket in the dressing-room——"

"Oh!"

"When the fellow was changing, he missed it. There was a lot of money in it. The money was never found again——"

"But why should they think——"

"Because," said Wilmot, with a ghastly face—"because the notecase dropped out of my pocket before them all, when I was putting on my jacket."

"Oh!"

"They'd been cheering me—clapping me on the back—but you should have seen their looks then!" groaned Wilmot. "It was our skipper—man named Raleigh—chap I'd always liked —but his face—when he picked up that wallet——"

He broke off with a shudder.

The chums of the Remove stood silent.

Wilmot's voice went on, almost in a whisper:

"He asked me for the money—the wallet was empty! I—I lost my temper, and hit him. I was a fool, of course. Then I went off by myself. I was a fool to do it—but—but—in the state of mind I was in—but I suppose you don't understand——"

"I think I do!" said Harry softly.

"Well, I cleared—I got back to Topham on the railway—feeling like a fellow in a bad dream! But—but that finished it! You—you see, they supposed I'd cleared off like that to get rid of the money. If I'd let them search me, in the dressing-room at St. Jude's, it would have been all right— it couldn't have been found on me, as it wasn't there! But—but clearing off, like that—it looked——"

He broke off.

"I mightn't have played the fool like that, but Crawley—that cad Crawley was there—he said he wouldn't travel home with a thief. That did it! I went out and left them——"

Wilmot dragged himself from the chair.

"Now you know!" he said. "Tell all Greyfriars—it can't matter much— I shall have to get out now!"

He went unsteadily to the door and left the study. The chums of the Remove were left in a grim, uncomfortable silence. On the table the sosses and poached eggs were quite cold!

THE ELEVENTH CHAPTER.

Shirty !

"LOOKING for you!"

The Bounder spoke quite amicably.

There was a glint in his eyes and a compression of his lips which revealed that he was not feeling so amicable as he chose to appear. But his manner was quite friendly and civil, as he stopped Harry Wharton on the stairs.

Wharton stopped—reluctantly.

He could guess what was coming— Smithy's claims to play in the match at Rookwood. He did not want to hear any more about that. But he had another reason for wanting to get away. He was going down to look for Wilmot.

"Well, what?" he asked. "Cut it short, Smithy—I'm in a hurry."

"You may have noticed that I was in the football practice this afternoon, before you went out on your bike?"

The Bounder wanted to be amicable; but he could not help being sarcastic.

"Of course I did, ass!"

"If you condescended to give me the once-over, you may have noticed that I've picked up some form again?"

"Yes, I noticed that."

"Well, what about me for Rookwood on Saturday?"

"Nothing!" answered Wharton tersely.

The Bounder set his lips. He was trying to be friendly, though he was not feeling so. But he kept his temper.

"Look here, Wharton, I'm not denying that you were right in chucking me for a time. I conked out at football— I know that. I've picked up since. I——"

"Only a week ago you cut games practice, to go blagging with Pon & Co., of Highcliffe. I told you that day that if you cut footer, footer would have to cut you. I haven't changed my mind since."

"Then you're against me—on any terms!" All pretence of civility was thrown aside now, and the Bounder knitted his brows over gleaming eyes. "You're determined to play your pal

THE MAGNET LIBRARY.—No. 1,460.

Nugent in my place, even if it means a beating at Rookwood!"

"Nothing of the kind—and you know it, or ought to know it!" answered the captain of the Remove scornfully. "A man like you in the team is enough to turn a football skipper's hair grey. But if you were back in your old form I'd play you—and Nugent would have to stand out. You're not! You've condescended to put in some practice, and I dare say you've kept off smoking for a week or so—but you can't pick up in a week all you've chucked away in a month!"

"Better than Nugent——"

"Not at all! You've picked up—and I dare say you're as good as Frank now—if you keep it up! That's no reason for turning out a good and reliable man, who's as keen as mustard, to play an unreliable man who's no better."

"So I'm out, anyhow?"

"Yes; stick to the game and keep off playing the giddy ox, and your old place is ready for you—next time. Not on Rookwood day, though."

"It's some days yet—and if I improve——"

The Bounder was unusually patient. As a matter of fact, he was realising, as he generally did when it was too late, that he had played the fool.

Wharton shook his head.

"It's not possible now. Besides, to tell you something I wasn't going to mention yet, I've got an eye on another man——"

"Leaving out dear Franky?" sneered the Bounder.

"Nugent will be glad to stand out for a better man—he's not your sort!" snapped Wharton. "Besides, he's got home leave for the day, as it happens."

"And who's the man?" demanded the Bounder. "I thought you'd been over the Remove with a small comb, hunting for a man to replace me."

"So I have; but——"

"Well, who's the man?"

"It's not settled yet. Anyhow, you can fix up one of your appointments with the Highcliffe cads for Saturday—you won't be wanted for the Rookwood game."

With that, the captain of the Remove walked round Vernon-Smith and went on his way down the stairs.

Herbert Vernon-Smith stood staring after him as he went, with a black scowl on his face.

Having thrown up his place in Remove football by sheer carelessness, and disregard of any consideration but the whim of the moment, the Bounder wanted it back—when it was too late! For some days now he had been trying his hardest to get back into his old form, scarcely believing that his skipper would venture, when it came to the test, to leave out a man who had always been a tower of strength to the side.

But the Remove men took Soccer seriously, and it was not a matter in which even the Bounder could play fast and loose. What he had done, he had done—and that was that!

He tramped up the Remove staircase at last, and went scowling along the passage.

"I say, Smithy——" Billy Bunter squeaked, blinking out of Study No. 7 through his big spectacles.

Heedless of the fat Owl, Smithy tramped into his own study—Study No. 4. His chum, Tom Redwing, was not there, which added to his irritation. Without quite realising it, he wanted

somebody to listen to an outburst of angry temper!

"I say, Smithy, old chap——"

Bunter's spectacles glimmered in at the door. The Bounder scowled round at him.

"Get out, you fat freak!" he snapped.

"Oh, really, Smithy——"

"Take your idiotic face away!"

Billy Bunter did not take his idiotic face away. As the Bounder turned his back to him, he proceeded to address Smithy's back.

"I say, what are you shirty about, old chap? I say, I'm in a bit of a fix, Smithy! That rotter Wilmot——"

The Bounder looked at him again. He disliked Wilmot intensely—and the new fellow's action in the Form-room, which had made most of the fellows think much better of him, had made no difference to Smithy. Smithy could not forget that Wilmot had knocked him out in a scrap. But he was surprised to hear this description of him from Bunter.

"Has he stopped lending you money?" sneered Smithy.

"I may have borrowed a few bobs from the chap!" said Bunter, with dignity. "He knows I'm going to settle out of my postal order when—when it comes. I don't owe him so much as I do you, old chap, anyhow."

"He hasn't been here so long!" agreed the Bounder. "You will, in the long run!"

"I say, he's let me down, Smithy!" said the fat Owl sorrowfully. "After all I've done for him, you know, he wouldn't help me pull Quelch's leg over some lines! Old Quelch came after those lines, and he's doubled them—I've got four hundred now, Smithy!"

"Go and do them!" suggested Smithy.

"How's a fellow to get through four hundred lines? I say, Smithy, you might help a chap!"

"I can see myself writing your lines!"

"I don't mean that! Skinner will do a fellow's lines, at half-a-crown a hundred—he's done lots for you. If you've got ten bob——"

"Ha, ha, ha!" roared the Bounder. It was true that the wealthy Bounder sometimes "tipped" the needy Skinner to write "impots" for him. But if he could not see himself writing Bunter's lines, still less could he see himself tipping Skinner to write them.

"Blessed if I see anything to cackle at!" said the fat Owl. "I say, I shall get a licking if those lines ain't done, Smithy."

"Good!"

"Beast! I mean, look here, old chap! You've got lots of money—your pater's a profiteer, reeking with it——"

"Wha-a-t?"

"And look here, you loathe Wilmot, because he thrashed you," said Bunter. "Well, now the cad's let me down I don't see why I should keep his rotten secrets. You tip Skinner to do those lines, old chap, and I'll tell you about Wilmot."

Billy Bunter was not, perhaps, a whale in tact. His description of Mr. Samuel Vernon-Smith as a profiteer reeking with money did not seem to gratify the son of that financial gentleman. And Smithy was very far from admitting that he had been "thrashed" by Wilmot, or that that episode had anything to do with his dislike of the fellow.

Instead of jumping at Bunter's offer, therefore, the Bounder jumped at Bunter himself.

He grasped the fat Owl by the collar.

"I—I say," howled Bunter, "I say, leggo! I'll tell you—I'll really tell you

about that cad who thrashed you, old chap——"

Bang!

Bunter's bullet head smote the door of Smithy's study.

Bunter's yell rang the length of the Remove passage.

"Yaroooh!"

Then the fat Owl was twirled round, and Smithy's foot landed. Bunter flew into the passage.

Bump!

Smithy's door slammed. The fat Owl scrambled up, in wild wrath.

"Ow!" roared Bunter. "Wow! Beast! Rotter! Cad! Sulking because you're chucked out of the football! Yah! I've a jolly good mind to thrash you like Wilmot did! You come out of that study, you rotter, and I'll mop up the passage with you."

The door-handle turned!

So did Bunter!

He flew!

On second thoughts, undoubtedly the best, he decided not to mop up the passage with Smithy. The Bounder, looking out of Study No. 4, had a brief glimpse of a fat figure vanishing into Study No. 7.

Inside Study No. 7, Billy Bunter jammed his foot against the door—and kept it there for several minutes, till it dawned on his fat brain that the Bounder was not pursuing him.

THE TWELFTH CHAPTER.
A Friend In Need !

"WILMOT!"

A pale face glimmered in the gloom under the old leafless elms.

The winter dusk was thickening over Greyfriars School. It was close on lock-up now, and most of the fellows were in the House. But Wilmot was still out, and Wharton had found him, pacing to and fro on the dusky Elm Walk.

The sulky, disdainful pride that had seemed a part of Wilmot's nature, was gone now. He was pale, troubled, utterly down and out. At Topham, only a few short weeks ago, his little world had fallen in ruins round him. Greyfriars had been his refuge—owing to his uncle's intervention with the Head. Now he was driven from his refuge.

"You!" he muttered. "What do you want?"

"A few words!" said Harry quietly.

"You want to rub it in?" asked Wilmot bitterly. "Well, I've been a rotten brute to you—you can take it out of me now. Get on!"

Wharton gave him a pitying look.

"Even if I believed you were a—a—a——" He balked at the miserable word and went on. "If I believed that of you, I shouldn't think of rubbing it in, I hope. But I don't—and my friends don't."

"What rot!"

"Eh?" ejaculated Wharton, startled.

"Don't you know a thing's true, if it's proved?" said Wilmot, with an accent of almost wild bitterness. "Wasn't it proved? How could it be proved more than it was? A stolen wallet dropping out of my pocket before a dozen fellows—and the money missing—haven't you sense enough to know what evidence is? You're a fool, then."

The wild words did not make Wharton angry. They only added to his compassion and concern for the unfortunate Topham fellow.

"I can't make all that out, of course," he said. "If you never did it, some other fellow did, and he seems to have fixed it on you. It sounds pretty black, but—but—I don't believe it of you,"

"Why not?" sneered Wilmot.

Wharton paused a moment.

"Well, I don't quite know!" he confessed. "But we've talked it over in the study, and we all agree that you're not that sort. Hacker believes in you——"

"He's my uncle——"

"He's a keen man, and he must have some reason, besides being a relation. He must have persuaded the Head that there was some sort of doubt—Dr. Locke must have felt you were entitled to a chance, if he let you come here. And —you've done nothing of the sort here!"

Wilmot started, as if a snake had stung him.

"Oh!" he gasped. "Could you think——"

"I'm looking at the matter as a sensible chap," said Harry. "I can't understand a thief—it's a sort of problem I can't find an answer to. But I know this, as every fellow does—if a man's a thief, it's because there's some queer kink in him, and he can't take normal views of things—and what he's done once he will do again. Every thief goes on till he gets spotted. He never has the sense to stop."

Wilmot stared at him.

"You think that?" he said. "I—I suppose you're right. Yes, I suppose you're right. If you are, there may be a chance for me yet."

"How do you mean?"

Wilmot gave a harsh laugh.

"The rotter who bagged Raleigh's currency notes, and planted the empty wallet in my jacket—if he goes on, as you say, he will get spotted in the long run, as you seem to think—then it may all come out."

"Oh!" said Harry.

That was a new thought to him. He pondered for a moment or two, and nodded.

"I think it's quite possible—even likely!" he answered. "Anyhow, you've shown no sign here of being such an awful beast—I can't believe it of you, and I won't."

"The school will!"

"Nobody knows!" said Harry quietly. "You couldn't have come here if it had been known. You couldn't stay if it got out. But why should it? The Head's given you a chance here—through your Uncle Hacker—Quelch must know; I'm jolly sure he does; but he's a just man, and if he's undertaken to give you a chance, he will do it. Nobody knows——"

"You and your friends——"

"We know; but we know how to hold our tongues, too!" said Harry Wharton. "Hold yours, and nothing's different from what it was before."

"But—it will get out that I was at Topham, and then——"

"I'm coming to that!" said Harry. "Let it get out about Topham—nobody here knows the place or the people— nobody will guess the facts. Shout Topham from the housetops, and they'll suspect less than ever that you have anything to hide there."

Wilmot smiled faintly.

"My uncle didn't think so!" he muttered.

"There is such a thing as being too cautious. Anyhow, it can't be helped now—Bunter is sure to tattle sooner or later, as you'd know if you knew him as well as we do—and any St. Jude's man who saw you would give the whole show away, without even knowing it. Take the bull by the horns."

"I dare say you're right—but——"

"I know I'm right, in that!" said Harry. "Make the best of your chance here, Wilmot. Think of your uncle, too! He's a crusty old stick, and has no tact; but he did a big thing for you,

getting you here. You don't want to hurt him. And your people, too——"

Wilmot winced.

"The poor old mater!" he said. "If I get kicked out of here as I did from Topham, it will break her heart." His voice faltered. "That—that's what I was just thinking of, when you came up——"

"That does it, then!" said Harry. "Your mother comes first—no fellow can have a right to think of himself before his mater. You've got to make good."

"But——" muttered Wilmot wretchedly.

"You've had rough luck, if what you say is true—and I believe it is, and my friends believe the same. No need to say a single word. Make the most of the chance you've got here. If you're innocent, as I believe, you've a right to keep such a rotten accusation dark. You'll keep it dark better by talking about Topham than by trying to keep it a secret that you were there. It can't be kept a secret, anyhow."

"But—you don't mean you're standing by me?" muttered Wilmot.

"That's exactly what I do mean."

"I've been a sulky brute in the study —I played a rotten trick on you the other day, getting off detention by pretending I was keen to play footer——"

"We'll wash that out with the rest."

"I can explain that—now. Crawley —that Topham fellow—insisted on coming over to see me. Goodness knows why, for he's no friend of mine, unless

---

DON'T FORGET

our First Grand FREE GIFT issue of the MAGNET will be on Sale FRIDAY, February 7th.

---

he wanted to borrow money. Anyhow, he came, and if I hadn't met him in Courtfield he would have come to the school. I was glad to lend him a couple of pounds, and get his promise not to come again. But—but you see, I had to meet him that day——"

"I see!" said Harry. "If I'd known it was anything like that——"

"Of course, you couldn't; and I couldn't tell you."

"We've had faults on both sides. Wash it all out! And the best way to begin is——"

"What?" asked Wilmot, with a docility that was new and strange in him.

Harry Wharton smiled.

"Take the bull by the horns about Topham," he said. "Join up for the football on Saturday, when the Rookwood men come over. I'll put your name on the list, and let everybody know you're picked because you were the Topham man who walked all over St. Jude's in the match there."

"You'll put me in the football—now you know?"

"Now I know you piled up four goals in a match at St. Jude's?" asked the captain of the Remove, with a smile. "Now you know what I was accused of at Topham?"

"I'm going to forget that—and so are you. If I believe in a fellow I can't do it by halves. Is it a go?"

Wilmot seemed to choke.

"I wanted to make no friends here," he muttered. "I had a rotten secret to keep, and I was afraid—afraid of being turned down if fellows got to know.

But you know now, and instead of turning me down you're taking me up! If I'd known you better——"

"We'll get better acquainted," said Harry, smiling. "There's the bell for lock-up! Come on!"

He linked his arm in Wilmot's and walked him away to the House.

By the time they reached the lighted doorway, and he glanced at his companion's face, he saw that it was cool and calm. There was nothing in Wilmot's looks to betray the stress of emotion through which he had passed. There was, indeed, a new light in his eyes, a new elasticity in his step. Sulky solitude had not been his desire; but it had seemed to him a necessity. It seemed now as if a heavy weight was gone from his mind and his heart.

They walked into the House together. The Co. joined them, and they went in to calling-over. And the whole Remove stared to see the outcast of the Form on such cheery and friendly terms with the Famous Five.

THE THIRTEENTH CHAPTER.

Bunter's Trump Card Trumped!

"I SAY, you fellows!"

Billy Bunter rolled along to Study No. 1 after prep that evening.

He blinked at the doorway in surprise.

Wharton, and Nugent, and Wilmot had been at prep together, as usual. But other things did not seem quite as usual.

Generally, prep in Study No. 1 went on in grim silence, and Wharton and Nugent left the study immediately it was over, if Wilmot remained, while, if they remained, Wilmot left it immediately.

Now, after prep was finished, the three juniors sat round the table in cheery conversation. Wilmot's face had lost its dark and sulky expression. It was brighter and happier than it had ever been seen before since he had become a Greyfriars fellow. And it was clear that he was on the best of terms with his study-mates.

Which caused astonishment to the fat Owl and afforded him no satisfaction. For Bunter was wrathy!

His "pal" had let him down! And Bunter was not the man to be let down with impunity. He had come to Study No. 1 to make that fact clear to the cheeky new fellow!

Once before, Wilmot's patience had run out, and he had so far forgotten friendship as to sling Bunter out of his study! On that occasion Bunter had brought him to order. He had talked about Topham!

Talking about Topham had been enough! In his uneasy dread of the fat Owl "spilling the beans," Wilmot had come round and endured once more the fatuous friendship of the fat Owl.

Now, Bunter—in happy ignorance of the change in the circumstances—was going to play the same game again.

"Cut off, Bunter!" said Harry Wharton over his shoulder, without looking round.

Bunter rolled in.

"You seem to be jolly friendly here!" he remarked sarcastically.

"Quite, thanks!" said Frank Nugent, laughing.

"Well, look here, I've got four hundred lines for Quelch!" said Bunter. "I want to know what's going to be done."

"The lines, I should think."

"It's all your fault, Wilmot——"

"Mine?" said Wilmot, smiling. "How's that, fatty?"

"If you'd stood by me it would have been all right. Now Quelch has doubled my lines. If you think I'm going to be treated like that, after all I've done for you, you're jolly well mistaken—see?"

"Shut the door after you!"

"Wha-a-t?"

"Getting deaf?"

Bunter blinked at the new fellow. Deep, dark wrath gathered on his podgy brow. This was sheer cheek! If the fellow was getting his ears up Bunter was the man to make him put them down again.

"I don't want any cheek, Wilmot!" he hooted.

"What a coincidence!" remarked Wilmot.

"Eh? What do you mean?"

"I mean that I don't want any, either!"

"Look here——" roared Bunter.

"Excuse me!" said Wilmot politely. "Would you mind getting a new set of features before I look there? I don't like looking at that lot!"

"Why, you—you——" gasped Bunter. Wharton and Nugent chuckled.

They knew the card that Bunter had up his sleeve—the card that had hitherto been a trump, and which he was not aware had now become, as it were, a chicken that would not fight. So they were rather amused.

Bunter blinked in amazement at Wilmot. He could not understand the change in the fellow.

He seemed to have turned from a glum misanthrope into a cheery and light-hearted schoolboy. And it was a startling change.

Still, Bunter knew what he knew!

Very fortunately, he had not the faintest idea why Wilmot had wanted to keep Topham "dark." But he knew that he had wanted to! He had brought him to order before by talking about Topham! He was going to try to bring him to order again—at all events, so he fancied.

"I—I say, you fellows," gasped Bunter. "Talking about Topham——"

"Ha, ha, ha!" yelled Wharton and Nugent.

Wilmot grinned.

Bunter, expecting him to wince, could only blink in amazement at his handsome, laughing face.

"Go it, Bunter!" said the captain of the Remove. "Let's hear about Topham!"

"Oh, do!" said Nugent.

"Get on!" said Wilmot. "I don't think you know a fearful lot about my old school, Bunter, but talk about it as much as you like!"

Bunter jumped, and his spectacles nearly fell off his fat little nose. Never had the fat Owl been so astonished.

Here was Wilmot babbling out the secret which for several weeks he had kept dark, at the heavy cost of accepting Billy Bunter as a "pal."

Bunter could scarcely believe his fat ears.

"Oh crikey!" he exclaimed blankly. "Have—have—have you told them?"

"Ha, ha, ha!" yelled Wharton and Nugent.

The expression on Bunter's fat face was worth a guinea a box at that moment.

"I say, you fellows, has that chap told you he was at Topham?" gasped Bunter.

"Why shouldn't he?" asked Harry.

"Eh? I don't know, but he was keep-

ing it dark, for some reason. He jolly well asked me to keep it dark!" gasped Bunter. "Why, the day he came here I knew him at once! I knew he was the Topham fellow I saw playing football at St. Jude's, and he asked me not to mention it." He gave Wilmot an accusing glare. "You jolly well know you did! And I kept it dark out of sheer good nature. You lending me ten bob had nothing to do with it, as you jolly well know!"

"Did I lend you ten bob?"

"You jolly well know you did!" hooted Bunter.

"And have you come here to square?"

"Eh?"

Wilmot held out his hand.

"Shell out!" he said cheerfully. "I can do with that ten bob, if you're keen to square."

"Oh! No! I—I wasn't thinking of that!" stuttered Bunter. "I'm going to square when my postal order comes! It—it hasn't come yet!"

"Ha, ha, ha!"

"Blessed if I see anything to cackle at!" snorted Bunter. "Wilmot made out that he wanted it kept dark about my seeing him at St. Jude's, so that the fellows wouldn't know where he came from. If he was pulling my leg, I don't see why."

"Do you ever see anything?" asked Harry.

"Oh, really, Wharton——"

"See that door?"

"Ha, ha, ha!"

"Well, if the silly ass has let it out——" said Bunter, puzzled and greatly annoyed. He realised that the power had departed from his fat hands. If Wilmot no longer cared whether the fellows knew that he had come from Topham, it was clear that he was not going to be brought to order by talk on that topic. "I say, he really asked me——"

"Never mind what Wilmot asked you—I'm asking you to get on the other side of that door!" pointed out the captain of the Remove.

"So you know that chap was at Topham?" said the puzzled Owl. "You know he was the Topham man who played football at St. Jude's?"

"Well, rather!"

"You never knew it before!" howled Bunter. "He can't have told you very long ago—you never knew—and I don't see now why he's let it out, after keeping it dark all these weeks. I think——"

"Hallo, hallo, hallo!" came a cheery roar from the passage. "Bunter telling whoppers again!"

Bob Cherry and Johnny Bull and Hurree Singh arrived at the study doorway.

Bunter blinked round at them.

"Who's telling whoppers?" he snorted.

"You are, old fat bean, if you were saying that you think!" answered Bob. "You can't, old chap! At least, you never do!"

"The thinkfulness of the esteemed fat Bunter is not terrific!" grinned Hurree Singh.

"I say, you fellows, did you fellows know that that chap Wilmot was at Topham?" demanded Bunter.

"The knowfulness is preposterous!" chuckled the Nabob of Bhanipur.

"Did you know he was the chap who played football at St. Judes?" gasped the perplexed Owl.

"Of course we know, as that's the reason why Wharton's putting him in the team for the Rookwood match!" said Bob Cherry.

"Oh crikey! Is he?" gasped Bunter.

"Making up the list now," said

Harry, laughing. "Anything more you want to know before you travel?"

"Well," said Bunter, blankly, "I'm blowed!"

"Blow away!" suggested Nugent.

"Well, look here," said Bunter. "I can't make it out, but I jolly well know he was keeping it dark, and I jolly well know he wanted me to, and I jolly well know——"

"There's one thing you don't jolly well know," remarked Johnny Bull, "and that is when your company superfluous!"

"Oh, really, Bull——"

"Roll that barrel out!" said Wilmot.

"I say, you fellows—— Yaroooooop!" roared Bunter, as he rolled out.

The door of Study No. 1 slammed on the fat Owl! In that study, now prep was over, the Famous Five and Eric Wilmot devoted themselves to the subject of football and the Rookwood match.

Billy Bunter rolled away in a state of great astonishment and annoyance. What it all meant he could not understand, but one thing, at least, was clear to Bunter—he had lost his "pal," and talking about Topham would never bring him back again! That pal had gone for good! The Owl of the Remove had played his trump card, and it had been trumped—and that was that!

THE FOURTEENTH CHAPTER.

Smithy Is Not Pleased !

HERBERT VERNON-SMITH looked—and looked again. At the first glance, the Bounder doubted whether he had seen aright.

The Rookwood list was posted in the Rag.

Perhaps with a lingering hope of finding his name there, Smithy gave it a look when he came in after prep.

His name was not there. But another name was there that made him stare blankly—the name of E. Wilmot!

Nugent's name was not there. In the place of F. Nugent was written E. Wilmot—amazing, but perfectly plain!

Smithy looked, and looked again, and drew a deep, hard breath. Wharton had told him that he had his eye on "another man," and the Bounder had been puzzling a good deal to guess which man it was. But Wilmot had never occurred to his mind for a moment.

He looked round the Rag! Harry Wharton & Co. stood in a cheery group by the fire, Wilmot with them. Smithy had heard already, with perplexity and irritation, that the outcast of the Remove had, somehow, established friendly relations with the Famous Five. But certainly he had never dreamed that it would go to this length.

He strode across to the group at the fire. He was enraged; but he was more astonished and puzzled than enraged.

"What does this mean, Wharton?" he asked, between his teeth.

"What and which?" inquired the captain of the Remove.

"Wilmot's name is up in the footer list."

"Yes, that's right."

"Is it a joke?"

"Hardly! Footer isn't a funny subject."

"You're playing an out-and-out dud in the Rookwood game?"

"No—you're left out!"

"Don't be a cheeky fool!" roared the Bounder, as there was a laugh from the fellows in the Rag.

"May I ask the same of you?" inquired Wharton politely.

With his back to the Form-master, Bunter did not see Mr. Quelch coming out of the House. "Quelch isn't an old toad like your uncle, Wilmot," he rattled on. "He may be a crusty old stick, but Hacker's really the limit, you know! A regular acid-drop! Crusty old toad——" "Bunter!" exclaimed Mr. Quelch, angrily.

"You were going to leave me out, to play the soft ass Nugent——"

"Thanks!" interjected Frank.

"Now it seems that you're leaving Nugent out, to play that dud—that foozler—that slacking rotter, who has to be kicked down to games practice!"

"Thanks!" said Wilmot.

"Do you think the team will stand it, Wharton?"

"I think so," said Harry cheerfully. "I've told all the men my reason. You'd have heard it if you'd been here when I put the list up. A first-class footballer like Wilmot can't be left out."

"A—a what?"

"First-class footballer!"

"That dud!" gasped the Bounder. "That idiot who lurches about the field like a sack of coke!"

"He won't lurch about like a sack of coke when Rookwood come over! Will you, Wilmot, old bean?"

"I'll try not to!" said Wilmot, smiling.

"You've seen him on Little Side—a dud, a slacker, a fool, a clumsy ass——" gasped Smithy.

"That was only his little game!" said Bob Cherry. "He fancied he didn't want to play Soccer here—but he's changed his mind."

"Rubbish! Rot! You know he can't play!" yelled the Bounder. "Has any man here ever seen him play footer?"

"Yes; Bunter has."

"Fat lot Bunter knows about Soccer! Anybody else?"

"No; but we're all going to see him to-morrow. We're fixing up a pick-up, just to show what the new man can do."

"You dummy——"

"Thanks!"

"You fool——"

"Thanks again!"

"Smithy, old man!" Redwing had just come into the Rag, and he caught the Bounder by the sleeve. "Don't be a goat, old man! Wharton wouldn't put a man in the team unless he knew——"

"Shut up, you ass!" Vernon-Smith shook off his chum's hand. "Look here, Wharton, you dolt——"

"Keep it up!"

"You howling dummy——"

"Is that the lot?"

"Will you tell me what you've put Wilmot into the team for?" almost shrieked the enraged Bounder. "You've always called him a dud!"

"Certainly! That was when I didn't know that he was the man from Topham who kicked four goals in a match with St. Jude's."

"He never did——"

"If you can't take my word, and Wilmot's, old bean, ask Bunter, who saw him doing it!" said the captain of the Remove. "Bunter was there! You've heard him talk about a Topham man who was a wonderful goal-getter! Well, Wilmot's the man!"

"Bunter's idiotic lies——"

"Well, Lunn told us the same. The St. Jude's skipper ought to know!"

"Lunn told you?" stuttered the Bounder.

"Yes. We met him this afternoon; and Wilmot came along, as it happened. So we found out we had been entertaining an angel unawares," said Wharton, laughing. "Wilmot seems to have been too jolly modest to tell us what a wonderful man he was; but as soon as I heard it from Lunn I made up my mind at once to bag him for the Remove eleven. And I can tell you

we've got a prize-packet, Smithy! You'll see when you see him play."

"I don't believe it."

"Well, seeing is believing—and you'll see to-morrow."

"If he can play Soccer, what has he been pretending to be a slacker and a dud for all the time he's been here?"

"Just temper," said Wilmot—"rotten, sulky temper! Not unlike your own, Vernon-Smith; but the difference is that I've got over it and you haven't."

"Ha, ha, ha!"

The Bounder clenched his hands.

"It's all rot, spoof, lies!" He almost choked with rage. "The fellow can't play, and he's too sulky and slack to play if he could! If you put him in a pick-up to-morrow he will foozle about, as usual——"

"Well, if he does, out he goes again," said Harry. "Can't say fairer than that, Smithy."

"Look here——" roared the Bounder.

"Give a man a chance," interrupted Bob Cherry. "If Wilmot foozles in the pick-up to-morrow you can turn on the megaphone then, old bean."

"Ha, ha, ha!"

The Bounder panted. He could not and would not believe, and his angry temper broke out fiercely. He made a spring at Wilmot.

"Put up your hands, you cad!" he panted. "Put up——"

Instantly the angry Bounder was grasped; the Famous Five closed round him like one man and seized him on all sides.

"Chuck that, Smithy!" said Harry Wharton tersely. "You can't punch a man because his skipper's picked him to play footer—and you're not going to damage my new recruit. Keep cool, you ass.''

"Oh, let him come on!" said Wilmot, with a flash of his old disdain. "He won't do a lot of damage."

Wharton gave him a look; Wilmot coloured.

"Sorry!" he said at once. "Look here, Vernon-Smith, don't play the goat! We've had one scrap—and I don't want another, if you do. Keep your temper."

"Let me go!" yelled the Bounder, struggling.

"Will you chuck it?"

"No!"

"You'll chuck it, or you'll be chucked out!" said the captain of the Remove. "Take your choice."

The Bounder's reply was a desperate wrench to free himself. The next moment he went whirling to the door in the grasp of the Famous Five. Lord Mauleverer opened the door, and Smithy went spinning into the passage.

"Come back when you're cool," said Harry. And the door slammed on Smithy.

Apparently Smithy did not get cool; at all events, he did not come back.

———

THE FIFTEENTH CHAPTER.

An Unlooked-for Chance !

"FEELING fit?"

Harry Wharton asked that question, with a smile, on Saturday afternoon, and Wilmot smiled as he answered:

"Fit as a fiddle!"

It was a cold, dry, keen February day, glorious for footer—as all the Remove men agreed—and the Removites were looking forward very keenly to the match that afternoon.

Even the Bounder did not doubt now that Wilmot was a good man for the side. He had seen him play in the pick-up, in which he had been put to the test for the general satisfaction of the footballing fraternity.

Smithy had watched him with angry, jealous eyes; but, angry as he was, he was no fool, and he had to admit that the fellow could play Soccer.

Whether it was sulky temper or any other reason that had made him show up as a dud hitherto, it was gone now, and the fellow from Topham put up a game as good as any man in the Remove—better than most—and quite equal to Vernon-Smith when he was at the top notch of his form.

The Bounder had to admit it, but the knowledge only made him the angrier. Frank Nugent displaced by the new recruit, had taken it with perfect good-humour, glad that his chum's worries over the Rookwood match were ended. The Bounder was far from taking it in good-humour.

Smithy was a sportsman in his own way, but the unexpected discovery that the fellow he loathed—the fellow who had licked him in a scrap—was a first-class footballer was too bitter a pill to be swallowed easily. The Bounder had had the solace, at least, of despising him as a dud at games; now that solace was taken away.

He had not even the solace of seeing the fellow unpopular, as he had hitherto been. He had no handle against him. It was useless to revive the old story of "greasing to the beaks," which had been so thoroughly disproved. Even Skinner & Co. had dropped that, and were rather ashamed of the part they had taken, in view of what they had escaped by Wilmot's refusal to give them away. Bolsover

THE MAGNET LIBRARY.—No. 1,460.

major was heard to declare that the chap was a jolly decent chap. Billy Bunter, it was true, displayed rather a resentful and disdainful attitude towards Wilmot—but to be barred by Bunter was rather a compliment than otherwise. If Wilmot had not exactly become popular, he was, at least, regarded with friendly eyes and greatly admired as a footballer.

Some fellows in the quad smiled as they glanced at the Bounder's face. He tramped into the House and went up to the Remove passage. Skinner and Snoop, loafing on the landing, winked at one another.

The Bounder gave them a black scowl, stopped at Study No. 1, and threw the door open. He had noticed that Wilmot was not in the quad with the other fellows just then, and he was in a mood for a row and a scrap. The idea of giving Wilmot a swollen nose to take on the football field with him was rather attractive to Smithy at the moment.

But Wilmot was not in the study. Frank Nugent was there, putting some things together on the study table, apparently for packing. He glanced round as the door flew open.

"Got it?" he asked.

"Eh, what?" asked Smithy, scowling. "Got what?"

Nugent smiled.

"I thought it was Wilmot. He's gone up to the box-room to fetch a bag for me."

The Bounder stared at him.

"Aren't you going to stop in and see the wonderful man playing in your place?" he sneered. "I remember Wharton mentioned you had home leave, but——"

"I'd like to, but I've got leave to go home for my sister's birthday; and as Wharton doesn't need me I'm going. You can watch Wilmot bagging goals, and tell me about it afterwards," suggested Nugent, with a grin. "I shall be back on Monday morning——"

Slam !

Frank Nugent laughed as the Bounder shut the door with a bang that rang the length of the passage.

Vernon-Smith tramped away up the Remove passage towards the box-room stairs. He almost ran.

His mind at that moment was full of bitterness and evil. Nugent's words had put an idea into that angry, bitter mind.

Already it had been in the Bounder's thoughts that he would put a spoke in his enemy's wheel if he could. There was little at which he would have stopped to prevent Wilmot's triumph on the football field that day. Now, as if to tempt him, at the moment when he was overcome with bitterness and rancour, it seemed as if the fellow was playing right into his hands—giving him the chance he had not dared to hope for. He ran up the box-room stairs—and reached the landing above just as Eric Wilmot came out with an empty suitcase in his hand.

Wilmot glanced at his bitter face, and would have passed him. The Bounder stepped aside for him.

But as Wilmot passed he made a sudden snatch at the suitcase and jerked it from his hand.

Wilmot, taken quite by surprise at what seemed to him a childish trick, stared at the Bounder as he ran up the upper stairs with Nugent's bag in his hand.

"You silly ass, what sort of a game do you call that?" exclaimed the new junior. "Chuck that bag down!"

"Fetch it if you want it!" retorted Vernon-Smith.

"You utter ass!" exclaimed Wilmot.

The Bounder laughed mockingly and ran up to the upper landing. Above the box-room was a disused garret. The Bounder swiftly took out the key, which he jammed into the outside of the lock.

Wilmot, angry, but more surprised than angry at what seemed to him an absolutely infantile prank, followed him up. The Bounder stepped into the garret.

"Give me that bag, you fathead!" exclaimed Wilmot. "Nugent's waiting for it—he's got a train to catch; he's going home this afternoon."

"Come and fetch it!"

"I'll do that fast enough!" snapped Wilmot, and he came into the garret, his hand outstretched. "Now, you silly ass—— Oh!"

The Bounder swung the suitcase round, catching him on the shoulder. Wilmot staggered across the garret.

In an instant Vernon-Smith leaped to the door and slammed it after him as he leaped out. The next instant the key turned in the lock. And in a moment more Wilmot was thumping on the inside of the door.

"Let me out, you fool!" he shouted.

"All serene—I'll take Nugent his bag!" The Bounder chuckled breathlessly. "You can stay there, you rotter!"

"I'm wanted at the footer, you fathead——"

"Not by me!"

Thump, thump! came angrily on the door.

"You rotter!" came Wilmot's angry voice. "If you don't let me out at once I'll shout for help, and you'll take the consequences."

"Why do you think I got you up to this garret, you fool?" jeered the Bounder. "You can shout till you're tired, but nobody will hear you from here! Shout away!"

With that the Bounder went down the stairs, grinning, with the bag in his hand. The thumping on the door died away as he descended the lower stairs. He strolled along the Remove passage, a grin on his face, though his heart was beating rather fast.

"Wilmot—— Oh, you again!" exclaimed Nugent, as the Bounder opened the door of Study No. 1. "Is that my bag?"

"Yes; Wilmot's gone down to the changing-room," answered the Bounder carelessly. "He asked me to bring it along."

"You're getting jolly obliging, old bean," said Nugent. "Thanks!"

"You'll want some things from your box in the dorm if you're staying over the night," remarked the Bounder. "Like me to help you pack?"

"If you like!"

They went to the Remove dormitory together. Ten minutes later Frank Nugent came out of the House, and his chums joined him, to walk down as far as the gates. The Bounder watched them with a cynical smile on his hard face.

Nugent was gone! Wilmot was locked in a garret at the top of the House, out of hearing if he shouted at the top of his voice. It looked as if Herbert Vernon-Smith might be playing in the Rookwood game, after all.

THE SIXTEENTH CHAPTER.

Neck or Nothing !

"OH, the rotter!" panted Wilmot. He thumped and thumped on the garret door.

But he soon gave that up. The Bounder was gone, and it was clear that Smithy did not mean to let him out. And the fact that he had taken the trouble, and the risk, to lock him in the garret at all was pretty conclusive proof that it was impossible for a prisoner there to make himself heard.

Wilmot clenched his hands.

What would the fellows think if he failed to turn up for the match? That it was another sample of his sulks and disdain? That he was treating an important fixture as he had treated the pick-up of a week ago—letting them expect him and then failing to turn up?

What else could they think?

The thought of that made him desperate. With the friendship and faith of the cheery Co. to help him through he had resolved on a new life at Greyfriars—and a few days of it had made him more than satisfied with his resolve. Wharton had been right in advising him to "take the bull by the horns" with regard to Topham! Everybody knew now that he had been at Topham—and thought nothing at all about it! Even the vengeful Bounder had extracted the information from Billy Bunter, too late to realise that there was anything in it to harm his enemy.

For several days now Wilmot had been almost as happy as in the old days at Topham. He had made friends—he was booked for the game he was keen on—the miserable past faded into the background.

Now was it all to be thrown away to gratify the malice of the scapegrace of the Remove—the fellow who had let the team down himself and yet was unwilling to see another man play in his place?

Wilmot gritted his teeth.

Minutes were passing—and minutes were precious. It was only half an hour to kick-off—Rookwood might arrive any minute.

With considerable difficulty Wilmot opened the window and put his head out. But he realised at once that the loudest shout could never be heard so far below with intervening roofs and buildings.

Far in the distance, toy-like, he had a glimpse of the gates, and saw several fellows there, one with a bag in his hand.

He gave a start. Nugent, of course—he was going! He would not be available if Wilmot failed his side! Wharton would be left a man short; he would have to pick up some stop-gap at the last minute——

Then the whole of the Bounder's scheme flashed into his mind.

Smithy knew that Nugent was going! All the Remove knew that Nugent had leave to go home for his sister's birthday party that day, and only playing in the Rookwood match would have kept him. As he was not wanted, since Wilmot had been put in, he was going. He would be wanted now—but he did not know it—and he was going! The Bounder was counting on that! Nugent gone and Wilmot tricked out of the way, Smithy was banking on being shoved into the vacant place—his old place in the team! Chance had played into his hands—and with reckless unscrupulousness he had jumped at the chance.

"Oh, the rotten rascal!" breathed Wilmot.

He stared at the distant gates.

Frank Nugent was gone! The other fellows who had seen him off came back from the gates and the buildings hid them from Wilmot's eyes. Had they looked up at that tiny window far over the roofs they would hardly have seen him there. But they naturally did not. Now they were lost to his sight.

He clenched his hands desperately.

Already they would be missing him! What would they be thinking of him? He craned his head out of the little window, trying to get a glimpse of the playing fields. He had a partial view and could see fellows gathering there. Then he had a glimpse of a pink-and-white shirt, and he knew the Rookwood colours. Jimmy Silver & Co. had arrived then!

He crossed to the door again and beat on it savagely. But only the echo of the knocking answered him. Even if the noise reached as far as the Remove passage no fellow was there in the studies to hear.

Again he went to the window.

Six feet below it was a roof ridge, with a steep slant of slates on either side. At the other end of the ridge was a window of some attic. For a long minute he stood looking, and then he moved. To drop to that narrow stone ridge, and work his way along, was to risk life and limb—but he had made up his mind to do it.

He had already changed for football, and had a coat on. He threw the coat off, and his slim figure squeezed through the window easily enough without it, small as the aperture was.

Holding on to the narrow sill, he could just feel the stone ridge below him with his football boots.

For a second he hesitated. If he failed to make good his hold—if he slipped—— A sudden slide down the slanting slates—a rush through the air, a fall of seventy feet or more to hard earth. Was it worth the fearful risk?

He let go his hold.

His heart was beating; but his head was cool. An instant, and he was astride the ridge.

On either side, space—and death! Carefully, steadily, he avoided looking down on either side, as he worked his way, slowly but surely, along the stone ridge.

It was slow progress. The studs of his football boots scraped lines on the damp slates. Inch by inch, foot by foot, his eyes fixed steadily on the attic window before him, he worked his way on.

It was minutes—but it seemed hours—before he reached the end of the roof ridge. Cold at it was, the perspiration was breaking out on his forehead.

But his nerve was steady as steel as he rose upright on the narrow ridge, and reached the attic window-sill above him.

He got his elbows on the sill, and hung there, his feet in space. The window was fastened within.

Holding on with one arm and hand, he cracked a pane with his other elbow. The shattering fragments fell within.

He groped for the fastening, and unlatched it. Even then it was difficult work to get the long-disused window open.

But it was open at last. He crawled through and dropped, almost exhausted, on a bare floor.

For a minute he lay there to recover. Then he was on his feet again, and dragging open the door. Outside was a staircase. He ran down, and found himself in the Fourth Form passage.

Temple of the Fourth, in his study doorway, stared at him.

"Hallo! Aren't you playin' footer?" drawled Cecil Reginald Temple. "I heard that you were in Wharton's team, old bean."

Without delaying to answer, Wilmot cut down the passage, and flew down the stairs, and out of the House. Cecil Reginald was left staring.

THE SEVENTEENTH CHAPTER.

Victory!

"WILMOT!"

"Where's Wilmot?"

"Where's that ass?"

"Where the dickens——"

A dozen fellows were asking those questions on Little Side. The Remove men were there—Jimmy Silver & Co., from Rookwood, were there—but the new recruit in the Remove Eleven was not there.

He had changed for the game when the other fellows did. Some of them had been punting a ball about when Wilmot went into the House with Frank Nugent, and he was not missed till the footballers were ready to gather for the kick-off.

Up to the last moment, Harry Wharton expected to see him come cutting down to the field. But he did not come.

The Bounder, lounging with his hands in his pockets, watched the captain of the Remove curiously. He had no compunction. If Wharton wanted him, he was ready to play—if not, the captain of the Remove could do his best without

(Continued on next page.)

him. Wilmot, at all events, would not be there.

"Where the dickens is the man?" muttered Bob Cherry.

"The wherefulness is terrific!"

Harry Wharton stared towards the House. There was no sign of Eric Wilmot coming. Other fellows were to be seen, coming down to the football ground to look on. But Wilmot was not among them.

The captain of the Remove knitted his brows. Was it possible—was it barely possible—that the fellow had failed him, after all? He remembered the pick-up of a week ago. Was it possible?

Potter, who was acting as referee, came up to Wharton.

"You can't hang about for ever, kid! If your man hasn't turned up, put in another man, and get going, for goodness' sake!" he said.

Harry Wharton gave a last look in the direction of the House. Then he made up his mind. He could hardly keep the Rookwooders waiting any longer for a man who did not choose to turn up.

He looked at Vernon-Smith.

"You get changed, Smithy! Thank goodness you're here, as Nugent's gone!"

The Bounder cut off towards the doorway of the changing-room with the speed of a deer.

"Only a few minutes now, Silver!" said Harry, biting his lip.

"Right as rain!" said the Rookwood junior cheerily.

"Hallo, hallo, hallo!" roared Bob Cherry. "Smithy's changed pretty quick!" His eyes were on an active figure, in football rig, racing down to the field. "Why—great gum—it's not Smithy—it's Wilmot!"

"Wilmot?" gasped Wharton.

"The esteemed and idiotic Wilmot!" exclaimed Hurree Jamset Ram Singh.

The Bounder was in the changing-room—changing fast. He was still there when Wilmot reached the group of footballers, panting for breath.

Wharton gave him a grim look.

"Sorry!" panted Wilmot. "I got delayed! I'm awfully sorry! If I'm not too late, Wharton! It wasn't my fault, really!"

"What the dickens—— But never mind that now! You're here!" Harry Wharton's face cleared. What had happened to keep Wilmot away, he could not guess; but, at the moment, it mattered little, as he had turned up in time. "Get into the field, you men!"

The footballers went into the field. Potter blew the whistle, and the ball was sent rolling. The game had already started, and was going strong, when Herbert Vernon-Smith came cutting down to Little Side—changed for football.

He gave almost a convulsive jump at the sight of the players in the field.

"What!" he gasped. "What!" For the moment he did not observe Wilmot there.

"Wilmot turned up, old man!" said Tom Redwing.

The Bounder staggered.

"Wilmot?" he repeated.

"Yes, at the last minute!"

"Don't be a fool!"

Redwing stared at him.

"He did, Smithy! There he is, on the wing!"

Vernon-Smith fixed his eyes on the graceful, athletic form, the handsome face, flushed and keen. He felt as if his head was turning round. He had left Wilmot locked in an inaccessible

garret—the key was still in his pocket! And Wilmot was there—playing football!

As he stared almost stupidly at that unexpected and amazing sight, there was a roar from the Greyfriars crowd:

"Wilmot! Wilmot!"

"Oh, good man!"

"Goal! Goal! Goal!"

"Wilmot! Oh, bravo, Wilmot!"

"By gum, that man can play football!" said Redwing.

The Bounder did not speak.

He could not.

With starting eyes, he stared at Wilmot. The Topham man had put the pill in in the first six minutes of the game. The Greyfriars crowd roared.

Harry Wharton clapped his new recruit on the shoulder as the players went back to the centre of the field. His eyes were dancing.

"Keep that up, Wilmot!" he said.

Wilmot smiled cheerily.

"I'll try!" he said.

He did try—and succeeded. Jimmy Silver & Co. had come over from Rookwood, expecting a hard game on the Greyfriars ground. But they had not expected quite so hard a game as this proved to be. They had never seen Wilmot before; but now that they saw him, they were not likely to forget him.

Another goal came to the new man in the first half. And one came to Harry Wharton, as the result of a pass from Wilmot.

Mornington put the ball in for Rookwood just on half-time. When the whistle went, Greyfriars were leading three to one.

In the interval Harry Wharton ran across to speak to the Bounder.

"Sorry, Smithy!" he said. "Wilmot turned up, and so—— You understand?"

"Oh, quite!" sneered Smithy. "Has he told you how he managed to turn up?"

"Eh—no."

"I'm rather curious about that!"

"Blessed if I know what you're driving at, Smithy!" said the captain of the Remove, puzzled.

"You will!" sneered the Bounder.

Wharton shrugged his shoulders, and went back to the players. When Potter blew the whistle again, the game went on hot and strong, the Greyfriars men in great spirits. Jimmy Silver & Co. fought hard; and they were good men, with plenty of fight in them.

But it booted not. Another goal came to Wilmot, and another to Wharton! After which the Rookwooders packed their goal, and defended successfully till the final whistle blew. For once Jimmy Silver & Co. were rather glad to hear it. Five goals to one was enough to satisfy the greediest!

*   *   *   *   *

Herbert Vernon-Smith watched the game to its victorious finish, and then went back to the House and to his study.

No one came up to the studies; but he could hear sounds later of a celebration going on in the Rag.

The Rookwooders were gone, with a tale of unusual defeat to tell. In the Rag, Wilmot was the hero of the hour—once the outcast of the Form!

The Bounder—gloomy, half-repentant, half-defiant—waited. He knew that they would come for him sooner or later. As soon as they knew the treacherous trick he had played—as soon as Wilmot told them why he had been kept away—the Remove footballers would deal with him. He knew that. Keeping a man who was wanted away from a football match was not an

offence the Removites were likely to forgive. He had failed, and he knew that Wilmot must have risked life and limb to make him fail. And when the Remove knew——

A record ragging, and "Coventry" for the rest of the term—that was the least the Bounder had to expect. He had risked it, with cynical recklessness, and he had at least the hardihood to stand it when it came. But the prospect was not attractive.

There was a step in the passage, a tap at the door. It opened, and Eric Wilmot came in.

The Bounder gave him a glance.

"Are they coming?" he jeered.

"Who?" asked Wilmot quietly.

"Oh, do you think I don't know what to expect?" exclaimed Smithy scoffingly. "Haven't you told them yet?"

"No."

"You prefer to keep it hanging over my head?" sneered Vernon-Smith.

"Well, it's like you!"

"I hope not!" said Wilmot in the same quiet tone.

"What do you mean?" snapped the Bounder roughly.

"No harm was done, after all," said Wilmot. "If I'd been kept away, I should have had to explain; but I got through. I've said nothing, and I'm not going to say anything. If you have the sense to hold your tongue, nobody will know what you did."

The Bounder stared at him blankly. He doubted whether his ears had heard aright.

Wilmot smiled faintly.

"Look here, Vernon-Smith," he said, "we've had rows, and we've had a scrap—my fault as much as yours, as I'm willing to own up. I made a bad start here; but the other fellows are willing to wash it out, and give a man a chance. Why not you? If we can't be friends, we needn't be enemies."

The Bounder still stared.

"Is that what you came up to say?" he stammered at last.

"Yes."

"After what I did——"

"Wash it out!"

The Bounder was silent for a long moment.

"Wash it out!" he repeated at length. "I—I'll tell you now, as you take it like that, that I'm sorry for what I did. I acted in a rotten temper, and I jolly well know that I ought to be booted for it! But if you're willing to wash it out——"

"More than willing!" said Wilmot.

"Well, I'm not the man to refuse a good offer!" said the Bounder, with a grin. "It's a go! But I'm really sorry!"

"I guessed you would be. Come down to the Rag. There's a feast of the gods going on. Let's get down before Bunter clears the table!"

The Bounder laughed, and went down with Wilmot. Harry Wharton & Co. gave him a cheery welcome as he came in, glad to see him on friendly terms with their new friend.

It was a great celebration of a great victory, and there were a good many bright faces in the Rag. But the brightest of all was that of Eric Wilmot, once the outcast of the Remove, the shadow of the past that had haunted him cast firmly behind him now, and his eyes fixed on a brighter future.

THE END.

(*Next week's* MAGNET *will contain the first of a splendid new series of stories featuring Harry Wharton & Co., entitled:* "THE TRAIL OF ADVENTURE!" *As there will be a great rush for next week's* DOUBLE FREE GIFT NUMBER *of the* MAGNET, *order your copy NOW!*)

DAN of the DOGGER BANK!

By David Goodwin

The Escape!

KENNETH GRAHAM, son of a millionaire shipowner, is rescued off the Dogger Bank by the crew of the fishing trawler, Grey Seal.

His past life a blank, he is given the name of "Dogger Dan," and signed on as fifth hand, under Skipper Atheling, Finn Macoul, Wat Griffiths, and Buck Atheling.

Aware of his nephew's fate, and knowing that he will come into the shipowner's money when his brother dies, Dudley Graham engages Jake Rebow and his cutthroats of the Black Squadron to get Kenneth out of the way for ever.

Rebow's efforts prove fruitless, however. A series of exciting adventures follow, after which Dan and Buck Atheling find themselves aboard Dudley Graham's yacht. Dan's memory returns, as the result of meeting his uncle, but Dudley denies relationship.

In Dan's possession is a chart, disclosing the whereabouts of a hidden treasure, worth £5,000. Knowing full well of his uncle's treachery, Dan makes friends with Jack Ward, the yacht's mate, gets him to broadcast a message telling of his whereabouts, and then fixes a dummy figure in his bed. Suddenly, in the darkness, a trapdoor by the side of the bunk opens, and a hand, gripping the haft of a knife, is thrust through the aperture. Springing forward like a panther, Dan grips the wrist, and then yells for his chum, Buck.

There was a savage wrench as Dan grabbed the protruding hand, but he hung on with all his might. The knife dropped upon the bunk.

A strong panting and gasping came from the other side of the panel, as though someone there were struggling with all his strength. The strain was terrific. There was a hurried rush outside in the alley-way, and in a moment Buck burst into the cabin.

"I've got him!" panted Dan. "Ah, he's slipping! I can't hold him!"

Buck, taking in the situation at a glance, came swiftly to the rescue and grabbed at the wrist.

But there was not room for both, and the boys hampered rather than aided each other.

Frantic wrenches came upon the wrist from its owner, and a running fire of oaths, muffled by the bulkhead, broke the silence.

"No good!" whispered Dan hoarsely. "Scoot round to his cabin, break the door in, and nail him, while I—— Ah!"

He staggered backwards. The hand broke from its hold with a jerk—Dan could get no purchase on it from where he was—and struck the top of the trapdoor, cutting the flesh deeply from wrist to knuckles. A moment later it disappeared, and the trapdoor closed with a snap.

Buck had dashed round to the other cabin like lightning before Dan had recovered himself. He was soon back, however, looking very crestfallen.

"There's no one there," he said—"not a soul!"

"I'm sick of this death-trap of a steamer!" said Dan bitterly. "Nothing but tricks and dirty work!" He picked up the knife that had fallen, and stowed it away. "Let's go on deck! Dudley won't be there, that's one blessing!"

The two chums walked the decks till breakfast-time, talking in a low voice.

Dudley turned up for breakfast, after all, much to the boys' surprise. He was even more cool and self-possessed than usual; but his long dressing-gown sleeve could not entirely cover his bandaged right wrist.

"You have a damaged wrist, I see," said Dan.

"Yes," returned Dudley. "I struck it against a stanchion last night."

"I should be careful next time," murmured Dan. "Stanchions are tough things."

The meal ended, and the rest of the day passed without any special incident.

When night was once more shutting out the daylight, Dan and Buck went below to settle on a plan of campaign.

"It's plain," said Dan, after they had been below for some time, "that we can't go on like this without—— Hallo!" He broke off suddenly. "The yacht's slowing down, isn't she? Great Scott, who's that?"

There was a stir in the cabin next door, and from behind the bulkhead came the sound of a harsh, grating voice the boys knew only too well.

"Aboard here, are they? Gosh, mon, why ha'e ye not settled them?"

"That's all very well," said Dudley's voice irritably. "I'm not a North Sea cutthroat, like you, Rebow. Can't you see I'm well known, and if I do anything shady it's easy to lay hands on me, to say nothing of this dago crew, who'd give their ears for a chance to blackmail me afterwards!"

"Ye could ha' done it withoot makin' a mess before the crew," said Rebow.

"I've tried, and they got to windward of me, the cursed cubs! Confound it, Rebow, you've got nothing to brag about yourself! You've had a thousand pounds before your nose, and two months to track the cubs down in, and you've failed a dozen times!"

"De'il tak' them!" growled Rebow. "It's not your bit siller that I'm followin'! Four o' my craft ha'e I lost since I started the chase!"

Buck nudged Dan, an appreciative grin on his face. Every word came, muffled but audible, through the panelling.

"Well, listen, and don't chatter!" continued the yacht-owner's voice angrily, "and don't tell me you care nothing for the money! I'm not a fool! You shall finger it; but the job mustn't be done here. It must be done on Baltrum Island!"

"Ah!" said Rebow. "What d'ye ken o' Baltrum Island, ma mannie?"

Dudley's voice sounded lower than ever.

"I know where Jan Osterling's treasure lies. I have the chart!"

"I'm wi' ye!" said Rebow, with an oath. "Let's have your plan!"

The voices sank to an inaudible whisper.

"Come, Dan!" breathed Buck. "Out of it—quick! To Jack Ward's cabin!"

They stole away without a sound, and were soon telling Ward what they had overheard.

"Great Scott!" ejaculated Ward. "The Wasp must be alongside. She's come up in the skipper's watch. Come on!"

They gained the deck and stood for a moment in the shadow of the charthouse.

A hundred yards away, rocking on the swell, lay the Black Fleet trawler, Wasp. The yacht's longboat lay alongside the Ercildoune, two of the dagos in her, and they were holding on by the yacht's davit-falls, which hung down to the water. Five of the Wasp's crew were on the Ercildoune's deck, talking earnestly with the deck-hands. A low chorus of laughter arose from time to time.

The mate looked round keenly. Then, turning round, he vanished down the engine-room. There was a squeal, and the sound of a heavy hammer striking upon solid steel.

Ward reappeared later, panting.

"There's but two on her," he said fiercely, pointing to the Wasp, "an' a pair o' dagos in the boat! The rest are here, palavering. Are ye game to take the trawler? It's your last chance!"

"Come on!" said the boys.

A moment later they were swarming down the davit-falls into the boat. One of the men aboard her looked up and gave a startled yell:

"Help, help! Dey ees-cape!"

Hampered!

THE mate let go the davit-fall and dropped lightly into the boat. The broken English of the terrified dago boatman stopped with a gasp as he looked down the barrel of Ward's revolver.

"That's right, sonny," said the mate —"dey ees-cape! An' if they don't, you don't, either, for I'll drill a hole in your saddle-coloured skin! So push off, an' pull for that smack quicker'n lightning!"

As the boat pushed off, the yacht's crew, with the Black Fleet visitors, made a startled rush for the rail and stared over it.

"Give way, you mongrels!" cried the mate, as the scared boatmen pulled out for the Wasp, where she lay to leeward. "If you slacken stroke, you're dead meat!"

The men wanted no reminding. They knew the mate of old, and guessed he would be as good as his word.

"Well done, Jack!" said Dan. "You did that smartly! They haven't tumbled to the game yet on the Ercildoune."

"They don't know it's us!" put in Buck. "They think we're some of her crew gone off to palaver without leave. Ah! They know now! They've gone below for Jake and Dudley."

"We'll reach the trawler before they're on deck!" said the mate, gleefully. "An' there'll be a change of ownership! Go on, you snuff-coloured sweeps! Put your backs into it!"

The Wasp nodded drunkenly on the swells. There were only two men on her, and they were drowsily waiting for the return of Jake and their comrades, who were on the yacht.

Swift and noiselessly, the boat slipped alongside.

One of the Wasp's men roused himself.

"Back already, skipper?" he said. "What! Hallo! Who the blazes are you?"

A yell of rage arose astern from the decks of the Ercildoune as Jake Rebow came up from below and learned the truth, and Dudley Graham's curses at the negligence of his crew were soon added.

Before the noise was thoroughly started, Dan seized the oars from the dago rowers and flung them away. Then it was that the Wasp's watch on deck said in his alarm:

"Who are you?"

"We're the new crew!" said the mate grimly, as he sprang aboard. "See?"

Without another word, he grappled with the astonished Black and flung him clean over the rail into the sea.

His companion turned on the newcomers with a yell, but he was soon overcome by Dan and Buck, and slung overboard like a sack of coal. He swam to the boat, where his companion was already hanging on.

The two dagos, furious but helpless, dragged them on board.

"Now, then, boys," said the mate, "fore-sheet over, an' let her rip! Here's the yacht down on us!"

There was hardly enough wind to move the trawler four miles an hour, and her new crew looked anxiously behind them.

A bell clanged deep in the Ercildoune's engine-room, and, with a long hoot of triumph from her whistle, she circled round, and came swooping down upon the Wasp.

"They won't run us down!" said Buck. "It's their own blessed boat, this!"

"Won't they?" retorted the mate, putting his helm up. "That's all you know! It's worth fifty old twopenny trawlers to them if they can wipe out our young millionaire here, eh, Kenneth Graham?"

"Dogger Dan's my name, Mr. Mate!" said Dan. "But you're right.

They've got the three of us on board here, an' they can make a clean job of us without any knifing, an' swear it was an accident. But I thought you'd snaffled the engines?"

"So I did," said Jack Ward, glancing at the towering steamer as she came hurtling down upon them. "They're bound to break down in a few dozen revolutions, but it's touch and go whether the steamer hits us first."

"The engines are sick already!" commented Buck. "I can hear 'em coughing."

The usual steady beat of the yacht's screws was changed to a groaning, clanking noise, and, by the shouting and bell-ringing aboard her, it was plain that those on the bridge were not pleased with those in the engine-room.

"We've got ye, ye loons!" roared the hoarse voice of Rebow from the yacht's bridge. "Give her mair steam, Mr. Dudley!"

The Ercildoune's stem was barely a dozen yards away, when there was a sudden grinding, crashing uproar in her bowels, and she rolled past, splintering the edge of the Wasp's taffrail as she went.

Slowly she came to a standstill, and her crew yelled with rage and disappointment.

A spattering storm of shots rattled on the Wasp, as spit after spit of flame leaped from the yacht's deck. One chance shot drew blood from Dan's wrist; but he had flattened himself behind the mast.

The smack glided away, and in a few minutes was out of range, leaving the Ercildoune crippled.

The Last Of The Narwhal!

"HOW long before they start after us, Jack?" cried Dan.

"Long after we're out o' sight," said the mate, "if only this night breeze'll hold. They'll take three hours, at least, putting things right. I'd say we've done pretty well in that deal. They've always a card up their sleeve, though. See there——"

From the dark hull of the yacht, now

half a mile away, gleamed the Black Fleet's signal—two short flashes and one long.

"There's the answer!" put in Dan, as a faint triple flash shone far out on the weather-beam.

"Ay," said Ward. "Hope it ain't the Thresher! We can deal with a trawler; but the tug would do us in, sure as a gun, in this breeze!"

"The Narwhal's dismasted," said Dan thoughtfully, "and her bows are stove in. Can't be her."

"That was a week ago," retorted Buck. "You can bet they ran her in sharp and put a new stick in her. The Blacks do repairs mighty quick."

"Then it's her," said the mate; "for it's a trawler, right enough. See her topsail! There's the yacht talkin' to her."

A constant flicker of flashes, dot and dash, gleamed from the yacht, whose hull was now out of sight in the dark distance, and when she paused the faraway trawler answered.

"Gettin' her orders," said Jack. "They've a fine system, them Blacks, an' that's a fact."

A great funnel of light came staggering across the sea, its thin end a blinding point far away astern, and its wide end a great ring of radiance that rested on the Wasp and lit her up as though a gigantic bullseye-lamp had been turned on her.

"A searchlight from the yacht!" cried Dan, when the ray of light had wandered round for a few moments and then settled steadily on the smack. "Didn't know she had one!"

It was not long before the nodding topsail of the Narwhal came bearing down upon the Wasp. The beam of light from the yacht rested on the newcomer for a moment, showing her new mast, unvarnished, and a rather rough patch on her port-bow where she had suffered from her collision on the night of the thunderstorm. The light gleamed on the barrels of four rifles levelled over the rail, and then the glare shifted from the attacker and settled on the Wasp again.

"They've got Service rifles," said Buck; "but there may be some aboard here, too!"

"Rout 'em out, lad, an' quick about it!" said Ward, gripping his tiller. "Don't fail to find 'em, or we're done! It's too long a range for pistol-shooting!"

The Narwhal ran down within a hundred yards of the Wasp, and then shifted her helm and ran parallel with her, just keeping outside the line of the searchlight, while her intended prey was in the full glare of it.

The first rifle spoke. A bullet screamed close over Jack Ward's head.

"Ay," he said, stretching himself out on the deck and steering with his left hand on the tiller, "they've got it all their own way, the swabs!"

"Here you are!" cried Dan, tumbling up the hatchway with a couple of rifles under his arm. "Buck's bringing up more, an' these are loaded!"

"Let her come up close," said the mate, holding his revolver at the ready, "and both of you keep under cover. See the patch on her bow! It's rottenly put on—not even let into the wood."

"I see," said Buck. "Fancy putting to sea like that! But what good will it do us?"

"It's white deal," said Jack. "Pour in a sharp fire on it, an' it'll crack up an' splinter, an' leave the breach open. We've two magazine rifles. She's down by the head as it is. She'll fill in ten minutes if we can strip it, short-manned as she be!"

Jack shifted his tiller. Straight at the Narwhal he went, and the searchlight followed him. Viciously the rifle-bullets pattered about the Wasp, but her crew were well sheltered, and in another twenty seconds the glare of light covered both vessels together.

"Now," cried Jack, thrusting his helm hard up, "let her have it!"

A blast of lead struck the crazy patchwork on the Narwhal's bows as the two magazine-rifles and Jack's revolver poured in a rapid fire. The deal patch withered and collapsed under it like a sheet of gelatine before a hot fire, and as the trawler dipped heavily to the next swell, she took a hundredweight of water through the open breach.

"Up forrard, ye fules!" shrieked the Narwhal's skipper to his men. "Stanch her, or we shall founder!"

But as two men started forward, Jack's revolver spoke. One of them yelped, while the other fled aft, for a bullet had passed through his hair.

The Narwhal made a plunge, the water pouring into her by the ton, and when the next wave passed, her bow did not rise.

"She's gaun!" yelled the captain, in a frenzy. "Oop, an' pour a volley intae them before she sinks! They shall gang tae their death with us!"

But even as they rose to their feet, the long black trawler hove up her stern to the sky, wallowed heavily in the trough of the sea, and dived into the depths. The seething waters closed over her!

Dan Means Business!

"STAND by!" said Dan. "Can't leave the poor beasts to drown! Heave her round, Mr. Ward!"

"It's more'n they deserve," said the mate. "But rope's cheap, so's Dartmoor Prison, an' the situation's fine and healthy. We'll pick the dirty dogs up, if you say so!"

Dan and Buck were leaning over the rail, ready to help any struggler in the water, as the Wasp passed over the scene of the wreck.

There was nothing to be seen, however. The silent sea had swallowed up the Narwhal and her crew of gunmen.

The Wasp stretched herself out to the eastward, and all night she sailed till the grey dawn began to grow over the sea. The yacht was nowhere in sight, and Jack Ward opined that the dago engineers were still pinching their fingers among the machinery.

Hunger and the cold of dawn began to weigh on the crew of the Wasp, and, routing out the smack's stores, they made a breakfast off hot coffee and bully-beef.

After the meal, Buck climbed leisurely to the cross-trees and peered out over the horizon.

"Land-ho!" he hailed. "Baltrum right ahead, by the look of it! Bring up the glasses, Dan! Ay, there's the hut and the old tree, too! We'll be there in two hours!"

He came down jubilantly; the smack began to hiss through the water. The wind was freshening, and the morning was dark and lowering.

"Dirty weather coming," said the mate, looking to windward. "What's that away on the quarter? Patrol boat, ain't it?"

"Gosh!" exclaimed Buck, staring at a long, low, grey vessel, almost invisible through the smother. "That's the old German gunboat that stopped the Seal last week. She's after the Wasp!"

"What!" said the mate blankly. "It's all up for us, then!"

GREYFRIARS INTERVIEWS

This week's brilliant verses by our long-haired poet are written around
EDWIN MYERS,
an inky-fingered member of the Second Form.

(1)
The inkiest of Friars
In Fagdom's happy land
Is known as Teddy Myers,
Of Dicky Nugent's band;
He has the reputation
(A gruesome one, I think)
Of taking recreation
By wallowing in ink.

(2)
If you should wish to spot him
And find a little swell
Whose face is clean—that's NOT him;
No fear! We know him well!
Find some untidy slacker
Who's just one mound of grime,
And if there's no one blacker,
Well, you'll be right this time!

(3)
I saw the young ass playing
At Soccer in the Rag,
With energy displaying
Much prowess for a fag!
The Second in full muster
Were kicking at the ball
(An old discarded duster)
Towards the goal—a wall!

(4)
Although not scientific
The game was hard and fast.
The clamour was terrific,
It smote me like a blast!
I scrambled on a table
In case I might be slain,
And shouted through the babel
To Teddy Myers—in vain.

(5)
The din was most appalling
As Dicky Nugent scored!
Some players started bawling,
And those that didn't, roared!
"Offside!" They cracked the ceiling!
The tumult made me deaf;
I found they were appealing
To me—"Offside there, ref!"

(6)
So I was ref! Well, clearly
The goal had been offside.
I told them so severely,
At any rate, I tried!
But they were then re-starting
Their soul-destroying row!
And I, before departing,
Exclaimed: "I'll stop that—now!"

(7)
I whistled long and shrilly.
They stopped the game and stared.
They asked: "What's that for, silly?"
And, "Time's up!" I declared.
"I'm ref, so just you stop it!
The game is finished—see?
And all save Myers can hop it!
And you, Myers, come with me!"

(8)
My words were quite unheeded!
They started up again!
And that was all I needed!
I smote them might and main!
Instead of swiftly fleeing
They seized me, one and all,
And I stopped refereeing
And started as—the ball!

Up came the gunboat, flying an urgent signal to heave-to. She had every right to stop a Black Fleet vessel that was plying her trade in German waters.

Seeing no notice taken of her signal, she threw a stronger one. She was nearly two miles away.

Boom!

A mushroom of white smoke blossomed against the gunboat's side, and a shell screamed across the bows of the Wasp.

"No need for you to worry, Dan," said the mate sadly. "You'll be all right, but it's ruin for me. This is a Black Fleet ship—the one they're looking for. I've been mate of a steamer for a month past, in close touch with the squadron all the time, an' you can bet when they're scooped in—as they will be—they'll swear I was one of them. They'll get even An' those dagos of the Ercildoune—there'll be some of those brought in as witnesses, an' they'll swear 'emselves blue to get their own back on me! It means a German gaol for me, my lads!"

"Rot!" said Dan. "We can bear witness you kept clear of the Blacks and helped us."

"Dudley Graham'll save himself by jumpin' on me, too; an' even if I wasn't

shoved in quod, I'm done for!" said the mate gloomily. "My ticket'll be dirtied, an' I'll never get another ship. However, it can't be helped, an' I'm glad you're out of your troubles, Dan. Here goes!"

He put the helm down, and waited in silence for the gunboat to come up.

"He's right, Dan," said Buck. "It's tough on old Jack!"

"Then, by gosh," cried Dan, springing to the tiller, "we'll run for it, neck or nothing!"

He wrenched the helm up, and the Wasp fell away before the wind and filled her sails.

Boom!

A second shell shrieked overhead as the tearing breeze sent the Wasp rushing along as fast as the gunboat herself.

"Let him fire, and be hanged to him!" cried Dan. "There's Baltrum close under our lee, an' we'll give him the slip and unearth the treasure yet! Give her sheet, there!"

Boom! Z-z-z-z!

A shell tore past within a dozen feet and smacked the top off a high wave just to leeward.

"That's his sighting shot!" said Buck, setting his teeth. "He'll blow us to THE MAGNET LIBRARY.—No. 1,460.

blazes with the next! He's training his gun dead on! Let's give in!"

"No!" said Dan savagely. "Let her rip!"

And as the gunboat surged clear of a white-topped wave, the gun-layer pulled his lanyard.

The Friendly Fog!

BOOM! Z-z-z-z-z!

The smoke leaped from the gunboat's side, and the shell screamed past so close to the Wasp that Dan felt the wind of it on his cheek.

"Smack through the mainsail!" cried Buck.

Boom-z-z-z!

Another shell whistled through the air, and over went the topmast like a reed snapped by a blast of wind. It hung over forward like the broken wing of a bird, and plunged and swayed with the kicking of the trawler.

"Cut it away!" cried Dan desperately. "Up aloft with you!"

The gunboat was coming up fast, and as Buck sprang up aloft to cut away the wreckage, Jack Ward turned upon Dan.

"Nothin' on the seas can save us now," he said. "The gunboat has the legs of us. We're only makin' it worse."

Dan glanced at the gunboat, and saw, with a sigh, that the mate was right. The sinking of the Wasp with a few more shots was a certainty. He had no right to throw away his comrades' lives.

"Here goes, then!" he said, luffing the trawler-head to wind. "Fore-sheet a-weather, and heave her to! I'd rather have gone on and taken what came. But they've got us now!"

Up came the gunboat. An angry, red-faced lieutenant was stamping on the bridge as he brought his vessel to a standstill close by.

"I guess we're in for it!" muttered Buck. "Whatever might ha' happened before we ran for it, we've done for ourselves now. Here comes the quarter-boat."

The davit-tackles of the gunboat screeched as they ran out, and the boat came pulling towards the Wasp. There was nothing to be said.

The bow-man was reaching out with his boathook to hook on to the Wasp's rail, when Dan, looking astern, gave a gasp of excitement.

A great billowy mass of dark mist—the thick wind-fog of the North Sea—came driving down upon the trawler and the gunboat like a curtain. A rush of damp wind came with it, and in a few seconds the gunboat seemed a mere filmy outline in a shroud of haze.

Dan sprang to the tiller.

"It's our turn now!" he cried hoarsely. "By George, we'll slip them yet! Smash that boathook! Let go the foresheet!"

Jack Ward, fired with new hope, snatched up an oar and snapped the boathook even as it touched the Wasp's rail.

Buck leaped into the bows and swung the fore-sheet over, and, amid a volley of angry shouts from the boat's crew, the black trawler laid her side down and leaped away into the fog.

"Fooled again!" shouted Buck, hauling madly on the bowline.

"Shut up that row," hissed Dan, "and pray that this fog doesn't lift, or we'll

be at the bottom of the sea in ten seconds, boat and all!"

The fog held. Anxiously the little crew watched it, for they knew their lives depended on it. One rift in the haze, and the gunboat would open fire.

"He'll think we've put to sea," muttered Dan, shifting his course. "An' for that very reason we'll make straight in for Baltrum, an' see if we can find the entrance of the gatway."

"He'll see our mast, even if we're anchored inside, when the fog lifts," said Buck. "An' he'll send a party ashore to capture us."

"I reckon not!" said Dan, closing his lips tight. "We'll cut the mast down and sink her in the creek!"

"Good lad!" said Ward. "The very thing! But how shall we get off again? S'pose the Ercildoune or the Fleet tug turns up, an' they're on the way to the treasure? They know where we've gone."

"The gunboat'll keep the Fleet off!" chuckled Dan. "One good turn deserves another. They thought we were one of Rebow's lot, an' I fancy we've made things hot for the Fleet if she does catch 'em. And the Valhalla—dad's yacht—ought to be here in twenty-four hours if that message you sent has gone through."

"Ah!" said Jack Ward eagerly. "An' there's the treasure in front of us! Let her go!"

Dan stood at the helm; the mate went into the bows and began to heave the lead, and Buck shinned up aloft and sat in the cross-trees.

"It's a bit clearer up here," he said, "an', by George, I can just see the beach!"

"In she goes!" cried Buck, as the narrow creek between the islands, white with tumbling surf, opened just ahead of them. "It's high water, an' a big tide, too!"

A minute later the Wasp was tumbling and plunging through the broken water over the bar, her decks washed like a half-tide rock, and her mast whipping like a reed. Dan's steady hand brought her through it, and she drew clear and glided up the sheltered waters of the creek, where the boys had already seen such stirring events.

"There's the old Vulture's topmast stickin' up though the water," said Buck. "We'll sink this hooker alongside her for company."

"Look sharp, then; the fog's clearing!" said Dan. "Down all sail and let go the anchor. If the gunboat spots our mast over the dunes, we're done!"

Down went the anchor, biting into the very ribs of the departed Vulture. The boat was launched and the rifles, cartridges, and all the available provisions bundled into her. Then a dozen strokes of an axe on the skin of the hold did their work, and as the fog drove away on the wings of a rising gale the Wasp settled down and joined her old comrade on the creek-bottom.

"And now for the treasure!" said Dan. "Give way!"

The Treasure!

THE boat grounded on the sand. Dan, Buck, and the mate unloaded her, dragged her right up the dunes, and then put the provisions back again.

"She ought to be well out o' the way there," said Dan. "It's going to be a

mighty big tide. It's over high-water mark now, an' coming in fast. Gosh! How it blows! We got here just in time!"

The high wind had cleared the last trace of fog, but a snorting gale was lashing the sea.

They raced down the dunes to the spot where the spades lay. The hole that Dan and Buck had made was undisturbed.

Without another word they fell to and dug furiously. No tide had touched the spot for many years; but the conditions were just right for a big flood, and things looked threatening. There were no dunes opposite the place where the treasure lay, nothing but a long slope of sand.

Nearer and nearer crept the surf.

"The breakers'll be over the dunes soon!" said Dan. "What on earth shall we do if the sea sweeps the island? Hallo! There's a tongue of smoke in the offing. It's the gunboat come back!"

Buck leaped up, gave one glance, and whistled in the teeth of the gale.

"Gunboat?" he said. "No, by George! It's the Ercildoune!"

He jumped down, seized Dan's spade, and began to dig frantically.

One glance showed the mate that Buck was right.

"Shall we let up till they've gone?" said the mate.

"No!" cried Dan. "Keep on with it! Get it, an' hold it!"

Furiously they dug, shovelling the sand like madmen and building up a rampart as best they could against the seething waters. The smoke to seaward thickened as the twilight grew, and the long, black hull of the Ercildoune, bearing with her the finest crew of scoundrels on all the bosom of the North Sea, came racing up through the gloom.

"They'll never make the gat!" said Dan, watching. "Her engines are half crocked and the gale's got her tucked under its arm. She's driving ashore!"

The Ercildoune drove far up the sands and struck with a crash; the seas poured over her and stripped her clean as a hulk. A swarm of black figures poured over her bows in twos and threes, leaping into the boiling surf, swimming for their lives.

"Dirty dagos!" growled the mate. "Ah, we're done!"

"No!" cried Buck, as his spade rang upon metal. He dropped to his knees and gripped a rusty handle of thick iron that peeped through the sand. Even as he did so the seething brine poured in, nearly swamping him. "Dan—Mr. Ward, give a hand here! I've got it!"

They bent down and felt wildly for a grip of the chest. Ten seconds of aching suspense, a wallowing struggle, and up through the sandy water came an iron chest that was more than one man could lift.

Over the sands, yet some distance away, a crowd of black figures came running towards the boys.

Dan snatched up the rifle.

Before the wrecked men had time to reach them, however, a mightier power intervened. The crests of the dunes crumbled under the battering of the breakers, a fierce swirl of waters broke through the gaps, and the North Sea rushed in upon Baltrum Island.

"To the big knoll, and quick, if you value your lives!" shouted Jack Ward. "Bring the chest along! Give me hold!"

Already the foaming water was nearly up to their knees.

Printed in Great Britain and published every Saturday by the Proprietors, The Amalgamated Press, Ltd., The Fleetway House, Farringdon Street, London, E.C.4. Advertisement offices: The Fleetway House, Farringdon Street, London, E.C.4. Registered for transmission by Canadian Magazine Post. Subscription rates: Inland and Abroad, 11s. per annum; 5s. 6d. for six months. Sole Agents for Australia and New Zealand: Messrs. Gordon & Gotch, Ltd., and for South Africa: Central News Agency, Ltd.—Saturday, February 8th, 1936.

Hoisting the treasure-chest up, they forged ahead with all the speed they could muster towards the higher, rising hill of sand in the centre of the island.

The men of the Ercildoune did not follow. The encroaching sea reached them first, and they were nearer to a second hill, whose crest lay a hundred yards away from the one the boys were trying to reach. Towards this, the tall figures of Dudley Graham and Rebow leading them, they struggled desperately.

Jack and his men threw themselves down at full length, sheltering behind the iron chest, and a heavy fire was poured in by Rebow's men. Buck and Ward lay flat, firing quietly now and then into the heart of the smoke, whence came a choked cry or an oath.

Dudley Graham stopped and stared out to sea as if petrified. His face was white and rigid, his breath came sharp between his teeth. Rebow followed his gaze.

"We're done, anyhow," he said. "This tide's finished us!"

Out of the morning haze, shouldering through the swells, the smoke pouring from her funnel, came a large shapely white vessel. She gave a blare from her siren that echoed over the wastes.

"It's the Valhalla!" shouted Dan, flinging his cap into the air.

All's Well !

DONALD GRAHAM, the man of millions had come back to demand his son from the sea. He was within an ace of coming too late.

Buck, Dan, and the mate were cut off completely from the lower sandhill on which the Ercildoune's crew had gathered. That was no refuge now, but a swamped hillock that was fast going under as the conquering sea ravaged it in a turmoil of foam and breakers.

No question of a fight now. The North Sea was master. Already the Ercildoune's men were up to their waists in water. A tidal wave swept a dozen of them away.

"Swim for the hut!" yelled Rebow, for the roar of the gale was deafening. "There's enough of us yet to mop up those deevils yonder and stop their mouths if we make the sandhill. It's drown or hang!"

"Keep by me!" screamed Dudley, as a breaker bore him off his feet. "Give me a hand; I'll never swim through that!"

"Every man for himself!" snarled Rebow. "You an' your fool games got us into this mess—get yoursel' oot of it!"

The tide and the surf swirled over them. A fierce inrush of the sea swept the Ercildoune's crew and the Blacks away together. The current swept them relentlessly, wide of the hut's hillock by hundreds of yards. No man could strive against that tearing tide nor keep afloat long in the boil of surf.

A score of black heads bobbed among the foam. One by one they went down, blotted out by the wrath of the sea.

By the hut Buck and Jack Ward watched, helpless and awestruck. A struggling swimmer, on the point of sinking, was swept past the hillock, far out, but no human power could have helped. The last of the Ercildoune's crew and the Blacks had vanished; nothing but a waste of wide, tossing waters and the scream of the gale.

"That's saved 'em from the hangman. So I'll say nothin' more," said Ward.

The long black trawler hove up her stern to the sky, wallowed heavily in the trough of the sea, and dived into the depths !

Dan took one look round at the empty sea and sank down on the sand, shivering.

In half an hour the water was falling steadily, the wind easing. The island began to reappear, one hillock after another showing.

Away off the island, the Valhalla was fighting the gale. As soon as the tide fell and the surf eased, she stood inshore and smartly lowered her two white quarter-boats.

Dan ran down to the beach. He was staring with wild eyes at a big, bronzed man in the bows of the foremost boat as she came in with lashing strokes of her six ash oars.

Without slackening an ounce of speed, she took the sands with a surge and a heave. The bronzed man leaped out of her and took Dan by the shoulders, his voice shaking.

"Kenneth!" he said. "Kenneth, my son!"

.   .   .   .   .

The evening sun gilded the swells, as the s.y. Valhalla steamed swiftly for the West, her tall bows turned towards Britain. By her quarter-rail sat Kenneth Graham and his father, and beside them Jack Ward and Buck. And from Dogger Dan fell the last words of his strange tale.

"It's like a nightmare to me—that Dudley should have come down to that," said Donald Graham, after a long pause. "He was crooked by nature, and he found his own level when he met up with the Black Fleet.

I've heard something of their doings before now. But that my own brother should——" He stopped dead. "Well, we won't talk of it, Ken. Nothing matters now I've got you back!"

He gripped his son's hand in his own.

"I own a fleet of liners, but you're the best thing I've got, or ever shall have. I'm proud of you! Proved yourself a better man than I ever reckoned. I spoiled you a bit ashore, being an only son. And your two mates, here—you're lucky to have such friends!"

He turned to the mate.

"You hold a master's ticket, don't you, Mr. Ward? My skipper is quitting the sea after this voyage—retiring for good! Most of my skippers seem able to do that, after a few years!" He chuckled. "I'm offering you a nice, fat bonus, right away—and the command of the Valhalla. How's that?"

Jack Ward flushed, and then grinned with delight.

"That's how, sir! I want to tell you I——"

"Never mind about thanking me! Now, Buck, what about you?" Old Graham clapped a hand on Buck's shoulder. "You're too good a sailor to give up the sea. I'm going to set you on the road to the biggest job afloat, and a fortune. I dealt with men and things before you were born, and I know the man I want, when I see him. I want to meet up with the Grey Seal, and your father, and his crew, right away. Think you can find her for me?"

"I bet I can pick her up, sir," said Buck, "if you'll let me give the skipper his course!"

"Do!" said Mr. Graham. "And tell him, from me, to whack up the ship to full speed!"

Dan went below. Almost too tired to eat, he staggered into a luxurious cabin berth and slept soundly for ten hours.

When he came on deck again the yacht was hove-to, with engines stopped, thirty miles south of the Dogger. Rocking in the warm rain, he saw a smart, red-sailed trawler lying with her fore-sheet a-weather. He gave a rousing whoop at the first sight of her.

"The Seal!" he shouted. "The old Seal!"

"Seal-ho!" said Buck, grinning. "Said I'd pick her up, didn't I? Gave the old skipper the tip, and we cruised around till we sighted her topsail!"

In ten minutes the Seal's crew—all but Griffiths, who was left to steer—climbed aboard the Valhalla. The handgrips, the questions, the whoops of surprise, filled the entire ship.

"Well, I'm busted!" said Atheling, for the fortieth time. "So you're a copper-bottomed millionaire, Dan! An' I thought you wasn't anything but a liar! Well, the laugh's on me!"

"There's one more laugh coming, skipper!" chuckled Kenneth. "What hit me was that you didn't believe in our little treasure-hunt—Buck's and mine. Got it right aboard here. Real, hard stuff! Pretty good voyage, eh? What d'you say if I come back with you on the Seal, and we'll lead the Valhalla to Lowestoft? I want to feel the heave of a trawler's deck under me!"

"Come on, lad!" cried Atheling. And over the side they went.

As soon as Griffiths had greeted him, Kenneth helped to crack on all sail, and away leaped the Seal, her head laid for Lowestoft. To Kenneth's huge delight, she held her own with the yacht—for it was just her day—and entered the harbour a quarter of a mile ahead of her. When the Valhalla came in the crew of the Seal had snugged their vessel down, and were ready to bear a hand.

That evening Mr. Graham, Kenneth, Ward, and all the Seal's crew sat down to a sumptuous banquet in the Valhalla's cabin, and in the centre of the table stood a rusty iron chest, that held £5,000 in Dutch gold.

Kenneth announced that according to Dogger rules it was to be divided equally among the crew of the Seal, including Jack Ward.

"I was wrong," admitted Skipper Atheling. "I was wrong, Dan—Kenneth, I mean. I ought to ha' listened to ye. But if ye came to me with such a yarn again I'd rope's-end ye, all the same!"

Donald Graham laughed. He put his hand on Atheling's shoulder.

"What do you think of it all, captain?" he asked.

"I'm thinking," said Atheling slowly, "that it's a pity Kenneth's got a job as a millionaire, for he's the best seaman o' his age that ever trod a deck on the Dogger. If ye'd seen the luck he brought us, trawlin'——"

"He'll bring you better luck yet. I want to have a talk with you, Skipper Atheling."

A wink passed between Kenneth and Buck. They slipped away on to the pier and gazed thoughtfully out on the starlit sea—the sea that the holiday-maker and the landsman know.

As Kenneth gazed out over the sleeping waters towards the vastness beyond he sighed.

"Buck," he said, "it's a fine breed of men they grow out there on the big waters. I bet Ken Graham'll never have as good a time as Dogger Dan did!"

THE END.

(See below for particulars of our grand new serial commencing next week.)

COME INTO THE OFFICE, BOYS!

Always glad to hear from you, chums, so drop me a line to the following address: The Editor, The "Magnet" Library, The Amalgamated Press, Ltd., The Fleetway House, Farringdon Street, London, E.C.4. A stamped, addressed envelope will ensure a reply.

WELL, chums, having read the announcements in this issue concerning our

FREE GIFTS,

there is no doubt you will all be bubbling over with excitement and waiting anxiously to get possession of the

MARVELLOUS MAGIC SPECTACLES

and the first sheet of

PICTURES THAT COME TO LIFE!

To look through the Magic Spectacles and see the pictures come to life, is a most fascinating experience.

These grand Scientific Gifts, which will put all previous free gifts entirely in the shade, will be PRESENTED FREE with next week's record-breaking issue of the MAGNET.

Further pictures will be given free in subsequent issues.

In order to give all my regular readers the chance of being able to

STEP IN FIRST

and secure these FREE GIFTS I have arranged to publish next week's issue of the MAGNET one day earlier than usual—Friday, February 7th. If you are wise, you will get your newsagent to deliver, or reserve, you a copy. Failing this, be sure and get your copy early Friday morning, for you will find boys and girls alike flocking round the newsagents' like bees round a jam-pot!

Though I have been very busy lately preparing these grand Free Gifts, my time, of course, has not been occupied solely with the FREE GIFTS. I have also been working hard on a

BUMPER PROGRAMME OF STORIES,

which I am confident will surpass any yet published in the good old MAGNET.

The piece-de-resistance is:

"THE TRAIL OF ADVENTURE!"

By Frank Richards,

the first of a grand new series of rattling fine school stories, telling how the world-famous chums—HARRY WHARTON & CO., of Greyfriars—pick up a trail that is destined to lead them into the most amazing adventures in far-off corners of the world. To say more would give the plot away and deprive you of the splendid treat in store. Geo. E. Rochester, well-known to you all, as one of the most famous and popular authors of the day, is contributing yet another masterpiece—a pulsating story of dare-devil adventures on land, sea and in the air. The powerful opening chapters next week are only a foretaste of what is to come. The "Greyfriars Herald"—which is unavoidably held over this week—will reappear with a burst of merriment. Our Rhymester's verses are also worthy of special praise—his "Interview" next week is really brilliant.

A final word of warning—next Friday is a red-letter day—the day when our BUMPER FREE GIFT NUMBER of the MAGNET will be on sale!

YOUR EDITOR.